Inherit the Skies

INHERIT
THE SKIES

Janet Tanner

$\overline{C}$

CENTURY

LONDON   SYDNEY   AUCKLAND   JOHANNESBURG

Copyright © Janet Tanner 1989

First published in Great Britain in 1989 by
Century Hutchinson Ltd
Brookmount House, 62–65 Chandos Place
London WC2N 4NW

Century Hutchinson South Africa (Pty) Ltd
PO Box 337, Bergvlei 2012, South Africa

Century Hutchinson Australia Pty Ltd
20 Alfred Street, Milsons Point, Sydney, NSW 2061
Australia

Century Hutchinson New Zealand Ltd
PO Box 40–086, Glenfield, Auckland 10
New Zealand

British Library Cataloguing in Publication Data

Tanner, Janet
Inherit the skies.
I. Title
823'.914 [F]

ISBN 0 7126 2595 X

Typeset by Deltatype, Ellesmere Port
Printed in Great Britain by
Mackays of Chatham PLC,
Chatham, Kent

To Terry with all my love

BOOK ONE – THE PRESENT – 1965

Exercise caution in your business affairs; for the world is full of trickery. But let this not blind you to what virtue there is.

Desiderata

Chapter One

Something has to be done.

The thought repeated itself over and over in Sarah Bailey's head with the insistence of a primeval religious chant as the Rolls-Royce Silver Cloud accelerated smoothly through the bends of the Somerset lanes; seemed even to be echoed by the swish of the tyres and the soft purr of the engine as Reakes, her chauffeur for more than twenty years, drove swiftly along the familiar road home.

Something has to be done. But what . . . what . . . ?

Beside her on the beige leather seat her briefcase lay unopened, further evidence of Sarah's preoccupation this March afternoon. Usually after the monthly board meeting of Morse Bailey Aero International she was only too anxious to get to grips with the sheafs of papers, peppered with her own notes, which kept her in touch with the company that was still her life's blood even though she no longer played the same active part in its running that she had once done.

Today however the sheafs of papers lay neglected while Sarah sat motionless, staring unseeingly out of the smoked glass windows of the Rolls-Royce as the hedges, still winter brown above the lushness of the green fields, flashed past. No amount of perusal of columns of figures could alter the disturbing facts that she had learned at today's meeting; the answer, if there was one, lay not in the black and white outpourings of computers and typewriters, but within herself.

Sarah gave her head a small impatient shake then raised a hand to smooth her soft silver curls back into place. Wasn't that the way she preferred it – the way she had always preferred it? Self-reliance, not dependence on others – and particularly not on mere machines, wonderful though they may be. If for a moment the problem seemed insoluble that was only because she had not applied herself to it sufficiently. She could not allow herself to be beaten. There was too much at stake. Everything her husband – and her father – had worked for. The very identity of Morse Bailey.

The Rolls swept around a bend in the gently sloping lane and as the house came into sight Sarah felt a familiar leap of comforting warmth. Chewton Leigh House. The sight of it never failed to lift her spirits. It had been her home now for more than thirty years and a haven for much longer than that and she loved every weathered grey stone of its imposing Queen Anne façade, every tendril of creeper which clung to the walls on the east side, every arch and timber.

To the side of the house some of the park had been fenced to allow a small herd of deer to graze and breed, behind it, hidden from the house by a copse, were the calm waters of a lake where moorhens and ducks sailed tranquilly and fish darted in the cool green depths. When she was nine years old Sarah had thought it a magic place, the most wonderful house in the world, and nothing that had happened in the intervening years had made her love it one jot less. On the contrary, with all her happiest memories contained like sweet ghosts within its walls it was the one place where she could feel truly content.

Now as the Rolls slowed to turn into the gravelled drive Sarah was seized with impatience for the tranquillity the house could offer. Already the raised angry voices and the tensions of the boardroom were beginning to recede in her senses. The problems were still there, yes. The battle she had still to fight was as daunting as ever. Yet Sarah felt that once ensconced in Chewton Leigh House nothing would seem so bad and its peace would enable her to recharge her batteries for the struggles ahead.

2

The Rolls drew up at the foot of the short flight of stone steps which led to the front door and Reakes came around to assist her out of the car. From long habit she allowed him to place his hand beneath her elbow and smothered the stab of irritation she could never help feeling at his solicitude. He was afraid of course that after the drive the arthritic knee that troubled her from time to time might have seized up and she would stumble. She accepted that whilst hating the one evidence of infirmity. At seventy-three years old Sarah was proud of her robust good health and she was keen to point out to anyone who assumed her slight stiffness was as a result of her age that in fact the troublesome knee was the legacy of a riding accident.

She straightened now with a swift impatient movement and drew her cream cashmere coat closely around her slender frame. After the warmth of the Rolls the March wind cutting across the valley was bone-chilling. Chewton Leigh House would be warm as well as welcoming. It was one comfort Sarah insisted upon.

A smile touched her lips as she remembered the way it used to be in the old days – roaring fires in every room and the corners and corridors as cold as charity. It used to be scorched faces and knees in the drawing-room, shivers in the bathroom, she recalled. And without warning her memory was slipping back further still – to a bedroom where the only sensible thing to do was to undress as quickly as possible and slip between icy sheets warmed in one spot by the round stone hot water bottle; a cold nose peeping out above the covers; cold linoleum between her toes when it was time to get up again; intricate frosted patterns on the window – the very thought of it sent a shiver prickling across her shoulders now.

The central heating she had installed at Chewton Leigh House ensured that Sarah would never be cold again. Sheila, her daughter, was invariably critical about it when she came to visit. 'Good heavens, Mummy, this entire place is like a hothouse! Surely you don't need every room heated, living alone? It's such a waste!' To which Sarah replied, with slight tartness, that she would spend her

3

money any way she chose – and being warm was one of them. She had no need to penny-pinch these days after all and Sheila did not feel the cold as she did. Sheila was country through and through; she gained her warmth from the body heat of a horse as she mucked out stables or cantered across a frosty meadow. Sarah could scarcely ever remember seeing her shiver even as a child. Well, give her time. . . .

Reakes opened the front door for her and as the warmth came out to meet her Sarah was once again glad that she was not possessed of Sheila's frugal nature. Odd, really, that a girl brought up to want for nothing as Sheila had been should be so . . . yes, admit it, *mean*. But then, it's probably that she wants her share of my personal fortune for her beloved horses, Sarah thought with a smile. If I have diminished it by keeping every corner of my house warm there will be less for hay and oats, liniment and vet's bills and stud fees. But there was no malice in the thought. Sarah was very fond of Sheila in spite of the fact that there was very little common ground between mother and daughter.

But then what do I have in common with any of my children? Sarah wondered. I bore them and gave them life yet they might almost be a brood of aliens, so different are they.

The thought somehow triggered once more the great core of unease within her, and Sarah's attitude returned full circle to the situation which had been presented to her at this afternoon's board meeting. Not that it had been either of her own sons who had put the suggestion up, though Roderick was playing a bigger and bigger part in the running of the company these days and Miles too had at last been persuaded out of the testing sheds into the boardroom for the once-monthly meeting at least. No, it had been Guy Bailey, revelling in his position as Managing Director, who had presented her with a virtual *fait accompli* of which he must have known she would never approve. But could Sarah count on her own sons for support? Each of them would have their own reason for going along with Guy. And as things stood even if she could persuade one of them to her point of view it would not be enough.

4

Sarah frowned and crow's-feet deepened the web of tiny lines around still-beautiful blue eyes as the insistent chant repeated itself once more inside her head. *Something has to be done*. But then she was aware of a treacherous floe of regret: why now? Why should I have to be fighting again now just when I thought I could relax a little. Sometimes it seems my life has been one long battle and I am tired, so tired. . . .

She crossed the hall, the heels of her smart town shoes clattering on the polished floor as she skirted from habit the exquisite Aubusson rug in muted pinks and blues which lay in the centre like a patch of spring flowers in a winter-dulled garden. Often she paused in the hall to drink in the essence of the house, in some ways unchanged from the time she had first known it, yet in a thousand other ways her own creation. The George Jack chest stood at the foot of the sweeping staircase as it had always done but now it was brightened by a vase of flowers – daffodils today – lending a splash of colour to an otherwise dark corner, the walls were hung with the precious tapestries she had discovered gathering dust in an attic room and a heavy gilt-framed mirror. A grandmother clock in a hand-crafted case of dark oak now filled the once-echoing silence with a gentle and comfortable ticking and on the refectory table one of Sarah's favourite pieces, a graceful T'ang horse, arched his thoroughbred's neck proudly.

Today however she passed him by without a second glance, making straight for the study. Once the study had been a retreat of Gilbert Morse, whose foresight, business flair and money had been the foundation of Morse Bailey, and it was one of the few rooms in the house which Sarah had left virtually unchanged. There was so much essence of Gilbert here and she could not have borne to remove the stamp of his powerful personality. The bookshelves that lined the walls were still full of the books he had loved, the antique swivel chair, upholstered in soft dark green leather, was the same one where he had sat to ponder problems in the early days, the heavy oak desk bore the scars of a cigar which had sometimes rolled unheeded from the ashtray

5

onto its polished surface. Flowers graced the desk now – a small crystal vase of snowdrops – and the ashtray was empty and sparklingly clean, but Gilbert's leather tooled blotter still occupied pride of place and his collection of antique maps still decorated the pale cream walls.

One picture dominated the room – a water colour in a frame of light oak and gilt. It portrayed an aeroplane – a quaint unstable construction with an open fuselage and intricate framework of white wood and piano wire – a monstrous kite on bicycle wheels which would surely never fly. But the artist commissioned by Gilbert had painted those wheels rising above the green meadow grass and the portrayal had been neither mere wishful thinking nor artistic licence. For this was MB1 or 'The Eagle' as the family had affectionately named it, the very first of the Morse Bailey aeroplanes and forerunner of a string of aircraft whose reputation had spread around the world.

Chewton Leigh – 1909 read the inscription but it might have been just yesterday, Sarah thought as the memories crowded in. She shrugged out of her coat, dropped it carelessly on the leather swivel chair and crossed to look more closely, as she so often did, at the painting.

Designed and flown by her own beloved Adam, paid for by Gilbert's money and foresight, the aeroplane in the picture epitomised all she was fighting for, and looking at it now only served to strengthen her resolve. Whatever happened she could not allow all this history, all these dreams and hard won achievements, to fall into the hands of the one person who had once come close to destroying it. Something had to be done. And there was no-one but her to do it.

'Granny! I thought I heard you come in!' The voice was light, bright and brimming with youth, and Sarah, her reverie shattered, swung round, a smile of surprise curving her lips.

'Kirsty, my dear, what are you doing here?'

'Well I've come to see you, of course! Only I'd forgotten it was the day for your silly meeting so I've had to while away the afternoon in the kitchen chatting with Grace.'

'Oh my goodness, I hope you haven't been interrupting

her!' Sarah said anxiously. 'I'm having a dinner party this evening so she has a great deal extra to do.'

'Granny! You know perfectly well Grace is more than capable of producing a banquet fit for royalty and chattering nineteen to the dozen at the same time. She's had a lifetime's practice at it. No, I'm the one likely to suffer. She's been feeding me all the delicious bits and bobs plus some freshly made scones and cream and I shall soon be as fat as a house.'

She came into the room to kiss her grandmother, a slender pretty girl in an oversized man's sweater and tight fitting denim jeans, and Sarah was unable to suppress a smile of amusement. Kirsty – fat? Never! She had always been thin – too thin, Sarah had thought – as a child and now, in the ridiculous uniform which young people who were also students seemed to adopt she looked small and waif-like.

'Let's go into the drawing-room and make ourselves comfortable, shall we?' Sarah suggested. If Grace knows I'm home she will probably be bringing in a pot of tea at any moment and we don't want it to get cold. Besides, a nice cup of tea is exactly what I could do with after an afternoon spent listening to Guy and the others all trying to outdo one another.'

'Guy!' Kirsty snorted, her tone expressing more eloquently than any words her distaste for the man who now headed the board of Morse Bailey, and Sarah smiled, a little grimly.

Her own feelings exactly. Guy had a good head for business, he was decisive and generally far-seeing and he gave the impression of being altruistic. He could be charming, if a little pompous, and he commanded respect among employees and competitors alike. But Sarah had long suspected he could also be ruthless and venal where his ambitions were concerned and this afternoon's meeting had only confirmed this. But then of course he was very much Alicia's son. With a mother like that it was only surprising he was not a great deal worse. . . .

At the very thought of Alicia it was as if the door had

slammed shut inside Sarah. Perhaps later she would have to think of Alicia. With things the way they were after this afternoon's board meeting there might very well be no alternative. But for the moment she was unwilling to let business worries mar Kirsty's visit. The time she could spend with her granddaughter now was all too short – and much too precious. The golden days of Kirsty's childhood when the family had teased her for practically *living* at Chewton Leigh House were gone now and when she graduated, found a job, married, perhaps moved away from the area, she would have less and less time for visiting however good her intentions. Knowing this saddened Sarah and filled her with a sense of urgency and determination to make the most of every moment.

'Let's not talk about the business,' she said now gaily. 'I want to hear all your news, Kirsty. How is college?'

'Oh fine. Though how anyone can believe an art degree is a soft option, I can't imagine. I'm permanently snowed under by work. But at least I'm lucky enough to be doing what I want to do and I know I have you to thank for that. I don't believe Mummy and Daddy would ever have let me go to art school if you hadn't persuaded them. I think they saw it as a den of deepest iniquity.'

Sarah smiled. 'There's good and bad everywhere, Kirsty. It's all a matter of what *you* make of it.'

'Of course it is – and you have the sense to see that, Granny.' Kirsty linked her arm companionably through Sarah's. 'Now come and sit down. You look all in.'

She propelled Sarah out into the hall in the direction of the drawing-room and Sarah felt some of her anxiety evaporate in a warm glow of love. From her earliest childhood Kirsty had been devoted to her grandmother, spending far more time at Chewton Leigh House than she ever did at her own home, Chorley Manor, on the other side of the valley, and showing far more interest in the aeroplanes which were a constant topic of conversation there than she did in the horses which were her mother's life.

'I don't think I like horses that much,' she had confided

to Sarah once. 'They frighten me a bit, though Mummy gets cross with me if I say so. And they do *smell* so.'

Sarah had laughed. She could imagine Sheila being very cross indeed with Kirsty if she had been unwise enough to mention the smell which Sheila preferred to any expensive perfume. Such a criticism would be regarded as the sheerest heresy. But she could understand Kirsty's fear. If she was truthful she had to admit that horses frightened her a little too, though she had always been ashamed of the fear which she considered to be a weakness. She had been a reasonably competent horsewoman until the fall had given her the excuse she needed not to ride again.

'What I'd really like to do is learn to fly,' Kirsty had said wistfully and at once Sarah had experienced this strange heady empathy which occurs when two minds, two personalities, reach out to one another.

Flying – yes. Flying was different. She felt no fear when piloting an aeroplane – except perhaps that sharp shaft that strikes when things go wrong. And even then it was a different sort of fear. Whatever the circumstances, at the controls of an aeroplane Sarah always felt she was the mistress of her own destiny, holding her fate in her own hands. Which was more than she could say for the terror she had experienced more than once on the back of a horse – and the uncomfortable, ever present knowledge that if the mount took it in into his head to do things *his* way there was nothing whatever she could do to stop him.

'You shall learn to fly, Kirsty, just as soon as you are old enough,' she had promised, and seen the child's eyes light up.

She had kept her promise and Kirsty had gained her licence in record time. She flew whenever she could, which was less than she would have liked now that the degree course in graphics at the West of England College of Art was absorbing more and more of her time.

Kirsty looked like her grandmother, some people said – and when she studied early photographs of herself Sarah was forced to admit it was true. Those high cheekbones and the small straight nose, the neat heart-shaped chin, the clear blue eyes. Her hair was lighter in colour than Sarah's, which had once been deep, almost reddish brown, and her mouth was fuller and wider, but the likeness was still there and it added to the closeness which Sarah felt to her granddaughter.

The drawing-room lay across the hall from the study, a large pleasant room which overlooked both the lawns to the front of the house and the deer park to the side. Furnishings in shades of gold, cream and apricot seemed to bring sunshine into the room on even the darkest of winter days, and the deep brocaded sofa and chairs were bliss to Sarah's tired bones at the end of a long business session. The family portraits which had once lined the walls, Sarah had relegated to the dining-room where they now presided over formal entertaining and family meals alike and Sarah had replaced them with art works of her own choosing – a Turner, a Hogarth, two lovely misty Monets and some more up-to-date paintings by artists whose names were not yet household words. An exquisite Chinese rug covered the polished wood floor, an ebony boule commode with a beautiful serpentine front stood in one corner, a plinth displaying a bronze bust occupied another. Although the velvet window drapes had not yet been drawn, the lamps in their delicate apricot shades had been lit to give the room a golden glow and in the hearth a log fire blazed a cheerful welcome.

As they entered Kirsty gasped a groan of mock horror.

'Oh my goodness – more scones!'

Clearly Grace had indeed heard Sarah arrive home. The sofa had been drawn up close to the fire and before it a small table had been laid with a plate of dainty sandwiches, a cut-and-come-again fruit cake and a dish piled high with buttered scones. A crock of thick yellow cream and a dish of home-made strawberry jam was close by.

Sarah sat down thankfully on the sofa and indicated that Kirsty should join her.

'I'm sure you can manage some more, darling. Though I must admit all I want is a nice cup of tea.'

'And here we are, Mrs Bailey! I had the kettle singing on

the hob ready for you.' As if by magic Grace appeared in the doorway bearing a heavy silver tray which held a gleaming Georgian tea service. She set it down on the second of the small tables which stood ready and waiting. 'Would you like me to pour for you, Ma'am? If you don't mind me saying so I reckon you could do with it. You look all in to me.'

'Thank you, Grace, that would be very nice. And yes, I am tired. It was a long meeting.'

She reached for a small linen napkin and spread it over the softly pleated skirt of her deep blue dress, then sipped gratefully at the searingly hot tea which Grace poured into the fine porcelain cups. As the housekeeper left the room she became aware that Kirsty was looking at her anxiously.

'Grace is right, Granny,' Kirsty said, her voice concerned. 'You *do* look all in. Are you sure you haven't been overdoing things?'

'No, darling, I haven't. You know they don't allow me to these days. Your Uncle Roderick is very firm about that.'

'Quite right too,' Kirsty said vehemently. 'But something *is* wrong, isn't it? I can tell just by looking at you. What is it? Did something happen this afternoon?'

Sarah hesitated, on the point of denying it, then changed her mind. It would be nice to talk to somebody about her worries and who better than Kirsty? There was nothing she could do to help of course but the very fact that she was one step removed from the machinations of the business and not directly involved as most of the family were made her an ideal confidante. And she would have to know sooner or later. They all would.

Sarah set down her cup and the slight tremble in her hand made it rattle against the saucer.

'Yes, darling, something did happen. Or, to be more precise, I was informed of something that might be *going* to happen.' She hesitated. 'There is talk of a merger, Kirsty.'

'A merger? Morse Bailey?'

Sarah smiled in spite of herself. 'Of course. Who else?'

11

'Whew!' Kirsty's breath came out in a soft whistle. 'Who are they proposing to merge with?'

'That's just it,' Sarah said. 'To be truthful I would look very carefully at *any* merger. Morse Bailey is quite big enough in my opinion.' And that was no more than the truth, she thought wryly – besides the parent company there was Morse Bailey Aero Engines and Morse Bailey Air Speed as well as the Canadian, Australian and South African companies. 'No, I wouldn't be very happy about any further involvements,' she repeated, 'but in this particular case it's the company it is proposed we should merge with that is worrying me.'

'Well?' Kirsty persisted. The scones and sandwiches were forgotten now; she sat tensely on the edge of her sofa regarding her grandmother with a piercing gaze. 'Who is it, Granny?'

'De Vere Motors,' Sarah said simply.

Kirsty's blue eyes widened still further. 'De Vere Motors? You mean *Leo* de Vere's company?'

'The same,' Sarah said and added drily, 'is there another de Vere?'

'But they make motor cars,' Kirsty protested.

'Yes. It hardly makes sense, does it? At least not in my opinion. But Guy disagrees. He's very keen to push it through – and he has enough sway to do it. Quite apart from his own voting shares and the others he can carry along with him he has his mother's proxy to vote with her shares in any way he thinks fit. It's years since Alicia has taken any active interest in the running of the company. That gives him power. Using Alicia's shares in concert with his own he can outvote me and the real support I can count on any time he chooses. It's been worrying me for some time though he has never before proposed anything which I felt really detrimental to the company. I have always been able to accept his decisions as in our best interests. This is different. I'm totally opposed to it, Kirsty.'

'I should think so!' Kirsty raised a slender, long-fingered hand to brush her light brown hair behind one ear in a gesture which betrayed the sense of shock she was experiencing. 'As you say any merger is something that needs really careful consideration. But merger with Leo de Vere . . . it's unthinkable! How can he *do* it?'

'Very easily by the sound of it,' Sarah said wryly. 'I had heard rumours that Guy had been seen with Leo – dining with him at his club, that sort of thing. But I discounted it as mere idle gossip. Now it seems I should have taken more notice. Guy is in Leo's pocket – not a doubt of it. I don't know what Leo has promised him if the deal goes through, but it must be good. A seat on the board at de Vere Motors, certainly, and more too if I'm not mistaken. Guy would never sacrifice his autonomous position at Morse Bailey unless he was getting something even bigger in return. But whatever the deal is, whatever he promises, you can be sure of one thing. The end result will be the same – Leo de Vere will effectively gain control of Morse Bailey, just as he's always wanted, with Guy as his puppet. That is how serious the situation is, Kirsty.' She shook her head slowly, her lips a tight-drawn line. 'My God, your grandfather and great-grandfather would turn in their graves if they knew about it. Leo de Vere back in Morse Bailey – and in a position of power that even they never dreamed of. With him at the helm it would be the end of the company as we know it, make no mistake of that.'

Kirsty sat silent for a moment, lost in thought. She knew very little about Leo de Vere, except that he was the step-son of Gilbert Morse, founder of the Morse Bailey empire. The Morse and Bailey family trees were complex and intertwined and their feuds did not help matters, cutting off some of the members of the family altogether. Leo de Vere fell into this category. For as long as she could remember Kirsty had noticed that Leo de Vere was spoken of in scathing tones or not at all, and though like every other citizen of the United Kingdom she had heard of de Vere Motors she had been almost grown up before she had realized he was actually related in some way. What she did know, of course, was that he was rich and powerful – and that practically everyone she held dear hated him. On the occasions when she had seen him on television, discussing

13

business, or when his photograph had been in the newspapers as it often was, she had looked at him curiously, marvelling that the handsome old man with the aristocratic face and thick snowy white hair could inspire such hatred. Leo de Vere did not look like a monster. He did not even look like a prominent businessman, but more like an aging nobleman or exiled prince whose throne in some obscure state had been snatched by revolutionaries. Yet hate him they did, including her beloved grandmother, who, in spite of her strong character and business acumen, was one of the kindest, most generous women alive.

Now, it seemed, there was a chink in the armour. There was one of the family who did not hate him, and that someone was Guy Bailey.

'What *did* happen when Leo was drummed out of the company?' she asked now. 'It couldn't have been that he wasn't good at his job, whatever that was. If he hadn't been good he couldn't have built up a successful company of his own. So what was it? What went wrong?'

Sarah made a small impatient gesture. 'Oh Kirsty it's much too long a story for me to go into now. And besides it all happened nearly fifty years ago. It's ancient history. Suffice it to say that this is what Leo has always wanted. I dare say he's spent the biggest part of his life scheming for it one way or another. He has always had to accept defeat before. Now, with Guy on his side, it looks as if he's about to get it.'

Kirsty thought for a moment. 'What about Uncle Max? Can't he help?'

Sarah's face softened slightly. Max Hurst, *Sir* Max nowadays, had always been her closest ally. He had been Adam's original partner; he had been in Morse Bailey from the beginning. But Max was an old man now. That was the trouble. They were all growing older – those that were left.

'Max has been very sick,' she said. 'He's never really recovered from that last bout of pneumonia. And though I'm sure he'll vote with me his shares are not sufficient to make any difference. No, I'm afraid there's nothing Max can do to help.'

For a moment Kirsty sat turning it over, then she spread her hands eloquently. 'I don't believe you'll lose Morse Bailey now, Granny,' she said. 'You'll think of something.'

'That's what I keep telling myself. But so far I have come up with only one solution.'

'There you are, Granny!' Kirsty said triumphantly. 'One solution is all you need – provided it works.'

'Exactly,' Sarah said drily. 'I should save your enthusiasm, Kirsty, until you've heard what it is.'

'Well – go on.'

Sarah touched her hand to her forehead. Suddenly she was feeling tired again.

'I shall have to appeal to Alicia,' she said. She raised her eyes and caught the shocked surprise reflected in Kirsty's face.

'Aunt Alicia? But you haven't spoken to one another for years and years. Not since . . .' she broke off, not wanting to re-open old wounds and Sarah let the sentence hang unfinished in the air.

'That was only the last straw,' she said at last. 'Alicia and I never got on.' She paused, thinking what an understatement *that* was. Never got on . . . bland words to mask a lifetime of resentment and rivalry that had finally culminated in bitter hatred. Alicia, whom she had wronged and who had wronged her in a hundred ways; Alicia, whom she had once admired and envied until attitudes and events had alienated the two women for ever. . . . Well, there was no point raking over old coals now. 'I can see no other way,' she went on slowly. 'As I say, Alicia has given Guy proxy to vote with her shares any way he thinks fit. But she wouldn't want this merger any more than I do. She loathes Leo, just as I do. And if I could persuade her to come to the meeting and throw in her voting shares with mine, then we could carry the day. Alicia and I still have sixty per cent between us – that was the way Gilbert intended it.' She smiled wearily. 'He was a wily old bird, you know, Kirsty. Perhaps he realised that one day just such a situation as this might arise. No, Alicia is the only one who can help me. I think after all this time I have to swallow my pride and ask for her assistance.'

15

Kirsty shook her head. She looked as worried now as her grandmother.

'She'll refuse to see you,' she said. 'She will, Granny. And even if she *did* see you – well, just think how upsetting it would be for you.'

'Not half as upsetting as seeing the company that has been my life fall into the hands of the one person its founders would never contemplate in a position of power,' Sarah said decisively. 'I've been in upsetting situations before, Kirsty. I've survived – and I'll survive again. It would be worth it, just as long as I can persuade Alicia to my point of view.'

Kirsty remained unconvinced.

'How can you hope to talk her round even if you do see her?' she demanded. 'Guy will have her on his side – he's bound to. He is her son, after all. She'll want to do whatever is best for him.'

'That is a possibility, yes,' Sarah admitted. 'Alicia dotes on Guy, it's true. But when she hears what I have to say she may change her mind. Morse Bailey is bigger than any of us. We *are* Morse Bailey – you must see that.'

'Yes, but will Alicia?' Kirsty asked. 'Even if she does agree to see you, surely the fact she hates you will go against her giving you any support? Why, she may go along with the merger simply to spite you, if for no other reason.'

'That is a chance I shall have to take,' Sarah said crisply. She glanced down at her tea, gone cold now while they talked. 'Pour me a fresh cup, Kirsty, there's a good girl, and have one yourself. And for heaven's sake do try to eat some of these sandwiches or Grace will be terribly hurt.'

'I couldn't eat a thing now, Granny. I feel far too choky,' Kirsty declared, but she poured fresh cups of tea and as Sarah sipped hers she began to feel her energy returning.

'You're not to let this upset you, Kirsty,' she admonished. 'I shouldn't have burdened you with my worries.'

'I'm glad you did, Granny. No wonder you look so tired. Oh, when I think of it . . .'

'It will be all right, Kirsty. It has to be. Now, let's forget it, shall we?'

Kirsty was silent for a moment and with some surprise Sarah thought she had acquiesced. But the thoughtful look was still there in her blue eyes and a moment later she said: 'There may be another way, Granny.'

'Another way? What do you mean?'

'Maybe if *I* talked to Guy . . .'

'*You*?' Sarah said in astonishment. 'What could *you* do?'

'I'm not sure. But I think Guy likes me.' Kirsty's face had gone very pale but there were high spots of colour burning in her cheeks. 'In fact I'm sure he does. He's made that plain on more than one occasion.'

'*Guy* has?' Sarah exclaimed. 'But he's old enough to be your father!'

'I know. Unfortunately – or maybe fortunately – he has something of a penchant for much younger women,' Kirsty said drily. 'You'll just have to take my word for it, Granny.'

'But you've never so much as mentioned this before, Kirsty!' Sarah said, shocked. 'You mean Guy has actually – made advances to you?'

Kirsty shrugged, adopting her woman-of-the-world pose, though those high spots of colour in her cheeks belied her attitude. 'I wouldn't put it quite that strongly. But I think I might be able to influence him, yes.'

'Well I absolutely forbid you to do anything of the kind!' Sarah stormed. 'It's a dreadful thing to suggest!'

Kirsty's flush deepened. 'Just now *you* were ready to do the unthinkable in a good cause.'

'My dear child, that is quite different! I wouldn't dream of allowing you to compromise yourself with Guy. Even if I thought it would do any good, which I'm quite certain it would not. Guy might like his fling but he is a businessman through and through, ruthless where his ambitions are concerned. He might make you promises if he thought it would get him anywhere with you but it's almost certain he would fail to keep them. For goodness sake, Kirsty, put such a notion right out of your head or you really *will* upset me.'

Kirsty said nothing.

'Promise me!' Sarah demanded.

'Oh very well,' Kirsty said, but her eyes did not meet her grandmother's and Sarah thought: she's not so easily dissuaded. She is as wilful and headstrong as I was when I was her age – and she's worried about me. Oh, why did I tell her? Why didn't I keep it to myself, at least until I'd exhausted every possible avenue?

Kirsty finished her tea and set down the cup.

'I'm going to have to go, Granny. I hate to leave you like this but . . .'

Sarah nodded. 'I know. You expected to spend the afternoon with me, not half the evening. Have you got a date?' she asked, hoping still to forestall the nonsense of any ideas Kirsty might still have about Guy.

Kirsty laughed. 'Not in the way you mean it. But a crowd of us are going to a Blues Session down in the Cellar Bars.'

Sarah wrinkled her nose. 'That sounds perfectly dreadful, but I dare say you'll enjoy it. Anyway, sad as I am to see you go, I suppose I musn't sit too long over tea either. As I said earlier I have a dinner party tonight and there are still one thousand and one things to see to.'

'And you need a rest first too,' Kirsty said solicitously. 'Don't worry, Granny, I'll see myself out. My little Mini is parked around at the back.' She dropped a kiss on Sarah's forehead. 'Take care, Granny. And don't worry too much. I'm sure everything will work out.'

'Yes. Drive carefully, darling. And come and see me again soon.'

'I will.'

When Kirsty had gone and Sarah had watched her little white Mini disappear up the drive she stood for a moment at the window looking out at the falling dusk. How beautiful it all was – the grey misty light softening the curve of the hills, the daffodils making splashes of brightness beneath the trees whose bare branches were, she thought, beginning to sprout tender green. Out in the deer park the small herd clustered together; from the grass a single magpie rose, shiny black and white, flapping up with lazy grace. One magpie. The old adage rose unbidden in her mind: One for sorrow, two for joy . . .

Oh what nonsense! Sarah thought. Luck does not depend on magpies! Luck depends mainly on our own actions.

For a moment the events of the afternoon weighed heavily upon her once more, then with a determined movement she shrugged them off.

If before she had been determined to save Morse Bailey now she had an extra reason – one which demanded urgent attention. She must do what she had to do quickly and so forestall any stupid heroics on the part of her beloved granddaughter.

With a decisive step, her arthritic knee forgotten, Sarah left the dining-room and crossed the hall to the study. Settling herself in the big comfortable swivel chair she reached for the leather covered address file and opened it to the page she required.

Strange that Alicia's number should still be listed here though it was so many years since she had spoken to her. It was almost as if she had subconsciously known she would need it one day.

Drawing a deep breath Sarah reached for the telephone.

She knew what she had to do. She supposed she had known ever since the meeting.

Though the tension was singing in her ears her fingers were quite steady as she began to dial.

Chapter Two

Alicia, Countess von Brecht, had already finished afternoon tea when the telephone rang in her Kensington town-house. Its shrill insistent note carried up the staircase to the small sitting-room where she sat in one of a matching pair of wing chairs idly smoking a Black Russian cigarette and stroking the ball of soft fawn fur which was curled up on her knee. Ming was her Pekinese and the term lap-dog might have been coined especially for her. Until Guy, Alicia's son, had given her Ming as a birthday present four years earlier, Alicia had had little time for small dogs, preferring the labradors and retrievers which had always been part of the scene when she had lived in the country but which would have made impractical pets in the heart of London. But after her initial reservation she had simply fallen in love with Ming. She was so intelligent and affectionate and her small pushed-up face made Alicia feel fiercely protective towards her.

'She's my baby,' she would say self-deprecatingly to friends who came to visit and remarked on the fact that they had never seen Alicia and Ming separated for more than a few minutes, but in truth it was more than that. Alicia's life had been marred by a series of turbulent relationships; Ming was an outlet for all her frustrated affection, a living creature who was excellent company and loving friend, who demanded little more than warmth, comfort and love – and the most tempting delicacies Fortnum and Mason could provide. Ming was a far more satisfactory companion than either of her husbands had been, Alicia often thought, for Adam Bailey, with whom she had fallen in love when she was no more than a girl, had been far more interested in producing and flying aeroplanes than he ever had been in her and the Count von Brecht, whom she had married after the collapse of her union with Adam, had been a wastrel whose taste for the high life had almost ruined them. Whereas Ming . . .

Alicia's heart softened with love. She stretched out a be-ringed scarlet tipped hand and extracted a chocolate from the box which stood open on the small pedestal table beside her chair. She seldom ate chocolates herself but Ming adored them; the hand-made Belgian confections had been purchased especially for her. Alicia offered Ming a rum truffle and the dog took it delicately from her fingers without the least suggestion of a greedy snatch.

'Good baby,' Alicia cooed. 'Did you like that?'

For answer Ming snuffled gently in her hand and Alicia reached for another chocolate.

Behind her the sitting-room door opened and Irene, her maid, entered the room.

'Telephone, Madam, for you.' Her voice was stiff and deferential; Alicia had never chosen to encourage the slightest hint of familiarity with her servants.

'Who is it?' Alicia asked, holding the second chocolate within reach of Ming's eager mouth.

'I don't know, Madam. They wouldn't say.'

Alicia raised one well-defined eyebrow a fraction.

'How very odd. Is it a man or a woman?'

'A woman, Madam. A *lady*, if her voice is anything to go by.'

The eyebrow arched a shade higher and Alicia stood up, tucking Ming beneath her left arm.

'Thank you, Irene, I'll take the call in here.'

She set her Black Russian down in the bell-boy ashtray and crossed to where the telephone sat on the bureau in front of the window, a slender woman in well-tailored grey slacks and a coral blouse. Alicia was now seventy-five years old but she had retained the striking looks of her youth; her hair, which had once been so black, shining and straight that one of her more romantic suitors had likened it to a raven's wing, was twisted into a sleek chignon at the base of her neck and was streaked only lightly with grey where it was strained tightly away from her temples; her forehead was remarkably unlined – perhaps a lifetime of that severe

21

style had helped to keep it smooth and taut. The coral of the blouse, the collar of which was finished in a large soft bow to hide the slight crepiness of her neck, flattered her pale skin, as did the matching lipstick which defined the slightly too-thin lines of her mouth, and only the web of fine lines around her eyes and the deep creases linking nose and mouth undeniably showed the passage of the years.

It had often been said that Alicia looked a little like a retired prima ballerina and because such an idea flattered and amused her she had decided to play the role to the full.

Now she reached for the telephone, waited a moment until the door had closed after Irene, and then spoke into it.

'Alicia von Brecht.'

'Alicia. I expect this will be something of a surprise to you.' The voice was familiar yet not immediately recognisable, a teasing echo of the past. 'It's Sarah.'

Breath seemed to catch in Alicia's throat. My God, she thought, I don't believe it. Someone is playing a joke on me.

'Sarah?' she said woodenly. 'Sarah Bailey?'

'Yes, I'm sorry to spring myself on you unannounced but I thought it was the best way.'

It's not a joke, thought Alicia. It *is* Sarah. A small tremor of shock ran through her and with it a stab of annoyance that her composure could be so completely shattered and the beginnings of something very like outrage. How dare Sarah telephone without warning, after all this time, in spite of all that had happened between them? How dare she cheat her way into Alicia's private sitting-room? Small wonder she had declined to give her name to Irene. She must have known Alicia would certainly have refused her call had she announced herself.

'What do you want, Sarah?' she asked, her tone icy.

There was the slightest of hesitations at the other end of the line and Alicia felt Sarah's reluctance to begin as an almost tangible entity. Her confidence grew and sensing an opportunity to dominate her old adversary she demanded haughtily: 'Are you still there, Sarah?'

Her attack brought immediate response. 'Of course I am, Alicia.' No hint of hesitation in Sarah's voice now. It was the old Sarah, firm, determined, confident. Sarah the go-getter, Alicia thought, surprising herself by her own bitterness.

'Well?'

'I must confess this isn't easy after so long,' Sarah said disarmingly. 'And I'm well aware I've taken you by surprise. However, I think it's insulting to you to waste your time on too many preliminaries so I'll come straight to the point. I wanted to ask if you would be prepared to meet me.'

Alicia froze and she was gripped by an overwhelming feeling of revulsion. She had no desire to see Sarah ever again and she had thought Sarah felt the same way. For a moment words escaped her and into the silence Sarah said: 'Something has happened, Alicia – something which makes it imperative that we talk.'

Alicia found her voice. 'What could we possibly have to say to one another?' she demanded.

'I really would prefer not to discuss it over the telephone for all sorts of reasons. It's something which needs to be talked about face to face. That's why I was hoping you would agree to meet me, though I realise it is asking a great deal.' Sarah's voice was level, utterly calm and reasonable, but it only served to infuriate Alicia still further.

'I'm sorry, Sarah, but you cannot seriously expect me to see you after all this time without having a single inkling of the reason for it,' she said decisively.

There was another slight pause then Sarah said briskly: 'Very well, Alicia. It's about the business. I want to talk to you about Morse Bailey.'

'I have nothing to do with the business these days,' Alicia snapped, surprised and irritated. 'Guy deals with my interests. You must know that.'

'Yes, I'm aware of it,' Sarah countered smoothly. 'But this is something I think you should know about before it's too late.'

'Are you implying there is something my son is keeping from me?'

'I'm not implying anything. I'm simply saying it's vital

that we should be able to talk. Oh Alicia, I know we've not been the best of friends these past years. But I beg you, in the interests of Morse Bailey, please agree to meet me. I'm willing to travel up to London to put you to the least possible inconvenience and I'll meet you wherever and whenever you choose. Only please don't refuse. This is too important to both of us.'

In spite of herself Alicia was aware of a twist of curiosity. Sarah Bailey – begging to see her? Sarah, who to her knowledge had never begged for anything in her life? Stolen, perhaps. Taken wealth and power – yes and people – to whom she had no right. But *begged*? It was totally foreign to her nature.

What the hell can it be that is so important to her? Alicia wondered. But the antagonisms of the past were still too strong, the pattern too indelibly set, to be ignored.

'I'm sorry, Sarah, but I don't wish to meet you,' Alicia said with cold decision.

'Alicia . . .'

'That is my last word on the matter,' Alicia snapped, 'except to say I do not appreciate you contacting me in this arbitrary manner. I trust I make myself clear. Goodbye, Sarah.'

She replaced the receiver with a thud and only then realised her hand was trembling. Tucked still into the crook of her arm Ming shifted restlessly as if she was aware of her mistress's change of mood and Alicia set her down on the sofa and crossed the room to her own chair. The Black Russian had burnt down now; Alicia stubbed it out, took another from the rosewood cigarette box and lit it, drawing deeply on the strong-tasting smoke. She felt shaken, more shaken than she could remember feeling in years. But that was hardly surprising. To take a telephone call, totally unprepared, and to hear Sarah's voice . . . after all this time. The sheer bare-faced nerve of the woman was breathtaking. Alicia sat down, stood up again and crossed to the window, looking out into the fading light of the March evening, at the familiar skyline of roofs and chimney pots silhouetted dark against the misting grey sky, and saw

only the face the years had taught her to hate. Sarah Bailey
–Sarah Thomas as she had been when Alicia had first set
eyes on her, beautiful, bold, determined. Sarah who had
come into her life as unexpectedly as this afternoon's
telephone call and taken as her right everything she had
wanted.

Abruptly, Alicia turned away from the window. It was
dim inside now. She crossed to the door, flicked the light
switch and three pairs of wall lights came on, illuminating
the room with soft brightness. A slightly austere room,
perhaps, but this was the way Alicia liked it – the walls and
drapes a rich rust red, the wall-to-wall carpet palest beige.
When she and her husband the Count had first bought the
house it had been filled to overflowing with the various
pieces he had loved to collect – oriental china and jade, an
ivory elephant from India, an ornate French anniversary
clock, Victorian bric-a-brac, some bought at auction for
thousands of pounds, some picked up for a song in out of
the way antique shops and stalls in Petticoat Lane or the
Portobello Road. Alicia had found the collection claustro-
phobic and she had not been sorry as the pieces disappeared, one by one, to pay for her husband's gambling
debts. It was for her the one saving grace of his addiction.
Klaus may have come close to ruining them; at least it
meant she no longer had to live surrounded by what she
regarded as clutter.

For the most part of course his degeneration into virtual
mania had been something of a nightmare, his physical and
mental deterioration causing her as much pain as his
increasingly manic behaviour. Towards the end she had
rarely seen him – he was at his various gaming clubs and
casinos from the time they opened their doors until the
small hours and he would then sleep until well into the
afternoon. But he had not always been able to keep from her
the demands of his creditors, although it was only after his
death that the full scale of his losses had become apparent to
her.

Why did I marry him? Alicia wondered sometimes – and
told herself it was one more disaster that could be laid at

Sarah's door. Alicia had been lonely, more hurt than she would ever admit, and Klaus had been charming, the perfect Teutonic gentleman, last in line of one of the oldest and noblest German families. He had kept his penchant for excesses well hidden from her until it was too late. But at least marrying him had helped her to salvage something of her fierce pride. No-one in the family, with the exception of Guy, her son, had known what a disastrous mistake she had made, and at least Klaus had had the decency to die before completely devouring her personal fortune.

Poor Klaus, she had thought in moments when his charm was clearer in her memory than his vices, he had not been a happy man. To the end he had missed his beloved fatherland; perhaps it was homesickness that had driven him to drink and gamble and find solace in the arms of as many different women as possible. But the fact that he had been estranged from his family for many years pointed to some old indiscretion of which she knew nothing and she was aware that to make excuses for his behaviour was like making excuses for Old Nick himself.

Klaus's death had brought her freedom and she had made up her mind she would never lose it again. Men had brought her nothing but trouble, husbands were a source of unhappiness and disillusion. As if to exorcise Klaus forever she had disposed of as much of his collection as his creditors had left and the town-house had ceased to be an oppressive place. Furnished in the way in which she liked it, run on the ordered lines which suited her, Alicia had begun to feel that at least now, in what might have been her declining years, she was mistress of her own fate. Her business interests, which had always bored and irritated her, she had turned over to Guy, her son, and she occupied her time now with her small circle of friends and the charity work which had become her life. Her name appeared as patron on the headed notepaper of countless charities, she headed at least half a dozen committees and her home was thrown open several times a year for coffee mornings and the private soirées for which she was famous to raise funds for her favourite causes.

All in all it seemed to her that at last she had put the past behind her, successfully eliminating every link with events – and people – who had caused her pain.

Now, in the space of a few brief minutes, old wounds had been reopened and the past was with her once again, sharp and painful as it had ever been, invading the present and digging with deep and tenacious claws into the fragile fabric of her peace.

For a few minutes Alicia moved restlessly about the room, drawing deeply on her cigarette and returning occasionally to tap ash into the bell-boy ashtray – one of the few pieces of Klaus's collection which she had retained. The bell-boy stood waist high, his painted outstretched arm proffering a small brass receptacle as he had proffered it to the patrons of some high-class Victorian establishment, standing on the pavement in all winds and weathers like the figurehead on the prow of a ship. She had an affection for the bell-boy which she could not explain; his shiny black face and jaunty pillbox hat amused her. He was a silent ally, she sometimes felt; his presence in the room was as comforting as that of Ming and even less demanding.

Alicia returned to him now, stubbing out the second Black Russian in the brass tray and running her fingers lightly across the hard line of his shoulder. Two Black Russians in the space of one hour. She would have to curb herself. Living with the Count had taught her to despise excesses and she would no more tolerate them in herself than in others. But today was something of an exception. Had she been a drinking woman Alicia felt she would probably have poured herself a large stiff whisky or gin. But she was not a drinking woman. She relied on the cigarettes to calm her jangling nerves and if they did that then where was the harm in one more than her usual allocation?

The trouble was that the extra cigarette had not calmed her. She was still tight-drawn and edgy; she could feel the tendons stretched taut in her neck and shoulders and her mind was racing.

Why? Why had Sarah telephoned? Why did she want to see her? All very well to dismiss her summarily – now that her initial anger was subsiding curiosity was creeping in once more and with it a sense of foreboding that settled in her stomach in a hard tight knot. For some reason Sarah had been prepared to humble herself, though humility and Sarah were not compatible. And she had said it was to do with Morse Bailey.

Alicia touched her fingers to her forehead, smoothing it up and out between those dark arched brows.

Purely as a business she had little or no interest in Morse Bailey. An aircraft empire spanning the world it might be but talk of expansion and profit margins, full order books and foreign co-operation deals had always left her cold. As for the intrigues and the boardroom squabbles, she had found them energy-sapping as well as time consuming, and she had been only too happy to abdicate responsibility to her son. Let Guy do what he thought best; he knew far more about the day-to-day running and the epoch-making decisions than she ever had. He was Managing Director – let him manage.

But on another quite different level Alicia was aware of Morse Bailey as a powerful force which had shaped her world – and an enduring monument to Gilbert Morse, her father, and Adam Bailey, who had been her first husband. They had created this empire and in turn the empire had created them – put their names at the forefront of aviation along with de Havilland and Shorts, the White family of Bristol Aeroplane Company fame and Hawker Siddeley, and made them legends in their own lifetime. For as long as she could remember now, it seemed, Morse Bailey had been more, far more, than simply a company or group of companies. It was an entity which in spite of her indifference to its daily machinations nevertheless remained so close to her heart that its well being was essential to her very existence.

It was years since it had even crossed her mind that Morse Bailey might be in any kind of trouble. Now the thought wormed its way into her consciousness and nagged like an aching tooth. Sarah had said something was wrong at Morse Bailey and unless the whole thing was a gigantic ploy it must be something serious to warrant her holding out an olive branch after all this time. If that was the case then Alicia wanted to know about it. Sarah was the one person left who felt as she did. The one person to whom Morse Bailey was far more than a great profit-making machine.

For a moment longer Alicia stood deep in thought then she reached for the telephone again. She would not be able to rest until she had got to the bottom of this, she knew, and for the first time in years she regretted that she lived in London, so far from the hub of the family empire. Not that the regret would last long, of course. Alicia loved the vitality of the city; though she seldom took advantage of the high life it could offer nowadays she was energised by the electric impulse which it seemed to her filled the air, crackling and buzzing beneath the ceiling of grey cloud as if it was the accumulated emission of a million busy brains and active bodies, the adrenaline of the masses released to short circuit and flash until it could once more be harnessed to the great machine of human kind. The country had always made her feel mummified; she experienced no sense of peace alone in an idyllic landscape. Born and raised in the heart of Somerset Alicia had known from the outset that she was a city girl at heart. Bristol had brought her to life; London even more so. No, she could not bear to bury herself in a soft green grave again, even if it did mean she had more immediate contact with her only son.

Alicia glanced at her watch, thought for a moment, then dialled the number of the office. The switchboard would be closed down by now but Guy always insisted his line was left plugged through to his office for he often worked late into the evening.

Thinking of Guy, Alicia experienced a slight pang. She would have liked to picture Guy leaving the office to go home to a caring wife and adoring children. Astute businessman he might be but Guy had always been quite incapable of managing his private life. He needed someone to love and care for him. But Guy's marriage, to a young WAAF he had met during his war service, had failed – doomed from the beginning, Alicia had always thought,

29

though she had the grace to acknowledge that she was not the best person to judge, with two failed marriages of her own.

She stood holding the receiver and listening to the clicks and buzzes on the line, then the sound of the telephone ringing unanswered in the offices of Morse Bailey. Another minute and I'll put the phone down and try him at home, Alicia thought. Her finger hovered over the receiver rest ready to disconnect; then there was a click and a girl's voice came on the line.

'Hello – Mr Bailey's office.' She sounded slightly breathless.

'I'd like to speak to Mr Bailey, please,' Alicia said.

'Oh I'm sorry. The office is closed now. If you'd like to call again in the morning . . .'

'Mr Bailey is there, is he not?'

'Well yes, but . . .' the girl sounded flustered. 'I'm not sure whether he is available. Who is that?'

'The Countess von Brecht,' Alicia said shortly. 'I am sure Mr Bailey will speak to me.'

'Oh – oh yes, of course . . .' The poor girl sounded more flustered than ever but Alicia felt no spark of sympathy for her. These flippertyjibbet office types thought they could get by on a pretty face and a handful of certificates in shorthand and typewriting. They had no idea of social graces. None. And Guy's latest acquisition was unlikely to learn any letting him chase her around the office when the rest of the staff had gone home. Good gracious, he ought to know better!

She tapped the telephone impatiently with her thumb nail, waiting.

'Hello, Mother.' Well at least *he* did not sound out of breath, she thought. Probably the game of squash he played regularly twice a week kept him in trim for other strenuous activities. 'You were lucky to catch me. Another minute and I should have left.'

Liar, she thought. Aloud she said: 'I thought I'd try the office first. I know what a fiend you are for working late.'

'You know Morse Bailey, Mother. There's always work to catch up on.'

'I do indeed. I'm only glad I'm not the one who has to spend long hours sorting it all out.'

'Mother . . .' Guy hesitated, 'I don't want to rush you but I do have a great deal to get through here before I can go home. Did you have some special reason for calling or is this just a social chat?'

'I had a reason.'

'What? Nothing is wrong is it, Mother?'

'I certainly hope not.'

'Then why?'

'I had a telephone call just now, Guy, which I must admit took me totally by surprise. It was Sarah Bailey.'

'Sarah?' She knew she had his full attention now. He sounded as shocked as she herself had been. 'What did she say?'

'Very little except that she wants me to meet her. There's something she wants to talk to me about.'

'Good God, Mother, you're not going to, are you? Meet her, I mean?'

'I refused of course,' Alicia said. 'She had intimated to me that whatever it was she wanted to talk to me about was connected with Morse Bailey. I told her in no uncertain manner that you handle all my business affairs. Nevertheless I can't help wondering if there is anything I should know.'

'*Know*, Mother? What do you mean?' Alicia heard the slightly uncomfortable note in his voice and her lips tightened a shade. She did not like it when Guy blustered. It usually meant he was hiding something.

'What I mean, Guy, is – have you any idea why Sarah should be so anxious to see me?'

There was a slight hesitation. In the momentary silence she thought: There is something. 'Well?' she demanded.

'I think I know what might be on Sarah's mind,' he said smoothly. 'There was a bit of a disagreement at the board meeting this afternoon. Sarah, as usual, is out of line with the rest of us.'

'About what?'

'An expansion we have in mind,' he said glibly. 'It's not

31

even settled yet and you can take it from me we will only go for it if we believe it to be in the best interests of the company. Surely you know that, Mother?'

'What sort of expansion?'

'Mother – it's not easy to discuss this sort of thing over the telephone. One never knows who may be listening in.'

'You mean your line might be bugged? Oh surely not!'

'One can never be too careful these days. Industrial espionage is growing to epidemic proportions. Didn't you read the case the other day . . .'

'Guy!' Alicia said sharply. 'If you are in a hurry I suggest we stick to the topic of Sarah.'

'Sarah!' Guy exploded vehemently. 'That woman is nothing but a damned nuisance, Mother, and has been for as long as I can remember. It's time she retired and left the business to those of us who know what we are doing. As for telephoning you – she's simply trying to make trouble.'

'And you are quite certain that what she wanted to tell me isn't something I should know?'

'Don't you trust me, Mother?' Guy demanded.

'Guy, I have trusted you with my voting shares for the last ten years . . .'

'So why are you questioning me now – on the instigation of a woman with whom you wouldn't normally even pass the time of day! Now promise me you'll put this right out of your mind and leave it all to me. And I shall have words with Mrs Sarah Bailey when next I see her and tell her that if she bothers you again she will have me to reckon with.'

'Very well, Guy,' Alicia said. 'I'll leave you to get on with your work now. But you must understand I had to know.'

'I don't see why, Mother. But still, as long as I've set your mind at rest. Just forget Sarah ever telephoned. And tell Irene to be sure not to put any more of her calls through to you.'

'I'll do that.'

'Good. I'll see you soon, Mother.'

'See you soon.'

She replaced the receiver but stood motionless, her fingers still resting on the cold black bakelite. A phone call to Guy should have satisfied her. On the contrary it had not.

Guy was keeping something from her, she was certain of it. His initial discomfort, his anger at Sarah, the glib way he had tried to turn the conversation, his insistence that she should not communicate with Sarah again – oh without a doubt there was something. Hopefully it was of little importance; as Guy had said Sarah was perfectly capable of blowing up some quite trivial disagreement to suit her own ends. But why had Guy been so unwilling to discuss it?

Alicia shook her head. Far from feeling satisfied she was more anxious than ever and the anxiety was a tight knot in her stomach. She reached for yet another Black Russian and lit it. Then she lifted the telephone once more.

She knew what she was going to do. Perhaps she was mad; perhaps she would live to regret this. But she had no intention of being deliberately kept in the dark, by Guy or anyone.

The number, unchanged through all the years, was still there in her memory. She dialled it and stood smoking while she waited. When the maid answered she was ready.

'I would like to speak to Mrs Bailey,' she said calmly. 'You can tell her the Countess von Brecht is returning her call.'

Chapter Three

'Mrs Bailey. What a pleasure to see you!'

The head waiter at Rules Restaurant, just off the Strand, greeted Sarah warmly. Sarah invariably dined at Rules when she was in town. She loved its atmosphere of gentility and its aura of history, loved the impeccable service she could be sure of getting there – and loved the memories it held for her.

When Alicia had telephoned to agree to the meeting she had at once suggested Rules as the venue for she liked the feeling of being on home ground. With a meeting as difficult as this one was likely to be it could prove a distinct advantage.

'I have reserved your usual table, Mrs Bailey,' the head waiter fluttered around her solicitously. 'May I take your coat?'

Sarah allowed him to relieve her of her cashmere coat. Beneath it she was wearing a softly tailored Chanel suit in a light navy; the pink flounced bow at the neckline lent a little colour to her pale cheeks.

'It was a table for two, I believe,' the head waiter murmured.

'Yes, my guest will be joining me shortly.' Sarah cast a quick apprehensive look past the head waiter as the thought occurred to her: perhaps Alicia was already here. There was no-one at her regular table, no sign of the autocratic old lady whose very presence commanded attention. Sarah experienced a moment's relief. She wanted to be composed and ready when Alicia arrived.

'May I ask . . . ?' the head waiter ventured.

Sarah hesitated. He must be aware that she and Alicia had not met either privately or publicly for more than thirty years. But he would have to know sooner or later – perhaps it was better that it should be sooner.

34

'My guest is the Countess von Brecht,' she said evenly.

She saw the momentary gleam of shock in his eyes before it was eclipsed by his professionalism.

'I will tell her you are here as soon as she arrives, Mrs Bailey.'

As she was shown into the restaurant Sarah glanced back over her shoulder and saw him murmuring something to one of his staff. A tiny smile lifted the corner of her mouth. If she could discomfit the immovable head waiter at Rules by telling him who her guest was to be it was certain that Alicia's arrival would cause something of a stir amongst the other diners, many of whom would know, as he did, that the two women scarcely acknowledged one another's existence.

Already the restaurant was quite full; businessmen sipping aperitifs, a couple, no doubt on some discreet assignation, lost in one another's company, waiters hovering or gliding away with their orders. Sarah was aware of a moment's doubt. Had she made a mistake in suggesting such a public place for their discussion? She anticipated a frosty atmosphere between them – suppose instead things should become heated? But no, Alicia was too well-bred to make a scene. Far more likely she would think better of agreeing to the arrangement and not come at all.

'Would you care for an aperitif, Madam?' the waiter enquired.

On the point of ordering her usual sherry Sarah changed her mind. Today she could use something stronger, she thought.

'Gin and tonic,' she said. 'And a bottle of Perrier, please.'

The waiter departed and Sarah sat, her hands folded in her lap, trying not to watch the door. The gin and tonic arrived and she sipped it sparingly, aware that she needed a clear head for the encounter to come. The minutes ticked by and anxiety began to creep in. Was it possible Alicia *had* changed her mind and decided not to come? Sarah wondered fleetingly what her next move would be if that were the case, then pushed the thought away. Concentrate on now. Worry about other possibilities later.

The outer door opened and someone came in. From

where she was sitting Sarah could not see who it was, yet the small stir that ran around the restaurant gave her the answer. She straightened, setting her aperitif glass to one side and as she did so Alicia came into the restaurant.

Dear God, she hasn't changed one scrap! was Sarah's first startled thought. Tall, dark, elegant in stark black and emerald green, Alicia stood for a moment as if she knew that every eye was on her. Her full length mink she had left with the head waiter yet the aura of it still clung to her like the misting of Givenchy perfume, her face was expressionless except for the slight curve of her mouth, a set smile which did not reach her eyes. Without doubt Alicia still knew how to make an entrance!

Leaning slightly on the table to facilitate her arthritic knee Sarah rose and Alicia moved slowly towards her. It seemed to her the whole restaurant had fallen silent – or was it just a silence imposed on her by the pounding of blood behind her own eardrums?

'Alicia. I'm very glad you could come,' she said levelly.

The cool hazel eyes, so bright and hard they could have been chips of topaz, met hers, but she could read nothing in them.

'Sarah.' Nothing else – no word of greeting. She is not going to make it easy for me, Sarah thought.

'Won't you sit down, Alicia? Can I order you something to drink?'

'No thank you.' No hint of a smile. No grasping of the olive branch. But when she had seated herself on the opposite side of the table Alicia took out an embossed leather cigarette case and placed one of her favourite Black Russians between her scarlet painted lips. A waiter hurried forward with a light and Sarah thought: so she still smokes in moments of stress. She is as apprehensive as I am. The thought gave her heart.

A waiter approached the table to present them with menus.

'Shall we order?' Sarah suggested.

Alicia glanced briefly at the menu then lowered it to the table placing her hand upon it with a decisive gesture.

36

'No, I'd like to talk first if you don't mind. When I know why you wanted to see me I'll be ready to order.'

Sarah looked at the waiter but he had already taken his cue and merged into the background.

'As you like.' She fingered the stem of her glass but did not drink. 'As I told you on the telephone something has happened which I think you should know about.'

'You mean the proposed expansion?' Her eyes were laser sharp and watchful.

'Is that what you choose to call it?'

Alicia raised one eyebrow a fraction.

'What would *you* call it?'

'The Board call it a merger. Personally I would think the term "take-over" might be more apt.'

She saw the slightly veiled look come into those sharp amber eyes.

'Take-over? My dear Sarah, who on earth would attempt to take over Morse Bailey?'

Sarah lifted her head. Light from the overhead lamps gleamed on her soft silver hair.

'The one person who has always wanted just that, Alicia,' she said steadily. 'Leo de Vere.'

The moment the words were out she knew they had had just the impact she had intended. Alicia's immobile face appeared frozen, only the amber eyes widened slightly to give her an expression of incredulity.

'Leo de Vere?' All the old enmity was there in her tone as she repeated the hated name. If anything, Alicia loathed Leo de Vere even more than Sarah did. She had known him longer, resented him and his intrusion into her life before she and Sarah had even met.

'The same,' Sarah said levelly. 'He has come up with proposals for a merger, Alicia – but you and I both know that he would never be satisfied with that. Leo has never wanted anything but to gain control of Morse Bailey. It was his downfall once and he has had to wait a lifetime for his opportunity. Oh no, Leo will not be satisfied with anything less than total control and I thought you should know about it.'

37

'My God,' Alicia said. 'Guy . . .'

'Guy is backing him,' Sarah explained. 'You know what that means.'

There was silence for a moment as Alicia digested what Sarah had said.

'I can't believe that,' she said at last, taking out another Black Russian and lighting it from the stub of the first. 'Guy knows my feelings on the subject of Leo de Vere. He would never play into his hands.'

Involuntarily Sarah felt a stab of pity for Alicia. It was not pleasant to be betrayed by one's own children, especially when one doted on them as Alicia did on Guy. She had trusted him totally. I am destroying her, Sarah thought, but it has to be done. Morse Bailey and all it stands for is more important than any of us.

'I'm sorry, Alicia, but it is true,' she said simply. 'I don't know what Leo has offered him but I assure you Guy is backing the merger all the way – and backing it with your votes as well as his own. This is why I telephoned you. I was fairly confident you did not know what was going on and I believed you had a right to know.' Alicia said nothing, and gaining confidence Sarah went on: 'The only way for me to stop this going through was to appeal to you direct. Use your own votes, Alicia, in concert with mine. Together we can prevent Morse Bailey from falling into Leo de Vere's hands.'

For long moments Alicia remained motionless, so still she might have been carved in stone. Then, abruptly, she leaned forward, stubbing out her cigarette with a quick angry movement.

'What are you trying to do, Sarah? Drive a wedge between me and my son? My God, haven't you taken enough from me already? Do you want to take him from me too? Is that what is behind asking me here?'

'Of course not,' Sarah said quickly. 'I know how painful this is for you, Alicia, but . . .'

'Guy would never do such a thing – never!' Alicia stated with conviction.

'I'm sorry, Alicia, but he is doing it.'

'Then he must have some very good reason.'

'If there is then why hasn't he explained the position to you – asked your blessing on the merger?'

Alicia's fine nostrils flared. 'Quite likely he prefers not to have me worried by all this.'

'He knew such a move would upset you, you mean.'

'Exactly. But I am certain he would never give merger with Leo De Vere a second thought unless it was absolutely necessary.'

'Or unless it would advance his own career,' Sarah said – and regretted the rash words the moment they were out.

There was fury in Alicia's eyes. She pushed back her chair.

'I think, Sarah, that this meeting is at an end. I came here today against my better judgement because I thought it was possible that we might, after all these years, have something to say to one another. I never, for one moment, expected to hear you make wild accusations against my son. Surely even you should have known better than that?'

'Alicia, please!'

'As far as I am concerned, Guy makes the business decisions now and you should have known I would never align myself with you against him. If he believes merger with Leo de Vere is in the interests of the company then I am prepared to back his judgement. Perhaps he is less blinkered than we are. Perhaps it is time to forget what Leo did. It's the future that matters now – the future as Guy sees it. The past is dead and gone.'

Is it? Sarah thought, seeing the flame of hatred in Alicia's eyes and knowing it was for her. The past may be gone but it is certainly not dead – not as far as you and I are concerned. I must have been a fool to think even for a moment that it might be. But I can't give up Morse Bailey and all that it stands for. I must fight it to the bitter end.

'Alicia, please, will you at least think about what I've said?' she pleaded. 'Talk to Guy by all means. Ask him for his version of what he plans to do. But don't just hand Morse Bailey to Leo de Vere on a plate. It's not just the family heritage that is at stake, though heaven knows, when you think what it cost in blood and sweat to those who were very dear to us, that should be enough. But there's more – much more. You speak of the future. Have you thought what Leo would do? He could decimate Morse Bailey. Hundreds of jobs might be at stake as he creamed off our profits for the benefit of his own companies. He may want to move the head offices out of Bristol – hundreds more jobs, the daily bread of local people, as well as the whole history of Morse Bailey. I beg you, don't let this happen simply because it is me who is asking you – and you hate me. Try for once to forget our differences. Let us work, just this once, in harmony – the way Gilbert intended us to.'

For a brief moment she thought she saw a gleam of indecision in Alicia's eyes. Then the older woman rose.

'You'll excuse me if I don't stay to lunch with you, Sarah,' she said, her tone cold and level. 'I will talk to Guy but I make you no promises. I believe this is just your latest attempt at mischief making. If it is, you should know that I look upon it with the utmost contempt. If it is not – well, you know, I believe, that I stand shoulder to shoulder with my son.'

'Even if what he is doing is detrimental to Morse Bailey?' Sarah asked desperately.

Again she saw that flicker that might have been uncertainty in Alicia's eyes. Then they hooded once more.

'I don't think that remark requires an answer,' Alicia said coldly. 'Goodbye, Sarah. I wish I could say it has been pleasant to see you again. Unfortunately I cannot – and even if I did I doubt you would believe me.'

Sarah smiled sadly. She felt very tired suddenly.

'That's true. Thank you, anyway, for coming, Alicia. I still hope I may hear from you when you have had time to think about this.'

A waiter, who had seen Alicia rise, hovered attention.

'Thank you, I am not lunching,' Alicia informed him. 'Would you kindly find my coat for me?'

As she moved away between the tables, where more than one diner watched with covert curiosity as she passed, Sarah felt the tiredness increase, an ache behind her eyes throbbing up into her temples.

So – the lunch had been the unmitigated disaster Kirsty had predicted it would be. She had gambled on Alicia's hatred for Leo being stronger even than the hatred she felt for her, Sarah. She had gambled – and lost.

Or had she? Alicia had originally turned down her request for a meeting and later changed her mind. Perhaps pride had made her react violently – pride and shock that her precious Guy could behave so treacherously. Maybe when she had had time to talk to him and time to think she would realise that now, for the first time ever, she and the woman she hated so much must become allies for the sake of the company.

Dear God, how did I ever manage to instil such hatred? Sarah wondered. I never meant to. I never meant to hurt anyone. And yet she knew that was exactly what she had done, always.

Thoughtfully she lifted her glass, draining the remains of the gin and tonic, and as she stared into its crystal depths it seemed suddenly that her whole life was reflected there with its triumphs and heartbreaks, its turbulent loves and its bitter hatreds.

And what a life! What would I change if I could? she wondered and the answer came back to her: not a great deal. I have lived for seventy-three years and each one of them fully. And even if I wanted to – *could* I have changed it?

Certainly not the beginning – and it was from that beginning that every thread flowed. In the beginning she had been just a child, a pawn in the hand of fate, and afterwards it was probably much too late. . . .

Sarah sipped her drink and let memory take her back in time to a past so real, so vivid, it might have been happening *now*.

BOOK TWO – THE PAST – 1901

You are a child of the universe, no less than the trees and the stars. You have a right to be here.

Avoid loud and aggressive persons – they are vexations to the spirit. If you compare yourself with others you may become vain and bitter for always there will be greater and lesser persons than yourself.

Desiderata

Chapter Four

'Billy Stickland, will you come on please!' Sarah begged. 'Pick your feet up and stop kicking every stone you see. We'll never get home at this rate.'

She tugged impatiently at the hand of the small boy who was lagging along beside her, trying to hurry him, but he only pulled back and dug in his toes more determinedly.

'Aw, Sarah, it's hot – and me boots are pinchin'. Why can't we go down by the stream?'

'Yes, Sarah, you promised we could fish for tadpoles . . .' The girl, Phyllis, was a year older than her brother and even more inclined to show signs of rebellion. Sarah might be bigger than they were but Phyllis resented having to do as Sarah told her. It wasn't even as if they were related; Sarah just happened to live next-door-but-one to them in the row of cottages at Starvault and when their mother had been growing fat and clumsy with yet another baby Sarah had been asked to take Billy the mile and a half to the village school and back each day. 'He'd never do what you told him to,' Phyllis had been informed by her mother when she protested about the arrangement and although she knew in her heart that it was true, Phyllis did her best to salve her wounded pride by ensuring that Billy did nothing Sarah told him to either.

'You said yesterday we could fish for tadpoles,' Phyllis persisted. 'I brought a jam jar with me to school and our Billy's been looking forward to it all day.'

'I didn't promise,' Sarah said. 'I only said we might, but now we can't.' She gave Billy's hand another tug in an effort to make him keep pace with her.

'Stop it, Sarah, you're hurting me arm!' Billy whimpered and Phyllis took up his cause.

'You're mean and bossy, Sarah. I shall tell our mum you hurt our Billy.'

'You can tell your mum what you like. I don't care. Only come *on*, will you?' Sarah said, fighting back tears of sheer desperation. 'If you don't I shall leave you here, both of you.'

'Then you *will* be in trouble.'

'I don't care, I tell you. I've got to get home.' But she did care. She knew and they knew she would never leave them – not when they had been entrusted to her care. Not Sarah. She might be only nine years old, skinny as a bean pole in a blue cotton pinafore, but her sense of responsibility was well developed. However anxious she was to get home she would make sure she took Phyllis and Billy with her if she had to drag them every inch of the way.

'Why do you keep making us run?' Phyllis asked complainingly. 'Why are you in such a hurry today?'

For a moment Sarah did not answer. Most of her breath had been used up struggling with the unwilling Billy and she felt hot, flustered and close to tears. But Phyllis was a friend – *almost* – and she was so very worried. . . .

'It's our mum,' she confided. 'She's ever so bad, Phyll. I started to tell you this morning but you kept going on about your six-times-table.'

'Yes, 'cos we had to know it by today. Miss Keevil said she'd give us three strokes if we didn't get it right and . . . Well, what's wrong with your mum anyway?'

'I don't know,' Sarah said, and felt more like crying than ever. 'That's just it, Phyll. I don't know what's the matter with her and I don't think *she* knows either. She's got this really bad pain in her tummy and . . .'

'P'raps she's going to have a baby,' Phyllis suggested. 'My mum had a pain in her tummy just before we had our Frank.'

'Don't be silly,' Sarah said scathingly. 'I haven't got a dad, have I?'

'No, but I don't see . . .'

'Babies don't get delivered to houses where there's no dad,' Sarah said. 'I don't know why but they just don't. And anyway, this is different. She keeps being sick. I heard her moaning and retching all night. And this morning she was too bad to get up at all. She just lay there.'

'Ooh!' At last Sarah had impressed Phyllis. Her eyes went round with horror. Children like her and Billy and little Frank were often sick, but mothers . . . when mothers were sick the world seemed to have fallen off balance. Phyllis experienced a small stab of guilt and she took her young brother's other hand. 'Come *on*, can't you, our Billy? Why are you so slow?'

Billy scowled and kicked defiantly at a small piece of gravel but he knew better than to argue. When the two girls put up a united front it was worse than useless.

For a few moments the three of them hurried along in silence while the sun beat down from a clear blue sky onto their bare heads and arms. Sometimes, on afternoons such as this, they would take off their socks and boots and wade through the lush green grass that grew along the edge of the lane, sometimes they would stop to pick handfuls of golden celandines and purple cock-robins, snow white feathery heads of cow parsley and scarlet silk poppies, fine and delicate as butterflies' wings, sometimes they would take a stick and poke into the ditch that lay between hedge and verge to see what treasures might be uncovered in its overgrown depths. It was so good to be free after a whole day of sitting on hard forms in the sunless schoolroom, constantly nagged at by Miss Keevil's piercing voice and threatened by the cane she kept propped up in the corner, and they loved to make the most of that freedom.

Not so today. Sarah's anxiety had at last transmitted itself to the other two children and even Billy stopped whining

44

and marched along between them, his pinching boots forgotten as a strange sense of urgency flowed like an electric current from the girls' hands into his own.

From the village school the lane wound steeply upwards for the first half mile, then followed the curve of the hill until it dipped away to where Starvault Cottages nestled in the lee. From the last bend before the lane began its descent they were plainly visible, looking like dolls' houses in the narrow valley below – three stone-built dwellings set at right angles to the lane with tiny patches of flower garden and a cinder path separating them from the long strips of vegetable garden which sloped up the hillside. The houses were identical except that Sarah's – closest to the lane – had a little wooden porch and a honeysuckle creeping around the door, while the small patch of garden outside Phyllis's house was surrounded by a low wall which dripped great cushions of clematis and snow-on-the-mountain.

Often as they rounded that last bend one or other of the children would cry: 'There's our house!' or 'See – there's our mum in the garden. Wave! *Wave!*' for the first sight of home at the end of a long day seemed to them every bit as welcome as an oasis to a traveller who has been lost in the desert. But today there was no pleasurable sensation of homecoming, only a creeping foreboding which seemed all the more oppressive because of the brightness of the sunshine, and in the cottages and gardens nothing stirred.

Billy was beginning to drag again and Sarah felt the tears of frustration threatening once more. Just why she was so anxious she was not sure, but the fact that this black dread which had been closing in around her all day was nebulous only served to make it more frightening. Perhaps if there had been someone she could talk to it would not have been so bad – a bigger girl at school, maybe, or the teacher. But the bigger girls, about to go out into the world and earn their living, tended to think themselves above talking to a nine-year-old, drawing into a huddle and turning their backs if they saw her approaching, and Miss Keevil was a daunting figure. No child ever dared to speak to Miss Keevil unless they were first spoken to and even then there

45

was always the danger of attracting three strokes from that ever-ready cane of hers if they were careless with their choice of words. And at home there was no-one. No-one but Mum. They only had each other. . . .

Unable to bear the delay a moment longer Sarah let go of Billy's hand.

'You'll be all right now, won't you? Look – we're almost home.'

'Yes, we'll be all right, Sarah,' Phyllis said. 'You go on.'

'Sure?'

'Yes, sure. Come out later and play five-stones or hopscotch.'

'I will.' But there was no comfort in the illusion of normality.

She began to run down the hill towards the cottages. The ribbon bow tying up her curls came loose; she pulled it out and thrust it in the pocket of her pinafore without stopping, and her booted legs almost ran away with her on the last steep slope. The impetus kept her going as she turned into the cinder track and down the short path that led across the square of flower garden to her front door.

Often on afternoons such as this the door would be open to let the fresh air and sunshine in and the heat of the fire – kept burning whatever the weather for cooking and boiling a kettle – out. Today however the door was closed. Sarah's foreboding deepened. She lifted the latch and went in.

The door opened directly into the small living-room with its low ceiling and flagstoned floor. It was empty. Worse, the fire had gone out and nothing appeared to have been done since Sarah had left for school this morning. The breakfast was still laid, the neat checked cloth covering the scrubbed wood table, the loaf of bread on the blue china bread plate, the mug of tea Sarah had not had time to drink with the milk congealed on the top in a creamy skin.

Sarah ran to the door that concealed the staircase and opened it.

'Mum!' she called. 'Mum – are you all right?'

No reply.

'Mum!'

She started up the stairs, her boots clattering on the bare narrow boards. The door at the top of the stairs was ajar, letting out some light; behind it lay Sarah's bedroom and beyond that, her mother's.

Sarah loved her little room with its freshly starched curtains and bright rag rugs which she had helped to make with remnants of material from her mother's 'piece box'. Most children she knew had to share their room with several brothers and sisters, some even had to sleep with their parents, but because Dad had died in India when she was just a baby she was an only child and this room was hers and hers alone. Today however she sped through it without so much as a second glance, her heart beating hard in her thin chest.

'Mum!'

She had drawn back the curtains before going to school and the light, streaming in at the window, glared harshly upon the narrow bed and the woman who lay there. Rachel Thomas was twenty-eight years old but now she looked twice her age, her skin waxy and shining with a faint film of moisture, her thick brown curls tangled and lacklustre against the vomit-stained pillow. Pain had etched great dark circles under her eyes so that they looked sunken and even her cheeks seemed to have hollowed beneath the high and delicate cheekbones.

Sarah caught her breath in a small frightened gasp. This haunted spectre did not look like Mum at all – Mum was pretty, her eyes were bright and sparkling, if a little strained, and she laughed a lot, even when she was tired. Only last week she and Sarah had gone for a walk in the woods behind the house; in the cool of the evening Mum had caught Sarah's hand and they had skipped together along the path, more like sisters than mother and daughter, until the pink colour had been whipped up in Mum's cheeks and she had leaned against the stile to catch her breath, tossing her head back and laughing with the lovely creamy skin stretched taut on her throat and her teeth showing even and pearly between red parted lips. Only her hands were less than beautiful, the once slim fingers calloused from the hours when she worked with her needle and a little puffy from the hard menial work of caring for a home and a child. But Sarah was not looking at her hands. She saw only full breasts beneath a striped cotton blouse, a narrow waist, hips lending flare to a flowing serge skirt and rich brown curls escaping from their pins, and thought: when I grow up I want to look just like Mum.

Now she gripped the doorpost, gazing with huge frightened eyes at the parody of all that life and beauty, and the almost nameless anxiety that had been growing inside her all day suddenly crystallised and gathered into a hard knot beneath her breastbone.

'Mum!' she whispered fearfully.

Rachel's head moved restlessly on the pillow.

'Sarah – is that you?' Her voice sounded oddly strangled.

Sarah took a half step into the room. 'Yes, Mum.'

'Sarah – come here – try to help me up – I can't . . . breathe.'

Reluctantly Sarah approached the bed, trying not to gag at the smell of vomit.

'Does your tummy still hurt, Mum?' she whispered.

'Yes – no – everything hurts . . .' Rachel choked. 'Help me up . . .'

She tried to lever herself up as Sarah put her arms around her shoulders, heaving, but the minute her head was raised she fell forward, dizzy and fainting, and in panic Sarah pushed her back onto the pillows.

'Mum – Mum, whatever is the matter with you? Shall I get the doctor, Mum?'

She had asked the same question this morning before she had left for school and been given an emphatic 'No'. Then, in spite of her pain, Rachel had thought of the bills a doctor's visit would bring – bills she could ill afford to meet. 'It's only a stomach upset, it will pass,' she had said and at the time, before the terrible foreboding had begun creeping up on her, Sarah had believed her. Mum knew best. If she said there was no need for a doctor then that was the end of the matter. She was a grown-up and she was always right. Now . . .

48

Sarah looked at her mother and knew with a horrible certainty that this time she had not been right.

Oh why didn't I tell someone? Sarah wondered fearfully. Even Miss Keevil . . . But Miss Keevil would not have done anything. Miss Keevil never helped anyone and certainly not Sarah or Sarah's mother. Miss Keevil seemed to reserve a special dislike for her, Sarah had noticed, and thought it probably had something to do with the fact that while Rachel was so pretty and full of life, Miss Keevil really was so dreadfully plain.

'Mum, shall I fetch the doctor?' she asked again.

Rachel's head moved feebly against the pillow and she whispered something unintelligible. Sarah leaned closer, struggling to understand.

'What is it, Mum? What do you want me to do?'

With a tremendous effort Rachel gathered her remaining strength. Her hand, cold and clammy, found Sarah's arm and closed around it in a convulsive grip.

'Tell Mr Morse,' she managed breathlessly. 'Do you understand? Tell Mr Morse.'

Sarah managed to nod but she was puzzled.

She knew Mr Morse, of course – Mr Gilbert Morse of Chewton Leigh House whose family had owned the whole valley for generations and who had factories in Bristol besides. Everyone in Chewton Leigh knew Mr Morse though Sarah felt with a slight sense of superiority that perhaps she knew him better than most for her mother was seamstress to his second wife, Blanche. In fact before that she had also been seamstress to his first wife, Rose, except that in those days she had been not so much seamstress as assistant seamstress for she had been apprenticed to Madame Dupont who had a dressmaker's shop in Bristol and a list of clients with impressive sounding names and even titles amongst them. Sarah never tired of hearing about those days and though she had begged the story so often that she could relate every detail by heart she still pestered her mother to tell her yet again of how she had first come to Chewton Leigh House as a girl of seventeen, charged along with Madame Dupont with making a new season's wardrobe for Mrs Rose Morse. Sarah loved to hear about the elegant dresses with their leg-of-mutton and puff sleeves and taffeta linings which rustled when they moved and which Mum and the exotic-sounding Madame Dupont had created together, making copies from the two or three models Mrs Morse had ordered from the Paris couturiers and staying in the big house for several weeks until the work was done. Sometimes when Mum was relating the stories she would delve into the treasure chest she called a 'piece box' and fish out odd-shaped remnants of the very fabrics they had used – the velveteens and satins, the silks and cashmeres and tulles, all in vivid shades of scarlet, magenta and electric blue.

There were more up-to-date scraps in the box too, of course, but they were in the quiet tasteful colours which were now in vogue and it seemed to Sarah there was less romance in them. Mrs Rose Morse was dead now and the second Mrs Morse – a widow with a son of her own – was not nearly as pleasant to work for as the first one had been, or so Mum said, for she was picky and complaining, forever changing her mind about this alteration and that, and keeping Mum working at the house long after she should have been at home with Sarah. Mum did not sleep at Chewton Leigh House now, of course. Since she lived in a cottage on the estate there was no need for that. And Madame Dupont had long since retired, her sight ruined from the years of close work. 'It will happen to me one day, Sarah,' Mum had said and the thought filled Sarah with dread.

'Why do you do it then?' she had asked and Mum had laughed.

'How do you think we would live if I didn't?' she had asked. 'Anyway it's better than washing clothes and ruining my hands or scrubbing floors and getting fat knees.'

Sarah had been doubtful. Eyesight seemed far more precious to her than either of those things.

'I'm lucky to have the job,' Mum had gone on. 'It's thanks to Mr Gilbert Morse, I'm sure. *She* would never have employed me if it had been left to her. She would have brought in another seamstress from Bristol with a fancy French-sounding name – though I've proved I can sew every bit as well as the best of them. But I'd never have been given the chance if it hadn't been for Mr Morse. He's been very good to us.'

'That's because my dad died in India in the service of his country I expect,' Sarah had said and Rachel's eyes had gone far away as they always did when Sarah talked about the soldier father she had never known.

'It's because Mr Morse is a gentleman – and a very kind one too,' she had said. 'There are those who hold grudges just because he owns most of the valley and nearly every man hereabouts depends on him for their living. But that's no more than common jealousy. Mr Gilbert Morse is a good man, Sarah, and don't you let anyone tell you different.'

Now, as she sat beside her mother's bed looking fearfully at the ashen face beaded with cold sweat Sarah remembered her words. Mr Morse was good and kind and Mum thought he could help. But for the life of her Sarah could not see how . . .

'Rachel! Rachel – are you up there?' a voice called from the foot of the stairs.

Sarah jumped up, relieved, freeing her hand from her mother's clammy grasp, and ran to the bedroom door.

'Mrs Stickland!' she called and heard the footsteps clattering up the stairs.

'Are you all right, Rachel? Our Phyll just told me Sarah said you weren't well . . .' She broke off abruptly as she reached the doorway and caught her first glimpse of the figure on the bed. 'Oh my lord, Rachel, whatever is the matter with you?'

'She's sick,' Sarah said in a small voice.

'I can see that! Why ever didn't you tell me? Has she been here on her own all day like this?'

Sarah could not reply. Dolly Stickland crossed to the bed, straightening the rumpled covers and brushing Rachel's tangled hair away from her grey face and Sarah's eyes filled with tears of relief that she was no longer alone.

'Why in the world didn't you get the doctor?' Dolly demanded. 'Lord help us, Sarah, *look* at her!'

51

Sarah looked, scrubbing the tears out of her eyes with her fists. Her mother's head had lolled to one side and her eyes were closed. For one terrible moment Sarah thought that she was dead.

Dolly Stickland brushed another wisp of Rachel's hair away from her face, as if by tidying her she could somehow work a miracle.

'She's gone unconscious,' she said. 'I won't answer for what will happen if she don't have the doctor to her quick sharp. She's been left too long already.'

'She said she didn't want . . .' Sarah began, unwilling to be blamed for her mother's neglect.

'Never mind what she wants or don't want,' Dolly interrupted roughly. 'You run down to the village and get the doctor *now*. Tell him to come quick. Tell him *I* said.' She bustled across the room, a big buxom woman with a comfortable manner, taking Sarah by the arms and bundling her towards the door. 'Go on with you now – and run all the way. Do you hear me?'

Sarah nodded. In the doorway she turned, looking back at her mother. The stillness was even more frightening than the restlessness had been.

'Go on!' Dolly ordered harshly.

Sarah fled, clattering down the stairs where her boots caught on the treads and through the kitchen and it was as if the momentum of her legs was echoed by the quickening beat of her heart. Phyllis and Billy were seated on the low stone wall outside their house, staring curiously at the door of the Thomas home but when Sarah came flying out she passed them without a word.

The lane climbed steeply in the direction of the village but she ran until her heart seemed to be bursting within her and her legs were trembling lumps of jelly. Then as she eased to a walk she seemed to move so slowly she could not bear it and somehow, sobbing with the effort, she was running again. By the time she reached the first straggle of houses she was gasping raggedly and when the lane sloped down again past the Plume of Feathers public house, the Chapel and Perry's little General Store a stitch was jabbing painfully at her side and her legs were running away with her.

The doctor's house was at the far end of the village, a pretty yet substantial house set back a little from the road and half hidden by a privet hedge. Sarah ran up the path and jangled the bell-pull set in the ivy around the front door. When there was no immediate answer she jangled it again and this time it was opened by the doctor's maid wearing her starched white afternoon cap and frilled apron. Sarah recognised her as one of the 'big girls' who had left school the previous summer to take up employment.

'Please, I want the doctor,' she managed with the little breath she had left.

Edie the maid sniffed. 'Sorry, but he's hout.'

The sense of nightmare began to spiral in Sarah once more.

'I've got to see him! It's my Mum – she's been took bad – really bad. Mrs Stickland said I was to fetch him right away.'

'I told you – he's hout.' Her voice was supercilious; she was enjoying her little bit of power. The door slammed shut.

For a moment Sarah stared at it in disbelief and a sense of utter helplessness added to her panic. Dare she ring the bell again? But if the doctor wasn't there he wasn't there. She pressed her knuckles against her teeth in an agony of indecision. And then she found herself forgetting Dolly Stickland's instructions and remembering only Mum's.

'Tell Mr Morse,' Rachel had said.

Of course! Mr Morse was power; Mr Morse could do anything. And he was good and kind, Mum said, not a bit the way people expected gentry who owned them body and soul to be. If only she had done what Mum had said and gone to Mr Morse in the first place! That stuck-up Edie would never have dared to slam the door in *his* face!

Sarah turned and ran down the path of the doctor's house as if all the demons in hell were after her. Edie, peeping through the curtains and wondering if she had exceeded her duty in sending Sarah away without a list of the houses where Dr Haley might be contacted saw her go through the gate in a flurry of petticoats and wondered what on earth had caused such a wild flight. But at least it salved her conscience a little.

'She came here for a dare, I bet!' Edie thought primly. 'And now she's hopping it quick before she gets caught!'

Unaware that Edie was watching her Sarah ran through the gate, leaving it swinging on its hinges, and started down the road.

Chewton Leigh House was more than a mile outside the village but the distance did not daunt her. She had walked it sometimes with Mum and she knew every step of the way. No, it was the need for haste that frightened her, bubbling inside her with more and more urgency like a kettle coming to the boil. She ran until she was breathless, her legs aching, her feet in their tight-fitting boots hot and sweating, and all the while the lane undulated, up, down a little, up again, a slow yet remorseless climb.

At last she reached the crest of the hill and the chimneys of Chewton Leigh House came into view, an impressive forest above the grey slate of the roof. The road wound down round this bend and that, the direct route lay across the fields. Sarah hesitated for a moment. The fields were part of the Chewton Leigh Home Farm and in summer there was always a herd of heifers in one or the other of them and sometimes a bull too. Though she was country born and bred Sarah was a little afraid of heifers, who tended to chase anyone entering their field like a pack of hounds after a fox, and she was utterly terrified of the big old black bull. But today she was prepared to risk anything to get help for her mother. She stopped at the gate and peered over. The heifers were in a far corner of the field, grazing and flipping their tails at the flies in the sunshine. Of the bull there was no sign. Sarah scooped up her skirts and clambered over the gate. She ran as fast as her aching legs would carry her, almost tripping over on the uneven turfs, afraid to look back in case she should see the heifers galloping in pursuit. When she reached the gate at the far end of the field she climbed it quickly and jumped down into the lane almost opposite the gates of Chewton Leigh House, landing with a soft thud on the grass verge and stumbling forward onto hands and knees.

'Hoi! Where do you think you've bin to?' The voice was gruff; Sarah jerked round to see a man working at the hedge where it had sprouted out to overhang the road. He was in shirt sleeves, the cuffs rolled back to the elbows to reveal thick forearms tanned nut brown by the sun, his trousers were fastened round the waist with a length of thick twine and an ancient hat was jammed on his head to shade his leathery face. The look of him could have been every bit as daunting as that gruff voice but Sarah felt only a rush of relief as she recognised him.

'Sorry, Mr Pugh, but I'm in a terrible hurry.'

'Sarah Thomas! You give me quite a turn shooting over th'ick gate like that!' Amos Pugh managed Home Farm and had done for the past twenty years and though on the whole he preferred the company of cows to humans and was as likely to carry on a conversation with a bramble bush as with a man, he was fond of children – so long as they did not damage the hedges, run paths through the best meadows of mowing grass or frighten the ewes in the lambing season – and he knew most of them by name.

'Sorry, but I wanted to get over quick in case the cows came.' Sarah picked herself up, rubbing her knee where a shard of gravel had bitten into it. 'Or the bull . . .'

Amos Pugh laughed, a dry sound like the creaking of a gate.

'He won't hurt you! He's gentle as a baby. And sweet natured, too, with all them lady friends to keep him company.' He broke off, noticing Sarah's hot and tear-stained face. 'What's the matter with you, my lovely?'

Sarah rubbed her nose with the back of her hand. She did not want to stop to explain.

'I'm all right. I've got to go . . .'

She began to run again, across the road, between the tall slanting shadows thrown by the twin gate posts, down the drive that led to the house. At the foot of the small flight of stone steps it forked and Sarah took the branch that curved away around the corner of the house and across a corner of the cobbled stableyard. She had come this way sometimes with Mum when Mum was working at the house and even in her haste it never occurred to her to go the shortest way – up the steps to the main door. Sarah might not yet be ten years old but she knew her place.

Here within the perimeters of Chewton Leigh House the afternoon lay as hot, heavy and still as it had across the meadows. The sun, lower in the sky now but still strong, seemed to bounce in waves of shimmering brightness off the grey stone walls and refract from the gleaming window panes, and across the cobbled yard the stable doors all swung open indicating that the horses were out in the meadow where they could feed on the sweet summer grass. Not a sound came from the open kitchen window to disturb the drowsy peace – no clatter of pots and pans, no voices calling to one another, no shrill litany as Cook yelled her dissatisfaction with Lizzie, the dim-witted scullery maid. The yard too was deserted; at this time of year there was less to do in the stables, unlike the hunting season when they were a hive of activity from morning to night, and somehow the almost unnatural quiet plucked another chord of unease in Sarah's tense little chest.

Suppose there is nobody here! she thought. Suppose I am the only person left in the whole world! She pressed her hand against her mouth as the fantasy momentarily overwhelmed her.

Then quite suddenly the peace of the afternoon shattered. The whole world seemed to vibrate with a low chugging sound descanted by a high pitched whine and around the corner of the house rattled the brass monstrosity on wheels which was known locally as Mr Gilbert Morse's 'motee car'.

When he had first acquired it a year earlier the 'motee car', a smart German Benz, had caused a great stir in Chewton Leigh. Children had run after it along the street, older folk had kept well back when it passed, half afraid that the juddering contraption would explode before their very eyes in a cloud of smoke, and Jem Stokes, driving his trap to market, had had to keep a tight rein on his frightened horse to keep it from bolting. The first time she had seen it Sarah had run all the way home to tell her mother and the excitement of it had remained with her for days. Since then the 'motee car' had become a familiar sight in Chewton Leigh and people had begun to take it for granted. It was even said that since Mr Morse's steam engine factory in Bristol was now making engines for 'motee cars' in all probability there would be other strange contraptions chugging around the lanes before long. But Sarah, who knew nothing of engines and cared less, had not bothered to listen to the talk and had never seen the car this close before. Now she drew back against the stable wall, her eyes round with apprehension as it rattled over the cobbles towards her.

The driver, perched on the black leather seat and clutching the steering wheel which rose on a long rod between his knees, was scarcely less frightening than his vehicle since he was almost hidden by a peaked cap, goggles and a voluminous white dust coat. The 'motee car' ground to a halt in the middle of the yard, juddering madly as the engine continued to run, and as the driver removed his cap and goggles Sarah realised it was Mr Morse himself.

Suddenly all the fears of the last hour fused into one and that fear was of Mr Gilbert Morse. All very well for her mother to say he was a kind man, all very well for her to instruct Sarah to run to him for help, and for Sarah herself to have seen him as her saviour when she was a mile away from Chewton Leigh House and almost weeping in despair. Now, faced with the flesh and blood reality of the man who was Squire to the whole valley, to whom grown men still tipped their caps or pulled their forelocks and women bobbed a half-curtsey, Sarah was overcome with terror. She stood, her back pressed against the stable wall, her fingers digging into the crevices in the rough stone, no more able to move or speak than a cornered rabbit.

Gilbert Morse did something to stop the engine of the 'motee car' and as the thunderous sound died away he turned to look at Sarah. She saw his eyebrows come

57

together slightly and cringed back even further against the wall, half expecting to be chastised for trespassing. After all, if Amos Pugh could scold her for running through the fields, how much more likely was Gilbert Morse to be angry with her for daring to venture into his stable-yard? And he looked so big and so frightening sitting up there in his 'motee car'.

'Hello, who are you?' Gilbert Morse asked. His tone was not unkind but the timbre of his voice did nothing to set Sarah at her ease. She was used to voices softened by the gentle Somerset burr; the lack of any noticeable accent made his voice sound cold and sharp like the crisp air on a December morning or the patterns the frost made on the window of her bedroom. She took a nervous step away from the sanctuary of the wall and stopped again, her eyes glued to the god-like man in his gleaming brass chariot.

He was very dark, she thought – dark hair, showing only the merest hint of grey where it had been flattened by the cap, dark brows, finely chiselled yet striking, neat dark moustache, all accentuated by the background of that voluminous white dust coat. Gilbert Morse was forty-two years old and most of his contemporaries privately thought he looked younger, for his complexion was fresh and the clear blue of his eyes lent him youthfulness, but to Sarah he looked as imposing as the new king, Edward, and as old as Methuselah.

'Come here!' Gilbert Morse instructed.

Reluctantly she crept forward, her damp palms clutching handfuls of petticoat. But her chin was held high and her eyes met his with a look that was almost defiant in spite of her nervousness.

As she came closer she saw his eyes narrow.

'It's Sarah, isn't it?' There was surprise now in that unfamiliarly cultured voice.

It was Sarah's turn to be surprised. The last thing she had expected was that Mr Morse would be able to identify her at a glance. She had been to the house once or twice with her mother, it was true, and once Mr Morse had come to the village school to present the prizes for regular attendance and good behaviour. But all the same . . .'

'Yes, it's Sarah Thomas, sir,' she supplied.

He got up, manoeuvring himself between that enormously tall steering wheel and another clutch of levers and swinging himself through the gap in the 'motee car''s side and down onto the cobbles.

'What brings you here, Sarah?' There was an edge to his voice which she was too frightened to wonder about. Standing there before her he seemed scarcely less of a giant than he had done sitting up high in the 'motee car', for Sarah, though tall for her age, barely reached up to his shoulder.

'Well?' His blue eyes were sharp, cool as his voice, with that same clear edge that made her think of frosty mornings.

'My Mum told me to come,' she said with a hint of defiance.

His eyes grew even sharper. 'Your mother?'

'Yes. She's seamstress to Mrs Morse . . .'

'I know who she is,' he said shortly. 'Why did she send you?'

And suddenly Sarah's anxiety for her mother was greater than her fear of Mr Morse – and it was all pouring out.

'She's bad – really bad – and the doctor wasn't there and that maid of his wouldn't tell me where to find him and I didn't know what to do. An' then I remembered Mum said to tell you an' . . .'

'What is wrong with your mother?' he enquired.

Sarah catalogued Rachel's symptoms. 'Please, Mr Morse, can you help? Because if you can't I think she's going to . . . I don't know what's going to happen!' she finished.

Gilbert Morse looked thoughtfully at the child who stood before him. She was a funny little thing, he thought, too thin by half, with her hair hanging loose around her face and her skirt stained with grass where she had fallen onto her knees. But her eyes, blue as cornflowers, were clear and honest and the consternation was written in them for all to see. She could be exaggerating, of course. Children sometimes did. But somehow he did not think she was exaggerating.

59

He turned back to the car, reaching for the cap and goggles which lay on the seat.

'I think I know where to find Dr Haley at this time of day,' he said wryly.

Sarah hung back, uncertain as to what he expected her to do, and he indicated the motor car.

'You'd better come with me.'

Still she hesitated. Her bravado was spent now and the thought of actually riding in this strange contraption along with the imposing Mr Morse was a daunting one.

'I can run home,' she said. 'It won't take me long. I can go across the fields, the way I come.'

He hid a smile. 'I'm sure you could, but it looks to me as if you have done enough running for one day. And besides, I shall need you to explain to Dr Haley what is wrong with your mother. Jump up, now.'

He caught her under the arms, swinging her up easily into the motor. The aroma of the sunwarmed leather and the petrolly smells emanating from the hot engine made Sarah wrinkle her nose but she sat obediently on the sofa-shaped seat, pulling her skirts down over her grass-stained knees. Gilbert Morse shouted for Joe, his chief stable lad, and to Sarah's surprise the boy emerged from one of the outbuildings where no doubt he had been idling away the summer afternoon.

'Start her up, Joe,' Gilbert instructed him, climbing into the motor beside Sarah. The boy cranked a handle at the front of the bonnet, puffing and panting with the effort. After a few tries it caught and the motor began to judder as it had before. Gilbert made some adjustments to the levers and as the motor began to move in a sweeping circle around the stable yard Sarah clung on tightly.

'Dr Haley will be at Little Orchard,' Gilbert shouted above the noise of the engine. 'He'll say it is a professional visit no doubt but it's my opinion his regular attendance there owes more to Cory Coombes' hospitality and his bottomless brandy bottle than it does to his lumbago.'

Sarah was silent, a little shocked and not certain how to respond to this statement. Captain Coombes at Little

Orchard was one of the most respected gentlemen in the district, only a peg or two down the scale from Mr Morse himself, and he was a retired colonial army officer, a fact that had always impressed Sarah immensely since her own father had been a lowly private.

Little Orchard lay between Chewton Leigh House and the village, with, as its name suggested, three quarters of an acre of apple orchard to hide it from the road. As the motor cleared the dense plot of gnarled old trees in full leaf Sarah saw that Mr Morse had been right – Dr Haley's pony and trap were indeed there, the patient pony hitched up to a convenient post, though Sarah knew he would wait all day for the doctor without any restriction at all.

Gilbert Morse brought the motor to a halt and she jumped down, running to jangle the doorbell. Now that Mr Gilbert Morse was there, a few yards away, ready to lend her support if necessary she explained herself with confidence to the captain's maid and a few moments later Dr Haley emerged from the house carrying his battered black bag, with the colour rather high in his whiskery cheeks.

'What's all this?' he demanded. Then, as he saw the motor: 'Why, Morse! What are you doing here?'

'Looking for you!' Gilbert said shortly. 'And it's a good thing I knew where to find you. Sarah's mother is very ill and you're needed there at once. You had better put that lazy pony of yours to a gallop if you don't want to lose a patient.'

'A patient? Rachel Thomas?' Dr Haley sounded almost indignant.

'What else would you call someone you are being asked to attend to?' Gilbert enquired with barely veiled sarcasm. 'And if it's payment you are worried about, I'll see to that. Rachel Thomas is an excellent seamstress – if anything happens to her before Blanche gets her autumn wardrobe, she'll never forgive you. So get a move on, man. Pay more attention to medicine and less to the brandy bottle!'

Sarah saw the doctor's face grow even redder and she wondered how many people would dare to speak to him in this fashion. But she felt no resentment at the suggestion

61

that Mr Morse's only reason for going to all this trouble was to safeguard his wife's autumn wardrobe. That was simply the way things were – everyone had their place in the scheme of things and to gentry like Mr Morse the lower orders would always be judged by their usefulness, assessed like the old bull who would one day be removed from his harem of heifers to make way for a younger, more virile, specimen.

Dr Haley unhitched the pony and climbed into the trap slightly unsteadily. He brought the reins down with a heavy flick across the pony's rump and she moved off at a trot, sensing her owner's mood. Sarah was about to run behind but Gilbert Morse called her back, a look of something like amusement playing around his well-shaped mouth.

'I'll take you, Sarah. Only let Dr Haley go on ahead a little. I don't want to overtake him in the lanes or that pony of his may take fright and they will end up in Bristol.'

When he had given the doctor time to get well ahead Gilbert drove slowly back to the road and turned in the direction of Starvault Cottages. Sarah did not think to wonder how he knew where she lived; it was only later that the thought occurred to her and even then she satisfied herself with the answer: a man like Gilbert Morse knows everything.

As the cottages came into sight she could see Dr Haley's pony quietly grazing the grass verge outside. Then as Gilbert Morse pulled the motor into the widest part of the lane she was amazed to see the door open and Dr Haley come out, tossing his bag into the trap. Her heart lifted with a great surge of joy. Mum must be better. The doctor was no longer needed.

Gilbert moved the motor across to the entrance to Starvault Cottages gently, so as not to startle the pony.

'Well?' His tone was brusque.

Dr Haley spread his hands and the expression on his face turned Sarah's joy to cold clammy fear. It spread through her veins and everywhere it touched was left weak and trembling. The dread debilitated her; she could not move a muscle.

'Well?' Gilbert said again.

Haley shook his head.

'Too late,' he said carelessly. 'She's gone.'

Chapter Five

The Chewton Leigh estate, which had been in the hands of generations of the Morse family since the dissolution of the monasteries, encompassed twelve hundred acres of rolling Somerset countryside between Bristol and the Mendip Hills. Bordered on three sides by Duchy land, the estate took in two copses and a small wooded lake, part of the village of Chewton Leigh and enough prime farm land to support five small farms. Four of these were let on long leases to tenant farmers, the fifth – Home Farm – was an acknowledged extension of the 'Big House'. When Gilbert's grandfather, old Robert Morse, had been Squire he had run it himself with the help of an agent and an army of labourers, somehow succeeding in making the necessary decisions and issuing his instructions in spite of riding to the hounds two and sometimes three times a week during the hunting season. His son, John, had shown little interest in the land, however, and less in hunting, shooting, and other 'gentlemanly pursuits'. His passion had been for the steam engines which as a child he had watched puffing down the newly constructed line in the next valley and when he had been the beneficiary of an unexpected legacy from a supposedly penniless grandfather on his mother's side, freedom had beckoned. John had stopped only to say a brief prayer at the Parish Church for the soul of the old man who had chosen to live in virtual poverty and decided for reasons best known to himself to leave every penny of his secret fortune to his favourite grandson, before riding into Bristol to join forces with two impecunious but equally besotted friends and set about actually producing some of the steam engines which so absorbed him.

Miraculously the venture had been successful – more than successful. Whether enthusiasm and backing alone had carried the day or whether John had in fact been a much shrewder businessman than his family had ever suspected was a much debated point; whichever, the factory flourished and Morse Engines was soon a thriving concern, employing upwards of fifty men at the now enlarged works site.

At the age of sixty Robert had met his death riding his usual headlong charge at a dangerous hedge in the hunting field and John had decided to install a manager to take over the running of Home Farm. This pattern had been allowed to continue for Gilbert, his only son, was no more inclined to interest himself in farming than his father had been. His heart too was in engineering though he dabbled in the City to satisfy his mother, who looked on the thriving little business empire as a rather grubby venture almost akin to 'trade' in its undesirability, and though after John's death he kept a paternal eye on the estate, Home Farm was left in the hands of the manager.

Amos Pugh had occupied this position now for almost twenty years and his solid expertise had ensured those three hundred acres were the most profitable and best run in the valley.

He was a countryman through and through, a reserved and softly spoken man with mild brown eyes not unlike those of the lumbering Friesian cows which grazed the pastures around Chewton Leigh House and a skin weathered to a leather tan by constant exposure to winter wind and summer sun alike. Amos rose before dawn and went to bed with the sun and if he had a single ambition beyond running the Morse farm to the best of his not inconsiderable abiltity then no-one in the valley ever got to know about it

His wife however was a very different kettle of fish. Bertha Pugh was a shrew, so local opinion ran, and how a decent man like Amos had come to fall into her clutches they could not imagine.

Bertha was a large woman with a bustling manner. Her hair, scraped into a loose bun, frequently escaped to hang in bushy tendrils around her rather stodgy face and she had big capable hands and enormous feet which she shod in the kind of sensible boots which coped easily with farmyard mud. Here however the resemblance to the archetypal farmer's wife ended. Bertha's eyes were small and mean and made smaller and meaner by the folds of flesh which surrounded them and her voice was shrill and complaining when she was not adopting the hectoring tone she so often used to her long-suffering husband.

Amos Pugh might be the most efficient farm manager on the estate; privately Bertha considered him a fool – and she treated him as such most of the time. He must be a fool, she reasoned, or he would own, or at least rent, his own farm instead of merely remaining an employee of the Morses. When she had married him, fifteen years earlier, he had already been installed as Gilbert's farm manager, but she had been sure he was destined for greater things and had believed that with her to push and encourage he would achieve what she felt was her right – a farm of their own which would be the envy of the neighbourhood. But no amount of bullying and nagging had been able to bring her one single step closer to her objective. Amos was perfectly happy as he was – and Amos with his mind set against something was as immovable as the craggy rocks of Cheddar Gorge some fifteen miles away to the south.

Nor was Amos's stubborn resistance to self-improvement his only failure in his wife's eyes. Fifteen years of marriage had failed to provide her with the family she felt would give her status in the present and insurance for the future. Never once did it occur to Bertha that their childlessness might possibly be her own fault. She blamed Amos fairly and squarely for her inability to conceive. Added to his total lack of ambition it seemed to her he had turned out to be a poor specimen of a husband and her frustration feasted upon itself and grew until it came close to being an obsession.

'Why ever I married you I don't know!' she would say to Amos whenever some action or omission irritated her into giving vent to the barely controlled fury which simmered inside her large ungainly body. 'You're the most useless man I ever met!' And Amos would fix her with those patient brown eyes, shake his head and find some job about the farm that demanded his urgent attention so that there were only the hens who strutted placidly around the farmyard and wandered into the kitchen when the door was left open to the summer sun to hear her.

That warm evening in late June however there was no escape for Amos though, with the hay almost ready to be cut in the long meadows beneath Home Farm, there were a hundred and one things he could think of that still needed doing. He stood at the window of the big flagged kitchen looking out at the sky that was deepening from blue to violet above the tall elms and listening to his wife's voice reaching scratchy fever pitch.

'*Why*, Amos? Why did you tell Gilbert Morse we'd have that Thomas child here?' she demanded and the fact that she had already asked the question half a dozen times since he had come in from the fields in no way detracted from the ferocity of the attack. 'What ever were you thinking of?'

'I didn't have no choice, Bertha,' Amos replied solidly. 'Mr Morse come to see me when I were working over in Top Meadow and he put it to me straight. The poor little soul's mother is dead an' she's got nowhere to go an' that's an end of it.'

'But why should he think we'd have her here?'

'Well, we've got plenty of room, I s'pose,' Amos reasoned. 'T'ain't as if we got nippers of our own, be it?'

The reminder only added to Bertha's annoyance.

'What's that got to do with it? She's nothing to us. Just because we haven't got family of our own that don't mean we've got to take in every waif and stray for miles around.'

'Not every one, Bertha. Just young Sarah.'

'I think it's a nerve to even suggest such a thing! And what's it to do with him anyway?'

'You know her mother worked for Mrs Morse – and Mrs Rose Morse before her. The Morses always look after them as work for 'em.'

The idea of patronage added fuel to Bertha's fire. Her ruddy countrywoman's complexion deepened to a blotchy unattractive puce and her heavy jowls quivered with indignation.

'If he's so bloomin' concerned, why can't he have her up there with them at the Big House?'

Amos half turned to look at her, his mild eyes expressing amazement that she should even think of such a thing.

'Up at the Big House o' the gentry? Oh, talk sense, Bertha, do!'

'And what's so daft about it I'd like to know?' She skirted the table, angrily banging the pickle jar which she had been too preoccupied to clear away after supper. 'I suppose Mrs High and Mighty Blanche Morse wouldn't want a common ragamuffin whose mother was no better than she should be. But I'm expected to take her in under my roof.'

Amos ran a hand through his thinning thatch of hair so that it stood on end like badly baled straw.

'It ain't like that, Bertha, and you know it. It wouldn't be fitting. Anyway, like I said, we got plenty of room. And I didn't think you'd take on like this. I thought you'd be . . . well, quite tickled to have a girl about the place to help you. You're always on about how much you've got to do and not having any nippers of your own an' that . . .'

For Amos it was a lengthy speech. He lapsed into silence as if surprised by his own verbosity.

'An' what good will a girl like that be to me I'd like to know?' Bertha demanded. 'I don't s'pose she knows the first thing about hard work! And what if she turns out like her mother? That would be a pretty kettle of fish!'

'Her mother was a nice enough woman.'

'Nice? *Nice*? Oh, she was nice to somebody, right enough.'

'Her husband died in India, didn't he?'

'So *she* said. Did anybody ever set eyes on him? No, they did not. She comes here to a respectable place with a baby and no husband, putting on her airs and graces and then . . . What did she die of, eh? That's something I'd like to know!' she added darkly.

The implication had the effect of sending Amos back into his shell. If there was one thing he disliked more than Bertha's constant nagging it was gossip and aspersions cast without foundation on the character of those against whom he held no grudge for Amos liked to think only the best of his fellow human beings. Perhaps it was this inherent good nature which had enabled him to endure Bertha's tantrums for fifteen years without ever turning on her and telling her to stop her clacking. Faced with a disagreement, or what he called 'unpleasantness', Amos simply walked away – or if he was unable to do that, retreated to a mental sanctuary where there were no decisions to be made except those that concerned the land, no enemies but the foxes, the crows or inclement weather and certainly no shrill-voiced Bertha.

'I hope the weather holds out for another day or two,' he said thoughtfully, gazing out at the purpling sky. 'Another day or two and we can get that hay in. But I don't care for the look of the sky. It's very black over Bill's mother's.'

The blatant change of subject infuriated Bertha past the point of control and she banged on the table in a frenzy so that the sugar basin rattled and the knives and forks jumped up and down on the plates.

'Amos Pugh, sometimes I don't think you'm all there! You let Gilbert Morse walk all over you and then when I'm trying to talk sensible to you about what you've gone and done all you can think of is your hay!'

Amos did not reply. He could have told Bertha the hay was the single most important thing at the moment; without it the animals would go hungry when winter came. And she had been a farmer's wife long enough to know that life revolved around the weather. But to point this out would be to add fuel to the fire; leave Bertha alone and she would burn herself out in the end, though she had worked herself up into a rare old tizzy this time and no mistake!

He was still staring solidly out of the window when he heard the bub-bub-bub of an engine and Gilbert Morse's 'motee car' turned into the farmyard. Gilbert was behind the wheel, clad in his cap, goggles and dustcoat, and beside him on the bucket seat was the small forlorn figure of Sarah.

'They'm here,' he announced impassively.

'*What?*' Bertha's voice reached a new pitch.

'They'm here – Mr Morse and young Sarah.'

68

She flew to the window as if refusing to take his word for it, her anger becoming something close to panic.

'*Here*? You didn't say nothing about them coming tonight! Oh my lord, just look at the state we'm in! Whatever is the matter with you, Amos?'

She rushed to the table, bundling the plates together with the knives and forks still between and depositing them hastily in the big stone sink. She could not bear to be caught at a disadvantage – she kept a good tidy house and she certainly did not want the Squire to think any different. As she dropped the half-eaten loaf of bread into the crock in the pantry she heard the knock on the back door; quickly she brushed the crumbs from the breadplate with her hand and stacked it on the slab behind the cheese dish.

Amos had gone to open the door and she returned to the kitchen untying the strings of her apron as she went.

'Ah, Amos, we haven't interrupted your supper I hope?' she heard Gilbert say.

'No. No, we had that some long time ago,' Amos said placidly and she experienced a fresh desire to strike him. Surely with the evidence of supper still on the table he could have had the sense to pretend they had only just finished! She bustled forward, bad temper conflicting with the lifelong habit of ingratiating herself with 'the gentry' she so despised.

'Good evening, Mr Morse. You'll excuse the mess, I hope. We've been so busy talking I'm all behind hand.'

'I wouldn't even notice, Mrs Pugh,' Gilbert said equably. 'May we come in?'

'Well yes – do!'

'Now, this is Sarah. You know Sarah, Mrs Pugh?'

Bertha lowered her eyes from the tall figure of Gilbert to the child at his side. She looked very small and forlorn standing there clutching a reticule and somehow the contrived neatness of her added to her vulnerability. Her hair was tied up with a length of slightly crumpled ribbon, her pinafore was freshly washed and starched and there was a shine on her boots as if she had spent a very long time making them presentable. But as Bertha scrutinized her the

69

small firm chin came up and the eyes that met hers held a look that might almost be defiance.

She's a little madam, I can see! Bertha thought. Aloud she said, 'I understand you want us to take her in, Mr Morse.'

'Yes. It's a great deal to ask, I know, but Sarah has no relations she knows of and nowhere to go. The Sticklands, her neighbours, have been taking care of her since her mother died but they don't have the room to make a permanent arrangement of it and unless some kind soul will give Sarah a home she will have to go into the Union until she is old enough to go into service. I'm sure none of us would want that for her. She has lost enough without having to leave her friends and familiar surroundings to go and live among strangers in . . . well, less than ideal conditions.'

Bertha gathered herself together, bristling slightly. Easy to see how Mr Morse had talked Amos into agreeing to his suggestion; he would not get around her so easily!

'Don't think I'm not sympathetic, Mr Morse – I am,' she began. 'But we're not used to children here. Amos is out all day and I . . .' she gave a little laugh, 'I've got my hands full. Wouldn't she be better off in a family where there are others her age? There must be somebody who . . .'

Gilbert Morse's elegant head tilted slightly as if he was perturbed.

'I was rather relying on you, Mrs Pugh. I gave the matter a great deal of thought before I approached your husband and I could think of no-one more suitable than yourselves. You have the room and Sarah won't be any trouble, I know. And there is something else,' he went on, lifting his hand to brook what had promised to be Bertha's interruption then letting it fall protectively around Sarah's thin shoulders, 'I really would like Sarah to be close enough to the house for me to keep an eye on her. Sarah's mother, as you know, worked for us for a good many years and I feel a sense of responsibility towards her. If Sarah is nearby I shall be able to take a hand, perhaps, in her upbringing. A sort of honorary guardian, if you understand me. I'd like to make

70

it clear I have no intention of simply depositing her at your door and taking no further interest. Sarah needs us – all of us. We are not going to fail her, are we?'

'Well . . .' Most of the wind had gone out of Bertha's sails. Almost without her realising it Gilbert had done exactly what she had accused Amos of allowing him to do – cleverly taken the very line which was most likely to penetrate her defences. Bertha cherished a high opinion of her own innate goodness and she was anxious that others should know what a generous and kindly soul she was at heart, if not a fool – no, certainly not that. Taking in an orphaned child was an act of charity which would impress all her neighbours, Bertha felt certain. Besides this there was an element of snobbery in her make-up which had only grown more dogged as her ambition to 'better herself ' had been more irrevocably thwarted. If Mr Morse himself was to take an interest in Sarah's upbringing then there would be an element of social contact the prospect of which Bertha found quite irresistible.

'I suppose we could manage it,' she said, cradling, her heavy chins in the palm of her hand and eyeing Sarah critically. 'Like I say there's no provision for children in the house and she'd have to be prepared to muck in and help with whatever wants doing. If you think she'd do that . . .'

'Of course she would, wouldn't you, Sarah?' He patted her shoulder, smiling at her encouragingly, but Sarah stood mute, her lower lip rucked by her teeth. 'It's uncommonly good of you, Mrs Pugh, I must say. You won't regret it, I'm certain.'

Bertha was unable to resist one last stab. 'I hope not, Mr Morse.'

He straightened. 'That's settled then. Run out and get your other bag from the motor, Sarah.'

She did as he bid and when she had gone Gilbert Morse said swiftly: 'There's one more thing. I'll make you an allowance to meet the child's keep, Mrs Pugh, but I'd rather she did not know about that.' He pulled out a wad of bank notes and pressed them into the astonished Bertha's hand. 'That should cover her food and perhaps buy any

71

clothes she may need. It seems to me she has very few possessions. Now . . .' As Sarah's returning footsteps clattered on the yard, 'put it away and not a word to Sarah.'

The child reappeared in the doorway clutching a small suitcase of scuffed brown leather. Gilbert smiled at her encouragingly.

'Come along in now, Sarah, and don't be afraid. Mr and Mrs Pugh will be kind to you I am sure.'

Bertha sniffed. Forlorn she might look, alone in the world she might be but fear was not an emotion she would have thought of attributing to the child whom Mr Morse seemed determined to foist upon them.

'I'll have to make up a bed for her,' she said. 'You had better come with me, Sarah, and I'll show you where it is.'

The room was small but painstakingly furnished; for it not to have been would have offended Bertha's sensibilities though she could not remember the last time anyone had used it. There was a tall narrow wardrobe, a matching chest of drawers and a marble-topped wash stand holding a jug and basin, a soap dish and a small china pot for hair pins. The wallpaper blazed with overblown cabbage roses, a large maidenhair fern in a pot sat on top of the chest of drawers and a framed worked sampler and a picture of Jesus, arms outstretched, with the text 'Suffer the Little Children to Come Unto Me' hung from the picture rail.

The picture brought a lump to Sarah's throat for it reminded her all too clearly that her mother, though not a little child, had gone to Jesus.

That was how Dolly Stickland had put it to her on the night that Rachel had died.

'Don't cry – don't cry!' she had said, clutching Sarah so close to her ample bosom that Sarah could scarcely breathe. 'She's gone to Jesus, my love. She's gone to a better place.'

But she had been crying herself, great noisy gulps and snuffles, and Sarah had been bewildered by the sentiments. How could her mother have gone to a better place? What could be better than Chewton Leigh in summertime? And if Jesus was all loving and all knowing as she had been taught in Sunday School, why had he taken Rachel when she did not want to go and when Sarah needed her so? Sarah's head ached from thinking about it, her heart ached with a leaden grief that was almost too great to be borne and her throat ached with the tears she was desperately trying not to cry.

'If you are going to stay here you'll have to do your bit,' Mrs Pugh said harshly. 'I haven't got time to wait on you hand, foot and finger. You'll make your own bed in the mornings and you can help me get breakfast. Mr Pugh gets up early and he likes to come in to a good feed when milking is done. And I shall find some other jobs for you, so be warned. You could black the grate for me for a start. And dust round the place. Then there's the flag floor in the kitchen – that gets in a terrible state with all the tracking in and out. That could be your job – washing it down every morning with a bucket of soapy water and a scrubbing brush. Do you know how to scrub a floor?'

Sarah nodded, daunted but not intimidated, and Mrs Pugh's mouth tightened so that it almost disappeared in the mound of flesh that seemed to join her cheeks to her shoulders.

'Well, I dare say what you don't know you'll soon learn. Now, you'd best have a good bath before you go to bed dirtying up the clean sheets.'

Sarah stared at her. Saturday night was bath night and in any case she was not dirty. She had a good strip down wash at the sink every morning and all that was necessary at night was to wash her hands, face and knees.

'I don't need a bath!' she protested.

'I'll be the judge of that, Miss. And you might as well know here and now I won't stand for any talking back. Children should be seen and not heard. That's how it was in my day and I don't reckon there's any call to change that now.'

A tin bath was brought into the kitchen and kettles set to boil on the open range. Mr Pugh went out for a last look around the farmyard but to Sarah's discomfort Mrs Pugh remained, watching as Sarah took off her neatly patched underwear, folded it and placed it on a chair, and tutting at the child's thinness.

As she washed and dried herself on a scratchy towel Sarah was aware of Mrs Pugh's continued scrutiny. Her eyes were like a pair of boot buttons, Sarah decided, small and hard and black. 'The eyes are the mirror of the soul,' Rachel had used to say and Sarah thought if this were true then Mrs Pugh could not have a soul – or if she had one it must be very small and mean.

'We go to bed at a decent time in this house,' she said briskly when Sarah had completed her toilet to Mrs Pugh's satisfaction. 'You won't be allowed out playing all hours here, so you might as well get used to it.'

She escorted Sarah upstairs and hovered in the doorway whilst Sarah knelt beside the bed to say her prayers. Then with a short 'Goodnight, then,' she was gone and Sarah was left alone.

Sarah climbed into bed and felt the tears squeezing out of the corners of her eyes. She had been unable to pray under Mrs Pugh's watchful eye and she was unable to pray now. She must have done something very wicked to be punished in this way, she decided. Bad enough to lose her beloved mother but now to be imprisoned in this awful place . . . But what had she done that merited such retribution? One day a week or so earlier she had slapped Billy Stickland's legs when he had tried her to the limits of her patience but surely it could not be that. Then there were the lilies of the valley she had stolen from old Miss Read's garden to take home to her mother. She had crept in at the gate and picked the flowers that the old lady had let go wild while Phyll watched the windows to make sure Miss Read was not watching. She shouldn't have done it she knew but even so . . .

Sarah swallowed her tears and her small mouth hardened. At least she had already suffered the worst punishment imaginable. She could do something much worse than stealing Miss Read's lilies and not have anything happen to her in retribution.

I think I'll do something really bad, Sarah thought. Only just for now I don't know what it is. But when the time comes I'll know. And I'll do it. I will!

The thought provided some small comfort and Sarah held onto it lying in the hard and unfamiliar bed waiting for the temporary release of sleep.

Chapter Six

Sarah struggled into the farmhouse kitchen with a gallon jug of water which she had drawn from the well in the farmyard, heaved it up and tipped it into the big stone sink. The can was too heavy for her to manage properly and some of the water slopped onto the floor. As she felt it splash her legs she pulled a face and continued pouring more carefully. Mrs Pugh would be annoyed if she found the floor wet but she would be even more annoyed if she came in from her expedition to the village to buy brown paper and sealing wax to find Sarah had not yet finished the jobs she had given her to do. Get those out of the way first and wipe the floor afterwards, Sarah decided, turning her attention to the basket of eggs which stood on the scrubbed wooden cupboard beside the sink waiting to be washed. Last week Mrs Pugh had accused her of not getting them clean enough and Sarah was anxious not to incur her wrath on that score again.

The trouble was Mrs Pugh really was a difficult woman to please. Nothing Sarah did seemed to find favour no matter how hard she tried. This past month since she had been at Home Farm she had worked harder than she had ever worked in her life and still met with nothing but disapproval. When she blacked the grate Mrs Pugh never seemed to notice how it gleamed – she only sniffed and said things like: 'Look at the state of you! There's more blacklead on your face and hands than there is on that grate!'; when she dusted Mrs Pugh would follow her round, running a finger across surfaces Sarah was unable to reach, clacking her tongue and shaking her head; when she scrubbed the flagged floor there was certain to be some corner or crevice which failed to meet with Mrs Pugh's satisfaction. Several times in the last weeks Sarah had been late for school because Mrs Pugh had insisted she re-did it though for the life of her Sarah could not see anything wrong with her first effort. Then by being late she would incur the wrath of Miss Keevil who would punish her by making her learn extra spellings or keeping her in when school ended to make up the time she had lost.

Sarah did not mind the extra work – she found learning easy and satisfying – but she did mind being kept in after the others had gone. She looked forward to walking up the lane with her friends and perhaps stopping for a game or two on the way. It was the only social contact she had now for though she could have gone back to the village to play in the evenings Mrs Pugh generally kept her busy until it was too late and the curfew she imposed meant that Sarah had to be in, and ready for bed, by nine o'clock. That in itself was horrid while the evenings were long and light for tired though she was Sarah found it impossible to sleep. Only during haymaking when they worked in the fields until dusk was the curfew extended and then, washing up a seemingly endless stream of crockery and glasses after they had served supper to all the labourers, Sarah had been so exhausted that her eyes had been dropping even as she stood elbow deep in suds. Yet still Mrs Pugh had not been satisfied.

'Sarah – there's pickle left on the edge of this plate! Can't you do anything properly?'

'Sorry, Mrs Pugh.'

'Sorry's no good though is it? If you did it right in the first place you'd save us both a lot of trouble. I don't know . . . dragged up she must have been!' she had added as an aside to one of the wives who had come to help but spent more time gossiping than making tea or sandwiches.

Sarah had heard the remark but remained silent. She had quickly learned that this was the best way but it rankled all the same and she remembered it now as she carefully took the eggs from the basket and placed them in the sink.

I wasn't dragged up! she thought. And anyway I've got better manners than Mrs Pugh. I know it's rude to talk about people in their hearing.

She scrubbed away at the eggs conscientiously but for all

77

her efforts bits of muck clung to the shells and Sarah began to feel desperate. They wouldn't do for Mrs Pugh, she knew. There would be another tongue-lashing in store unless she could get them cleaner than this. But cold water did not seem to be making any impression on those last stubborn bits of muck and straw which stuck like glue to the speckled shells. If only she had some warm water . . .

She glanced round. The big old kettle was settled on the hob where it sat most of the day. Sarah went across and lifted it. It felt heavy. She took it back to the sink and poured some hot water into the cold in the sink, then began to scrub the eggs again. Yes, that was better. The bits of muck were loosening now.

She had been working steadily for a few minutes when she heard the door open.

Bertha Pugh came in, puffing a little, and set her basket down on the table.

'Whew, it's warm this afternoon! How are you getting on, Sarah? Not finished yet?' She turned, wiping the film of perspiration from her forehead with one of Amos's large handkerchiefs, and noticed the pool of moisture beneath the sink. 'What's all this mess, eh? You've spilled water all over my clean floor!'

My clean floor, Sarah thought with a stirring of rebellion.

'I'll clean it up in a minute,' she said.

'In a minute! Well, in a minute might not be good enough!' Bertha snapped. Then, seeing the kettle standing on the cupboard top beside the egg basket, her small mean eyes narrowed. 'And what's *that* doing there, I'd like to know?'

Sarah dropped the egg she had been scrubbing back into the water.

'I'll put it back . . .'

She lifted the kettle but Bertha advanced, head poked forward, concertina chins jutting, so that she looked for all the world like one of her own broody hens.

'What's it doing here? That's what I asked.' She dipped a thick finger into the sink and withdrew it so sharply that spray splashed up onto the front of her blouse. 'Oh my lord, you haven't been washing the eggs in hot water, have you?'

78

'I'm trying to get them clean,' Sarah explained.

'You stupid girl!' Bertha's neck was turning turkey-cock red and as always when she was angry she began to gobble. 'You can't use hot water to wash eggs!'

'But . . .' Sarah broke off aghast as the terrible truth began to dawn. 'Oh!' she said in a small voice.

'You've coddled them, that's what you've done! Every one of them bloody eggs!' Bertha was not above swearing when she was angry and she was angry now. 'Two dozen eggs and you've gone and bloody coddled 'em!' she repeated. Then not even the unladylike language was enough to relieve the rage that was coursing through her body and throbbing in her temples and she set about Sarah, cuffing her sharply round the ears, then striking out wildly at her arms and chest. Sarah ducked and tried to move back out of the way of those flailing hands, her boot slipped on the wet flagstone and she went crashing down, grazing her knee on the corner of the sink. Bertha kicked out at her. Her toe caught Sarah in the ribs and she squealed like an injured puppy.

'Little Turk!' Bertha screamed at her. 'Are you stupid? Or did you do it o' purpose? You did, didn't you! You did it o' . . .'

She stopped mid sentence, hearing for the first time above the roar of the blood in her ears the alien sound floating in through the open door – the bub-bub-bub of a motor car engine. She straightened quickly, patting her hair into place and hissing at Sarah: 'Get up! Get up, do you hear me?'

Sarah scrambled to her feet just as Gilbert Morse approached the door. Her knee was stinging and there was a sharp pain in her ribs where Bertha had kicked her, but she felt only an acute sense of shame.

He stopped in the doorway, hand raised to knock, looking perplexed.

'Mrs Pugh. Is everything all right?'

'Oh yes, Mr Morse.' Her chins bobbed as she tried to hide her own embarrassment and fluster with a ripple of forced laughter. 'Well, Sarah slipped if you must know on the wet floor. That'll teach her to be more careful with the water won't it, silly child!' She laughed again.

Gilbert turned to look at Sarah. His expression was concerned.

'Did you hurt yourself, Sarah?'

'Oh no, no, they fall easy, the young, don't they? Not like you or me, Mr Morse, if we should happen to go down . . .'

Gilbert ignored her.

'Sarah?' he asked gravely.

Sarah swallowed at the tears that were gathering in her throat, raised her chin and met his eyes directly.

'I'm all right.'

He held her gaze for a moment longer and his look was thoughtful.

'Well, Mr Morse, and to what do we owe this pleasure?' Bertha prattled. 'You've come to see Mr Pugh I expect. He's in the cowsheds, I shouldn't wonder. It's just turned milking time . . .'

'No, I didn't come to see Amos,' Gilbert said. 'The purpose of my visit was to see how you are getting along with Sarah.'

He came into the kitchen, removing his cap, and Bertha fussed around him, anxious to dispel any remaining awkwardness.

'We're doing fine. She has a lot to learn, of course, but then I suppose that's only to be expected. A woman like her mother . . . raising her all on her own . . . she's missed out on a lot, stands to reason. But we shall win, I dare say.' She laughed again, a little too loudly.

'Hmm.' Gilbert was still looking thoughtful.

'Can I offer you something, Mr Morse?' Bertha gushed. 'A nice cup of tea or a glass of sherry?'

'No thank you, Mrs Pugh.' He turned to Sarah. 'You are settling in then, my dear? And how are you getting on at school?'

'That's something again, of course,' Bertha interrupted before Sarah could answer. 'She's been kept in a few times lately. Not learning her lessons properly, I dare say.'

'That's not true!' Sarah protested and Mrs Pugh flashed

80

her a warning glare before fawning again for Gilbert's benefit.

'Well of course it is! Why else would Miss Keevil keep you in when the others have gone home?'

'Don't you like school, Sarah?' Gilbert asked.

'Not much,' Sarah admitted honestly.

'Why not? You are a bright girl.'

'We do the same things day after day. Though I quite like it when I have to teach the little ones,' she added, brightening.

'You teach the little ones?'

'Yes – to read. Miss Keevil can't hear them all and I like reading. I'm good at it,' she said with pride.

'And what do you like to read?'

'*Lamb's Tales from Shakespeare*,' she said promptly. 'And *The Water Babies*. I feel really sorry for Tom, but when he falls in the river it's good. Everything comes right.'

Her face had come alight as she spoke but Bertha tutted and shook her head. She had no time for talking about such nonsense.

'That's as maybe,' she said shortly . 'It's your sums you should be concentrating on, my girl, if you're ever to balance your housekeeping accounts when you've got a home of your own to run.'

'I like sums too,' Sarah said quickly. 'It's just that they're too easy.'

A smile twinkled in Gilbert's eyes. What would Mrs Pugh make of *that*, he wondered.

She was shaking her head again.

'I don't know, I'm sure. Boastfulness is next to vanity, Sarah, and you know what vanity is, don't you? One of the seven deadly sins. Or don't they teach you that in Sunday School any more?'

Gilbert saw the light go out of Sarah's eyes.

'I didn't mean . . .'

'You're just showing off in front of Mr Morse. If you are so clever my girl why did you coddle two dozen eggs, I'd like to know?' She nodded at Gilbert, her chins wobbling as emphasis. 'Washed the eggs in hot water, she did! Hot

81

water! Now wouldn't you think her own common sense would tell her . . .'

'I was only trying to get them clean,' Sarah protested. 'You were angry last week because . . .'

'Don't answer back!' Bertha snapped. 'I've told you before, children should be seen and not heard!'

Sarah's lips clamped shut and she looked at the flagstone floor. When Gilbert had gone she'd be for it, she knew. Answering back was high on Bertha's list of serious crimes. Oh how she hated her! thought Sarah.

'I shall not impose on your time any longer, Mrs Pugh,' Gilbert said now. 'I must be getting along. Would you like to ride as far as the end of the lane, Sarah? You'll have to walk back, of course, but . . .'

'I don't mind!' Sarah cried. Her eyes were shining again at the prospect of another chance to ride in the 'motee car'.

'Well don't be long now. I shall be getting tea soon.' Mrs Pugh shot a meaningful look at Gilbert and continued: 'Eats me out of house and home, she does. You'd never think what a difference a skinny little thing like her makes to my grocery bill.'

Gilbert touched Sarah's arm. 'Out you go then and wait in the car for me.'

Sarah went. Outside the great brass motor car was gleaming in the sunshine and the wonder of it almost eclipsed the well of misery inside her. She climbed up carefully so as not to catch her petticoats, sat down on the warm leather seat and took the steering wheel in her hands, pretending she was driving it.

If only she could! If only she could start the engine and go rattling down the lane as Mr Morse did with the wind in her hair, steering carefully around the bends, feeling the jar of the wheels coming right up the long stick of the steering wheel and into her hands, drive and drive, faster than a horse could gallop, drive and drive and never come back . . .

One day I will, Sarah promised herself. One day I'll have a 'motee car' just like Mr Morse's and when I do I won't care about Mrs Pugh or Miss Keevil or anyone. They'll look up

82

to me when I rattle past and they'll say 'There goes Sarah Thomas in her motee car. Look! Look!'

Bertha's voice as she bade Gilbert Morse an effusive farewell invaded her dream and with a jolt Sarah returned to reality. She had just a short ride down the lane to look forward to and then it would be back to Bertha's bullying and nagging. But the pleasure of these few minutes would remain with her, warming her senses and making it easier to bear. For the moment Sarah knew that would have to be enough.

Chapter Seven

On a morning in July Gilbert Morse was pacing the floor of his study, deep in thought.

The study was his sanctuary, the one room which was truly his own. Generously proportioned Chewton Leigh House might be; with a large family such as his and an army of servants it often seemed impossible to find a room in which to be alone. A few moments' peace in the big sunny drawing-room was almost certain to be interrupted by either Lawrence or Hugh, his eldest sons, at home from their public school for the long summer vacation; the library was constantly invaded by Alicia, his daughter, who at eleven years old was an avid reader and likely to question him on any of the hundreds of valuable antiquarian books or leather bound classics which lined the walls; and for all the strict discipline Gilbert imposed upon him six-year-old James seemed able to engineer his escape from the nursery often enough to be able to appear, along with Blanche's son, Leo, whose shadow he was, in almost any room in the house where Gilbert happened to be. True, they always lapsed into a nervous silence and edged, straight-backed, for the door when they saw Gilbert, but he found this caution and overweening respect almost as irritating as their defiant presence would have been; he did not like either of them.

As for the bedroom, that was very much Blanche's domain now. She had added frills and furbelows to the decor and furnishings and a permanent haze of perfume hung in the air, even wafting in to invade his dressing-room so that he no longer felt that was his own. And it was not only her perfume that made the invasion but her voice, slightly nasal with that faint Transatlantic drawl he had found so fetching in the days when he had first met her, the well-bred English widow of a wealthy American banker, returned home for a visit with her young son. She had

captivated him then for he too was lonely after the loss of
Rose, his first wife, who had died giving birth to young
James, and Blanche was the very opposite to what Rose had
been – a gregarious and social butterfly where Rose had
been happiest in a quiet home environment, yet with a
sharp and enquiring mind and an interest in politics,
business and economics that was totally unusual in a woman
and might have been unseemly had it not been for her
considerable charm and grace. When he had first met her
Gilbert had considered Blanche an extraordinary woman
and she had so fascinated him that he had counted himself
the luckiest man alive to win her favour; now, three years
later, Gilbert was less certain exactly who had been the
victor.

In any event the study was his retreat, the one room
where none of them, not even the slippery James would
dare to intrude, and it was here in this typically masculine
domain that Gilbert came to be alone with his thoughts.

He strode now from desk to window and back again,
hands in pockets, head bent, so that he looked slightly less
than his five feet ten inches, an immaculately dressed,
compactly built man whose dark hair had greyed into
attractive wings at the temples and whose clipped moustache added a certain rakishness to his handsome face.
Beneath the neat moustache his mouth was full and verging
on the sensuous and his blue eyes were capable of the most
wicked twinkle. This morning however they were clouded
with thought. It was barely seven o'clock but Gilbert had
been awake for an hour or more and rather than disturb
Blanche he had risen, dressed and come downstairs to the
study in order to allow himself freedom to think. Yet even
here in the study with no interruptions and no diversions of
any sort he found his mind chasing in indeterminate circles.

The inability to define a clear line of thought and get to
grips with the problem irritated Gilbert and disconcerted
him. He thrived on problems. His capacity for taking a
problem which had seemed insoluble to everyone else and
turning it to his own advantage had been one of the
hallmarks of his success both in the City and at Morse

Engines – where his father had ridden hurdles and managed to surmount them with a combination of flexibility and sound technical knowledge Gilbert, by employing his own particular brand of intuition, was able to positively soar over them.

But this was not a business porism. It concerned Sarah, and Sarah was a much more complex problem.

Early sunshine soft and golden with none of the harsh glare that would come later in the day began to flood the study and Gilbert crossed to open the window. A faint cool breeze whispered in and with it a teasing whiff of the honeysuckle that clung to the grey stone walls on this corner of the house. It was a fresh scent, bearing the newness of the morning, and Gilbert breathed it in as he pondered the question of the orphaned daughter of his wife's seamstress.

When he first suggested to the Pughs that they should take her in it had seemed an ideal soluton. The Pughs were honest hardworking folk with no family of their own and the farm was close enough to the village for Sarah to be able to maintain her friendships and continue with her schooling without the upheaval of having to settle into a completely different routine. At least there would be some continuity in the shattered pattern of her life, he had thought.

But since his unannounced visit to the farm some two weeks ago when he had happened upon a fracas of some sort he had begun to have serious doubts. It was inevitable there would be teething problems in the arrangement of course, but how regularly did scenes of this kind occur? It had been serious, Gilbert was certain and he was unable to allay the suspicion that Bertha had been beating Sarah. Perhaps, he thought, it had not been so wise after all to expect her to accept a young girl into her home. Perhaps he had been so anxious to avoid Sarah being taken away to the Union that he had made light of the difficulties and deceived himself into believing the arrangement could work.

Then there was the matter of Sarah's schooling. After their conversation he had been to see Miss Keevil to ask why she had found it necessary to detain Sarah after school hours. Miss Keevil had told him with a malicious glint in her eye that it was because Sarah was now persistently late, but when he had pressed her she had admitted the child seemed constantly tired these days and was not achieving the results she had done previously. Remembering how Bertha Pugh had said she expected Sarah to 'do her bit' and having noticed on his last visit how red and puffy her hands had looked, Gilbert had begun to put two and two together. It was not outside the realms of possibility that Bertha was making the child get up early to do the chores before leaving for school – and chastising her if they were not done to her satisfaction.

Gilbert had begun to suspect there might be another side to Bertha Pugh – a dark side which she painstakingly hid from the world – and a slow anger had begun to burn in him. Hadn't the child suffered enough? Surely she was deserving of a little compassion to help her to come to terms with her loss, not the sort of treatment meted out to poor children in the dark days before modern enlightenment. With a growing sense of unease Gilbert had found himself remembering how eagerly she had cited *The Water Babies* as a favourite book. Could it be that she was identifying with Tom, the little chimney sweep? In this day and age, surely not. And yet . . .

He had failed her, he thought – and worse he had failed Rachel, her mother. For a moment it seemed she was there in the room with him, looking just as she had when he had first set eyes on her, a young apprentice dressmaker come to the house to sew a wardrobe for Rose, his first wife.

How lovely she had been! She had captivated him with her laughing eyes, her rich brown hair and her effervescent carefree youth, making him feel young again so that he had thrown caution and propriety to the winds, position and responsibilities forgotten in a fever of desire. He had loved her as he had never loved either of his wives, pale gentle Rose and worldly domineering Blanche, and that love reached out now across the years making him ache for what he had known for such a tantalisingly brief interlude.

Oh Rachel, Rachel . . . But those lovely eyes were not laughing now. Instead they reproached him. What had he ever done for Rachel beyond the barest financial support she had deigned to accept from him? What was he doing now for her child . . . for *their* child?

Gilbert straighened, removing his hands from his pockets and brushing the lick of dark hair just flecked with silver from his high forehead.

He could not remove Sarah from the care of the Pughs now. He had no plausible reason for doing so and in any case there was nowhere else that she could go. But there was one thing he could do for her. Blanche would probably oppose the plan, Alicia might resent it – but they could scarcely object too strenuously without showing themselves in a totally uncharitable light. And in any case, Gilbert was still very much master in his own house.

Across the valley the church clock chimed the half hour. With the breeze in this direction the sound floated through the open window of the study along with the scent of honeysuckle, faint yet melodious and somehow evocative of other summer mornings, long since past. Gilbert drew out his fob watch, checking it with the chimes.

Half past seven. Time, perhaps, for a stroll around the gardens before breakfast. And then, when they were all gathered together, he would inform them of his decision.

Breakfast was, for the Morse family, a sacred and carefully observed ceremony.

At lunch time Gilbert was usually out either at the works or his city office, while tea was a nursery meal for the younger members of the family who were then in bed before their elders gathered for dinner. At breakfast however there was no excuse for any one of them to be absent and Gilbert, always an early riser himself, would accept none. Even illness had to be dire in order to qualify for since Gilbert was scarcely ever ill himself he was impatient of what he looked on as a sign of either weakness or deliberate perversity in others. Little James, who suffered from bilious attacks, sometimes sat ashen faced and silent after a sleepless night with his head bent over the basin, and Alicia had presented herself one morning without making a single reference to the peppering of spots which had later been diagnosed as chicken pox. Only Blanche refused to pander to Gilbert's idealism; if she was unwell she did not hesitate to say so – but then Blanche rarely refrained from speaking her mind, Gilbert thought ruefully.

When he entered the morning-room after his stroll around the gardens he found her already seated at the foot of the table, an elegant woman whose dark green silk morning dress perfectly complemented the gingery brown of her hair and somehow managed to turn it from a nondescript shade to her undoubted crowning glory. Her skin was pale too; the dress made it appear creamy, and on closer inspection it could be noticed it was the exact same colour as her eyes.

When she saw Gilbert she smiled, but it was a smile without warmth, and her eyes retained the look of chips of green glass.

'Good morning, my dear,' Gilbert greeted her. 'You slept well, I trust?'

'Very well.'

He turned to the two boys, fifteen and thirteen years old respectively, who were also seated on opposite sides of the table.

'Good morning, Lawrence. Good morning, Hugh.'

'Good morning, Father.'

At first sight they were as alike as peas in a pod, more like twins than brothers whose birthdays were separated by thirteen months. Both had Gilbert's lean, straight build and his dark good looks. Both were neatly dressed in white shirts with deep turned down collars and knickerbockers. But the resemblance was superficial only. Whilst Lawrence, the elder, was so serious and conscientious that Gilbert sometimes feared that what little sense of humour he had been born with had been totally subjugated by his desire to do well at school and the seriousness with which he took his position as heir to the Chewton Leigh estates and the Morse Engine Works, Hugh was a merry lad whose razor-sharp intelligence and ready sense of fun was apparent in every shade of expression so that the same blue eyes that so often narrowed with anxiety in Lawrence's humourless face twinkled wickedly behind Hugh's thick fringe of dark lashes and his smile could be wide or mischievous rather than strangely anxious as Lawrence's tended to be. Already Hugh had attracted the attention of most of the girls in Chewton Leigh; in church on Sundays when he was home for the holidays Gilbert had noticed them eyeing him when they thought their parents were not looking and nudging one another and whispering.

It was a great pity Hugh did not put as much effort into his schooling as he did into enjoying himself, Gilbert sometimes thought, and it was a malicious trick of nature that whilst Lawrence was possessed of the ambition to do well it was Hugh who had the ability. He would have liked both of them to get a University education before embarking on their chosen careers but somehow he doubted that Lawrence would achieve good enough results to be offered a place and Hugh expressed a desire only to leave school as soon as he was able and put learning behind him. His heart was set on a military career and he had been following the fortunes of the war in South Africa with a jingoism which Gilbert found faintly alarming since he himself had every sympathy with the Boers who were, after all, only fighting for their own land.

At least Lawrence, however, displayed a gratifying enthusiasm for the family firm. Even as a little boy he had been fascinated by all things mechanical. He had striven to build a working model of a stationary steam engine and whenever he was missing for any length of time he could be sure to be found in the outbuilding which housed the engine, dynamo and accumulators which provided electricity for Chewton Leigh House. Now during the school holidays his greatest pleasure was to visit Morse Motors where he would attach himself to Frank Raisey, the General Manager, whenever he toured the works, dallying to watch the assembly of the intricate workings and pouring over the shoulders of the men in the drawing office.

'Are you going to the Works today, Father?' he asked eagerly as Gilbert took his place at the head of the table.

'I wasn't planning to,' Gilbert admitted. 'Frank Raisey has everything under control there and I have a great deal to do at my office.' Then, as he saw the boy's face fall, he smiled. 'I dare say I could drop you off there before I go into town if you'd like me to.'

Blanche sniffed. 'On a beautiful day like this I would have thought you would have been better off spending some time in the fresh air rather than in those stuffy workshops,' she commented.

'But aren't they working on a new engine for a motor bicycle?' Lawrence persisted. 'I'd really like to see that. In fact I was thinking if I could get hold of a bicycle frame I might be able to build one myself. It's the transmission that's bothering me. I've been thinking about it and . . .'

'Do we have to talk about engines and motor bicycles at breakfast?' Blanche enquired lightly. 'Evans is waiting to serve us and everything will be getting cold.'

She glanced at Evans, the butler, who was hovering beside the array of chafing dishes laid out on the sideboard. 'Please begin, Evans. We won't wait for the children. They will be here very soon, I am sure.'

'Where are they?' Gilbert demanded a trifle imperiously and almost as if waiting for their cue the morning-room door burst open and the three youngest members of the family came in led by Alicia.

She crossed to her father, a tall slender child of eleven whose hair was every bit as dark as his and whose classic finely chiselled features appeared slightly too mature for her years. In time Alicia would be a beauty, at present she looked a little too old, a little too sedate, and her sharp eyes, though missing nothing, gave nothing away either.

'Good morning, Father.' She kissed him on the forehead and moved to her place.

Behind her came the two boys, Leo, Blanche's son, who was just a year younger than she, a scowling boy with his mother's aristocratic nose and a mouth that was oddly epicene, and six-year-old James. As Alicia had kissed her father so Leo dutifully dropped a peck on his mother's cheek before taking his place at the table. But James hung back in the doorway then scooted for his own place, his eyes shooting quick nervous messages at the assembled family.

'James!' Blanche's voice arrested him before he could slip into his chair. 'You have not kissed your father! It's bad enough that you should be late for breakfast without trying to slip in in the hope that no-one will notice you.'

James crept towards his father and Gilbert did his best to conceal the irritation he could not help feeling for his youngest son. What was the matter with the boy? He was like a little shadow, slippery and without substance. Perhaps it was because his mother had died when he was born, Gilbert thought. But the very fact that this timid child had cost the robust Rose her life seemed incongruous.

'It's all right, James,' he said hastily, for the boy's very proximity made him shudder inwardly. 'You may sit down. And make up your mind what you want for breakfast today before Evans serves you. I don't want to see a plateful of good food going back to the kitchens again. There are plenty of children who would be only too glad of the chance to eat what you allow to go to waste.'

Evans began serving mounds of fluffy scrambled egg, lean rashers of bacon and small succulent kidneys, moving around the table with the inconspicuous grace which had been perfected through a lifetime of service at Chewton Leigh House. Evans came from a long line of highly skilled butlers, he had learned his business at his father's knee and when his turn had come to take on the exacting role he had been ready for it.

'I hear the Thomas child is settling in well at Home Farm,' Blanche said, beginning on her minuscule portion of scrambled eggs. 'It was extremely generous of the Pughs to take her in, I think. Her mother was an excellent seamstress of course. It could be Bertha Pugh thinks Sarah will develop the same talent.'

Gilbert, who had been glancing at the headlines of *The Times*, neatly folded as always beside his place, looked up. He had not intended to broach the subject of Sarah so early in the proceedings but now that Blanche had mentioned her he realised the moment had come.

'I believe it falls to all of us to adopt a Christian attitude towards Sarah,' he said, nodding to Evans to indicate that he should proceed with serving him. 'When a child is orphaned in such tragic circumstances it seems only right that we should do our best to rally round.' He saw Blanche's light eyebrows raise a fraction and continued: 'I have been doing some thinking about Sarah myself. She is a clever child and very willing and I believe her education is suffering as a result of all her misfortunes. Not that the village school has a great deal to offer in any case for although all children get at least a rudimentary education free since Salisbury introduced his government grant, a great many of them have no wish to be there and their parents resent them having to attend. No, I believe Sarah is worth more than that. I have decided to invite her here, to the house, to share her lessons with our children.'

For a moment there was complete silence at the breakfast table. Even the inscrutable Evans appeared to falter, the silver service hovering briefly over the chafing dish before continuing smoothly as before and Gilbert saw Blanche's green eyes widen with shock. It was Lawrence, however, who broke the silence.

'I say, Father, that's a bit extreme, isn't it?'

'No, I don't think so.' Gilbert reached for the condiments, liberally salting his eggs and kidneys. 'Richard Hartley is an excellent tutor – that is what I pay him for –but his talents are hardly used to capacity at present. And Leo will soon be going away to preparatory school and on to public school as you boys did. That means he will have only Alicia and James to occupy him. Sarah seems to me to be an exceptionally able girl who would benefit from a good education and I'd like to see she gets the opportunity.'

'But why, Father?' Lawrence persisted. 'I mean, what's the point? She's just a girl . . .'

'I thought you were conversant with my views on the education of girls, Lawrence,' Gilbert said a trifle tartly. 'I realise it is generally considered quite unnecessary but I fail to see why a girl should not receive at least a good enough education to fit her to be able to carry on an intelligent conversation with her husband and be mistress in her own house. There are women's colleges at both Oxford and Cambridge now, and have been for the last twenty years, to fit women to be teachers and governesses. It could be that Sarah could aspire to something like that given the opportunity. Besides I happen to think that we shall soon see some changes in attitudes to women generally. Women's suffrage is very much on the menu nowadays. It may be a long while yet before these free thinkers make any impression on the old order but I believe it will come. And when it does then all kinds of things will be open to women that people of my generation would never have believed possible. That is why I have ensured Alicia has received at least as good a grounding as you boys; why I might consider Cheltenham Ladies' College for her even.'

'But this Sarah isn't just a girl – she's a *village* girl,' Hugh put in. 'That's what you mean, isn't it, Lawrence? Her mother was a seamstress. You can't compare her with Alicia.'

Gilbert's mouth hardened.

'Obviously you have never listened very carefully to my views either, Hugh. I don't believe an accident of birth should make anyone unworthy. That should depend entirely on their abilities. And ability, unless nurtured, can never be given a fair chance.'

'An accident of birth!' Blanche repeated softly, unable to keep the scorn out of her voice. 'Really, Gilbert – you and your revolutionary views! It's bad enough that you support Campbell Bannerman and the Liberals when in your position it would only make sense for you to be a Conservative. But from the way you are talking you will be joining Keir Hardy and his group of cloth-capped upstarts next!'

Gilbert smiled. When Keir Hardy, the Scottish miners' leader, had been elected to Parliament nine years earlier he had caused a great stir by arriving at the House wearing a cloth hat instead of the traditional 'topper' and now, with

94

Ramsay Macdonald, he was set on forming a distinct group in Parliament to represent the interests of the unions and the working classes generally. Gilbert was himself a fair employer but he had long sympathised with the millions of men who worked in unspeakable conditions for a pittance below subsistence level and he thought the new rallying of the underdogs was no bad thing.

'I doubt I shall go quite that far, Blanche,' he said, beginning on his eggs. 'But I don't feel this is the moment for a discussion on my political views. This is no great matter of laws to change the course of history. All I am proposing is a small social experiment.'

'One which may well have a detrimental effect on your own children. You cannot seriously expect Alicia to share her lessons with a child of Sarah's upbringing,' Blanche said. Tiny high spots of colour had appeared in her pale cheeks and her eggs lay untouched on the plate in front of her.

'I see no reason why not,' Gilbert replied levelly. 'Alicia has a good many privileges. I don't believe it is too much to ask her to be generous with some of them. Besides, as the only girl in the family she is very much one on her own. A little female company in the schoolroom could only be beneficial to her.'

'I don't want female company,' Alicia said. It was the first time she had spoken since her father had made his outrageous suggestion and her voice, though quiet, had the ringing tones of conviction.

Gilbert flicked her a glance of annoyance.

'When I want your opinion, Miss, I'll ask for it.'

'But that's not fair!' Alicia protested. 'I'm the one who has to have lessons with this – this Sarah.' She had been on the point of saying 'slut' but the expression on her father's face made her think better of it.

'That is true, Alicia,' he said firmly. 'And it will do you no harm at all.'

'But I don't want . . .'

'What you want, Miss, is not at issue. You have had things far too much your own way and it is beginning to show. Your brothers spoil you and I must confess that although I was determined it would not happen I have spoiled you too. It stems from your being the only girl, I expect.'

'It isn't spoiling me to force me to have my lessons with a common village girl,' Alicia said defiantly.

'That will do, Alicia,' Gilbert said coldly. 'My mind is quite made up. And if this morning's performance is anything to go by I think you will learn as much from this experiment as Sarah will.'

She stared at him defiantly for a moment, her eyes holding his, her mouth puckered into a tight hard pout. Then she clattered her knife and fork onto her plate of scarcely touched egg, scraped back her chair and leaped to her feet.

'Alicia . . .' Blanche began warningly but Alicia ignored her.

'I won't!' she spat furiously. 'I won't have my lessons with her. Why should I? And if you make me I . . . I won't learn a thing!'

She pushed the heavy Victorian chair aside and flounced across the room.

'Come back here this minute!' Gilbert thundered.

She checked momentarily, twisting her head to look at him. He saw the quick flash of fear in her eyes then her jaw set and her mouth hardened again. 'Make me!' that look seemed to say and with a flash of insight Gilbert knew that he was facing a will as indomitable as his own. How ironic, he was to think later. None of his sons had ever openly defied him and although, for all his liberal and forward-looking views his authority where his family was concerned was very important to him, yet strangely their acquiescence and continual eagerness to please had disappointed him in a way he could scarcely understand. Somewhere inside him a boy should have the spark to make him rebel, his own individuality should occasionally surface as insurrection; as in nature the young buck should sometimes test his strength and make his play for the position of leader of the herd. Yet the boys did not do this. Lawrence was too anxious to be thought of as responsible by his elders, Hugh, for all his military aspirations, was too lightweight to care – not for him the family responsibilities that would come hand in hand with superiority. And James – James had no spine and no spirit, Gilbert decided, and wondered idly if young John, his third son, had lived if he would have had that dominance which was so lacking in the others. But John had died of whooping cough when he was just fourteen months old and the secrets of his character had gone with him to the tiny grave beneath the outstretched wings of the stone angel in Chewton Leigh Cemetery. No, Gilbert had sometimes thought, none of his sons showed the spirit he would have hoped for in them. And now, unexpectedly, there it was in the eyes of his daughter.

The challenge was brief and shocking yet for all his anger it excited him, firing some deeply hidden ambition for the continuity of family traits founded in the dark ages and for a future which might be even greater than the past.

Lawrence had half risen from his chair.

'Shall I fetch her back, Father?'

'No!' Gilbert spoke sharply, then regained his control. 'No, let her go, Lawrence. I shall speak to her later. This meal has already been interrupted quite enough.' He looked around at each of them in turn. 'Has anyone else anything to say on the subject or can we consider it closed?'

'It seems,' Blanche said evenly, 'as though you have made up your mind.' Her expression said that there was more she would have liked to discuss but she was too wise to do so and he took her words at their spoken value.

'Yes.' He lifted his fork and popped a piece of succulent kidney into his mouth. 'Yes, Blanche, I believe I have. Now I suggest we all forget Alicia's unpardonable behaviour and enjoy our breakfast.'

Chapter Eight

The schoolroom in Chewton Leigh House was situated on the first floor, a pleasantly sunny room which overlooked the open parkland to the side of the house. Alicia and James were the second generation of Morses who had sat there at the square, comfortably worn table to learn their lessons. Well away from the main living rooms, it provided the peaceful atmosphere necessary to do sums and grammar and learn the conjugation of Latin verbs. The walls were panelled in wood and hung with delicate watercolours depicting the various components of wild flowers and the curtains of dusky pink velvet had been altered to fit this room by Sarah's mother, Rachel, when new ones had been purchased for the drawing-room.

Sitting at the table one day in September, flanked by Alicia and Leo and under the eagle eye of Richard Hartley, the tutor, Sarah found herself looking at the curtains as the one friendly item in this alien place. She had come to the house with her mother when Rachel had been sewing them; she remembered the bright flush of colour they had made in the small bare sewing room and the way her mother's fingers had flown nimbly over the hems. She had been bored at the time, having quickly grown tired of the piece of needlework Rachel had given her to occupy herself, for Sarah had not inherited her mother's talent with a needle, but now looking back it conjured up for her a time when she had known nothing but warmth and happiness, carefree days forever lost in a barren desert of hostility.

It was bad enough at Home Farm, Sarah thought, for Bertha Pugh's temper had not improved with the passage of the weeks. If anything practice had put sharp barbs on her tongue and she demanded more, not less, from Sarah by way of assistance with the daily chores. But here at Chewton Leigh House it was infinitely worse.

From the moment Gilbert had brought her here Sarah had been aware of the resentment the family felt for her. Gilbert was kind enough, it was true, but even he was different here at the house, a total stranger displaying none of the warmth she had felt when he had first rescued her at the time of her mother's death. Lawrence and Hugh, who had been distant but not unfriendly, were now back at their boarding school. Only little James seemed not to object to her presence – and he was too young to count. A wraith of a child with none of Billy Stickland's rumbustious sense of fun and mischief, he spent most of his time with his Nanny, only entering the schoolroom for a few hours a day and Sarah was almost unaware of his existence.

'Sarah! Perhaps you would like to read the next passage for us.' The tutor's voice ended Sarah's reverie and she looked up to see his eyes, oblique behind his thick spectacles, on her.

'I – I'm sorry . . .' she faltered. *The Old Curiosity Shop* was open in front of her but what the next passage was she had no idea.

'Pay attention, Sarah, please,' he reproved gently. It was not in Richard Hartley's nature to bully or scold; the gentle and scholarly son of a parson, he believed firmly that encouragement was far more efficacious than compulsion and the carrot worked a great deal better than the whip. But he was well aware that Sarah's village school education had left her far behind both Alicia and Leo and even allowing for the difference in their ages he would have to work hard to raise her to a standard which would satisfy Gilbert Morse. Still, she was an able child – if only he could bring her to keep her mind on her work! At the moment she seemed to spend most of her time in a world of her own.

With a tremendous effort Sarah tried to concentrate on the pages in front of her. She had always enjoyed reading but many of the words in *The Old Curiosity Shop* were unfamiliar to her. Aware of Alicia and Leo's scorn she stumbled through the passage Richard had asked her to read, manfully deciphering the words though she had no real understanding of the sense of the piece.

99

'Is it too difficult for you, Sarah?' he asked, not unkindly.

Her flush deepened. She would never admit to failure – not in front of her young tormentors. 'No.'

'I think you are struggling,' he said. 'But there's no need to be ashamed of that. You are not as old as the others, remember.' He drew his fob watch out of his pocket and glanced at it. 'I think it is time we were finishing now, anyway. Your tea will be ready,' he said to the two Morse children, 'but if you can spare a little longer, Sarah, we will have another look at what we've been doing together. Perhaps if I explain the story and some of the vocabulary you will find it easier to follow next time.'

Leo sniggered but Alicia packed her books together without looking at him. At least there seemed to be no love lost between the two of them, Sarah thought. It was one point in her favour. Had they provided a united front lessons with them would have been unbearable. But she sensed a barely veiled antagonism between them, heard them vie with one another day by day, saw the cold arrogance Alicia displayed and noticed his reciprocal dislike.

Now they thanked their tutor politely and left but in the corridor outside Sarah heard the beginnings of an argument between them.

'Why should she have longer than us?' That was Leo, whining.

'Be quiet and think yourself lucky he didn't keep us, too.'

'But it's your father who is paying the tutor. She doesn't contribute at all.'

'It's my father who is paying for your education too.'

Their voices faded away. Sarah's cheeks were pink. She glanced apprehensively at the tutor and he smiled at her encouragingly.

'Now then, Sarah, let's begin at the beginning,' he suggested. 'You tell me what you understand of the story and what you find difficult. Then perhaps I can help you make sense of it.'

They worked together for half an hour and without the critical presence of the older children Sarah found herself enjoying her lesson. At last the tutor was satisfied they had done enough. He smiled at her kindly.

'You are a bright girl, Sarah. Don't be intimidated by the others. You have just as much ability as they have – more if I'm not mistaken – and you will catch them up in no time. Now pack up your things and run along home. You might as well make the most of what is left of the day.'

'Thank you,' she said demurely but she was thinking: home! The Pughs' farmhouse! Longing for the cottage at Starvault and for her mother overwhelmed her and with a sharp pang she realised that never again would she run down the lane to find Rachel waiting for her. Bitter tears stung her throat and she bent her head over her books so that he should not see them.

She left the schoolroom and walked along the dim corridor past the white-painted closed doors. At the end one stood open. The nursery. Her footsteps slowed and in spite of herself she peeped inside. There was no-one there; clearly tea was over and James and his Nanny must have gone outside to take advantage of the September sunshine. Sarah hesitated, drawn by overwhelming curiosity.

During the weeks she had been coming to Chewton Leigh House she had never once been inside the nursery. The very name held a fascination for her, a word which epitomised a world in which she had no place, a world of privilege and security undreamed of by ordinary folk. She glanced quickly around. The corridor was deserted, the schoolroom door still firmly closed. She took a step into the nursery and stopped, her fascination turning to wonder.

The maid had not yet been in to clear the tea things; they still littered the table – sandwiches, daintily cut, not the great doorsteps Mrs Pugh made, some bread and butter interleaved on a plate, a pot of honey and a dish of iced fairy cakes. Sarah looked around furtively once more and unable to resist the temptation reached out for one. It seemed to melt in her mouth. With relish she licked her fingers and continued her exploration.

Behind the door was a screen covered with bright pictures and scraps – perhaps Alicia had made it, Sarah

101

thought. Although she disliked Alicia for her unpleasantness yet at the same time she was fascinated by her and longed to be able to emulate her. In front of the window stood an enormous rocking horse with a mane and tail of real hair; as Sarah touched him he swayed gently on his stand. Growing bolder she went further into the room and there she saw the dolls sitting straight backed in a row on a shoulder-high shelf – beautiful dolls, more beautiful than any she had ever seen in her life before, dainty dolls with delicate china faces dressed in silk and lace. Shocked by her own daring yet quite unable to stop herself Sarah picked one up, stroking the fine hair and lifting the cream silk dress to reveal a pair of matching lace-edged drawers.

'Oh – you are beautiful!' she whispered. 'What is your name? Emily? Florence?' They were the grandest names she could think of yet they were still not grand enough for this perfect aristocratic doll. Then she remembered the name of Mr Morse's first wife. 'Perhaps you are called Rose,' she said.

She had not heard the footsteps approaching in the corridor and when the voice came, shrill with outrage, she almost dropped the doll in shock.

'What do you think you are doing? You have no right in here!'

She spun round to see Alicia in the doorway. Her face was dark with anger, her eyes blazing fire.

'Are these dolls yours?' Sarah asked.

'Yes, they are mine. How dare you touch them!' Alicia advanced towards Sarah snatching furiously for the doll and clutching it to her.

Sarah quaked but stood her ground.

'I wouldn't hurt them. I'm only looking.'

'You have no right. You're just a little slut. Don't ever touch them again!'

'I – I'm sorry . . . ' Sarah faltered.

'What is going on here?' Another figure materialised in the doorway, a tall dark figure immaculate in the cutaway coat of black broadcloth, grey waistcoat and grey-striped trousers which he wore for the city. Gilbert! Seeing him

Sarah was overcome by shame at being discovered trespassing.

'She has been interfering with my dolls!' Alicia shrilled. 'She has no right here, Father. Tell her!'

'I was only looking,' Sarah protested, anxious to establish her innocence. 'They're so beautiful.'

'Leave them alone!' Alicia spat. She banged the doll back into her place on the shelf. 'She lives here, you understand? Here!'

'Alicia!' Gilbert reproved. There was an expression on his face Sarah could not understand but in her terror she thought it must mean that he too was angry with her. Then to her amazement she realised it was Alicia at whom his anger was directed. 'I told you when Sarah came here that you would learn as much as she would and one of the things I intended you to learn was how to share. You have a shelf full of dolls you scarcely play with any more. Why should Sarah not enjoy them too?'

'Because they are mine,' the older girl returned stubbornly.

Gilbert's mouth hardened. 'And now one of them is going to be Sarah's,' he said coldly. 'Which one would you like, Sarah?'

'You can't give her one of my dolls!' Alicia shrieked in horror.

'I can and I will. I refuse to tolerate your selfishness, Alicia,' Gilbert said sternly. 'Choose, Sarah.'

Sarah recoiled in dismay. Much as she had admired the dolls the idea of taking one of them was horrific to her. They *were* Alicia's and she knew if they belonged to her she would not be able to bear having to part with any of them.

'No,' she whispered shaking her head so that the ribbon bounced in her curls. 'Oh no, I couldn't.'

Gilbert reached out and picked up the doll Alicia had returned to the shelf. 'This was the one you liked, I think. Take her.'

Sarah could see the tears sparkling in Alicia's eyes and felt them pricking at her own.

When he saw she was making no move to take the doll he

lifted her arm and tucked the doll beneath it. 'Alicia has plenty more, Sarah. Now run along home. We'll see you tomorrow. Mr Hartley says he is very pleased with your progress, by the way. I thought you'd like to know.'

She stood quite unable to speak. He put his arm around her thin shoulders, urging her towards the door.

'Off you go now. And Alicia – I want a word with you!'

Because there was nothing left to do Sarah went, clutching the doll tightly. She could still see the hatred that had blazed in Alicia's eyes, feel it following her along the corridor. It was with her as she descended the staircase and even outside as the fresh air cooled her burning cheeks she was aware of it.

Alicia had disliked her before and never hidden that dislike. Now Sarah realised with a twist of foreboding she had unwittingly made a sworn enemy.

In her sitting-room along the corridor from the nursery and schoolroom Blanche Morse was disturbed by the sound of raised voices.

She set down her pen, cocked her carefully coiffured head to one side for a moment to listen, then rose from the small Queen Anne writing desk where she had been sitting to answer some letters and crossed to the door opening it a fraction.

The voices belonged to Alicia and Sarah and they were quarrelling. Blanche's lips tightened in distaste. She hated vulgarity of any kind and always had done. There were plenty of ways of getting what one wanted without resorting to verbal violence and most of them were a great deal more efficacious. She was about to close the door again when she heard footsteps in the corridor and Gilbert's voice. She stood, poised to fly back to the desk if he came into the room, and listened.

Every word of the altercation carried clearly along the echoing corridor and as it came to an end and Sarah scuttled past the door Blanche's eyes narrowed thoughtfully. A door closed and she could no longer hear Gilbert's voice – obviously he had gone into the nursery with Alicia to give her a talking to. Blanche went back into her sitting-room but she was unable to return to her letter writing.

There was something odd about the way Gilbert was behaving towards the Thomas child – she had thought so for some time. She knew his altruistic views of course and whilst she did not agree with them at least she accorded him a certain amount of respect where they were concerned. It was, she supposed, praiseworthy to wish to see his tenants and employees were well looked after and without a doubt Gilbert was held in high regard by them all. Not for him the disaffection and resentment generally reserved by the working classes for their betters.

But Blanche was unable to dispel the suspicion that there was something more than simple generosity involved here. Sarah was an attractive child, of course, a pretty little thing in spite of being too thin, and her intelligence was not in question. In some ways it was very like Gilbert to be conducting his own social experiment and at the same time patting himself on the back for enhancing the expectations of a girl who could otherwise have had little to look forward to in life. But even so . . .

Blanche raised a hand and carefully eased out the tiny furrow between her thin eyebrows. Pointless to give herself worry lines over the issue. And at least the young upstart was a mere girl and no matter how far she wormed her way into Gilbert's affection she would be unlikely to pose any threat to Blanche's plans for Leo's future as heir to the Morse empire.

The thought pleased her and as she so often did she congratulated herself on how clever she had been. When she arrived in England, widowed and left penniless by her late husband's business failures and resulting suicide, friends had introduced her to Gilbert and she had wasted no time in planning a campaign to win him. Handsome, wealthy, with lands that belonged to the past and a business enterprise which looked to the future he offered a life style she desired, security for her old age and glowing prospects for her young son.

For Blanche had quickly realised that when the time

came Gilbert would look for his successor at Morse Motors from amongst the next generation of his family. But Lawrence was dull, Hugh had not the slightest interest in the business and James . . . well, James was James, dreamy and a constant annoyance to his father. None of them were suited to such a position of responsibility. And Blanche was determined that Leo should be the one to step into the breach. He had all the necessary qualities – and not least he had inherited his mother's ruthless ambition. It was only disappointing to Blanche that so far Gilbert had failed to take to him but she had attributed this to Gilbert's natural reticence. Now, out of the blue, had come this girl, this funny little nobody, and Gilbert seemed to be lavishing on her all the interest he had denied her son.

Blanche's lips tightened. She did not like Sarah, and liked even less the way Gilbert was treating her as his protégée. Something would have to be done if she was not to become even more of an annoyance. When the opportunity arose Blanche was determined she would see Miss Sarah Thomas got her come-uppance.

I hate her, Alicia thought and her hands made fists with her neatly cut nails digging into her palms. *Why did she have to come here spoiling everything? I hate her!*

But her hatred, though pouring like acid through her veins, was impotent and she knew that revile Sarah Thomas as she might the girl was not actually responsible for spoiling anything. That had happened before she had come, beginning with the death of Rose, Alicia's mother.

Sometimes Alicia looked back with longing to the days when she had been a little girl, the baby of the family, but they seemed so long ago now. Her mother was no more now than a lovely dream; the cherished memory of the warmth of her arms, the perfume of lavender water, the sound of her voice singing soft bedtime lullabies were the haunting echoes of another time, another life.

Life now was Blanche who had imposed herself on Chewton Leigh House like the cloying heat of a summer's day when a thunderstorm is brewing and that repulsive

Leo, intruding into the nursery which had belonged to her and James, taking up her father's precious time.

And now there was also Sarah. Another intruder, another call on her father's attention. And he had actually given her Alicia's doll, her lovely Sleeping Beauty, and not content with that lectured Alicia on being nice to the wretched Sarah.

Why, she doesn't even *speak* properly! Alicia thought in fury. Her accent is even worse than Leo's horrid American drawl. It sounds so common!

The thought gave her a little comfort for it made her feel superior but it did nothing to lessen the hatred bubbling inside her.

The door of the inner nursery opened and she turned to see James standing there, his thumb hovering uncertainly in his mouth.

'Is something the matter, Alicia?' he asked, speaking with a slight lisp.

Alicia spun round. 'James! What are you doing here?'

'I came up for my ball and then I heard shouting so I . . . I hid,' he admitted. He looked frightened, his face pale and drawn above the collar of his little sailor suit.

She crossed to him, kneeling down in front of him and gently taking his thumb out of his mouth. Sometimes Alicia thought James was the one person in the world she loved. He had never known the warmth and happiness that made up the lovely dream world she sometimes allowed herself to remember. In the six years that they had been motherless Alicia sometimes felt that she had almost become his mother and he her child.

'It's all right, James,' she said. 'That stupid Sarah was prying and Father was angry. That's all.'

'He wasn't angry with me?'

'No, James, he wasn't angry with you.'

He nodded but the shadows did not quite leave his eyes and she stood up.

'Did you find your ball? If you get it I'll come down and play with you for a while if you like.'

'Leo said he'd play with me.'

107

'Leo!' she returned scornfully. 'Who cares about *Leo*? Listen James, it's you and me, remember? Leo's not your brother so you can stop hanging around him. And that stupid Sarah . . . Forget about them, James. *I'll* look after you. And then when we are old enough we'll show them all. We're the Morses. We can do anything, James, you and I.'

She took his hand and in giving him comfort felt her own strength grow.

'One day we'll show them, James,' she said. 'One day we'll show the world!'

Chapter Nine

As autumn drew on and the leaves on the trees in the park turned scarlet, russet and gold against an intensely blue sky Sarah continued to take her lessons in the schoolroom at Chewton Leigh House with Alicia Morse and Leo de Vere. The hunting season began and sometimes the sound of the horn and the baying of the hounds would carry in through the schoolroom window; if they looked up and craned their necks a little the children could see the huntsmen in their scarlet and black streaming across the hillside. Gilbert hunted when he could spare the time as did Lawrence and Hugh when they were home from boarding school and Alicia and Leo continually tried to catch a glimpse of them.

'When I'm just a little older I'll be able to hunt too,' Alicia would say with a sidelong glance at Sarah, whom she knew could not ride. But Sarah refused to take the bait or even to take the slightest notice of the hunt. She was too interested in her books, too determined to make progress in her efforts to compare with the others, to be distracted by such silly ploys and besides her sympathy was fairly and squarely with the fox.

Soon her diligence was paying off and Richard Hartley was delighted with her progress. He was less pleased, however, with Leo and Alicia and he reported as much to Gilbert one crisp day in October.

'Alicia is a clever girl and Leo, though more of a plodder, is no fool. If they spent as much time and effort on their work as they do on sniping at one another they would do very well indeed. As it is Leo is causing me some concern and I have to say that unless he is prepared to knuckle down he may flunk the entrance exam for his prep school.'

Gilbert's face darkened. 'Bad as that? Very well, Hartley, I'll have a word with him.'

He strode out of the schoolroom and down the stairs.

Blanche was in the drawing-room arranging a vase of chrysanthemums which Dent the head gardener had cut for her and he determined to tell her of the tutor's concern for her son's progress. As he talked she continued to arrange her flowers and only the slow tightening of her features revealed her displeasure.

'I see,' she said when he had at last finished. 'Well, to be honest with you Gilbert I am hardly surprised.'

He looked puzzled. 'What do you mean by that?'

Blanche stripped a last untidy leaf from a chrysanthemum stalk, dropped it into the wastepaper basket and poked the flower into its place. Then she turned slowly, folding her hands on the skirt of her russet brown velvet dress.

'I dare say he is being distracted by Sarah Thomas,' she said coolly.

'Surely not!' Gilbert scoffed. 'Hartley is very pleased with her.'

'That is as may be,' Blanche said darkly. 'I don't think either Leo or Alicia can be being helped by her company.'

Gilbert thrust his hands into the pockets of his grey stripe trousers.

'I don't understand what you are trying to say, Blanche.'

She paused, choosing her words carefully. Since she had come to see Sarah as a threat to her son Blanche had been busy. For some weeks now she had been nursing the nugget of information she had unearthed, waiting for the right moment to bring it into the open. Now that moment had come and she intended to make the most of it.

'I am sorry to have to tell you this, Gilbert, but I have been making a few enquiries about Sarah. Perhaps you will disapprove but since she is being educated alongside my son I decided to make it my business. And what I discovered has disturbed me greatly.'

His eyes narrowed. He stood very still, the stillness from which his strength generally emanated, but now strangely it was as if even that strength was a carefully created illusion. Blanche was overcome with the ridiculous notion that she held in her hands the power to

110

hurt him, to hurt the great Gilbert Morse. Only in the bedroom did she experience this sensation of ascendancy, when he wanted her and she with-held her favours or afterwards when he lay sleeping, his handsome face boyish in repose. But now instead of exhilarating her as it did then the knowledge of her power frightened her a little and made her hesitate, aware she was treading a fine line across a potential minefield.

'I am afraid I have discovered that Sarah Thomas is illegitimate,' she said meeting his eyes squarely. 'I always had my suspicions about her mother. It seemed to me a little too convenient the way her husband was supposed to have died in India and yet nobody ever admitted to having set eyes on him. I decided to do a little investigation.'

He drew a silver cigarette case out of his pocket but did not open it.

'And what did you discover?' His voice was taut. The tone of it made her quake inwardly but she had gone too far to draw back now.

'Rachel Thomas was never married,' she said coolly. 'She came back here under false pretences and set herself up as a respectable married woman. That she never was.'

'And Sarah's father?' Gilbert asked. 'Who was her father?'

Blanche hesitated, wondering whether she dared confront him with the suspicion which nagged at her. She decided against it. 'Maybe he *was* a soldier – goodness knows there are always young women ready to throw themselves at men in uniform without a thought to their reputation – or the consequences,' she said shortly. 'In any case it makes little difference. Sarah Thomas is a bastard – and this is the child you see fit to educate alongside our own.'

'And why not?' Gilbert snapped the cigarette case open.

Blanche glared. 'She is hardly the company I would choose for Leo. And I would have thought you would have been more concerned with Alicia's moral welfare than to allow her to associate with a child like that. She could contaminate them both – if she has not already done so.'

111

'Good heavens, Blanche, don't you think you are making a little too much of this?' Gilbert said. His tone was as level as ever, yet she was aware that he was angry.

She held her ground. 'I don't think so.'

'Well I most certainly do! Sarah – *contaminate* Alicia and Leo? I never heard such nonsense. This is a child you are talking about.'

'A child whose mother was no better than she should be.'

'That,' said Gilbert angrily, 'is scarcely the child's fault. Surely she has as much right to life as any born in wedlock? No!' He raised his hand imperiously as Blanche opened her mouth to speak again. 'I won't hear another word on the subject. Sarah is a very nice child and it would do Leo no harm to emulate her in many ways. As for this visiting the sins of the fathers upon the children I find it singularly lacking in charity. If you wish Leo to be educated away from what you call Sarah's contaminating influence then that is your prerogative. I shall not interfere with any arrangements you may wish to make concerning him. But Sarah stays here.' He paused. 'As a matter of fact I have been considering integrating her into the family a little more. She has precious little fun with those Pughs. You have just made up my mind for me. I shall see that Sarah is taught to ride and next time we have a family outing I shall arrange for her to come along. Understand me, Blanche, I will not tolerate this sort of prejudice under my roof and the sooner you realise it the better!'

He strode to the door and threw it open to reveal James crouching there listening. He grabbed him by the collar and hauled him into the room.

'And what do you think you are doing skulking there? How dare you listen at keyholes?' He administered a quick cuff to James' ear, then turned and stalked out.

'How dare you, James!' Blanche echoed him. 'Go to the nursery at once!'

He scuttled away and left alone Blanche pressed a lace handkerchief to her cold lips to stop them trembling. She had never seen Gilbert so furious before and she realised she had made a bad mistake in attacking his patronage of Sarah.

Clearly for the moment she was going to have to suffer the child. But Gilbert's very stubbornness in the matter served only to heighten her suspicions and his anger was yet another factor. Altruistic Gilbert might be, in this case Blanche was beginning to be convinced there was more to it than that.

As a young girl Rachel Thomas had often stayed in this very house. From what Blanche had heard Rose, Gilbert's first wife, had been a dull soul and remembering Rachel's obvious charms Blanche thought it was quite conceivable that even a man as honourable as Gilbert might have been tempted to stray.

If her suspicions were correct then it would be that much more difficult to get rid of Sarah. But Blanche had never been one to give up without a fight. When the opportunity arose she would grasp it with both hands. She crossed to the window and the sky, grey and leaden now above the thinning leaves of the still brilliant-hued trees, seemed to reflect the steely determination in her heart.

'I don't believe you,' Sarah said. 'I don't believe you!'

She stood in the centre of the schoolroom, her hands clutching the folds of her skirt, her eyes huge in her small face.

Alicia glared at her maliciously. 'It's true. James was outside the door. He heard every word. You're a bastard!'

Sarah almost sobbed aloud. 'Don't say that word! It's bad!'

'But it's what you are. That makes you bad too.'

'It's not true! My dad was a soldier. He died in India . . .'

'Ha-ha!' Alicia said scornfully. 'That's what your mother told you because she was ashamed. He never married her, whoever he was. She was a fallen woman.'

'She wasn't. She wasn't!'

'Yes she was. I expect that's why she died. It was a judgement.'

'What about your mother?' Sarah sobbed. 'She died too. Was *she* a fallen woman?'

'No she was not!' Alicia's hands screwed into fists. 'Don't dare to say such a thing! She was married to my father.'

113

'I'll say if it I like. You said it. You said it about *my* mother!'

'Because it's true.'

'It's not. It's not!'

'You're a bastard.'

'I'm not! You are. You're the bastard!' She flew at Alicia, grabbing a handful of the thick dark hair and pulling and suddenly they were scrapping like a pair of young puppies, kicking, biting, tearing at one another's hair and clothing. For long seconds they fought, their hatred of one another finding expression in violence, and it was only when a voice from the doorway thundered: 'Girls! What are you doing?' that they parted, shame-faced yet still glowering at one another.

'It was her – she started it! She called me a terrible name!' Sarah sobbed.

'What name?'

'Bastard.'

His eyes behind his thick spectacles expressed his shock.

'Sarah! Where did you learn such a word?'

'She said it. She said I was . . . and my mother was . . .' Her eyes were wild, her blouse torn, her ribbon dangling loose.

Alicia drew herself to her full height. 'I never said any such thing!'

In spite of the scrap she looked miraculously cool, with only her slightly tumbled hair evidence of Sarah's attack. Richard Hartley looked from one to the other of them.

'I think we had better begin on our lessons,' he suggested, turning as always in moments of crisis to what he knew best. 'Sarah, go and make yourself look respectable. Alicia, tidy your hair and take your place. And both of you try to behave like young ladies.'

Stung and resentful still they did as they were bid. And if either of them noticed Leo, his epicene mouth twisted into a gloating expression as he watched them from the doorway, then for the moment at least they really did not care.

As if in defiance of Blanche's revelations Gilbert began

114

Sarah's riding lessons the following week. One of Alicia's old riding habits was altered to fit her by the seamstress who had succeeded Rachel and every day for an hour Sarah had to endure the torment of putting it on and presenting herself at the stables for an hour's tuition from Turner, the groom.

She did not like the stables. She did not like the smell and she was nervous of all the horses, even the gentle pony Blackie whom Turner had decided would be the most suitable mount for her. But Sarah was growing used to having to do things she did not like and she was determined not to give Alicia the pleasure of knowing she was frightened. She persevered, Turner persevered, and at last she became competent enough at balancing on the side saddle and handling the pony to be allowed to gallop and even take a small jump or two.

Once when she was riding with Alicia and Leo the boy managed to get close enough to her to take a surreptitious swipe at Blackie with his riding stick in the hope of making the pony bolt but Blackie was too good tempered to respond to such a ploy and since no-one but Sarah knew what he had done the incident never reached Gilbert's ears.

He kept his promise too to include Sarah in some of the family's activities but this did nothing to lessen her sense of alienation from them. They hated her, she knew, and she hated them, but she kept her own counsel. There was no-one she could turn to in any case. She belonged nowhere, she thought wretchedly, for the village children no longer treated her as one of them either. At Home Farm she did the chores which Bertha had allotted her uncomplainingly and if she ever cried she did it in the privacy of her room, her head tucked under the pillow to stifle the sobs so that no-one should hear. At the house she was constantly aware of the resentment she aroused and the antagonism between her and Alicia was almost tangible. Unwillingly she admired the older girl, envied her self-possession and her confidence, her pretty clothes and the fact that she was Gilbert's daughter – more because Sarah hero-worshipped Gilbert than because she had any conscious desire to be one of the Morse clan. But any overtures of friendship were quickly slapped down, any hint of an alliance which glimmered occasionally on the horizon when Alicia and Leo were engaged in their frequent clashes was quickly negated and Sarah realised that Alicia had not mellowed towards her one jot. Part of her was glad. She had not forgotten the terrible things Alicia had said about her mother and she did not think she ever would. The name Alicia had called her still haunted her in the night, making her cringe with its ugliness and filling her with a fierce hatred of the girl who had thrown it at her with such malice. Yet in spite of this there was an undoubted glamour about Alicia and perversely Sarah longed to be accepted by her, to be a part of her charmed world and no longer the butt of her spite.

They *should* be able to be friends, she thought. Both of them had lost their mothers and instinctively, with a maturity far beyond her years, Sarah sensed that Alicia was as unhappy as she. Sometimes when Gilbert was there Alicia would put on an act for him, drawing Sarah into the circle of her activity so that Gilbert looked at her with affection and Sarah dared to hope that after all things were going to be different.

Only they never were.

At Christmas when Lawrence and Hugh came home the atmosphere improved a little. Alicia was on her best behaviour for them and Hugh, at least, made quite a fuss of Sarah. She was grateful for his attention but also a little scared lest Alicia should be jealous and take it out on her later. Sarah was invited to the house for the festivities and she and Alicia trimmed the tree together with Gilbert looking fondly on. The tree was an enormous one, perhaps ten feet high, and Turner had to bring a step ladder into the drawing-room for them to be able to reach the top of it.

'Take care, girls,' Gilbert warned. 'We don't want any broken arms or legs for Christmas. Perhaps you should allow Leo to do it.'

Alicia tossed her head. 'Why? He's so clumsy he'd only break the baubles. He can put up the holly and mistletoe.'

So Leo was delegated to hang the mistletoe boughs from

116

the doorways and Sarah and Alicia took turns to steady the step ladder for one another to climb up with the dainty glass ornaments and the tiny lanterns each containing a minute candle.

It was when the presents were hung on the tree however that Sarah began to feel like an intruder again. There were so many for the others and she could not see a single parcel bearing her name.

There was though and when she opened it on Christmas day she was overjoyed to find a little silver bracelet inside of the finest filigree. Gilbert was smiling at her and for a moment joy spilled through her.

'Oh it's beautiful!' she whispered. 'I've never seen anything so beautiful!'

Then she became aware of the other faces watching her with thinly veiled hostility and her joy died. She clutched the bracelet to her as if afraid it might be snatched away and knew instinctively that if Christmas was meant to be the season of goodwill, as far as Blanche, Leo and Alicia were concerned at least the goodwill did not extend to her.

She treasured the bracelet all the same. Gilbert fastened it around her wrist and that night back in the bare bedroom at Home Farm she replaced it carefully in its tissue paper and laid it in the drawer with her few knick-knacks.

'You see, Rose?' she said to the doll which had once been Alicia's and who now sat on the cupboard beside her bed. 'I have two beautiful things now – you and my bracelet.'

The doll gazed back at her with unwinking glass eyes and silently Sarah promised herself that one day there would be other treasures, other beautiful things. And perhaps, if she was very lucky, there would be someone to share them with. She would have a happy home again, she decided, with all the love and warmth she had known in the cottage at Starvault but it would be encompassed by the sort of surroundings and possessions the Morse family took for granted.

One day I'll be *somebody*, Sarah promised herself. Not just the little outsider there because of the charity of others but a very special somebody in my own right.

Secure in her dreams Sarah slept.

117

Chapter Ten

On a warm summer afternoon in July 1906 Hugh Morse left Chewton Leigh House carrying a picnic basket which Cook had filled with all manner of delicious goodies and made for the yard where his father's latest acquisition, a Rolls-Royce Silver Ghost, was parked. The Rolls was a beautiful motor and Hugh had been longing for an opportunity to take it for more than simply a token spin ever since returning home from the public school where he had just completed his last term.

When he had driven with his father beside him Gilbert was continually warning him to 'Slow down or you'll have us over!' or 'Don't tax the engine so, my boy!' and Hugh had been impatient to be left alone to try out his own skill and the full potential of the motor. Now that opportunity had come. Gilbert had gone to France where he had been invited to take a look at the progress Santos-Dumont, the brilliant Argentinian engineer, was making in the construction of a flying machine and Hugh had been quick to seize his chance to drive the Rolls.

As he swung the picnic basket into the luggage dickey he whistled a snatch of Gilbert and Sullivan and his blue eyes twinkled merrily in his handsome face. But it was not only the prospect of driving the Rolls that lifted his spirits and made small spirals of excitement twist deep inside him. Unknown to his step-mother, who would certainly not have approved, he had invited Sarah Thomas to accompany him.

Still whistling Hugh jammed the starting handle into place and swung it effortlessly. Five years had seen him develop from a good-looking lad into a handsome and well-made young man. At five foot ten he was already as tall as his father and since he was still only eighteen years old there was always the possibility that he might yet grow another inch or two. Added to this his sporting activities had helped him develop a fine physique. At school Hugh had been a keen cricketer and rugby footballer, at home he rode regularly and swam in the lake and the deep river pools, and as a consequence his shoulders had broadened and muscles rippled across his back beneath the fine white lawn of his shirt and in his strong arms. His hips however had remained as narrow as they had always been and the light cream trousers he was wearing flattered both them and his long muscled legs.

Hugh took a pride in his strong and healthy body and was now eagerly looking forward to the day when he would clothe it in the uniform of an army officer. He had passed the entrance examination for Sandhurst with flying colours and in the autumn he would be going there to begin his training. In the meantime he had the long hot days of summer to while away – and he intended to make the most of them.

The engine of the Rolls turned over and as the motor car began to tremble convulsively Hugh leaped up into the seat and gripped the steering wheel. A honk on the bulbous rubber horn to warn Brandy and Bet, two of the family's labradors who were lurking curiously in the yards, and he was off, bouncing over the cobbles and out into the lane, the wind streaming in his jet black hair.

This was the life, he thought, laughing aloud as a startled magpie rose from the road before his wheels in a flurry of outraged black and white feathers, and experienced a moment's pity for Lawrence, his brother, who would be wasting this beautiful afternoon away at the Works.

As Gilbert had anticipated the results of Lawrence's endeavours to gain academic qualifications had not been good enough to take him to University and when he had left school he had gone straight into Morse Motors. The move had suited him. On a practical level Lawrence was indisputably able, he was as enthusiastic about the family firm as Hugh was for the military, and was already establishing himself as a force to be reckoned with. Less adventurous in outlook than either his father or grandfather had been and without their flare for recognising the forward trends of progress perhaps a decade before they occurred, yet he had a solid and reliable base of practical knowledge and sound common sense. This, coupled with his capacity for hard work, inspired confidence in the work force; they might think him a dry stick for a young man barely out of his teens, but they respected and liked him all the same and believed, with reason, that the future of the company was safe in his hands.

Thank heavens for Lawrence! Hugh thought gratefully as he steered the Rolls around a bend in the lane. Without him his father might have been less ready to allow Hugh to fulfil his own ambitions. Frank Raisey might be an excellent general manager and quite capable of overseeing the running of the works, Joe Isaccs, in his dusty little office, might keep the accounts in apple pie order and advise on each point of legality which arose without ever bothering the firm's solicitor, but Hugh knew that Gilbert would consider it unthinkable that there should not be a member of the Morse family at the helm. Fortunately Lawrence was perfectly happy to take on that responsibility and Hugh was left free to pursue his own fortune, wherever it may lead him – and to enjoy his pleasures.

This afternoon those pleasures could hardly have been more enticing. A drive in the Rolls with no-one to criticise or curb – and the prospect of impressing Sarah with his driving ability into the bargain.

At the thought of Sarah his spirits rose another notch. She was a little peach and no mistake! Hugh had almost forgotten now what a pathetic little thing she had been when his father had first introduced her to Chewton Leigh House; he only knew that when he had come home last year for his Christmas vacation he had been amazed to find such a lovely young girl beneath his very roof.

The change of course had been gradual. Years of tuition from the conscientious Richard Hartley had sharpened her already quick mind and expanded her knowledge, and continued proximity with the gentry had refined her speech, eliminating the sloppy syntax and reducing her accent to an almost unnoticeable burr which she was capable of losing altogether in the company of the Morses and their friends although she still retained it as a defence mechanism when she was with her adopted family, the Pughs, or her old village friends, the one passport to belonging still available to her. She had gained in confidence, her manner was now easy and positive and she had learned well from Alicia so that slowly, almost imperceptibly, she had ceased to stand out like a sore thumb amongst the well-bred Morses and begun to behave as if to the manner born.

Her physical development had been longer in coming and then more shockingly sudden; almost overnight it seemed her figure had blossomed from that of a skinny child into the curves of young womanhood.

Now Sarah was tall and slender with long legs and nut brown hair which streamed free of the ribbons she had worn as a child. Her breasts were firm and high, her waist as small as it had ever been and her hips, not yet rounded to the fullness of maturity, had a neat streamlined flair that was pleasing to the eye. Good food and plenty of it had put roses in her cheeks and her eyes, blue as cornflowers, sparkled with health and with fun. But perhaps it was her freshness that was most appealing of all to Hugh.

Since his early teens Hugh's startling good looks had made him the object of attention of practically every girl with whom he came into contact. In spite of his youth he had been pursued relentlessly in every possible way and he was familiar with – and immune to – every flick of the eyelashes and every sidelong glance that told him he had made yet another conquest. And it was not only young women. There had been one or two older ones too, more subtle and yet at the same time more provocative, who had expressed their interest in a variety of ways as old as time. But not Sarah. Never once had she showed the slightest interest in him except as a friend and the omission inflamed him as none of the coquetry of the others had done.

Why didn't she notice him, dammit? Was she still so much a child inside that new and voluptuous body that she did not experience the slightest curiosity or desire? Alicia was only a year or so older and she had flirted shamelessly with Hugh's friend Oliver when he had brought him home for the holidays. But then Alicia was very aware of the power of her body. Once or twice they had conducted experiments of their own – the memory was enough to bring the blood rushing to the surface in a hot flood, pounding at his temples and suffusing his skin with a rosy glow. But he knew experiments with Alicia were dangerous. If Father ever so much as suspected he would take the horsewhip to Hugh, big as he was. And besides, how could one's own sister be half as interesting as this lovely young woman who had blossomed unnoticed?

Hugh had done his best to engage her attention without success. She remained warm towards him but in an even more sisterly way than Alicia and he cursed the fact that he had been the one to establish the friendly relationship in the first place. He had done it because he felt sorry for her, of course, so little and lost and with everyone hating and resenting her. Now he wished he had been more distant – cruel even. That way she might have admired, rather than liking, him, and he would have had a base from which to work when even the slightest courtesy or kindness would have been noticed and remarked upon. As it was he was 'good old Hugh' – and that was not an enviable position nor the way to raise interest for an amorous encounter. When he smiled at her she smiled back just as she always had, apparently quite unaware of the way she was making his heart pound, when he drew her into conversations she responded with her customary unaffected eagerness. Even when he touched her she seemed unmoved and totally oblivious of the havoc she was wreaking in him. Only when he had once been bold enough to brush his hand against her breast had there been any response; the colour had rushed to her face like an echo of the blood that was congesting his body and for a heady moment he had thought she was excited as he was by the contact. That delightful notion had been quickly dispelled. Her eyes had flipped up to meet his briefly but they expressed horror, not coquetry, and she had turned away in something like panic.

122

Far from discouraging Hugh this reaction had stirred new depths of excitement. Nobody had ever touched her breasts before, he was certain of it. He had been the first. The dark excitement ran through his veins like a current of electricity from the transformer in the outbuildings, making his skin prick and his bones turn to water. He began to wonder how those breasts would feel without several layers of material to mask the contact and what they would look like. Hugh had never seen a woman unclothed – except of course Alicia, and she was as flat chested as a boy. He and some of his friends at school had pored over a collection of photographs one of the chaps had smuggled in – half-naked girls in strange poses which the photographer had clearly thought erotic but which to the boys had seemed faintly ridiculous for all their avid and vociferous appreciation of the female form. But the girls in the photographs had all been plump with voluptuous bottoms and big solid thighs and their uncorseted breasts had been heavy as over-ripe melons. Sarah, he had decided, fell somewhere between these two extremes, and he began to be obsessed with the desire to explore her.

When he had suggested the trip out in the Rolls he had held his breath, terrified she might refuse. But she had accepted eagerly with only the one small hesitation: 'Are you sure your father won't mind?'

Anticipation coursing through him had made him bold. 'Why should he? I'm allowed to drive the Rolls.'

She knew this was true. What she did not know was that he had never before driven it unsupervised and was hoping that Gilbert would not learn he was going to do so now.

'I'd love to,' she had said, smiling so that the dimples played in her cheeks and he felt the familiar heat prickling at the most sensitive parts of his body.

Now as he turned into the Home Farm track he saw her waiting for him outside the house. She was wearing a gingham dress and a wide straw hat tied under the chin with a chiffon scarf. She waved and he accelerated in a cloud of dust, unable to resist showing off his prowess, then slowed to a juddering halt beside her.

123

'Hello there! You're all ready then.'

'I've been ready for an hour,' she said ingenuously. 'You don't know how nice it is to get away from Mrs Misery for an afternoon. I was terrified she'd find some job for me to do that would make me late so I've kept well out of her way.'

'Mrs Misery' was Sarah's name for Bertha; she had names for everyone and it amused him. Lawrence was 'Sobersides', Leo was 'Creepy Crawlie'. Privately she also called Alicia 'Miss Wasp' but she had not dared tell Hugh of this label for she was afraid he would not take kindly to it. He and Alicia were very close.

Mrs Pugh however was fair game for a shared joke. He laughed as he climbed down from the motor with fluid athletic grace.

'If she had I'd have dealt with her personally,' he said airily. 'Now, you had better put on this dustcoat, Sarah. I brought a spare one especially for you.'

He held it for her while she slipped her arms into the voluminous white sleeves. The dust coat reached almost to the ground and laughing she did a little dance for him. He laughed with her, a little regretfully, for the dustcoat completely hid her lovely figure but it was essential to wear it if she was not to get her dress filthy especially on a dry day like today when the wheels sent up a fine haze of dust at even the slowest of speeds.

'Where are we going?' she asked as he helped her up into the Rolls.

'Do you know Bury Woods?'

She shook her head. She knew every inch of the countryside within walking distance but with a motor it was possible to go much further afield. Hugh had planned and scouted; Bury Woods was, he thought, the perfect place.

As he drove Sarah watched intently.

'I wish *I* could have a turn,' she said.

'Perhaps you can later.'

They were on a straight stretch of road now and he built the speed up steadily until they were travelling at almost forty miles an hour. He stole a glance at her; the wind was whipping up the colour in her cheeks, her eyes were shining and the chiffon scarf framed her face, accentuating the heart-shaped bone structure. He looked away quickly. At that moment driving the motor required all his concentration. There would be plenty of time later for drinking in Sarah.

'Fancy your father going to France!' she shouted over the noise of the engine. 'Do you really think this Mr Santos What-ever-his-name-is will be able to build a machine that will fly?'

'I don't see why not,' he shouted back. 'The Wright brothers are doing it in America.'

'*Really* flying? Like a bird?'

'They are only doing short hops at the moment. I think they thought they had cracked it a couple of years ago when they invited all the newspapers to watch them but that was a bit of a flop and no-one seems to take them seriously any more. But yes, I'm sure it will come. It's only a matter of time now, a few refinements and lots of trial and error. One of these days we shall see men up there with the birds – and not too far in the future if you ask me.'

'And this Santos man is doing it too?'

'Yes. Father was really excited at the chance to see the progress he is making.' He broke off to slow down to execute a bend. The Rolls was really living up to his expectations and he was enjoying himself immensely.

'You know what I think?' he said when they were safely around the bend and onto another straight stretch. 'I think Father would like to build engines for flying machines.'

'Your father? At Morse Motors?' She sounded incredulous.

'Why not? Someone has to. Father has always been one to look to the future. Mind you,' he added, 'he doesn't have so much to do with the works these days and I can't see Lawrence being very keen to take that sort of risk. You know what a stick-in-the-mud he is.'

'Old Sobersides?' Sarah said, laughing. 'He would do what your father told him to though, surely?'

'Oh yes, he'd do *that* all right. Lawrence always does what Father tells him.' There was faint sarcasm in his voice.

Her brows came together.

'We shouldn't make fun of Lawrence, Hugh. He's really nice. And he can't help it if he's a bit . . .'

'A bit of a sobersides?' Hugh suggested.

She laughed again. 'Well – yes!'

The hedges, thick with tall white cowparsley, sped by; in some of the banks there were flashes of purple willow herb and mallow and pale clusters of dog roses. From the elevated seat of the Rolls they could see over the hedges to the meadows where herds of cows grazed, black and white Friesians like the cows at Home Farm and some reddish brown Jersey cattle, sleek and handsome. There were cornfields too, brilliant gold in the sunshine and dotted with vermillion silk poppies, and beyond them the hills were varying patches of green and gold that reached up to touch the periwinkle blue of the sky. The road was almost deserted; once they passed a wagon lumbering along and once a smart brougham, otherwise they might have been the only two people in the world.

Another bend, another dip, and the hedges on one side of the road became trees, thickening gradually into an area of natural woodland. The sun filtered through them in dizzying patterns and Sarah raised her hand to shade her eyes as the kaleidoscope of light and shade assailed them. Half a mile or so further on Hugh slowed the car and turned in between a space in the trees, steering carefully along the natural path between the bushes and gnarled old trunks, then coming to a stop in a clearing.

'This is as far as we can go. It gets thicker in a minute.'

Sarah rose from the seat and leaped down before he could come around to help her. She had enjoyed her ride, now she was eager to stretch her legs and explore. She ran a few yards, her boots scuffing the covering of last year's dead leaves, stretched out her arms and spun in a circle.

'What a lovely place! It's so quiet – and so cool!'

'Aren't you going to take off your dustcoat?'

'Oh yes!' She skipped back to the motor, slipped off the voluminous dustcoat and laid it on the seat. 'See, I'm already such a seasoned motorist I quite forgot I was wearing it!'

126

I didn't, Hugh thought, relieved to be treated once more to a view of those delectable curves as she pirouetted beneath the trees.

'Wait for me!' he called, his voice not quite steady. 'I have to get the picnic basket. Besides, you don't know the way.'

'Does it matter?' she called gaily.

He unloaded the picnic basket and they started down one of the leafy paths walking Indian fashion. As he watched the sway of her trim hips his heart began to thud again. The wood grew thicker, the sun only a glimmer now through the branches of the tall trees, and the ground began to slope downwards. At one point it became a steep bank; she scrambled nimbly down and he followed more slowly, balancing himself by holding onto branches as he manoeuvred the heavy picnic basket. Then all at once the wood ended and they were back in a sunlit meadow, encompassed by the curve of the wood and sloping gently towards a lazy ribbon of river.

'This will do, won't it?' he said.

'I want to explore!'

'Let's eat first. I don't want to have to lug this basket around all afternoon.'

'All right then!' The fresh air had made her hungry. She threw herself down on a tussock of grass, spreading her skirts and lifting them high enough to expose a pair of neat calves. The blood pounded at his temples. He turned away setting down the picnic basket.

'Let's see what Cook has packed for us,' he suggested.

'You open it.' She was untying the chiffon scarf, tossing her hat down onto the grass beside her, shaking out her lovely nut-brown hair. He could not look at her, so hard was his heart beating.

On top of the food was a checked tablecloth and a tartan carriage rug.

'No wonder the basket was so heavy!' he remarked. 'I suppose Cook thought I might get a chill sitting on the damp grass.'

'It's not damp,' she objected.

127

'No, but you know how cautious Cook is. *Ne'er cast a clout till May be out*,' he quoted.

'May's been out a long time. It's July now.'

'That wouldn't make a bit of difference to Cook!' They both laughed. 'Do you want to sit on the rug?'

'No. I'd rather feel the grass tickling my knees.'

'It's all right for you. I'll probably get grass stains on my trousers. Come on, we may as well since she has put it in for us.' He did not add that sharing a rug was a good excuse for getting closer to her. He spread the rug and the tablecloth and began setting out the goodies – sandwiches and slab cake, cut into thick slices, some hand-raised pork pie and a flagon of dandelion wine.

'What a spread!' Sarah commented enthusiastically.

Hugh uncorked the flagon and poured some wine into the two mugs which had been carefully packed into linen serviettes.

'Have some, Sarah.'

'Thank you. I must say I'm quite thirsty.' She drank, then giggled. 'Shan't we get tipsy, though, on this stuff?'

'I shouldn't think so. Cook would never have given it to us if she thought it was that strong,' he said but it was a pleasant thought all the same – if Sarah was slightly tipsy she might be less likely to object to what he had in mind.

They began tucking into the food though for once Hugh found he was unable to eat as heartily as usual and he marvelled at the enthusiastic way Sarah was disposing of a slice of pie. Alicia ate so sparingly, forever thinking of her waistline, but Sarah had no such inhibitions. When at last they had finished he threw himself back full length on the rug, luxuriating in the warmth of the sun on his face, but Sarah leaped to her feet.

'Come on, lazybones, I thought we were going to explore!'

'Not for a minute.'

'Yes! Come on!' She grabbed his hand, tugging. For a moment he resisted thinking how easy it would be to pull her down beside him. Then before he could act on the idea she let go his hand, dancing away. 'Well I'm going to if

128

you're not!' she called over her shoulder as she made for the river. He watched her flying hair and petticoats then got to his feet and ran after her, catching her easily with his long athletic strides.

By the river it was cool again. Sarah took off her boots and waded in, squealing as the pebbles tickled her toes and bunching up her skirts. A moorhen scuttled from the opposite bank; in the shallows minnows darted beneath her bare feet. He rolled up his trousers and followed suit, still wondering if the opportunity to touch those lovely rounded breasts would ever come. She kicked up a little water at him, laughing, teasing, but not in a flirting manner, and he began to despair. A whole afternoon alone with Sarah and still she was behaving like a child let out of school . . . though he laughed with her, frustration was beginning to smoulder within him.

'You're making me wet,' he objected.

'It'll soon dry in the sun,' she scoffed. 'You sound more like old Sobersides. Don't say you're going to grow up like him – to be no fun at all!'

He made a grab for her then but she eluded him, wading back to the bank, standing there tantalisingly while he followed more slowly to avoid soaking his rolled-up trousers.

Surely she knew what she was doing to him! he thought with mounting irritation. Not even Sarah could be that naive.

She led the dash back up the field, reached the rug and threw herself down on it wringing the water out of the hem of her dress.

'And you were worried about getting wet!' she teased. 'Just look at me!'

'I am looking,' he said.

She jerked her head up, startled, and he saw the guarded look that was suddenly there in her eyes. She dropped the hem of her skirt abruptly.

'We had better pack up the picnic things.'

Again he cursed. He knelt beside her, more aware than ever of her nearness, yet still apprehensive about her

129

reaction if he should make a move. The easiness between them was momentarily lost. He banged the plates into a corner of the picnic basket and heard her squeal. Swivelling his head he saw that she had lifted the remains of the fruitcake and disturbed a wasp; it was now buzzing angrily around her. He grabbed a serviette and flapped at it.

'Don't!' she ordered, her voice a little panicky. 'You'll make it angry and it will sting!'

'I'll kill it.'

'No you won't – you'll just make it angry. Cook says . . .'

The wasp flew out of range of Hugh's flailing serviette and suddenly he knew what he was going to do.

They continued packing up the picnic basket, Sarah bending over it to arrange things neatly. Her hair was swinging over her shoulders; where it had parted he could see the nape of her neck, smooth, pale and enticing.

'Don't move,' he said, his voice uneven.

She froze. 'What . . . ?'

'That wasp. It's in your hair. No!' as she made a quick panicky movement, 'stay quite still or it will sting you. I'll get it.'

She froze again, shoulders tense, neck rigid. He reached out and touched her hair. It felt silky soft. His throat was so tight he could scarcely breathe. He spread his fingers and felt a tremor run through her.

'Hugh . . .'

'It's all right,' he said. 'It's gone.'

She began to turn her head but he left his hand where it was, feeling her hair slip through his fingers. She was trembling but in his excitement he scarcely noticed. He caught her shoulder, turning her into his arms and she buried her face in him, half-sobbing. Slowly he moved his hand around her neck, astonished at the softness of it beneath his fingers, stroking, gentling. For a moment they remained there, kneeling together and he let his other hand slip down a little from her shoulder towards her breast. The desire was pounding in him now. As his fingers touched her breast she stiffened, drawing back a little, as though startled yet unwilling to believe the contact was deliberate

130

and he could restrain himself no longer. He grabbed her breast, cupping it and squeezing, and felt the shock wave reverberate through her body.

'Hugh!'

He held her firm. 'Don't move! Oh Sarah . . .'

'No!' she breathed, wriggling away.

The movement of her breast beneath his hand only increased his fever. It felt even better than he had anticipated in his wildest dreams, firm yet soft, like a ripe peach, filling the palm of his hand.

'Stay still!' he ordered. 'I won't hurt you.'

She continued to wriggle.

'Hugh, don't, please! Stop it!'

He ignored her. Her face was close to his; suddenly feeling her breasts was not enough. He wanted to kiss her. His fingers tightened on the nape of her neck, spreading out to immobilise her twisting head and his lips found hers. They were sweet, tasting faintly of the dandelion wine. He kissed her hard and felt them move, unwillingly returning the pressure. For a moment he drank her in then he could no longer endure the throbbing demands of his body. He pushed her back so that she was lying half on the rug and half on the grass, kneeling astride her and fumbling at her skirts.

She began to flail then, half sobbing. 'Hugh stop it! Hugh please – stop it!'

He ignored her pleas. The firm flesh of her long legs felt too good. His seeking hand found the vee between her thighs, the warmth emanating through the thin cotton drawers inflamed him still further.

'Lie still!' he ordered her, covering her mouth with his again. This time there was no answering response from her lips, her head twisted and her body writhed as she tried to escape. Keeping her shoulders pinned to the ground he fumbled with his clothing and tore at her drawers. A madness seemed to have taken control of him now; he had never intended that the encounter should go this far but now her very resistance was driving him on. With his knee he wedged her legs apart and began to thrust and plunge

131

between them. He heard her sob and scream softly then her back arched towards him and the madness was all-consuming so that his body seemed almost not to belong to him and hers was no longer that of little Sarah but simply an object of his crazed delight. At the end it was all he could do to keep from crying out as she had done for the shock waves seemed to reverberate to the very core of him and he covered her face with kisses. She lay beneath him like a trapped butterfly and it was only when he tasted the salt of her tears that he realised she was crying.

He felt a moment's horror at what he had done but the exhilaration and the feeling of power and ascendancy was too great for it to last.

'Sarah?' he said raggedly.

She did not move, lying there with the sun on her face and her hair tumbled in the grass. He sat up, looking down at her, and felt the strength regenerating in him.

'Why are you crying?'

She opened her eyes and looked up at him. She did not speak. He reached out and pulled her blood-flecked skirt down over her splayed legs.

'You're mine now, Sarah,' he said and there was a note of triumph in his voice. 'You're mine and don't you forget it.'

Her eyes held his. He could not read the expression in them. After a few moments she sat up. He half-expected her to run but she did not. Instead without a word she resumed packing the remains of the picnic basket.

Puzzled he watched her. She stood up, tidying her hair with her fingers and smoothing her crumpled skirt.

'It's time we were getting back,' she said.

Her calm almost unnerved him and as an unwelcome new thought struck him he turned cold.

'You won't tell my father?'

An expression close to scorn twisted her features.

'Of course not!' she said. 'But don't try anything like that again, Hugh. Not ever again.'

A slow smile crossed his face. The sight of her was stirring him again, his body was remembering the delights

132

of a few moments ago. He felt young and strong and invincible. She was better than Alicia. Much better.

They carried the picnic things back to the motor without speaking. The brightness was dying out of the day now, the sun sinking towards the horizon in a ball of deep orange fire.

It was only as they were driving home that he remembered he had still not seen Sarah's breasts though he had had more, much more, than he had expected. But he would. Oh yes, he would. The whole summer stretched invitingly before them and in spite of Sarah's warnings he knew there would be other times. As he had said, she was his now. And he had not the slightest intention of letting her go.

Chapter Eleven

Sarah walked across the yard at Chewton Leigh House towards the stables. In her hand she carried a paper bag filled with sugar lumps. Sweet Lass, the mare Gilbert had bought for her when she had learned to ride, was in foal and her time was near. Sarah visited her whenever she could, bringing her little treats such as the sugar lumps which she bought from the village shop since Bertha had complained about her helping herself to the ones she kept in the kitchen.

As she passed the windows of the house she looked in nervously but saw no-one and the quick beat of her heart steadied a little. No sign of Alicia or Leo, and more importantly no sign of Hugh. Since that afternoon, three weeks ago now, when she and Hugh had taken the Rolls to Bury Woods she had avoided him whenever she could but still he sought her out and the confusion in her emotions was such that she both dreaded the encounters and yet was strangely disappointed when they did not occur.

Why she should feel this disappointment Sarah could not imagine. After what had happened she had thought she would never want to see him again and the prospect of facing him, particularly in the presence of other members of the family, had made her feel physically sick. But after a few days when she had hidden herself away at Home Farm, her attitude towards the events of that afternoon had begun to undergo a strange metamorphosis. She recalled them now not so much with horror as with a creeping fascination, pondering on the way that Hugh had changed from the merry boy who had brightened her days at Chewton Leigh House and whom she had sometimes thought of as her only friend to something approaching a wild beast and marvelled that in some way it had been her body which had caused that change.

The knowledge was frightening and yet at the same time oddly exciting. She had taken off all her clothes and looked at herself in the slightly mottled mirror on her dressing table, noting with a critical eye the swell of her young breasts and the trimness of her waist, and remembering how she had once heard one of the 'big girls' at school complaining in the seclusion of the privy block that her chest was sprouting and she did not want it to. 'I don't want those ugly things' the big girl had said, almost weeping, but Sarah had been unable to understand her attitude then and she could not understand it now. For as long as she could remember she had admired her mother's breasts and hoped that when she grew up she would look just like Rachel; now, examining her reflection in the mirror, she knew her ambition had been realised. She ran her hands over them and felt prickling sensations trickle like silken cords from them to the very core of her being, the same sensation she encountered whenever she remembered Hugh and what he had done to her. She let her hands run on, across the flatness of her stomach to the firm columns of her thighs, then to the soft insides and up to the tuft of baby fine hair which grew there, and was aware of a strange feeling of power, unidentifiable yet very real.

This feeling puzzled her; Hugh had been the aggressor, she had been quite unable to prevent him from doing as he willed. So why should she now feel, even for a moment, that it was *she* who was the powerful one?

These secret thoughts did nothing to lessen the mortifying embarrassment she had felt on seeing him again, however. Her whole body had seemed to blush, her heart had pounded painfully against her ribs and she wished she could die. Alicia and James had also been in the room and with a tremendous effort she had behaved normally, desperate not to let them gain any inkling that things between her and Hugh were any different than they had ever been. Then Hugh had looked at her and she was sure the game was up. It was all there in his knowing narrowed eyes and the slight triumphant curve of his mouth, a look which made her blush all over again and started her heart

135

beating so fast she could scarcely breathe, a look which sent the tiny shivers flickering through the deepest parts of her body and made her want to run and hide, and also to feel his hands on her again, both at the same time. So obvious was the look to her that she could not believe the alert Alicia had not noticed it. But it seemed she did not. When she left Hugh had come with Sarah to the door and his hand had rested for a moment on her back before slipping around and giving her breast a quick squeeze. Again her heart had lurched and he whispered, his breath hot on her ear: 'Tomorrow in the copse by the lake. Ten o'clock.'

Of course she had not kept the appointment though at ten o'clock she was looking out of her bedroom window, her emotions swinging between the wistful and the tumultuous as she imagined him by the lake waiting for her.

The following afternoon he had come to the farm. She had seen him coming and run up to her room but Bertha had called her down.

'Here's Master Hugh come to see you.'

'I don't want to see him. I've got a headache.'

'Don't be so rude, my girl. Come down this minute!'

She had come down, meeting his eyes defiantly, and again been aware of the sensation of power when she realised he was slightly non-plussed.

'I came to see if you'd like to go for a walk, Sarah,' he said.

'No thank you. I don't feel very well.'

'It's this heat, I expect,' Bertha said, making excuses for her, and Sarah was for once grateful for the older woman's presence.

Hugh had left and as Bertha scolded her, saying she did not know what was wrong with her, Sarah had experienced that strange contrary little feeling of disappointment. She did not want to be alone with Hugh, did not want to place herself in circumstances when a repeat performance of the other afternoon would be possible, yet was aware of a restlessness yawning in her almost like hunger.

Since then he had sought her out whenever possible and although they were not alone for long enough for any

136

serious developments yet he managed to touch her sometimes on her breasts or bottom or between her legs, starting the quivers of prickling excitement inside her at the same time as arousing embarrassment and panic and afterwards she experienced again the peculiar sense of anti-climax and a perverse longing for more.

Her greatest regret was the loss of their former easy friendship. In many ways the years had exacerbated Sarah's isolation for her continued absorption into life at the big house had meant she no longer had any friends among the village children. The girls she had known had all left school now and had positions of one kind and another in service but even before they had gone away the gap between their world and Sarah's had grown for they looked on her as someone who had got 'above herself'. She had tried to rekindle at least some of the relationships, particularly with Phyllis, who had grown into a plump pretty girl with an enviable carefree attitude to life, but they no longer had anything in common and imperceptibly Sarah was beginning to grow impatient with her old friends even while longing to share their secrets and their celebrations. The comprehensive education she was receiving and her taste of life at Chewton Leigh House was changing her, setting her sights higher than theirs and making her search for something more than they could give her, yet she was not a part of the 'gentry' either. They were kind enough to her, her every need was catered for, and yet she was not one of them.

Sometimes Sarah felt she belonged nowhere.

Only Hugh had treated her as a person in her own right, a girl he teased as he teased his sister, made a fuss of and actually liked. Only with Hugh had she felt neither ashamed of the remnants of her Somerset burr nor embarrassed by the more genteel tones she had unconsciously adopted. Only with Hugh could she relax and be herself. And now that ease had gone forever, lost in a sunny field along with her innocence.

Still there was always Sweet Lass, Sarah comforted herself as she left the cobbled yard and slipped in at the open door of the stables. Though she had never completely overcome her nervousness of some of the big powerful hunters in the stables she loved the little mare dearly. Sweet Lass was a strawberry roan, game and willing yet as gentle as her name implied and from the moment Gilbert had introduced them Sarah had known she could never be afraid of Sweet Lass. Now as she entered the stable the mare heard her and whinnied softly, pawing the floor gracefully in greeting.

Sarah crossed to her stall and the big nose came out to nuzzle her. Sarah stroked it gently.

'Hello, my love! And how are you today? I expect you wish you could be out in the meadow with the other horses. Never mind it won't be long now and you will be. Tom says you'll have your foal before the week is out.'

Sweet Lass prodded at Sarah gently but insistently. Sarah laughed.

'I know what you are looking for. It's cupboard love, isn't it? Just cupboard love!'

She opened the paper bag and took out a sugar lump, offering it to Sweet Lass on the palm of her hand. The mare took it, crunching delicately, and Sarah gave her another.

Dim as it was in the stable she did not notice the shadow as someone entered and with the straw underfoot his boots made no sound.

'Well hello there, Sarah! What are you doing inside on such a fine day?'

She swung round, her hand still outstretched to Sweet Lass with yet another sugar lump. Hugh was standing in the doorway leaning nonchalantly against the wooden post.

'You made me jump!' she said accusingly but her heart had begun to pound and her voice was not quite level.

'You haven't got another headache, I hope,' Hugh said. The mock solicitude was not lost on her.

'I came to see Sweet Lass,' she said defensively. 'She's due to foal any day now.'

'Rubbish,' he said. 'You came to see me.'

'I did not!'

She could not see his face because of the shadow but she knew from his voice that he was smiling.

138

'Of course you did. At least – I hope so! Though I must confess I was beginning to think you were avoiding me.'

'I told you I came to see Sweet Lass!' she snapped. 'But now I have to get back. Mrs Pugh will be expecting me.' She thrust another sugar lump at the mare and started towards the door. He did not move. His tall frame half filled the doorway. 'Please let me pass.'

'You are not in such a hurry, surely,' he drawled. 'You've only just come.'

Unable to leave without brushing past him she turned back to the horse, rubbing the nose that was still resting over the top of the stall.

'When is your father coming back?' she asked, trying to change the subject and defuse the situation though knowing she was effectively trapped.

'Oh, he'll be away for a couple of weeks yet,' Hugh replied. 'Blanche received a letter from him this morning. He is very impressed with Santos Dumont's work and he has been invited to stay on a little longer. Santos Dumont thinks his flying machine will be ready for a test flight very soon.'

'It must be very exciting for him.' The breath was tight in her throat; she could scarcely breathe.

'Yes. But we don't want to talk about Santos Dumont, do we? We've got better things to do.' His tone was overlaid with meaning. In the humid atmosphere of the stable she could almost smell the desire on him. Panic, pure and simple, swept over her. How could she have wished even for a moment to be alone with him again after that afternoon at Bury Woods? It had been wrong, really wrong. She must ensure it did not happen again.

She made a determined effort to get to the door.

'I really have to go, Hugh.'

His hand shot out, imprisoning her wrist.

'Not until you tell me when you are going to come out with me again.'

'I'm not.'

He pulled her close, so close she could feel his breath on her face and the heat emanating from his body.

'Oh yes you are. I told you, Sarah – you're mine!'

His lips found hers and his hand took her breast squeezing roughly. For just a moment the dangerous dark excitement rose in her and against her will she found herself wanting him to handle not just one breast but both, not just her breasts but her whole body. The pressure of his lips was brutal yet exhilarating; she felt herself draining into him. Then as his hand moved down between her legs the panic returned, contradictory yet undeniable and all-consuming.

'No!' With one hand she tried to stop his exploring fingers, with the other she pushed at his chest, trying to thrust him away. 'Will you stop, please! We mustn't!'

'Why not?' His breath was ragged; she could feel the tension mounting in him.

'Because it's wrong. Because I don't like it!'

'Oh yes you do,' he contradicted her. He had her blouse open now though she had not been aware of him undoing the buttons. His hand crept inside her camisole and the palm, hard against the rose pink tip of her erect nipple made the weakness flood through her again. 'You do like it, Sarah!'

'I don't! I don't! You're bad, Hugh!'

'No worse than you. You could have stopped me if you had wanted to. But you didn't.' He was kissing her again, speaking disjointedly between those kisses, his lips moving down her throat towards the breast which he had now freed from the covering of her camisole. 'Oh Sarah . . . Sarah . . .'

He was drinking her in now, the feel of her, the taste of her, the sight of her, beautiful, just as he had known she would be, even here in the dim stable. She struggled in spasms as the conflicting emotions swayed her, for in spite of the growing eagerness of her body she knew it was wrong . . . wrong . . .

'You're mine.' His lips tugged at her nipple and he hoisted up her skirt; to Sarah it seemed he had become an octopus with hands everywhere.

'Hugh, stop!' she screamed. 'Leave me alone!'

'You're mine!' he grated. His arm slid down behind her

140

knees and he lifted her bodily, carrying her as easily as if she had been a child, back into the stable. There at the far end a few bales of hay formed a low ledge. He put her down on it, holding her down with one hand and tearing at her dress.

'Hugh – my frock!' she protested, almost weeping.

'Take it off!' he ordered, towering over her.

'No! Please!' she was screaming.

Neither of them heard someone else enter the stable. The first Hugh, demented with desire, knew of it was when a hand grabbed his collar from behind, hauling him off her. Taken by surprise he could offer no resistance; he stumbled blindly, falling against the half open door of one of the stalls, and Lawrence's fist, connecting with his chin, jerked his head back and sent him flying backwards into the stall.

'What the hell do you think you are doing?' Lawrence yelled.

For a moment Hugh lay half-stunned in the mucky straw then he was on his feet, passion turning to blinding anger.

'Stay out of this, Lawrence!' He tried to push past and Lawrence hit him again. This time Hugh was more prepared. He rode the blow and went for his brother like a bull. Within seconds they were fighting, trading blows as they had not done since they were children, racketing around the walls of the stall.

Sarah cowered briefly against the bales of hay, then as the full horror of what was happening came home to her she scrambled to her feet. The two young men were on the floor of the stall now, rolling over and over in the straw.

'Stop it! Oh please, stop!' she sobbed, vainly trying to separate them.

It seemed to her the fight would never end. Lawrence was perhaps the bigger of the two but Hugh's athleticism eventually told and he scrambled up, standing over his brother threateningly.

'Get up, Lawrence. But if you hit me again so help me I'll kill you!'

Lawrence sat up slowly, his hand covering his face. Between his fingers his nose streamed blood. It poured down over his white shirt front; even in the dim stable Sarah could see the spreading stain.

'How dare you interfere!' Hugh spat at him, his voice trembling with rage and unsatisfied lust.

'You were hurting Sarah!' Lawrence said nasally. Already his normal truculence was returning in the face of his brother's angry ascendancy.

'I wasn't doing anything Sarah didn't want. Why did you have to come in here, poking your nose into what didn't concern you?'

'I heard voices. I heard Sarah screaming . . .'

'What Sarah and I play at is our own business.'

'But . . .'

'Sarah wasn't screaming. She was laughing. Don't you know the difference, you big oaf?'

'It sounded like screaming to me.'

'How would you know?' Hugh asked sarcastically. 'What do you know about anything? How many girls have *you* had, I'd like to know?'

'You know damned well I haven't had any. *I* treat them like a gentleman.'

'More fool you. You think they admire you for it? Do you know what Sarah calls you? *Sobersides* and *Stick in the Mud*. Isn't that true, Sarah?'

She could not answer. She was close to tears now from shock and fear and the sight of Lawrence sitting there in the straw, his nose streaming blood, as if he and not Hugh were the one in the wrong was too much for her. It was wrong, all wrong – and not least because in spite of all he had done she could still feel Hugh's animal attraction, the more so because he stood there crowing, undisputed leader of the herd. 'Isn't it true, Sarah?' he insisted, determined not to relent until his victory was complete. 'You do call him those names?'

'Yes, but I don't mean it unkindly,' she whispered.

'There. Now get out – brother!' Hugh ordered. 'Get out and leave us alone.'

She wanted to run then. She wanted to follow Lawrence, thank him for interfering on her behalf and wipe the blood away from his face, but her legs seemed to have become lumps of jelly. She leaned against the corner of the stall watching him go and when Hugh's arms came around her roughly she had no resistance to offer.

'Now, Sarah, I believe we have some unfinished business,' he grated at her.

In the dim stable Sweet Lass whinnied in distress but there was no-one but Hugh and Sarah to hear her and they were otherwise occupied.

'Sarah, please come to my sitting-room. I wish to speak to you,' Blanche said.

It was the next day. Sarah had been summoned to the big house and she had gone there dressed neatly in her best gingham, her heart quaking, for she was sure the summons meant trouble.

The moment she had entered the door she had known she was not mistaken. She had passed Hugh in the hall just going out. He was wearing his riding clothes and his face bore the scars of yesterday's scrap – a black eye and a swollen lip. He looked at her without smiling, raised one eyebrow sardonically and lowered it quickly as if the facial movement was painful to him, and went on out of the door.

Like the other half of the couple in the weather-house which stood on the Pughs' mantlepiece, Blanche had appeared in the doorway of the dining–room. Her expression was inscrutable as always but if anything her lips were tighter and her voice, commanding Sarah to accompany her to her sitting-room, was cold as charity.

Wretchedly Sarah followed the straight line of her back up the stairs.

Blanche's sitting-room was off her bedroom, a study in cold blues and greys. Not even the profusion of ornaments and knick-knacks could give it warmth. Sarah had never been inside the room before, now although too nervous to notice a single detail she was aware of its general ambience and her spirits sank still lower.

Blanche swept across to the window, a stately figure in a chiffon blouse of dove grey and full gored skirt in rich blue poplin. Blue velvet bows on the blouse swayed gracefully, blue ear bobs skimmed the high lace collar. So completely did Blanche seem to blend with the room that Sarah found herself wondering incongruously if she changed the decor to match her clothes.

'Now, madam.' Blanche turned abruptly, hands folded in front of her, cold eyes fixed on Sarah, and all such foolish thoughts fled the girl's mind. 'I think it is high time you and I had a little talk.'

Sarah stood quite still, returning her gaze.

'What have you to say for yourself?' Blanche demanded.

'I . . . I suppose it is about yesterday,' Sarah faltered.

'You suppose correctly,' Blanche snapped. 'How do you explain your behaviour?'

'I – it wasn't my fault,' Sarah said lamely. 'I only came to the stables to see Sweet Lass and . . .'

'Really!' Blanche snorted. 'Would that that were all there were to it! Unfortunately it is not. You came here deliberately to try to throw yourself at Mister Hugh. Isn't that closer to the truth?'

'No . . .' Sarah broke off, wondering how she could explain without denouncing Hugh to his stepmother. Even now, frightened as she was by the turn their relationship had taken, she felt a fierce loyalty to him. Blanche had always treated her as an intruder while Hugh . . . 'No, it's not true,' she said, trembling.

'Please don't compound your behaviour with lies!' Blanche snapped. 'The boys have already told me what happened since I demanded an explanation of their injuries. You lured Hugh into the stable and attempted to seduce him, something I believe you have aspired to for some time now. I was afraid of something of the sort happening one day. I foresaw it from the moment Gilbert brought you here and I tried to tell him so, but he would have none of it. Well now I have been proved correct. Oh!' She raised a slim hand, gesticulating at the empty air, 'I suppose you are not entirely to blame. That sort of behaviour was born in you. It's in your blood. Your mother . . . Gilbert could not see it. He is a good man – too good – and he mistakenly believed he

144

could do something for you and prevent you from falling into her ways. Well, he was wrong, wasn't he? Blood will out!'

Sarah's brow furrowed. 'I don't understand . . .'

'Don't you? I think you do. Just what you had in mind I am not certain. Perhaps you meant to compromise Mr Hugh, inveigle yourself into a position where he would feel compelled to make an honest woman of you, something your mother, with all her wiles, was never able to accomplish. Perhaps you merely wanted an adventure. I don't know – and neither do I very much care. All I do know is that I cannot – will not – have you behaving in this way under my roof. Quite apart from leading Mr Hugh astray I have to consider the effect you could have on the others. Mr Hugh will be off soon to Sandhurst but in his absence you might turn to Leo or even James. And your influence on Alicia could be quite disastrous.'

Sarah gazed at Blanche almost unable to comprehend what she was saying. Not only was she accusing her of being the instigator of what had happened between her and Hugh, was she truly suggesting that she might become involved with the hateful Leo or little James, still scarcely more than a child? It was monstrous! And as for influencing Alicia – it would be almost amusing if it were not so ridiculous – and serious. Alicia despised her. She would sooner die than copy Sarah in anything she did.

If I *had* done anything, Sarah thought. And I haven't – I haven't!

'I have thought this over carefully,' Blanche was continuing, 'and I have come to a decision. If Gilbert were here he could deal with the situation but he is not. He is still in France and likely to be there for a few weeks yet. I have decided this matter is too serious to await his return. It needs to be dealt with immediately. You cannot be allowed to remain in proximity to this family for another day, Sarah.'

'What do you mean?' Sarah asked, trembling.

'I mean that I am going to send you away,' Blanche said coolly.

145

'Send me away? But where?'

Blanche raised a hand to smooth her elegant chignon. Her hand gleamed palely as the sun, streaming through the window, caught the creamy skin and the gold rings she wore.

'Since this appalling story was relayed to me I have been busy,' she said. 'I have friends in Essex. They recently lost one of their maid servants when she married and was foolish enough to find herself in the family way. I have spoken to them and out of friendship to me they have agreed to take you on in her place. You start there immediately.'

Sarah was speechless. The unfairness of this entire interview had left her shell-shocked and she was frighteningly aware that nothing she could say would make a scrap of difference now. Blanche had made up her mind that she was to blame for the whole incident and she would not be swayed.

'Go back to the farm and get your things together,' she said coldly. 'Tom will take you to Bristol and put you on a train. Perhaps well away from this family you will come to your senses, though I doubt it.' She glanced at her watch, pinned to the chiffon blouse. 'Tom will come for you in an hour. You had better be ready. Now this interview is at an end.'

Sarah drew herself up, distraught but determined not to humble herself before Blanche. She raised her chin and her eyes met Blanche's squarely.

'What will Mr Morse say when he comes home and finds me gone?'

Blanche shrugged. 'I believe he will be of the opinion I have acted in the best interests of all concerned. Especially when he hears how you have abused his kindness and generosity.'

Horror flooded through Sarah. She could not bear the thought of Gilbert hearing this appalling story – believing it even. Let Blanche think what she liked – but not Mr Morse! Oh, not Mr Morse . . .

'Please – you've got it all wrong . . .' she whispered.

Blanche's mouth tightened and she reached for the bell pull.

'I do not wish to hear another word. Now – will you leave of your own accord or must I ring for someone to show you out?'

Sarah turned, lifting her chin again.

'It's all right, Mrs Morse. I'm going.'

'Good. And I can only hope, Sarah, that you have the grace to be thoroughly ashamed of yourself.'

With those parting words ringing in her ears Sarah left Blanche Morse's sitting-room.

The tears were pricking at her eyes as she emerged from the house and she blinked them fiercely away. She would not cry. She would not! Bad things had happened to her before. Worse. Nothing could be as bad as her mother dying.

It was Mr Morse thinking badly of her that really hurt. And having to leave without ever seeing Sweet Lass's foal.

I must say goodbye to her, Sarah thought.

She went around to the stables, half afraid of entering them again after what had happened there yesterday yet determined to overcome her fear.

In the dim interior Sweet Lass poked her nose over the door of her stall enquiringly, muzzling Sarah and looking for her usual sugar.

'I haven't got any, Sweet Lass,' Sarah said. 'I won't be bringing you any ever again.' A tear escaped and rolled down her nose. She wiped it away and buried her face in the mare's neck. 'Goodbye, my darling horse. They'll look after you and your foal. You'll have her soon, you'll see.'

The tears were blinding her. She could not bear to prolong the goodbye. She dropped a kiss on Sweet Lass's muzzle and left the stable without a backward glance.

Hugh was in the stableyard on Satan, his hunter. He saw her and looked quickly away. A shaft of desperation lent her courage. She ran towards him.

'Hugh – oh Hugh, she's sending me away!'

He bent to check his girth fastening, unable to meet her eyes.

'I know.'

'Hugh, she's got it all wrong! She thinks that I . . . Oh Hugh, please, you've got to tell them it wasn't my fault!'

147

He looked up. She saw the evasion in his face.

'What do you mean?'

'You've got to tell her I wasn't to blame! She said I . . . seduced you!'

His mouth lifted at one corner but without any of his usual humour.

'Well – didn't you?'

'You know I didn't!'

'You could have stopped me,' he said stubbornly. 'You wanted it, Sarah, just as I did.'

'But I didn't seduce you! You must tell them . . .'

He looked away again.

'My father would kill me if he thought that I . . .'

'And what about me?'

'I'm sorry, Sarah,' he said. 'There's nothing I can do that would make any difference.'

He touched Satan with his heels and the horse began to move away.

On the point of running after him, Sarah checked herself. It was as useless to plead with Hugh as with Blanche. He would never admit to his father that he had been the instigator. Well she wasn't going to beg. At least she still had her pride.

'All right, Hugh, but I hope you're satisfied,' she called after him. 'I hope you can sleep at night. And I hope at Sandhurst they make you into an officer *and* a gentleman!'

He did not answer. With a quick proud flick of her head Sarah tossed her hair back over her shoulder. She turned on her heel and walked out of the yard. Hugh did not see her tears, nor she his.

Chapter Twelve

Deedham Green, the home of Blanche's friends the Carsons, stood bleak and isolated on the Cooling Marshes, silent and morose but for the whistling of the wind in its tall chimneys and the mournful cries of the curlews, its grey walls seeming to merge and blend into the swirling mists which crept up the estuary with the tides. When she had been there a day Sarah knew she hated it, after a month she felt that its desolation was invading her very soul.

The house was dark and draughty, pervaded by a dank chill which emanated from the centuries-old walls and the flagged floors even on those rare days when the sun broke through the thick river mist and a musty smell hung in the rooms, overcrowded with Victorian bric-a-brac and faded glories of days gone by which she was required to clean, polish and dust until she felt her arms would drop off.

Each morning she rose with the dawn, washing and dressing herself in the little attic room which looked out over the marshes and hurried down the back stairs to the cheerless flagged kitchen to begin the endless round of tasks which had been allocated to her. There were floors to scrub and grates to be blackleaded, heavy scuttles of coal to be filled and endless piles of dishes and stacks of greasy pots and pans to be washed and all beneath the eagle eye of Mrs Edgell, the Carsons' ill-tempered cook-housekeeper, whose nature seemed to have been soured by the loneliness and the creeping mists until she was virtually impossible to please, and Mr Smith, the pompous fault-finding butler whose chief mission in life was to make himself important by belittling others.

Apart from Emily, the ladies' maid, who never demeaned herself by undertaking any of the menial tasks below stairs, and a greasy looking woman who came in from the nearby village to assist when the Carsons entertained, Sarah was the only servant so she was not only lonely but also run almost literally off her feet and she sometimes paused to wonder how it was that her predecessor, whom she had never heard referred to by name, had found the opportunity to meet a young man at all, much less become pregnant by him. But she felt no spark of envy for the unknown girl who had, she considered, merely exchanged one form of slavery for another. More fool her! Sarah thought scornfully. More fool her to let a man near her! And fury at Hugh and what he had done to her burned in her so fiercely and painfully it almost frightened her, along with relief that she had not shared the unknown girl's fate.

Sometimes, lying in bed too tired to sleep, Sarah wondered about the connection between Blanche and the Carsons. They were, she thought, the most unlikely people for the worldly and sophisticated Blanche to have selected for her friends. The Misses Carson, Catherine and Olivia, were a strange pair, stiffly correct and depressingly dowdy in their dresses of heavy grey and bottle green serge which no doubt helped to keep out the creeping cold of the marshes but which would, in Sarah's opinion, have been more suitable for a housekeeper of years gone by than for gentlefolk of means in the bright new century, while their brother, Sir Percy, was choleric and gouty. All three lived strictly celibate lives, Sir Percy taking his comfort from the brandy bottle, *The Times* crossword and the form pages of the racing papers, the women working at needlepoint and maintaining their position as pillars of the local church. As young women they had been engaged to be married, Emily their ladies' maid had told Sarah when in a rare communicative mood, but their beaux had been killed in the Crimea. As for Sir Percy, he had been married once, but his wife had had a weak heart and an even weaker mind and she had died young leaving no children. Frankly Sarah found it difficult to believe the Misses Carson could ever have been young and in love and since faded portraits in the drawing-room were the only evidence that any of the three had ever existed Sarah sometimes wondered if they had been dreamed up, figments of the imagination, like characters in the novels of

Jane Austen and George Eliot with which they peopled their otherwise barren lives.

During those first weeks at Deedham Green two things kept Sarah going. One was the anger at the way she had been treated. The other was the faint hope that when he returned from France and found her gone Gilbert would seek her out and whisk her away from the prison to which Blanche had sentenced her. How he would accomplish this she did not know for clearly there was no place for her now at Chewton Leigh but she could not believe he would abandon her totally. He had saved her once before when she had been in the depths of despair and Sarah had implicit faith in his ability to do so again if he chose to do so. But as the weeks passed with no word from him hope began to fade. It revived briefly when one morning Sarah overheard Mr Smith reading to Mrs Edgell from his newspaper that a Mr Santos Dumont had made a short flight in an aeroplane somewhere in France. Perhaps, Sarah thought, Gilbert had extended his visit in order to see Mr Santos Dumont get his aeroplane into the air, and as yet knew nothing of what had happened during his absence. But her hopes that he might yet seek her out when he found her missing were clouded by the sickening certainty that Blanche would justify herself at Sarah's expense. Every time she thought of the story Blanche would tell, of the distorted version of the truth she would present, Sarah felt as if the whole of her inside was curling up like a piece of paper crinkling and shrivelling in the heat of a fire. She thought she would have died rather than have Gilbert believe that she had betrayed his confidence in her in such a despicable way, and as the weeks passed with no word from him she was forced to the unwilling conclusion that this was indeed the case. Blanche had told him of her disgrace and he had believed her version of events. The knowledge was a leaden weight in her heart, dragging her down, shackling her. And when hope was gone there was nothing left but the anger.

It sustained her now through the long days and nights, burning in her veins like a potent drug even when she was exhausted, when her hands were red from constant immer-

151

sion in hot water and her legs felt like lumps of lead. And it was directed now not only at the Morses but also at the unlovable Carsons, at Mrs Edgell and Mr Smith. One day, she promised herself, one day I'll leave this place and never come back. One day I'll show them all! But the endless round of chores left little time for planning and her meagre wages held out no hope of independence. The weeks passed and, too tired to fight, Sarah drifted with the tide.

'We've gentry for dinner tonight,' Mrs Edgell said, puffing out her mountainous bosoms like some obscene turkey cock. 'So I hope you've a clean apron to put on, my girl, because it will be for you to serve them.'

'Gentry?' Sarah experienced a moment's panic. To her 'gentry' was synonymous with the Morses and it was highly unusual for the Carsons to entertain. 'Who is it?'

'You mind your business, my girl, and get on with what you're paid for,' the cook snapped. Then, unable to resist parading her superior knowledge, she added: 'It's our prospective member of parliament, if you must know, though anyone would think it was the King himself for all the fuss that's being made.'

Sarah heaved a sigh of relief. Of course she should have known it was much too far from Somerset for the Morses to be dinner guests.

'Tendrons de Veau à la Jardinière and Roast Goose!' the cook grumbled. 'Who ever heard of such a thing? Why they couldn't put on a good piece of boiled mutton and caper sauce I don't know. And apple soufflé and meringues! A nice bread and butter pudding would go down a darn sight better. It wouldn't keep them awake with indigestion half the night and it might put a bit of flesh on Miss Catherine. She's been looking very peaky lately.'

Being somewhat overweight herself Mrs Edgell had a hearty disdain for anyone who was less than ample, regarding thinness as a personal affront.

As the afternoon wore on and the hour of reckoning approached Mrs Edgell grew more and more flustered and she sent Sarah scuttling from one job to the next while Mr

Smith, wearing a green baize apron to protect his clothing, countermanded her every move with instructions of his own.

'You can get the table set now.'

'*After* the fire has been lit, Mr Smith, *if* you don't mind. We don't want the guests catching their death of cold in that dining-room.'

'Make haste, Sarah! I don't know what's the matter with you, girl. You're like a snail! Have you washed the best china – and the glasses? And the silver will need cleaning afresh. We can't use dirty silver.'

As usual Mrs Edgell was determined to have the last word.

'Come here and stir this sauce for me, Sarah. I don't want it sticking to the pan and going lumpy.'

She waved the spoon threateningly in Sarah's direction. Sarah went to take it and slipped on a patch of grease which Mrs Edgell must have spilled from the roasting tin while basting the goose. She grabbed at the table to save herself and a cullender of diced carrots, left too near the edge, fell off. Carrots rolled all over the floor.

'You clumsy fool! Now look what you've done!' Mrs Edgell expostulated.

'Oh – I'm sorry . . .' Sarah dropped to her hands and knees retrieving the small neat dice which she had chopped so painstakingly a half-hour before. Suddenly Mrs Edgell exploded in fury.

'There! And now my sauce has gone all lumpy!'

She swung at Sarah with the wooden spoon which she was still holding. It caught her behind the ear and as she reeled in shock and pain the cullender tipped again, depositing the newly retrieved carrots over the floor once more.

'You little fool!' Mrs Edgell screamed, beside herself with rage. 'You're useless – useless!' She struck at Sarah again, catching her this time on the temple. 'Pick them up. Pick them all up. And then you'll have to do some more. We can't serve carrots all covered in bits and hairs.'

Sarah straightened, her eyes blazing in her pale face, a

153

dark lump already rising on her temple. Her ear was stinging too, a sharp throb which sent needles of pain down her neck, and suddenly it was as if she had been transported back in time to the kitchen in the farmhouse at Chewton Leigh when Mrs Pugh had struck her for coddling the eggs.

She had been a child then. She had had no redress against her tormentor. But she was not a child any longer. She was fifteen years old and she owed this horrible woman nothing.

'Pick them up yourself!' The words were out before she could stop them; they hung in the air like the echoes of a thunderclap and as she saw the horror and disbelief on the faces of Mrs Edgell and Mr Smith Sarah was intoxicated by her own daring. Then as the two of them converged on her she knew she had gone too far.

'How dare you!' Mr Smith thundered. 'How dare you speak to your elders and betters in that way?'

She might be my elder but she is certainly not my better, Sarah wanted to say, but this time she let discretion be the better part of valour.

'You will pick up those carrots this instant and do as you are told, my girl. Or you'll have me to answer to. And if you ever dare to cheek Mrs Edgell again you will be reported to Sir Percy for instant dismissal. Then where will you be, I'd like to know?'

For a moment Sarah held his eyes rebelliously then as a wave of dizziness washed over her she realised this was not the moment for outright confrontation. She bent over, retrieving carrot dice and returning them once more to the cullender and satisfied with his victory Mr Smith stood over her, supervising what he took for her compliance, whilst Mrs Edgell, huffing and puffing, scraped the spoiled sauce into the dustbin and set about making some more.

Neither of them knew what was going on in Sarah's throbbing head. Neither of them had an inkling of the determination which was welling up and giving birth to a boldness that was encouraging her to throw caution to the winds.

Instant dismissal! Sarah thought. Well, I won't wait for that. I'm going to leave this place just as soon as I can pack my few things together. Where I will go and what I will do I don't know. But I'll find something. Oh, I'll find something. I'll make something of myself. *Be* someone. And when I do no-one will ever strike me or speak to me in that manner ever again!

BOOK THREE – 1909–1910

Enjoy your achievements as well as your plans . . . Be yourself.
Especially do not feign affection.

Desiderata

Chapter Thirteen

On an evening in the spring of 1909 Gilbert Morse was ensconced in his favourite deep leather chair in the library at Chewton Leigh House with a copy of the day's *Times* spread out on his knee and the current *Illustrated Weekly News* and *Punch* lying on the low rosewood table beside him.

It had been a perfect spring day but now the curtains had been drawn against the fading light, a fire crackled cheerfully in the grate to banish the winter chill which would return when the sun finally fell over the fold of Somerset hills and Gilbert had retired to spend the hour before dinner relaxing after the rigours of the day with a whisky and soda and the newspapers he had not had time to read before leaving for the office that morning.

He turned the pages, searching for news on the subject which interested him most – the progress being made in the construction of flying machines. Reports appeared almost daily now; the scepticism with which the press had so recently treated the new inventions had turned to a flush of excitement as fantasy became reality. The *Daily Mail*, for so long the one newspaper to take the possibility of powered flight seriously, had now offered prizes of £1000 to the first pilot to fly the English Channel and £10,000 for the first to link their two publishing centres, London and Manchester, by air. At first the very idea had been laughed to scorn but now fewer people were laughing. Already Bleriot, the Frenchman, had made a cross country flight of twenty-five miles, it was said, though he had had to put down three times before completing the distance, and Wilbur Wright had covered an incredible seventy-seven miles in Auvours in December to win the Michelin prize and set up a new world record.

Ever since he had been to France almost three years earlier to see Santos Dumont's efforts to get a flying machine into the sky, Gilbert had been fascinated by the idea of powered flight. He had extended his visit in order to be there at the magic moment when the wheels left the ground for the first time, and back in England he had paid more than one visit to Brooklands as the guest of Alliott Verdon-Roe, who had managed some short hops in his own Avro Biplane with a borrowed Antoinette engine the previous June. For a time Gilbert had toyed with the idea that Morse Motors might themselves be able to produce engines of the same calibre, light yet reliable, and he had gone so far as to mention it to Lawrence, who was now effectively in charge of the works.

Lawrence, however, had merely frowned.

'That is a little ambitious, isn't it, Father? This flying business is still very much in its infancy. No-one knows yet whether it will ever be a viable proposition. I believe if we are to keep the firm on an even keel we should stick with what we know well and do best.'

His tone was reproving and faintly patronising and for a moment Gilbert felt uncomfortably as if he was the younger man, foolishly carried away by youthful enthusiasm, while Lawrence was his sensible senior, gently pointing out his folly. It was by no means the first time he had experienced this feeling of role reversal; since Lawrence had taken over the works the mantle of responsibility had drained him of every vestige of humour and the thirst for adventure. It was a pity, Gilbert considered, that he should have lost his youth in this way and sometimes he reflected that if the genes which gave Lawrence and Alicia their characters had been more thoroughly mixed both of them might have felt the benefit.

Alicia had grown into a wild and wilful young woman whose circle was composed mainly of the young bucks of

157

the hunting set who seemed to spend even more of their lives drinking and partying until dawn than they did setting their mounts at hedges and ditches in pursuit of the fox. But Gilbert could not see much harm in it – better to sow their wild oats while they were young than to conform too soon and become rakes and roués at forty as King Edward had done when he was Prince of Wales. Without a doubt the years would quieten down Alicia's rebellious streak – but he doubted they would do anything to mellow Lawrence. If at twenty-three he could give the impression of a solid stick-in-the-mud of twice his age, what in heaven's name would he be like by the time he was fifty?

For once Gilbert was unable to find any mention in his newspaper of the doings of the aeroplane men and he folded the paper neatly, put it aside, and opened the *Illustrated Weekly News*. There was, so the front cover promised, an article on ballooning and though Gilbert considered it an outmoded form of flight it still interested him nonetheless.

He had just begun to search for the article when there was a knock at the library door. 'Yes?' he called, a trifle impatiently.

The door opened and Hugh looked in.

'Could I have a word with you, Father?'

'Yes – yes, of course.' Gilbert laid the *Illustrated Weekly News* down on the table beside him. 'Come in, Hugh.'

Hugh did so but although he treated his father to his usual flashing smile there was something hesitant in his manner and Gilbert's heart sank. He knew that look of old. When Hugh had been a little boy it had heralded a confession of some kind – the charming smile intended to disarm his father into sparing him a hiding for his latest piece of mischief.

Hugh was no longer a little boy to be walloped, of course. He was twenty-one years old now, taller than his father by two inches, with the dashing good looks and debonair manner that set feminine hearts beating wherever he went and brought a gleam of serious intent to many a hopeful mother's eye. But none of them had been able to trap Hugh as yet. He was still footloose and fancy free and the trail of dashed hopes and broken hearts stretched behind him ever longer, for the uniform he now wore only added to his glamour.

Hugh had done well at Sandhurst, passing out with honours, and Gilbert had been able to secure him a commission in the Life Guards. A short spell with the Household Cavalry had just ended; now Hugh was home on an embarkation leave before sailing for India.

Gilbert had looked forward to Hugh's furlough, anticipating the talks they would be able to have and the man-to-man humour they would be able to share, but Hugh had been curiously reticent. On the surface he was the same young man he had always been, charming, open and merry, but more than once Gilbert had surprised a thoughtful, almost brooding, expression on his face and he felt certain that Hugh was hiding something. Several times he had been on the point of asking Hugh what was troubling him but he had thought better of it. It was not the first time Hugh had behaved in this way and it would not be the last. He would tell Gilbert what was on his mind in his own good time if he wanted him to know – and in all probability he did not.

It has something to do with a young woman if I am not mistaken, Gilbert thought. I only hope the young hothead has not done anything dishonourable. Well, if he has and there's an angry father after him with a double barrelled shotgun he will have to be man enough to stand up and face the music.

'Well, Hugh, this is pleasant,' he said, giving no indication of his thoughts, 'I see far too little of you. I suppose it is unavoidable with you going straight from school to Sandhurst and straight from Sandhurst to a regiment but all the same . . .' He paused, then continued: 'I'm having a whisky and soda. Will you join me?'

'Thank you, Father, I will.' Hugh's voice was a fraction too eager and when Gilbert handed him the tumbler he tossed half of it back with one quick gulp.

Gilbert sighed inwardly. There was something, not a doubt of it. Well, he might as well come out with it, and quickly.

159

'What's wrong, Hugh?' he asked, countermanding his decision to wait for the boy to raise the subject of what was troubling him.

Hugh hesitated, a little taken aback by the directness of the question. 'Nothing really, Father.'

'Don't play the fool with me, Hugh. You wouldn't be here downing my whisky with that look on your face if there wasn't something wrong. What is it – a girl?'

Briefly a curious expression flickered in Hugh's eyes, a look of guilt surprised which convinced Gilbert momentarily that he had been right. Then Hugh's brow cleared and he laughed.

'No, Father, it's not a girl. Not this time. I'm afraid it's much more humdrum than that. I wondered if I might borrow some money.'

Gilbert's eyes narrowed. 'Money? What for?'

Faint colour rose in Hugh's cheeks. 'Well, Father, a chap has to live . . .'

'I'm aware of that,' Gilbert said, turning his whisky glass between his hands. 'But I thought we had taken everything into account when I organised your commission – the upkeep of your horses and polo ponies and an allowance for you to be able to live comfortably . . . How much do you want to borrow?'

Hugh drained his glass and turned away, unable to meet his father's eye.

'Five hundred.'

'Five hundred!' Gilbert repeated, stunned, then as the figure came home to him he repeated it again, more loudly and with angry emphasis. 'Five hundred pounds! Did I hear you aright, Hugh?'

'Yes, Father, I'm afraid you did.'

'But what in heaven's name do you want with five hundred pounds? That is more than double your annual commission!'

'Yes,' Hugh agreed uncomfortably. 'But I'll pay it back, Father, I swear I will.'

'Out of what may I ask? And you still have not answered my question, Hugh. Why do you need five hundred pounds?'

160

'I owe it to one of my brother officers,' Hugh admitted, having the grace to look a little shamefaced. 'We had a game of poker and I'm afraid I lost.'

Gilbert frowned. 'Five hundred pounds – in one game? I find that a little difficult to believe, Hugh. Unless you are more of a fool than I thought.'

'Well yes – but what does it matter exactly how many games it was?' Hugh asked. 'I've lost it and there it is. And I've got to raise the cash somehow to pay it back before I leave for India. Debts in the regiment are regarded very seriously.'

'You should have thought of that before you ran them up then, shouldn't you?' Gilbert said, beginning to be annoyed by Hugh's irresponsibility. Lawrence a dullard, Alicia wild and perhaps wanton for all he knew and Hugh calmly asking him for five hundred pounds to settle a gambling debt. What in the name of heaven was wrong with them all?

'I'm sorry, Father, I'm in the wrong I know,' Hugh said, sounding a little pained at being taken to task. 'But I really do need the money. I've said I'll pay it back. What more can I do?'

Gilbert sighed. 'You can make damned sure, Hugh, that such a thing never happens again! I don't suppose a lecture will do one bit of good but I'm afraid I don't feel able to hand over five hundred pounds to you without at least pointing out the error of your ways. Gambling is the most ludicrous form of sport. You would do well to remember the old maxim – a fool and his money are soon parted. That is what happens ultimately to everyone who gambles.'

'It didn't happen to old Willoughby,' Hugh said ruefully. 'He's five hundred pounds better off.'

'On this occasion, maybe.'

'Every occasion. He's cleaned out practically everyone in the Mess at one time or another.'

'Then he's either a cheat or he has the luck of the devil. Either way you'd do well to avoid him like the plague.' Gilbert rose. 'All right, Hugh, you shall have your five hundred pounds – but as a gift, not a loan. I shouldn't like you to be tempted to a repeat performance with your next month's allowance in the hope of winning enough to repay me.' He crossed to the small oak bureau which stood in an alcove to the right of the fireplace and took out his cheque book. 'To whom do I make this payable?'

Hugh did not answer. Gilbert was assailed by an unpleasant suspicion that Hugh had not been entirely truthful as to his reasons for wanting such a large amount of money.

'Hugh? Are you sure you are not misleading me? This money is for a man named Willoughby, I believe you said?'

He turned to see Hugh staring as though transfixed at the *Illustrated Weekly News*.

'Hugh?' he said again, the suspicion deepening. 'I intend to pay the money direct to your creditor – you might as well know that.'

'Hang my creditor!' Hugh said and the note of suppressed tension in his voice dispelled all Gilbert's doubts instantly. The colour had drained from his face and he was clutching the periodical with hands that shook slightly. 'Have you seen this?'

'No – what is it?' Gilbert asked, crossing to his son, and Hugh thrust the paper into his hands.

'See for yourself!'

Gilbert took the paper which was open at the ballooning article. The heading, bold capitals, leaped up at him but imparted nothing.

'THE SWEETHEART OF THE SKIES' it proclaimed.

Beneath this, taking up a full half page, was a photograph of a young woman in the costume of an acrobatic balloonist and parachutist – natty knickerbocker suit, front laced calf-length boots and small cap, standing in front of an inflated balloon.

'The young lady who has been delighting the crowds at air displays the length and breadth of the country with her thrilling aerobatics,' he read and glanced again at Hugh who was still looking as if he had seen a ghost.

'One of the daredevils who risk life and limb for the entertainment of the masses,' he said easily. 'What of it?'

'Yes – but do you see who it is?' Hugh asked. He was

162

recovering himself a little now but there was still a tremor in his voice. Gilbert returned to the feature and read on.

'Miss Sarah Thomas, popularly known as The Sweetheart of the Skies, has been performing now for the past two seasons with the renowned Dare Brothers. Miss Thomas, seen above in her ballooning costume, is second only in both ability and popular charisma to Miss Dolly Shepherd of the Gaudron team and makes her daring ascents attached to her small swaying trapeze with all the grace of a ballerina of the air. Once aloft, high over the heads of the watching crowds, Miss Thomas detaches herself and floats effortlessly to earth beneath her billowing parachute. And how the public love her! "Without a doubt is is Sarah they come to see," Captain Eric Dare, himself an experienced and extremely daring balloonist, told our correspondent. "When beauty and bravery go hand in hand, who can resist the spectacle they provide?"'

'Sarah!' he said, as shocked now as Hugh had been. 'I don't believe it!'

'It's her all right,' Hugh said, poring over his father's shoulder. 'But what the devil is she doing ballooning?'

'Heaven knows.' Gilbert looked again at the photograph, examining the face of the young woman more closely. At first glance it had appeared to bear no resemblance to the child he had taken into his care and who had left in such mysterious circumstances three years previously; now, with confirmation of the name to guide him, he accepted reluctantly that it could indeed be Sarah. She had grown up in the intervening years of course – stupidly whenever he had thought of her he had pictured her as being unchanged from the last time he had seen her. Now he looked at the small face beneath the jaunty cap, at the even features and wise smiling mouth and felt something close up inside him. By George, she was the image of her mother – why had he not noticed it at once? And yet why should he? Without the accompanying article it would simply never have occurred to him that Sarah and 'The Sweetheart of the Skies' could be one and the same.

'I've seen these ballooning displays,' Hugh was saying.

'They are pretty damned spectacular. But they can also be dangerous. I've heard of all kinds of things going wrong with the apparatus and more than one parachutist has been killed or badly injured when they have been blown off course. Why in heaven's name should Sarah get involved with something like that?'

Gilbert took a cigarette from the box that stood on the table and lit it.

'I don't know, Hugh, but I mean to find out.'

'Why should you do that?' Hugh asked, the colour draining from his face.

'Because I have never understood why she left us as she did,' Gilbert said. 'Don't you ever wonder about it?'

'I suppose so,' Hugh said edgily. 'But I assume she must have had her reasons.'

'True. And I would like to know what they were. I thought Sarah was happy with us. When I left for France there was nothing to suggest anything different. Yet when I returned she had gone.'

He paused, remembering the shock he had experienced at the time when Blanche had told him that Sarah had simply packed her bags one night and disappeared, leaving not one single clue to her whereabouts. 'She must have been planning it for months,' Blanche had said. 'Either that or she had some other secret life that she did not want us to know about.' 'Don't be ridiculous,' he had protested. 'A secret life – Sarah? She is as open as the day is long!' But Blanche had merely shrugged and remained totally un-moved by the disappearance of the girl who had shared their lives for five years. 'I don't know why you should be surprised,' she had said. 'A girl like that . . . Don't waste a second's thought on her, Gilbert.'

But Gilbert had thought about her long and often and in spite of Blanche's protestations he had made every effort to discover her whereabouts. All very well for Blanche to insist she had simply run away and that was the end of the matter. Blanche had resented Sarah from the beginning. But each of his lines of enquiry had drawn a blank and at last he had been forced to concede defeat. Sarah had disappeared like a stone in a deep pond leaving not so much as a ripple on the surface.

It was not only Blanche who seemed glad to see the back of Sarah, however. The rest of the family were clearly equally relieved that his efforts had proved fruitless and it had occurred to Gilbert to wonder if he had been told the whole truth. Since none of them would admit to any knowledge beyond the story as Blanche had related it and it was impossible to ask Sarah herself for an explanation he had eventually had to let the matter rest though it had continued to bother him, like a tiny splinter of glass buried deep in the flesh. Now, looking at Hugh's pale face and listening to his protests, the suspicion that there was indeed more to Sarah's disappearance than he had been led to believe reared its head once again.

'Don't you think it would be a good idea for me to go and see Sarah?' he asked, watching Hugh closely.

'I certainly do not!' Hugh said. He removed a handkerchief from his pocket and mopped his brow; Gilbert saw that it was glistening with a fine haze of perspiration.

'Why not?'

'Because if Sarah had wanted to see you or any of us she would have come back before now,' Hugh said. His voice was eager – too eager. 'Good grief, you must see that, Father. She has made a new life for herself. The last thing she will want is to be reminded of her roots. Look at her – "The Sweetheart of the Skies". It wouldn't suit if the truth were to come out about her, would it?'

'What truth?'

'That she is the illegitimate daughter of a seamstress,' Hugh blustered.

'Why should she be ashamed of it? And in any case there is no reason for anything to "come out" as you put it. I intend to see her in private, not seek an interview with the world press looking on.'

'Well I think it is a pointless idea,' Hugh repeated. 'No good will come of it. And besides, how would you know where to find her?'

Gilbert stabbed at the article with his forefinger. 'It says

here that when she is not ballooning Sarah works with the
Dare Brothers at the balloon factory at Alexandra Palace,'
he said. 'I shall visit her there.'

Hugh wiped another bead of sweat from his face. He
knew that further argument was useless with his father in
this mood.

'Well I suppose it is up to you,' he said truculently.

Gilbert's lips tightened. If he had been undecided before
about his course of action Hugh's attitude had removed
every last vestige of doubt.

'Yes, Hugh, it is,' he said. 'I shall visit Sarah immediately. And I only wish something like this article had come
into my hands long ago.'

Hugh did not reply. He was wishing heartily that he had
been alone when he had seen the article – and that he had
consigned the *Illustrated Weekly News* to the bonfire.
Ghosts which had seemed to be laid for the past three years
were about to rear up and begin haunting him again. Still, at
least he would soon be in India and well out of the way. He
had no wish to be anywhere in the vicinity when his father
discovered the truth about Sarah's departure from Chewton
Leigh.

Chapter Fourteen

Bright spring sunshine bathed the vast pleasure ground that was Alexandra Palace in a warm golden hue. It dappled through the leafy branches of the lime and cherry trees which shaded the tables in the open air restaurants, it reflected from the shining metal and bright paintwork of the rides in the fairground in arrow-sharp shards and glanced off the water of the boating lake in myriads of diamond and sapphire-like light. Between the lines of booths where the sideshows were situated the shadows lay tall and distinct across the hoardings proclaiming the attractions and the warm air hummed with the mingled shouts of the barkers, the strains of a brass band playing Sousa and the shouts of laughter and the constant chattering hum of people intent on enjoying themselves.

As Sarah made her way across the park she smiled to herself. All the world, it seemed, flocked to Alexandra Palace – or 'Ally Pally' as it was popularly known. Some came for the entertainments and the concerts, some came to see the horse racing on the magnificent race course, some simply to sit and watch the world go by. But all were set on pleasure, determined to enjoy every moment to the full, and although after almost two years Sarah was familiar with every corner of the place it never failed to give a lift to her spirits to see the smiling faces and feel the air of excitement that prevailed, just as it had been when she had first come seeking employment as a waitress.

How long ago it seemed now, she thought as she skirted the tables where once she had served pots of tea and long cool glasses of lemonade, ice cream in shallow silver dishes, plates of pastries and sticky buns. Sometimes it was difficult to believe she had been that young girl, overawed by the enormity of the world into which she had launched herself, alone and a little frightened, but determined to stand on her own two feet and make something of herself. Now she had a circle of friends, a life style which took her to the best suites in the best hotels, a wardrobe of fashionable clothes and a degree of fame. She was no longer little Sarah, orphan, scullery maid and waitress. She was Sarah Thomas, Sweetheart of the Skies.

Sometimes as she mingled with the crowds wearing her natty ballooning costume of red and gold braid-trimmed knickerbocker suit and cap and knee-high laced boots of softest black leather someone would recognise her and point her out. The knowledge that she was a personality never failed to please her; she walked jauntily now, her head held high, a small smile ready on her lips, for although it was three hours yet until the ballooning display of the day and she had not yet changed into her costume, that air of readiness to be recognised had become a part of her everyday demeanour, contributing to her natural grace and drawing attention to her striking good looks – her figure, as slender now at seventeen as it had been three years earlier and curved in all the right places, her eyes, sparkling blue and fringed with long lashes, her nut brown hair swept up into a loose pompadour from which ends escaped to frame her neat featured face. Sarah had always had the promise of beauty – now she possessed an aura too. In her own way, in the world of aero-acrobatics, Sarah was a star.

Sarah skirted the bandstand, moving with that easy grace between the crowds who had gathered to listen to the stirring music and made for the banqueting hall which housed the aeronaut's workshop.

To her it was and always had been a magic place where a potent alchemy turned canvas, hemp and wicker into gondolas which could float and soar on the wind and mere mortals into demi-gods of the skies. From the first day she had come here and learned of the work which went on in the vast and mysterious hall she had been drawn to it like a moth to a flame for ballooning had always seemed to her a most romantic activity. As a child she had listened eagerly when Richard Hartley had talked of it, lapping up the stories of the first-ever passengers in a balloon – a cockerel, a sheep and a duck who had been sent two miles high by the Moltgolfier brothers over a hundred years earlier, watched by a crowd of some 30,000 including King Louis XVI and Queen Marie Antoinette – and Vincent Lunardi, secretary to the Neapolitan ambassador in London, who had made the first manned balloon voyage in Britain with a pigeon, a cat and a dog to keep him company. The names of the pioneers had become as familiar to her as any of the great figures of history and she had been enthralled to learn that some of the modern giants of the air were based here – Henry Spencer, a third generation balloonist of the famous Spencer family, his brother-in-law, Captain Gaudron, who headed a full team of stunt parachutists, and most out-rageous of all, Samuel Franklin Cody, who had used his sharp shooting act *The Klondike Nugget* to finance his serious business of building a kite strong enough to carry a man into the air until he had been lured away by the challenge of building and flying aeroplanes. Sometimes the balloon men came into the restaurant where she worked, drinking gallons of tea and absentmindedly tucking into pastries as they discussed the latest innovations, and when she could be spared from her duties Sarah slipped away to watch the parachutists giving their daring displays of aerial acrobatics. The balloons gave joyrides too to those who could afford to pay for the pleasure; watching them float away over the tree tops Sarah had made up her mind to save her pennies until she could afford to make a trip herself.

That day seemed very distant however. Her wages, though better than the meagre three shillings she had earned as a kitchen maid at Deedham Green, were swallowed up each week by the day to day expenses of living. There was food to buy, for she was too sensible to try to exist on the buns and pastries she served at the restaurant, shoe leather to be replaced, for the constant traipsing back and forth meant it wore thin at an alarming rate, and the rent to pay for the room she had taken over a teashop in a suburban high street. Sarah considered herself fortunate to have found the room – Molly Norkett who owned the teashop was a widow and a motherly soul and soon she had suggested that Sarah should share her meals with her and keep her company in the evenings. But Sarah felt obliged to contribute towards the good wholesome stews and roasts, cooked in the same oven that Molly used to bake buns and teacakes for her shop so that the little apartment was always redolent of delicious mouth-watering smells, and though she helped Molly in the teashop on her days off from her regular work at Alexandra Palace in order to increase her income money still seemed to flow out of her purse every bit as fast as it went in and her savings for her balloon ride grew so slowly that she began to doubt she would ever have enough.

It was when Dolly Shepherd, star parachutist of the Gaudron team, had come into the restaurant one day that Sarah had realised there was 'more than one way of skinning a cat' as Bertha Pugh might have put it. Dolly was a pretty girl with bubbling curls and a warm smile. In her ballooning costume of royal blue she drew glances of admiration from the men and frank envy from the women and she was brave and resourceful as well as pretty. But fame had done nothing to spoil her. Dolly had a smile and a friendly word for everyone and as Sarah watched her chatting unaffectedly to the autograph hunters who sought her out Becky, one of the other waitresses, nudged her arm.

'She used to work here, you know,' she confided.

'Dolly Shepherd did?' Sarah asked, surprised.

'Yes. She was a waitress just like us. One night Sam Cody had a mishap in his sharp shooting act. He used to shoot a plaster egg off his wife's head blindfolded and this particular time something went wrong and the bullet grazed her scalp. Dolly had the nerve to offer to act as stand in. Of course that got her in with Cody and his cronies and the next thing any of us knew was that she was making parachute descents with the Gaudron team.'

'Really?' Sarah's eyes widened and she looked at the pretty girl in the blue knickerbocker suit with new interest.

'That's how it all began – and look at her now! A celebrity in her own right. Not that I'd want to do it, mind you. Imagine launching yourself out of a balloon with nothing

170

but a bit of silk between you and the ground! The very thought of it makes my hair stand on end. But Dolly seems to enjoy it – and look where it's taken her!'

A customer had signalled for Sarah's attention and the conversation had come to an abrupt end. But as she hurried to take the order a small pulse of excitement was beating deep inside her. The thought of parachuting certainly did not frighten her as it frightened Becky – she could think of nothing more exciting. And knowing that Dolly had once been a waitress just as she was made her feel for a moment as if some of the glamour of Dolly's exciting life had somehow rubbed off onto her. Her feet flew as she hurried between the tables, glancing over her shoulder from time to time to catch another glimpse of Dolly, and feeling that first prickle of excitement hardening into resolve.

What was to stop her from trying to become one of the Gaudron team? She was young, she was fit, and, without so much as a trace of false modesty, she knew she too would look good in a ballooning costume – something audiences expected whether the performer was an actress, a singer on the halls or a parachutist. Why it had not occurred to her before she did not know – perhaps because the starry aura of the display team had made them seem different somehow from mere mortals. But now Sarah's mind was made up. If Dolly Shepherd could do it – so could she!

During the next few days Sarah had watched for Captain Gaudron to come into the restaurant. He did not and when she enquired she learned he was away performing at a gala somewhere in the north. The delay annoyed her for she was impatient to put her plan into action. A week later she caught a glimpse of his dapper figure in the crowds but he was with several other men and there was no opportunity to speak to him. As she scurried between the tables with her tray Sarah's sense of frustration deepened. If she waited for him to come into the restaurant and sit at one of her tables she might wait for ever. There was only one way to be sure of gaining an audience with him and that was to visit him at his workshop.

The boldness of the idea set Sarah's veins tingling for the

171

workshop seemed to her to be cloaked in an air of mystery and importance. She was very much afraid Captain Gaudron might be annoyed at the intrusion and would show her the door without even listening to what she had to say, much less offering to give her the chance she was seeking. But at least she could try. Sarah was a firm believer in taking her fate into her own hands. To sit back and wait for something to happen was, in her opinion, the next best thing to making sure nothing happened at all.

By the time she had served the last customers and cleared the last table it was too late to visit the aeronauts' workshop and in any case after a long day waiting at tables Sarah knew she did not look her best. Much better to come in early tomorrow and make the visit before starting work for the day. Next morning she took extra care over her toilet, brushing her hair until it shone, pinching colour into her cheeks and lips and dressing in a pretty yellow gingham which seemed to echo the early sunshine.

'My goodness, you look a picture today and no mistake!' Molly said when she came down to the shop. 'And you're early this morning, too. What's it in aid of, I'd like to know? A young man?'

Sarah had smiled at the sharp knowing look in the bright button eyes which always reminded her of the currants in one of Molly's homemade buns. Molly made no secret of the fact that she thought it was high time that a pretty girl like Sarah had a sweetheart and was puzzled by her disinterest in the opposite sex.

'No, Molly, it's not a young man,' Sarah said but she did not elaborate. She knew instinctively that Molly would disapprove of her plans.

When she reached Alexandra Palace Sarah made straight for the banqueting hall which accommodated the aeronauts' workshop. Her pulses were racing and there was a tightness in her chest but she walked briskly into the banqueting hall with head held high.

Although it was early the aeronauts' workshop was already a hive of activity. As Sarah's eyes grew accustomed to the dimmer light after the bright sunshine outside she became aware of the wicker baskets which seemed to fill every corner of the hall, the yards of coiled rope and cord and the acres of netting strung from the high ceilings. There was a busy hum of sewing machines, sounding for all the world like a swarm of angry bees, and the dust in the air tickled Sarah's nose, making her want to sneeze. There was a smell about the place unlike anything she had ever encountered before – a pungent pot pourri of canvas, hemp and glue. Carefully Sarah picked her way over the coils of rope which littered the floor and spoke to a girl who was seated at a sewing machine stitching a canvas envelope.

'I'm looking for Captain Gaudron. Do you know where I can find him?'

The girl hardly paused in her task.

'Over there,' she shouted above the hum of the treddle and jerked her head to indicate the far end of the hall.

Following her glance Sarah saw him, a neat dapper man in shirt sleeves, deep in conversation with a fellow aeronaut. Her mouth took on a determined set and although her heart had begun hammering uncomfortably against her ribs she made her way directly across the hall and positioned herself in front of him.

'Excuse me, Captain Gaudron, but could I have a word with you?'

He broke off his conversation and she felt the full force of his gaze sweeping over her. His eyes were piercing in his lively intelligent face and his moustache so expertly waxed it seemed positively to gleam in the light of the overhead carbide lamps.

'Yes?' he asked briskly.

Sarah's courage almost deserted her and she drew a deep steadying breath.

'I know this may seem a frightful nerve but I would like to become a parachutist and I wondered if you would take me into your team.'

She thought she caught a gleam of amusement in those sharp eyes.

'Did you now. And what makes you think you could be a parachutist?'

173

'Why shouldn't I be?' Sarah countered boldly. 'What special attributes do I need that I couldn't learn?'

Again she was aware of that gleam of amusement.

'Courage for one thing – though it seems you do not lack that. Strength, for another.' He glanced down at her hands, took one and examined it, circling her slim wrist with his fingers. 'Your bones look like a bird's, Miss . . . ?'

'Thomas,' Sarah said. 'And there is certainly nothing wrong with my bones. I've never broken one in my life.'

'Hmm.' A faint smile lifted one corner of his mouth beneath that neatly waxed moustache and he indicated a bar contraption which swung from the ceiling. 'See if you can swing on that.'

Sarah stared at him for a moment uncertain as to whether or not he was having a joke at her expense but he returned her gaze steadily.

'My girls have to be able to support themselves on a trapeze,' he explained. 'Try it.'

'Very well.' Sarah took the bar between her hands, flexing her fingers, and lifted her feet off the ground.

'Hold on,' he said, checking his watch.

Grimly Sarah did so. At first she was merely annoyed at the undignified picture she was sure she was making, then as the seconds ticked by and the weight of her body began to drag on her arms she could think of nothing but the effort of hanging there. She flexed her fingers feeling as if her arms were being dragged from their sockets and small beads of perspiration rose on her forehead. At last, just as she thought she would be forced to give in, he nodded.

'Good. You are stronger than you look, Miss Thomas. Very well, you can come down now.'

Relieved Sarah released her hold on the bar and lowered herself to the ground.

'Well?' she said, gently chaffing the life back into her tingling fingers and trying to appear composed. 'Do I pass your test?'

'With flying colours. Five minutes – very good for a first attempt.' He smiled. 'Unfortunately however I have a full team at the moment. I do not need any more girls.'

Sarah experienced a stab of anger.

'You mean I went through that for nothing?'

His teeth gleamed very white.

'I'm afraid so. Unless something happens to one of my girls – an accident – or perhaps one of them may decide to give up . . . But ballooning is a drug, Miss Thomas. Most of them stay for quite a long while.'

Sarah drew herself up. Disappointment was a hard knot inside her; she was afraid if she remained there a moment longer she would disgrace herself by bursting into tears. After all her high hopes she hated to give up so easily yet her fierce pride would not allow her to beg and besides she knew instinctively it would do no good. She summoned her remaining reserves.

'In that case, Captain Gaudron, I am sorry to have taken up your time,' she said stiffly and turned away before he could see those treacherous tears shimmering behind her long lashes.

'Just a moment!' It was the other man, Captain Gaudron's companion, who spoke. Sarah stopped, holding herself stiffly. She did not dare to turn around. 'You really want to parachute?' he asked.

He had a gentle voice, lacking Auguste Gaudron's natural authority. She blinked away the tears and turned, looking at him for the first time and seeing a slightly built man a few inches taller than herself. Sandy hair was slicked away from a narrow, interesting face, a moustache, so light in colour as to be almost indistinguishable etched a light shadow on his upper lip and above the high cheekbones his eyes gleamed, tawny as a cat's behind a pale fringing of lashes.

'Well of course I want to parachute,' she said, disappointment and the still-threatening tears making her voice sharp. 'That's why I'm here.'

'Then perhaps I can help you,' he said. 'In fact, we may be able to help each other.'

'*You?*' No sooner had the exclamation left her lips than she realised how rude it had sounded and she flushed. 'I'm sorry. How can we help each other?'

175

The amused curve had returned to Captain Gaudron's lips. He clapped a hand around his companion's shoulders.

'Allow me to introduce you. This is Captain Eric Dare. Perhaps you have heard of him. He and his brother Henry are also balloonists. The Flying Dares.'

'Oh, yes,' Sarah said faintly. She had indeed heard of the Flying Dares. It was simply that she had paid little attention to them. Here at Alexandra Palace in the shadow of the most illustrious balloonists they had seemed of little account. Even in appearance Eric Dare was pale by comparison with the great Auguste Gaudron.

'I realise flying with me is a pretty poor substitute for the famed Gaudron team,' he said wryly. 'But as you may know my brother and I also entertain with displays of aerobatics to help us finance our serious research work. I have thought for some time that what we lack is a little glamour. However impressive my stunts there is no doubt the public like to see a pretty face and a trim figure.'

Sarah nodded, accepting the compliment in the spirit it was meant, although she was aware of Eric Dare's eyes appraising her.

'Yes,' he continued affably. 'I think we might very well be able to come to some arrangement. Why don't you come with me and meet my brother Henry and we'll see what he has to say.'

Sarah's heart sank. The young man's offer might yet be vetoed by his brother. As if reading her mind Eric smiled.

'Don't worry – he's not an ogre. In fact as long as Henry has the resources to continue with his work perfecting his very own dirigible model very little bothers him. I'm sure I can convince him of the advantage in my plan.' He slapped Auguste Gaudron lightly on the upper arm. 'I'll see you later, my friend. Come along, Miss Thomas. Let me show you the way to our corner of the workshop.'

He placed an arm on Sarah's waist to guide her through the maze of equipment and for the first time since her experience with Hugh Sarah did not shy away from the touch of a man. It was a pleasant touch, friendly and unthreatening, and Sarah warmed to it. He might not be

Captain Gaudron, leader of the famous Gaudron team, but he was a very nice young man. And if he could help her achieve her ambition then really she could ask for no more. Excitement throbbed in her, touching her cheeks with colour and bringing a sparkle to her eyes.

It looked as if her boldness was going to pay off after all – and she intended to gain every possible advantage from it.

Now, two years later, as she made for the aeronauts' workshop, Sarah found herself remembering that first momentous visit with amusement – and not a little pride. From that day on she had never looked back. From her first tentative jump from the edge of the balloon basket she had progressed to advanced ascents on the small swaying trapeze, and graceful well-judged descents. She had gained acclaim wherever she went and although it was the Dares who had made it possible, Sarah knew that it was her own audacity and initiative that had taken her from her humble life as a kitchen maid and the humdrum day-to-day routine of waiting at tables to her present enviable station as one of the undisputed queens of the sky.

As she entered the vast hall the noise of the sewing machines, the busy chatter of the ballooning fraternity and that indefinable dusty smell enfolded her just as it had done on that first day but now it was as familiar to her as her own breath and she picked her way with accustomed ease between the wicker baskets and coils of rope towards the corner which the Dares had made their own. As she went some of the men called a greeting and she acknowledged them with a wave of her hand but most were totally absorbed in their work. It was always this way; ballooning was a way of life which demanded total allegiance, body and soul, from those who loved it.

At the far end of the hall she could see the slim whippy figure of Henry Dare as engrossed as any of them and she smiled to herself. As Eric had told her that first day she had met him, Henry was one of the most fanatical of the balloon fraternity, a man totally dedicated to the pursuit of excellence and without a single interest unconnected to the passion which was his life. In some ways he reminded her of a professor or boffin for often he would arrive at the balloon centre so eager to put some new idea or theory to the test that he would have quite forgotten to comb his hair or the light thready moustache and side whiskers which were even paler in colour than his brother's or even to button his shirt correctly. On one famous occasion he had arrived wearing no shirt at all – his waistcoat and jacket pulled hastily on over his thick flannel vest – and wearing odd shoes, one black, one a brown elastic-sided boot. But where ballooning was concerned there was nothing in the least absent minded about Henry. Every detail was checked and rechecked and he could work out complicated calculations at lightning speed barely jotting down a single figure on one of the scraps of paper that he could produce from his copious pockets like a magician producing a rabbit from a hat. Meteorology and aerodynamics were the breath of life to him – whilst he seldom knew what day of the week it was and Eric was forced to remind him of every appointment, every high day and holiday including Christmas and his own birthday, he was a fount of knowledge on air speeds and cloud movements, on the relative attributes of a few extra pounds ballast on drift with an accuracy that left Sarah breathless.

'Good morning, Henry,' she greeted him. 'How are you this fine morning?'

He glanced up, acknowledging her with a birdlike nod of the head before bending once more to examine some imagined fault in the burner he was holding.

'Me? I'm fine! I wish the same could be said of these components. The standard of workmanship these days – appalling!'

'I'm sure there's nothing wrong with it,' she soothed. 'You are a dear old fusspot, Henry.'

He looked up again, his light eyes darting over her face.

'And it's thanks to me for being a fusspot that you are still alive and sound in wind and limb, Sarah. You can't afford to take chances up there, my dear – and don't you forget it!'

'I won't, Henry,' Sarah placated him. 'Where is Eric?'

'Hmm?' Henry had returned his attention to the burner once more and his tone registered his impatience with the irrelevance of her question. 'Oh, he's gone to get a cup of coffee, I think he said. Always thinking of his stomach, that boy.'

'I'm sure that's not true, Henry,' Sarah chided. 'He knows that anyone – even you – can work better after a nice strong cup of coffee. I hope he thinks to bring one for me too.'

She neither expected, nor received, a reply, but after a moment Henry glanced up again.

'There was someone asking for you just now. A man.'

'Oh – who was that?' Sarah enquired without much interest. As Sweetheart of the Skies she was not unused to a steady stream of admirers, usually headed off by Eric.

'I couldn't say. I told him you would be arriving shortly so he'll be back no doubt.' Henry brushed aside a limp strand of sandy hair which had fallen over his forehead and peered, eyes narrowed, past Sarah. 'Here is Eric now. And the man who was asking for you is with him.' He sounded vaguely surprised as if he had half believed the enquirer to have been a figment of his own imagination.

Sarah turned, following his gaze, and felt the breath catch in her throat.

'I don't believe it,' she whispered faintly.

'What's that?' Henry asked mildly.

Sarah did not reply. Her mouth had gone dry and she raised a hand which trembled slightly to cover her lips. It couldn't be. Not after all this time. Not here at Alexandra Palace . . .

He walked towards her with the long measured stride she knew and loved so well. He was wearing a suit of fine dark blue wool; above the stiff shiny white collar of his shirt his fresh-complexioned face was grave. There was a little more silver in his hair than there had been, etching feathery wings in the crisp jet black, and it showed too in his neat dark moustache like a sprinkling of hoar frost on a dark winter garden. But his eyes were as clear and blue as she remembered them though there was a slight wariness in them that she did not understand and his height and the indefinable presence of him were as imposing as they had ever been.

She stood quite still, feeling her legs turn to jelly, but there was an eagerness bubbling in her so that in spite of the shock, in spite of the tumultuous inexplicable emotions that were making her dizzy, it was all she could do to stop herself from running to him and throwing herself into his arms.

'Well, Sarah,' he said in that cool sharp voice that had always reminded her of frosty mornings. 'So I've found you at last!'

She removed her hand from her lips and locked it with the other in the folds of her skirt to keep it from trembling. She lifted her chin, returning his gaze, and her face was as grave as his, not betraying for an instant the tumultuous delight that had begun to course through her in warm rushing waves.

'Mr Morse!' she said, and her voice was little more than a whisper.

Chapter Fifteen

'How you have grown up, Sarah!' he said. 'I confess I would have scarcely known you.'

They were sitting at a table in the very open-air restaurant where Sarah had worked as a waitress. It was the best place, Sarah had thought, for them to be able to talk away from the curious eyes of Eric, Henry and the others – and besides she had been desperate suddenly for fresh air, as if the closed-in, dusty atmosphere in the workshop was suffocating her.

In the restaurant Gilbert had ordered them a coffee each and a plate of pastries but the food lay untouched on the lace-doilied plate, and when Sarah raised her cup to sip the strong dark liquid she was annoyed to realise her hand was still trembling.

'I'm seventeen now,' she said defensively.

'Yes, I suppose you are.' He sighed, almost inaudibly. 'Seventeen! It's strange but somehow I continued to think of you as you were when I last saw you – as if time had stood still. But of course that's nonsense. And look at you now! Not only a young woman but a very successful one. A balloonist, no less. How did that come about?'

'Oh, it's a very long story.' A little haltingly because of the slight awkwardness that still lay between them she related how she had come to Alexandra Palace, met the Dare Brothers and begun to work with them. She made no mention of the time she had spent at Deedham Green. It was still too painful to her and she had no wish to sour this meeting by referring to it or even thinking of it. It hurt her still that Gilbert had made no effort to contact her during those dreadful months and though the memory of the despair and sense of degradation had dimmed, it was still there, a disturbing prickle beneath her skin like the fading yet persistent irritation of a virulent rash.

181

Gilbert listened with interest while she talked, his eyes scarcely leaving her face. Occasionally he interjected a question, once he drew out his cigarette case and lit a cigarette and it was then that Sarah knew he was as affected by the interview as she was. Gilbert rarely smoked before luncheon unless something was disturbing him.

'I must say I am impressed. It sounds as if you have a good life here, Sarah,' he said at last.

'I do,' she said simply. 'I get a tremendous thrill from ballooning. It's wonderfully peaceful up there, high above the ground and you hardly seem to be moving at all. Even during an ascent it's as if it is the ground that is falling away, not the balloon rising.

'And parachuting?'

'Oh – that's wonderful too,' she said, wondering how she could describe the first moments of exhilarating free-fall when the wind seemed to drive all the breath out of her, the little shock that ran through her body as the parachute opened, the effortless drift back to earth. She had no words to explain the way trees and bushes mutated, changed shape and dimension, from the tiny replicas which might have been models from James's wooden farmyard, through enormous distorted mushroom shapes until at last they took on their normal appearance and proportions, albeit upside down as she landed, rolling backwards the moment her feet touched the ground as she had been taught in order to minimise the danger of damage to her spine.

'And dangerous,' Gilbert said thoughtfully, tapping ash from his cigarette. 'Plenty of people have been killed or badly injured parachuting from balloons. Wasn't one of Captain Gaudron's team killed recently?'

'Violet Kavanagh? Yes.' But she did not want to dwell on it. A deep shadow had fallen over the ballooning fraternity when Violet had been lifted from a factory roof on which she had inadvertently landed, dashed to the ground and killed. But thinking of such things did no good. After the initial shock they were seldom discussed. For a while extra caution would be exercised, more thorough checks made of equipment and prevailing weather conditions, but no

182

mention would be made of the reason for this, no concern admitted. And there was no great show of grief. That was kept for the dark watches of the night. In public the fraternity put on a show of hearty unconcern as if the disaster had never happened.

'But how long is it all going to last?' Gilbert asked, sensing her withdrawal and turning the conversation deftly. 'I believe the era of ballooning is coming to an end. It won't be long now before powered flight takes its place. You must have heard of the progress being made by Bleriot and the others. I don't think it will be long now before he, or someone else, manages to cross the Channel and the *Daily Mail* prize is won. Then there will be no stopping. Even I have thought of building aero engines at Morse Motors. At present Lawrence is not enthusiastic but as things progress I shall be keeping a close watch on what is needed and I may yet persuade him to see things my way.' His voice grew firm and vibrant with his enthusiasm for his own particular interest. 'Aeroplanes will go ahead in leaps and bounds and balloons will be as outdated in the air as the horse and cart is becoming on the roads. And what will you do then, Sarah? Have you thought of that?'

She sipped her coffee, which had cooled as they talked, not answering for a moment. The end of the golden age of ballooning was another subject she did not care to think about yet she knew in her heart he was right. Already there were fewer demonstrations and acrobatics than there had been – racing was the thing of the moment with big meets arranged at suitable sites all over the country – and it was the progress being made in the construction of powered aircraft which excited the pioneers now. She had mentioned this to the Dares once or twice but Henry had refused point blank to discuss her suggestion that the balloon might soon be obsolete. Let the crackpots try to fly in their heavier-than-air machines if they thought they could, was his attitude; engines were noisy and smelly and spoiled the perfection of flight. Sarah respected his view though she did not agree with it and now she smiled and voiced what had so far occurred to her only as a vague impossible dream.

'If aeroplanes replace balloons I dare say I shall have to move with the times. I learned to balloon and parachute – why not learn to fly an aeroplane?'

He laughed aloud, amused by her temerity yet as always delighted by the sheer vital force which drove her. She had not changed, he thought. She was still the same Sarah in spite of the physical changes, still bold and courageous, still refusing to be bound by any of the limits with which others found themselves shackled to their own narrow worlds.

'I don't think you know what you are saying, my dear,' he said, still smiling at the thought of Sarah wrestling with the controls of a contraption of matchwood, brown paper and string, such as he had seen Alberto Santos-Dumont do. 'It's still beyond most men at the moment. And even more dangerous than your precious ballooning.'

'But if things progress as you say they will and men do build aeroplanes that can fly then why shouldn't a woman do it too?' she demanded, a little defensive in the face of his amusement. 'Anyway, I shall continue to make the most of ballooning as long as I can. I enjoy it and I enjoy the rewards too. When we go off to do displays we always stay in the best hotels and have receptions given in our honour. There is good food and plenty of it and champagne corks popping everywhere. Do you wonder that I don't want it ever to end?'

His eyes had grown thoughtful again and he lit another cigarette, looking at her steadily.

'And what about the times when you are not cavorting about the countryside living the life of a celebrity?' he asked. 'What do you do then?'

'Oh, sometimes I help Henry and Eric here.'

'The Dares. They are the two young men I met earlier?'

'Yes. Their name isn't Dare really – it's Gardiner. But they think Dare is a better name for a balloon team. When I first jumped with them they wanted me to call myself Mam'selle Valla or some such Frenchy name, but I refused.' She smiled at the memory. 'It seemed a bit silly to me.'

'Yes, I dare say it would,' Gilbert agreed. There was a

down to earth streak in Sarah's nature which would pour scorn on such pretentiousness. 'Eric Dare, is he your . . . ?' He broke off, not certain how to frame the question. 'Is there anything between you?'

Sarah shook her head with such vehemence that he realised he had unwittingly trodden on some nerve ending.

'Certainly not. We are good friends – that's all.'

'So where do you live when you are not being feted at some grand hotel?' he enquired mildly.

'With Molly Norkett. She owns a teashop and I have a room above it. So does Molly,' she added quickly, afraid he might be about to cast doubts on her morality. 'We share meals and I help her in the teashop when I am not working here. Molly has been very good to me though she makes no secret of the fact that she does not approve of me ballooning. She does not think it is a very ladylike thing to so.'

'She sounds like a good woman.'

'Oh she is. She treats me like a daughter,' Sarah said seriously.

Gilbert drew smoke and blew it out in a thin stream. His hand was quite steady now and his eyes held hers.

'I thought *I* treated you that way,' he said quietly. 'I think I must tell you I am most disappointed that you have not repaid me by behaving like one.'

During the last half hour she had relaxed, now, quite suddenly, all the awkwardness returned. She had thought he was going to be content to let the past lie. Now the old hurts and resentments flared again as she realised he was not. She looked away quickly for she felt sure they were mirrored in her eyes and she did not want him to see them.

'Why did you run away, Sarah?' he asked. 'Why did you leave without so much as a word of explanation?'

Her chin came up as a sudden anger blazed through her veins. How dare he ask such a thing? As if he had cared two hoots about how she had fared after being banished to Deedham Green! Not once had he contacted her – why should he think he had any right now to an explanation as to why she had left?

185

'Sarah?' he pressed her.

'Because it was terrible. I couldn't stand it a moment longer.' Her eyes met his defiantly and she saw the small frown pucker his well-defined brows.

'Terrible? Oh surely not! I always did my best to see you were well treated. You must know that. I was shocked, yes, shocked, when I returned from France to find you had simply run off without a word to anyone – not even a note to explain your reasons. And in all this time you have never seen fit to make contact even once to let us know where you were or even if you were alive. Surely you must have known how worried I would be? I felt responsible for you, Sarah, whether you like it or not. And what I want to know now is *why?*'

As he spoke she remained motionless, the colour draining from her face and then returning in a hot flush as anger gave way to confusion and confusion to unwilling, mind-dizzying comprehension. Gilbert was referring not to her flight from Deedham Green but her disappearance from Chewton Leigh!

'Didn't they tell you?' she asked. Her voice was thready and faint.

'Tell me what?' He regarded her closely, his expression reproachful still, yet genuinely puzzled. 'What did you think I would have been told? Did something happen whilst I was in France? Something I should know about?'

She knew then without any more doubt what had happened. No-one at Chewton Leigh had ever told him of the circumstances of her leaving – not even their own distorted version of the truth. They had given him to understand she had simply run away without any word of explanation so that all this time he had believed her guilty of behaving in a callous and ungrateful fashion. No wonder he had never contacted her – he had no idea where she had gone. She looked into his troubled eyes knowing how much it must have hurt him and felt a rising tide of anger at the deceit that had been perpetrated. Yet at the same time she was glad that he had not been misled into thinking that she was an adventuress taking advantage of his hospitality to

186

seduce his son. Now she could present her side of the story and he would believe her, she knew. The bond between them had always been based on perfect honesty. And if he had any doubts he could always verify her version of what had happened after she left by checking with the Carson family.

'Well, Sarah?' he demanded, looking at her expectantly and for a moment the words trembled on Sarah's lips. Yet for all his concern his air of confidence was unshaken. Whatever he thought she might say it bore no resemblance to the ugly truth and with a sudden flash Sarah knew there was no way she could enlighten him.

Your favourite son raped me, not once but twice. He lied to cover his guilt, not caring how much he blackened my character. Your wife passed sentence on me and then she too lied and schemed and deceived. What would it do to Gilbert if she told him that? He would know of course – if he believed her – that she had not walked out of the life he had welcomed her into with callous lack of gratitude. But he would learn that his family, those closest to him, were treacherous and deceitful, lacking in compassion and even common decency. If she spoke now the family could be torn apart, with trust and respect shattered and relationships damaged beyond repair. Sarah did not care very much if the foundations of Blanche's world were shaken, and she had longed to take her revenge on Hugh for what he had done. Now suddenly she knew that revenge would not be sweet as she had imagined but hollow, for in taking it she would hurt the one person who meant more to her than any other – Gilbert Morse himself. And the hurt would go far deeper than any he might feel in the rejection he believed her guilty of. For they were his family while she was only the orphan he had taken in and treated with a kindness for which she was eternally grateful.

As she saw, too clearly, the consequences of speaking out, Sarah made her decision. She could not tell him now or ever what had happened during his absence. She alone must bear the responsibility for leaving Chewton Leigh.

'There was an argument,' she said lamely. 'I thought it best that I should leave. That's all.'

187

'An argument? What about?'

She experienced a moment's panic. The sun was growing hot now; its brightness was beginning to make her head ache.

'Oh we don't have to go into it all now do we?' she begged. 'It's so long ago. It's past history.'

For a moment Gilbert's eyes held hers and she thought that even now he was going to refuse to let the matter drop. Then he sighed and nodded, a trifle brusquely.

'Very well. If you do not feel able to confide in me then I suppose we must leave it at that.'

The silence hung awkwardly between them for a moment and illogically Sarah felt bereft suddenly as if she had closed the door for the last time on her life at Chewton Leigh. As a drowning man sees his past life flash before his eyes so all the things she had known and loved were suddenly there like the pieces of a jigsaw puzzle, bittersweet and hauntingly evocative – the rolling green hills and the cool shaded lake, the winding lanes thick with cow parsley, the meadows, yellow with buttercups, where she had run and played as a child and later cantered with Sweet Lass. The thought of the horse she had loved was the most poignant of all; she was overcome with longing to feel the gentle nose nuzzle her again, searching for the sugar lumps Sarah always took to her, and to bury her face in the firm column of the strawberry roan's neck.

'How is Sweet Lass?' she asked before she could stop herself.

A small muscle moved in Gilbert's cheek. His expression was inscrutable. 'She still misses you, I think. She had a fine foal – Baron, we called him. Alicia took him over. She broke him herself and rides him whenever she has time.'

Sarah nodded. It hurt to think of Alicia taking Sweet Lass's foal for her own. But Alicia was good with horses. It was one of her redeeming features. And since she was no longer there herself . . . She swallowed at the lump which had risen in her throat.

'I suppose,' Gilbert said suddenly, 'that it would do no good if I asked you to come home?'

188

Her heart leaped. Home! Yes, in spite of everything it was still just that and something deep within her yearned towards it as if drawn by an unseen magnet. But too much had happened. The barriers were too great to surmount. Her life was here now.

'I can't do that,' she said quietly. 'But thank you for asking me.'

He nodded. His throat was full suddenly.

'I understand, Sarah. But don't forget, will you, that we still care for you very much. Any time you feel ready to come home we shall be ready to welcome you. And if you ever need anything, or are in any sort of trouble, don't hesitate to contact me.'

'Thank you,' she said huskily, realising the interview was coming to an end and wishing with all her heart that she could throw her arms around Gilbert and tell him how grateful she was for all he had done for her and how much it had meant to her to see him today. But theirs had never been a physical relationship and the barrier of habit was yet another which was insuperable.

'Take care, Sarah,' he said, rising and smiling down at her with a wistfulness that tugged at her heartstrings.

'I'll come with you to the gate,' she offered, jumping to her feet.

'Don't trouble. I am sure I can find my way – and don't you have a demonstration to do?'

'Oh yes, I do!' she cried, horrified that she could have forgotten. 'Won't you stay and watch?'

He shook his head. 'No. I'll leave you now. But don't forget what I said, will you? The door is always open, Sarah. You have only to say the word.'

He smiled at her once more, turned, and was gone, swallowed up in the crowds. For a moment she stood trying to catch a last glimpse of him, then resigned she started to make her way back towards the banqueting hall. Some people in the crowd recognised her, pointing her out and waving. But for once Sarah did not even notice. Her professional smile was set stiffly on her lips and if her eyes shone more brightly than usual it was because they glittered with unshed tears.

Chapter Sixteen

The moment she re-entered the banqueting hall Eric Gardiner could see that something had happened to upset Sarah. Eric was a perceptive young man, as sensitive as he was resourceful. He was also in love with Sarah and had been from the first moment he had laid eyes on her when she had come to ask Auguste Gaudron for a chance to parachute with his team. But in spite of their intimate working relationship and the friendship that had grown and blossomed from it, in spite of the bond that was inevitable between two people who held one another's life in their hands almost daily, Eric had never been able to get close to her. God alone knows, he had tried. But always he had come up against a barrier and beyond it a bleak no-man's land behind which the heart of her was hidden like a vista in teasing, swirling mists. Sometimes he thought he caught a glimpse of the real Sarah behind the smiling, confident, public exterior, but as quickly it was gone again and he was left with the unsolved enigma. Who was Sarah? Where did she come from? Where were her relatives and why did she never talk about them – or indeed about anything from her past. She had been hurt, he suspected, by something or someone, hurt so deeply that she had withdrawn into the persona of The Sweetheart of the Skies like an actress living a part.

Because he loved her he wondered about it often, asking himself what it was that could have so affected her that she had locked herself into this ivory tower from which occasionally, like Rapunzel, she let down her hair just a little, only to jerk it back in panic when she thought her fortress might be breeched. She did not like being touched, that much was certain. If ever he made the slightest advance towards her he felt her immediate withdrawal the moment a friendly arm became a little more than friendly, yet he also

190

sensed that there was a great warmth within her, untapped, which she controlled with the same iron will which controlled all her emotions. The casing might be cold and hard, unbreakable as tempered steel, within it burned the embers of a fire which some day some lucky man would be able to fan to life. Eric hoped with all his heart that he might be that man. But he believed that patience and gentleness were the only keys which would unlock that secret heart and free her from whatever memories and experiences had caused her to retreat to her private sanctuary.

Sometimes when they were alone together in some hotel sitting-room after a successful display it was all he could do to control the powerful longing to take her in his arms. Inevitably Henry would take his noggin and retire to bed early while Sarah and Eric would linger, discussing the events of the day over a bottle of champagne. Sarah would be relaxed, shoes discarded to allow her to wiggle her toes in luxurious carpets or tuck her feet up beneath her as she curled in totally unladylike fashion in some deep wing chair, and the mood would be the pleasurable awareness that settled in after the adrenaline ceased to flow, like the drowsy contentment that follows satisfying love making. On these occasions and glowing from the effects of the champagne, Eric felt his love pounding through his veins with his blood, a fever that almost burned him up with its intensity. But he knew that a wrong move on his part could shatter the mood – and with it the whole structure of their relationship and the trust between them which he had taken such pains to establish. Adoring her, he suffered for her and prayed that one day his patience would bring its rewards, the relationship would deepen from loving friends to lovers and the ghosts which haunted Sarah would be exorcised forever.

Now as she walked towards him across the banqueting hall at Alexandra Palace he saw the shadow of those ghosts on Sarah's face and some sixth sense told him that whoever her visitor had been he had touched deeply on whatever it was that was secret and unmentionable in her past. The knowledge caused him a moment's anxiety, a creeping

191

sense of unease that he could not have explained, even to himself. The man in himself had posed no threat. He was clearly a gentleman with the easy manners of his station and a set to his face that was totally without malice or Machiavellism. His eyes, very blue, had seemed almost familiar to Eric; when enquiring for Sarah he had sounded concerned, not in any way threatening. And Sarah had clearly been delighted to see him if a little shocked. Yet all the while she had been gone Eric had been on tenterhooks and now knew his concern had been justified. His visit had touched Sarah as nothing else had done in the two years Eric had known her. Somehow, almost imperceptibly, a crack had appeared in the iron fortress and Sarah's vulnerability was peeping through.

He hurried towards her taking her arm in friendly fashion and she did not draw away.

'I was beginning to think you were lost!' he said.

'Were you?' She sounded pre-occupied.

'Yes, who was that man, Sarah?'

'Oh . . .' Emotion flickered briefly across her face before she retreated once more into a world of her own thoughts. 'Just someone I used to know.' Her voice was faint.

He glanced at her quickly. 'Are you all right?'

'Yes, of course.' But her eyes still held that faraway look. He was alarmed suddenly at the realisation that in less than an hour they would be making their parachute jump of the day. Jumping required complete concentration, anything less could spell disaster. Sarah was an experienced parachutist now of course with a totally professional approach. In all likelihood she would be able to put aside whatever it was that was troubling her for the duration of the display at least. But if she did not . . . Eric felt his blood run cold at the thought of some mishap or error of judgement. If anything happened to Sarah he did not think he could bear it.

In the aeronauts' workshop it was hot and dusty and the noise of the sewing machines was deafening.

'Let's go and get some fresh air,' he suggested.

She allowed him to lead her outside. They found a bench

192

on the shady side of the banqueting hall and sat down, Sarah staring into space, her lower lip rucked by her teeth.

'Whoever he was he seems to have upset you,' Eric commented.

Sarah came back from her reverie, her eyes expressing surprise.

'Mr Morse? Oh no, he hasn't upset me! He couldn't! He is a wonderful person. It's just that he . . . reminded me of some things I would rather forget.'

'But who is he?'

'Gilbert Morse. Have you ever heard of Morse Motors? If you haven't I dare say you soon will. He is thinking of going into the manufacture of engines for aeroplanes and knowing him as I do I should think he would make a tremendous success of it. He is so forward looking and everything he touches – well, he seems to touch it with success.' Her face was glowing, suddenly she looked alive. A terrible suspicion assailed Eric.

'Are you in love with him?' he asked before he could stop himself.

She swung round and the sheer amazement on her face dispelled his doubts instantly.

'Good heavens no! He has been like a father to me. He took me in when I was orphaned – arranged for my education – everything.'

'So you are an orphan?' Eric pressed her gently.

'Yes. My mother died when I was nine. I never knew my father. I was always told he had been a soldier and died in the service of his country but I'm not so sure that is true. Alicia said something once – Alicia is Mr Morse's daughter. She called me . . . a name. I didn't want to believe it then. I was very young and I didn't care to think that my mother was "no better than she should be" as they say. But now . . . well, I think it is very likely the truth – or something close to it.'

He nodded almost afraid to reply in case he stopped her flow. It was the first time Sarah had ever talked about herself and he felt that at last he was getting some insight into what made her the person she was.

'How did your mother die?' he asked at last when it became clear she had relapsed into silence.

'I don't know what was wrong with her. She wasn't ill for very long. I came home from school one day and found her in a coma.' Her hands were making baskets in the folds of her skirts. 'I blame myself, you know. If I had fetched the doctor before I went to school she might be alive today. But I didn't. She said she would be all right and I believed her.'

'You were nine years old,' he comforted her. 'You couldn't have known. And maybe there was nothing anyone could have done in any case.' She was silent. 'So where does Mr Morse come in?' he pressed her gently.

Softly, haltingly, as if she were talking to herself she sketched in the details of her story and as he listened the love he felt for her began to swell inside him until he felt he would burst with it. He wanted to hold her and comfort her as she spoke of that last vain dash for the doctor; his hands balled into fists when she described Mrs Pugh and the treatment she had meted out. But he heard the genuine affection in her voice whenever she mentioned Gilbert and as she finished her story and fell silent, looking down at her twisted hands, he had no way of knowing there was a great deal more which she had omitted to tell him and the real reason for her withdrawal into that ivory tower was still a secret between her and certain members of the Morse family.

No wonder she withheld affection, he thought – she was desperately afraid that she would be hurt again. Maybe even this Morse man had exacerbated the situation for she plainly adored him and perhaps had hoped that he might take the place of the father she had never known. Eric was no psychologist but his love for her made him long to understand and his sensitive nature provided an instinctive insight. He reached out and covered one of her hands with his own, tenderness and concern for her sweeping aside all restraint.

'Sarah – let me take care of you. You have had a very hard time. I'd like to make sure nothing bad ever happens to you again.'

'Oh Eric!' She turned her hand over so that her fingers clasped his. 'You are sweet. But that would be a pretty tall order.'

'I suppose so.' He laughed a little self-consciously. 'But no trouble seems so bad when there is someone to share it with. And I swear I would do murder before I would let anyone hurt you. I love you, Sarah. You must know that. If you would marry me I would be the happiest man alive. And I promise you would never be alone, unwanted or pushed from pillar to post again.'

His voice was low and eager and Sarah experienced a quick stab of guilt. It was true – she had known how he felt about her for a long while and although she had done nothing to encourage him she had not discouraged him either. It was agreeable to bask in the adoration of an attractive man, particularly one who set the hearts of the ladies aflutter wherever he went. But to have him propose to her . . . Unexpectedly a lump rose in her throat. Eric was a good man and a wonderful friend. In the two years she had come to know him she had come to rely on him in a hundred ways and he had never let her down. She was fond of him – more than fond, she loved him like a brother. But that was all.

'Eric – I don't know what to say. I'm flattered and, yes, surprised. But it's no use pretending. I don't love you. Not in that way. I'm sorry.'

She glanced at him, knowing she was hurting him and hating herself for it. But it seemed that having taken the bull by the horns Eric was determined not to let the matter rest.

'You may grow to,' he said earnestly. 'You don't dislike me, do you?'

'Oh no, of course I don't! It's just that . . .'

'I wouldn't rush you, Sarah,' he promised eagerly. 'I wouldn't . . . well, demand anything that you felt you were not ready to give. I just want to take care of you and make you happy. And I don't want you to feel you are alone and friendless ever again.'

She nodded, her heart full. After the emotional turmoil

of the last hour the pressure of his hand on hers felt good and safe and she wondered if perhaps she was making a mistake to turn down his offer out of hand. She did not love him it was true but perhaps there were worse things than a marriage without romantic love. He would be good to her, she knew, and do everything in his power to make her happy just as he had promised. In many ways it was a tempting prospect.

'Will you at least think about it, Sarah?' he begged her and again she found herself nodding.

'Very well, Eric.' A new thought occurred to her, catapulting her back to reality with a small shock. 'What is the time? Shouldn't we be getting ready for our parachute jump?'

Eric took out his watch and looked at it.

'Good lord, Sarah, you're right! Henry will be wondering what has happened to us!'

'Knowing Henry, I doubt it, but we'd better be getting back all the same!' She stood up and moved out into the sunlight which seemed to put a golden aureole all around her. 'Thank you for asking me, Eric,' she said softly. 'And I promise I won't keep you waiting too long for an answer.'

The air was crystal clear and very still. Swaying in her small sling beneath the balloon basket Sarah waved at the crowds far below. But for once there were other things on her mind than the simple exhilaration of silent flight and appreciation of the scene laid out beneath her like an intricate crazy paving or mosaic. Automatically with the ease born of long practice Sarah watched her height on the aneroid waiting for the moment to launch herself free from the balloon so as to land on the designated site below. But she could think of nothing but Eric's proposal and her promise to give him an answer very soon.

What should she do? she asked herself and the currents of air lifting her hair and rustling the skirts of her pantaloon suit seemed to toy with the possible answers tossing them hither and thither. If she refused life would most likely go on much as before though she doubted if she and Eric would ever quite regain their former easy relationship. If she accepted she would be his wife and everything would certainly be changed. She believed him when he said he would not rush her into a physical union until she felt she was ready but she hardly considered that as an option. Such an arrangement would be grossly unfair to him and though some women might be only too glad of an excuse to avoid that side of marriage Sarah dismissed such an idea as unthinkable. No, whatever her feelings, if she agreed to marry him she must become his wife in the full sense of the word and do her best to make him happy. It would be the least she could do in return for all he would do for her, for she had no doubt he would prove to be a wonderful husband, kind, generous and understanding, and she would at last have a measure of security in her life which she had so far been unable to find. Never again would she need to feel isolated and lonely, never again need she worry about her future – or her past. What more could she ask for?

A small wistful smile played at the corners of Sarah's mouth as the breeze tossed the answer to her. Was it greedy of her to wish that she might also be in love with the man she married? Perhaps it was. Nothing in life was ever perfect, she of all people should know that. She liked Eric, respected him and believed she could submit to his love making without being constantly reminded of Hugh and how he had used her. Perhaps it was wrong of her to feel that there should be something more than mere submission, that with the right man there should be joy in giving, in sharing . . . not only physical love making but every other aspect of life too.

Sarah looked down at the ground, a world in miniature spread out beneath her feet and tried to clear her mind as she prepared to jump.

It was unlikely that the man who could make her feel that way existed – and if he did it was too late for him now. She was going to accept Eric's proposal. Her mind was made up. The minute she landed she would tell him and she would back up her decision by doing everything in her power to make him as good a wife as she was certain he would be a good husband.

Sarah checked the aneroid once again. Three thousand feet. Resolutely she put all thought of Eric and private matters from her mind and pulled the cord that would release her from the balloon.

Chapter Seventeen

'There is someone I want you to meet, Sarah,' Eric said, setting down his teacup on the glass topped cane table that graced Molly Norkett's minute sitting-room and glancing at Sarah who sat curled up on the comfortable sofa beside him.

Sarah's heart sank. Since she had agreed to marry Eric he had proudly introduced her to a seemingly endless stream of relatives and she was beginning to grow a little tired of fobbing off the inevitable question – when was the wedding to be? All very well for Eric to assure her he would not rush her until she was ready – aunts and cousins, eager for an excuse to buy a new hat and join in a celebration were less patient and she did not care for the raised eyebrows and the exchanged glances when she explained that the date had yet to be agreed upon. But she had the grace to feel a little guilty at the stab of irritation. Eric was sweet, patient and kindness itself to her. The least she could do was to meet his relatives with good grace.

'You must have the largest family in England, Eric,' she said, hiding her dismay with a wry smile.

'No, it's not a relative this time, Sarah,' he said. 'It's someone I think you may be able to help. You remember the man who came to see you the day I asked you to marry me? You told me that his firm was called Morse Motors and that he was interested in building engines for aeroplanes.'

'Yes, that's right. But what . . . ?'

'The other day I ran into an old friend – Adam Bailey. He is an engineer and draughtsman and he works for a motor car company. But he and another chap – a Maximillian Hurst – are working in their spare time to design an aeroplane.'

'Really?' Sarah said, interested but not unduly surprised. Since entering the world of ballooning she had met a great many men who attempted the seemingly impossible; new inventions were all part of the normal round of everyday life.

'Yes. They are very enthusiastic. Adam believes they have come up with something rather special though he insists that Max is the brains behind it. But it seems the man is not only interested in the structure – he also has his own ideas for an engine. And the pair of them are looking for someone to build it for them.'

'Surely the motor car firm they work for would be the ideal people to do that?' Sarah suggested.

'I said the same thing, but apparently they are not altogether keen on two of their best men burning the midnight oil on a project of their own. Adam seemed to think it unwise to draw their attention to the fact by asking them to build the engine. It was then that I remembered what you had said about your friend Mr Morse and I suggested the three of us might have dinner together sometime and talk the matter over. Would you be agreeable to that?'

'Well yes,' Sarah said. 'I don't see what I could do but if you would like to . . .'

Eric reached for her hand and twisted the ring he had bought her so that the row of perfectly-set diamonds sat squarely on her finger.

'Good. In that case I will arrange it,' he said.

Eric had booked a table at *Rules*, the oldest restaurant in London and one of the most prestigious. Here writers, artists, lawyers and actors met to enjoy the company and the fine food in congenial surroundings, upstairs at a table beside a lattice window the King had wined and dined the beautiful Lily Langtry when he was Prince of Wales, it was said, though a special door had been put in to enable them to enter and leave without having to walk through the restaurant in full view of the other patrons.

As a deferential waiter relieved her of her wrap and led them between the tables where the finest crystal and silver gleamed on starched white napery Sarah smiled to herself.

Eric would never be a rich man, that much was certain. He was too fond of luxury and the good things of life, spending the rewards that came his way without a thought for the future. Not even their engagement had curbed his habit. Money burned a hole in Eric's pocket and it worried her slightly. She remembered only too well what it was like to have nothing and sometimes when Eric lavished on her the fruits of his success she thought of her mother, eyes crinkled with strain, fingers sore and bleeding as she sewed far into the night to earn enough to keep body and soul together. But there was no point chastising Eric about it. He would simply look glum, the light going out of his merry eyes, apologise profusely – and continue in exactly the same way as before. When they were married she would take care of the purse strings, Sarah decided. In the meantime she might as well simply relax and enjoy the luxuries which Eric showered on her.

The waiter pulled out her chair with a flourish and hovered attentively.

'Would Madame care for an apéritif?'

'Why not?' Eric said expansively. Sarah, guessing the price of the drinks here, thought she could have made out a very good case for waiting for their guest but said nothing.

'We were lucky to get here first,' Eric said, settling himself comfortably and lighting a small cigar. 'When Henry started telling me about the latest problem with his dirigible I thought we would be late and Adam would be here before us. That would have been unforgiveable.'

'What is he like?' Sarah asked, sipping her sherry.

'Adam? Oh, he's a decent chap. A bit of a mystery in some ways . . .'

'A mystery? What can you mean?'

'Ah!' Eric laid his cigar down in the crystal ashtray. 'You'll soon be able to judge for yourself. Here he is now!'

He pushed back his chair, rising to his feet, and Sarah followed his glance to see the waiter ushering a man towards them.

Her first impression was that he was very tall, then she realised it was the shortness of the waiter which accentuated his height. In reality he was perhaps no more than six foot, lean and muscular in his dark well-cut suit. Lamplight gleamed on a fine head of hair, almost aggressively fair; beneath it his face was strong boned and handsome with a square jaw and slightly hooked nose that suggested it might have been broken at some time. There was a faint arrogance about the set of the mouth, though the full lower lip conveyed an impression of sensuality; the eyes, wide set and hazel in colour, were direct. Sarah felt a small stab of surprise along with an inexplicable quickening of her pulses. Though she had wasted little time wondering what he would be like she had somehow expected an impoverished engineer to be nondescript and a little shabby. This man had an undeniable presence and a look which made her instantly glad that she was looking her best. Whatever else he might be Adam Bailey was all male and it evoked an immediate response in any woman who crossed his path.

Totally unaware of her confusion Eric greeted his guest.

'Adam! you're here. Good to see you. May I introduce you? Sarah – Adam Bailey. Adam – my fiancée, Sarah Thomas.'

The eyes met hers, appraising and, she felt, slightly mocking. Disconcerted yet determined not to show it she smiled.

'Mr Bailey.'

'Miss Thomas. Delighted to meet you at last. I have heard so much about the famous lady balloonist.' There was the faintest hint of amusement in his tone.

'Hardly famous,' Sarah returned.

'Oh, I wouldn't agree. I have read a great deal about your exploits.' But again there was that suggestion of amusement and Sarah bristled slightly. When introduced people usually greeted her with interest if not outright admiration whilst this man seemed almost to be laughing at her.

'A drink, Adam,' Eric suggested.

'Thank you. A Scotch would be very nice.'

The waiter, attentive as ever, brought Adam's drink and the menus.

'Shall we order first and talk afterwards?' Eric suggested. 'I recommend oysters to begin. *Rules* began as an oyster bar, you know – porter, pies and oysters – at the end of the eighteenth century when it was frequented by rakes, dandies and superior intelligences.'

'My ancestors, no doubt,' Adam said drily.

'The superior intelligences?'

'Good heavens, no! The rakes.'

They all laughed and as they studied the menus Sarah relaxed a little. The sherry was running trickles of warmth down her throat and into her veins and Eric's attentiveness and obvious pride in her went some way to restoring her dented confidence. The oysters arrived winking invitingly in their silvery shells. Sarah eased one out and tasted it – delicious.

'Eric tells me you are building an aeroplane, Mr Bailey,' she said, dabbing at the corner of her mouth with an ivory damask napkin.

'That's right.' The mocking light had gone out of his eyes; suddenly he was completely serious. 'Maybe it sounds like an impossible dream but Max – my partner in crime – is a bit of a genius and we are certain that between us we can get a machine into the sky. We have studied all the layouts that seem to work, from the Wright brothers to Henry Farman's Voison and come up with our own version – a biplane with the engine mounted in the fuselage and the crankshaft parallel with the wings. It will have two propellors but we believe we can improve on the Wright brothers' method of a crossed chain for opposite rotation by using bevel gears.'

'Good gracious!' Sarah said faintly. The catalogue of technicalities had quite lost her but she was unwilling to admit it for his amused dismissal of her ballooning feats still rankled.

'It's not brilliantly original,' Adam admitted, 'but we wanted to begin with something reasonably safe and improve by trial and error as we go along. But the most important thing is the engine. It's that which causes most of the problems – it needs to be powerful enough to get

203

airborne yet at the same time as light as possible. That's where Max's genius comes in. He has done all the drawings and tracings for a design he believes answers those requirements. Now we have to find someone to build it for us.'

'And I suggested your friend Gilbert Morse,' Eric put in. 'He is in the business and you told me he is interested in the concept of flying, Sarah.'

'He certainly is,' Sarah said, glad to be able to contribute something to the conversation. 'He was in France when Santos-Dumont made his first flight.'

'Ah – Santos-Dumont!' Adam laid down his fork and again Sarah caught a glimpse of that amusement which she found so disconcerting. 'The back-to-front pioneer.'

'What do you mean?' she demanded.

'Poor old Santos-Dumont's design meant he had to stand up in his box kite and stagger into the air facing backwards,' Adam said with a smile. 'I must confess I would prefer to look where I am going.'

'At least he flew,' she returned a little sharply. 'I hope you will be able to say the same some day.'

Adam raised an eyebrow. 'Touché!' His eyes held hers and the challenge in them was unmistakeable. 'I am sure we will.'

Confused she looked away. She could make no sense of the effect he was having on her; she could not make up her mind whether she liked or detested him. She should not have been tempted into sherry on an empty stomach, she decided.

'Without a doubt the engine is the problem,' Eric was saying seriously. 'Everyone says the same – though of course it's one thing we don't have to worry about with balloons!' He laughed a little self-consciously and went on swiftly, 'Alliott Verdon-Roe solved the problem by borrowing an Antoinette from a friend, I understand.'

'That's right. But Max is convinced his design is best for our aeroplane and I have implicit faith in his judgement. I shall be only too happy to put my life in his hands, as it were, when the time comes.'

'*You're* going to fly the aeroplane then are you?' Sarah asked before she could stop herself.

A corner of his mouth lifted. 'That is the part that really excites me, yes. As I say I am only a mediocre engineer compared to Max but when it comes to trying the thing out then I can provide the brute force and ignorance.'

'Don't be so modest, man!' Eric chided and Sarah thought scornfully: he's not being modest at all. He'll let his friend do all the brainwork while he takes the glory!

A waiter whisked away the plates of empty oyster shells; another served the main course from gleaming silver platters – roast beef, pink and rare for the men, a tender escalope of veal for Sarah. When their plates were full Eric took up the conversation once more.

'So – do you think your Mr Morse could help, Sarah?' he asked.

Sarah nodded. 'I am certain he could. He would probably be pleased to. Though I am not so sure about Lawrence . . .'

'Lawrence?'

'His son. He's in charge of the works. He's a very conservative soul.'

'I am sure *you* could persuade him, Sarah,' Eric said, pride in his voice.

Sarah looked down at her plate, remembering the last time she had seen Lawrence – on the day he had tried to intervene between her and Hugh. Like slides in a magic lantern show she caught glimpses of the scene – the two boys fighting, rolling over and over in the straw of the stable, Lawrence, his nose streaming blood, Hugh crowing over him, the victor and the vanquished. 'How many girls have *you* had?' 'Do you know what Sarah calls you? Sobersides and Stick in the Mud. Isn't that true, Sarah?' The ugly words rang in her ears and she cringed inwardly as she had cringed then. Once perhaps she could have influenced Lawrence. They had never been as close as she and Hugh had been but she had liked him well enough even if she had thought him a 'sobersides'. Now she was uncomfortably sure Lawrence would not wish to see her. She had witnessed his humiliation. He would not readily forgive her that.

'I don't know . . .' she said.

'Come now, Sarah! I have assured Adam you have tremendous influence with the Morses!' Eric's voice was almost pleading; she looked at him and saw anxiety in his light eyes that puzzled her. Why should it matter to Eric whether she talked to Gilbert and Lawrence on Adam's behalf? Surely if he wanted an engine built he could contact them himself? She was about to say as much when Adam spoke.

'Please don't trouble yourself on my account, Miss Thomas. Eric suggested the approach might come better from you but if you would prefer not to be involved then don't give it a second thought.'

His eyes held hers and she saw the unmistakeable challenge in them. It was almost as if he was looking inside her, she thought, seeing that she had a deep and secret reason for not wanting to approach the Morses and even knowing what it was. Briefly she felt naked, vulnerable. No-one had ever made her feel quite that way before. She did not like it but at the same time it aroused an instinct to fight. She did not relish the thought of contacting Lawrence but it was preferable to allowing this man to read and dismiss her so lightly. And besides . . .

Ever since the day Gilbert had sought her out she had longed for an excuse to see him – and perhaps Chewton Leigh – again. Eric and Adam had just provided her with that excuse – if she had the courage to use it.

Adam's eyes were still holding hers; a tiny pulse that was half excitement, half determination, throbbed within her.

'It's all right,' she said, taking up the gauntlet he had thrown down to her. 'Leave it to me. I will write to Mr Morse. If I ask I am sure they will build your aeroplane engine for you, Mr Bailey.'

A faint smile lifted one corner of his mouth but he had one more challenge to make.

'Please call me Adam,' he said.

In the breakfast room at Chewton Leigh House Lawrence Morse ladled a good sized portion of scrambled eggs onto his plate and carried it to the table. The years had done nothing to change the family custom of eating the meal together. Blanche was already in her place picking delicately at a wafer thin slice of toast while Alicia, her eyes dark shadowed from yet another night spent partying with her friends of the county set poured herself another cup of strong coffee and avoided the disapproving glances of her stepmother.

Lawrence took his place and began on his eggs without speaking to either of them beyond the briefest of 'good mornings'. His mind was busy with the problems of Morse Motors and he preferred to spend the hour before leaving for Bristol in preparing himself for the rigours of the day ahead.

Lawrence took his responsibility for the running of the works with the utmost seriousness and though his diligence was regarded by many as a natural extension of the steady-going and unadventurous traits of his nature, in reality it was more than that. Deep down, well hidden by the suet-duff exterior, Lawrence suffered from a basic insecurity and a lack of confidence in his own abilities. He was well aware that compared to his brother Hugh he was a dull fish. As a child, although he was the elder, he had always felt himself to be in Hugh's shadow, obliged to gain the approval of adults by good behaviour and sensible attitudes rather than by a winning personality. He had envied Hugh, who had been able to be outrageously mischievous and sometimes downright wicked and yet still be universally liked, and longed for some of that easy charm to rub off on him. But as they had grown to manhood nothing had changed. It was Hugh who excelled at sport and achieved better results with schoolwork without even trying, Hugh who attracted the attention of young ladies – and their match-making mamas – in spite of the fact that he treated them disgracefully, and Hugh who was the apple of his father's eye.

It was perhaps the knowledge that Hugh was Gilbert's favourite which hurt Lawrence most. He hero-worshipped his father and craved his approval. When he left his public school, having failed to distinguish himself in any way, and Gilbert had suggested that the best place for him to carve out a future career would be in the family business he had seen his chance. If only he could do well enough perhaps at last he would be able to please and even impress his father. Lawrence threw himself wholeheartedly into learning the business. For the first time in his life Hugh was not on his heels offering direct competition and soon his hard work was paying off. Gilbert, busy with his city concerns, came to the works less and less and nominally at least control passed into Lawrence's hands. He was under no illusion about the completeness of his power, of course. Behind him, rock solid, stood Frank Raisey, the Works Manager, who had been with Morses man and boy for close on forty years. But Lawrence was determined that in this field at least he could be a success. By the time Frank hung up his keys for the last time and collected the gold watch which Morses presented to all long serving employees he would be ready, having gradually shouldered the great decisions along with the day to day responsibilities. Even more important, his father would know he was ready.

But success had never come easily to Lawrence and it did not come easily now. Maintaining and improving on his position was a constant struggle with countless facts to be assimilated and strategies to be decided upon. And he was uncomfortably aware of another threat to his position hovering on the horizon and growing larger with each passing year – a threat in the shape of Leo de Vere.

Lawrence did not like his stepmother's son any better than the other Morses did and he was fairly certain that Gilbert did not care for him either. But Leo was clever and ambitious – and he had the backing of his mother. As yet he was only eighteen years old and still at boarding school but he would be leaving at the end of the school year. The talk was that he would win a place at University, perhaps even Oxford or Cambridge, and if he did Lawrence would be granted a stay of execution before Leo came snapping at his heels, eager to make his mark on the family firm. But it would also mean that he would eventually arrive in a blaze of glory, the undisputed brains of the family, with all the vigour of a young man confident of himself and his ability. In nightmares Lawrence saw himself usurped by Leo, waking he was determined to make his position impregnable before the time came to face the assault.

His obsession with Morse Motors and his position there became complete. What outside interests he had had were forgotten and he had no time for forming friendships or even courting a girl. Time enough for that when his future was secure. As for the trivialities of family life, he dismissed them as intrusions on the all-important business matters and this morning was no different. Blanche and Alicia, used to his withdrawn silences, made no attempt to engage him in conversation as he tucked into his eggs. But as the breakfast room door opened and Gilbert entered he raised his eyes eagerly.

'Good morning, Father!'

'Ah Lawrence! Just the man I want to see!' Gilbert's tone was jaunty. He laid his *Times* and something else – a letter – beside his place and crossed to the sideboard to serve himself with kidneys and bacon.

'Anyone would think you were not in the habit of seeing Lawrence at breakfast,' Blanche observed acidly. 'I hope that remark does not mean we have to endure a long discussion on business affairs.'

Gilbert raised a quizzical eyebrow at her but his good humour remained intact. 'Yes and no.'

'What is that supposed to mean?' Blanche snapped.

'Exactly that, my dear. Yes – there is a business matter I want to discuss with Lawrence. But it does not end there. What I have to say concerns all of us.' He looked from one to the other of them, gathering their attention. 'I received a letter in my morning mail. From Sarah.'

There was a moment's total shocked silence at the table, then Alicia set down her cup abruptly so that it clattered on its saucer. Lawrence made a small choking sound as he swallowed a mouthful of egg too quickly. Only Blanche's expression remained inscrutable.

'The nerve of the girl! Why should she write to you?'

Gilbert removed the letter from beneath the copy of *The Times*, laying it where he could see it though after reading it several times he was already familiar with every word.

'You are aware I went to visit Sarah some weeks ago?' he began.

'Yes indeed,' Blanche snapped, giving no hint of the disquiet she was feeling. She had spent a few uncomfortable days when Gilbert had announced his intention of seeing Sarah for she had been sure the girl would tell him at least something of the circumstances of her leaving and she had decided the best way to deal with it was to pretend utter shock and outrage and counter with a direct denial if Gilbert came home demanding an explanation. But that had not happened. It seemed that Sarah had said nothing. But her silence had puzzled Blanche and now she found herself wondering whether the storm had not been averted but merely postponed. 'What of it?' she demanded in an effort to retain at least part of the initiative.

Gilbert was demolishing his bacon and eggs; he did not look like a man about to launch into an accusation.

'You remember I told you she is with the ballooning fraternity?' he said equably. 'Well, it seems one of her friends is also a pioneer of powered flight. He is designing and building an aeroplane. Sarah has written to ask if we would be prepared to fulfil an order for the engine.'

'Good heavens – an aeroplane engine!' Lawrence said.

'There's no reason to sound quite so startled, Lawrence,' Gilbert said. 'I have talked to you before about the possibility of Morse Motors entering the field. We have to move with the times, you know.'

'So you say, Father,' Lawrence said, torn between his natural conservatism and the desire to please his father. 'But *Sarah*! It is hard to believe she could be involved with something like this.'

'Why?' Alicia asked. Her eyes were glittering. Just the mention of Sarah's name had evoked old animosities. 'It is just the sort of thing I can imagine her being involved with. She was always ambitious.'

'And dreadfully ungrateful,' Blanche said, taking the

opportunity to press home her version of Sarah's leaving. 'I must confess to a total disgust with the girl.'

'I am sorry you feel like that, Blanche,' Gilbert said, 'because I intend to invite her and her friend to Bristol to discuss the matter.'

'You intend to invite her *here*? After what she did?' Blanche demanded.

Gilbert's eyes held hers. 'What did she do, Blanche?'

Blanche crumpled up her napkin impatiently. Inwardly she felt very cold but she had no intention of letting Gilbert know that.

'She behaved disgracefully. After all you did for her – to run off like that.'

'It wasn't entirely her fault,' Lawrence said.

They all turned to look at him and he felt the colour rush into his face and neck. The very mention of Sarah revived unpleasant memories for him, painful echoes of an incident he would prefer to forget. But alongside his secret insecurities Lawrence nursed a deep-rooted hatred of injustice. Though the loss of his pride had made him anxious to put the matter behind him he believed Sarah had been wronged. No matter how often he had told himself that Hugh had spoken the truth and he had mistaken screams of laughter for cries for help he knew it was not so. The family had closed against her in a conspiracy of silence and to his undying shame he had gone along with it. Now he knew if he did not speak out on her behalf his self-esteem would be damaged beyond repair.

'What do you mean, Lawrence?' Gilbert asked.

Lawrence opened his mouth, caught Blanche's eye, cold with fury, daring him to speak out, and lost his nerve. To tell the whole story now would be to open a Pandora's box of mischiefs and focus attention on his own inadequacy. Perhaps it would be enough to take Sarah's part.

'I simply mean we should not judge her too harshly,' he said lamely. 'Things weren't easy for her, particularly when you were away, Father.'

For a moment Gilbert continued to look at him as if he knew there were more to it than that. Then he nodded.

'Very well. Then it is up to us to make her welcome when she is here. Anything less will meet with my hearty displeasure.' He refolded the letter and placed it in his breast pocket. 'Before you leave, Lawrence, we will discuss the matter of the aeroplane engine. And now perhaps we had better all of us get on with our breakfast.'

He opened his copy of *The Times*, forking bacon into his mouth, and Lawrence, Alicia and Blanche each knew that for the moment the subject of Sarah was closed. But each was equally certain that the curtain had not fallen on that particular episode in their lives.

Chapter Eighteen

Sarah stood at the window of Gilbert's office at Morse Motors looking out at the sunlit expanse of countryside. The works were situated on the outskirts of Bristol with 'the front door in the city and the back door in the country', as Gilbert had once described it so that, though it occupied a prime position conveniently placed for accessibility to all the amenities provided by the centuries-old port and business centre and the labour force who lived in the narrow streets of back-to-back houses, yet it commanded fine views of the rolling hills and valleys that stretched south and west, almost unbroken, for the ten miles to Chewton Leigh itself and beyond.

This afternoon the June sunshine bathed those fields and hillsides in soft golden light so that the vivid green took on a freshness that was accented by pools of deeper colour where the hillocks and hollows undulated gently, and away towards the horizon where blue-tinted hills met bluer sky, white flecked with small fluffy clouds, Sarah could see a herd of lazy cows grazing peaceably and a threshing machine, pulled by a pair of sturdy horses, pursuing its plodding progress across a meadow of sweet deep mowing grass.

She breathed deeply, sniffing at the air which wafted into the office through the open window – air which smelled of the grass, the wild flowers and new mown hay with only the slightest whiff of the metallic oily smells from the workshops below to taint it and knew without a shadow of a doubt that she had come home.

Motoring down from London with Adam she had been aware of the turmoil of emotions within her. Firstly there had been the disturbing presence of the man himself, for without doubt he had an effect on her which no other man had ever had, making her aggressive and oddly defensive both at the same time for though she disliked his self-assurance and the amused challenge of his attitude towards her she also found him almost disturbingly attractive – a fact which oddly seemed only to reinforce her feelings of antagonism and resentment. She wished heartily she had not had to travel alone with him but a crisis in the balloon factory had forced Eric to remain behind and she had been left with the task of going to Chewton Leigh with Adam to make the introduction. Then there was the creeping apprehension she was unable to quash at the thought of facing the Morse family, coupled with a tingling eagerness to see Gilbert again. Taken all together and shaken into a cocktail by the jolting of the motor the warring emotions had settled into a hard knot of nervousness in the pit of her stomach and woven a gossamer web of unreality around her. But as the wide flat expanses of the Wiltshire Downs had taken on the soft curves of the Somerset hills she had been aware of a strange stirring in her veins and all the nagging doubts and irritations, all the edgy apprehensions, had ceased to matter.

She loved Somerset with a fierce love whose roots were in the distant past, not a past marred by the ill temper of Bertha Pugh or the spite and resentment of Blanche and Alicia but a past when she had run and laughed and played in woods and fields very like those through which they were driving, a child secure in a carefree world bounded by love with no presentiment of what lay ahead. And deeper still, for her love of the country had been born in her, in genes passed down from generations of ancestors who had lived and loved, worked, played and died here. It was a part of her whether she liked it or not; here she belonged, here she felt a sense of rightness which only a soul in its element can experience. And now, standing at the window and gazing out across the peaceful vista her responses crystalised and took shape so that she knew without doubt that this place was not only her past but also her future.

The men were discussing the aeroplane, Adam explaining, Gilbert asking innumerable questions, Lawrence occasionally venturing a comment in his earnest way. Sarah was aware of the rise and fall of their voices but she was not really listening. The idea of flight fascinated and excited her, the melange of technical details did not. She thought they were making progress however – for all Lawrence's reservations the suggestion that Morse Motors should build the engine had not been dismissed out of hand. Then she heard Gilbert say: 'Does £225 sound fair to you?' and realising they were about to reach an agreement she swung around in time to catch a fleeting expression of surprise and delight on Adam's face before it was replaced by his usual nonchalant smile.

'Very fair.' He extended his hand swiftly. 'I know I can speak for my partner when I say we shall be happy to accept your quotation.'

'Good.' There was a gleam in Gilbert's eye which reminded Sarah of the look of a child who has just unwrapped a Christmas parcel to discover a much-coveted toy inside. Lawrence however was attempting to conceal his disapproval behind a rather false smile and Sarah, who knew nothing whatever of the costings of such a project, decided that the price Gilbert had quoted was probably more than fair – because the idea fascinated him Gilbert had been generous in the extreme. Morse Motors would not be making much profit, if any, on the deal.

'Where do you propose to do your flying trials?' Gilbert asked Adam.

'I must confess we have yet to find a suitable site,' Adam admitted. 'So far all the design work has been done in a room at our lodgings which we have converted into a drawing office and a vacant railway arch we rented to use as a workshop. But we can hardly taxi an aeroplane on the public highway and ideally we are looking for a shed close to a suitable field so that we can simply push the machine out for trials rather than having to move it out in bits and reassemble it again each time.'

Gilbert took out his cigarettes, lit one and drew on it thoughtfully. 'Does it have to be in the London area?' he asked.

'Our jobs are in London and we only work on the

aeroplane in our spare time,' Adam confirmed. 'Why do you ask?'

'Because I think I know of just the place – a field at the rear of my house at Chewton Leigh. It's open apart from a clump of elms at the far end and it's on a slight slope – ideal for the extra impetus that might help get a flying machine into the air. And there is a barn close by which could be used as a shed. The roof needs some repair but apart from that it is sturdy and fairly spacious. I think it would suit your purpose admirably.'

'Is it not in use?' Adam asked.

'The barn is empty except for a few bits of farm machinery and though we do graze the Home Farm cows in Long Meadow it would be easy enough to move them out when you wanted to do tests. What's more they would keep the grass short enough for taxiing on. But of course it is a good long way from London,' Gilbert said eying Adam speculatively. 'Unless of course you could find employment in the Chewton Leigh area,' he added after a moment.

Sarah suppressed a smile. Try as he might to hide his feelings she could see how eager he was to have an aeroplane taking shape in his own back garden.

'You wouldn't want to leave your present employer, I take it?'

Adam shrugged. 'Speaking for myself I owe them no particular allegiance and I don't believe Max does either. Our main concern is our aeroplane. Unfortunately we depend on our everyday jobs to keep us going. Even pioneers have to eat.'

'Lawrence – do we have any suitable vacancies at present?' Gilbert enquired.

Lawrence's rather puddingy face was set stubbornly; already this interview had taken more than one turn that he did not approve of.

'No, Father, I don't believe we do.'

'Pity,' Gilbert said regretfully.

'Good gracious, I certainly could not impose on you to provide us with employment!' Adam said swiftly. 'You have been more than kind already. But your suggestion is certainly worth looking into. I'll talk to Max about it. Do you have any other motor car works in this part of the world?'

'No, but there are coach builders, ship builders and engineers of every kind. Perhaps one or the other of them might be able to accommodate you.'

'I shall certainly discuss it with Max,' Adam said. 'What sort of figure would you be thinking of for the rental of your field and barn?'

Gilbert shrugged. 'Nominal. I wouldn't bankrupt you, Mr Bailey. I would look on it as my small contribution to progress in the field of aviation. I suggest we run over to Chewton Leigh now so that you can have a look at it. And if you decide to transfer to this part of the world then you will know the offer is open to you.'

'Thank you very much, sir,' Adam said.

Lawrence rose still looking disgruntled and Sarah felt a moment's sympathy for him. His life had been a series of such setbacks, she suspected.

'If you don't need me any more, Father, I have a great deal to do,' he said now.

'No, please carry on, Lawrence,' Gilbert said smoothly. 'Will you ride with me to Chewton Leigh, Sarah?'

'Of course,' Sarah said, pleased he should have asked yet almost sorry she would have to wait to discover what Adam thought of Gilbert's offer.

'I will lead the way,' Gilbert suggested. 'Chewton Leigh is not difficult to find but the country lanes can be confusing.'

They went down to the front drive where Gilbert's gleaming Rolls was parked and waited while Adam started up his much older Panhard. Soon they were bowling along the open road leaving the mean streets behind them. Birds, disturbed by the chuntering of the motor, fluttered in the hedgerows and the sweet haunting perfume of the country-side sent small quivers of aching nostalgia through Sarah's veins.

'I hope you didn't mind me writing to you,' Sarah said.

'Mind? Good heavens I was delighted!' Gilbert shifted the gear stick and smiled at her. 'For one thing I am very pleased to be involved in this project, for another it is more than good to have you here, Sarah. I told you when I came to see you – nothing would please me more than if you should decide to return to Chewton Leigh – permanently.'

'And what would the others say about that?' Sarah asked, nervousness at the thought of meeting them again creeping in once more.

'Whatever differences you had with them, my dear, it was all a long time ago,' he said easily. 'Blanche is fond of you and it is good for Alicia to have the company of another young woman. She misses you, you know.'

Sarah said nothing. Was Gilbert merely being kind, or was he really unaware of the antagonism between her and Alicia?

'You cannot balloon for ever,' Gilbert continued, steering the motor around a lumbering horse and cart and raising his hand in greeting to the driver. 'When the thrill of it palls I hope you will remember your home is here with us.' He glanced along at her. 'I take it Mr Bailey is a good friend of yours,' he said.

His tone was light, his eyes hidden behind his thick motoring goggles but Sarah was in no doubt as to the meaning hidden behind the seemingly casual words. So that was it – Gilbert had yet another motive besides his interest in aeroplanes in encouraging Adam Bailey to move his workshop to Bristol – he thought there was something between him and Sarah and he hoped his hospitality might go some way towards enticing her back.

'I scarcely know Adam,' she admitted. 'And in any case I am engaged to be married to someone else – Eric Gardiner, my partner in The Flying Dares.'

'Ah!' His voice betrayed nothing of what he might be feeling. 'I see! I saw your ring and assumed . . .'

Colour rose in her cheeks. She had quite forgotten she was wearing her engagement ring. Gilbert had noticed it and jumped to the wrong conclusion.

'I'm sorry, I should have told you,' she said. 'I didn't think.'

He did not answer for a moment, concentrating on

urging the car up a small sharp incline. Then he said: 'I would have thought a recently betrothed girl would have had her fiancé very much on her mind. Do you love him, Sarah?'

His perceptiveness shocked her. 'Yes – yes, of course I do,' she said quickly. She did not want to admit the myriad of doubts that still assailed her when she thought of marrying Eric.

'I hope so,' he said seriously. 'A good marriage can be a wonderful thing but marriage to the wrong person can be a living hell. I wouldn't want that for you.'

'Eric is good and kind,' she said, embarrassed. 'Being with him could never be hell.'

'In that case I am happy for you. And I hope this Eric knows what a lucky man he is. Perhaps I may meet him again sometime.'

'Oh yes. He would have accompanied us today only he is very busy. And Max too – Adam's partner, you know. But Adam says he does not care for long journeys,' she said, eager to change the subject for she did not trust herself to hide the truth from Gilbert for very long.

The countryside was becoming steadily more familiar; she recognised the lane along which she had driven with Hugh on that fateful afternoon and turned her head so as not to look at it. Then they rounded a bend and as Chewton Leigh House came into view, dreaming in the heat of the June afternoon, her heart came into her mouth.

How beautiful it was, its ancient stones turned almost golden by the sunshine, tall chimneys reaching up into the blue of the sky. Around it the trees provided patches of welcome leafy shade and dappled the drive with pools of light. Gilbert turned into the stable-yard and moments later Adam pulled in behind him.

'We'll go straight out to Long Meadow,' Gilbert said, handing Sarah down from the high fender. 'Would you like to come with us, my dear?'

Sarah was looking longingly towards the stables.

'Do you mind if I don't? I'd really like to see Sweet Lass and . . . well, Long Meadow is just Long Meadow.'

Gilbert nodded. 'She is in the paddock with Baron, her foal. You'll be surprised by him. He is a fully grown three-year-old now. When we come back from Long Meadow we'll all have some tea before you leave. If I can't persuade you to change your mind and stay the night, that is.'

'Thank you but I am expected back at the motor works in the morning – and besides I am most anxious to discuss matters with Max,' Adam said.

Sarah found herself fervently hoping she would not run into Blanche or Alicia before they returned. But somehow the prospect, however daunting, was quite overshadowed by the desire to see her beloved mare.

She set off in the direction of the paddock. The air was fresh and sweet; it carried on it the scent of grass and new mown hay. She sniffed appreciatively. These things had once been part of her everyday life which she had taken as much for granted as breathing; in the busy hustle of her life with the Dares she had not realised just how much she had missed them.

In the paddock Sweet Lass was gently cropping grass but of Baron there was no sign. She called to the horse and the moment she heard Sarah's voice she raised her head and whinnied, then came trotting across, pushing her nose out across the picket fence and nuzzling Sarah. A mist of tears rose in Sarah's eyes and she buried her head in the horse's rough neck.

'Oh Sweet Lass, I've come home!' she whispered – and found herself wishing with all her heart that she need never leave again.

'Here's to the success of your aeroplane, Mr Bailey,' Gilbert said. He raised his teacup as if it were a glass of champagne and his blue eyes shone with enthusiasm. 'Since we were unable to persuade you to stay for dinner we shall have to make do with toasting your enterprise in China tea. But somehow I don't think that will have the slightest effect on the enterprise.' He turned to Sarah. 'Are you sure you wouldn't like to remain with us for a few days, my dear?'

Sarah experienced an ache of longing. If only she could!

But Eric was expecting her back– they had a display booked for the following day. And besides . . . Sarah glanced at Blanche, sitting very taut, very straight, on the Louis XV chair beside the low, heavily laden tea table. When Gilbert had introduced her to Adam she had been sweetness itself, the very essence of charm and politeness, but there had been a cold gleam in her eyes when she greeted Sarah and Sarah was in no doubt that as far as Blanche was concerned nothing had changed.

'Thank you but I must go back with Mr Bailey,' Sarah said.

Gilbert nodded, resigned. 'Very well. But I hope we shall see something of you before too long. And I am anxious to meet this fiancé of yours again too.' He turned to Adam. 'I take it you would like the engine completed as soon as possible. This whole business is becoming something of a race, isn't it?'

Adam nodded. 'Things are moving very fast now. I expect either Bleriot or Hubert Latham will manage to cross the Channel before long.' He paused and added ruminatively: 'I must say I'd rather like it to be Hubert Latham. He only took up flying because his doctors told him he only had a year to live and he thinks he may as well live it dangerously.'

'The true pioneering spirit,' Gilbert smiled. 'I see it in you too, Mr Bailey – and I am certain you will succeed with your plans.'

Adam's eyes were steely. 'I intend to. You know the Bible says the meek shall inherit the earth – and who am I to argue with that? But I will make a prediction. It is the bold who will inherit the skies.'

A small shiver of excitement ran through Sarah and she thought: if anyone can do it, it is Adam Bailey. Arrogant he might be – but perhaps arrogance was an essential in a man who believed he could conquer the laws of nature. Infuriating he might be in the way he could make her feel insignificant and even faintly ridiculous with a word or a glance, but he was also possessed of an undeniable strength and just a hint of the buccaneer. If anyone could get an aeroplane into the skies it was him.

221

The strange dark excitement tingled deep within her as she looked at him and as if feeling her gaze upon him he glanced up. Their eyes met and the amused challenge in his was so potent she felt momentarily as if she had been struck by lightning.

'Who do you believe was the first man into the air?' Gilbert asked Adam. 'Sam Cody has the credit for it, I know, but I have heard it said that Alliott Roe beat him to it at Brooklands, though he had no witnesses to prove it.'

Sarah bristled slightly. She knew Sam Cody from his ballooning days at Alexandra Palace and liked the eccentric showman.

'Possibly,' Adam agreed. 'Poor old Roe has had more than his fair share of problems. Rodakowski, the racing manager at Brooklands, is determined to get him banned from there. But at least both of them are genuine pioneers – unlike Monsieur Bellamy.'

'Monsieur Bellamy?' Blanche queried, offering him a scone.

'A charlatan who fooled the entire district into believing the only reason his contraption of bamboo rods and calico would not leave the ground was because the air at Brooklands was different to the air in France. His second brainchild, an aero catamaran, fared little better. It phuttered to a stop halfway across Hugh Locke King's private lake. Then Monsieur Bellamy, who had unpaid bills owing to practically every tradesman in Weybridge, went up in a balloon and never came back.'

A sudden thunder of hooves outside made them all look towards the window. The drawing-room overlooked not only the lawns to the front of the house but also the parkland to the side. A horse and rider were crossing it at a gallop, the royal blue of the rider's habit spread out across the pale flanks of the horse, her jet black hair streaming in the wind. They cleared the picket fence that divided park from lawns without even breaking stride and hardly slowed as they passed the drawing-room windows.

'Alicia!' Blanche muttered. 'Why must she ride like that?'

222

Gilbert shook his head but his smile was indulgent. 'She is a superb horsewoman, my dear.'

'Perhaps. Nevertheless she will end up breaking her neck.'

'I doubt it. One of these days she will meet a man who will tame her.' He glanced at Adam. 'Alicia is my daughter, Mr Bailey, and she is I confess a little wild. Blanche worries about her but personally I find her spirit refreshing.'

'She certainly rides well,' Adam said and Sarah found the admiration in his tone slightly galling after the way he had appeared to find her own ballooning exploits merely amusing.

'Let us hope then that she contents herself with exhausting her high spirits galloping Baron into the ground,' Blanche remarked acidly. 'At luncheon she was threatening to run off and join the suffragettes.'

Gilbert smiled in amusement. 'Wild she may be but Alicia is too fond of her creature comforts to risk being manhandled, thrown into jail and force fed. The suffragettes are brave women fighting for a just cause and they have my sympathies. But somehow, whatever she may say, I do not see my daughter becoming one of them.'

As he spoke they heard the sound of footsteps outside, the door flew open and Alicia stood framed in the doorway. Her hair which she had not bothered to put up was tumbled into a halo of jet black, the wind had whipped fresh colour into her pale ivory cheeks and her lips were parted into a smile by the excitement of the ride. Sarah saw Adam's eyes narrow appreciatively as Alicia came into the room with a swish of her blue velvet riding habit, tearing off her gloves and looking from one to the other of them.

'I didn't realise we had company!' Her glance slid coldly over Sarah and came to rest on Adam. 'You must be Mr Bailey. I am Alicia Morse.'

Adam had risen. 'It's very good to meet you, Miss Morse.'

'Alicia, please.' She held his glance briefly then turned away to help herself to a neat triangle of cucumber sandwich, but not before Sarah had seen the look in her violet eyes.

223

Alicia had not changed one iota, Sarah thought. She still knew how to command attention, still knew how to captivate with that strange brew of straight-forwardness and coquetry, all the more potent now that she was a beautiful young woman. She held centre stage now, eating her sandwich with a mixture of delicacy and delight that was somehow unquestionably sensuous, a graceful figure with the trim and tightly tucked waist of her riding habit giving the impression of curves which were in reality absent for Alicia was still almost as flat chested and slim hipped as a boy.

'I understand you are building an aeroplane, Mr Bailey,' Alicia said, running a finger around her lips to brush away crumbs. 'Have you persuaded my father to construct the engine for you?'

'He has indeed.' Gilbert assured her. 'In fact you may very well see the prototype fly. I have offered Mr Bailey the use of Long Meadow for his trials.'

'And has he accepted?' Oh the cool challenge in those violet eyes!

'That depends on whether my partner and I can find employment here,' Adam said. 'We need to work to finance our project, I am afraid.'

'Has Father not got a job he could offer you?'

'Lawrence says not – at the moment anyway,' Gilbert informed her.

'Oh – Lawrence!' she said impatiently. 'Surely you can over-rule him?'

'Lawrence is in charge of the works,' Gilbert said firmly. 'I wouldn't undermine his position in that way, Alicia.'

She tossed her head and the small gesture said more clearly than any words what she thought of her brother's stick-in-the-mud attitude.

'Well, I do hope you will be building your aeroplane here, Mr Bailey. And who knows – if you do get it into the air perhaps you will take me along as a passenger – or even teach me to fly it myself!'

'Alicia!' Blanche said, scandalised. 'I never heard of such a thing! A woman – flying! It is quite ridiculous!'

'Why?' Alicia demanded. 'I ride a horse as well as any man and better than most – and sidesaddle too! Why shouldn't I fly an aeroplane?'

'I agree,' Sarah said. She felt Alicia had had things her own way long enough. 'I'd love to fly an aeroplane – and I can tell you, being high up in the air is wonderful!'

'In a balloon. That's different,' Alicia said dismissively. 'Anyone can ride up in a basket and jump out. But to fly an aeroplane . . .' She let her voice tail away, emphasising the difference which existed in her opinion between the supreme achievement and the brainless.

'I am quite sure you would both make excellent aeronauts,' Gilbert said with a smile, and to Adam: 'You can see the two of them were brought up together, can't you? A little sibling rivalry, you might say.'

Alicia's expression left Sarah in no doubt but that she was infuriated by the remark. But she smiled at Adam artfully.

'You see? Father has every confidence in us.'

'Which I am sure is justified,' Adam said. 'But first we have to build an aeroplane that will fly.'

'You'll do it,' Sarah said confidently. 'What was it you said earlier, Adam? The bold will inherit the skies. That's you, I'm certain of it.'

'I hope so.' Adam stood up. 'I think, if you will pardon us, Mr Morse, we should be leaving. We have a long way to go and I would like to cover as much of the journey as possible before dark.'

'Certainly. Take good care of Sarah, won't you? And I hope we shall meet again very soon, Mr Bailey.'

They completed their farewells and Gilbert accompanied them out to Adam's Panhard. As Sarah settled herself on the bench seat she realised she was leaving Chewton Leigh with feelings as mixed as when she had arrived.

She loved the place, loved Gilbert, loved Sweet Lass. And on the other hand she hated Alicia and Blanche as much as she had ever done, perhaps more because now she understood them better. Alicia was shallow and an exhibitionist, Blanche a cold and ruthless schemer. Sarah

225

felt a sudden stab of sympathy for Gilbert, trapped in marriage to such a woman.

The sun was low in the sky now, a ball of fire over the distant hills. As the Panhard chuntered away up the drive Sarah turned for one last look at the square impressive façade of Chewton Leigh House, its windows reflecting the scarlet light of the dying sun.

I will be back, she promised herself, and knew that in spite of the antagonisms and frustrations, the ill feeling and the outright hostility, it was a promise she would keep.

Chapter Nineteen

'Alicia is quite a girl isn't she?' Adam said conversationally.

They were bowling along the open road in the fading light. Now that the sun had fallen over the horizon the colour seemed to have faded from the countryside. Blackbird and thrush swooped low in the hedgerows, martins and swallows arced and wheeled, and far out across the rise of open meadowland a hawk hovered on the still air, intent on gaining one more morsel for its supper.

Sarah, who had been watching the hawk, as mesmerised as any field mouse or rabbit by its graceful stillness, looked at him sharply, her hackles rising.

'I dare say that would be one way of describing her.'

He raised an eyebrow and his mouth took on that lift of infuriating amusement.

'It doesn't sound as though the two of you got along.'

'We didn't.' But she had no intention of elaborating and the silence between them was less than companionable.

Now that they had left Chewton Leigh behind she was once again regretting the fact that she was alone with Adam and the long journey back to London stretched ahead interminably. To begin with they had travelled in silence, Adam considering the implications of the meeting, Sarah wrapped in her own thoughts, and what conversation they had was polite and conventional. Now his remark about Alicia caught her on the raw and she wondered irritably just why she should be so infuriated by it. Perhaps it was because she had suffered so much from Alicia's superiority in the past and had thought that at last she had raised herself to become her equal, perhaps it had to do with the fact that, however unwillingly, she admired Adam and found him almost disconcertingly attractive. Whichever, the thought that he had fallen prey to Alicia's rather obvious charms was galling, especially as he seemed to consider her own achievements something of a joke.

'What time do you expect we shall be back in London?' Sarah asked, attempting to change the subject.

'Oh – another hour or so, provided my motor continues to behave itself,' Adam said. 'Why – aren't you enjoying my company?'

His tone did nothing to soothe Sarah's ruffled feathers. The impertinence of the man!

'Your company is neither here nor there,' she said tartly. 'I'm very tired and I have a long day in front of me tomorrow. Besides, Eric will be anxious about me.'

'Oh surely not. He knows you are in good hands.'

'He could still be anxious about me. On a long journey like this anything could happen.'

'Highly unlikely. If he was so worried about you why did he let you come?'

'He's not my keeper. In any case I came to introduce you to Mr Morse in case you have forgotten.'

'I'm sure a letter of introduction would have been sufficient. After all when it comes to a business arrangement it really is between me and Mr Morse.'

And Alicia! Sarah thought furiously. You'd have liked that, wouldn't you, a chance to make up to Alicia. Aloud she said: 'Well if that's all the thanks I get I'm sure I wish I hadn't troubled!' and was instantly annoyed with herself for she knew she had sounded pettish. What on earth was the matter with her, she wondered, allowing him to rile her in this way?

They travelled in silence for a while, then quite suddenly Adam asked: 'Are you in love with Eric?'

The baldness of the question shocked her. She glared at his profile, very strong, very aloof in the fading light.

'I'm engaged to him, aren't I?'

He continued to drive, not removing his eyes from the road for a single second.

'I'm aware of that but it does not answer my question.'

'Eric is a good man!' she said sharply. 'Of course I love him. How dare you suggest I don't?'

'Oh I agree he's a good man,' he said evenly. 'I have never

228

for one moment doubted it. Very likely it is his sheer goodness that persuaded him to allow you to travel alone with me to Bristol – he simply cannot conceive that either of us would do anything to betray his trust.'

Quite suddenly she found that her hands were trembling. 'I don't know what you are talking about!'

He glanced at her and even in the fading light the challenge in his eyes was unmistakeable. 'Don't you?'

'Most certainly I do not! Just because Alicia flaunts herself and throws herself at you does not mean that I would do the same. Why – I don't even like you!'

'Ouch!' he said, but there was still a good measure of amusement in his tone and it infuriated her almost to fever pitch.

'If you must know, Mr Bailey, I find you quite insufferable!' she snapped.

'Oh dear,' he said ruefully. 'What have I done to warrant this?'

The fact that she could not think of one single concrete thing did nothing to improve her temper.

'It's your attitude!' she snapped. 'You always seem to be laughing at me!'

'Perhaps that is because you take yourself so seriously,' he said lightly. 'And you must admit there is something slightly comic in what you do.'

'There you go, you see – laughing at me again! I don't find ballooning in the least comic.'

'And there *you* go – taking yourself so seriously! You have plenty of spunk, I admit, Sarah – a cool nerve and a hot temper. I admire you . . .'

'Well, I don't admire you!' she returned. 'If you must know I find you arrogant and rather rude!'

'I am sorry to hear that. But I am afraid you will have to put up with me for a little longer. Until we get back to London at any rate.'

'Not necessarily.'

'What do you mean?'

'I could always ask you to stop the motor now and let me out.'

'But you wouldn't. You wouldn't want to be stranded in the middle of nowhere.'

'Even that might be preferable to the next hour spent bickering with you.'

'All right.' He slammed on the brakes and the car ground abruptly to a halt. 'If that's the way you want it, you may get out of my motor, Miss Thomas. Arrogant I might be, rude I might be – a jailer I am not. Please feel free to avail yourself of the opportunity to take a nice long walk on a warm summer's night.'

A bolt of horror shot through Sarah. This was ridiculous! It was all over nothing – a storm in a teacup because she had allowed him to rile her. She certainly had not expected him to take her at her word. But here he was looking at her with that infuriating challenge in his eyes, daring her to do as she had threatened. And now she had put herself in the impossible position of either admitting ignominiously that she had not the slightest inclination to get out of the car and walk alone into the fast-falling night or sticking to her guns and doing just that!

Well, she would not give him the satisfaction of knowing the very idea terrified her. Her fierce pride simply would not allow it. With a toss of her head she got up and climbed down out of the car. He wouldn't leave her. He couldn't! When he saw she was actually prepared to do as she had said he would insist she got back into the car . . . wouldn't he?

But the moment her feet touched the ground he opened the throttle and the motor began to move away. Panic constricted her throat and she almost screamed at him to wait, but again pride prevented her and moments later she was standing on the grass verge watching the motor disappear into the fading light.

For a moment she stood quite still, almost paralysed by horror. 'Beast!' she whispered, and then louder: 'Beast – beast!' The sound of her voice disturbed a bird in the hedgerow; it rustled urgently, startling her, and her quick intake of breath became a sob: 'Oh, how could you? How *could* you just *leave* me here?'

The quiet of the night gave no reply. In the few moments she had stood there it seemed the darkness had become more complete, the hedges taking on dark and threatening shapes, the sky closing in to obscure even the ribbon of road. Well, there was nothing for it – she would simply have to set out in search of a cottage or farm, knock on the door and ask for refuge. But it was so humiliating – and all so stupid!

Somewhere across the dark fields an owl hooted and Sarah felt the skin on the back of her neck prickle. She was a country girl, used to the sounds of nature, but never before had she felt so totally alone. Then suddenly, close by, on the other side of the hedge a cow lowed, an unearthly sound in the silence of the night. Her carefully controlled panic erupted and Sarah began to run.

She did not notice the bank at the edge of the road until she ran into it. One fleeing foot followed the other, her ankle twisted and she staggered and fell headlong. She heard her skirt rip, her hands skagged on brambles and as she tried to rise she lost her balance again and rolled helplessly into the drainage ditch at the bottom of the bank. There had been no rain for some days but the ground was low lying and the ditch was clogged with last year's dead leaves and muddy with water that had seeped down from the higher level of the field.

'Oh!' she sobbed.

And at that very moment saw the lights of a motor coming towards her down the road.

Her first thought was overwhelming relief. She scrambled out of the ditch and into the road, waving her arms wildly at the approaching motor. Then as it slowed to a stop beside her relief turned to outrage, humiliation and anger.

'What on earth have you been up to?' the driver enquired mildly.

It was Adam.

She drew herself up, not the easiest thing when she was scratched, bedraggled and trembling all over.

'I thought you had gone without me!' she said accusingly.

'Did you really? And how do you suppose I would have faced Eric and told him I'd left you God-knows-where? Come on, you little idiot, get in!'

She glowered at him.

'Are you going to get in – or shall I leave you here again?' he asked.

She knew she was beaten. She had no doubt now but that if she refused he would simply drive away again. She took a step, her ankle almost gave way beneath her and pain shot through it, white hot. He heard her gasp, and realising she was hurt, was down in a flash lifting her as effortlessly as if she weighed no more than a child and setting her up on the seat. She wanted to protest but no words would come. It was a supreme effort to hold back the tears.

'Oh Sarah!' he said, looking at her. 'What a state you are in! And I only left you for five minutes. You didn't really think I'd go back to London without you, did you? What do you take me for? No – don't answer that. An arrogant swine. That's what you said, wasn't it?'

'And so you are,' she said through gritted teeth.

'I couldn't agree more. I shouldn't have done it.' There was no mockery in his tone now, only real regret. He fished in his pocket for a handkerchief and handed it to her. 'Here – clean yourself up with this.'

She took the handkerchief and suddenly the tears she had been struggling to hold back were coursing down her cheeks.

'It was horrible!' she wept.

'Oh come now, not so bad for a girl who jumps out of balloons, surely?' But it was not said unkindly and the gentle teasing was somehow quite different.

'Look at me! Look at the mess I'm in!'

'Sarah,' he said, 'you still look beautiful.'

'Will you stop making fun of me!' she cried.

'I am not making fun of you. I am simply telling you the truth.' His voice was low and vibrant; the sound of it sent a sudden tingle up her spine.

She looked at him sharply. The moon had risen, a pale bright orb, and in its light and the smattering of reflected light from the headlamps of the motor his face was deeply shadowed, his eyes mysterious pools of darkness. Yet somehow they beamed her a message, a message so powerful that she received it with every pore of her body and every nerve ending rose in tingling response. She was aching now not from the effects of her fall but from longing – a longing she could not comprehend and did not attempt to – and the trembling in her limbs ceased momentarily as if frozen by some powerful emotion. She looked at him, breath catching in her throat, and felt the whole of her being drawn up into that one point of contact.

'Sarah,' he said softly.

His hand was in her hair, combing the tangled curls away from her temple, then it slid down to her chin, cupping it firmly and lifting. His face was close, inches from hers, and a tremor ran through her. She knew now what that ache of longing meant. He was going to kiss her – and she wanted him to. She closed her eyes, giving herself up to the longing, then suddenly just as his lips brushed hers sanity came rushing in on a wave of panic. What was she *doing*? She was engaged to be married to Eric – she had no business being here in the arms of another man.

Abruptly she pulled away. 'No!'

For a moment longer he held her and she wondered in panic if he might be going to force himself on her as Hugh had done. Then he released her and she shrank back against the leather seat.

'Well, Sarah . . .' That familiar infuriating amusement was back in his voice.

'Please take me home,' she said, pressing his handkerchief to her trembling lips. The unfamiliar smell of it evoked more small shocks and yearnings in her inflamed senses and she sat rigid, resisting them.

Without another word Adam depressed the accelerator and the motor shot forward in the darkness. And the tears which were still so close and threatening squeezed out from Sarah's eyes and began to roll silently down her cheeks.

Chapter Twenty

In the small attic room at his lodgings which he had converted into a drawing office Adam Bailey laid down his pencil for at least the tenth time that evening, took a long pull from the mug of half cold coffee which stood at his elbow and ran his hands through his thick fair hair, staring into space.

Damn it, he simply could not concentrate on water-cooled engines and crankshafts this evening – had not been able to for the past two evenings either in point of fact. His mind kept wandering however hard he tried to channel it and each time he looked at the careful calculations on the sheet of paper in front of him he seemed to see nothing but a mop of rich brown hair and a pair of sparkling blue eyes. Sarah Thomas had got under his skin, not a doubt of it, but wonder about it as he might Adam could not say why.

She was a very pretty girl, of course, but she was far from being the first to have crossed his path and in all honesty he could not say she was the prettiest – at twenty-four, handsome and eligible, Adam had known his share of beauties. She had courage. It would have been obvious in the tilt of her chin and the set of her small well-shaped mouth even if he had not known of her ballooning exploits, the very thought of which would have been enough to make most girls swoon. And she had dignity, determination and a kind of crystal clear honesty which shone out of those lovely blue eyes. But he could not see that any of those things, attractive though they were, were enough to distract him from the obsession that had been his life now for almost as long as he could remember.

Adam sighed, lit a cigarette and crossed the attic to set the kettle on the small phuttering gas ring. He could not afford to waste precious time in this way – especially now when they were so close to perfecting the design for their very own aeroplane. Yet here he was unable to do a stroke of work for thinking about a girl who had given not the slightest indication of even returning his interest.

In all likelihood it was that which made her so attractive, Adam thought wryly. In his experience young ladies from barmaids to the flighty well-heeled daughter of his employer had fallen over themselves in an effort to make him notice them and favours had been offered to him with an eagerness he had begun to take for granted. But although he enjoyed their company not one of them had touched his heart, let alone moved him sufficiently to interfere with the project that was the great and flaming passion in his life.

Forget her! Adam told himself crossly. She is engaged to someone else and clearly has not the slightest interest in you.

But he could not forget her. Since meeting her there had not been a single waking moment when she had not been there, coming between him and any coherent thought, and even when he slept it seemed she invaded his dreams.

The sound of footsteps on the bare wooden stairs brought Adam out of his reverie; he turned from the kettle which was already beginning to sing merrily to see the door open and Maximillian Hurst came bursting in.

'Great news, Adam! Not working? By God, you will be, and harder than ever before when you hear what I have to tell you!'

'Max!' In spite of his own strange mood Adam found himself smiling at his friend's obvious high spirits. 'You look as if you've lost a farthing and found a shilling!'

'Better than that.' Max came into the room with a bouncy stride, a short thick-set young man with a face that was far from handsome yet agreeably pleasant, mobile and expressive with a large humorous mouth.

Though they were as different as chalk and cheese, he and Adam had been firm friends from the moment they had met, both raw young apprentices in the drawing office at the firm of motor engineers. Talking one day they had discovered their mutual fascination with the pioneering of powered flight and from there it had been a short step to

235

deciding to work together on their very own design. When Adam had discovered Max was thoroughly wretched in the lodgings he rented from a shrewish old woman he had persuaded his own kindly and easy going landlady to let a room to Max and the proximity had done nothing to sour their friendship. If anything it had deepened it for now they were able to talk into the small hours over the dying embers of the fire, discussing and dreaming with only one flight of stairs to climb before they could fall exhausted into bed.

As their ideas took shape Mrs Hicks, the landlady, had been persuaded to allow them the use of the attic as a drawing office though Adam suspected, quite correctly, that she believed the work they did there was no more serious than a child's game. Even when they acquired a small workshop under the railway arches to begin the construction of their brainchild she continued to treat them with good-humoured indulgence and a smile that said that sooner or later when they realised the true seriousness of life they would grow out of their far fetched notions and behave like normal adult men.

'One of these days we will build a plane that will fly,' Adam had told her. 'And when we do you shall be our first passenger.'

But Mrs Hicks had only thrown up her hands in horror.

'Get on with your nonsense! My feet are staying right here on terra firma – and I've no doubt yours will be too, Mr Adam!'

Her scepticism did not upset them and they sometimes chuckled over how surprised Mrs Hicks would be to find herself one day dragged unwillingly into the twentieth century with all the fruits of progress waiting for her.

'Well, what is all the excitement about?' Adam asked now as Max entered the attic and shut the door behind him.

'Is the kettle on the boil?' Now he had whetted Adam's appetite Max was determined to savour his moment of triumph. 'Make me a cup of tea, my friend, and when I've got my breath back I'll tell you all about it.'

'Make yourself one, you lazy good-for-nothing,' Adam

retorted. 'I've been working while you have been out gallivanting.'

'That is not quite how I would put it,' Max returned, his monkey-face mock serious. 'What I've been doing is securing our future. Now, do I get that tea or don't you want to hear my news?' He crossed to the chintz-covered rocking chair, lowering himself into it and grinning at Adam encouragingly.

'All right, I'll make your blasted tea,' Adam agreed. He emptied cold dregs from the pot, spooned in three good measures and added the now-boiling water. When the tea was ready he carried it across to Max and settled himself back into his upright chair, turning it to face his friend. 'Come on then, tell me your news. I'm all agog.'

Max took a sip of scalding tea and wiped his mouth on a large scarlet spotted handkerchief. 'What would you say if I told you our troubles are over? That we can give notice to the company and go down to Bristol to work full time on our project?'

'I'd say you'd finally taken leave of your senses.'

'And you'd be wrong,' Max said. 'Do you know where I have been this evening, Adam?'

'No. You were very secretive about it.'

'Because I didn't want to raise your hopes in case things failed to work out as I hoped. But since that is not the case I can now tell you I have been to see my Great Uncle Winston. Do you remember you came with me once when I went to visit him?'

'I certainly do,' Adam said recalling a shrewd old man clad in a velvet smoking jacket, his knees covered by a tartan rug as he held court in his cluttered parlour surrounded by innumerable cats. 'What of it?'

'I asked him for a loan,' Max said simply. 'I told him of our plans and our problems in getting the project off the ground. And the old boy turned up trumps. It seems he intended to leave me £1000 in his will but when he heard how desperate we are he agreed that I should have it now – provided of course I don't expect any more later. He is going to see his solicitor tomorrow and have the thousand

237

transferred to my bank account. So you see that should buy all the equipment and bits and pieces we need and pay us both modest salaries for long enough to get our flying machine into the air. Do you wonder that I am feeling pleased with myself?'

'Good Lord!' Adam sat in silence for a moment pondering the full implications of what Max had said. A thousand pounds – enough to cater for all their needs and to spare! 'And you are proposing we should both give notice and work full time on the aeroplane, are you?' he asked after a moment.

'Of course. We've always been a team, you and I.'

'But it's your money – your inheritance, Max. It wouldn't be right for you to use it to keep me as well.'

'I guessed you would say that and I have given it some thought,' Max said easily. 'There are two ways around it as I see things. Either you work for me and I pay you a wage. Or – and I must say this is the solution I favour – we'll split the money and the costs fifty/fifty and call it a loan. You can pay me back when you are able. Though if I am right and we make as much money out of our aeroplane as I think we will I shall probably be too rich to care much whether you pay me back or not.'

'I certainly would pay you back,' Adam said decisively. 'I don't like being indebted to anyone, Max – even to you.' He was silent for a moment reflecting on the irony of the situation. Once there had been enough money in his family to make Max's £1000 look like small change. His mother's family had been Irish nobility with estates and properties that had amounted to a small fortune. But her father, third son of the Earl, had been a profligate. His share of the inheritance had been squandered on gambling and high living and eventually he had fled to England pursued by his creditors. When she had married Adam's father, a down-to-earth Liverpool ship owner, he had given her the first security she had known, but it had been short lived. He had been ruined by a series of devastating losses and died a poor and broken man, leaving nothing but the crumbling ruin of their once impressive home and just enough money to keep

238

it habitable for the duration of his wife's life. Apart from two good suits, a gold ring, a pocket watch and a hip flask still half full of fine old brandy Adam had not benefited at all. But this latest downturn in his family's fortunes had served to reinforce Adam's dislike of owing money. *Neither a borrower nor a lender be*, his mother, mindful of the follies of her ancestors, had used to say and Adam could see the sense in it. He had no wish to follow his grandfather into ruin and disgrace or his father into bankruptcy.

'Well, are we agreed?' Max asked and Adam nodded.

'Yes. I must admit it's a heaven sent opportunity. Everything seems to be going our way and if we can give the project our full attention I reckon we should be in the air in say six months.'

'You mean *you* can be in the air.' Max's face grew serious. 'I envy you, Adam, and I don't mind admitting it. I only wish I could be the one to try out the aeroplane when it's ready.'

'Maybe you will be able to,' Adam said, pouring tea.

'With this arm of mine?' Max shook his head sadly and as if to prove his statement used his right hand to lift his left onto his lap. It lay there, withered into a permanently hooked claw, half the size it should be. Max had been the victim of infantile paralysis as a child; the withered arm was its legacy. But it had not bred self-pity in him. Max was as adept with one hand as most men were with two and his brilliant mind more than made up for his disability. The most innovative aspects of design were due to his genius and Adam accepted that without Max it was unlikely the aeroplane could ever have been more than a dream.

Flying it however would be a different matter. The present design meant two hands were needed to manage the rudder bar and as yet they had been unable to come up with a workable alternative.

'One day maybe – but not yet,' Max said firmly. 'We can't waste precious time looking for alternatives simply to suit me. Let's work with what we've got and get the machine into the air with you at the controls, Adam. There will be time enough for me later.'

'I dare say you are right,' Adam admitted reluctantly.

Max drained his cup.

'Which brings us to your problems, Adam,' he said equably. 'If anyone is wasting time just now it is you. I can't see one single change of any significance in the plans you were so busily *not* poring over when I came in.'

'I was thinking,' Adam said a touch irritably.

'But not about our aeroplane, I'll warrant.' Max cast him a shrewd glance. 'What you were thinking about was that young lady who is occupying so much of your attention unless I am very much mistaken.'

'You mean Sarah Thomas I presume.' Adam said steadily.

'I do indeed. You are besotted with her, Adam.'

'Rubbish! All I did was travel down to Bristol with her. Now can we drop the subject?'

'No,' Max said evenly. 'I don't think we can. You'll never put your whole attention to our project while you are mooning about her. For heaven's sake go and see her and fight your suit.'

'I would have thought the last thing I wanted just now was a woman to distract me.' Adam ran a hand through his thick fair hair.

'You'd work a great deal better if you had a satisfactory love life,' Max persisted. 'Look at me and Annie if you have any doubts.'

Adam smiled wryly. Annie was Max's young lady, a sweet-natured girl whose sole role in Max's life seemed to be providing endless cups of tea and coffee and operating the heavy old industrial sewing machine they had acquired for stitching canvas. Adam could not imagine Sarah Thomas standing for that sort of treatment. She was a girl who was used to being at the centre of things, not some kind of willing unpaid servant. And in any case . . .

'Sarah Thomas is not interested in me,' he said bad-temperedly. 'She is engaged to Eric Gardiner.'

Max shook his head, laughing.

'Adam, the woman who is not interested in you is not yet born,' he said. 'Engaged or not you could get her if you wanted her. And you do. Listen to Uncle Max.'

Adam slammed down his cup. 'I've listened enough. I don't need your lectures or your advice.'

'Oh yes you do,' Max said quietly. 'And I will put it to you straight, Adam. Either you make an effort to woo the lovely Sarah or you'll get not a penny piece of my £1000 either as a wage or a loan. Do I make myself clear?'

Suddenly Adam's bad temper disintegrated. He gave a snort of laughter.

'Max, you are nothing but a blackmailing swine. Though what it is to you I can't imagine.'

'My peace of mind and both our futures,' Max said equably. 'Will you do it?'

'All right. Just for you and to prove that you are wrong. Sarah Thomas will turn me down flat, I promise you,' Adam said lightly.

But for all his levity he was aware of a core of determination hardening within him. Like hell she'd turn him down! He did want her – Max was right about that. And by George he meant to have her!

When she left Alexandra Palace two nights later he was waiting. She saw his Panhard parked in the road and her heart lurched uncomfortably.

'Why hello,' he said when she drew level with the motor.

'Hello. If you are looking for Eric I'm afraid you're out of luck. He and Henry have gone over to visit the Short brothers at their factory.'

'I'm not looking for Eric. It's you I came to see.' His tone was light but his eyes held hers and she felt the colour rushing into her cheeks.

'I thought you could make use of a ride home since you are without your usual transport,' he said and she thought: so he knew! He knew all the time that Eric was not here today – and that is why he came!

'Thank you but I quite enjoy a walk on a pleasant summer evening,' she said stiffly.

'Oh dear. There were several things I wanted to discuss regarding your friend Mr Morse and I thought driving you home would be an ideal opportunity to talk. But of course if you prefer to walk . . .'

Her flush deepened. She hoped he had not read her thoughts.

'Very well,' she said ungraciously, climbing up into the motor. 'What did you want to talk about?'

'Max and I have decided to accept Gilbert's kind offer. We are giving notice at the motor works and moving our project lock, stock and barrel to Somerset.' He glanced at her. 'I thought you would like to know.'

'Oh yes . . . good.' She couldn't decide whether she was glad or sorry. Gilbert would be pleased she knew and it was nice to think of the aeroplane being built at Chewton Leigh. But if Adam went to Somerset it meant she would not see him very often if at all. It should not matter to her; if anything she should be relieved, considering the unbelievable turmoil he caused in her, but she felt only a creeping dismay.

'Why don't you come too?' he said. His voice was as light as before but the words brought her up with a shock.

'Me?'

'Why not? It's your home isn't it? Gilbert made it clear they would welcome you.'

'Gilbert might. The others certainly would not . . .' She broke off, biting her lip. She had no intention of laying her history bare to him. 'In any case my life is here.'

'Ballooning? That will soon be a thing of the past. You should be looking at the future, Sarah. And the future is aeroplanes.'

She was silent for a moment remembering. Gilbert had once said something of the kind to her . . .

'It is going to be a very exciting time,' he said. 'Wouldn't you like to be a part of it?'

Still she was silent. His words were painting pictures in her mind; pictures she knew she had no right to be seeing and a small spiral of excitement was twisting within her. Oh yes, she would have liked to be a part of it all – but it was out of the question.

'I couldn't possibly,' she said.

242

He swung the car off the road into a small leafy park. Two little boys were bowling hoops along the path and a nanny, out for an early evening stroll before putting her charge to bed, pushed a perambulator on the sunny side of the road. Adam cruised the motor to a halt and turned to look at her.

'What are you afraid of?' he asked.

'I don't know what you are talking about. And why have we stopped?'

'We have stopped to make it easier to talk. Come to Bristol, Sarah. You don't have to move back into the big house if you don't want to. Annie, Max's fiancée, is coming with us and we shall have to find lodgings for her. The two of you could share a room.'

'Don't be ridiculous! I don't even know her.'

'But you will and you will like her, I am sure. It's going to be an adventure – I thought you had a taste for adventure.'

'I have but . . . why are you trying so hard to persuade me? You want me to act as go-between with Gilbert, I suppose?'

His mouth quirked. 'Is that what you think?'

'I can't do it, Adam. It's crazy. What would Eric say?'

'I don't suppose he'd be very pleased. But that's beside the point.'

'I have to consider him. After all I am supposed to be marrying him.'

There was a tiny pause. Then he said: 'That, of course, is your mistake.'

The blood rushed to her skin again. She could feel it tickling and prickling at every pore.

'What do you mean?'

'You shouldn't be marrying him.' His voice was even. 'You don't love him.'

Her chin came up. 'That is none of your business.'

'Perhaps not. But I intend to make it my business.'

'Really? And who do *you* think I should be marrying?'

His eyes held hers; she felt the breath constrict in her throat.

'Well, me of course,' he said.

Somehow she had known exactly what he was going to

say yet the words still shocked her. The nerve of the man! The sheer bare-faced cheek of him! And yet . . . oh, when he looked at her in that way, the crazy response it evoked in her! – her heart hammering so that it echoed in each and every pulse, the spiralling excitement within so sharp it was like the twist of a corkscrew, the prickling of her skin, sensitised, drawn towards him like a pin to a magnet though they were sitting the car's width apart. Involuntarily she found herself remembering the way it had felt the night he had almost kissed her – the rocklike strength of his body, the trembling eagerness of her own. For a moment suspended in time she imagined what it would be like to give herself up to these churning emotions, launching herself into the unknown as she had done the first time she had jumped from the edge of the balloon basket. Then her fingers, twisting together in her lap, encountered her ring and fastened on it, and reality came rushing in. Her breath escaped in a gasp that was half laugh, half sob.

'You're crazy!'

'Maybe we should all be a little crazy once in a while. And nothing is as crazy as marrying a man you don't love.'

'Why do you keep saying I don't love him? I thought you were supposed to be Eric's friend!'

'I am. But you are not doing him any favours marrying him the way you feel.'

'How do you know how I feel?'

'Oh believe me, Sarah, I do.'

There was no mockery in his face now. He was looking at her directly, not making the slightest move towards her, just looking – she felt as if he was able to strip away every pretence and see her very soul. Her fingers tightened on her ring, the only contact with normality. She was panicking now; it was as if she had launched herself into space only to find her parachute cord was jammed.

'Please, Adam, take me home,' she said. He made no move. 'If you don't take me home this very minute I shall get out of the car again. And we are not in the middle of nowhere now but in the heart of London.'

Her tone left no room for argument. Without a word he got out and swung the starting handle. She sat stiffly trying to hide the fact that she was still trembling. Neither spoke until he had parked at the kerb outside Molly Norkett's tea shop.

'Thank you,' Sarah said stiffly.

'My pleasure.' His features were hard – no smile now, no teasing. She felt inexplicably bereft.

'Adam . . .'

'No, Sarah,' he said, 'your life is your own. You have made your decision – don't apologise for it.'

She drew herself up. 'I wasn't going to!'

'Good. I only hope you don't live to regret it.'

Then he was gone and she was left staring after the cloud of exhaust fumes while the sense of loss spread through her body and it was all she could do not to take to her heels and run after him.

Hellfire and damnation! he was thinking as he pressed his foot down hard and the car hurtled joltingly across the cobbles. You made a pig's ear of that, my lad. But then, as the saying goes – you can't win 'em all . . . And the fact that Sarah was the only one you have ever really wanted to win is neither here nor there.

So – go back to the drawing board. Give all your attention to building an aeroplane and learning to fly. And make up your mind to forget Miss Sarah Thomas once and for all.

But even so, determined as he was, single-minded as he could be, Adam knew it would not be that easy.

Chapter Twenty-One

Night after night in the long silent hours she lay sleepless, thinking of Adam and Eric and her own confused emotions and wondering what she should do.

She had only herself to blame for the fiasco, of course. She should never have agreed to marry Eric. She had been fooling herself to think it would be enough to feel safe and cherished, content with the companionship of a man who loved her. She should have listened instead to the small voice of doubt which had warned her that one day there might be a man who could stir her deeper emotions. Now she had met that man and she knew with certainty that however well Eric might treat her, however much she liked and respected him, it was not enough.

She would have to tell him – it was not fair to either of them to keep up the charade. But how . . . how? And when she had told him – what then? Would she be able to continue with The Flying Dares? To do so might be awkward to say the least and painful for Eric, but it was the only life she knew and she enjoyed it too much to want to give it up.

As for Adam . . . though just thinking about him sent her senses reeling she could not believe he had any serious intention towards her. He was arrogant, conceited, too sure of himself by half, and it would be quite in keeping with what she knew of him if the things he had said had been simply a game he was playing for his own amusement, safe in the knowledge that she belonged to someone else. Yet for all that she felt herself drawn like a moth to a flame, drawn by the same sense of danger that ballooning had once excited in her. And she knew that now she had experienced this attraction for a man – attraction so powerful that the very air seemed to snap and crackle with electricity when they were together – she could not settle for less.

There was nothing for it. Much as she hated the thought of hurting Eric, it had to be done. And the sooner the better.

The balloon rose skywards a little less smoothly than usual for the breeze had turned suddenly gusty. In her sling beneath it Sarah hung with her customary grace, smiling and waving a small Union Jack to the crowds who craned their necks to watch her.

There was always certain to be a good crowd at a Miners' Gala and this one, in the heart of the Yorkshire coalfield, was no exception. First there had been the procession with the colourful banners and the marching bands followed by the stirring speeches from the platform. Now the emphasis had moved from politics to entertainment, the highlight of which was to be Sarah's parachute descent. Today, with no prospect of the patrons being able to afford to ride in the basket as better-off spectators did, Sarah was to use an unmanned balloon which would gradually deflate after she had jumped and drift back to earth.

As always the adulation of the crowd was obvious in the upturned faces but today Sarah was scarcely aware of it. In her mind's eye she could see only one face – Eric's – white with shock and disbelief when she had told him earlier that she could not marry him.

'I am so sorry, Eric,' she had said wretchedly. 'But you did know I didn't love you. I never pretended otherwise.'

'It's true you didn't,' he agreed, 'but that didn't stop me hoping, Sarah.' He paused then asked tautly: 'Is there someone else?'

'It's not a question of there being anyone else,' she said, avoiding the direct lie. 'It's *me* – the way I feel. It's just not right, Eric.'

'But I thought we could be happy together. We *are* happy together, aren't we?'

'Yes, we are. But I'm not sure it's a strong enough basis for marriage. I thought it was but . . . oh Eric, I'm sorry. Please don't *look* like that!'

He turned away but not before she had seen what looked

247

like tears glittering in his eyes. His back was very straight, his shoulders presenting her with a hard line. 'Well,' he said without looking at her, 'whatever you decide, Sarah, I suppose I shall have to accept it. But I'd like you to know that nothing has changed as far as I am concerned. I still love you, idiot that I am, and I think I always will. If you change your mind I shall be waiting. No matter how long it takes, just say the word.'

If he had been angry it would have been easier, Sarah thought now as the balloon rose higher. At least she would have felt less guilty for hurting him. But paradoxically the very *niceness* of him seemed to support her decision. Eric deserved far more than she could give him. However painful, she had done the right thing . . . hadn't she . . . ?

'For pity's sake concentrate – or you will be killed!'

Though she was all alone high in the sky the words suddenly echoed through her mind with the clarity of a voice speaking directly in her ear, catapulting her back to reality with a start and making her shudder as she realised just how little attention she had been paying to what she was doing. Usually she was so careful. Before each ascent she made a point of checking her equipment thoroughly and thinking through every aspect of what could go wrong, and although she knew that despite every care luck still played its part, yet she prided herself on never having had an accident in the air. Today, however, totally preoccupied with her interview with Eric she had given her parachute only the most cursory of glances before stepping into the sling and now, drifting high above the crowds, she wished heartily she had not taken for granted something upon which her life depended.

Here, high up, the swirling gusts were less noticeable but the movement of the trees and bushes surrounding the gala field reminded Sarah of their strength and she found herself remembering how Violet Kavanagh had been killed, blown onto a roof and off again, and Auguste Gaudron himself seriously injured – again as a result of high winds. Putting the uncomfortable thoughts out of her mind Sarah checked her ancroid – 3000 feet – and pulled sharply on the ripping cord. To her dismay nothing happened. She pulled again, harder. Still nothing.

The cotter pin must be jammed. It was the only explanation. Sarah had heard of this happening before though she had never experienced it herself. She glanced at the aneroid and was alarmed to see that she was now at 6000 feet and rising. If she did not free herself soon goodness knows where she would end up – she could even be carried out to sea before the balloon deflated and ditched with her still attached to it.

With all her strength she yanked on the ripping cord and to her relief she felt it give. The first exhilarating free fall sucked all the breath out of her body, then as the parachute billowed open she felt the tug on her arms and the headlong plunge became a more sedate drift. But because of the delay in freeing the pin the balloon was no longer over the gala field where she had planned to land. The ground beneath her now was rough moorland – steep slopes strewn with boulders and bisected by a small gushing stream. It would be so ignominious to arrive back with her natty pantaloon suit hanging around her like limp wet rags.

A few feet above the ground the first gust of wind took her, filling her parachute and lifting her like a toy. She gasped as breath blew back in her throat. Her feet kicked into the rough turf but before she could roll over backwards another gust filled the collapsing parachute like a sail on a racing yacht. It bowled across the uneven ground and, unable to release herself from her safety harness, Sarah was dragged helplessly along in its wake, grazing herself on sharp stones and boulders and feeling brambles scag at her hair and clothing. Suddenly to her horror she caught a blurred glimpse of a low stone wall beyond the billowing silk of the parachute and realised she was going to crash head first into it. Desperately she grabbed at the tussocks of grass, twisting herself round, and then her shoulder and hip hit the wall. The parachute bowled on and Sarah was lifted bodily up the rough stone face before the jagged coping frayed the cords of the parachute. One moment she was suspended two feet above the ground, the next she crashed back onto the rough turf.

The fall knocked what little breath she had left out of her lungs. For a moment she lay gasping helplessly, the whole of her body numb and her head spinning. Automatically she tried to stagger to her feet but a wave of excruciating pain shot through her shoulder and she fell back again. The sky, it seemed, had turned black, studded with a million flashing stars, and a roar like the sea filled her ears, drowning the sound of her own scream. Briefly the black world swam around her, then Sarah knew no more.

Gilbert was in his study when he saw the telegraph boy pass the window. Immediately he stiffened. Marconigrams were not unusual but they did tend to mean bad news. He set down the papers he had been working on and drummed his fingers on the desk top, waiting. The doorbell jangled and moments later there was a tap at the study door. It was Evans, the butler.

'Marconigram, sir.'

'Thank you, Evans.' He took the envelope from the silver salver on which it lay, ripping it open and anxiously extracting the message sheet which was tucked inside.

'Is there any reply, sir?' Evans enquired.

'No. No reply.'

When the butler had left Gilbert re-read the Marconigram, his face grave. He thought for a few moments, then left the study and crossed the hall to the drawing-room where Blanche was taking tea. She glanced up from her plate of buttered teacake, smiling faintly.

'Why Gilbert, what a pleasant surprise!'

'I have just received a wire from Sarah's fiancé, the ballooning fellow,' he told her. 'It seems Sarah has been involved in an accident at a display in Yorkshire.'

Blanche smirked. 'I can't say I am surprised. If she must engage in such an unladylike activity she must expect catastrophe. Is she badly hurt?'

'It is serious according to the wire but of course I have no further details. I shall ask Evans to find out about trains for me and leave for Yorkshire immediately.'

'Really? What can you do?'

250

Gilbert suppressed his irritation with difficulty.

'I want to see her for myself. And I think I should warn you, Blanche, that as soon as she is fit I intend to bring her here to Chewton Leigh to convalesce.'

'Here?' Blanche echoed faintly.

'Of course. She will need looking after and where else would she go? You must remember, Blanche, that this is her home.'

'Oh yes,' Blanche replied drily. 'How foolish of me!'

And silently, but with bitterness, added: as if I could forget!

Chapter Twenty-Two

Sarah lay on the elegant velvet chaise in the drawing-room at Chewton Leigh wriggling fretfully against the cushion which had been placed behind her head in an effort to make herself more comfortable and balancing a well thumbed copy of *Tess of the d'Urbervilles* against the back of the chaise with her good hand. But although occasionally she summoned up the energy to turn a page Sarah was not really giving the book much attention. *Tess* was such a sad story it depressed her and besides she was bored with reading. Since her accident she had done little else and what had once seemed a luxury to her now made her skin crawl with frustration.

She should be glad to be at Chewton Leigh, she knew. It was a great improvement on the bleak loneliness of the private room Gilbert had arranged for her in the hospital in Bradford. There, when she had emerged from the semi-conscious trance of the first days, there had been nothing but the pristine white ceiling and walls to gaze at and no company except for that of the briskly cheerful nurses who bustled in from time to time to check her temperature and pulse rate and change the dressings on her badly gashed leg, and the slightest movement had caused her so much pain that she had lain as still as possible, hardly daring even to draw breath. Here at least she was in the hub of the house and Gilbert had thoughtfully arranged for the chaise to be turned towards the window so that she could look out at the garden. But the enforced inactivity was anathema to her for Sarah had always loathed wasting a single moment.

She sighed deeply, let the book fall shut and tried to channel her thoughts towards what she would do when she had recovered sufficiently for Dr Haley to allow her to get up and about but even marshalling thoughts was too great an effort for her. Each and every possibility which occurred to her was nebulous, slipping away the moment she tried to grasp and pursue it and the stultifying conviction that she no longer belonged anywhere plunged her into depression. Perhaps this mental morass was another legacy of the accident, she thought, but it was of no comfort to her. One thing only was she certain of – that she had finished with ballooning forever. She had known it, she believed, from the moment that mysterious voice had spoken inside her high in the air and what had followed had only served to convince her of her own mortality and the chances she took with it each time she jumped. Too many display team members were dead or maimed and she had come close to being one of them. Once she might have dismissed the risk. She had enjoyed ballooning too much to care about the dangers. But now she realised that the intensity of the thrill had long since palled; parachuting had become as much a part of her life as falling out of bed each morning and brushing her hair each night – only a million times more dangerous. With the thrill removed the risk was no longer acceptable. She was young – her whole life lay before her and she wanted to live it, whole, fit and ready for whatever adventure might come her way, not die before her time or perhaps survive, a helpless cripple. Suppose she had broken her back out there on the Yorkshire moors instead of merely dislocating her shoulder and fracturing her collar bone? She could have found herself confined to a couch, not just for a few weeks but for the rest of her life! The thought made Sarah shudder.

Voices impinged on the periphery of her trance. It sounded like Gilbert, she thought, surprised, but he had looked in to bid her goodbye before he left for the office a few hours earlier with Leo, who was home for the vacation and filling in time at Morse Motors before going up to University in the autumn. Footsteps crossed the polished stone floor of the hall and she wriggled up so as to be able to see over the high back of the chaise.

'I've brought you a visitor, Sarah.' It was indeed Gilbert –but he was not alone. Behind him stood a tall figure, fair and handsome – Adam! a small tremor shivered over her skin and the colour of confusion rushed to her cheeks. She had not seen him since that night he had waylaid her outside Alexandra Palace but how often she had thought of him – thoughts that had made her blush even when she had been alone. Now he was here, no dream, but only too real. She tried to raise herself, pain shot through her shoulder and she subsided again. Her heart was pounding uncomfortably, breath caught somewhere beneath her bruised ribs.

He came around the end of the chaise, immaculate in well cut light trousers and a white shirt.

'Well, Sarah, so you came to Chewton Leigh after all!' he said.

The amusement in his voice annoyed her.

'So it seems,' she said icily. 'How are you?' he asked.

'Oh, I expect I'll live.' She was aware of Gilbert's puzzled expression and she guessed he was wondering what had precipitated her rudeness. 'I must be getting better,' she said more civilly. 'I'm bored out of my brain.'

A corner of his mouth quirked. 'I expect you are. You were always a do-er, Sarah. I've never seen you as one to sit quietly with a piece of needlepoint.'

'I couldn't do needlepoint even if I wanted to,' she returned. 'My shoulder wouldn't let me. All I can do is read and I must confess at this moment I wouldn't care if I never saw another book again.'

Gilbert crossed to the window where he stood, hands folded behind his back, regarding her thoughtfully.

'Perhaps it is just fiction you are tired of, Sarah,' he said. 'Perhaps what you need is something you can really get your teeth into.'

'What do you mean?'

'Why don't you use this time to learn something about business? I don't know what you plan to do when you are recovered but you have always been quick and clever and I have long thought you are wasting your talents – and your education. I know it is unusual to suggest such a thing for a girl but I believe that things are beginning to change. We have a lady typewriter at the office now and very good she is too.'

Sarah smiled wryly. 'I could hardly learn to use a typewriter lying here on the chaise.'

'True. But there are other things. Accounts, for instance, and business law.'

'You have a book keeper,' Sarah pointed out.

'But we haven't,' Adam said unexpectedly. 'Max and I have no-one to look after the business side of our enterprise at all. Why don't you take it on for us, Sarah?'

'Me?' She stared at him in blank amazement. 'But you are only building an aeroplane, not running a business. Why should you need help?'

'Because building the aeroplane demands all our attention,' Adam said. 'We have a pile of bills unpaid for one thing because Max and I each think the other has dealt with it and correspondence to be answered. And although it may seem like a pipedream at present things are progressing fast. The engine is very nearly ready for testing and we hope to have the aeroplane in the air by the end of the summer. If we are successful who knows where it will lead us?'

Sarah was silent.

'We have to work flat out now,' Adam continued. 'You know Bleriot crossed the Channel last week? Another milestone in aviation. If we are not to be left hopelessly behind there is not a moment to lose. It's a great adventure – if you would only do as Gilbert suggests and learn something about business affairs you could be a part of it.'

For once there was not the slightest hint of teasing in his tone and quite suddenly she realised the truth. They had cooked this up between them – Gilbert because he wanted to keep her at Chewton Leigh, Adam for some small reason of his own. But knowing it made no difference. A small dart of excitement tugged at her stomach. It *was* a momentous time – the birth of a new age. And yes, she would like to be a part of it . . .

Sarah lifted her chin and her features set into an expression of resolve.

'Very well,' she said, almost defiantly. 'Tell me what I have to do.'

*

As her strength returned and the waves of pain began to recede Sarah began to work as she had never worked before.

The chaise was no longer a velvet prison to her, it had become her library and schoolroom. The books that Gilbert brought her were spread all around within her reach; she pored over them until her eyes ached and worked at the exercises that Gilbert set her, resting the papers on a board balanced on her knees.

Sometimes Gilbert worked with her, explaining and tutoring, sometimes Joe Isaacs the accountant at Morse Motors came to take over her lessons. When she was well enough she could go to the office to gain some practical experience, Gilbert had said, and Sarah, filled with enthusiasm, could hardly wait.

Adam came sometimes, bringing her letters to be answered and bills to be paid, and she looked forward to his visits. But always the conversation was strictly business and Sarah began to be convinced that any interest he had in her had existed only in her imagination, or alternatively that she had been successful in convincing him that she had no interest in him. Occasionally there was a flash of that biting humour that could make her face burn, especially since she was still so acutely aware of him as a man. She wondered if he had noticed she was no longer wearing her engagement ring but if he did he made no mention of it. He seemed totally preoccupied now with the progress of the aeroplane and she supposed that was scarcely to be wondered at. He and Max were spending every available minute working on it and it occupied all their thoughts as well as their time.

When she was strong enough he took her to the converted cowshed at Long Meadow that was now the hub of their activity. There he introduced her to Max and Annie and she had her first sight of the framework of wooden struts and piano wire which went to make up the frame of the flying machine. To the uninitiated it might have appeared an unwieldy and unprepossessing structure but to Sarah, used to the trappings of the balloon factory, there was a comfortable familiarity in the way it lay there like the skeleton of a great wooden bird waiting for the power of the wind to give it flight. Her heart lifted with excitement and she picked her way around the framework of struts taking care not to damage any of them while Adam pointed out the features of their design.

Max welcomed her warmly enough, shaking her hand with a grip that was pleasantly firm, but Sarah was disconcerted by the shrewd way he was appraising her when he thought she was not looking and by his shrivelled left arm. It was wrong to take notice of such a thing, she knew, yet it bothered her all the same for the more she tried to ignore it the more conscious of it she became, her eyes pointedly fixed at the level of his face. But Annie she liked instantly.

Perhaps it was her face, sweet and friendly beneath her broad flower-trimmed hat which was so attractive, perhaps it was her voice, low and soft. But somehow Sarah did not think it was either of these things. Annie was not a beautiful girl – her features were too square and ordinary for conventional beauty – but she had great warmth and there was a kind of innate goodness about her which shone out of her wide set eyes and curved her full mouth. Annie thought the best of everyone, always managing to find some saving grace however obscure and wished only good to all, even those who wronged her. She had not an enemy in the world and Max and Adam in their different ways both adored her. Sarah, meeting her for the first time, knew only that she wanted to be her friend.

In one corner of the shed a heavy duty sewing machine at which Annie had been working disgorged yards of neatly stitched wing canvas, in another a billycan bubbled merrily on a primus stove. At Adam's suggestion Annie brewed tea and the three of them sat on a low wooden form to drink it while Adam leaned casually against the workbench.

'So you are going to organise us into a viable company when we are successful, I hear, Sarah,' Max said affably.

'I wouldn't quite say that. But I would like to be of what help I can.' She glanced up to see Adam's eyes on her and flushed. 'Of course when I know enough I expect Gilbert

257

will allow me to work at Morse Motors. But that is a long way off yet.'

'And I hope it does not mean that you will neglect us,' Annie said warmly. 'I can't tell you how nice it is to have another girl to chat to. These two are always totally absorbed in technical details and I don't understand the first thing about them.'

'No, but you are the best seamstress I know.' Max gave Annie an affectionate hug.

'Sometimes I think that is all you want me for!' she retorted, tossing her head so that the flowers on her hat bobbed fetchingly, and Sarah felt a small pang of envy. Tease one another as they might, there was obviously a very strong bond between Annie and Max. They were in love and it showed.

'Why don't you come over and visit me sometime?' Annie went on. 'I have a nice little room at my lodgings but it can get lonely when Max and Adam are working late and I can't help wishing I could be with them at the Plume of Feathers.'

'You know your father would never let you lodge in a public house, however respectable,' Max said seriously. 'You would not have been allowed to come with us if he had thought you would be staying in a place where there was strong drink on the premises – and where my room was just along the passage from yours!'

Annie wrinkled her nose. It was a pretty nose, tip-tilted and far and away her best feature.

'I expect you're right. Anyway we shall be married just as soon as you can spare the time and then I shall do as I please.'

'Oh no you won't, my girl. You'll do as I tell you!' But the warmth was obvious in his voice and she gave him a small playful push.

'Oh – you! Now you see what I have to put up with, promise you'll come and visit me, Sarah.'

'I promise,' Sarah said laughing.

As they finished their tea the talk turned to the big aviation meeting being held in Reims – la Grande Semaine d'Aviation de la Champagne. Gilbert had gone to France to attend and it was said that all the great names in the flying world would be there.

'I only wish we could have gone,' Max said wistfully. 'The latest aeroplanes will be on display, and new records will be set. But at present our place is here. We couldn't have spared the time, even if we could have afforded to go. But perhaps next year . . .'

'Perhaps next year we will be there with our own aeroplane,' Adam said and once again Sarah was aware of the feeling of excitement that unwieldy framework of struts and piano wire could generate.

'Perhaps I should be taking you home, Sarah,' Adam said. 'For someone who has been as unwell as you have I think this is quite long enough for your first outing.'

Regretfully Sarah agreed. She had enjoyed herself enormously but now she was beginning to feel tired.

Dusk was falling as Adam drove her home, the soft dusk of an early August evening, and the headlamps of the motor made a golden path along the narrow grey ribbon of road between the burgeoning hedgerows.

'That was fun,' Sarah said. 'Annie and Max are nice, aren't they?'

'The best.' He glanced along at her, his face taking on that faintly quizzical expression she was coming to know. 'Aren't you glad now that you decided to come to Chewton Leigh?'

Instantly her defences came up.

'It wasn't my choice, you know. If it hadn't been for my accident . . .'

'So why did you break off your engagement to Eric?' he asked.

She had no answer and confusion made her sharp.

'That is absolutely no business of yours.'

'Isn't it?' he asked softly. 'Are you sure of that, Sarah?'

She was trembling, the blood hammering in her veins.

'I don't want to talk about it.'

'Perhaps not. But I think you should.' He stopped the

motor and turned to look at her. 'Why do you insist on fighting it, Sarah?'

'Fighting what? I don't know what you mean.'

'Look.' His voice was steady, no hint of sarcasm now. 'I honestly don't know how we came to get off on such a bad footing. It seems whenever we are alone together we end up quarrelling. I really don't know why. But if we are going to be working together don't you think we should call a truce?'

She looked at him. In the half light his face was all planes and shadows. A muscle contracted in her throat.

'I'd like to go back to the beginning and start with a fresh slate.' he said. 'Would you be agreeable to do that, Sarah?'

The muscle contracted again. 'Yes – yes, I suppose so.'

'Good. And this time I intend to make my intentions clear from the very start.'

And then almost before she knew what was happening, she was in his arms. For a brief moment she tried to pull away but he was holding her firmly and the trembling of her own limbs made her weak. Beneath her outstretched hands his chest felt rock hard, the faint soapy smell of his skin and the tang of tobacco on his breath made her senses swim. As his mouth covered hers she remained motionless, trapped in time and space by the strength of his body and her own tumultuous emotions, then as the pressure of his lips parted hers a tremor ran through her like the whispering sigh of the wind in the grass and she let her hand slide around his shoulder to the nape of his neck. As her fingers encountered the corded muscles there beneath the thick line of his hair, the trembling increased and she found her lips moving beneath his, responding to his kiss. It was as if all her pent-up longings, all the dreams and desires she had hardly dared admit to, even to herself, were released by his touch and she clung to him, drowning in the sea of her own emotions, wanting only to be close, closer, and for the magic of this moment to last forever.

When at last he lifted his mouth from hers he did it so slowly that even when the pressure was no more their lips still clung then hovered, so sensitised that the very air between them was a caress. Then he released her, sliding his hands up her neck to cup her chin tenderly and those hazel eyes looked down into hers so deeply that she felt he was seeking her very soul.

'Oh Sarah,' he said – no more.

She could not move. She was spellbound, helpless in her longing. Somewhere out across the darkening countryside an owl hooted, herald of the night. The sound floated on the edges of her consciousness.

'That is why you could not marry Eric,' he said simply and she knew it was the truth.

Adam would never be hers as Eric might have been. He was too hard, too independent. There would always be that other side of him that she could not reach and certainly could not tame. But he was all she had ever wanted in a man.

'I think perhaps I should take you home,' he said roughly. Still holding her chin cupped in his hands he bent and kissed her again – a restrained kiss as sweet and chaste as the other had been darkly passionate.

'Remember,' he said, 'that this is our fresh start.'

He got down to crank the engine; in the light of the headlamps she watched the powerful ripple of his shoulders as he swung the handle and longed to feel them beneath her fingers again. Then without another word he climbed back up into the Panhard and drove her home.

The first thing she heard when she woke was the song of the birds outside her window clamouring in the dawn chorus. Sleep had come easily and quickly, now despite the earliness of the hour she had woken feeling refreshed. For a moment she lay wondering why it was she felt so happy, then memory came flooding back and she let herself savour again the sensuous delight his kiss had brought, the potency of the chemistry that had been worked between them.

Adam! she thought and his name was like an aria soaring in her heart.

She loved him. Useless to deny it any longer. Why had she ever tried to? Because she did not trust him – or because she did not trust herself? He was such an enigma, he raised such a welter of conflicting emotions in her, frightening as

261

well as delighting her. But it was a fact she could no longer ignore, no longer try to hide, even from herself. She loved him with all her heart, with all her body, with her very soul, and she thought she had done from the first moment she had laid eyes on him. Why else should she have reacted to him with such vehemence if he had not stirred her in a way that no-one had ever done before?

Did he love her? He wanted her, yes, but that was not necessarily the same thing. He was a man used to his power and she knew instinctively that many women had fallen prey to it. Easy to believe, when she so much wanted to, that unless he felt as she did that force field of desire could never have come into being. Might it not simply be that his desire was purely physical, as Hugh's had been, coupled with a desire to dominate?

No, don't spoil it! she wanted to cry. Take what you have and be grateful. God alone knows such perfect happiness is rare.

She pushed aside the bedclothes and padded softly over to the window, drawing back the curtains and looking out into the freshness of the August morning. The sun had not yet cleared the hills but the park was bathed in soft golden light and a faint haze hung over the copse that hid the lake. The grass of the lawns sparkled darkly with dew, the haunting perfume of the bushes of flowering currant and the stocks in the neat beds beneath her window wafted up on the sweet fresh air. In the trees the chorus of the birds rose to one last clamouring crescendo before dying away almost as suddenly as it had begun. Sarah thought the song and the ensuing silence were the most beautiful sounds she had ever heard.

Chapter Twenty-Three

The gelding cantered across the meadow with flowing grace, lithe muscles rippling beneath his shining coat, mane and tail streaming in the brisk wind of an early September afternoon. On his back Alicia Morse sat with an ease which echoed the perfection of movement of the horse, back straight, slim hands controlling the reins with just the right blend of strength and gentleness, chin lifted so that the wind whipped colour into the ivory of her cheeks. Her royal blue riding habit was spread out against Baron's pale flanks and today she wore a little hat set at a jaunty angle on her upswept hair. Alicia was something of an exhibitionist – even when doing something she enjoyed and excelled at as she did at riding she liked to strike a pose so that the people she passed would stare in admiration and report to their families: 'I saw Alicia Morse out riding today – she looked magnificent!'

There was a low brush hedge at the perimeter of the field; Alicia set Baron at it and he cleared it easily, landing on the other side with the sure-footedness of a cat and finding his stride again at once. For another hundred yards she let him have his head then as the ground began to drop away she pulled him up. From this high point the valley spread out below in a panorama of green with only the copper beeches to lend a touch of the hues that would soon transform the entire vista with the russets of autumn. Away to the left a herd of Friesians grazed, to the right the chimneys of Chewton Leigh House were just visible over a fold of the hill. But Alicia was not looking at any of these things as she sat there relaxing for a moment against the pommel of her sidesaddle. Her gaze was directed at the converted cowshed immediately below her and the contraption which had been pushed out onto the grass in front of it, a contraption which at this distance looked no more than a child's toy, a flimsy

263

framework of wooden struts, brown paper and canvas. But even this miracle of modern engineering did not interest her much. It was the man bending over to inspect some detail of the structure who held her attention, and her pulses, already racing from the excitement of the ride, beat a little more insistently at the sight of him.

From the first time she had met him Adam Bailey had excited Alicia in a way no man had ever done before though she was at a loss to know why. He was very handsome, of course, but then so were many of the young men in her circle and beyond it who had tried unsuccessfully to pay court to her and he had none of their wealth or social standing. He was pleasant enough but so totally absorbed in his work that he made no effort to charm or even to observe social niceties and for all her efforts he seemed hardly to have noticed she existed. Yet the very thought of him could set her senses aflame and Alicia had spent a great deal of time thinking about him.

Perhaps it was the essential maleness of him which stirred her – beside him other men paled into insignificant shadows. Perhaps it was the sense of purpose that charged him with an electric impulse impossible to resist. Or perhaps it was the very fact that he seemed impervious to her charms, paying more attention to Sarah than he did to her. All her life Alicia had been used to having what she wanted; so far as she could remember nothing had ever been denied her. Now she wanted Adam, wanted him with a ferocity which startled her. And she was determined that she would have him, come what may, just as she had had everything else she had ever set her heart on.

Alicia's eyes narrowed and the lines of her mouth hardened slightly. So far Adam had eluded her but she would get him in the end. Failure was not a word in her vocabulary. As she watched he straightened up, the sun catching the golden lights of his hair, and moved towards the shed. At this distance she could only imagine the strong lines of his face and the clean muscular litheness of his limbs but the imagining was enough to send a thrill tingling through the core of her and her mouth softened to a secret smile. For a moment she savoured the sensation then the wanting was a fever in her veins and she touched Baron's side with the heel of her riding boot and started down the field.

As she trotted up to the shed he emerged once more wiping his hands on a piece of rag.

'Alicia!'

'Hello, Adam.' Her voice was cool, not betraying a vestige of the emotion which was making her tremble, but when he came over to help her dismount she held his eyes for a moment with a look of smouldering enticement and allowed her hand to rest on his arm briefly before turning away to twist Baron's reins around a metal bracket on the wall of the shed. 'How are things going?'

'Slowly. Much too slowly for my liking but I suppose I am impatient by nature. I imagined when we got the engine we would be flying within days but each taxiing trial seems to throw up fresh problems. First there was trouble with the gear box casing, then the carburettor developed a fault, now I'm not sure whether we should think again about the propeller arrangement . . .'

'Oh dear,' she said lightly. 'It all sounds very trying.'

'It certainly is frustrating when we are so close to a breakthrough. The other day when I was taxiing I felt she was almost on the point of taking off.'

'Are you all alone today?' she asked, looking around.

'Yes. Max and Annie have gone into Bristol to pick up some things we need,' he replied.

Alicia's lips curved, giving her the look of a kitten who has just spied a saucer of cream. 'I chose just the right time to visit you then didn't I?' she said and when he made no response she went on, slightly irked: 'I didn't think Max drove. That hand of his . . .'

'He doesn't. But I have given Annie instruction. It's not practical for me to be the only driver.'

'Lucky Annie!' she said lightly. '*I* would like to learn to drive. Perhaps one day when you have more time you will teach *me*.'

'Perhaps – but if you are impatient to learn I suggest you

find another tutor. This project looks like keeping me fully occupied for some time yet.'

'Oh I'd much rather wait and let *you* teach me.' Again she held his eyes for a moment before dropping her own demurely.

'You must excuse me Alicia, but I have a great deal to do. If Max returns and finds me slacking there is likely to be a falling out of partners.' He moved away and she experienced a stab of frustration. Coquetry seemed to have no effect whatever on Adam. Well, she would have to go for a more direct approach.

'Father was wondering whether perhaps you would like to dine at Chewton Leigh one evening,' she said, following him across to the aeroplane. 'It's a very long time since you were up at the house and however busy you are you must make time to eat, at least!'

'That is true, though we do often depend on a sandwich or a piece of cold pie at the inn.'

'Then a good meal would give you more energy to enable you to work even harder next day!'

'How kind. Does the invitation extend to the others?' he asked without a flicker.

'Of course,' she replied, hiding her annoyance.

He was bending over the aeroplane again inspecting the propeller.

'You see – this should run symmetrically. I am afraid there is a weakness somewhere. If it failed in the air it could be disastrous . . .'

'Adam, would you mind terribly having a look at my finger?' she said, drawing off one of her gloves and making a great show of examining it herself. 'I think I have a thorn in it – or maybe a splinter. The wood on some of the stable doors is very rough . . .'

He straightened. 'My hands aren't too clean.'

'I'm sure they won't do me any harm!' She laughed lightly. 'See – just there. Does that look like a splinter to you?'

'I can't see anything.' He was holding her hand. The touch of his fingers on hers made the excitement twist in her again. She laid her gloved hand on his arm.

266

'Just there – see?' She leaned forward so that her breast brushed against him. He looked up quickly. As their eyes met she smiled at him, a slow tantalising smile full of invitation and briefly she saw the response flicker across his face, the enduring primitive response of a man to an attractive woman. Triumph soared within her along with the overwhelming compulsion. At last she had made him aware of her – though heaven knew she had had to practically throw herself at him to do it!

'Adam . . .' she said silkily – and heard the approaching phutter of a motor car engine.

She looked up in fury to see the Panhard shuddering around a bend in the lane. Annie was driving, sitting up very straight and holding tightly to the wheel as if she expected the monstrosity to break away from her at any moment like a mettlesome horse. Max was sitting beside her and in the rear seat sat Sarah. The wind had got into her hair, loosening it from the pins, so that it stood out in a brown cloud around her head and her cheeks were pink.

Alicia swore silently but her smile was unwavering and she allowed her hand to remain on Adam's arm as the car turned in at the gateway and ploughed across the uneven ground.

'Sarah!' Adam said warmly. 'What are you doing here? I thought Gilbert was keeping you busy at the works these days.'

'Yes, but I decided to ride back with Annie and Max to see how the aeroplane is getting on,' she said, smiling back at him.

Alicia saw the look which passed between them and it only served to strengthen her determination. How was it Sarah could get a look like that from him when she could not? An idea occurred to her – one more devious than anything she had so far tried in her efforts to win Adam's attention.

'I am very glad to see you are allowed some time off from your studies,' she said smoothly. 'Heaven knows we see little enough of each other for two girls who live under the same roof.' She saw the puzzled look come into Sarah's eyes and knew what she was thinking: even during the weeks that Sarah had been laid up Alicia had barely found the time to spend an hour with her – and neither of them would have wanted her to. 'You work far too hard,' Alicia went on smoothly. 'You scarcely ever exercise Sweet Lass any more. Now, I am going to make a suggestion. Take an afternoon off tomorrow. First we will lunch together and then we will ride. And if Father objects you can refer him to me!'

'Oh Alicia, I don't know. Mr Isaacs has promised to go over the ledgers with me tomorrow . . .'

'I insist!' Alicia said sweetly.

'You should, Sarah,' Adam put in. 'It's true, you are working far too hard. A ride would put the roses in your cheeks and blow away the cobwebs.'

'Thank you, Adam, for backing me up.' Alicia smiled at him as if the two of them were conspirators, then removed her hand from his arm with a deliberate movement that implied relinquishing possession, if only temporarily. 'I must go now. But don't forget, Sarah, I shall hold you to our arrangement.'

She unhooked Baron's reins and mounted with easy grace. Sitting there sidesaddle she made a picture and she knew it. She raised one gloved hand and smiled at them, then turned Baron and kicked him into a trot. The determination was as fierce in her as ever and her pulses were still hammering from the excitement of the encounter. But she set the horse up the field and though she knew they were watching her she did not look back.

'Well, Sarah, this is exceedingly pleasant,' Alicia said.

'Yes it is,' Sarah agreed.

They were walking the horses single file through a copse in the bottom of the Chewton Leigh valley, Alicia leading the way on Baron, Sarah following with Sweet Lass and in spite of her dislike for Alicia, Sarah was glad she had come. She had enjoyed the leisurely trot along the lanes and the brisk canter across the meadows for riding provided a wonderful means of relaxation and Sarah resolved she would find the time to do it more often. Provided of course

268

that dear Sweet Lass was her mount. She did not fancy the idea of managing the mettlesome Baron one bit and she was filled with generous admiration for the easy way in which Alicia controlled him.

But then control was something Alicia was very good at. The way she had inveigled Sarah into riding with her this afternoon was a case in point. But Sarah was puzzled by her motive. Alicia had never made any secret of her disdain for Sarah – why this sudden change of heart? There is bound to be a reason, Sarah thought, and I think I know what it is. She wants Adam and she thinks the way to get to him is through me.

From the moment she had been introduced to him it had been obvious that Alicia was setting her cap at Adam, but it was only when she had come upon the little scene at Long Meadow the previous afternoon that Sarah had realised just how serious Alicia was in her intentions. A splinter in her finger indeed! She must think we are green as grass! Sarah thought scornfully. But Adam seemed to have been taken in by it – or perhaps he had *wanted* to be taken in . . .

Sarah gave her head a small impatient shake, trying to dispel the sudden doubt that had assailed her. But still it hung over her like the shadow of the trees across the woodland path.

If only they had been able to spend more time together! If only there had been more moments of passion and tenderness like the one they had shared on the way home from that first meeting with Annie and Max! But work on the aeroplane was claiming all his time and most of his attention.

Max was as bad, of course. Annie was forever complaining that if it were not for her visits to the shed to stitch wing fabric she would have quite forgotten what he looked like. But it was different for Annie. She was secure in the knowledge of Max's love, his ring was on her finger and he left her in no doubt that she figured in all his plans for the future. Whilst Adam . . .

Maybe he thinks that kissing me until I am weak is enough – but it isn't, Sarah thought. I am more crazily in love with him than ever but I still don't know for sure how he thinks of me. Or how he thinks of Alicia for that matter . . .

Here under the trees where the sun could not reach the breeze was cool, even chilly, and Sarah shivered.

'Shall we go back along the lane?' Alicia called over her shoulder. 'Yes, if you like,' Sarah called back, and her tone gave no indication of her thoughts.

Leo de Vere was feeling annoyed. This was not unusual – Leo spent most of his life experiencing either annoyance or resentment or downright jealousy. Long ago he had decided that fate had dealt him an unfair hand and the conviction had eaten deeply into him, destroying any humour or compassion that might otherwise have tempered his rather dour nature and imbuing even his triumphs with a satisfaction that owed more to bitterness than pleasure.

As a child his world had been torn apart by the death of his father and though Leo had not missed him much since he had seldom been in evidence even when he was alive he soon became aware of the privations that came with his death. Cornelius de Vere had been a wealthy and respected banker who had been unable to face the disgrace and ruin when his empire suddenly crashed about his ears; he had taken a double-barrelled shotgun and put a bullet through the roof of his mouth, ending his life and Leo's comfortable existence in one fell swoop. The luxurious house on Fifth Avenue had been the first thing to go, along with his riding lessons and exclusive prep school and Blanche had taken Leo and fled to the picturesque, but in Leo's opinion, paltry, house in New Hampshire which was the home of Cornelius's sister Elinor. He had hated the place, hated the unfamiliar accents and the remoteness, hated his mother's enforced preoccupation with survival where before she had been principally concerned with his welfare. Most of all he hated the fact that he could no longer have all the things that money could buy at the merest snap of his fingers. During the year they spent in New Hampshire Leo had learned many things but the education had not made a better person of him. Instead it had set him on the downward spiral of resentment and bitterness.

At first he had looked forward to the visit to Blanche's family in England as the cue for matters to improve. He had soon been disappointed. He liked England even less than he had liked New Hampshire and when his mother had told. him she intended to marry Gilbert Morse and settle there he had been enraged.

Life in the Morse household had done nothing to make him happier. Money was no longer scarce it was true but once he had come to take the relaxed state of finances for granted he quickly began to find other things that were unsatisfactory. He was no longer the sole object of his mother's attention for one thing. Her new husband was far more demanding of her time than his father had ever been. And there were the Morse children, all older than him with the exception of James, all bursting with a confidence which only exacerbated his own feeling of inferiority, all far better looking than he. Leo had never been an attractive child, with his narrow face, prominent nose and cheekbones and rather thin lips, but he had never been as aware of his own lack of beauty as he was when he looked at the Morses with their good features and clear blue eyes. They disliked him and looked upon him as an interloper he knew and he felt they were united against him, again with the exception of James who attached himself to Leo like a shadow. But far from being grateful to James for his obvious adoration Leo despised him. James was 'wet', preferring his paint box to any rough and tumble game, always whining, often sickly, and prone to bursting into tears. Alliance with him, Leo felt, would be a reflection on himself yet friendship with the others was impossible. They treated him with thinly veiled resentment and he hated them for their overflowing confidence and for excluding him from all the things they took for granted.

Alicia he hated most of all. Because she was closest to him in age she took her lessons with him and he had thought that since she was a mere girl his position as kingpin was impregnable. But Alicia had had other ideas. Her pride and disdain were apparent in everything she did and the fact that James hero-worshipped him made him a target for her spite also. He did not want James's adoration, yet perversely he was hurt and annoyed when Alicia made it clear that at a snap of her fingers she could take even that from him.

Matters had deteriorated still further when Sarah Thomas came to Chewton Leigh. Again he had felt that now, at least, he would no longer be last in the pecking order, again he had been disillusioned. Gilbert, who had no time for him at all, doted on her and even the tutor, Richard Hartley, seemed to favour her. Briefly he had formed an alliance with Alicia, whose hatred for Sarah was obvious, but he had been unable to capitalise even on this for the defects in his character made him seem more sly than bold, and Alicia was too strong and independent to wish to include him in any of her plans and schemes to disenchant her father with Sarah.

Boarding school had taken Leo away from his enemies the Morses but he had made no lasting friends there either. The chip on his shoulder made him sour and truculent when things went wrong and he crowed unpleasantly over his successes so that not surprisingly no-one ever seemed genuinely pleased for him. But he was a clever boy and with no chums and no schoolboy larks to distract him he produced a set of examination results which would have been the delight of his schoolmasters had they been able to summon up even a cursory liking for him.

Only his mother seemed willing to fight his corner. She championed him to such an extent that it only had the effect of making the others dislike him more and he relied on her encouragement as heavily as he had done as a small child.

'Go to university, Leo,' she had advised him. 'Then you will be in a position to head Morse Motors one day. Lawrence might be Gilbert's eldest son but he is a thick head. You can run rings around him. Hugh will never take the slightest interest in the business and neither will James, unless I am much mistaken. He is talking, believe it or not, of becoming an artist. As for Alicia, she is only a girl. She will marry and spend her time raising a family and entertaining her husband. But you are clever. If you do well Gilbert will come to realise it is to you he must look to carry on the family empire.'

This advice had echoed precisely Leo's own thoughts. He was aware that his intellect was his greatest asset and he had long harboured an ambition to beat the Morses at their own game. How wonderful it would be to take control of the family firm! He could see himself sitting at the head of the long polished oak table in the boardroom, taking the decisions, controlling all their destinies. And oh, how sweet revenge would be! When he was in charge he would make them pay, all of them, for their treatment of him. They would discover then the frustration of having to wait on *his* pleasure, of knowing that it was he, not they, who reigned supreme in this world of theirs. He would do things his way; he would have all the money and power he wanted. And he could do it. His mother was right. There was not one among them fitted for the throne. All he had to do was play his cards correctly, gain the qualifications to impress Gilbert and the experience he would need of the running of the firm, then sit back and reap his rewards.

Gilbert might have slighted him in the past but this time he would not be able to afford to do so. Not if he wanted to keep Morse Motors successful – and in the hands of the family.

These thoughts had spun a strong skein of ambition in Leo de Vere. It became his driving force and sustained him through all his depressions and moments of self-doubt. Each real or imagined slight only served to strengthen it until it became an obsession with him. Revenge – the revenge of being all powerful whilst they were forced to be as puppets in his hands. Day by day he had seen his goal coming closer. He would be going to university soon – three more years and he could begin to insinuate himself into a striking position at the works. Lawrence was not fit to take the reins, he had spent time there during the vacation and seen with his own eyes how slow and indecisive Gilbert's eldest son was. His mother was right, just as she always was. With her help it would be easy.

And now, just when it seemed he was moving inexorably towards his goal, someone had appeared on the horizon whom he recognised as a threat.

At first he had not taken undue notice of Adam Bailey, dismissing him as something of a crackpot who, as a friend of the upstart Sarah, was barely worthy of consideration. The first seeds of disquiet had been sown when he had recognised Gilbert's enthusiasm for the young man and his outlandish project but he still had not fully understood why he experienced concern. Adam was nothing more than a customer to whom Gilbert had given a certain amount of backing. He was not, and never would be, a member of the Morse dynasty.

But this morning he had had a conversation with James which had caused him to think again.

Relations between James and Leo had never changed much since their childhood days – Leo still disliked the quiet artistic young man and his airy-fairy notions; James still seemed totally unaware of that dislike. This morning both of them had been late for breakfast, Leo because he had been working late into the night at the books he thought would stand him in good stead when he started at Cambridge, James because he had been drinking and playing cards with some of his wilder friends. As they helped themselves to kidneys and bacon from the silver chafing dishes on the sideboard Leo had attempted to avoid conversation but James had had other ideas.

'I say, I do believe Alicia is in love at last,' he remarked cheerfully.

'Really?' Leo said discouragingly, opening the copy of the day's *Times* which Gilbert had left on the breakfast table. Alicia's affairs of the heart were not of the slightest interest to him.

'Haven't you noticed?' James enquired, pouring himself black coffee from the silver coffee pot. 'She has taken a great shine to this Adam Bailey fellow. In fact I have never seen Alicia set her cap at anyone with such determination.'

Leo grunted, his eyes still roving over the columns of financial news.

'He's a clever fellow,' James continued unabashed. 'Father is impressed with him I know. But I don't think it's his cleverness Alicia is interested in. She's fallen for the chap, not a doubt of it.'

Leo was aware of the first niggle of disquiet. 'He's shown no interest in her has he?' he said, his tone surly. 'I thought he was Sarah's friend.'

James grinned. 'That is hardly likely to stop Alicia, is it? You know as well as I do what Alicia is like when her heart is set on something. She invariably gets what she wants. And she wants Adam Bailey – I'd wager a month's allowance on it. As for Adam – well he'd be a fool to upset her, wouldn't he? He and that friend of his with the withered arm have scarcely two half-pennies to rub together from what I hear of it. They're scraping the barrel to finance this project of theirs. Think what a difference it would make to them if he was to take up with Alicia! It would ensure father's backing. He wouldn't want Alicia married to a penniless adventurer. He'd pull out all the stops to make sure Adam had whatever he needed to be successful. Even take him into partnership if they were to get married, I shouldn't wonder. Oh yes, Adam would be a fool to ignore Alicia's interest – and he is no fool. There will be wedding bells before the year is out, mark my words, unless Alicia changes her mind. And somehow I don't think she will.'

Leo swallowed hard. The succulent kidney seemed to have turned to cardboard in his dry mouth. Alicia and Adam. If James was right and she wooed him with the promise of Morse backing for his project it could be the undoing of all Leo's carefully laid plans. There was no Morse fitted to take over the family empire – but supposing Adam became Alicia's husband? Then things could be very different. Of course, as yet it was nothing but mere hypothesis. But as James said, Alicia was a very determined young woman. What she wanted she invariably got.

He set down his knife and fork with a clatter and pushed back his plate. He was no longer hungry.

'I'm going to the works,' he said. 'I'll see you at dinner, James.'

'Oh!' James looked disappointed. He had been enjoying Leo's company, oblivious as ever of the other's impatience with him. 'In that case I think I shall take my easel and go out to do a spot of painting. It's a nice day. The light is just right.'

Leo left the room without replying. He got himself ready and drove into Bristol and all the while the thoughts which their conversation had stirred up rankled in him like the sour taste left in the mouth after a night's hard drinking. It would be just his luck if Alicia were to upset the applecart now. Why was it that things always went wrong for him?

At the works he chatted with Frank Raisey, the general manager, and nothing that was said did anything to improve his humour. Raisey was raving about Adam and Max and their flying machine and the progress in powered flight in general. Since Bleriot had crossed the Channel in July, skimming a few feet above the water, losing his way for lack of a compass and finally landing in a meadow behind Dover Castle things had moved apace. A revolutionary new aero-engine had been designed in France and Raisey felt sure it would not be long before the £10 000 prize for linking London and Manchester would also be won. And he believed Adam and Max with their home-grown version would not be far behind.

'And with an engine made here at Morse Motors,' he said, swelling with pride. 'Makes you proud to be a part of it, eh lad?'

Leo turned away. He did not feel proud. He felt bitter and envious. Reflected glory meant nothing to him. It was his own success he was interested in.

When Raisey mentioned that Sarah had left the works early today to go riding with Alicia Leo was puzzled – and suspicious. The girls despised one another. They would never have sought one another's company unless they had very good reason to. The arrangement seemed to smack of a conspiracy of some kind and Leo did not like it one bit.

He left the works in a foul temper. Never the most sympathetic of drivers, today he drove fast and badly, crashing gears and swearing when he hit a pothole or bump

276

in the road. Damn the Morses. Damn all of them. He'd show them yet!

He was almost back at Chewton Leigh when he rounded a bend in the lane and saw the two horses ahead of him – Alicia on Baron, Sarah on Sweet Lass. Another wave of fury roared in his ears. He put his foot down hard and rocketed towards them. Why the hell should he slow down for them? They could just get out of his way. As he approached them Baron sidestepped nervously and he honked raucously on his horn. Stupid animals. Stupid girls. He honked again, pulling out to pass them and roaring off down the lane. Faintly, above the noise of the engine, he was aware of Baron's frightened whinny and the raised voice of one of the girls. Just ahead of him the road forked obtusely – left to Chewton Leigh House, right to the farms in the valley bottom. With a smile of grim satisfaction curling his lips Leo took the left fork and did not look back.

To lose control of the horse you are riding is a frightening thing. When sixteen hands of solid horseflesh and corded muscle decides to take fright and go its own way there is virtually nothing you can do about it. The very size of the animal, previously comforting, now works against you and you know you have no more chance of stopping it than Canute did of holding back the tide.

It was the highly strung Baron who was most upset by Leo's thoughtless behaviour. For a few moments Alicia fought to steady him without success. Eyes wild, nostrils flaring, he took off, galloping madly along the road as if the devil himself were after him. And Sweet Lass went with him. Already upset by Leo, her foal's panic communicated itself to her and she raced with him, shoulder to shoulder while Sarah vainly tried to stop her.

At the fork in the road the terrified horses veered to the right. Soon the lane narrowed, sloping steeply, but they galloped on. At the bottom it curved sharply, ahead of them was a hedge, six feet high and thick with the brambles of autumn. Baron leapt it like a cat, Sweet Lass attempted to follow, but her stride was all wrong. Her flailing front legs crashed into the branches and she fell back into the ditch. Her scream was one with Sarah's and then she was still. In the quiet of the September afternoon the thunder of Baron's galloping hooves echoed for a few minutes more before his panic began to subside and Alicia was able to bring him under control. Then the only sound was the distant phutter of Leo's motor heading up the hill to Chewton Leigh.

'Where is she?' Adam asked. His voice was rough with anxiety; it carried across the great entrance hall of Chewton Leigh House and into the drawing-room where once again Sarah lay on the velvet covered chaise. Had she ever left it? she wondered. The fall had set her shoulder throbbing again. Dr Haley had been and prescribed complete rest for a day or so at least to ensure there was no further damage to the old injury and in any case once again movement was too painful to attempt. But the pain in her collarbone, coldly numbing and fiery sharp as it was, was nothing to the pain in her heart.

Adam appeared in the doorway, crossed the room in two strides.

'Sarah!'

'Hello,' she said faintly. Her voice seemed to belong to someone else.

He dropped to his haunches beside her taking her hand and shaking his head. 'I don't know what I shall do with you. If you're not falling out of balloons, you are falling off horses!'

He had expected this riposte to spark off her usual quick retort. It was so easy to get Sarah going. But today she made no reply – seemed hardly to hear him even. She lay staring into space, eyes unfocused, and she was deathly pale.

'Sarah,' he said more seriously. 'Are you all right?'

She turned her head slowly as if coming back from a long way off.

'Me? Yes, *I'm* all right. Sweet Lass isn't. She's dead.' Her voice was flat and the lack of emotion was chilling. Somehow one knew that it was all there, bottled up deep inside, grief too terrible to express.

'Oh sweetheart!'

The longed-for endearment passed unnoticed. 'She broke her neck. That stupid Leo frightened the horses. Baron bolted and Sweet Lass followed.'

'I know. The idiot. If I lay hands on him I'll horsewhip him . . .'

Her brows knitted together. She looked merely puzzled.

Dear God, he thought, she is in deep shock, and anger at Leo de Vere coursed through his veins. If he could get hold of him now he would not merely horsewhip him but kill him. But that would not help Sarah. Somehow he had to bring her back from this strange world inside herself into which she had retreated or he did not know what would become of her.

He put his arms around her, turning her face into his shirt front. 'Oh Sarah, Sarah, poor Sweet Lass! How you will miss her!' he whispered against her ear. 'She was always your horse, wasn't she? When you were a little girl . . . ?'

How long it took he did not know. Time had ceased to be of importance. But at last to his relief the dam burst. The tears she had not yet shed began to roll down her cheeks, slowly at first then hotter and faster and her whole body racked with sobs. He held her, distressed at the storm he had unleashed, yet thinking that anything, anything, was better than that awful remoteness, that lack of emotion. He took out his handkerchief, wiping the tears away as they rolled down her cheeks, and tenderness for her almost superseded his anger. Almost – but not quite. If Leo de Vere were to walk in now he would still like to kill him with his bare hands for what he had done.

Neither he nor Sarah noticed Alicia standing in the doorway. For a moment the tightness within her held her rigid, neither able to announce her presence nor turn to go. Jealousy consumed her, a jealousy so fierce it seemed to rage in her veins like a forest fire and the heat it generated burned on her skin. With difficulty she controlled her breathing, pushed the door open and went into the room.

'Sarah, my dear, are you all right?' she asked, her voice dripping honey.

Adam straightened. 'She is very upset.'

'Don't worry,' she said silkily, 'I'll look after her. I'm sure Max will be wondering what has become of you. But she will be all right with me.'

His hand was still on Sarah's; Alicia wished she could tear it away.

'Are you sure, Alicia?' he asked.

'Oh yes,' she said and the grim determination sounded a fair imitation of concern. 'You can quite safely leave Sarah to me.'

Time passed but the grief refused to go away. Sarah wondered how it was possible to feel such grief for an animal. Sweet Lass, the dearest horse who had ever lived, was gone. Never again would she nuzzle Sarah and poke an enquiring nose into her pocket in search of a sugar lump, never again carry her through the dew fresh fields. The loss ached in her endlessly; not Gilbert, not gentle Annie, not even Adam could make it less. Life was going on. But something had gone from her world which was irreplaceable. Nothing would ever be quite the same again.

Chapter Twenty-Four

'I am determined to get that aeroplane off the ground tomorrow,' Adam said. 'We have wasted enough time on taxiing trials. If we don't make it tomorrow we never will.'

'I agree. If the wind is in the right direction in the morning we'll go for it.' Max reached for Annie's hand, squeezing it. 'What do you say, Missie?'

Annie smiled. 'If you think you are ready, Adam. Only don't take any foolish chances, will you?'

'Don't worry, I won't.' Adam glanced at Sarah. 'Are you coming out to the field to watch?'

The four of them had shared supper in Annie's room and now Sarah was clearing away.

'Yes, I think I will,' she said, piling plates together, 'if you really think something is going to happen.'

'I feel in my bones it is. Leave those things now and let's go for a walk. I could do with a breath of air and I want to talk to you.'

'Max and I will finish the dishes,' Annie offered. 'Take Adam out and make him relax for heaven's sake. He has a big day tomorrow.'

Sarah fetched her wrap and she and Adam went down the rickety iron stairway that led from Annie's room to the street below. It was a fine clear October evening with the smell of bonfires and of damp leaves in the air and in the cottage windows oil lamps shed their auroras of welcoming golden light. Sarah linked her arm through Adam's.

'Do you really think you can fly tomorrow?'

'I do. I've felt her almost ready to lift several times already. If I can get up enough speed I'm certain I can take off.'

She glanced at him, anxious suddenly. 'You will be careful, won't you?'

'Of course. Stop worrying.' He looked at her seriously.

281

'Now listen, once we have done what we set out to do and built an aeroplane that will fly I have other plans in mind. I mentioned them to you once before but I didn't get much response. This time, when I am a successful aviator, I hope I shall merit serious consideration.'

'What are you talking about, Adam?'

'I intend to ask you to marry me. Correction. I intend to marry you.'

They had reached the end of the lane, cottages became fields and at the entrance to them was a five-bar gate. Adam leaned against it and pulled Sarah into his arms. His mouth sought hers, his hands encircled her small waist beneath her wrap.

'Oh Adam . . .' *I love you*, she wanted to say but somehow she could not. The words hung on her tongue like thick honey and she could not speak them. Then he was kissing her and she was whirling in the vortex of desire which was becoming familiar but none the less exciting for all that.

'Well?' he teased. 'What have you got to say for yourself, Miss Thomas?'

She tossed her head, happiness lending her the ability to tease in return. 'Fly your aeroplane tomorrow, Mr Bailey, and I'll tell you!'

He laughed aloud. 'Very well, it's a deal. And I shall hold you to it.'

She smiled. Her whole being was a shout of joy. So Adam thought he could fly tomorrow. Great heavens, she was flying now!

'It looks as if tomorrow could be a momentous day,' she said.

The box kite bumped and lurched over the rough ground as Adam taxied to the top of the rise. There in the vastness of the field she looked small and fragile, a child's toy made of wood, fabric and bicycle wheels and held together with piano wire. But the wind was just right – when Max had held up a handkerchief to test it the fabric had barely stirred in the light breeze – and the engine sounded good and throaty. Listening to it Gilbert nodded his satisfaction.

There was no mistaking the tension in the air however, Sarah thought, looking from one to the other of the small group of watchers. In their own way each of them was so aware of the importance of the moment and the vulnerability of the aeroplane that it was almost unbearable. Max was bobbing up and down like a cat on hot bricks, Gilbert was tight-coiled as a wire, and although Annie's expression was serene as always her tightly clasped gloved hands betrayed the tension she was feeling. Only Alicia appeared to be enjoying herself. Her eyes were glittering, her lips parted in an expression that was almost feline. She had no fear for Adam's safety, no dread of disaster, for the failure would not be hers, though she would not hesitate to grasp her share of any triumph. Sarah looked away quickly, concentrating on the aeroplane which was now silhouetted against the cold clear blue of the sky.

She could never remember feeling quite this way before, not even before her very first parachute jump. Then she had been at the centre of the action and the danger had been her own. Now she could do nothing but watch, wait and pray. Silently her lips moved.

Please God let it fly. Don't let them be disappointed. And please God keep Adam safe. Most of all keep Adam safe . . .

From the top of the rise the view was stupendous. Beneath him the valley was laid out in a patchwork of green and the trees, russet and gold for autumn, made splashes of brilliant colour against the brittle blue of the sky.

There was a tension in him, pumping with the adrenaline through his veins yet at the same time he felt calm and utterly controlled, more determined than he had ever been in his life before. If willpower alone could take the box kite into the air then she would certainly fly – but mere willpower would not be enough. This was the moment to put to the test all their hard work and theorising, the design they had dreamed up together, the modifications they had agonised over. And they had it right. In his heart he was certain of it. Now it was all up to him.

He completed his turn so that the box kite faced down the slope into the valley. He could see the small group of watchers standing near the shed, he waved to them and saw Max raise his arm in reply.

I have to do it for Max, Adam thought. The aeroplane is his brainchild and he has backed it with every penny he is ever likely to have – now, it has to be said, almost all gone. If I can make his aeroplane fly it will make it all worthwhile – and he and Annie will be able to get married at last. And Sarah. I have to do it for Sarah too . . .

The thought gave added impetus to his determination. He drew his goggles down over his eyes and jammed his cap down firmly on his head. Then he set the nose of the aeroplane down the slope and opened the throttle wide.

The box kite began to move, slowly at first, bumping over the uneven turf, then gathering speed. The twin propellers were whirring now, scarcely more than a blur in the clear air; the ground raced by beneath the wheels and the wind blew the breath back into his throat. The sheer speed made him feel alive as never before, his brain sharp and crystal clear, his nerves and muscles ready for instant response. The moment of decision was his and his alone. He was taxiing now as fast as was safe. There was nothing between him and disaster except . . . flight!

His hand was steady on the stick, his grip firm. Now! He pulled back hard and felt the front of the machine rise. Excitement made him rash, too late he realised he had lifted too sharply. The nose was pointing skyward, his weight wrongly distributed. For a moment it felt as if he would tip over backwards and the force seemed to attach his stomach to his spine. For brief seconds he fought to control the bucking aircraft then he heard the sharp crack of splintering wood and felt himself falling. The aeroplane hit the ground again with a devastating crash and disintegrated around him. For a moment he knew nothing but a sense of shock, then, as he climbed gingerly from the wreckage, he realised the extent of the damage and felt sick with horror. The aeroplane lay like a broken bird, framework smashed to matchwood, fabric torn, propellers twisted. Gone – all gone – months of painstaking work and loving care now reduced to splinters.

Sarah was leading the others in a charge up the field, skirts bunched up to free her flying feet.

She threw herself at him. 'Adam! Are you all right? Oh my God!' Her voice was shaking, her face ashen.

'I'm fine.' He held her briefly, then as Max came panting up he put her aside. 'Max, old man, I'm sorry. I took her up too sharply . . .'

But Max was not looking at the devastation. His rubbery face was wreathed in smiles and he clapped Adam on the back.

'Never mind that! We can build it again. The thing is you flew. You realise that? You *flew!*'

And suddenly Adam was laughing with him.

'I did, didn't I? Great heavens, Max, we did it! Our aeroplane flew!'

Like a pair of whirling dervishes they grabbed one another, capering madly. And Sarah, trembling still from the tension and the shock, clasped her hands together and thanked God that her prayers had been answered.

Their elation was short lived. All very well to know that the aeroplane they had designed was capable of flight. All very well to relish those heady moments when the wheels had left the ground. All very well to be grateful to have escaped unhurt and knowing how to prevent a recurrence of that fatal but wholly understandable error in manipulating a giant man-made bird for the first time. The indisputable fact was that the aeroplane had been damaged beyond repair and there was no money left for building another.

'I think we have come to the end of the road, my friends,' Max said gravely as they sat around the huge old table which dominated Annie's little room glumly eating the meal that she had prepared as a celebration supper.

'But you can't give up now when you are so close!' Annie protested.

'We have no choice, my dear. The money left in the bank will barely support our living expenses for a few more weeks. It simply will not stretch to buy the things we should need to start rebuilding.'

Annie looked pleadingly at Sarah, who nodded gently.

'It's true, Annie.' Since she had become adept at book keeping she had taken on the settlement of accounts and she knew as well as Max did the paltry amount still lodged with the bank -- and the pile of invoices for goods still waiting to be paid. 'Short of a miracle I'm afraid it's all over. We shall be bankrupt in a matter of days rather than weeks.'

Adam said nothing. He sat gloomily in the overstuffed easy chairs, depressed by the knowledge that he was responsible for their predicament. The aeroplane was nothing but a heap of matchwood and it was all his fault.

'I can't believe you are going to give up now,' Annie said wretchedly.

Max put his arm around her shoulders. 'We won't give up. But first Adam and I will have to find jobs to keep our heads above water and save enough money to begin again. Isn't that right, Adam?'

Adam nodded, thinking of the family fortune which might have been his and experiencing, for the first time in his life, resentment towards his profligate ancestors. Just a small portion of the money that had been squandered and gambled away would have paid for the fresh start they needed.

'You can't afford that kind of delay,' Annie argued. Tears were shining in her eyes. 'You have said often enough that it is a race and you will be left miles behind. The Short brothers, Geoffrey de Havilland, A V Roe – they are all pressing on. I've even heard that George White of the Bristol Tramways Company is taking an interest. Oh Max, it's not fair!'

'Fair or not, I'm afraid that's the way it is. We simply do not have the money.'

Sarah looked from one to the other of them and knew suddenly what she was going to do.

'There might be a way,' she said. Three pairs of eyes turned to her. 'Don't ask me any questions for the moment,' she said, 'but don't despair just yet. Leave this to me.'

She sought Gilbert out in his *study next day before he left for the office.

'I want to talk to you about the aeroplane.'

'Of course, my dear. Sit down.' He indicated the low visitor's chair opposite his own deep leather swivel. 'What happened yesterday was a great shame but we must be thankful Adam was not hurt.'

'It was more than a shame – it was a disaster,' Sarah said. 'They were working on a shoestring and there is no more money for them to rebuild.'

'Oh dear.' Gilbert shook his head sadly.

Sarah knotted her hands tightly together in her lap. 'Before I go any further I must tell you they do not know I am speaking to you,' she said. 'It's entirely my own idea. But I can't stand by and see everything they have worked for thrown away. And so I want to ask you to back them.'

Gilbert sat back in his chair looking at her narrowly.

'And why should I do that, Sarah?'

Determination flared in her face. It was not the answer she had hoped for but she was not going to give up so easily.

'Because it would be to your advantage. They have designed an aeroplane that will fly but that design is useless unless they have the finance to rebuild it. Now if you would help them they could do it. A wonderful special aeroplane built here in Bristol. Think of the prestige for Morse Motors! Why, it could be the start of a whole new industry. I've been awake all night thinking about it and I'm sure I am right. Flying is the thing of the future. And you could be associated with it, not just as the builder of one engine, not just as the owner of the field where it first took off, but as the man with the foresight to finance it!'

Gilbert regarded her with a mixture of pleasure and pride. She had come to him for help but she had not come begging on bended knee but with a proposition which she had put with confidence and eloquence as well as good sense. He had been right to foresee a great future for Sarah. One day she would be quite a business woman. A smile lifted his mouth and twinkled in his eyes; Sarah saw and misinterpreted it.

'Don't laugh at me!' she said passionately. 'It is a good design – I know it is. And if you back Adam and Max I know you won't be sorry.'

His smile broadened. 'I happen to agree with you, Sarah,' he said.

Her strained expression became one of surprise and delight. 'You do?'

'Indeed. I must confess I have had thoughts on the same lines myself. Morse Motors needs to move with the times if it is not to be left behind. Max and Adam are two very clever – and brave – young men, and I would be proud to be associated with them. The only reason I have not suggested such an arrangement before is that I feared they might feel I was interfering. However if their situation is as dire as you say then it puts a whole different complexion on the matter. Ask them to come to Chewton Leigh to dine tonight and we will discuss it fully.'

Sarah hesitated. 'I don't suppose *you* could ask them? I would prefer them to think it was entirely your idea.'

'Very well. If you think it best. Now,' he glanced at his fob watch, 'I must be getting on. I have a full day ahead of me – including a meeting with my stock broker. If I am to finance this operation I can't afford to be late for that, can I?'

'No.' Her face was alight now. She rose, and almost without thinking, leaned across the desk and kissed him on the cheek. 'Thank you. Thank you for everything.' Then, embarrassed by her own action, she turned and hurried out of the study.

Chapter Twenty-Five

An hour later Sarah climbed the rickety staircase to Annie's room for she wanted to forewarn her friend about the dinner invitation. It might be late in the afternoon before the men got around to telling her about it and Annie would want to sort out something decent to wear.

When she tapped at the door there was no response and after a moment she tried it. It gave. 'Hello! Are you there?' she called. Then as her eyes grew accustomed to the dim light she saw Annie bent double over the little sink. After a moment the girl straightened up, wiping her mouth with her hand, and as she turned Sarah was shocked by her pallor.

'Whatever is the matter?' she asked.

'Nothing.' Annie smiled wanly.

'How can you say that? Are you ill? Is it something you ate?'

'No. Neither of those things.' Annie steadied herself against the sink. 'I'm pregnant, Sarah. I am going to have a baby.

'*What?*' Sarah stared in disbelief. 'But you can't be!'

Annie laughed but it sounded a little hollow. 'I'm afraid I am. Oh, don't look so shocked, Sarah, please. I know everyone else will be. But not you. I couldn't bear it.'

Sarah shook her head. She still could not believe her ears or the evidence of her eyes. Pregnant – Annie?

'But when . . . ? How . . . ?'

'It just happened,' Annie said simply, crossing to collapse into the overstuffed chair. 'I know it was very wrong. But we love one another so much and we've waited so long. I expect you think I am very wicked.'

'Oh don't be so silly!' Sarah said sharply. 'Of course I don't think you are wicked. Heaven knows, given the chance I might be in the same position myself . . .' She broke off remembering the electric tension that was there between her and Adam, the longing to be close, to give, that was so powerful it was almost unbearable. How could she be sure that given the right circumstances she would have been any stronger than the generous, affectionate Annie?

'Does Max know?' she asked.

Annie shook her head. 'No. I didn't want to worry him when he has so much on his mind. But I don't know how much longer I can keep it to myself, Sarah.'

'You goose!' Sarah said fiercely. 'You should have told me at least!'

'I didn't want to tell anyone – not even you, dear, until I'd told Max. I thought if the flight was a success I'd break it to him then. But now everything has gone wrong. And I'm not going to be able to hide it much longer, Sarah. My skirt was too tight to button up properly this morning so I'm going to begin to show soon.' An expression of pure panic crossed her face. 'Oh Sarah, what am I going to do? I can't be a burden to Max just now. I thought of trying to get rid of it but – oh, I couldn't do that.'

'I should think not!' Sarah exploded. 'Risk your life in the hands of some backstreet butcher? Annie, really!'

'It's not me I am worried about,' Annie said simply. 'If it would help I'd be ready for anything. But I couldn't destroy my own child – Max's child . . .' Her lip trembled. 'I thought of leaving him and running away somewhere he couldn't find me. But I can't do that either. Oh Sarah, I'm so afraid! I don't know what to do for the best . . .'

'Everything is going to be all right, you'll see.' Sarah crossed to kneel on the floor beside Annie's chair, taking hold of her trembling hands. 'Listen, I am going to tell you something – as long as you promise to keep it a secret. I have just been talking to Gilbert Morse. He has agreed to back Max and Adam by providing them with enough capital to rebuild the aeroplane and maybe pay them wages as well. He is very enthusiastic about the whole project and I know he is right to be. So you see things are not nearly as black as they seem. But the suggestion must come from Gilbert. I don't want Adam or Max to know I had anything to do with it. That's why I want you to promise not to breathe a word.'

'Oh Sarah!' Annie covered her face with her hands but the tears that trickled through her fingers were tears of relief. 'That would be wonderful! If things work out Max and I will be able to get married!'

'That's right,' Sarah agreed. 'Wait until Max knows the project is safe again, then tell him and we'll have a double celebration. But remember – not a word about my part in it.'

'I think they should know what you have done for them,' Annie said loyally. 'But if that's the way you want it, Sarah . . .'

'It is.'

Annie clasped her hand. 'Oh Sarah, I'm so glad that we are friends! And I hope that one day you will be as happy as I am now. You and Adam . . .'

Sarah smiled. 'I'll let you into another secret, Annie. Adam has asked me to marry him.'

Annie's face lit up with delight. 'That's wonderful! And you have accepted?'

'Not yet. I do love him but after being engaged before and hurting poor Eric so much I want to be quite sure this time.'

'But you are sure! You must be! You two make a perfect pair. And he adores you, I know he does. I've never seen Adam care for any girl the way he cares for you.'

A glow of warmth spread through Sarah's veins.

'Perhaps like you I was just waiting for the moment to be right,' she conceded.

They smiled at one another and in that moment it seemed to them both that nothing could go wrong in their world again.

Dinner at Chewton Leigh was over, the men had retired to the library for brandy and cigars and Blanche, pleading a headache, had gone to her room. Annie, still feeling unwell, had not joined the party and to Sarah's relief Max had accepted her excuse that she thought she was suffering from

291

a stomach upset without pressing her too far. The dinner had been a pleasant affair, the food and wine superb as always and the conversation easy and undemanding. But now Sarah and Alicia were alone.

'Well, Sarah, what shall we talk about to amuse ourselves?' Alicia asked facetiously. She was looking beautiful in a gown of cerise pink, her jet black hair drawn into a shining pompadour which served to emphasise the finely chiselled lines of her face.

'Do we have to talk at all?' Sarah countered. Her thoughts were very much with the men in the library where she guessed Gilbert would at this very moment be putting the terms of his propostion to Adam and Max.

As if reading her mind Alicia smiled, a trifle smugly.

'I dare say we both know why Father issued the invitation to dinner tonight,' she said, perching on the edge of the chaise and arranging her skirts around her.

Sarah turned to see the shrewd eyes, like chips of cold glass, upon her. 'I do, certainly. I did not know you were aware of it.'

Alicia's lips curved slightly. 'Father tells me everything. You of all people should know how close we are. His only regret, I think, is that I am not a boy.'

'I'm sure that's not true. He has three sons, after all.'

'And all of them a disappointment to him in one way or another. James should have been the girl and I the boy. But that is one of the tricks nature delights in playing, I suppose. And I intend to make sure that I, at least, do not disappoint him.'

Sarah made no reply and after a moment Alicia continued: 'Yes, I think father is determined to back the aeroplane. He even mentioned to me that he might think of setting up a separate company if the new tests are successful.'

'Really?' Sarah felt a prickling of excitement. This was more than she had even dared to hope for.

'Yes.' Alicia was watching her reaction closely, her features more feline than ever. 'It could mark an important step forward for them, Sarah. Provided of course that you do nothing to rock the boat.'

'Me?' Sarah said, surprised. 'What have I to do with it?'

'More than you realise. Father has two passions in life – the family empire – and me. If he could see the two merged together he would be a happy man.'

'I don't understand.'

Alicia lifted a slim hand to smooth her sleek pompadour. Rubies and diamonds, family heirlooms, glittered on her fingers and wrist.

'Come now, Sarah, I am sure you do if you only stop to think for a moment. It is Father's dearest wish that Adam and I should . . . form an alliance. Don't you see what it would mean to him? He would set up a company with himself and Adam as partners. A new *family* company, a generation of Morse Motors especially created for me, my husband and our children.'

Sarah's eyes widened. 'Your *husband*? You mean . . . Adam?'

'Of course. I made up my mind to have him, Sarah, a long while ago. And I would have won him by now if you had not stood in the way.'

'You are mad, Alicia,' Sarah said furiously. 'You have been spoiled, I know. You have always had everything you ever wanted. But even you should know you cannot buy love.'

Alicia's lips curved. 'Everything and everyone has a price, my dear. Adam wants to succeed with his flying machine very much.'

'Adam would never . . . You've got the wrong man. He is upright and honourable. And perhaps I should tell you that he and I . . .'

Alicia waved her to silence with an imperious gesture.

'Oh yes, I know all about you and Adam,' she said dismissively. 'I know he has eyes only for you – at present. But if you were not here I'd like to see how quickly he would change his tune.'

Suddenly, unaccountably, Sarah felt frightened.

'What are you saying, Alicia?'

Alicia was very still and in that stillness her power was more apparent than it had ever been.

'Go away, Sarah. You did it once before – you can do it again. No-one would be in the least surprised. Go away and leave Adam to me and I will see that his future is assured with all the scope and backing he needs to build a dozen aeroplanes and a position in his own company – our company – commensurate with his ability. I've even thought of a name for it – Morse Bailey. It sounds good, doesn't it? Adam will never regret it if he does as Father wishes and marries me. He is a generous man – you know that – and how much more generous would he be to his own daughter's husband? No matter how many expensive failures there may be along the way he will stand them. And eventually Adam will have all the success he has ever dreamed of. More probably. So you see, Sarah, it is not only my way you stand in by remaining here. It is Adam's.'

She smiled and the cold certainty of that smile infuriated Sarah.

'You bitch!' she said.

Alicia raised an eyebrow. 'My goodness, Sarah, wherever did you learn such language? Of course on reflection it is probably true but I don't mind you calling me names. Not when I hold all the cards.'

'You do not hold all the cards. Adam loves me.'

'And you love him. Which is why you will do as I say.'

Sarah was shivering in spite of the heat of the room, her blood like rivers of ice in her veins.

'And if I don't?'

'Then I will ruin him,' Alicia said calmly. 'I will make certain he does not get a single penny of Father's money. I can do that, make no mistake. However interested Father may appear to be now I assure you by the time I have finished he would not be prepared to allow Adam house room, never mind backing and accommodation, soft deals for engine building and a nice secure future. He and that crippled friend of his would be out of here so fast their feet would not touch the ground – and they would be lucky to find suitable work anywhere ever again. Father is very influential, you know.'

'Alicia you wouldn't!' Sarah cried, aghast.

'Don't try me, my dear. I think you know me well enough to be quite sure that I certainly would. And there is something else, too, just for good measure. Father never did hear the truth of what happened between you and Hugh, did he?'

Sarah was white now except for high spots of colour flaming in her cheeks.

'The truth of that matter is very far from what your stepmother made it out to be,' she said furiously. 'Perhaps it is time I told *my* version of it.'

Alicia smiled. As she had said, she held the winning hand – and she knew it.

'Who would believe you?' she asked. 'You attempted to seduce Hugh – succeeded for all I know – and you were packed off in disgrace. The truth was kept from Father to spare the pain of knowing that a girl he had befriended and treated with kindness and generosity could behave in such a despicable manner. Perhaps now it is time he learned exactly what a little viper he nursed in his bosom.'

'It is my word against Hugh's and Hugh is not here,' Sarah said. 'I was a child then but I am not a child any longer. Gilbert would know the truth when he heard it.'

'That his son was a rapist? That would make him very happy, Sarah. A nice way to repay him for all he has done for you.'

'Alicia, you are despicable,' Sarah said, her voice low and trembling. 'I always knew it but I never thought even you would stoop to this.'

Alicia's mouth quirked but her eyes had a faraway expression in them.

'Father gave you my doll once, do you remember? My lovely Sleeping Beauty. I vowed then, Sarah, that never again would I lose what I wanted to you. I intend to keep that vow.'

'Adam is no doll to be passed from hand to hand, Alicia.'

'Perhaps not. But if you care about him you will think about what I have said. You know what will happen if you do not.' She cocked her head. 'Listen! I believe the gentlemen are returning. You don't need to give me an

295

answer, Sarah. I shall know by your actions what you decide.'

The door opened and the men came in. Max and Adam looked pleased, Leo was scowling.

'Well,' Gilbert said expansively, 'we have had a most fruitful discussion. I hope you young ladies have enjoyed one another's company.'

'Oh yes,' Alicia said smoothly, 'Sarah and I have had a fruitful discussion too. Isn't that true, Sarah?'

For a moment Sarah was unable to reply. The bright hope that was shining out of the faces of Adam and Max seemed like the final nail in the coffin of her own dreams. Somehow she summoned a tight smile.

'We have had a long talk, yes,' she said.

The night seemed endless, sleep refused to come. At last Sarah rose from her bed and crossed to the window, looking out at the fields and hills that had been drained of all colour by the cold moonlight.

She had no choice. She had known it from the moment Alicia had laid down her ultimatum. She would do as she had threatened, Sarah had no doubts, if she was thwarted, for Alicia was totally ruthless. There would be no money for Adam and Max to build their aeroplane, no company to give them security, no future for any of them. Perhaps she and Adam could be happy together without those things but she knew she could not risk robbing him of all he had worked for. If she did she would never forgive herself. And there was Annie to think of too. Remembering her own childhood Sarah knew she could not sentence Annie's baby to a life of insecurity. It deserved a better start than that.

'I'll see they never work again,' Alicia had said and it was a threat Sarah dared not take lightly. There was nothing for it but to do as Alicia demanded, though how she could bring herself to say goodbye to Adam, and where she would go or what she would do she could not even begin to imagine.

In the trees below her window a gust of wind brought down a shower of leaves, a portent of coming winter, and the bare branches seemed to echo the bleakness of Sarah's heart.

She ran to the only haven she could think of, the only person in the world who could give her an excuse that would satisfy both Adam and Gilbert. And he welcomed her back with open arms just as she had known that he would.

'I know I treated you badly, Eric,' she said, 'but I promise I won't hurt you ever again.'

And happy only to have her back he asked no questions, made no demands, beyond asking if her return meant she would, after all, marry him.

'Oh yes, Eric, of course it does,' she whispered, and although she felt her heart was breaking, Sarah vowed that she would keep her promise. Eric must never know that there was someone she loved as she could never love him, never have the slightest inkling that she had come to him because it was the only way she knew to secure the future for Adam and for Annie and Max. She would be a good wife, make a home for him, bear his children. And she would do it with a smile on her face that would hide the pain inside. It was not the future she had hoped for but it would be – must be – enough.

Chapter Twenty-Six

'You flew, Adam! Sweet heaven you flew!' Max came running across the field at Chewton Leigh as fast as his short legs would carry him, tearing his cap from his head as he ran and tossing it high into the air. His face was alight with excitement and when he reached the box kite he capered around it like an animated puppet, almost beside himself in his moment of triumph. 'You were a good foot off the ground for at least forty yards. I was lying flat on the grass and when you went past me you were airborne, not a doubt of it!'

Adam eased himself out of the basket seat and climbed onto the field. He felt relieved but not elated; he had waited for this moment for so long that now it had come it brought with it almost a sense of anticlimax. He was tired from the long days and weeks he and Max had spent rebuilding and modifying and curiously joyless. The light had gone out of his life when Sarah had left and even progress with the aeroplane had almost ceased to matter. It had sustained him, it was true, and working on it to the point of exhaustion had kept some measure of sanity in his life. But the dedication had gone and the driving sense of purpose. He still wanted to fly, still wanted to be a pioneer in this new and demanding field, but the wanting was dull habit now not fiery obsession, and the setbacks had made him bad-tempered and depressed instead of grimly determined as they had done before.

Adam gave little thought to his changed attitude for he could never be accused of being introspective. His was a simple personality, painted in bold primaries, not with a palette of subtly blended shades. Now an uncharacteristic greyness had descended on him and though he refused to think of Sarah when he was working, yet she had a habit of creeping up on him unawares so that suddenly he would seem to see her face or hear her laugh and the pain of knowing that she was no longer his would overwhelm him, all the more potent for having taken him by surprise.

It hit him now as he climbed down from the aeroplane, the sudden treacherous falling away of his stomach at the realisation that his triumph was almost unimportant with Sarah not here to witness it. Max was clapping him on the back and he smiled briefly at his friend's delight, but it was as if he stood back from the scene somehow, a spectator rather than one of the chief participants, and he kicked at a turf torn up by the wheels of the aircraft with a sudden flash of impatience.

Damn it, how could she do this to him? Before he had met her he had been his own man, sure of his ambitions and untouched by anything but the most transient of affections for any of the women who had come his way. Then Sarah had come into his life and everything had changed. He had wanted her with a ferocity that had shocked him, he had wooed her, and he had thought he had won her. But all the time she had still been hankering after Eric Dare – and now she was married to him. He had heard the news from Annie, who corresponded regularly with Sarah, and again from Gilbert. Second-hand news of a second-hand love, he thought bitterly – and hated himself for caring so much.

'Are you going to give her another run?' Max asked.

Adam glanced towards the shed where Gilbert and Alicia stood watching, huddled up in overcoats and stamping their feet against the sharp clear cold of the December morning.

'Might as well give the audience something to make their visit worth their while,' Adam said and was surprised at the bitterness in his tone. Gilbert had every right to come to the field to watch – it was his money which had made this possible. And Alicia was an even more frequent visitor than he had been, her beauty and her expensive and fashionable wardrobe lending glamour to the proceedings.

'Now?'

'Why not?' He climbed into the basket seat while Max swung the propeller then taxied back up the field. Over the last weeks the feel of the rebuilt aeroplane had become familiar to him, he was beginning to know the sound of the engine in all its moods and the responses of the stick and rudder bar were now second nature to him. At the top of the rise he turned the aeroplane. The air was still with no threat of the sudden gust of wind which could prove disastrous; the scene laid out before him was rural England at its most peaceful – the trees, bare now for winter, stretching bony fingers towards the ice blue of the sky, a flock of sheep white woolly dots on the neighbouring hillside.

He thought again of Sarah who had first introduced him to this place and wished with all his heart that she was here now. Then with a stab of impatience he dismissed her from his mind, concentrating on the job in hand. He had taken the aeroplane off the ground once – for a good forty yards, Max had said. Now he must do it again, a little higher and for a little further. Sixty yards, maybe? Seventy? That would be about the limit he could safely achieve until he could get enough height to clear the hedge and take in the next field. He could get the height he was sure. It was simply a matter of easing back the stick gently and easily not with a jerk as he had on his first attempt at flying which had upset the balance and put too great a strain on the flimsy frame. But the more height he had, the more difficult landing would be. None of the hours of taxiing practice had equipped him for that tricky manoeuvre. He knew what he had to do, of course – reduce the propeller revolutions and pull back on the stick until just the right angle was reached, then stall the engine a foot or so above the ground. This was the theory he had evolved and he was sure it was the right one. But putting it into practice would be a difficult matter with only his own judgement to rely upon for both speed and height. Stall too high and disaster would follow, with the machine crashing down as she had done on the first flight trial, stall too late, touch down with the engine still running and she would bounce and buck like a bronco in Buffalo Bill's Wild West Show causing untold damage. No, landing after a flight of any height and distance was going to be tricky; he was glad there was no question of attempting it today with Gilbert and Alicia there to watch. Time enough for that when he and Max were alone and the aeroplane had proved herself skimming just above the ground.

He began his run down the slope, concentration now controlling every fibre of his being. At exactly the right moment he pulled back on the stick with the firm yet gentle pressure to raise the nose smoothly and felt the aeroplane lift. This time, more confident, he was conscious of a feeling of exhilaration. The rush of air felt good on his face, the smoothness of movement now that the ground was no longer bumping past beneath his wheels gave him the brief sensation of weightlessness. Encouraged he pulled on the stick a little more and knew without doubt this time that the aeroplane was responding. He was flying – he looked down at the grass and saw that his wheels were at least a foot clear. But there was no time to relish the sensation or the triumph before he had to put her down once again, bumping to a halt on the rough turf.

This time as he climbed down he saw that Gilbert and Alicia were making their way towards him. Gilbert looked pleased, Alicia, as always, wore an expression of inscrutability. She looked beautiful this morning in her coat of dark red wool, a small fur cap covering her glossy dark hair. With the release of tension singing in his veins he was aware of her for almost the first time as an extremely attractive woman.

'Well done!' Gilbert greeted him. 'That was magnificent!'

'Thrilling!' Alicia placed a small gloved hand on his arm; he looked at her and her eyes met his levelly. There was something in them he could not read – challenge, and something else . . . the hint of an invitation? The maleness in him responded to it briefly sending a surge of power through him and warming his loins. He looked away.

'You see, sir, I don't think your confidence in us was misplaced,' he said. 'That was only a brief hop but it is just the beginning.'

'I am sure it is,' Gilbert said. 'And I have two propositions to put to you gentlemen. One concerns you both, the other only you, Adam.'

A cold and unexpected blast of wind cut across the open field. How lucky it had not sprung up a few minutes earlier, Adam thought!

Gilbert shrugged his overcoat around him. 'By God it's cold all of a sudden! Shall we go into the shed to talk?'

Adam nodded his agreement. In spite of the wind he was not cold; heat was still coursing through his body in waves, making his skin glow. But he had felt a slight tremor in Alicia's hand, still lying on his arm, and he was suddenly solicitous for her well-being.

The shed was now scarcely recognisable as a byre, equipped as it was with work benches, a couple of chairs and Annie's sewing machine, and littered tools, discarded parts and wing fabric.

'I appreciate this is not the place for a full-scale business meeting,' Gilbert said, 'but I will outline what I have in mind so that the two of you can discuss it before we have more formal talks. I backed your venture because I had faith in it and the display I have witnessed today has proved me right – the machine is a success. Now I would like to see things on a more permanent footing so that we can begin to plan confidently for the future.' He paused, looking from one to the other, then continued: 'When the machine is perfected I want to put it into production. We have been building engines of one sort or another for three generations. Now I want to produce aeroplanes at Morse Motors –aeroplanes that will be recognised the world over as masterpieces of engineering. But I appreciate that the design – and the achievement – are yours. All I have done is provide backing – and build the engine to your specifications. Now what I propose is this. That we should set up a new company, incorporating the two of you together with myself and perhaps Lawrence and Alicia as directors.'

Adam glanced at Alicia. He had been expecting something of this sort; what he had not expected was that she would be included. But her expression remained serene, a small smile lifting the corner of her mouth. She had known about this, he realised, and she was in full agreement with it.

'It sounds a very sound plan to me,' he said smoothly. 'What do you think, Max?'

Max shrugged. 'I am a designer, not a businessman. I leave that side of things to you, Adam.'

'You do not have to give me an answer now,' Gilbert said. 'I realise you will want to think about it and talk it over. But I do urge you to realise the potential of what you have here. You are not a businessman you say, Max – and I dare say, truth to tell, neither is Adam – whilst I have at my disposal all the experience and expertise of finance and marketing as well as production facilities. Together we could take the world by storm with this aeroplane of yours. Alone . . . well, frankly I think you would soon find yourselves struggling.'

'I agree,' Max said. 'Though as you say, obviously Adam and I need time to discuss this together.'

'Of course. Now as I told you I have another proposition. You have been living alone, Adam, since Max married. I suggest that whilst we are working closely on the production of the aeroplane you should move into Chewton Leigh House. You would be a great deal more comfortable than at the inn, besides being close to the shed and it would be a great deal easier for us to iron out any problems. What do you say?'

'It's very civil of you, sir,' Adam said. He was surprised by the suggestion and he was not certain whether he liked the idea of surrendering his independence. But he could see the sense in it all the same and it did have a certain appeal. The room at the inn was poky and often tainted with the smell of stale beer and cigarette smoke which wafted up the stairs, the landlady's cooking was not always as appetising as it might have been and sometimes when the customers in the bar downstairs were rowdy it could be noisy – not the most congenial conditions for working or relaxing at the end of a hard day. In addition he missed Max's company and what he had taken easily in his stride when his friend was there to share it and joke about it became depressing and annoying now that he was alone.

'You may need to think about that too,' Gilbert said.

'But we shall be very disappointed if you refuse,' Alicia put in, and her cut-glass eyes left him in no doubt as to her meaning – for '*we* shall be disappointed' substitute '*I* shall be disappointed'. Once again, almost in spite of himself, he felt his quick response and a faint smile twisted his mouth. Sarah was the only woman he had been in love with and he loved her still. But Sarah was married to another man. Now here was the wealthy, charming and undeniably beautiful Miss Alicia Morse, toast of two counties, making him a tempting offer. Sometime, somehow, he had to burn Sarah out of his heart. Might he not just as well begin the exorcism now?

'I am not a man to take a lot of time weighing pros and cons,' he said. 'I am very grateful for the offer, sir, and I would like to take you up on it – for the time being at least.'

'Good.' Gilbert smiled. 'And if we are to be partners I suggest you drop the "sir". I think it is high time you began addressing me as Gilbert.'

He was flying now almost every day when the weather allowed, hopping further, gaining height, practising the tricky landing technique which he had planned, even banking the machine to execute big uneven figures of eight over the test field. Max was always there to inspect the machine after he had put her through her paces and he tried to remain patient and interested as Max deliberated, even putting forward some suggestions of his own. But he was becoming less and less interested in design except as a means of keeping him in the air for now at last he had confirmed to himself what he had always known in his heart was true – all he really wanted to do was fly. The glorious sensation that assailed him every time his wheels left the ground intoxicated him; like a drug addict desperate for his next fix, from the moment he landed he longed only for the moment when he could take off again. He fretted and fumed over time spent working on modifications although he knew how necessary they were and days when the weather prevented him from flying were sheer torture.

Up there in the skies he could forget Sarah for a little

while. Back on earth everything, even the tantalising Alicia, served only to remind him.

The day after that first momentous flight he had given notice to the landlord at the inn that he no longer required the room and the following week he had moved into Chewton Leigh House. The room which Gilbert had had prepared for him was in reality a small suite – bedroom, sitting-room and a dressing-room – and after the spartan conditions in which he and Max had lived at the inn it seemed the very height of luxury. Luxurious accommodation was not something Adam had been used to – or cared about very much but he looked forward to the evenings when dinner was over and the men retired to the library for Gilbert's customary brandy and cigars. The brandy was the finest old French cognac, the cigars panatellas which filled the library with a heady sweet aroma. But it was the conversation which Adam found most stimulating after a long day spent testing and refining in the company of Max.

Now that he had thrown the weight of his business empire behind their endeavours Gilbert's enthusiasm for the new venture was growing by the day. Good as his word he had formed the new company and was busy making plans to set up workshops adjoining the works and negotiating to buy the adjoining land so that tests could be carried out there. He was planning to transfer some of his most experienced engineers and craftsmen to the new project and had made tentative enquiries of his contacts in France to ascertain whether he might be able to persuade some of the experienced continentals to join the new team on a short contract basis at least. In Europe the French were still leaders in the race for the skies and their expertise would be invaluable. A carefully prepared statement had been issued to the press, the local newspapers had shouted the news that Morse Motors was moving into the new and exciting world of flying, and the national dailies, though more sceptical, had picked up the story and sent a reporter to Chewton Leigh to interview Gilbert about his plans.

Adam was slightly bemused by this turn of events. He and Max had scarcely looked beyond getting their first aeroplane into the sky; there had been no time for wondering where they would go or what they would do with it once their objective had been achieved. But Gilbert had set his mind to exploring all the possibilities and he outlined them one December evening to Adam, Lawrence and Hugh, home on leave from his regiment, over their customary brandy.

'As I see it there are two directions we can take once we have established a good sound base. The first is to look at the possibilities of aircraft for commercial use.'

'I don't quite follow you,' Lawrence said. Like Adam he was a little bemused but for different reasons. All his life he had known Morse Motors as manufacturers of engines; now with the planned expansion changing everything at the works he felt a little like a man who has started out for a quiet ride on a solidly plodding donkey only to find his mount had become a mettlesome stallion. Events were racing away from him and he felt disturbed and out of control. 'What sort of commercial use did you have in mind?'

'Every sort,' Gilbert said expansively. 'Think what a boon it would be to be able to airlift packages and mail direct from one given place to another! And eventually it won't only be correspondence and inanimate objects but human cargo too. When flying can be made safer and more comfortable there will be no shortage of passengers, mark my words.'

'Do you really think so?' Lawrence puffed on his cigar looking doubtful.

'I do indeed,' Gilbert confirmed. 'I dare say the steam engine was once treated with the same scepticism. But your great grandfather didn't let that stop him. Our business has been built on looking to the future, Lawrence, and we would do well not to forget it.'

'You mentioned a second use for aircraft,' Adam said, sipping his brandy. 'What else did you have in mind?

'Military reconnaissance,' Gilbert said.

In the startled silence that followed Hugh gave a short laugh.

306

'Is that a dig at me, Father? You know reconnaissance has always been the job of the cavalry.'

'Not entirely. Balloons have been used for the last hundred years to give men an aerial view of the enemy, as you are well aware. But balloons have to be tethered. What can be seen from them is limited. Now supposing an aircraft could actually fly far enough to scout out the lie of the land and what the enemy were up to and report back! Think what an advantage that would be to those planning strategy!'

The sense of the argument excited Adam. Gilbert was right – a bird's eye view of an opposing army would be a tremendous advantage in time of war. But Hugh, the dedicated cavalry officer, remained unconvinced.

'The noise would frighten the horses,' he said flatly.

'Perhaps the horses will have to get used to it,' Gilbert suggested. 'I have thought about it a great deal and I am convinced that supremacy in the air will play a great part in the wars of the future.'

Hugh laughed again, shaking his head in frank disbelief.

'You will be telling us next that one day wars will be fought in the air instead of on the ground or the seas.'

'I believe that is a possibility,' Gilbert replied simply. 'But it is up to us to convince the government of it. Do you know they set aside only £5000 to aeronautics this year?'

'£5000 too much if you ask me,' Hugh said rudely. His years at Sandhurst and with his regiment had served only to make his cavalier attitude more apparent – in the officers' mess he was regarded as a wag, the master of the sharp put-down, and the adoration of his men had increased his natural self-confidence so that it now verged on conceit.

'That is your opinion, Hugh, and I dare say you are entitled to it,' Gilbert said equably. 'It is not however the view of the German government. Whilst we had to be content with our miserly £5000 they were investing £400000 for the development of aeronautics.'

'More fools them.'

'I think not. Whatever the Germans might be they are not

fools. And if they – or any other nation – manage to get a good lead in that field I think we shall all rue the day.'

'Give me a good horse and a scout who knows the land any time. It's no use chasing the shadow and neglecting the substance.' Hugh drained his glass and grinned engagingly. 'Is there any more brandy, Father, or is that rationed too?'

'You know very well it is not. Help yourself, Hugh,' Gilbert said, shaking his head in mock exasperation. Hugh was still the apple of his eye and he regarded his outbursts with the same tolerance that had so often allowed him to escape punishment when he had got into scrapes as a boy. 'Just don't give yourself a hangover,' he added as an afterthought. 'Aren't you riding with Clarissa Beamish-Browne tomorrow morning?'

'I certainly am!' Hugh's eyes lit up at the prospect. Clarissa was one of the belles of the district. She liked fast horses and fast men – and she was always pleased to see him and ready to show her pleasure in a variety of ways, all equally agreeable. Why old Lawrence hadn't made some effort to sweet-talk her in his absence he could not imagine – but Lawrence seemed totally disinterested in the fair sex, preferring his own plodding pursuits. Ah well – each to his own, Hugh thought dismissively.

'Shall we rejoin the ladies?' Gilbert suggested when Hugh had finished his brandy.

They went back to the drawing-room where Blanche and Alicia were listening to some music on the phonograph Blanche had recently acquired and Adam could not fail to be aware of Alicia's quickening interest the moment he entered the room. She had been glancing through the latest edition of the *Englishwoman's Domestic Magazine* between winding up the phonograph; now she laid it aside on the small octagonal table.

'Well and what have you gentlemen been discussing?' she asked lazily. 'No – don't tell me – let me guess. The future of our new venture – Morse Aeroplane Company. Well, as a director I really think you should enlighten me on your deliberations.'

'For heaven's sake, Alicia!' Blanche protested. 'Can't we forget the business whilst we are relaxing?'

Alicia threw her a shrewd glance. She knew Blanche was irritated by the fact that she had been included as a director of the company – she believed that if another member of the family had had to be named it should have been Leo.

'Don't you think you are taking your position just a little too seriously?' Blanche continued lightly.

'I agree,' Hugh said. Unnoticed by his father he had brought the brandy decanter into the drawing-room with him; now he refilled his glass surreptitiously and swigged at it. 'We have had quite enough of flying for one evening.'

'Well if the rest of you refuse to tell me what has been discussed I am sure Adam at least won't be so mean.' She leaned forward, her violet eyes narrowed in her pale face, and touched his arm lightly with her slim fingers. The tight bodice of her dinner dress emphasised the curve of her small firm breasts, light from the overhead chandelier made her glossy black hair gleam with midnight blue highlights.

'Don't dare, Adam,' Hugh cautioned him jokingly.

Alicia shrugged her narrow shoulders. 'Oh well, if you are going to be so tedious Adam and I will have to talk on our own sometime, won't we, Adam?' she said without removing her hand from his arm and her look left him in no doubt that it was not only business she wanted to discuss when they were alone.

Again he was aware of the quickening deep inside him. One of these days . . . he thought, one of these days, Miss Alicia Morse, you are going to get what you are asking for.

'Now you have returned, gentlemen, I suggest one of you might wind up the phonograph,' Blanche said.

'Very well, I'll do it,' Lawrence said good naturedly, moving towards it whilst Hugh poured himself yet another brandy and Gilbert crossed to warm himself by the roaring fire. But Adam remained where he was, drawn against his will by the magnetism Alicia exuded and the pleasurable sensation her touch had started in his stomach, warming it as the brandy had done.

She was not Sarah. Oh no, there was only one Sarah. But

she was a very attractive woman – and he was a man. She did not stir his heart, but by God she could stir his body. After the havoc Sarah had wreaked with his emotions he had little desire for anything else. Perhaps, he thought, it would be enough.

Chapter Twenty-Seven

The snow came in the night, covering the countryside in a soft white blanket. The moment he awoke the strange luminous light it cast through the gap in his curtains announced its arrival to Adam and he swore softly, turned back the covers and padded across to the window.

It lay unbroken as far as the eye could see, deep and smooth over the parkland, whipped into long flowing ridges and waves by the wind further out on the slopes of the meadow. The thick crust on his window sill gave him some idea of the depth of it and the way the bare branches of the trees hung low beneath its weight confirmed the assessment. This was not just a passing flurry but the onset of a sudden harsh spell. What was more it was still snowing, small firm flakes falling steadily from a leaden sky.

Adam swore again. There would be no flying today – or for some days to come if the look of the sky was anything to go by. They had been very lucky with the weather so far this winter and it was unreasonable to expect the mild spell to continue for ever. But it was infuriating to have to suspend tests now, just when things were going so well.

Adam shivered, padded into his dressing-room and pulled on his trousers. His obsession with teaching himself to fly was such that he was jealous of every hour of every day; the thought of a spell of enforced inactivity was anathema to him. But perhaps at least they could usefully employ the time attempting to fix a passenger seat to the aeroplane. Some time ago Max had expressed the desire to be taken up for a flight as soon as possible but so far other modifications had taken precedence. Maybe today while Max attended to the finer technical details Adam could be working out the best position for a passenger seat and deciding how best to construct it.

This plan was short lived, however, for when the family

311

gathered for breakfast Adam learned to his dismay that the snow had almost certainly made him a prisoner in the house for the day at least.

'Bloody annoying!' Hugh was saying as he helped himself to kidneys and bacon from the silver chafing dishes. 'I'm only here for a few days and I have to choose the very week when we get snowed in!'

'Surely there is some way out?' Adam said.

'If there was I promise you I'd know about it!' None the worse for his excess of brandy the previous evening Hugh was piling his plate high. 'I have an appointment with Clarissa this morning, remember. No, the way this place lies in the fold of the hills we get drifts, God knows how deep, on every side. If the snow comes during the day we can at least have a crack at keeping the road open, though we can't always guarantee it. But when it comes at night we haven't a cat in hell's chance.'

'Can't we dig ourselves out?' Adam suggested.

'Until it stops snowing there's no point. As fast as we clear one bit another will drift over and you might as well resign yourself to it.'

'But for how long?'

Hugh shrugged. 'Who knows? It doesn't often last down here like it does further north. But I remember once we were cut off for a week. Sickening, isn't it?'

Adam made no reply but he resolved that whatever conditions might be he had no intention of remaining marooned for a week. There was far too much to do. If only he could get to the shed it would not be so bad – but if the roads were impassable common sense told him it was quite out of the question to even think about reaching the shed. Fuming with impatience he helped himself to bacon and coffee.

They were soon joined by Gilbert, Lawrence and Alicia. Both men were as annoyed as Adam by the vagaries of the weather but Alicia seemed merely amused by their incarceration. She was looking lovelier than ever this morning, Adam noticed, in a warm red woollen gown, her clear skin seeming to reflect the whiteness of the snow. Since today

312

there was no reason to hurry they lingered over breakfast but when the last of the coffee had gone Gilbert and Lawrence departed to the library to work on what papers they had with them and Adam put on his boots to investigate conditions outside.

He soon discovered they were every bit as bad as Hugh had predicted, deep drifts making it impossible to get much further than the stable-yard, and after exchanging a few words with the grooms who were plodding through the swirling whiteness to attend to feeding and watering the horses he had to admit defeat and go back indoors.

All morning the snow continued to fall and after lunch Adam decided to spend the time making some drawings that would help with the construction of the passenger seat on the aeroplane. It was warm and cosy in his small sitting room with a log fire blazing in the grate and sending showers of sparks up the chimney. He sat at the writing table, absorbed in his work, and when he heard the door opening softly he looked up in surprise to see Alicia standing there.

'May I come in?' she asked.

'Yes, of course,' he said, though he was annoyed at the interruption.

She came in, closing the door behind her, and crossed to the fire to warm her hands.

'You look very busy,' she said conversationally. 'What are you doing?'

He explained and though she listened he sensed her mind was not entirely on what he was saying.

'I think it is most amusing the way you men all mind so much about being snowed in,' she said at last. 'I should have thought you would be only too pleased to take an enforced break. I can understand Hugh's annoyance of course – he is furious at not being able to enjoy Clarissa's company, but the rest of you . . . Father and Lawrence have locked themselves away in the library and here are you, still thinking about nothing but your aeroplane even though it will probably be weeks before you can fly it again.'

'I certainly hope not!' he said with feeling. 'And judging

by what you were saying last night I should have thought you would be as frustrated as we are.'

She turned, cocking her head to one side. Firelight gleamed on her raven hair.

'Oh no, Adam, I can think of nothing nicer than being cut off for weeks and weeks from the outside world – especially if I am cut off with you!'

In spite of the veiled invitations of the past weeks her boldness startled him. She smiled, pretending not to notice.

'You promised last night to initiate me into the mysteries of what is going on in the company of which I am a director,' she said silkily. 'I thought that since we are alone now was as good a time as any to begin.'

I promised nothing of the kind, he thought, but the blood was beginning to pound at his temples and congest in his body.

'You know you don't give a fig for the business, Alicia,' he said roughly.

'That is not true!' she protested. 'I am very proud to be a director.'

'Perhaps, but it is only a game to you. Just as I am. Why do you persist in trying to make me seduce you?'

She smiled again, standing there quite still before the fire.

'Perhaps because I want you to,' she said softly.

He felt the breath ragged in his throat.

'You don't know what you are saying.'

'Oh yes I do. And you are wrong when you accuse me of playing games with you, Adam. I have never been more serious in my life. Come here.'

He almost did as she bade, so great was the power of her magnetism and the response throbbing through his body. But his very masculinity stopped him. He was not a man to be manipulated and seduced by a woman, however attractive. When he took her – if he took her – he would make sure that he was the initiator. He got up, leaning back against the desk, arms folded.

'You want to know about the business, Alicia. Very well – I shall tell you. I expect it will bore you to tears, knowing

314

as I do your scant interest in it. But you can hardly admit that now, can you?'

Inwardly she swore yet his unyielding dominance was inflaming her. She had planned to use her sexuality to possess Adam body and soul, now to her chagrin she found herself hoist with her own petard. As he talked, outlining plans, describing laws of aerodynamics, she sat on the chintz covered chaise, hands folded tightly to keep them from trembling, eyes demurely lowered because to look at him would have been unbearable torture. Beneath her petticoats her thighs were pressed together as tightly as her hands; they were sensitised and she felt small prickles of desire flickering over them to the congested and most secret places of her body. Why ever was it said that a woman could not enjoy these sensations? she wondered. Why ever was it whispered that sex was a disgusting animal activity which a woman must endure in order to satisfy a man's basest instincts? She raised her eyes from his shining brown boots, stealing a glance at the long hard columns of his legs which the narrow cut of his trousers did nothing to conceal and longed to feel them wrapped around her, another upward glance at his body, lean yet undeniably powerful beneath the matching jacket and waistcoat, and her breath was so tight in her throat she could scarcely breathe. She lowered her eyes quickly again, not daring to look him in the face. He was still talking, endlessly it seemed, and she had heard not a single word, yet she knew she could have gone on listening to that dark brown voice forever, caressing every rise and fall, intoxicated by the harsh masculinity of it. Her flesh rose and crept in willing response to the tumbled thoughts which seemed to come not from her brain but from the very core of her being and the curious white light reflecting into the room from the snowcovered landscape outside the window imbued her every thought, every emotion, with a dreamlike sense of unreality.

Suddenly she was aware that his tone had changed. He was not lecturing her any more but asking her a question.

'Well? How did you enjoy your lesson on the birth of the aeroplane industry?'

315

Her eyes flicked up. He saw something akin to panic in their violet depths. 'It was very interesting . . .'

The corner of his mouth curled. 'Good. Come here then.'

'But . . .' After all her planning, all her longing, the panic he had glimpsed suddenly paralysed her. She sat very still, hands and thighs still pressed tightly together. He stretched out his hand.

'Come here, I said.' There was no tenderness on his face or in his voice. In that moment he looked almost cruel. She stood up, took two steps towards him. 'So, one lesson is over. Now it is time for the other.'

He caught her hand, pulled her towards him and kissed her on the mouth. The brutality of his lips made her gasp but the weakness in her thighs was spreading now so that she felt oddly formless. After a moment he held her away, looking at her, and his eyes were dark and unfathomable. Then very deliberately he unfastened the top button at the neck of her dress and then the next. She stood motionless. This was not the way she had planned it – not at all! She had seen herself seducing him slowly, easing his shoulders out of his jacket, running her hand lightly but firmly over the rippling muscles of his back, teasing his nipples with her lips . . . But how could she protest? She had offered herself to him, after all.

One more button and he was still completely in control. 'Take it off,' he ordered.

She could not tear her eyes away from his. They remained locked, the dark brown and the violet, as she unfastened the remaining buttons and let her dress whisper to the floor. His eyes left hers then, running down the length of her body, taking in the whiteness of her shoulders and the curve of her small breasts above her chemise, her tiny tightly corseted waist and the resulting sweep of her petticoats, two layers of white muslin topped by scarlet taffeta. She saw a muscle move in his cheek. For seemingly endless moments they stood there, then he moved, lifting her bodily as if she weighed no more than a feather and carried her to the chaise. She lay transfixed against the cushioned arm while he towered over her, unbuttoning his

316

waistcoat and his trousers. Then his weight was upon her, one hand freeing her breasts from the covering chemise, the other removing her frilled cotton drawers. She gasped as his mouth took her breast, gasped again as he entered her. And suddenly her body came alive again and she arched towards him, relishing the sharpness of his teeth and the grinding strength of his body, giving herself up to a paroxysm of passion the like of which she had never experienced before. He was in her and around her, suffocating, possessing. Alicia felt the beginnings of a scream rise in her throat but it was a scream of pleasure now. She twisted her fingers in his hair and raked his back with her nails. Even when he was still she moved against him until her own need climbed to its zenith, hung poised for a moment in exquisite heart-stopping abandon, then descended on a sobbing sigh to the planes of reality. Yet reality was not as it had been before. Now there was a warmth and a languorousness which was all-encompassing and far deeper than any fleeting moment of triumph and a desire to be with him for ever, to feel his weight pressing her into the chaise for ever, to sleep here with him and in sleeping to die because that way alone could she be sure that there would never be anyone else for either of them, no other stolen moments to detract from the glory of this moment, no intrusion of everyday life to mar its wonder.

'Adam . . .' she whispered. 'Oh Adam . . .'

He moved, rolling away from her and standing up. His back was towards her, he was dressing himself, and the sense of abandonment ripped at her heart. 'Adam!' she said again.

'Would you excuse me, Alicia? I have work to do.' His tone was cold and hard; she could scarcely believe it. He couldn't be speaking to her like this – not after what they had just shared.

She reached for his hand. 'Adam, please . . .'

He drew it away. 'I thought your purpose in coming here was to seduce me,' he said. 'Haven't you got what you wanted?'

'No – no!' she sobbed. She had never been less in control of herself.

'Forgive me,' he said coldly. 'But that was certainly the impression you gave me.'

She was trembling now, her dreams falling about her ears.

'You can't leave me like this . . .'

'Why not?'

'You wanted me, just as I wanted you.'

'Perhaps. In that case we should both be satisfied. It was a pleasant interlude, Alicia, nothing more.'

Suddenly she was angry, her passion and desire turning to a cold fury. She was Alicia Morse. No-one treated her like this, no-one – certainly not this arrogant upstart.

'We'll see about that,' she said. 'You wanted me then and you'll want me again. As often as I choose.'

He laughed. The sound of his laughter roared like the sea in her ears.

'Oh, Alicia, I'm afraid you have had your own way too often and for too long. If I want you again it will be when *I* choose. I should have thought this afternoon would have taught you that at least.'

She drew herself up. Even standing there clad in nothing but her disarrayed corset and petticoats she had a dignity which was awesome.

'You are forgetting something, Adam. My father holds the purse strings. Without his support you would be nothing – nobody. That is what you were before and that is what you will be again unless you do as I want. What would my father say if he knew you had just raped me?'

'I did not rape you. I gave you what you have been begging for for weeks.'

'That is not what I shall tell Father. And we shall soon see which of us he believes. Are you willing to take that chance, Adam?'

He looked at her coldly. She could scarcely believe that such a short time ago they had been united in passion. Perhaps this was what they meant, the old wives, when they said it was a man's world, she thought. Perhaps they did not mean that a woman could not enjoy making love, but that afterwards she was unable to detach herself from the act as

318

Adam seemed capable of doing. *Man's love is of man's life a thing apart, 'Tis woman's whole existence* . . .

He was fully dressed now and more distant from her than he had ever been.

'Good afternoon, Alicia,' he said politely as if they had done nothing more than share a pot of tea together. 'I really must ask you to excuse me.'

Her fury at his rejection drove iron splinters into her heart. She would show him! Oh yes, she would show him he could not treat her like this!

She stepped into her dress, fastening it with fingers that trembled. In the doorway she paused. Already he was back at his desk, head bent over the pages of diagrams and calculations. He was not even bothering to look at her.

'Very well, Adam, I will go now,' she said and her calm voice belied the turmoil within her. 'But don't think it's over. Because I assure you it is not.'

Then without waiting for his reply she went out and closed the door after her.

She came to his room again that night because she could not stay away. She had lain for a while listening to the house grow quiet under the mantle of snow but unable to sleep for the fire which burned again in her veins and across her skin in slow rashes of desire and at last she rose, pulled on her wrap over her nightgown and crept along the silent corridor, terrified he might reject her yet quite unable to resist another attempt to initiate the closeness she longed for and this time hoped to prolong.

His light was still burning as he sat at his desk working on yet more calculations but this time when she entered the room he showed no surprise. He got up without a word, took her hand and led her to the bedroom. Again the encounter was tumultuous, his mastery of her complete as he knelt astride her, taking her with thrusts which made her writhe in painful ecstasy, but afterwards he did not dismiss her but lay beside her, stroking her hair as it spread out on the pillow in a shining cascade with a hand lying on her naked belly in a gesture of careless possession.

For a while she lay glorying in the rosy glow which suffused her body and the wetness between her thighs, then she began to be afraid they might fall asleep here together and be discovered in the morning and reluctantly stirred herself. As she slipped away his breath was deep and even and only then did she realise he was already asleep.

She crept out of his room and back to her own. Hardly a word had passed between them but her resolve was stronger than ever. He did want her, just as she had known he did, just as she wanted him! And she would have him, not just on odd stolen occasions but all the time – as her husband. She had made up her mind to that long ago, now his desire for her, though without a single gesture of commitment, had given her the power that she needed.

Back in her own bed Alicia ran her hands over her body which his hands had so lately touched, cupping the place where the wetness had now dried to stickiness, as if by so doing she could keep something of him within her and relishing the drowsy dreaming contentment until she fell asleep.

Adam was in the library next day when Gilbert came in.

'Adam, my boy, I am glad to see you alone. I understand you wish to speak to me.'

Adam, who had been deep in thought, looked up, puzzled. There was an unmistakeable twinkle in Gilbert's shrewd blue eyes and the first alarm bell began to ring in Adam's head. 'At least, Alicia told me you did.' Gilbert qualified.

'Ah!' Adam said guardedly. He crossed to the window. 'No break in the weather yet then,' he said to give himself time to think.

'No, it will be another day at least before the roads are passable,' Gilbert agreed. 'But from what Alicia said I did not think it was the weather you wanted to talk to me about.'

He joined Adam at the window. 'I know this sort of thing isn't easy,' he said, wry amusement in his tone. 'I remember how nerve-racking I found it when I had to speak to Rose's father. Rose was my first wife, you know. Thank goodness Blanche was a widow whose parents were long since gone so I did not have to go through the whole performance again. But I certainly recall how embarrassing such conversations can be and I am glad Alicia had the good sense to tell me herself what you had in mind – though I suppose it's hardly etiquette, I don't think we should let that bother us, do you?'

Adam was suddenly filled with the firm conviction that he knew exactly how a shipwrecked mariner must feel when a strong tide takes control of his flimsy raft.

'Alicia has spoken to you?' he repeated. 'What did she say?'

Gilbert smiled. 'That the two of you had fallen in love and would like to be married, of course – and that you intended to seek my permission. Well, I am saving you the trouble, Adam. I was delighted at the news and most relieved that Alicia is ready to settle down at last – and with a man like yourself, not one of those scallywags she has brought home in the past. There is no-one I would be more happy to have as my son-in-law. When you are one of the family we shall be able to work together admirably and I know if anyone can tame Alicia it is you. So you see, my boy, I don't expect you to plead your suit and I shall not be interrogating you as to your prospects. As far as I am concerned, you have my blessing.'

'Thank you,' Adam said faintly.

'One other thing,' Gilbert continued. 'I dare say it is a little early to be talking of wedding presents when the engagement is not yet announced. But I would like to tell you all the same what my personal gift to you will be. I intend to change the name of the new company to include your own. It has long been my hope that Alicia could be a part of the family firm – that was the reason I made her a director, though I realise it is an unusual step for a woman. And if you are to be my son-in-law then I feel it it is only right that you should have proper acknowledgement. Morse Bailey Aeroplane Company sounds quite impressive, don't you think?'

'I do indeed,' Adam said.

Dumbfounded as he was he could not help admiring the sheer audacity of Alicia's move. Little minx – she had promised him it was not over and backed up her promise with a shot that was almost breathtaking in its audacity. She knew he was not a man to be manipulated or threatened, but she had done it so cleverly, baiting a sweet trap with such tempting inducements that the steel teeth were all but hidden.

Adam shook his head, unexpectedly aware of a sense of exhilaration. A minx she might be, but Alicia had an attraction that was all her own. Her determination and daring in going after what she wanted made her a worthy adversary and the thought of the battles ahead excited him suddenly. At the moment it was she who was calling the tune. But it would not always be so. Already he had two distinct choices – to call her bluff and take the consequences, fighting every inch of the way, or to go along with the plan and marry her, taking advantage of the obvious benefits which would come his way as Gilbert's son-in-law whilst clawing back the initiative from her in other, subtle ways. The prospect of regaining the ascendancy was almost an aphrodisiac, and he found himself remembering the pleasures of the previous night and the eager response of her body. Dammit, maybe I am a little in love with her, he thought. Maybe I was so blinded by Sarah I could not see it.

Sarah. The mere thought of her was painful to him and quite suddenly he knew his mind was made up. Sarah was lost to him. She was married to Eric. If he continued to moon over her he was a fool. Forget Sarah. And what better way to do it than to marry Alicia who had so much to offer?

'Well, Adam, we shall be able to tell Alicia we have had our little talk, shall we not?' Gilbert held out his hand; when Adam took it his touch was firm and cool. Not for the first time Adam thought how much he liked Gilbert. 'Welcome to the family, my boy.'

Chapter Twenty-Eight

Sarah read and re-read the letter and still the words blurred before her eyes. Adam and Alicia were going to be married. Tears ached in Sarah's throat and she crumpled the letter into a ball and tossed it onto the fire which blazed in the hearth.

Stupid to be upset – or surprised. It was her own decision to leave which had left the field clear for Alicia. Stupid to have hoped, almost without realising it, that Adam might still care for her too deeply to allow Alicia to win him over. And more stupid still to feel disappointed that he was not wise enough to see the real Alicia behind the charming mask. When she so chose Alicia could be as amusing as she was tantalising – and she had so much to offer. Marrying her would be much to Adam's advantage. Why, already his name was linked with Gilbert's in the title of the new company – Morse Bailey Aeroplane Company. It sounded so grand, so important – and without a doubt it would be highly successful.

I am being selfish, Sarah thought, selfish and greedy. I have so much it is quite unreasonable for me to begrudge Adam the chance of happiness.

'Sarah – are you there?' Eric called to her from the hall and he came in carrying a bunch of deep yellow and bronze chrysanthemums. He smiled as he presented them to her, the pleasant smile that came so readily these days since she had become his wife. 'I got these from the flower seller outside the railway station. She didn't have red roses, I'm afraid, but the sentiment is there just the same.'

'Oh Eric, you are too good to me!' Sarah put up her face to be kissed, and her smile did not betray anything of the heartache she was feeling. She had grown quite good at pretending, she thought with some pride, and she had kept her secret promise to Eric that she would do nothing to make him regret having married her.

It was her good fortune of course that she had always been fond of Eric and enjoyed his company so the charade was not as difficult as it might have been and he was so besotted with her and so happy to have her back that he made no undue demands. He was content to have her with him, helping him at the Alexandra Palace workshops by using her newly acquired skills to keep the books for him and Henry, accompanying him to ballooning meets and sometimes going with him on ascents or races though she no longer took part in aerobatic displays as she had once done, and sharing his bed. He did not notice the wistful look that came into her eyes when the new aeroplanes were discussed, he did not know that sometimes after they had made love she would lie awake, staring into the darkness, her cheeks wet with tears. When he turned to her she was always there and it was more than he had dared to hope for. He loved her, took care of her and gentled her, and in return he received the warmth of which he had always known she was capable. And now there was an additional reason to bring them close and make him glow with happiness and pride. Sarah was going to have a baby – their baby. It was not due until the summer but already he could see the thickening of her waist, the new fullness in her breasts, and he could hardly wait. Always tender towards her, always solicitous of her welfare, he swelled now with a love which made him doubly attentive; the flowers he had brought her were simply one more gesture, one more tangible way of expressing that love.

'How are you feeling?' he asked now. 'When I came in I thought you looked a little peaky.'

'It's nothing really.' She smiled at the flowers, pulling the wrapping paper aside to expose the full beauty of the blooms. 'I must put these in water.'

She went through to the kitchen, small and compact like the rest of their house, yet at the same time bright and neat, reminiscent of the cosy rooms at Molly Norkett's which had always seemed to Sarah the very epitome of what a home should be. As she filled a large china jug with water Eric followed her into the kitchen.

'The news stands are full of the election,' he informed her. 'It seems that the results were something and nothing. Asquith has been returned again but without a clear-cut majority it's doubtful he'll be able to govern for long without going to the country again.'

Sarah broke the stem of a chrysanthemum and propped it in the vase. Politics had never interested her greatly but she remembered Gilbert's somewhat surprising espousement of the Liberal cause and the memory heightened her feelings of poignancy.

'I had a letter from home today,' she said, putting the last flower into the vase and standing back to admire the effect. 'Alicia and Adam are to be married. In May. We are invited to the wedding.'

'Oh really?' His tone was as light and casual as hers. 'Will you feel like travelling by then do you think?'

'I see no reason why I shouldn't. I am disgustingly fit, Eric, as well you know, and I should like to go. For one thing, Annie's baby will be born by then, for another . . .' She broke off, aware of how close she had come to putting into words the perverse longing to see Adam again even while she shrank from the thought of watching him exchange marriage vows with Alicia. 'I think Gilbert will expect me to be there,' she said. 'Unless of course you think it will be embarrassing for me to be seen in public in my condition . . .'

'Embarrassing? For whom? Certainly not for me! You know how proud of you I am, my dear.' He caught at her hand, pulling her into his arms, and she laid her head against his waistcoat, glad he could no longer see her face. All very well to pretend; when her heart was breaking it was such a dreadful effort to conceal it!

'I love you, Sarah,' he whispered into her hair. 'You have made me a very happy man. Never forget that.'

She nodded silently, unable to reply. Her throat was constricted by tears.

And then suddenly she was aware of the tiniest of flutters deep within her. At first, lost in her thoughts, she failed to recognise the significance of it, then as it came again she stood quite still, her hand flying to her waist. The baby had moved. Where a moment before there had been only bleak despair now a sense of wonder began to creep in. She held her breath waiting to see if the flutter would come again. When it did she gave a little gasp. Concerned, Eric held her away.

'What is it, my love?'

'The baby! It moved!' The wonder was spilling into her voice; for the moment Adam and Alicia were forgotten. 'See if you can feel it!'

She caught his hand, pressing it against her waist, and for a moment they waited.

'I can't feel anything,' Eric said at last, disappointed.

'No. It was very faint. But it was there!'

'Our baby!'

'Yes.' She held tight to the thought. Somehow it seemed a little like an omen that she should have felt the baby move for the first time today, just when she had learned of Adam's impending marriage.

An old saying of Molly's crept into her mind. Whenever God closes a door somewhere he opens a window.

That part of my life is finally over, she thought. Now I have to look to the new beginning, not just with my mind and my body but with my whole heart. For my baby's sake if nothing else.

She laid her head on Eric's chest again and experienced a moment's complete peace.

Adam and Alicia were married in the full flush of May-time when the trees that surrounded Chewton Leigh were full with fresh green leaf and the apple-blossom hung against the clear blue sky in clouds of lacy white. The wedding was the grandest the village had seen in decades and as a topic of conversation it vied with the news that the King had passed away, providing a spectacular and happy celebration in the village church to efface the solemn service which the Vicar had hastily arranged to mark the royal death. Few people in the village had ever so much as set eyes on the King, and though the carnal excesses which had caused so much

326

disquiet when he had been Prince of Wales were more or less forgotten now and he had proved, in the end, a popular monarch, the long faces and black armbands which some of the older folk felt obliged to wear as a mark of respect were gladly enough discarded with the wedding of the daughter of the local 'gentry' as an excuse.

Initially, when he heard the news of the King's death Gilbert wondered if he should cancel the supper dance and firework display which he had arranged to mark the occasion and to which all his tenants and employees had been invited, but after some deliberation he decided this would cause too much disappointment and in any case there was always the accession of the new king, George, to honour.

On the day of the wedding the village turned out in force to watch Alicia, resplendent in cream lace, arrive at the church on the arm of her father. Inside, with the candles radiating a golden glow and illuminating the flowers that were banked around the stone pillars and the base of the pulpit, Sarah sat in a daze of unreality. From her pew on the left-hand side of the aisle she had a perfect view of Adam as he stood at the altar rail waiting for his bride and when the organ announced her arrival and he turned around to watch her approach their eyes met briefly. Sarah felt the hot colour rush into her cheeks and she looked down quickly, fixing her eyes on her order of service so that she missed seeing Alicia glide by, her heavy lace veil and demure expression barely masking the glorious swell of triumph she was experiencing.

The wedding breakfast was to be held in the banqueting room at Chewton Leigh House; here were more banks of flowers, tables laid with crisp white napery, gleaming silver and crystal and a dais for a trio of musicians to play chamber music. Again, as she moved down the receiving line, Sarah was aware of the strange feeling of unreality, as if she were swimming in a warm and sticky pool. Alicia kissed her theatrically but Adam's greeting was that of an old friend. Sarah smiled stiffly and moved on into the vast hall.

'Are you feeling all right?' Eric murmured solicitously. 'You look a little pale.'

Her lips tightened; her eyes were hard and bright.

'I'm fine – and I shall be even better after a glass of champagne.'

'Do you think you should?' Eric asked doubtfully but without much hope. The fact that she was his wife and was carrying his child had made no difference to the wilful trait of doing exactly as she pleased.

Sarah and Eric had been seated with Annie and Max.

'I don't look too much like a fairground exhibit do I?' Sarah whispered to Annie as they took their places.

'Good heavens no! That loose coat is very flattering. No-one would ever guess you are about to become a mother.'

Sarah smiled. 'I think you are being a bit kind in saying that, Annie, but still . . . What's it like? Being a mother, I mean.'

'Wonderful.' Annie's glow was confirmation of that; though she was now a little plumper than she had used to be there was little doubt but that motherhood suited her. 'I can't wait for you to see John – you'll adore him.'

'John. I've always liked that name.'

'We called him after Moore-Brabazon. He had to be called after one of the pioneers, Max insisted on it. And who better than JTC?' Annie leaned closer. 'There is something I wanted to ask you, Sarah. I wondered if you would do us the honour of being godmother to little John.'

'Oh Annie – I'd love to! How nice of you to ask me! Though don't you think living in London I'm rather a long way away to be a proper godmother? I'll hardly ever see him.'

'I wouldn't be too sure of that,' Annie said mysteriously but when Sarah pressed her she refused to be drawn further.

Several glasses of champagne helped Sarah through the wedding breakfast but its anaesthetising effect was rendered totally useless by the pain of having to watch Adam and Alicia leave together for their honeymoon in Switzerland and when the evening's dancing began Sarah felt she could not keep up the pretence of enjoying herself a moment longer.

'I think I've done enough for one day,' she said, summoning all her remaining control in an effort to make her voice bright and cheerful. 'I shall go to bed.'

'So soon?' Eric looked regretful, torn between solicitude for his wife and the desire to stay a while longer. He and Max were getting along famously and he was enjoying the opportunity to talk about aeroplanes. Balloon man he might be – the new technology of powered flight was beginning to win him over.

'There's no need for you to leave on my account,' Sarah said. 'There's not even any need for you to see me to our room. I used to live here, remember.'

'Well, if you're sure . . .'

'I certainly am. Just as long as you won't mind if I'm asleep when you come to bed.'

As she said her goodnights she was aware of Annie's eyes on her, watchful and a little sad. I believe she knows, Sarah thought, and she lifted her chin and smiled, the same smile she had been forcing all day until her cheeks ached.

Alone in her room, however, there was no longer need for pretence. Wearily Sarah went through the motions of preparing for bed, for her whole body felt as heavy as her heart. She put out the light and lay staring into the darkness but in it she seemed to see Adam's face, glowing, yet a little blurred around the edges as the lamp had been. Pain ached through her like a paralysing cramp so that every bit of her seemed to be drawn up into one tight ball somewhere at the heart of her and the pain had a name – Adam. She stretched out her arms towards the image of his face, there in the darkness, but there was another face beside it, an oval of pale ivory framed by jet black hair and smiling a smile of triumph. Sarah's fingers tautened and stretched then crumpled into fists. She drew her arms tight around herself and sobs, torn from the heart of her, shook her body. The tears that came were hot tears, burning her eyes and doing nothing to alleviate the agony.

Oh Adam, Adam . . . oh Adam . . .

In the quiet dark Sarah wept and when at last all her tears were spent and there was nothing left but emptiness and

329

exhaustion she turned her blotched and crumpled face into the pillow and slept.

She was woken by the sound of cheery whistling. She opened her eyes. They felt heavy and the sunlight, creeping in at the half-open curtains, hurt them a little. She turned towards the sound of the whistling and saw Eric shaving at the heavy mirror propped up on the wash-stand.

'Oh – you're awake then.' He turned, razor in hand, to smile at her. 'You were sleeping the sleep of the just. You didn't hear me come to bed last night and you didn't hear me get up this morning.'

'What time is it?'

'Eight o'clock.' The cut-throat glided effortlessly through the lather of shaving soap cutting a wide pale swathe. 'There's no need for you to get up yet though. I want to have a chat with Gilbert before breakfast.'

'*Gilbert?*'

'Yes. I want to finish off a conversation we were having last night.' He put down the razor and came towards the bed, one half of his face still all over lather. 'Oh hell, I might as well tell you now, mightn't I, as be mysterious until all the details are worked out. Gilbert has offered me a position with Morse Bailey.'

'What?'

'I know. I must say I was surprised too. Hang on a minute while I finish shaving and I'll tell you all about it.'

He drew the blade over his face with a few swift strokes, deftly avoiding his moustache, swilled the cut-throat in the jug of water and towelled his chin dry. Slightly stunned by the revelation Sarah lay against the pillows watching him.

'That's better,' he said, tossing the towel aside and rolling down his sleeves. 'Now – where was I?'

'Gilbert offered you a position with the new company.'

'That's right.' Even now Eric was unable to remain still. He searched for his cuff links and fastened them as he spoke. 'Gilbert has great plans, you know, for the expansion of the company. He wants to demonstrate the aeroplanes Morse Bailey are building all over the world and

330

he intends to set up flying schools so as to increase the number of potential customers. I know – it all sounds like pie in the sky, but I honestly believe he can do it. When he talks about it it doesn't sound far fetched at all but very, very plausible. He's a wonderful man!'

'Yes, I know he is,' Sarah said drily. 'Gilbert has a talent for firing others with his own enthusiasm. But where do you come in? You don't know anything about aeroplanes.'

'I know more than you think. This may be powered flight but it's still aero-dynamics. Sam Cody made the change successfully and so did the Short brothers. Why shouldn't I?'

'Doing what?'

'Well, flying of course! If he is to expand as he plans Gilbert needs to recruit people in every field and he reckons I'd be a natural to learn to fly. Don't look so surprised, my dear! It's not very flattering.'

Sarah was silent. She could hardly tell him the thoughts that were racing through her mind – that if he were to come to Chewton Leigh to fly she would have to face seeing Adam with Alicia not just for one day but practically every day of her life and she did not know if she could bear it.

Seeing her expression he crossed to the bed and sat on the edge of it.

'What's wrong, Sarah? I thought you would be pleased. You are always saying how much you love this part of the world.'

'Yes – yes, I do. But . . . are you sure, Eric? What will Henry say?'

'Henry knows life must move on. As a matter of fact there's something I haven't told you for fear of worrying you. Henry has had an offer from the Army Balloon Factory at Farnborough and he's keen to go there. I was thinking of seeing if I could do the same but I like the sound of Gilbert's offer better. And it would mean you were near friends, Sarah. I think that will be very important when the baby is born.'

'You've accepted then, have you?'

'Yes.' Eric put his arm around her. 'I have you to thank

for this, Sarah. Gilbert would never have thought of asking me to join him if it hadn't been for you. I think he wants you home again. And I can't say I blame him. Anyone who didn't want you near them would be a fool.'

'Oh – rubbish! Eric you are getting to sound very banal.'

'Sarah, I love you and I want you to be happy. I'm delighted with Gilbert's offer but if you're against it, then I'll turn it down. It's up to you.'

'Oh Eric!' She felt almost angry with him for making the decision her responsibility for she was very afraid of what would happen if she came back. Chewton Leigh had always been a catalyst to her, she thought. When she was here emotions became charged, situations developed, that were quite out of her control. It had always been so and she knew instinctively it always would be. But her destiny was bound up with Chewton Leigh; try as she might there was no escaping it. 'Of course we'll come back,' she said. And hoped she would not live to regret the decision.

BOOK FOUR – 1914–1918

Nurture strength of spirit to shield you in sudden misfortune. But do not distress yourself with imaginings. Many fears are born of fatigue and loneliness.

   . . . everywhere life is full of heroism.

Desiderata

Chapter Twenty-Nine

'Mama! Mama! Come and see! Come and see!'

The small boy squatted on his haunches to peer into the rock pool, mesmerised by the darting movement of some tiny sea creature marooned in its clear depths. Carefully, with great concentration, he broke the surface of the water with his index finger, surprised by its warmth, but as the ripples spread the little creature darted again, so fast he did not see it go, only the shimmering ribbon of disturbed water in its wake, and he withdrew his finger again so quickly he almost lost his balance and toppled over backwards in the untidy rabble of rocks.

'Mama!' he called again urgently.

Sarah, kneeling with Annie on a rug spread out on the sand to unpack the picnic hamper, looked around at him and felt her heart fill with love. Stephen was four years old now and a miniature version of Eric. His body and limbs were wiry, his face almost elfin with its high cheekbones and small pointed chin, his eyes dark and bright as boot-buttons. Only his eyebrows were Sarah's, delicate arches, and his lashes were long and thick as a girl's. His was an inquisitive nature, he had a bright and lively intelligence, but there was not a bad-tempered bone in his body and he had never been known to throw a childish tantrum though his curiosity had often led him into one scrape after another. Sarah adored him with a fierce protective love stronger than she could have imagined she was capable of and sometimes it seemed to her that every breath she drew, every dream she dreamed, was for Stephen. He was the focus of her life now in a way that Eric could never be, though she had kept her vow to be a good wife to him, and when her heart ached for Adam, as it still did, she reminded herself that if she had not left Adam there would be no Stephen.

She looked at him now, crouching beside the rock pool, his face bright and eager, and smiled.

'Be careful that you don't fall in, Stephen,' she warned.

'But Mama – look!'

'Not now, darling. Auntie Annie and I are just getting the lunch out. Show John instead.' She glanced at the other small boy, plumper and fairer skinned than Stephen, who was digging happily in the sand. 'John, why don't you go and see what Stephen has found?'

'Yes – go and see, John,' Annie echoed, sitting back on her heels to unwrap a packet of sandwiches.

John's eyes strayed longingly towards the food but he picked himself up obediently and trotted over to join Stephen at the rock pool. Annie watched him go, smiling contentedly.

'Isn't it nice, Sarah, that they are the same age and can amuse one another? I think we were very clever, don't you? Even if we were less clever in our choice of husbands. Honestly, I never heard of such a thing – crying off the holiday after it had been planned for so long and leaving us to come alone – and all because of work. They seem to think of nothing else these days. Though I suppose if we are honest it has always been the same.'

Sarah smiled wryly. It was true that aeroplanes dominated their lives but she did not mind that – in her own way she was as obsessed as the men were and as excited by the progress they had made. Sometimes when she cast her mind back it was hard to believe it was less than five short years ago that the first prototype had hopped and skimmed over the field at Chewton Leigh, for in that time the project which had once seemed little more than a wild dream had grown from its humble beginnings in a makeshift shed to a company of worldwide renown.

334

Under Gilbert's guidance and with his wealth to back it expansion had been breathtakingly rapid. He had acquired the land adjoining the motor works for an airfield along with an almost derelict mansion which he had renovated to provide central office accommodation for the new company. Skilled fitters and mechanics, draughtsmen and engineers had been brought in to work alongside the cream of the craftsmen from Morse Motors, producing the aeroplanes at the rate of two a week, and fliers who had learned their expertise on French Voisins and Farmans were persuaded into the fold for the purpose of demonstrating the prowess of Morse Bailey monoplanes and biplanes to potential customers all over the world.

Orders had come flooding in and soon the name of Morse Bailey was ranking with the best – Shorts and Vickers, Avro and Sopwith and Morse Bailey's closest rivals, Sir George White's British and Colonial Company with their Bristol Boxkites.

To Gilbert's credit, however, he had ensured that the original team were not elbowed aside. Max had been appointed Chief Designer and his was the final word on any new innovation; Adam, now a highly skilled self-taught pilot, was regarded as the expert in the air. He still loved nothing better than to fly and when Gilbert set up the first of his flying schools on Salisbury Plain Adam became its chief instructor.

There were three flying schools now where both civilians and army officers could learn the skills of piloting an aeroplane, though the army officers had to foot the bill from their own pockets and hope to be reimbursed afterwards – a scandal, Gilbert said, for he believed the military authorities were still failing to see the potential of air power – and with other countries ready to place orders for the Morse Bailey models a chain of schools had been set up across Europe too – in Spain, Italy and Germany.

It was in this ever widening market place that Eric had found his niche. He had taken to flying an aeroplane as readily as he had to piloting a balloon and soon he was travelling the world with the team which staged demonstrations for potential customers. There was scarcely any part of the globe now which had not been visited – India, Australia, New Zealand and even Turkey, and when Eric travelled to Malaya and Singapore for demonstrations to the British garrisons there, Sarah had longed to go with him for the lure of foreign parts was very strong. But with Stephen so young she had known her duty lay at home for she remembered her own motherless years too well to leave him in the care of others while she was away on such a lengthy trip and she had to content herself with her new found role working on the design of the catalogues which extolled the virtues of the Morse Bailey machines.

It was work she enjoyed for she had discovered an unexpected aptitude for words and she was able to write prose which managed to be both informative and lyrical, and, remembering something Adam had once said, she had devised an advertising slogan: 'Inherit the skies with Morse Bailey – the aeroplanes of the future'. Gilbert had been delighted with her work and before long she had her own little office in the renovated mansion which had now become the hub of the empire. Details of every new innovation were deposited on her desk and she had the last word on the production of every catalogue and press release, much to the chagrin of Leo de Vere, who had joined the company on coming down from University and who had expressed an interest in taking overall control of marketing when he had sufficient experience of the business.

Sarah's involvement had not been limited to desk work, however. Once or twice she had flown as a passenger on demonstration flights – 'to add a touch of glamour and prove how much faith we have in the safety of our aeroplane', Gilbert had said when he had suggested it. Sarah had enjoyed every moment of the experience and considered it every bit as exciting as ballooning, if not more so. It was not as peaceful, of course, but it had a thrill all its own and Sarah had climbed down from the rickety passenger seat on the framework of wooden struts and piano wire minus her hat, which had been blown away by the wind, but breathless with excitement.

'Do you think *I* could learn to fly?' she had asked Max when she rejoined him and Max, smiling at her enthusiasm, had replied that he saw no reason why not. Flying was not so much a matter of strength as skill, concentration and co-ordination – already a few daredevil women had gained their licences. But when she had pursued the idea she had come up against not one, but two, stumbling blocks.

The first, surprisingly, was Eric. Though he had been quite prepared to allow her to risk life and limb as a parachutist when she was Sweetheart of the Skies he took quite a different view now that she was his wife and the mother of his child. Flying was still far too hazardous, he insisted – far too many things could go wrong, even for seasoned fliers. There had been thirty-three deaths during 1910, including the Honourable Charles Rolls, killed when he crashed in the sea at Bournemouth during the first aviation meeting there, and another sixty-five in 1911. Sarah was too precious for him to allow her to risk her life in this way. Sarah had argued and pleaded and because she was still capable of winding Eric around her little finger she might eventually have got her way had not another obstacle arisen, one which she was reluctant to face in spite of her eagerness to learn to fly, and she learned of it when, in defiance of Eric's stubborn refusal, she raised the subject with Gilbert.

There was only one person, he told her, with whom he would trust her as a pupil – and that person was Adam.

Sarah had heard this pronouncement with dismay. Marriage to Eric had done nothing to change her feelings for Adam. When he came into a room she still felt a little as if she were standing too close to the edge of a very high cliff; there were still times when she dreamed of him and woke bathed in a rosy glow of happiness until she remembered the reality – that she had lost him forever. For the most part she believed that she concealed her feelings successfully. They met seldom for he was away from Chewton Leigh a good deal and on the occasions when they were unable to avoid one another they each maintained a chilly politeness. But how different it would be if he were to be detailed to teach her to fly! They would be alone then for long periods with no-one else to break the awkward silences, no barrier of habit or protocol for protection. The prospect was at once tempting and terrifying and Sarah knew it would be the turn of the screw which would be quite unbearable. She loved Adam still; she simply could not trust herself to be alone with him. Regretfully she had abandoned her dream.

Now, sitting on the beach at Weston-super-Mare, Sarah remembered it briefly. But Annie was chattering on, oblivious as she always was these days to anything outside her world of domestic contentment.

'It would have been so nice, wouldn't it, if Max and Eric had come with us as planned. Max sees so little of John I sometimes think one of these days John is going to ask me who his father is and why he doesn't come with us on holiday like other boys' daddies. And what am I to tell him? I don't understand myself what was so important just now that he and Eric had to cry off at such a late stage. It's so disappointing. After all, you got away, didn't you, Sarah? You didn't say work was more important. So why did they?'

Sarah refrained from answering. She did not wish to spoil her friend's enjoyment of the longed-for holiday by telling her now of the rumblings of international crisis she had been privy to at Morse Bailey or mentioning her own unease at the developing situation. It was disappointing, of course, when well-laid plans had to be disrupted but there were worse things. And Sarah had the uncomfortable feeling that this time, at any rate, Max and Eric had been right to put work before pleasure.

Sarah glanced along the beach at the thronging crowds. Everywhere, it seemed, people were making the most of the glorious weather. Family groups were gathered in deck-chairs and on rugs around laden picnic baskets, young people shrieked with laughter as they ran down the long expanse of muddy beach to splash and gambol in the fast retreating tide, older folk, with wide-brimmed hats or even knotted handkerchiefs to protect their heads turned their faces to the sun. A constant procession of girls emerged coyly from the ladies-only bathing machines in their gaily-coloured and voluminous costumes to the admiring glances of the young men. On the pier couples strolled arm in arm, some tucking into dishes of cockles and prawns which they had purchased from the sea food stalls, the men jaunty in their straw boaters, the girls keeping pace with them with some difficulty as they minced along in their up-to-the-minute 'hobble skirts'. The entire scene was one of jollity and good carefree fun but somehow it did nothing to lighten Sarah's mood. Instead it served only to increase her creeping sense of foreboding.

'Ah well, even without the men it's been a good holiday, hasn't it, and I dare say we shouldn't complain.' Annie lifted a pork pie from the picnic hamper. The crust shone with glaze and it was decorated with small pastry flowers. 'Goodness, this looks delicious! The cook at our hotel is a wonder. I shall be going home fat as a house if I'm not careful.'

The sound of a newsboy's cry was blown along the beach by the stiff breeze and Sarah looked past Annie to see him plodding along the sand. 'Evening Post! All the latest! Evening Post!'

'I'm going to buy a paper.' Sarah reached for her bag but was arrested by Annie's touch on her arm. She looked up, surprised, and as her eyes met those of her friend she saw her own anxiety mirrored there.

'Don't, Sarah. This is all so perfect. Don't spoil it.'

'But I want to find out . . .'

'Whatever it is we'll know soon enough. Oh, I expect you think I am just burying my head in the sand but we need good days, like this one, to make us strong for the bad ones. It's a little like having a post office savings account, except that we are banking happiness instead of money.' Annie's voice was urgent and reluctantly Sarah gave in. How strange, she thought, that for all Annie's apparent serenity the same dark fear was hovering around her heart.

'All right, Annie,' she said, 'we'll try to forget what's going on in the big wide world and just enjoy today.'

Annie nodded, relieved. The shadow left her eyes and as she called to the boys her tone was as carefree as it had been before.

'John! Stephen! Lunch is ready now.'

The newsboy was wending his way back along the beach, his cries almost lost now in the shrieks of laughter from the holidaymakers and the plaintive cries of the seagulls as they wheeled above the receding tide and swooped in for crumbs thrown by the picnickers. But Sarah was unable to shut out reality as Annie seemed capable of doing. Deep inside a small voice was whispering to her that today would be forever burned into her mind and not for the carefree pleasures of a Bank Holiday spent on a sandy beach beneath a clear blue sky.

As usual Sarah's instincts were correct.

The day was 3rd August, the year was 1914. It was a date which would go down as one of the blackest ever in the annals of British history.

In Gilbert Morse's large and well-appointed office at the headquarters of Morse Bailey Aeroplane Company world events were also under discussion but here there was no drawing a veil over the harsh and threatening reality as Annie had done.

'There is no doubt about it,' Gilbert said, lighting a cigarette and crossing to the window that overlooked the expanse of flat open land where the aeroplanes were tested, 'things are looking very black indeed. If Germany proceed with their plan to violate Belgian neutrality then there will be no alternative but to keep our promises to King Albert and go to his assistance. Our ultimatum to the Kaiser expires at midnight their time. If he fails to agree to withdraw by then there will be no options left. We shall have to declare war on Germany.'

There was a moment's silence in the room. The bald statement came as no shock to them for they had watched helplessly all summer as the situation in Europe had grown steadily worse but to hear their darkest fears put into words, and by Gilbert Morse, the most far sighted and least sensational of men, put flesh on the skeletons of their nightmares.

After a moment Adam Bailey eased his long frame away from the table on which he had been perched.

'I suppose it was inevitable it would come to this,' he said, thrusting his hands into his pockets. 'The Germans have been getting too big for their boots for some time. After the Archduke Franz Ferdinand was murdered I suppose the chance to show their might by backing Austria against Serbia was too great a temptation for them.'

There was a murmur of agreement from the others assembled in the room but Leo de Vere thumped on the table petulantly.

'That is all very well but I fail to see why the rest of Europe has to be drawn in. Let the Croats fight their own battles, I say.'

Gilbert threw him a look of distaste. Try as he might to like his wife's son he had no more patience with him now than he had when Leo had been a boy.

'It's not as simple as that, Leo. First we have Germany supporting Austria and Hungary, then Russia come in on the side of the Serbians, dragging France and England along with it. I have no doubt Sir Edward Grey has done his best to keep the peace but if you want my honest opinion I believe that there are those in Europe who are set on war and matters moved too far too fast. It's a damnable business, of course, but we cannot desert our allies. If we do, God help us all, for the Kaiser is not so far from us either, just the other side of the North Sea – or the German Ocean as they insist on calling it – and if we fail to present a united front he will simply pick us off one by one.'

'He'll do that anyway,' Leo argued. 'The trouble is Germany is prepared for war and we are not.'

'He's right there,' Max said. For once his mobile face wore an expression of extreme seriousness. 'The German army is a well-trained, well-equipped fighting force. Haldane has done his best to bring the Territorials up to strength and get the regular army up to scratch but the fact is we are heavily outnumbered. Thanks to Winston Churchill's foresight the fleet is gathered in the North Sea, of course, and that is something of a comfort. But no-one knows better than we do how many aeroplanes and trained pilots the Germans have compared to us. Not to mention their Zeppelins.'

341

Again there was a moment's silence while they ruminated on the unpalatable truth of Max's statement. Britain had lagged far behind the continent in the development of air services and although public opinion had forced some improvement the combined force of the Royal Flying Corps and the Naval Air Service could still muster less than 150 aircraft while the Germans were able to boast many times that number, in addition to the nine rigid airships Max had mentioned – the Zeppelins.

'The trouble is I don't believe anyone at the Ministry quite realises how important air power is going to be in a war,' Gilbert said bluntly. 'It seems to me they are all rooted in the past, each jealously guarding whichever wing of the fighting forces they happen to favour. Just look at the fuss and palaver last year when Seely took £86000 from Army funds to help build up the military wing of the RFC – ridiculous! Instead of working together and seeing the pattern as a whole they engage in their petty squabbles like dogs fighting over a bone. And none of them seem to realise it is air power which will be the deciding factor in any conflict now.'

'How can you say that?' Leo sneered. He was still smarting from Gilbert's dismissal of his views on British involvement. 'They have been a little tardy I admit but things have changed lately. Haven't we just been given a good contract to supply BE2c's for the services?'

'That is true,' Gilbert admitted. 'And though I would prefer to be building aeroplanes that we had designed ourselves rather than simply making up the brain children of the boffins at the Government's Royal Aircraft Factory at Farnborough I am very glad we were considered for the order. No, I'm not knocking the planes. I believe Geoffrey de Havilland was responsible for their design and he is a young man who should go far. I wish I could get him to join our company – he and Max would make an unbeatable team. But BE2c's are reconnaissance aircraft. And reconnaissance aircraft alone will not be enough to win a war nowadays.'

'But you have always been such a keen advocate of planes

for reconnaissance purposes,' Lawrence said, speaking for the first time.

When the new company had been formed, Lawrence had remained with Morse Motors and the years of nominal authority had only served to make him more ponderous and pedantic. He disliked joint meetings with the board of the Aeroplane Company, considering them an uncomfortable mix of crackpots and hustlers and the smoke-filled atmosphere irritated the cough that had troubled him since the winter and which not even the hot summer weather seemed able to cure. He viewed the success of their enterprise with a certain amount of suspicion, but with world events taking such a serious turn Gilbert had insisted he should be present at this afternoon's deliberations.

'Of course aeroplanes will revolutionise reconnaissance,' Gilbert said now, unconsciously adopting the patient tones he habitually used when addressing his eldest son. 'But it won't stop there. One only has to take the argument a stage further to see how things will develop. If both sides are using aeroplanes for reconnaissance there will be only one way to preserve the security of operations – other aeroplanes, equipped to fight off the scouts. There will be a fight for supremacy in the air. It is inevitable.'

'You are right of course,' Adam said. 'And where, I ask myself, are they coming from? As far as I know there are only two gun-carrying aeroplanes in service, both of them belonging to the Navy.'

'Just so.' Gilbert stubbed out his cigarette and immediately lit another, a sure sign of his preoccupation. 'Now what I propose is this. That we set to work immediately with a view to producing an aeroplane to help offset the problem.'

'Put our money into a prototype the Ministry may not even be prepared to consider, you mean?' Leo asked incredulously.

'That is hardly a new departure,' Gilbert returned tartly. 'Practically every advance in aviation has been made thanks to private enterprise. We would still be in the dark ages if it had been left to the Government. In any case I am quite prepared to use what resources we have if it is for the good of the country. None of our lives will be worth living if we don't win this war. Better a little spent on the defence of our island now than stand aside, do nothing, and see it all appropriated by the Kaiser.'

Max leaned forward. Gilbert's suggestion had fired his enthusiasm; already he was itching to begin plans for a fighting plane.

'You want me to design it, Gilbert?'

'Who else?' Gilbert smiled, if a little bleakly. 'I have complete faith in your ability, Max. There is one thing, though. I think you should work in complete secrecy, well away from the rest of the company staff.'

'Don't you trust them?' Lawrence asked.

'Of course I do. But we must not lose sight of the fact that this is war – or will be if the Kaiser does not respond to our ultimatum by midnight. If – when – it comes, everything will be different. A great many people work in the Aeroplane Company building now – it would not be so difficult for an infiltrator to penetrate the place. I would prefer it, Max, if you moved into an office well away from the main house – in the old Morse Motors buildings, perhaps.'

'If you think it is necessary,' Max said.

'I do. It may sound alarmist, Max, but I believe this is a case when it would be infinitely better to be safe than sorry. And there is something else to consider. It is quite possible that if war comes the Ministry will decide to take control of all aircraft manufacture – monopolise the factories and orchestrate production. I would fight such a move every inch of the way, through the courts if necessary, but if I failed it would suit our purpose better if Max was officially deemed to be working for the Motor Company.'

Max nodded. 'Agreed.'

'Good. We'll hope it does not come to that, of course, and I shall do my utmost to persuade the powers-that-be to begin looking a little further than their noses.'

'If anyone can do that, Gilbert, it is you,' Adam said. 'But there is one thing you haven't thought of. If war comes and we are as short of fighting men as you say we are then there is going to be a campaign to swell the ranks urgently.'

'Conscript, you mean, Adam?' Leo asked. He had gone very white.

'Not necessarily – though it may come to that. I would imagine they will try persuasion first. Either way we could find ourselves losing a lot of skilled men just when we need them most.'

'You are right,' Gilbert agreed. 'Some young hotheads are bound to rush off to enlist. We shall just have to do our best to persuade them – and the War Office – that they are more use to the country where they are, doing what they know best. Well, I don't think there is a great deal more we can usefully discuss at the moment. We may as well get back to work – if we can work this afternoon with this threat hanging over us. Though I dare say it is a pressure we shall have to get used to.'

In sombre mood they dispersed, Max going back to the Motor Works with Lawrence to decide upon an office for his future use, Leo excusing himself to deal with what he mutteringly called 'urgent paperwork'. Adam however remained in Gilbert's office, looking out of the window at the rolling Somerset hills, green and sunlit beneath the clear blue sky, while Gilbert took his leave of the others. When they had gone Gilbert closed the door and crossed to the oak cabinet which stood behind his desk.

'Let's have a drink, shall we, Adam? I dare say we could both do with one. Unless you're anxious to get back to Chewton Leigh and Alicia, of course. You haven't seen much of her these last months, have you?'

'That is true,' Adam agreed. He had been supervising intensive pilot training courses at the three British based Morse Bailey Schools in his capacity as chief instructor, but since he was seldom in one place for long Alicia had remained at home. 'I must get back and spend a little time with her. But you're right, I certainly could do with a drink, and in any case there is something I want to talk to you about.'

'Scotch or brandy?' Gilbert asked, unlocking the

345

cupboard to reveal a row of bottles and an array of crystal glasses.

'Scotch, please. Neat.'

Gilbert poured the drinks, generous measures, and brought one across to Adam.

'This is a damnable business and no mistake.' He gulped his brandy with the air of a man recently rescued from the snow by a life-saving St Bernard. 'Well, what was it you wanted to talk to me about?'

Adam sipped his whisky, equally grateful for the bite of the alcohol on his tongue.

'I thought I should warn you,' he said directly. 'If this conflict comes – and like you I am almost certain it is bound to – I intend to volunteer for the RFC.'

Gilbert looked up sharply. His glass shook in his hand.

'Good God, man – why?'

'Because I believe I could be of most use to the war effort if I did. I am a pilot, first and foremost. It's what I am best at. And the Flying Corps is going to need every competent man it can get.'

Gilbert was silent for a moment whilst he digested Adam's words.

'But surely you could be of most use training others,' he said at last.

'I dare say. But I would be able to do that inside the service as well as outside it and I could fly myself too,' Adam reasoned. 'Besides I wouldn't be at all surprised if the Government take over our flying schools the moment war is declared.'

Gilbert nodded. 'Yes, they will see central control as a necessity – though I am bound to say I find it galling after all the years of batting our heads against a brick wall while they shilly-shallied. The best we can hope for is that there will be someone with a little intelligence and foresight in charge at the War Office. Kitchener would be a good man. It is fortunate that he is in the country at the moment, though I understand he is due to return to his duties as Agent-General in Egypt. I only hope Asquith will have the good sense to appoint him Secretary of State – though heaven knows even he will have his work cut out. This war is going to be a terrible one, Adam, mark my words.'

'And the sooner we can get it over and done with the better.' Adam drained his glass. 'I'm sorry if my news has come as a bombshell to you, but I just wouldn't feel right at a time like this not being in uniform. Call it patriotism if you like or simply damn-fool recklessness. Perhaps there are times in history when they amount to much the same thing.'

Gilbert smiled thinly. 'I can't pretend that what you propose pleases me, Adam. It's bad enough knowing that Hugh is bound to be in the thick of things without seeing you rush off like a lemming as well. I could ask you to think of Alicia, if nothing else. As her father I think that is my duty. But I dare say it will do no good.' He glanced at Adam, his eyes narrowing. 'Perhaps this is none of my business, but things are all right between the two of you, are they?'

Adam crossed to the table, setting down his empty glass. He did not meet Gilbert's eyes.

'Of course. But at a time like this personal considerations have to take second place. As you yourself said unless we can win this war and quickly life won't be worth living for any of us. I have to do my bit, and do it in the way I know best.'

Gilbert nodded. Adam's answer had not entirely satisfied him. He was not convinced that everything was as it should be between Adam and Alicia. Adam took his absences – necessary to his work though they were – too lightly, and there was a brittleness about Alicia which suggested she was not entirely happy. But then Alicia had always been something of an enigma, and that fierce pride of hers meant that she was good at hiding her true feelings.

Gilbert sighed. Alicia, Blanche and even Sarah were all liable to behave in inexplicable ways. The only woman he had ever truly understood was Rose – sweet natured, open, warm hearted Rose – and the tragedy of it was that though he had been exceedingly fond of her and honestly deva-stated by her death, before then she had long since ceased to interest him as a woman. Perhaps it was complexity, the

347

mystery and the intrigue that constituted the spark of attraction, Gilbert thought. Unfair it might be, yet inescapable, primitive as the law of the jungle, yet able to influence a man as civilised as he considered himself to be. Had it not been that way with Rachel?

'Well, Adam, I won't try to dissuade you. I can see your mind is made up. If I were twenty years younger I would probably feel just as you do. That is the trouble with growing older. The spark goes and caution sets in. I look on war now as something which will bring about suffering on a scale it is almost impossible to imagine – whilst to the young I suppose it is a shining crusade, a tremendous adventure. Thank God for the young men with the courage and vigour to fight – and thank God for the older ones who may have the wisdom to know when to hold back.'

'There can be no holding back this time,' Adam said.

'No, but it makes me very sad. Even though I dare say it will mean progress for our industry at a rate we should never achieve in time of peace. Do you want another drink?'

'No thank you. I think I will get over to Chewton Leigh. Alicia will be expecting me.'

'I shouldn't drink at this time of day either,' Gilbert admitted. 'It makes me maudlin. Very well, Adam, I'll see you at dinner. We may have more news by then.'

'Let us hope so,' Adam replied. 'Otherwise we can do nothing but wait for midnight.'

Gilbert shook his head. 'I feel as if we are waiting for Armageddon,' he said grimly.

The atmosphere around the dinner table at Chewton Leigh was tense for the strain of these last hours, waiting for what they all believed to be the inevitable declaration of war, yet still hoping for some miracle to avert it, had taken its toll on all of them and matters had not been improved by Adam's announcement that he intended to volunteer for the RFC.

Eyebrows were raised all around the table but it was Leo who voiced what they were all thinking.

'Good grief, man, how are we supposed to produce aeroplanes if you set that kind of example to the work force?

348

It's bad enough the reservists have all been called up – if you go tearing off into uniform half the factory will think it's all right for them to do the same. Already I've heard enough jingoism on the shop floor this afternoon to sink a battleship and if the call goes out for volunteers the only thing we shall be able to do to stop them rushing out in droves is to appeal to their loyalty.'

'I can only do what I believe to be right,' Adam said evenly.

Leo bristled. 'Right indeed! Well all I can say is that your idea of what is right and mine certainly do not coincide.'

'And never have, Leo. I take it you will not be volunteering?'

'Most certainly I will not. No-one with any sense will. Why, you admitted yourself this afternoon that we cannot afford to lose skilled men just now, so why set them such an ill-advised example?'

'Adam must do as his conscience dictates,' Gilbert said quietly. He had drunk a good deal of brandy since the afternoon meeting but it had done nothing to lift his depression. If anything it had only served to make him more morose. 'When it comes to defending honour and freedom then that is all anyone can do.'

'Honour and freedom!'

'That is what this war is about, surely? It is the only thing that justifies such desperate measures.'

'No war can be justified,' James said. They all turned to look at him briefly, a little surprised, for they had almost forgotten he was there. The years had not made James any less of a shadow – he spent much of his time alone, painting and scribbling poetry, and seldom contributed anything to family discussion so that when he was away at university he was scarcely missed.

'What are you talking about?' Gilbert asked, irritated as always by his youngest son.

'Nothing can justify killing and maiming,' James replied, his face very pale and set. 'Leo is quite right to be against it and refuse to volunteer. So shall I. I would refuse absolutely to have any part in it.'

'Oh for heaven's sake!' Gilbert exploded, thoroughly annoyed.

'I'm sorry but it's the way I feel,' James said defensively, aware that he had managed to arouse the hostility not only of his father but also the rest of the assembled family. 'You understand, don't you, Alicia?'

He turned to his sister for the backing she invariably gave him but for once he was disappointed. Alicia seemed barely to have heard him. She sat white-faced, her meal untouched since Adam had shocked her with his announcement.

It could not be true! she was thinking. Surely Adam could not have made such a decision without even discussing it with her? Bad enough that he should be prepared to abandon the company which, as Leo said, needed his full support. But her hurt went deeper than that. Far, far deeper.

'Alicia, are you feeling well?' Blanche enquired. 'You look very pale.'

Alicia laid down her fork, only her iron control preventing it from clattering onto her plate. 'I do have a headache,' she said. 'If you will excuse me, I think I will go to my room.' She rose from her chair.

'Of course, my dear. Millie can bring you a cup of hot milk if you would like it. Millie . . .' Gilbert's concern was obvious and Alicia felt high spots of colour begin to burn in her cheeks. Did he know this was the first she had heard of Adam's decision? The humiliation of it – learning along with everyone else what one's own husband planned to do!

'Thank you, but please don't trouble Millie.' She glanced at Adam, but he was eating steadily, totally oblivious to the furore he had caused.

Propelled by anger she swept up the staircase and into her room. She and Adam shared a suite – a pair of bedrooms linked by a small sitting-room. On her instructions the curtains had been left open to allow what air there was on this hot August night to circulate more freely, but the sheets had been turned down and her most glamourous nightgown laid out ready for her. Her lips tightened when she saw it, remembering with what high hopes she had selected it for

350

Adam's first night home after two weeks' absence touring the flying schools. So much for her plans to seduce him all over again! The fact that he could humiliate her this way showed how little he cared for her – and his eagerness to join the colours without a thought for her wishes was confirmation of it – if confirmation were needed.

Alicia wriggled to unfasten her dress, determined not to summon Millie, stepped out of it and kicked it contemptuously into a corner. Let the maid hang it up in the morning and if it was creased well then she would have to iron it. Why should Alicia care? She stripped herself of her undergarments, dropping them with the same careless abandon, and slipped into the nightgown and matching peignoir. After the restrictions of her corset the filmy silk felt good against her hot skin and when she sat down at her dressing table to unpin her hair she was slightly mollified by the picture her reflection made.

There was no doubt about it, the ivory silk flattered her, setting off the blue-black sheen of her hair and making her look pure, though not in the least virginal. But the flush of pleasure did not last. She drew the brush through her hair for the first of the hundred strokes that she had performed every evening since she was a child and reflected on the pathetic sham her marriage had become.

Perhaps things might have been different, she thought, if she had been able to carry to full term the child she had conceived in the first months of heady unfettered love. But it was not to be. She had miscarried in the fifth month and Dr Haley had warned that he would not be responsible for the consequences if she fell pregnant again before at least a year had elapsed.

Lovemaking had been the one real point of contact in their troubled marriage – Alicia knew her expertise was the trump card which kept him interested in her. Without it he had taken to coming home later and staying away longer and though he pleaded pressure of work Alicia was under no illusions.

The knowledge hurt her, for winning his love had long since ceased to be the game it had once been. She had come

351

to care too much for him. But she had thought that to a certain extent at least she had come to terms with it. Now, brushing her hair with a vigour that did nothing to relieve her feelings, she knew she had not.

The bristles of the brush scraped her forehead. She winced and watched the small red weals criss cross the white skin. Then, reflected in the mirror, she saw the door open. She did not turn but sat very still, the hairbrush resting against her cheek.

'Alicia – I came to see if you were all right.' It was Adam, looking very tall, very handsome in his evening dress suit. In spite of herself she felt the familiar excited quickening of her pulses and tightened her grip on the handle of the brush.

'To what do I owe this sudden flush of concern?'

His eyes narrowed. 'From your tone I assume it was not simply a headache that was the cause of your leaving your dinner unfinished.'

'You assume right.'

'So what was the cause?'

'Oh how can you be so obtuse?' she blazed. 'Don't tell me you thought I would be *pleased* to learn my husband has decided to go off to war without a single reference to me and learn it only at the same time as the rest of the family. What kind of a fool do you think that made me look?'

'Alicia.' Adam's tone was conciliatory. He came into the room, closing the door behind him. 'I am sorry I didn't have the opportunity to discuss it with you first. I came home early with that very intention but you were out riding and by the time you returned I was fully occupied with your father again.'

'As always.'

'We are in business together. And this is a time of crisis.'

'Hmm!' she snorted. 'And don't you think we have a crisis in our marriage when you never pay the slightest consideration to my feelings?'

He loosened his tie so that it hung in a black ribbon beneath the stiff white collar of his shirt.

'You are behaving like a child.'

352

'All you ever think of is business! You seem to forget that it is thanks to me that you are a part of it.'

A muscle moved in his cheek. 'Oh no, I could hardly forget that. And I really don't know what you are complaining about. You got what you wanted, after all.'

She began to tremble again, a tremor of cold fury. 'What do you mean by that?'

His face was hard, his eyes very cold. 'I married you, didn't I?'

The fury exploded. Her fingers tightened on the handle of the brush, she turned and with one swift movement flung it at him. It caught him on the cheek, rebounded and fell, knocking over a small china ornament.

'Bastard!' she screamed.

His eyes narrowed. He raised a hand to the sharp stinging spot. She stood up, hands clenched, eyes blazing.

'Oh yes, you married me.' Her voice was low and trembling. 'And much good has it done me. Do you think I don't know how it is with you? That I don't know who it is you would prefer to be married to? Do you think I don't see the way you look at her? I'd be a fool not to see! But is that all you do, Adam – look? Or is there another reason besides business which keeps you away from me – stops you from wanting me. Is *she* satisfying you? Is that what it is?'

'Don't be ridiculous!'

She tossed her head. 'Not so ridiculous, Adam. I know Sarah of old. She has the morals of an alleycat.'

He took a step towards her. She thought he was going to strike her. She stood her ground, eyes glittering with all her accumulated disappointments and years of hatred and resentment of the girl who had always been a thorn in her flesh.

'Oh yes, I am afraid it is true, Adam. Perhaps you don't know why your precious Sarah was sent away from Chewton Leigh as a girl. I'm sure you don't – she wouldn't have been likely to tell you. But I will. She seduced my brother. Lawrence found her with Hugh, rolling in the hay like a common whore. Which of course is exactly what her mother was. Like mother, like daughter.'

353

His hands shot out, imprisoning her wrists. 'Alicia!' His tone was threatening. She threw back her head and laughed.

'True, all true. Has Sarah mentioned her father to you? No – I'm sure she hasn't. She doesn't know who he is – and neither did her mother, I should think. So you see the girl you put on a pedestal does not exist. She never has. And for her, for this trollop, you are ruining our marriage!'

He was still gripping her wrists so hard that his fingers raised red weals in the white skin but there was a dazed expression in his eyes as if he had been struck in the face by a brick. She laughed again, lips parting to show her teeth, head thrown back so that her raven hair cascaded over the ivory peignoir, her throat stretched long and creamy and her breasts thrust enticingly against the silk and lace.

'Oh Adam, don't waste your time. Not now, when it is so short.'

For a moment longer his fingers bit into her wrists then with a movement so swift it startled her he drew her to him. His mouth came down on hers, choking off her laughter, his teeth raking her lips. The smell of the whisky on his breath mingled with the scent of honeysuckle wafting through the open window in her nostrils and the old familiar desire rose in her, blotting out anger and despair in a tide of passion. Roughly his hands tore away the silk and lace so that her body was exposed, smooth and creamy in the moonlight.

Briefly he towered over her, divesting himself of his clothes and she lay waiting in an agony of delight. Then his weight was upon her and within her and she gloried in the union with the one man who could truly dominate her, body and soul.

All too soon it was over. For a few minutes he lay beside her then he levered himself up and rose from the bed, gathering his clothes from where he had dropped them. She wanted to protest, to beg him to stay, to sleep with her tonight at least in her bed and be there beside her when she woke in the morning. But no words came and she lay helplessly, passion and anger spent.

In the doorway he paused, looking back at her, at the whiteness of her body and her raven hair spread out across the pillow.

'Goodnight, Alicia.'

There was a finality in the words. He might have been saying goodbye.

The door closed after him and she was alone. Tears of frustration ached in her throat but her eyes were hot and dry.

Somewhere in the stillness of the night a clock struck twelve.

Chapter Thirty

War fever gripped Chewton Leigh as it gripped the rest of the country. As Gilbert had feared some of the best of his workforce rushed off, young and keen, to join the queues at the recruiting offices which had been hastily set up and Eric decided to follow Adam's lead and volunteer for the RFC.

'You will be able to manage while I am away won't you?' he said to Sarah. 'It's not as if you are miles from family and friends. And anyway, they say if we make a concerted effort the war could be over by Christmas.'

'I think that's a bit optimistic,' Sarah said doubtfully. 'Of course I shall be all right. The question is – will you?'

'Oh, I expect so,' Eric said breezily. 'You know me, Sarah. I have the luck of the very Old Nick. And besides, I shall take good care of myself, knowing I have you and this young man to come home to.' He ruffled Stephen's tousled sandy head, smiling with pride. 'You wouldn't like to grow up thinking your daddy shirked his duty, would you, Stephen?'

'I'm sure he would never think that,' Sarah said a little sharply for she was suddenly filled with a dreadful feeling of desolation. Everyone, it seemed, was going to war. Adam, now Eric, and Hugh had already left for France with a composite regiment drawn from the various Guards Brigades. Not that she cared about Hugh, but his going had made all the other departures seem very real, very threatening. But Eric was right, of course. If he could best serve the war effort by being in uniform then it was only right that he should go. She would not have expected him to do otherwise. She could never have loved a man who was afraid to place himself in a little danger, and she certainly could not have married one, however kind and considerate he might be. 'Where do you think they will send you?'

'I don't know. We shall have to wait and see. But I hope

356

it's France. I quite fancy the idea of scouting over the German lines and I think Adam feels the same way.'

Sarah turned away, busying herself with looking over the bowl of raspberries she had just picked from the bushes that grew against the south-facing wall of the garden. She still did not trust herself not to give away some hint of her feelings whenever Adam's name was mentioned.

'You're fools, both of you,' she said shortly. 'Anyone would think this was some kind of game. Scouting over the German lines, indeed! It will be no more than you are asking for if they start taking pot shots at you!'

Eric's eyes twinkled. He seldom loved Sarah more than when she 'got on her high horse' as he described it.

'I think we are both anxious to show Hugh the way modern methods can work,' he told her. 'He still thinks reconnaissance is the job of the cavalry. But the days of the horse on the battlefield are numbered.'

'And a good thing too!' Sarah said grimly. The Government had been requisitioning horses to reinforce the numbers of both the cavalry and the mounted wings of the infantry – many hunters from around Chewton Leigh had been taken already and she knew Alicia was living in fear that Baron would go too. Much as she hated Alicia, in this she had Sarah's unbridled sympathy for as Sweet Lass's foal Baron was the last link with her own beloved mare. 'It's horrible to think of horses being shot at and blown up.'

'And quite all right for men to suffer the same fate?' Eric asked, amused.

'At least they are there from choice, unlike the horses. And at least they understand what is happening to them.' Sarah popped a raspberry into her mouth and held one out for Stephen.

'I suppose you are right,' Eric smiled and held out his hand. 'Are those rationed or can I have one too?' She passed him the bowl and he caught at her juice-stained hand. 'Or maybe I could have a kiss, seeing I am going to France.'

She glanced at Stephen who had returned to twirling his spinning top and smiled coquettishly. 'Maybe you could – seeing you are going to France!'

'Come here then, Mrs Gardiner and send a poor man happy to his death,' he teased, pulling her into his arms. 'Or at least with a memory to keep his resolve strong when faced with all those jolie mam'selles!'

In the event neither Eric nor Adam were destined for France, for the time being at any rate. Instead Eric found himself sent to Brooklands, which Hugh Locke King had offered to the government the moment war was declared and which had quickly been designated an Aircraft Acceptance Park, whilst Adam was posted even closer to home – the Central Flying School at Upavon on Salisbury Plain. Both, though they did not admit it, felt vaguely cheated, both secretly envied Hugh, away in the thick of things.

But Hugh's days in France were numbered. After being plunged into combat almost at once Hugh's company found themselves bound for Wytschaete where they were involved in fierce fighting during the last day of October and the first of November. When the battle was over both the CO and the Squadron Leader of the 1st Life Guards were numbered amongst the dead, many men had been wounded and many more taken prisoner. Hugh was amongst those who managed to return to the English camp in spite of having been wounded in the shoulder and knee, and after a brief spell in a field hospital in France where the shot was removed and a month in a London hospital he was sent home to Chewton Leigh to convalesce.

Alicia, who had always been close to Hugh, set herself the task of nursing him and was glad of the diversion. The thing she had feared most had happened, the military had taken Baron in spite of all her efforts to make them think he was too highly strung for their needs, and with Adam away too she was desperate for something to take her mind off her loss. Nursing Hugh was exactly the tonic she needed. She quickly learned to dress his wounds and take care of his medications and she was quite prepared to sit with him while he talked of the horror of the battle, the therapy which was the best possible treatment to heal his mind, while Dr Haley – and nature – took care of his body. She was less happy to carry trays up and down the back stairs from the kitchen or light the fire to warm his room on the cold December mornings, but she did it all the same for the war had left them desperately short of servants. Bert, who had assisted Evans the butler had gone off to join the Somerset Light Infantry and Mabel the 'tween maid had given notice and gone off to work in a munitions factory. Alicia fervently hoped they would find replacements before long but Gilbert did not hold out much hope, and so Alicia took on the tasks in order to make her brother's convalescence more comfortable.

Christmas was fast approaching – the Christmas beyond which the pundits had prophesied the war would not last – but there was no sign of a speedy end to hostilities. Far from it, everything seemed to point to an embarrassing deadlock in France, where a continuous line of trenches now ran from the Swiss frontier to the sea. And always, it seemed, there was news of casualties. Several of the young men who had rushed into uniform leaving their jobs at the works would never be coming back – their photographs appeared in the evening paper under the banner headline 'LOCAL HEROES DIE AT YPRES' – and Will Bennett, son of the local postman, a stoker on the *Audacious* had been lost when the battleship was struck by a mine at the end of October.

Naturally enough it was the contribution to the war effort of the newly formed air squadrons which aroused most interest at Chewton Leigh House for already Gilbert's predictions that their part would not be limited to scouting and reconnaissance had proved accurate. At the end of September the Eastchurch Squadron of the RNAS had carried out a raid on airship sheds at Cologne and though they had been shot at from the ground they had returned virtually unscathed.

A problem had arisen however – the Union Jacks that were painted on the tails of the aircraft could all too easily be mistaken for the German Iron Cross and a new identification had to be found to ensure the British guns did not attack their own.

'I understand it is being replaced by a roundel,' Gilbert

told Lawrence over breakfast one morning. 'Circles of red, white and blue that even a blind man could identify.'

'Good idea . . .' Lawrence broke off, clapping his hand over his mouth as one of his spasms of coughing overtook him and Blanche regarded them both with profound disapproval.

'Do we have to talk about the war at breakfast? I must say I am becoming heartily sick of it. And Lawrence – that cough of yours is no better is it? Don't you think it's high time you saw Dr Haley and got something for it?'

'I'm sorry . . .' Lawrence managed between spasms.

'Do something about it then! It is irritating, to say the least . . .' She broke off as the door opened and Alicia came in. 'Ah – Alicia, at last. I was beginning to think you had decided not to join us this morning.'

Alicia glanced at her with dislike. She was wearing a plain dress of dark grey wool, very different from the flamboyant clothes that had once been her trademark, and her hair had been scraped up hastily rather than carefully arranged as it had used to be. As she served herself with coffee Blanche noticed with distaste that her fingers were grained with the marks of coaldust.

'I have to attend to Hugh before I breakfast these days,' she said coolly.

Blanche's lips tightened. 'This shortage of servants is becoming intolerable.'

Alicia ignored her, turning instead to Gilbert.

'Father, I have been thinking. I am very glad to do what I can for Hugh but I am not sure it is enough. He was telling me last night about his friends – officers like him who have been wounded and need peace and quiet and country air to recover from their ordeal. But not all of them are as lucky as he is with a home like Chewton Leigh. I'd like to have some of them here.'

A small frown puckered Gilbert's forehead. A change had come over Alicia; even he, engrossed as he was in the business of running the works with all the increased pressures that war had brought, had not failed to notice it. Now, looking at her set and determined face, it struck him that she was not a happy young woman.

'What exactly had you in mind?' he enquired.

'We have plenty of room. Perhaps we could offer some of them a place to convalesce.'

'You mean turn Chewton Leigh into some kind of hospital?' Blanche asked incredulously.

'Not a hospital exactly. Obviously we couldn't cope with men still in need of proper medical treatment. But when they reach the stage Hugh is at, it is more a case of providing them with good food, a comfortable bed and a sympathetic ear. And a garden to walk in when the weather improves.'

'And who would look after them, pray?'

Alicia sipped her coffee. 'Perhaps some of the girls who are unwilling to take on domestic posts would see things in a different light if they were working to nurse men who have fought for king and country,' she said, not looking at her stepmother.'

'Ah! You mean it as a ploy!' Blanche smiled thinly. 'Well I would certainly be very much in favour of anything that brought our domestic staff back up to full strength. I suppose I could endure a few strangers in the guest rooms for a while if that were to be the case.'

Alicia eyed her stepmother with dislike. 'I didn't mean that at all. I was looking at it as our contribution to the war effort and thinking of the good we could do.'

And of the handsome young men you could have here in your husband's absence, thought Blanche, but even she did not dare say it.

'And what would your part be in all this?' she asked instead.

'I am sure if I spent a short while in a Red Cross hospital I would soon learn enough to be able to supervise the nursing staff,' Alicia said smoothly. 'Dr Haley would be prepared to act as medical officer for us I know and as I said we would be taking on convalescent cases only.'

'I believe you have taken leave of your senses!' Blanche declared.

'I think Alicia is right,' Lawrence said. He had recovered from his coughing fit now. 'If there is a need for convalescent homes and we can provide one then I think we should do it.'

'And what about those of us who live here?' Leo enquired raising his nose from his copy of *The Times*. 'We are working long hours to build the aeroplanes that are needed. We could do without the inconvenience of sick men in the drawing-room. If you ladies want to do something for the war effort I suggest you confine yourselves to knitting socks or running bazaars to raise money for the plum pudding fund.'

Alicia glared at him. 'Don't patronise, Leo. Well, Father, what do you say? It's your house – the decision is yours.'

Gilbert smoothed his moustache with his index finger. For once he had a certain amount of sympathy with Leo – coming home after a hard day at the works to have to be polite, if not sociable, to strangers suffering from various degrees of shell-shock was not the most engaging of prospects. But it was good to see Alicia taking an interest in something again and commendable that she should want to do her bit for the war effort.

'Well, Alicia, it would be up to you to make the arrangements,' he said. 'I want no part in it. And we must stipulate that the patients would be at the convalescent stage. I have no desire to be called from my bed to play Florence Nightingale. But if you think you can manage and your heart is set on it then you have my blessing.'

Alicia's face lit up. She set down her half-drunk cup of coffee and scraped back her chair.

'Oh thank you, Father! Will you excuse me? I must tell Hugh!'

She ran from the room leaving the other Morses to wonder just what she would be letting them all in for.

In the days that followed, those days which in other years had been filled with gathering holly and mistletoe to deck the house, supervising the trimming of the eight-foot tall fir tree which always occupied pride of place in the drawing-room, wrapping presents and penning greetings, Alicia was busy making preparations to receive her convalescent officers. Four of the bedrooms on the upper floor were made ready and the old nursery opened up to provide a day room. With fires blazing in the grates to thoroughly air the rooms the whole house seemed a little warmer and brighter. Two village women had been persuaded to come in to help with the preparation but they were amazed and not a little outraged to see Alicia with a scrubbing brush and bucket of water washing skirting boards and window sills alongside them.

'It's not right!' they whispered to one another. 'Miss Morse – well, Mrs Bailey as she is now – with her hands all red and spreathed!'

But times were changing. England was at war and Alicia was totally obsessed with getting her convalescent home operational as soon as possible. She had set her sights on receiving her first patients in time for Christmas but this was not to be. The Red Cross were unable to give her the basic training she required until the New Year and so the rooms, smelling of soap and polish and sweet woodsmoke, remained empty and Christmas was celebrated by the family alone.

Because Eric had not been given any leave for Christmas Sarah was invited to Chewton Leigh, she and Stephen motoring over in the smart new Morris which Eric had bought just before the outbreak of war when he had taught Sarah to drive.

'As far as I am concerned you could have stayed here,' Gilbert said when they arrived, warmly wrapped up and laden with presents, their faces rosy from the biting wind. 'But Alicia has taken over the spare rooms.'

'There is no-one in them yet,' Leo objected, taking the opportunity to register his disapproval of the conversion of his home into an infirmary.

'No, but if they are used they will have to be cleaned all over again,' Alicia said. 'We can't put wounded men in rooms where they might get some infection.'

'That is all very well, but it is an inconvenience,' Blanche said haughtily. 'Leo would have liked to invite Emily Sellers to stay for the holiday, wouldn't you, Leo?'

'Her father would never have allowed it,' Alicia said

scornfully. 'Not without Leo getting formally engaged – and he's not going to do that.'

For the past year Leo had been paying court to Emily, whose father, the Reverend Michael Sellers had the living of the next parish. But whenever the family teased him about the imminence of wedding bells Leo made it crystal clear that he had not the slightest intention of walking down the aisle with Emily or anyone else for a good long while.

'That is as may be but I still say it is an inconvenience. Rooms empty, people wanting to stay and not able to, and all because of a handful of officers who may not ever arrive.'

'Please don't worry on my account,' Sarah said hastily. 'I am quite happy to go home . . .' She broke off, suddenly aware of Hugh, sitting in the deep wing chair beside the roaring fire.

'Hello Sarah. My goodness, you are a sight for sore eyes.' His voice was light, amused as ever, but it was a parody somehow of the old gaiety and she thought how much thinner and older he looked, as if he had left the last of his boyhood rosiness in the mud of France. 'I'm sorry I can't get up. You'll have to come over here to wish me a merry Christmas!'

She did so, offering him her cheek because she knew it was expected of her but feeling a prickle of revulsion, nonetheless. Was it just imagination or was there a lecherous look now in those slightly sunken blue eyes? Was his true nature beginning to show through or was it simply that knowing him for what he was gave her the perception to see what had always been there?

'Mama – there's a present for me hanging on the tree! I can see it – it's got my name on it!' Stephen trilled.

'Is there? Just imagine, Father Christmas must have known you would be here!'

'Mama, I want to open it? Please may I?'

'Later. You must be patient, Stephen.'

'Have an orange, old chap.' Hugh took one from the bowl on the small pedestal table beside it and offered it to Stephen. 'Or would you prefer some nuts? I can't reach those, but if you'd like to bring me some and the nutcrackers I'll break them open for you.'

Stephen ran off in search of the nutcrackers and Hugh said: 'He's a fine boy, Sarah. Eric is a lucky man.' But the expression in his eyes told Sarah that it was not so much Eric's good fortune in having Stephen as a son that he was referring to as the fact that he envied the easy access to Sarah. She felt the colour rushing to her cheeks and spun round afraid the others might notice something amiss. But they were laughing and chattering with the effervescent good cheer of Christmas morning. Only Alicia was looking at them, violet eyes narrowed like a cat's, one corner of her mouth raised quizzically. This morning, in a cherry red skirt and high-necked white blouse trimmed with cherry ribbons she looked much more like her old self.

'Well Sarah!' she said playfully. 'Christmas without our husbands! What ever shall we do?'

But Alicia did not have to spend Christmas without her husband. To everyone's surprise Adam arrived in time for lunch having been given permission to leave the camp, where everything had stopped for Christmas, and drive over from Upavon.

When she heard his voice in the hall Sarah's heart began to pound unevenly and she wondered if he would ever fail to affect her in this way – especially when she was taken unawares. But at least she had become practised at concealing her feelings. When he came into the room she was sufficiently in control of herself to greet him as she would have greeted any old friend and when Alicia took his arm, leading him over to the fire, she was able to hide the sharp pain that could still catch her like a stitch in her side to see them together.

Adam was in uniform and very well it suited him, Sarah thought, the double-breasted cut of the jacket seeming to lend breadth to his chest and the high boots making his legs look long and muscular. The sight of the uniform fascinated Stephen too. He gave up bothering to be allowed to open his Christmas tree package and attached himself to Adam instead, pointing at the various buttons and buckles and asking: 'What is that for? Why have you got so many of those . . . ?'

'Stephen, do leave Uncle Adam alone for five minutes!' Sarah told him but Adam merely smiled.

'He's not doing any harm, Sarah. Did you know, Stephen, that your daddy has a uniform like this one?'

'And what is happening to the war whilst you are here enjoying Christmas luncheon?' Leo asked when the meal had been served.

'It has stopped.' Adam looked around the table, saw the incredulous faces and smiled. 'True. Hostilities have ceased, for today at least. Both sides have laid down their weapons and are celebrating Christmas behind their lines.'

'Good God!' Hugh said. Alicia had helped him to the table; now he sat between her and Blanche and, to her discomfort, opposite Sarah. As he toyed with his food she noticed a quiver in his hands that had not been there before and occasionally his head jerked upwards with a peculiar flicking movement. 'Good God!' he said again.

'Exactly.' Gilbert piled vegetables onto his plate and passed them around the table; there were not enough staff to serve them now, especially on Christmas Day. 'Christmas is, after all, a time of good will to all men.'

'Unfortunately it won't last,' Adam said. 'At the stroke of midnight it will all begin again.'

'I suppose you must be pleased about that,' James said. His tone was defiant.

'What the devil do you mean by that?'

'Exactly what I say. It would have been disappointing for you not to have the chance to do a bit of fancy flying over the German lines and perhaps to kill a few of your fellow men.'

There was a moment's shocked silence. Gilbert fixed him with a cold glare.

'There is no need to be offensive, James.'

'It's all right, Gilbert,' Adam said hastily. 'I know James has strong feelings on the subject of war.'

'Feelings which disgrace us all!' Hugh was less inclined to let the remark pass, and Alicia, laying down her knife and fork, joined in.

'How dare you say such things, James, with your own brother wounded in the service of his country?'

366

'I don't care what you say, fighting and killing are not the way to settle anything,' James defended himself. 'There have to be better ways.'

'Such as what?'

'Talking things over – compromise.'

'Standing aside and letting a bully walk all over you, you mean.'

'No, what the Kaiser is doing is wrong, not a doubt of it. But so is war. Two wrongs don't make a right.'

'Talking to a bully does no good. There is only one thing he understands – and that is force,' Hugh maintained.

'You would say that!' James's face was pink now. He disliked arguments almost as much as he disliked physical violence. 'You have always settled your arguments with your fists, Hugh. I haven't forgotten how you and Lawrence used to fight. There was one time – I shall always remember it – when the two of you had a fight in the stables and you made Lawrence's nose bleed and blacked his eye. What good did it do? I don't remember what it was about and I don't suppose you do either but . . .' He broke off. The hush around the table was no longer the silence of a family biting their tongues not to say something which would spoil the Christmas meal but a silence full of horrified embarrassment. The blood had drained from Sarah's face, Blanche looked thunderstruck, while Lawrence, Hugh and Alicia wore expressions of varying degrees of guilt and fury. Only Leo looked faintly puzzled and little Stephen, totally unaware of the impact of James's words, continued to munch happily.

Gilbert looked from one to the other of them. 'Whilst I am aware you boys were always scrapping when you were young I can't say I recall anything so serious.'

Alicia gave a short forced laugh. 'I expect James is exaggerating as usual. It is known as artistic licence.'

'But a bloody nose and a black eye! I'm sure I would not have forgotten something like that. Or does the artistic licence extend that far? Well, James?'

'Yes, sir. I mean . . .' James was stuttering now, realising that he had stumbled into forbidden territory.

'Yes you invented the bloody nose?' Gilbert persisted. 'You mean to say you are a liar as well as a coward?'

'Father, really!' In spite of her earlier outburst Alicia now rushed to his defence. 'James is neither a coward nor a liar. It's just that he has . . . convictions.'

'And illusions.'

'No. The fight he is referring to happened while you were away. In France. It was a very long time ago.'

'Not so long ago but that you all seem to remember it very clearly,' Gilbert said drily.

'I think I should have stayed at Upavon!' Adam remarked in an effort to restore a good humoured atmosphere. 'There is a good deal less shot and shell there!'

'How true!' Blanche said hastily, steering the conversation away from dangerous waters. 'Stephen has finished eating, I see. I suggest we allow him to open the present Father Christmas left for him on the tree. After all he has been a very patient little boy.'

'What a good idea!' Alicia leaped up, fetching the ribbon-trimmed package and helping Stephen to untie the bows. 'What is it, Stephen? Shall we see?'

As he tore aside the paper to reveal a toy merry-go-round, each horse on its barley-sugar pole beautifully carved, Sarah watched, but her hands were twisted tightly together in the folds of her skirt and her forced smile was making her cheeks ache. Feelings in this family ran as high as ever, memories were long. Not even a war could erase them. But at least they were all as anxious as she was to prevent Gilbert discovering the truth of what had happened that long ago day. Concentrating on Stephen and his new toy she avoided the eyes of the others and longed for the time when she would be able to take her son and drive home away from all of them.

From all of them except of course Adam.

She stole a glance at him, bending over to show Stephen how to wind the handle on the merry-go-round to make it turn and the horses rise and fall on their poles, and wished for a sharply aching moment that he was coming with her. But Adam was Alicia's husband and had been now for more than four years. In some ways it seemed a lifetime since he had been hers, in others just yesterday.

With a determination born of long practice Sarah pushed the treacherous thought away.

When the works resumed full production after the short Christmas break Sarah went to see Gilbert in his office. For some time now she had been feeling increasingly dissatisfied with the part she was playing – there was little need now for brochures and catalogues proclaiming the attributes of Morse Bailey machines for every aeroplane turned out by the works was to Government specification and the work which kept Max busy was more secret than the love letters of a king to a courtesan. Sarah hated to feel useless and her frustration had been fuelled by the discovery that Alicia had plans to do something positive for the war effort.

There must be something she could do, Sarah had thought, racking her brains in the long lonely hours when Stephen was in bed and asleep. But when the idea had come to her, it had set her pulses racing with excitement.

She would learn to fly. It was something she had longed to do from the first time she had seen an aeroplane but Eric had forbidden it. Now Eric was no longer here to stop her. Besides, how could he justify doing so when it would be her contribution to the war effort? For there must be jobs for anyone who could fly, even a woman – ferrying aeroplanes, perhaps, making deliveries and air drops of mail and supplies; when every trained man was needed for really dangerous and taxing missions there must be a niche for her . . . The more she thought about it the more enthusiastic Sarah grew and she resolved to take the matter up with Gilbert without delay.

She found him in his office poring over the latest set of instructions from the Royal Aircraft Factory. When he saw her he set them aside, sitting back in his chair and smoothing the tired furrows between his eyebrows with his fingers.

'Sarah, nice to see you!'

'I hope you still think so when I tell you why I'm here.'

369

He smiled wryly. 'That sounds ominous.'

'Not really. But I'm not quite sure if you will approve of what I am going to suggest – and I do so want you to.'

He laughed as he always did at her forthrightness. 'Well, Sarah, what is it you want?'

'I want to learn to fly.'

'Good Lord!'

'I thought you'd be surprised but . . .' She launched into the speech she had prepared and he listened, fingers pressed together.

'Sarah, I don't think it's possible,' he said when she finished. 'The flying schools are mostly occupied with training young men for the RFC and the RNAS. There is a civilian school at Hendon it's true. But I fail to see what use you could be, and I don't think it would be right for you to take up aircraft and instructors who would be better employed training pilots. No, I'm sorry but I couldn't approve such an idea.'

'But I feel so useless!' Sarah pleaded. 'Alicia has her convalescent home after all while I . . .'

'What would become of Stephen while you were away?' Gilbert asked. 'I know he is at nursery school now but didn't his nanny leave to get married last year? Isn't that one of the reasons you have been leaving the office early on the days you have been working?'

'Yes – it didn't seem necessary to replace her but of course if I were away I would have to make some arrangements. I realise a lot of suitable girls have gone off to become nurses but if I ran into difficulties I am sure Annie would be only too pleased to help me out. Stephen and John are very good friends and Annie adores him.'

'Hmm.' Gilbert looked thoughtful. 'In that case I am going to make a suggestion. Why don't you help Alicia with the nursing home?'

Sarah gazed at him in dismay. The idea was ludicrous – she and Alicia, sworn enemies, working so closely together! Worse, since the convalescent home was Alicia's idea, she would be the one in charge. The very thought of having to do as Alicia told her was anathema to Sarah. Yet Gilbert was quite serious in putting forward the suggestion. Would he never learn that the two girls could never be friends? Would he never stop trying to force them together?

'You don't have to make a decision now. I know it is not quite what you had in mind but it is altogether more suitable and if you wish to aid the war effort I know you will give it your serious consideration.' Gilbert paused, looking at her. 'Besides, there is something I would like you to do for me which would give you the chance to see something of what the work would be. Alicia is going to Bristol for a week or so to learn the rudiments of First Aid. Her convalescent home will not involve any real nursing, of course, but there are certain things she needs to know. I wondered if you would come to Chewton Leigh and look after Hugh while she is away. He is much better now but Alicia feels he should not be left alone.'

Sarah's hands and feet had begun to prickle uncomfortably.

'Surely Blanche . . .'

'Blanche is no nurse.'

'You said no nursing was involved.'

'Not as such. But convincing Blanche of that is quite another matter. Anyway she has other commitments.' He said it indulgently, with a twinkle that told Sarah he knew Blanche's 'other commitments' were nothing more than an excuse. 'I would be very grateful, Sarah, if you would do this – as a favour to me.'

With a sinking heart she knew he had her. The prospect of being alone with Hugh for a single hour, let alone perhaps days on end, was repugnant to her but when Gilbert put it like that it was impossible to refuse him after all he had done for her. She folded her hands tightly, conscious of his eyes on her as he waited for her answer.

'Very well. What do I have to do?'

'Alicia begins her course on Monday. Perhaps you could come to Chewton Leigh early enough for her to show you the ropes.'

Another wave of distaste made Sarah's skin prickle. Surely they did not expect her to attend to Hugh's personal toilet – wash him and dress him? She could not do it. Would not!

As if reading her thoughts Gilbert said swiftly: 'Don't worry – you won't have to do anything you might consider improper. Hugh is quite capable of doing everything for himself now with the exception of having his bath and Evans has proved himself most loyal in that respect. No, it is more a matter of being with him and preventing him from brooding too much. A good many of his friends died at Wytschaete, you know, and things were pretty bad. Hugh is more affected than he cares to admit.'

'Really?' she said, doubt creeping into her voice. Hugh the career soldier, Hugh the man – neither had ever struck her as being sensitive enough to be upset by the things he had seen and experienced, however horrible. She pictured him as he had been at Christmas, sitting there and sneering at her, and found Gilbert's statement even more difficult to believe.

'A man like Hugh believes emotion is a weakness,' Gilbert said and again she had the uncanny feeling he could read her thoughts. 'As for fear – he equates that with cowardice, not fully realising that it is only possible to be truly brave when one is afraid. Until now his boldness has all stemmed from lack of imagination. Now he has seen warfare at its most horrible and he does not need imagination to conjure it up. His memories are all too real and he has to come to terms with the emotions they evoke. Besides this he knows he has to return to France as soon as he is fit.' He paused, looking at her directly. 'Some of the stories he may tell you will not be very pleasant, but I believe you are strong enough to listen, just as Alicia is. You are strong enough, aren't you, Sarah?'

'Oh yes,' she said faintly, thinking that however gory Hugh's conversation might be it would be preferable to the personal things he might say to her.

'Good. As to this flying business, put it out of your mind. It is not practicable at the moment – and goodness knows what Eric would say if he knew what you were suggesting. Since he is not here it is only right that I should uphold his wishes.'

372

So much for your fine theories about the emancipation of women! Sarah thought furiously but she did not dare say it. Her respect for Gilbert was far too great.

'I shall tell Alicia to expect you first thing in the morning then,' Gilbert said and there was nothing she could do but nod impotently.

Chapter Thirty-One

On a bitter morning a week after Christmas Adam pushed aside his rough army blanket and crawled out of his narrow bed. Outside the hut which comprised his billet here at the Central Flying School the darkness was still complete and Adam shivered as he drew icy water for his bath and soaped himself vigorously.

If this was war then it was a tedious business! he thought irritably, and not for the first time he found himself envying the young men he tutored. They were a motley crew, some with the instant feeling for the controls which marked out the born flier, some struggling with grim determination to master the techniques and skills, a few who would never make pilots at all. But they all came to the Flying School brimming with enthusiasm, craving the excitement that trench warfare could never give them, ready to swank about their achievements and excuse their disasters, and Adam had found himself growing steadily more impatient with his own role. All very well to tell himself he was playing a vital part in the war effort – he could not rid himself of the feeling that instructing was an old man's job, and he was far from being an old man.

It was true, of course, that very little was going on in France just now. The hard European winter had settled in on the battlefields, freezing the mud in the trenches and restricting the flying. When pilots did manage to take off for reconnaissance they were at the mercy of strong westerly winds which blew them towards Germany. But when conditions improved in the spring it would be a different story. Then the squadrons would have plenty to do. As he threw on his clothes ready to begin another long day's instruction Adam made up his mind. He was not prepared to take a back seat any longer. When the show began again he wanted to be in the thick of it.

As soon as the opportunity arose he went to see the Commanding Officer and put his case. At first the CO tried to talk him out of it – Adam was one of the best and most experienced instructors he had. But Adam persisted and at last the CO agreed to put his request to the authorities. A week later the reply came back – granted. Adam was to be posted to one of the squadrons at present in France who had suffered losses. His place at Upavon would be taken by a Flying Officer who had been wounded when his Avro had been shot down but who was now well enough to return to light duties.

'You had better take a few days' leave and go home to say goodbye to your family,' the CO told him, squinting at Adam through his monocle. 'God alone knows when you will be back in England again.'

'Can't we be friends, Sarah?' Hugh asked.

It was her second day at Chewton Leigh House. Annie had agreed to look after Stephen and with some trepidation Sarah had moved in to be on hand whenever she was wanted. This morning she had been up with the lark to lay the fire in Hugh's sitting-room and bring him breakfast and the round of chores took her back to her days in service. But she minded this less than having Hugh's company forced upon her and now his silken request made her bristle, wary of what was to come.

'I don't know what you mean,' she said, avoiding his eyes.

'Yes you do. I believe you'd be nicer to me if I were a German prisoner of war!' he said ruefully. 'But since we are stuck with one another for the next couple of weeks don't you think we should let bygones be bygones? What happened was a very long time ago and before that we used to get along very well. You liked me then, didn't you?'

Briefly she was transported back to those sunny days of her youth before everything had turned sour. Yes, she had liked Hugh. He had often been her champion and she had enjoyed his company. It was what he had done to her that she could not forgive.

She glanced at him, sitting there in his chair with the breakfast tray on his knees, looking thin and frail almost in his paisley silk dressing gown, and wondered suddenly if perhaps she had been too hard on him. He had been young and headstrong, carried away by a young man's passions. As for his betrayal of her that was almost understandable. He must have been terrified of Gilbert finding out what he had done. It did not excuse him, of course, but all the same it was true that it was a long time ago now. Hugh was no longer the brash youth he had been – there were dark shadows beneath his eyes now and lines on his handsome face that had not been there before.

'I hate being bad friends with you, Sarah,' Hugh was saying, and the eagerness of his tone tore at her heart. 'Couldn't we at least be civil to one another whilst you are here? Otherwise we are in for a pretty miserable couple of weeks, aren't we?'

The door opened; it was Evans who had come to help Hugh with his toilet. Sarah made to leave but Hugh caught at her arm.

'Please?' he pressed her and she caught a glimpse of the old, charming Hugh.

'Oh very well, we'll see,' she said shortly.

It was impossible to dispel the grudges of a lifetime so easily but over the next few days her attitude towards him softened imperceptibly.

He was subject to wild swings of mood, she discovered. At times he could be amusing, entertaining her with anecdotes of life in the Officers' Mess, at others he became so silent and depressed she felt it her duty to prise from him those other, horrifying stories which upset him as much to tell as it did for her to listen, but which were a vital part of the healing process none the less.

He told of refugees traipsing wearily along with their few pathetic belongings heaped onto handcarts, of burning houses sending showers of sparks and clouds of acrid smoke into the clear autumn air, of a ravaged countryside where the trees, shattered by shellfire, stretched bare and broken arms to the sky. Worst of all he told of the friends he had seen die, of the thunder of the guns and the screams of terrified horses.

'Christ, don't ever tell Alicia what happens to the horses out there,' he begged. 'She'd go crazy if she knew. The battlefield, with all the modern weapons of war, is no place for them any more.'

Sarah pressed her hands together so tightly that the nails bit into the palms in an effort not to show her own horror at the fate of the proud and trusting beasts. Things must be very bad, she decided, if a dedicated cavalryman like Hugh had come to believe that the horse no longer had a place in warfare.

'The stuff they have now is almost beyond belief,' Hugh went on. 'Take the Jack Johnsons, for instance – they will blast a hole in the ground twenty feet deep and thirty feet across. And the "coalboxes" – where do these names come from? – can kill several men at once. It's a bloody war, Sarah – and I use the word advisedly, not as the adjective that figures prominently in our CO's vocabulary and is not fit for use in the presence of ladies.'

He smiled slightly as he said it but Sarah saw a muscle spasm begin in his cheek. Impulsively she reached over and took his hand.

'It must be dreadful,' she said inadequately.

'Yes, and it's going to get worse. This war isn't like any other, Sarah, yet it is being fought the old way. Whole companies rushing from cover, wailing like banshees, for all the world as if it were a battle back in the days of the Civil War, and getting mown down like flies. And the more the boffins work on producing newer, more effective weapons of every kind the more dire it will get – unless the puppet masters change their tactics. I tell you, I'm not looking forward to going back – and I am a trained soldier.'

'Do you have to go back?' Sarah asked.

'Dammit, of course I do!' Hugh replied, his nerves spilling over into irritation. 'As soon as I am fit I shall be in the thick of it again – unless it's over first, and I don't think it will be. Not while there are still men left alive to stand up and fight.'

His fingers tightened on Sarah's but she scarcely noticed; cold horror had replaced all other feeling. What was happening out there was almost beyond belief, certainly beyond understanding. How could human beings *do* this to one another? For the first time she felt a glimmer of sympathy for James and his pacifist views. But she knew better than to mention them now. She sat silently holding Hugh's hand and feeling more angry and more helpless than she had ever felt in her life before. All the crises and troubles of her own life seemed so trivial in comparison with this, mere pinpricks seen against this huge running sore of horror.

The days passed and Sarah found something of their old companionship returning as she did her best to keep his mind off the nightmares he had lived through and to which he must shortly return. And without a doubt she was good for him. Soon he was taking his bath before breakfast unaided and eating with the family, so much more like his old self that even Gilbert noticed and commented on it.

'You always knew how to bring a little sunshine into our lives, Sarah,' he said, smiling at her, and she felt as warmed by his approval as she had when she was twelve years old.

It was almost the end of the second week and they were in the drawing-room, Sarah reading to Hugh from *A Tale of Two Cities*. Since they had run out of topics of conversation it was a good way to pass an afternoon but Sarah's mind was not completely on the book. This morning she had received a letter from Eric telling her that he was moving to Northolt from where he would be doing a certain amount of operational flying, patrolling the coast to keep a look out for raiders. Ten days before Christmas the German battle cruisers which had carried out an abortive raid on Great Yarmouth six weeks earlier had come back to the attack and this time had met with more success. Scarborough, Whitby and Hartlepool had been shelled from the sea and more than a hundred civilians killed. Now aeroplanes were to be used as an early warning system in an effort to prevent such a thing happening again.

When she reached the end of the chapter Sarah looked up from the page to see Hugh's eyes on her. She had thought she had grown used to his company over the past week but now something in his expression disconcerted her, an echo from the past. She placed the bookmark between the pages, set the book down on the table beside her and stood up.

'Would you like a cup of tea?'

'Not particularly.' His eyes were still on her face and his gaze was disconcerting.

'Well I certainly would!' she said, a little too quickly. 'My throat is as dry as a bone.' She turned, intending to escape to the kitchen, but as she passed his chair his hand shot out, fastening around her wrist. 'What are you doing?' she demanded, startled.

'Come here!' His voice was low and urgent. 'I want you near to me.'

'Hugh, for goodness' sake!'

'Be nice to me,' he wheedled. 'It's not such an unpleasant thought, is it? You like me, don't you?'

'No, I don't.' She tried to free herself from his grasp and could not. Frail he might have looked but there was no mistaking his strength now. He laughed, holding her fast and levering himself to his feet so that he towered over her.

'Oh Sarah, don't you remember the way it was? I do. How could I ever forget?' His voice was slightly slurred as if he had been drinking though Sarah knew he had not.

'You're mad!' she managed.

His lip curled a little. 'Am I? Perhaps you make me mad.'

She began to struggle but somehow struggling only brought her into closer contact with him. His lips found hers and he kissed her brutally. She beat at him with her hands but he was too strong for her and he held her fast, laughing down at her.

'Oh Sarah, how you love to fight! You always did. But you mustn't fight too much now. I am a sick man, remember.'

'You are sick all right!' she grated and tasted the blood on her lips where his teeth had sunk in.

'You wouldn't send me back to France without something to remember, would you? Come on now, Sarah . . .'

'Stop it!' she screamed, memories of the past so fresh and sharp in her mind that she reacted with something close to hysteria. But her resistance only excited him more. His hand went to the fastening of her dress, tearing at it in a frenzy. 'Stop it!' she screamed again as the fastening gave.

And at that precise moment the door opened and a voice enquired: 'What the devil is going on here?'

Again it was *déjà vu*. Hugh released Sarah abruptly and she swung round, half expecting to see Lawrence, his fists raised to fight Hugh. But it was not Lawrence. It was Adam.

For a moment the shock of seeing him numbed her. Then reaction to Hugh's attack, shame, and horror that he should find her in such circumstances made her sob aloud. Her hands flew to the open neck of her dress, pulling it together over her exposed bosom. She heard Hugh laugh but recognised the trace of nervousness which was choking him.

'Adam, old man! Sarah and I were just having a bit of fun . . .'

Adam was staring in disbelief and her shame turned to fury. Once before Hugh had blamed her and she had been unable to defend herself; he was not going to do so again.

'How dare you, Hugh?' she spat at him. 'You might have been having fun – I certainly was not! If I had known you were capable of a repeat performance I would never have come here to keep you company, no matter how Gilbert begged me. And to think I felt sorry for you! You haven't changed. Not one iota. You are still the same. Well, I won't keep silent any longer. The only reason I have done so all these years is because I thought the truth would hurt Gilbert too much – and because I was afraid he might not believe me. Now . . .'

She whirled round to face Adam. 'Listen to what I have to say – and then see if you think I was enjoying myself with this monster!'

The room seemed to sing still and echo with her words. Hugh had turned pale, the blood draining from his face and

380

leaving it the colour of old parchment so that once again he looked sick and ill; Adam was staring from one to the other of them like a man who had seen a ghost. And suddenly the realisation of the hopelessness of it struck her like a thunderbolt. Whatever she said it would make no more difference now than it had then. Adam would dismiss it all as hysterical guilt. She could see the contempt and disgust in his eyes and she could bear it no longer.

'Oh, don't look at me like that!' she snapped.

She ran from the room but by the time she reached the staircase she was seeing it through a red mist. She lifted her skirt clear of her flying feet and raced upstairs as if a dozen devils were on her heels. She was using one of the rooms Alicia had prepared for her officers – there had been no alternative – and she rushed in, closing the door after her and leaning against it, her breath coming in sobbing gasps and the tears, hot and blinding, running down her face.

Oh the injustice of it! She had grown used to Lawrence, Blanche and Alicia regarding her as little better than a whore, but for Adam to think the same . . .

After a while she crossed to where her valise was stowed on the newly constructed luggage rack and laid it open on the bed. She had begun throwing her clothes into it when a tap at the door made her stiffen. 'Who is it?'

'Adam. May I come in?'

She almost called out 'no', she did not want to see anyone and especially not him, but she did not. She crossed to the door and opened it.

'Yes?'

His eyes took in her tear-stained face, looking past her he saw the suitcase open on the bed, her clothes strewn around it, her toiletries still arranged neatly on the dressing table, the only personal effects in that bare and sterile room.

'Are you all right?' His voice was rough.

'Yes.'

'But you are leaving.'

'I can hardly stay here now. In any case I came to look after Hugh and it is clear that he has recovered. He doesn't need me.'

381

'Sarah . . .'

'If that is all you came to say I'd be obliged if you'd leave me to get on with my packing.' She turned her back on him, crossed to the bed and dumped a day dress, unfolded, into the case.

He followed her into the room. 'What happened, Sarah?'

She swept up a handful of toiletries from the dressing table.

'You saw what happened.'

'No, I only saw *part* of what happened.'

'And drew your conclusions. I'm a whore, Adam. The daughter of a whore. Hasn't Alicia told you that?'

He ignored the challenge. 'What did you mean, Sarah, by what you said to Hugh?'

'Nothing.'

'Come now, don't treat me like a fool. There's more to this than meets the eye, isn't there? I have always known there was something. I want to know what it is.'

'Why?' She was fastening her case, avoiding looking at him.

'Because I care about you Sarah – very much,' he said quietly. 'I can't bear to see you so upset. I want to know what this is all about.'

She swallowed. Her throat felt dry and choky.

'Why don't you ask Hugh?'

'I did. He was very evasive. So now I'm asking you. Please tell me, Sarah.'

Her dry throat convulsed. She covered her face with her hands. 'I can't.'

'Yes you can.' He took her hands, holding them. His eyes seemed to be looking into her very soul. Gently he eased her down until she was sitting on the edge of the bed and she did not resist. Every bit of fight seemed to have gone out of her. 'Tell me.'

And suddenly she was telling him, the words tumbling out, confiding the secrets she had kept to herself for so long. When she had finished she looked up at him fearfully. His face was hard.

'Do you believe me?'

'Well, of course. Why shouldn't I?' He did not mention he had already heard another, different version of the story.

'No-one else did. Or perhaps they chose not to.'

'Perhaps. After all, Hugh is one of their own.'

He was making excuses for Alicia's part in it, she thought. For some reason it hurt all the more sharply when he was sitting there beside her, holding her hands, comforting her.

'I never thought he'd try it again,' she said. 'If I had I'd never have come here, not even for Gilbert. Or perhaps – perhaps I did suspect he might, but I thought I was capable of taking care of myself now.'

'Oh Sarah.' He shook his head. 'And you never told Gilbert.'

'No. I didn't want him to know. It would have hurt him so much, not only because Hugh . . . did what he did, but because the others lied to him. Promise me you won't tell him, Adam.'

'I wouldn't say anything. It's not my place. But I think he should know all the same. He never could understand why you went away.'

'I know and I'm sorry about that. But I still think it's best he should blame me rather than know his family . . .' She broke off, remembering that she was talking to Alicia's husband, then raised her eyes defiantly. For Gilbert's sake she had protected them all these years. But this was one sacrifice she was not prepared to make.

'Just as long as you believe me, that's all that matters,' she said.

'I believe you.'

Tears stung her eyes again. 'That's all right then,' she said. 'I don't care about anything else.'

'So why are you crying?' He said it very gently.

'Because I thought that you . . . oh Adam, I couldn't bear to think that you would think badly of me. Not you . . .'

'Sarah, I could never think badly of you . . .'

And suddenly, without knowing how it happened, she was in his arms.

383

It had been so long, so long. She had hungered for him so much, been so certain that he was lost to her forever, that never again would she feel the rippling muscles of his back and shoulders beneath her fingers, the roughness of his chin against her cheek. It was wrong, she knew. They each belonged now to someone else. But the depth of her desire, suppressed for so long, swept her through the barriers that drew the dividing line between comfort and love and she clung to him as little able to tear herself away as she had been to control her tears.

Adam – the whole world was Adam. It had been from the moment she had met him and nothing that had happened between, none of the ebbs and flows, none of the moments of despair and heartache, mattered any more. His lips touched her forehead, her cheeks, her throat, and she moved sensuously beneath them, relishing every contact. Then his mouth found hers, kissing her with the fervour of a drowning man gasping for air and she felt as if she were melting into him, losing all identity, all sense of time and place. The storms of the past hour were forgotten now, Hugh like the rest of the world had ceased to exist. There was only Adam and her love for him, stronger, deeper, more all-consuming than any other emotion she had ever experienced.

Her body ached for him, every nerve ending alive suddenly and singing. She felt his hands caressing her like the touch of icy fingers on fevered skin and the echoes sensitised every inch of her – breasts, stomach and her soft inner thighs so that she felt as if an electric current were passing through her. Adam . . . Adam . . . For long, precious moments she hung suspended in this vortex of unreality, knowing only that at last she was where she wanted to be, sheltered from the storms, home at last, warming herself at the fire of his love. Then perversely she was aware of the first tiny flicker of guilt and the awareness fanned the flicker into a fire.

'Adam, no, we mustn't. It's wrong. Eric . . .'

'You don't love Eric. You never did.' He continued to kiss her.

'Adam – no! Alicia . . .'

At the mention of his wife's name he raised his head, looking at her.

'Why are you determined to spoil this?'

'I don't want to spoil . . .'

'Then hush!' He kissed her again, his lips stopping her protests. But the first uncaring magic had gone. Alicia and Eric were there between them now, shadows of reality. Sensing her withdrawal he released her.

'Our marriage is nothing but a sham, Sarah. It was never really anything else. A marriage of convenience, you could say.'

'Why did you go through with it then?'

'Why? Because . . .' He broke off, answering her question with one of his own. 'Why did you run off and leave me?'

She hesitated. 'I'm not sure I should tell you that . . . I don't want to spoil what there is between you.'

'I told you – there is nothing to spoil. What feeling I had for Alicia died long ago. But it does matter to me very much to know why you . . . did what you did. Tell me.' His eyes seemed to bore into her.

'I . . . Alicia . . .' And still the words would not come. It was too dreadful.

'I think I already suspect the truth.' His face was hard. 'It was some kind of blackmail, wasn't it?' She nodded wordlessly. 'She threatened to tell Gilbert about you and Hugh, is that it?'

'That was part of it.'

'And the rest?' He took her chin between his fingers. 'Come on, Sarah, you are going to tell me if I have to crush it out of you.'

'Very well.' She could not look at him. 'If you are determined to have the truth, here it is. It was at the time you desperately needed Gilbert's backing. She said she would see you did not get it unless I did as she asked. She promised to see your future with the company was secure if I left the field clear for her. Otherwise she said it was the end of your dream of an aeroplane.' She glanced at him fearfully

385

as she finished speaking. The expression on his face was unreadable.

'You did that for me?'

'And for Annie and Max. Annie was having John and she was desperately afraid Max would not be able to afford to marry her. So I had no choice, did I? I knew simply leaving was not enough. So I went back to Eric.'

'You used him.'

'Yes, I suppose I did. But I have been a good wife to him, Adam. I've made him happy. And I'm going to go on making him happy. I owe him that much at least.'

His hands tightened around her chin. She could feel his fingers biting into her jawbone.

'You can't go back to him. Not now. I won't let you.'

Her eyes swam with tears. The temptation was so strong she did not know how to resist it. She swallowed at the knot in her throat.

'I have to, Adam. It's too late for anything else. Too many people are involved – innocent people who will be hurt.'

'Eric has had you for almost five years. If he hasn't been able to make you love him in that time then he doesn't deserve you.'

'And what about Stephen?'

'I'll take care of Stephen.'

'But he worships his father, Adam. And anyway, Eric might refuse to let me have him. I couldn't leave him – he's a little boy, he needs me. No, it's out of the question – impossible!'

'That's what they said about getting an aeroplane off the ground.'

'Oh – fiddle! Getting an aeroplane off the ground is nothing compared to what you are proposing.'

'Do you love me?'

'You know I do. I always have and I always will. But I can't do it, Adam. We have to forget this afternoon happened and try to go on just as before.'

Something in her tone must have told him her mind was made up. He let go of her abruptly and stood up.

'That is one thing I don't have to do. The reason I came home today was to break the news that I have been given a transfer. I am going to join a squadron. In France.'

She gasped, covering her mouth with her hands. 'Oh no!'

'Oh yes.' He smiled quizzically. 'I thought it was about time I did my bit for England. Now I see it is an even better solution than I imagined.'

'Oh Adam!' She stretched out her hands to him. 'Do you have to go?'

'I'm afraid I do.'

'But supposing you . . .' She broke off, biting back the words. 'Supposing you don't come back?'

He shrugged. 'That really would solve everything satisfactorily, wouldn't it?'

'Oh don't say such things!' She was in turmoil now. A moment ago everything had seemed so clear cut and she had known exactly what she should do, no matter how hard it might be. Now suddenly everything had turned topsy turvy again. He smiled crookedly.

'No, I dare say it's not such a bad thing that I am going away. It will give us a breathing space, won't it? Time to think. By the time the war is over you may feel able to change your mind.' His tone was very cool; she felt as if he had gone away from her already. The earlier closeness had all gone, now there was only confusion and despair. 'I take it you still intend to leave Chewton Leigh tonight?'

'Of course. I couldn't stay under the same roof as Hugh. Will you tell Gilbert? Say that I couldn't bear to be parted from Stephen for a moment longer.'

He raised an eyebrow. 'I shall tell Gilbert what I think fit.'

'Adam, you promised!'

'I promised not to tell him what happened all those years ago. I said nothing about this afternoon's episode. I don't see why he shouldn't be told that Hugh has recovered sufficiently to make a nuisance of himself. But if it will upset you I suppose I must be careful what I say. Now – if you are going perhaps I should leave you to finish your packing.'

'Very well.' She took her cool tone from him. It was after all what she wanted – was it not? But as he turned to the door she simply could not bear it. She ran after him, grabbing his arm. 'Adam – you will take care, won't you? Please, come back safely – oh please!'

For a moment their eyes met and held, love, pure and strong, passing between them like an electric current. Then he pulled her to him, very gently kising her again, pressing her to him as if to remember every line of her body with his own, and she felt as if her very soul was being drawn out of her, slowly, poignantly, leaving her an empty shell. Her arms were twined around his neck for she suddenly had the craziest feeling that if she could only keep him there in her arms everything would be miraculously changed and they could be together for ever. But with an abrupt movement he freed himself, turning again for the door.

'Goodbye my love.'

'Goodbye.'

Then he was gone and the bleakness and sense of loss came rushing in to engulf her. Nothing had changed. Circumstances were still conspiring to keep them apart just as they always had and perhaps always would.

Only now there was a new factor – the danger of war which could take him from her forever. And in that moment Sarah knew that nothing was important, nothing mattered, just as long as he came home safely.

Chapter Thirty-Two

The cold winter months had done nothing to help Lawrence's cough. Though he tried to hide from his family the fact that it was worsening he was beginning to be seriously concerned about the racking bouts he suffered which now occurred frequently and which sometimes kept him awake at night. And he was always so tired! Sometimes it was all he could do to muster the energy for everyday duties – especially since they were becoming more and more onerous as the war effort reached new heights of endeavour.

One day in February Lawrence decided to go to see Dr Haley. He had delayed the visit as long as possible partly because he objected to Blanche's imperious commands that he should do so and partly because he was secretly afraid of what he might hear from the now-ageing but still robust doctor, and when Dr Haley had examined him Lawrence knew from the old man's face that his fears had been justified.

'I don't care for it, Lawrence, I don't care for it at all,' Dr Haley said bluntly, easing his thumbs under the watch chain which straddled his portly chest. 'You should have come to see me before now.'

'With a cough? I'm not an old woman, you know!' Lawrence said in an effort to hide his anxiety. 'But now I am here, can you give me something to ease it?'

'I dare say I can do that but I have the gravest suspicion it is more than just a cough,' the doctor informed him. 'There is only one thing for it in my opinion and that is to get away from this damned climate of ours. I think a spell in a sanatorium is what you need, with good clear air and plenty of rest. I know of a very good one in Austria but with the war on I dare say it would make more sense to look to Switzerland. Leave it with me and I'll see what I can do.'

'Good Lord, that's out of the question!' Lawrence said, aghast.

'Why, man? There's no shortage of money, is there?'

'Of course not. But we are at full production at the works. I can't go haring off to Switzerland!'

'Well, Lawrence, it's up to you. But if you value your health you'll think about it – and soon.'

'Impossible!'

'You won't be much use to the works or anyone else if you put yourself in a coffin,' the doctor said flatly. He reached for his pen, thinking for a moment. 'I'll prescribe you something as you ask but I do urge you to give some serious thought to the sanatorium. And don't hesitate to come and see me again, or call me to the house, if things get worse.'

'Very well, I'll think about it,' Lawrence agreed. But already his mind was made up. He couldn't leave the works and go off to Switzerland for months, or even weeks. If he did he would return to find himself usurped by Leo de Vere. The damned fellow was always breathing down his neck – with a golden opportunity like that presented to him he would take over before Lawrence's chair was cool. No, whatever Dr Haley might say he would simply have to dose himself up, try to get a little more rest, and soldier on. After all it was no more than thousands of others were doing on both sides of the Channel.

Hoping his absence had not been noticed, Lawrence returned to the works.

Alicia's first 'guests', as she preferred to call the recuperating patients, arrived during the early part of the bleak cold month of February – two young officers who had been wounded at Ypres. One had lost a leg, amputated in a field hospital when gangrene threatened, the other, a gentle student who had left his studies at Oxford to rush with patriotic fervour into the army on the outbreak of war, had been blinded. Both had suffered as much emotional damage as they had physical – their nerves were so shot that the slightest sudden noise or even a raised voice could turn them into gibbering wrecks and when they suffered nightmares, as they did frequently, it was only the thick walls of Chewton Leigh which prevented them from waking the whole house with their screams.

Alicia was good with them. Her rather hard, autocratic manner seemed to reassure them and provided a crutch while they struggled to come to terms with the shattered wreck of their lives. But Hugh had little patience with them. For one thing he did not care to be reminded of the terrible wounds it was possible to suffer, for another his own nerve had recovered so well he found himself irritated by their babblings.

'Call themselves men? They'd never have got commissions in the regular army,' he said disgustedly.

'They aren't men – they are little more than boys,' Alicia pointed out. 'And they have suffered terribly.'

But Hugh, who seemed to have become even more arrogant, like a young plant which has weathered the winter storms and grown stronger because of it, refused to be sympathetic.

'No wonder we are not making any progress with this war with lillies like them fighting on our side. I'm glad to be going back, I can tell you.'

Alicia's eyes darkened. She was dreading the imminent departure of her brother. Bad enough to know that Adam was in France; when Hugh had gone too . . .

I am only glad I have the convalescent home to keep me going, Alicia thought grimly.

A few weeks later Hugh left to return to the front and scarcely had he gone than news began to come through that things were hotting up. The stranglehold of winter was easing now and there were new battles to be fought back and forth across the French countryside along the line where the name places, once obscure and unheard of except by the people who lived in them, were destined to be on every tongue and enter the annals of history. In March came the battle of Neuve Chapelle; in April the second battle of Ypres, which people had christened 'Wipers'; when Maytime was covering English trees in blossom those around Aubers Ridge were being blasted into shrivelled stumps. The casualty lists were depressingly long now, everyone, it seemed, knew someone who had been killed or wounded, and a depression seemed to hang over the countryside so that the sunshine had an aurora of darkness around it and the sky, though clear and blue, seemed heavy with threatening storms.

Stories had trickled through from the front too of a new horror – the Germans were using gas on the British troops. At first the suggestion was almost too obscene to credit, but at Chewton Leigh a letter from Adam confirmed that it was true. Flying over the Ypres Salient one April evening he had seen what looked like greenish yellow smoke wafting away from the German trenches; going down to take a closer look he had been able to identify it for what it was – gas. Gilbert, with his typically English sense of fair play, was shocked; he had not believed anyone, not even the Germans, could stoop so low. He much preferred to believe in the spirit of comradeship which existed between the aviators and which Adam had described in earlier letters.

One letter in particular had caused considerable interest when read aloud over breakfast:

We were in the Mess last night when someone came rushing in and said he had seen two German airmen being frogmarched along by some Zouave soldiers and a mob of French civilians. They were jeering at the two poor fellows, spitting and pelting them with anything they could get their hands on. We were outraged. The entire squadron piled into a lorry and went out to look for them. When we caught up with them we explained, politely enough, that as they had been shot down by the British they were British prisoners and we wished to take them over but the French would have none of it. They became very excited at the prospect of losing their sport and in the end there was nothing for it but for us to show them we meant business. There was quite a scuffle but we had our way. When we returned to our base we not only had the Germans but also the two Zouaves. We had to take some of the more belligerent of the French with us as prisoners too but had to release them later, a little the

392

worse for drink. I do not expect them to be quite so abusive to German aviators in future.

The letter had brought a little light relief but this was short lived. Perhaps, thought Gilbert, the Frenchmen had not been so wrong after all – if the Germans could descend to such brutalities as gas to win a hasty victory then they could hardly expect to be treated as gentlemen, aviators or not.

Because Adam's letters went to Chewton Leigh House Sarah had to be content to get news of him second-hand and each day when she went to the works she sought Gilbert out in a ferment of anxiety. She could not always ask if there was news of Adam of course; a little interest was understandable but to allow Gilbert to see that she thought of little else would quickly have aroused his suspicions. But at least simply talking with Gilbert could set her mind at rest for a little while, for the old maxim 'no news is good news' held good. If Gilbert was his normal self then all must be well with Adam. It was not much, but it had to suffice. And it was only when she was back in her own office that the thought would strike her: mail took at least four days to get through – a letter received today from Adam did not necessarily mean he was still alive. He could have been shot down in the meantime and they would not know.

But I would know, Sarah comforted herself. If anything happened to Adam I am quite sure I would know. And she would turn her mind determinedly to the papers she was working on – papers she had taken over from Lawrence, whom she knew was in truth no longer fit to be working at all.

Of all the family she was the only one who knew how seriously ill Lawrence was. She had gone into his office one day, rushing in unexpectedly as she so often did without knocking, to find him slumped in his chair with his head in his hands.

'Lawrence – whatever is the matter?' she had demanded, and caught at a low ebb he had told her.

'You *must* go to a sanatorium!' she told him when he had finished. 'If Dr Haley says so – you must!'

He shook his head. 'And have Leo step into my shoes? Not likely! It's bad enough now keeping the little rat from ousting me. I know Father doesn't like him but he's so damned persistent it's hard to refuse him especially when I know damned well I'm not on top of my work. Look at the pile of returns I have to do now! It seems to get bigger every day.'

'That's because you're not fit, Lawrence,' Sarah said. She was desperately worried by the drawn look of him but since she disliked Leo every bit as much as he did she could well understand his feelings. 'Look – can I help? I'm not exactly overloaded with work these days – in fact I had been wondering if I could take on other responsibilities. Just tell me what I have to do . . .'

And so she had become Lawrence's secret ally, her sharp brain quickly assimilating the knowledge and taking over much of the work which he had found demanding even when he had been well.

The extra work stimulated her; it took her mind off her worries about Adam – and about Eric, who was now flying patrols to watch out for the Zeppelins which had begun offensives on the east coast. This was another departure which had been received with horror and near disbelief – German bombs actually falling on English towns and killing people in their own homes – shocking! Where would it all end? But at least the peace of Somerset was relatively undisturbed. At least they could go to sleep at night safe in their own beds – it was something to be thankful for.

The long school summer holidays, when they came, posed something of a problem for Sarah, who had been unable to find a replacement nanny for Stephen. The whole servant problem was as bad as ever, as Blanche was only too fond of complaining, for most of the girls who had not turned to nursing had run off to work in munitions factories where there was more money to be made in a week than most of them had earned in a month in service, and they enjoyed personal freedom beyond their wildest dreams. The only applicants Sarah had interviewed for the post had been totally unsuitable and the problem seemed insoluble.

During term time, Annie was quite happy to collect Stephen from nursery school along with John, give him tea and entertain him until Sarah arrived to take him home, but Sarah was loath to impose on her friend's easy going hospitality from morning till night for the duration of the summer. If Annie had a nanny it would be a different matter, but she did not, for she had steadfastly refused to employ one in spite of pressure from Max who thought it would be a status symbol.

'I didn't have John for someone else to look after him,' she would say, her sweet face so set and determined that Max knew argument was useless.

Being aware of Annie's views on the subject made Sarah even more reluctant to beg her assistance for she thought Annie would think her a poor sort of mother not to want to spend the summer with her only son. But when she summoned the courage to raise the question she found Annie only too ready to oblige.

'Good gracious, Sarah, of course I don't mind! Stephen is wonderful company for John – they are just like brothers. Better than brothers, in fact, being the same age.'

'Bless you, Annie!' Sarah hugged her. 'You don't know what a weight you have taken off my mind. I was so afraid you wouldn't approve. I know how much store you set on a mother having a close relationship with her child.'

'Well, it's easy for me, isn't it? I haven't anything else to do, while you . . . you are working for the war effort, aren't you?'

Sarah refrained from saying she would hope to be doing something other than simply being a mother, war or no war.

'I know how busy you are,' Annie went on. 'What with all the aeroplanes that are needed – and the engines too. There simply aren't enough being built in this country, Max says, and they are having to be obtained from abroad. I think that's shameful. But I'll let you into a secret. I couldn't work now even if I wanted to because . . .' her round face flushed with pleasure, 'well, I'm going to have another baby!'

'You are? When?'

'In November. Don't sound so surprised!' Annie twinkled. 'Why shouldn't I have another baby? Married people do, you know.'

'Yes of course and I'm delighted for you, Annie,' Sarah said. 'It's just that . . . well, Max is hardly ever at home is he?' She broke off, flushing as she realised this was a rather immodest thing to say even to her friend, but if Annie thought so she gave no sign of it.

'Oh I know, he's so busy, Sarah, with this new project of his. Of course it's all top secret and he does seem to spend more time locked up in that office of his than anywhere else. Often I'm fast asleep long before he comes home. I only hope he'll have a little more time to himself soon or John will hardly know him – and the new baby will be practically fatherless!' She broke off, biting her lip. 'I suppose I shouldn't complain, though. At least I know he's safe at Chewton Leigh, not off halfway across the world, fighting Germans.'

Sarah's stomach contracted. 'So it's all right for Stephen to come to you during the holidays?' she asked quickly in order to change the subject.

'Of course it is. I'm only surprised you thought you had to ask.'

And so, when nursery school disbanded for the summer holidays, Sarah took Stephen each day to Annie's house and collected him each evening.

Though she was grateful for the arrangement and though she admitted she would have gone crazy with boredom if she had had to stay at home with him all day as Annie did, yet perversely she was slightly discomfited by the eagerness with which he left her, jumping out of the motor and skipping up the path to Annie's pretty little cottage where roses trailed around the door like the setting for a popular song without so much as a backward glance. Often Annie, coming out to meet him with John at her heels like a lively puppy, had to tell him to wave goodbye to his mother and sometimes when she arrived to collect him she was greeted with groans and cries of: 'Oh no! Can't I stay just a little longer? We were just going to . . .'

On occasions such as these Sarah heard her voice become very firm like a schoolmarm. 'No, you can't, Stephen. It's bedtime and you have been bothering Aunt Annie quite long enough.'

'But Mama . . .'

'No!' And she was truthful enough to admit that her sharpness stemmed partly from the fact that he seemed a great deal more at home with Annie and John than he did with her. Surely he should be at least a little pleased to see her? But he never seemed to be. She was just a nuisance – a killjoy, spoiling his fun.

Perhaps it is time we had a holiday, Sarah thought. Just a little one, just long enough for me to get to know my son a bit better.

A whole week was out of the question; she did not feel she could abandon Lawrence for that long. But perhaps a few days would be possible. She mentioned the idea to Annie who responded enthusiastically; a couple of days by the sea would be lovely. Neither did Gilbert raise any objections – Sarah had been working too hard in his opinion and a break would do her good.

At once Sarah set the arrangements in hand and on a lovely Saturday in early July the two girls and the children set off in Sarah's motor for the south coast. The sun was shining from a clear sky, the air was warm and calm, everything augured well for a pleasant break. But for some reason she could not comprehend Sarah felt uneasy. As she and Annie sat companionably side by side on the shingly beach watching the children run and play in the breakers and search for unusual shells and pebbles to outdo one another it nagged at her like a persistent rash, a nameless foreboding which refused to be stilled.

Perhaps, she told herself, it was an echo of that other day when she and Annie had been at the seaside with the children – the day war had been declared. But somehow she could not believe that that alone would cause her to be quite so apprehensive. She thought of Adam somewhere in France and wondered if some sixth sense was warning her that he was in danger; she thought of Eric, flying daily as both instructor and operational scout, and said a silent prayer for their safety. But the apprehension remained, feeding on itself until the very sunshine seemed darkened by it.

The beach was almost deserted – war time seemed to have kept people at home. The boys explored happily and even ran a small way into a tunnel in the rocks.

'Mama – there's a cave! It's very dark and wet – but there's light at the other end. Can we go and see where it leads?'

'No, Stephen. Stay here on the beach.' She sounded snappy and Annie frowned.

'Is anything wrong, Sarah? You seem very preoccupied.'

'I expect I've been working too hard. I can't unwind. I keep worrying about . . . I don't know really.'

'The holiday won't do you a bit of good unless you relax. Things will go on without you very nicely, you know.'

'Yes. I'm sorry.' But she made up her mind that she would seek out a telephone as soon as the opportunity arose and put through a call, if only to reassure herself that all was indeed well.

Towards the end of the afternoon they packed their things together and made their way back up the steep cliff path. The boys scrambled on ahead, their eager feet kicking up small showers of stones which cascaded to the beach far below.

'Be careful!' Sarah warned, still affected by the inexplicable feeling of unease.

The boarding house door stood ajar; they made the boys kick the sand off their shoes on the bootscraper and went into the hall. As they started up the stairs the woman who kept the boarding house came bustling into the hall, her face a little flushed.

'You're back. Good. This wire came for you . . .' She held out a buff envelope, uncertain which of them to give it to. 'Mrs Gardiner . . . ?'

Sarah's apprehension came rushing back, forming a nervous lump in her throat. 'I'll take it.'

'Not bad news, I hope?' The woman hovered, her small eyes beady in her plump pink face.

Sarah took the envelope. It was all she could do to keep from opening it immediately but she waited until she was away from the woman's curious gaze. Her fingers trembled slightly as she ripped it open and the bald words leaped up at her, then a combination of anxiety and relief made her go weak. Bad enough – but not as bad as she had feared. She looked up. The others had frozen a tableau around her, Annie, the colour drained from her face, chewing her nail and clearly afraid to ask the question that was burning on her lips, the boys, their naturally ebullient natures sobered by the mood of the adults, and the awesome sight of that sheet of buff paper which could inspire such fear.

'Is it . . . ?' Annie formed the words with lips gone dry as dust.

'No.' Sarah shook her head, answering the unspoken question. 'It's Lawrence. He collapsed at the office this morning.'

'*Lawrence?*'

'He's ill. He's been ill for a long time and I knew it. I should never have left him.' Her mind was racing. She folded the wire and replaced it in its envelope. 'Annie, would you mind very much if I went home? I'm the only one who really knows about Lawrence's work. I think I shall be needed.'

'Of course,' Annie said loyally, though she looked disappointed. 'We'll pack immediately.'

The boys set up a clamour of protest and Sarah said hastily: 'There's no need for you to come too unless you want to. Why don't you and the boys stay here as planned – if you think you can cope with them, that is.'

'I could cope, of course,' Annie assured her, 'and I dare say we could come home on the train to save you driving all the way back for us, Sarah. The boys would like that, wouldn't you, boys?'

'Yes! Yes!' Neither seemed unduly bothered that Sarah was leaving now that they knew their holiday was safe and the prospect of a ride in a steam train never failed to excite them.

Sarah nodded. 'That's decided, then. I'll pack right away.'

'Oh not tonight, Sarah!' Annie pleaded. 'You must have something to eat and a good night's rest first.'

Sarah considered and decided she owed this much at least to Annie.

'Very well. I'll go first thing in the morning.'

When the boys were in bed she and Annie sat in the comfortable lounge in the fading light, talking about the war and its implications – and about Lawrence.

'I'm sorry to leave you in the lurch, Annie, but I believe he is seriously ill,' Sarah said. 'I've kept what I knew about him to myself and I suppose I shouldn't have but it was what he wanted. Anyway, now it's all out in the open, but I do feel I owe it to him to keep an eye on things until he's able to take over himself – if he ever can.'

'That bad?' Annie asked gently.'

'I think so. Anyway, thank you for being so sporting about it – and thanks for staying on with Stephen. He would have been so disappointed if he had had to go home.'

'It's a pleasure. I'm not clever like you, Sarah, but I like to do what I can.'

'You are a wonderful person, Annie. Max and John are very lucky.' She hugged her friend, meaning every word she said. Annie was the sweetest, most unselfish person she knew and she very much wished she could be just a little like her. But she knew if she lived to be a hundred she never would.

Next morning dawned, another fine day. They all had breakfast together at the same table in the bay window. Above the craggy cliff top the sky was the same cloudless blue.

'I think you are in for a couple of really scorching days,' Sarah said.

'I think so too. Aren't we lucky?'

'Yes.' But she felt no envy now. She was only glad to be

going back. That was how important her work had become to her.

When she had loaded her things into the car dickey she kissed Stephen, cranked the engine to life and climbed in. As she drove off along the road she turned to wave to them, standing there on the steps of the guest house, Annie with John on one side of her, Stephen on the other. They looked, Sarah thought, more like a part of a family than she would ever be, and she experienced a wave of love, all the stronger because she was going away and they had no further claim on her.

Annie was a perfect friend, a perfect wife and mother. She is better for Stephen than I am, far better, Sarah thought, and for once felt not a tinge of jealousy.

The motor turned the corner and they were lost to sight.

Chewton Leigh was in a state of uproar. The seriousness of Lawrence's illness had come as a bombshell for they had come almost to take his hacking cough for granted and he had managed to hide from them just how tired and ill he had been feeling for many months now.

'The boy is in a bad way,' Gilbert told Sarah when she went to see him in his office on her return. 'Haley tells me he told him months ago he should go into a sanatorium. Why the devil didn't he do it? Why keep it to himself?'

'I expect he was worried about losing control of the office. You know how much it means to him,' Sarah said, not liking to mention that she had been in Lawrence's confidence.

'Well, whatever, it's immaterial now. He's off to a sanatorium whether he likes it or not. But he was asking for you, Sarah. He seems to think you know best what he's been doing. Is that right?'

'I have been giving him a helping hand, yes . . .'

'And you are willing to continue?'

'Of course. I'll do whatever is necessary to keep the wheels turning until he is fit again.'

The worried frown lines creasing Gilbert's brow eased; he smiled and there was a trace of pride in the smile.

'You are a good girl, Sarah. I know I can depend on you.'

'Mama – can we go into the tunnel – *please*?'

'No, John, play nicely on the beach, there's a good boy.'

'But there's nothing left to do on the beach. We want to explore.'

'*Please*, Aunt Annie!' Stephen added his voice to John's pleas and Annie shook her head in amused exasperation.

The holiday had been pleasant but not nearly as pleasant as if Sarah had been there too. Annie had read her way through two romantic novellas while the boys played, and enjoyed the sun and the bracing breeze from the sea, but now the novellas were finished, pushed to the bottom of her beach bag along with the apple cores and the remains of the sandwiches the landlady had made for them and Annie too, truth to tell, was becoming a little bored of the same stretch of beach.

Worse, another family had set up camp nearby, a rather common family in Annie's opinion – a man with a paunch which hung over the top of his trousers and a knotted handkerchief on his head, a shrill voiced woman and four noisy children who continually ran over the small fort of pebbles which John and Stephen were trying to build, knocking it down.

'Very well,' she said. 'But only if I come with you.'

She picked up her bag and followed the boys, who were already running towards the tunnel in the outcrop of rock. The pebbles cut into her feet, making walking difficult, and Annie thought she would not be sorry when it was time to go home to Chewton Leigh – and Max. Though he worked so very hard these days and spent so little time at home, yet it was a comfort to know he was near. When they were apart she always missed him but never more so than now, and she thought maybe it had something to do with the fact that she was pregnant. Though she had not been sick this time as she had been with John she felt heavier and more uncomfortable and at the same time desperately in need of someone to rely on if – just if – she should need them.

The boys disappeared into the tunnel and Annie followed, picking her way over the tumbled rocks and soft sludgy sand. It was chilly here out of the heat of the sun, a dank chill which made her shiver and she could hear the drip of water on the rock walls of the passage. The dark was complete, the tunnel much longer than she had expected, but as the boys had said there was a glimmer of light at the far end which was briefly eclipsed as first one boy, then the other, squeezed through the neck of the passageway, then slipped back inside to call to her.

'Mama! There's another beach!'

'Come and see, Aunt Annie! It's lovely!'

Gamely Annie struggled on. It was rather wet underfoot; she felt her shoes squelch in water and hoisted up the hem of her dress – too late. The soaked material flapped around her ankles.

I should have put my foot down and made the boys stay where we were, Annie thought. But it was too late now. They had disappeared again and moments later she emerged from the narrow cleft in the rocks to find herself on a narrow, secluded stretch of beach.

'See? Isn't it wonderful, Mama?' John shrieked, swooping towards her. 'See – it's *sand*. Stephen and I can make sandcastles and pies. Come on, Stephen! We'll build the biggest castle ever. One that not even silly old Kaiser Bill could knock over!'

They ran off again and, smiling at their excitement, Annie followed.

The tiny beach was indeed sand, much more fun for the children than the pebbles they had left behind. And it was so quiet – only the seabirds wheeling and crying as they came in to land on the steep cliffs which encompassed it and the gentle lapping of the tide to break the stillness of the summer's afternoon. The only trouble was the sand was not powdery dry to sit on but firm and slightly damp to the touch. Annie tested it and wrinkled her nose. She didn't want to catch a chill. It wouldn't be at all good for the baby.

She spread her rug and sat down, idly watching the boys digging with their hands and thinking about the baby. Would it be another boy – or might it be a girl this time? A girl would be nice – but there was something special in being the mother of boys. She glanced at John, taking intense pride in his sturdy body and limbs and the bright little face serious now with the effort of concentration on the task in hand. Another boy would be company for him too for though he and Stephen were like brothers Stephen would not always be there. But then again it might be fun to have a girl, to be able to buy pretty dresses and ribbons for her hair and never ever have to worry about her going off to war – if there should be another one. But there wouldn't be, of course. This was 'the war to end wars', that was what everyone said . . .

Annie found her thoughts growing slightly confused and realised she was getting drowsy. The sun was hot, beating down with such strength that it managed to make small trickling patterns of light through the straw of her wide-brimmed hat. She settled more comfortably on the blanket, resting her head against her loaded beach bag. The cry of the gulls and the sound of the waves were fainter now and a little muzzy; even the shouts of the boys seemed to be coming from a long way off. Annie put her hand up to shade her eyes and let herself drift. Just a little nap . . . just a little one . . .

'Mama!'

'Aunt Annie!'

The boys voices, urgent suddenly, woke Annie. She fought through the layers of sleep to feel them tugging at her skirts.

'The sea – Mama, the sea!'

'Aunt Annie, wake up! Wake up!'

She struggled to a sitting position, a prickle of alarm touching her spine. The tide had come in while she slept. It was now lapping around the sand castle they had built, no more than a yard from her feet.

'Come on, boys we had better go . . .'

But as she scrambled to her feet she saw to her horror that the way back to the tunnel was underwater – the opening in the cliff completely hidden.

'Oh my God!'

404

Hearing the panic in her voice John began to cry. 'Mama! Mama! The sea!'

She snatched up the rug, desperately trying to force herself to be calm.

'Be quiet, John. It's all right.'

She looked around. The beach was now no more than a strip of sludgy sand, already at its edges the waves were lapping the foot of the cliffs.

'Come on.' She retreated towards the central point of the beach, dragging them with her. Beneath her feet the sand was ominously firm, the rocks towards which they were heading looked shiny, frighteningly clean. Back, back, as close to the enclosing cliffs as they could go but in her trembling heart she knew it would not be far enough. The cliffs rose behind them, sheer and impassable, and in front of them the sea still encroached a little further with each creeping foam-topped wave.

'We must call for help,' she said. 'There were people on the other beach – remember? They'll hear us. Together now. Ready – HELP!'

But the roar of the sea was loud now and the wind seemed to take their reedy voices and blow them away.

The first wave lapped around John's toes; he clutched at her legs in terror.

'Mama! I don't like it! Mama!'

'Someone will come,' she said. 'Someone will find us.'

But even as she said it she knew they would not. Or if they did they would not be in time.

She dropped the beach bag, a wave lapped around it, depositing a layer of creamy foam. Annie drew the boys to her, one on each side with her arms around them, holding them in close to her skirts, and tears of pure panic stung her eyes.

'Oh Sarah – I'm sorry!' she whispered. And, 'Max – Max – I love you! Help us, please!'

But Max was a hundred miles away and so was Sarah. No-one heard her cries and no-one came.

And then there was only the sea, swirling deeper and

deeper. She lifted the boys clear of it as long as she was able. And then there was nothing left to do but wait.

'Drowned?' Sarah whispered. 'I don't believe you. What do you mean – drowned?'

'Darling, it's true.' Eric's voice was gentle, his hands held hers. And his face, ashen and haunted, was the confirmation of his words.

'No!' Sarah gasped. The protestation was wrung from her like a sob, tearing at the soft heart of her with a pain that seemed to tear her in two. 'Annie was with them. They can't be drowned!'

'Annie was drowned too.' There was no gentle way to say it.

'No – not Annie.'

'Yes. They were caught by the tide on this little beach.'

'What beach? What beach?'

'There's a tunnel that is accessible at low tide. They must have gone through not realising . . . a family on the main beach saw them go.'

'Then why didn't they say?'

'They didn't realise. Until they were found . . .'

'I don't understand! How could they? How could she . . . ?'

'We shall never really know.'

'All of them? *All* of them, drowned? Stephen and Annie and John?'

'Yes. Poor Max . . .'

'Never mind poor Max!' she cried with a flash of anger. 'Annie has killed my baby! She has killed Stephen!'

'Sarah, it's no good blaming Annie. Not now.'

'But I do blame her! I trusted her with my son!'

'Sarah – stop it!' His voice was tortured but firm. 'You can't blame Annie. You might as well blame me – or yourself – for not being there.'

Her eyes went wild. 'Yes!' she screamed. 'Yes – of course I should have been there! But I wasn't. Annie was. She's simple, Eric. She's not as bright as you or I. I should have known it. I should have known it!'

Her nails were tearing at her face in the paroxysm of her grief. He thought, mildly surprised, that he had not realised just how much she had cared for Stephen. Sometimes it had seemed to him she thought the child more of an encumbrance than a joy, a burden standing between her and all she wanted to do, just as he sometimes felt that he, himself did. But this . . .

He was not to know that it was Sarah's guilt that fuelled her terrible punishing grief. He did not realise when he told her she might as well blame herself for the tragedy how close he had come to the inner torture that was tearing her apart.

I never really wanted him, thought Sarah, and now I have lost him. This is God's punishment on me for being a bad mother, just as I was punished as a child by having my mother snatched away from me.

'Sarah . . .' Eric put his arms around her in an attempt to comfort her but she pushed him away.

'Don't! Leave me alone!' The venom in her tone made him draw back. He did not know this Sarah. Surely now in their grief they should have been able to draw closer, be – what was it the marriage service said? – of mutual comfort one to the other? But she was like a wild thing, flying, retreating from every other living soul, he could not reach her. Somehow in that moment he doubted he ever would again.

'Oh Sarah,' he groaned. It was a lament for more than a dearly loved lost son.

The darkness was complete. It closed in around her waking and sleeping. Sometimes for a brief moment when she woke with the dawn she found herself wondering just what was the weight around her heart, then memory would come rushing in and with it grief – and guilt. She had killed Stephen. She had signed his death warrant leaving him there with Annie. She had blamed Annie but in truth she had no-one to blame but herself.

For perhaps the first time in her life Sarah could see no glimmer of hope for the future for nothing else seemed to

407

matter. The love she had somehow failed to lavish on Stephen during his lifetime came on her now in a rush so that it seemed she was drowning in it as surely as he had drowned in the waves. Her son – the child of her body – was dead and she was to blame. She could scarcely eat, scarcely sleep, and the one solace she had turned to all her life seemed now to evade her for neither could she work. There was nothing, nothing but the blackness, nothing but the all-consuming grief and guilt.

And then just when she thought she would never surface again came the letter from Lawrence.

'Sarah – I know I have no right to ask it but I am relying on you. I am a little better I think and knowing you are looking after things for me is a great comfort. For God's sake, Sarah, don't let Leo take the reins. If he does we will never get him out.' And then a paragraph which touched her, probing through the thick layer of grief. 'I have never told you how sorry I am for what happened long ago. I could have saved you. I knew the truth. But I was weak, just as I am weak now. Be strong for me, Sarah – and forgive me.'

That day Sarah dressed, tidied herself and went to the works. She had wallowed for long enough. It was time to begin the long fight back.

The news reached them a week later. Lawrence was dead. She accepted it calmly – death was becoming commonplace. Only the irony of it struck her. Half the family had gone to war – one might conceivably have expected it was they who should have died. But they had not. No, it was those whom they had left behind in supposed safety who had gone. Dear sweet Annie, little John, Stephen for whom she would grieve to the end of her days and now Lawrence. Strange, how strange, the tricks of fate. And how cruel.

Somehow, inexplicably, Sarah began to heal. And with the healing came a new strength. Let fate do its worst. Hadn't it always? But she wouldn't be beaten or cowed down. Forged in the fire she would be tempered like steel. Sad but determined Sarah faced the future.

Chapter Thirty-Three

'You are looking positively radiant tonight, my dear,' Gilbert said to Blanche as they went in to dinner one evening shortly before Christmas.

Blanche smiled. There was indeed a glow about her which Gilbert might have suspected had come from a bottle of spirits if he had not known better – she looked almost intoxicated.

'Has something happened to please you?' Gilbert pressed her. Again she smiled, but said nothing, and he added: 'Well, whatever it is, I must say it suits you!'

Blanche turned, clapping a hand over her mouth in almost girlish fashion, then laying it on Gilbert's arm.

'I'll give you a clue, Gilbert. Leo has something to tell us at dinner tonight. But I mustn't say any more or I'll spoil the surprise. You will just have to be patient a little longer.'

Gilbert crossed to pour a small glass of sherry for Blanche and a brandy for himself.

'I'm not much good at guessing games, my dear,' he said passing her the drink.

'Hmm . . .' She sipped, regarding him over the rim of her glass. 'How have things been at the works today? Have you found an answer yet to that nasty new German plane – what did you call it – a Fokker?'

Gilbert almost choked on his drink with surprise. Blanche actually taking an interest in the business – amazing! She *must* be in a good humour!

'A Fokker, yes,' he confirmed, naming the fast, light monoplane fitted with a synchronised gun which was threatening British supremacy in the air. 'And the answer is no, we haven't come up with a definite prototype yet. But Max is working on it and I have high hopes. That young man has a touch of the genius: if anyone can produce a machine even more manoeuvrable than the Fokker it is him.'

The door opened and James and Leo came in. James was home from Oxford for the Christmas holidays and though he no longer attached himself to Leo like a shadow yet the impression remained.

'Drink?' Gilbert suggested. Leo accepted but James shook his head. What was the matter with him? Gilbert wondered. Was there nothing normal about him at all? Irritation made him testy.

'I understand you have something to tell us, Leo,' he said.

Leo's jaw dropped a shade. 'Well yes, but . . .' He glanced at his mother accusingly. Her smile had died.

'I – I'm sorry, Leo . . . I was so excited!'

'Excited about what?' Unnoticed by any of them Alicia had entered the room. None of her new batch of recuperating officers were yet fit enough to be downstairs and she had settled them in their rooms before coming down to dine with the family. 'What is going on here that I don't know about?'

'Leo has something to tell us.'

'You lot certainly know how to take the wind out of a chap's sails, don't you?' Leo said crossly. 'I was going to choose a more opportune moment but . . . oh well, I might as well tell you now, I suppose. I have decided to get married.'

'Good grief!' Gilbert said in a stunned tone. 'Who is the lucky girl – Emily?'

'Well, of course!' Blanche was smiling again, determined not to let the moment's awkwardness impinge on her happiness and pride. She crossed to Leo, linking her arm through his. 'Leo has already approached the Reverend Sellers and he has given his blessing. The wedding is to be on New Year's Day.'

'That's a bit soon, isn't it?' James ventured, then blushed, fearing he might have said something immodest.

'I must say it's a little surprising, Leo,' Gilbert agreed. 'I know you have been courting Emily for some time now but all the same . . .' He broke off, realising this was scarcely the moment to admit that he had suspected Leo of fighting

410

shy of marriage, and he knew that Reverend Sellers had long ago given up hope of seeing his daughter walk up the aisle.

Alicia, however, had no such scruples. Her expression was cold, her eyes glittered.

'I don't think it is surprising in the least,' she said haughtily. 'Really it is something we should have expected of Leo.'

'What do you mean by that?' Blanche demanded, recognising the venom in her stepdaughter's tone.

Alicia shrugged. 'Don't any of you read the newspapers? Surely you know that the Unionists are all for making conscription compulsory and Lloyd George is right behind them. If that happens the single men will have to go first. Men of Leo's age. Whilst married ones will be able to remain safely at home with their wives . . .' She let her voice tail away meaningfully.

'What are you suggesting?' Blanche let go of Leo's arm, her hands clenching angrily.

'It's obvious isn't it? Do you really think Leo would tie himself to that dull little Emily Sellers if it wasn't to save his skin? That is why the wedding is to be so soon – so that our dear sweet brother will be a married man before the legislation goes through parliament and he will be able to escape being called on to do his duty for King and country.'

'Alicia – how could you!' Blanche cried. There were high spots of colour in her cheeks and she looked close to tears now. 'How could you say such things?'

'Oh – be quiet, mother!' Leo snapped. 'I don't know why you have to make such a performance out of it.'

'But Leo – I won't stand by and hear you maligned!' she protested. 'Why shouldn't you marry Emily? Goodness knows you have been walking out with her long enough. And if it means that you will be saved from being sent off to France then it is only sensible. Don't you agree, Gilbert?'

Gilbert said nothing. The thought of a young man marrying so as to avoid conscription stuck in his craw. It seemed to him a despicable and cowardly thing to do.

A few weeks earlier, driving home one night through the

411

village he had come upon a most unpleasant scene – a crowd of women attacking young Ned Hucker, the baker's boy, and taunting him for having failed to volunteer. 'A dirty slacker,' they had called him, and though Gilbert had intervened, telling the women that the reason the rather slow-witted Ned had not volunteered was because he was reluctant to leave his widowed mother all alone, deep down he had understood how they felt.

This was even worse. To marry a woman with the sole intention of hiding behind her skirts . . . Gilbert was unable to conceal his look of disgust and Blanche, noticing it, reacted furiously.

'I don't know why you are all taking this view!' she stormed. 'And you are not in a position to be so critical anyway, Gilbert. At least everyone knows that Leo and Emily planned to marry one day. James has no such responsibilities but I dare say he will be looking for an excuse to get out of serving if conscription becomes law, all the same.'

James had sidled over to the window, taking no part in the argument. He hated harsh words almost as much as he hated war. Now he looked round, startled to find himself brought into it, and dismayed by the hostility on every face but Alicia's.

'Well, James, what have you got to say to that?' Gilbert barked, and suddenly James was angry, the slow-burning anger of a man without a violent bone in his body.

How could they glorify war in this way? Surely they couldn't approve of the horrors that were going on in the name of justice and freedom? Yet they seemed to, and that tacit approval helped to perpetrate it, encouraging raw untrained recruits as young as eighteen years old to rush off and offer themselves as fodder for the guns.

'I don't blame Leo as you seem to do,' he said. 'But if you are asking me whether I am going to do the same then the answer is no.'

'Really? I thought you would do anything to avoid going into the army,' Blanche sneered.

'I shall refuse to fight, certainly,' James agreed. 'There is

412

not much point in having convictions if one is not prepared to stand up for them. I believe war is wrong – all war – and I will not do anything to assist in it. Truth to tell, I find your involvement repulsive, Father.'

Gilbert almost choked with indignation.

'Because we build aeroplanes, you mean?'

'They are being used as weapons. It's wrong.'

'Don't talk rubbish,' Gilbert snapped. 'And how do you suppose you are going to avoid being conscripted if Lloyd George gets his way and the bill goes through? If you persist with this attitude you'll be arrested for breaking the law.'

'Yes,' James said. 'I know.'

'What do you mean – you know?'

'We have been warned of what might happen at the No-Conscription Fellowship meetings. I may very well be thrown into gaol and there is always the possibility that I shall be sent to the front by force and shot as a deserter when I refuse to take up arms.' His voice was low and matter-of-fact, betraying none of the welter of emotions he was feeling – the anger, the betrayal, the trembling fear.

'Great Scott!' Gilbert exclaimed. 'You can't be serious, James!'

'I am – perfectly. I can always appeal of course but to be honest I don't hold out much hope. The authorities are determined to misunderstand our views – just as you are.'

'And you would be prepared to go to prison or even die rather than compromise your beliefs?' Gilbert asked.

'Of course,' James said.

Gilbert shook his head, wondering if he really knew his youngest son at all. He had always looked on James as something of a weakling, now suddenly there was substance to the shadow. James might not be as bold and dashing as Hugh was but it took courage to stand up for his beliefs, particularly when they were so unpopular. Gilbert could not follow his reasoning and did not agree with him in even the smallest particular, but he felt the beginnings of unwilling admiration nevertheless.

At least James was not taking the coward's way out as Leo was. He was meeting the challenge head on and he was

413

prepared to face the consequences of his actions however terrible they might be. His own trembling determination was lending him an awesome strength.

For the first time in twenty years Gilbert was proud of his son.

Chapter Thirty-Four

In the autumn of 1916 when the Battle of the Somme was reaching its bitter and bloody end, floundering in the mud with no decisive victory one way or the other to avenge the loss of 420 000 British lives, and while James Morse, arrested eight months earlier for refusing to answer the call of his country, was languishing in a military prison, scorned and spurned by his guards and largely forgotten by everyone else, Eric Gardiner had his moment of triumph.

For Eric the war had been a quiet one. Like Adam he had spent much of it in a training squadron, but here the similarity ended for he was quite content with his lot. It was not that Eric was a coward, far from it, but he was a very peaceable man who did not care for the idea of being responsible for the death of any other human being, let alone a fellow flier. The fact that in training pilots to fight and bomb he was actually killing by proxy did not occur to him for a very long while and when it did he accepted it regretfully. Death in war was inevitable and the cause was a worthy one; at least he personally had not had to fire a gun and see a German aeroplane spiral down trailing deathly black plumes, and the look-out missions he had flown had all been uneventful.

But as the war dragged on into its third year he began to see things in a less comfortable light. Too many of the young men who passed through his hands were going straight to their deaths and Eric was unable to escape the conclusion that it was because they simply were not skilled enough to handle the situations in which they found themselves. The more the fighter squadrons were decimated the worse it became – the pressure was on for more and still more pilots to take the place of those who were lost so that some, mere boys of nineteen or twenty, were sent over the enemy lines with as little as ten hours' experience of solo flying on training machines, to fly two or even three missions a day through a hail of flak and engage the experienced German pilots in their vastly superior aircraft. Time after time he heard stories of how slow and unwieldy the British machines were by comparison with the German Fokkers and the newest model, the Albatros, and how difficult to fight from with the struts and wires limiting the field of fire and the pilot seated behind the observer who in turn was seated behind the engine. There were some new designs on the stocks, it was rumoured, including one that Max was working on in secret, but in the meantime all were untried and Eric had the uncomfortable feeling that when they were they might very well take the blame for the inexperience of the pilots he was turning out.

The knowledge gave him an edge of aggression that had been missing before. Dammit, how many more young men would he send to their deaths before this bloody war was over?

Occasionally Eric found himself seconded to the anti-Zeppelin patrols and he was experiencing a bout of this newly found aggression one night in early October when the message came through shortly after dark – Zeppelins approaching the south coast. The giant airships with their deadly cargo of bombs had been a menace for some time now, targeting munitions factories, explosives works and even the capital itself, sometimes in great formidable fleets, but since Leefe Robinson had brought down the first Schutte-Lanz over London at the beginning of September they were no longer regarded as invincible and that night as Eric hastily struggled into his flying jacket a feeling of deadly determination made his skin crawl and the blood pound in his temples.

Somewhat hampered by the heavy kit he ran across the airfield to where his ancient BE2c stood waiting on its chocks at the pole position of the make-shift runway – a lane of oil drums filled with burning paraffin which cast a smoky glow over the rough grass. As he strapped himself in, the mechanic was already thrusting at the propeller and after a few moments' superhuman effort the engine coughed into life.

The cold night air stiffened the muscles of his cheeks and hurt his lungs as he flew though he ducked his head down behind the windscreen of the open cockpit and before long he was shaking so much with the cold that it was difficult to keep his hands steady on the rudder. But gritting his teeth he flew on. Damned if the Zepps were going to drop their load of death and get away with it tonight. He wasn't going to go through this for nothing if he could help it!

Just when it seemed that he was the only living soul in the night sky he saw it – a pyramid of light away to his port side. So – the searchlights had found the Zepp if he had not. He turned towards it, flying steadily, and soon he could see the Zepp – small glittering speck caught in the pyramid of light like a moth in a candle flame. Excitement lit a fuse within him; as the adrenaline began to course through his veins Eric forgot the cold, forgot his aversion to playing the role of an angel of death, forgot everything but his over-whelming determination to get to grips with the airship.

As he came closer it seemed to take shape, a gleaming silver balloon hanging apparently motionless against the backdrop of black velvet sky. Tracers made bright streams around her and bursts of shellfire illuminated the blackness like an elaborate firework display as the ground defences attempted to stop the monster in its tracks, but Eric could see they were missing their target by miles. He flexed his hands on the controls, loosening his fingers sufficiently to enable him to be able to fire his gun when the moment came. They still felt stiff but he had no doubt they would react as he wanted them to. Needs must when the devil drives, he thought grimly.

They were closing fast now and he thought the Zepp must have seen him because she loosed her bombs to explode in a cluster of brilliant winking lights on the ground far below. But there was no resulting rush of flame and Eric thought with satisfaction that they must have missed any intended target. Then the Zepp began to rise swiftly, freed of the weight of bombs, and Eric knew that he had to act fast if he was not to lose her. He struggled on through the shells which exploded in the air around him, rocking the BE like a

417

small ship in a storm-tossed ocean and got a hand to his gun. He fired off a drum, raking the airship from nose to tail, steep turned after her and came in again. Tracer bullets shot from her car and gondolas but he ignored them. His teeth were gritted, sweat pouring down his half-frozen face, his fingers closed again on the trigger of his gun.

Get the bugger. Get him! he urged himself. Don't let him get away!

He fired another drum with the same grim determination then the breath came out between his gritted teeth in a sharp whistle.

The silver of the airship was suddenly suffused with a rosy glow then with a terrifying whoosh! a sheet of flame illuminated the blackness. The airship shot up like a rocket, hovered momentarily then plummeted down, ablaze from front to stern.

For a brief moment Eric could think of nothing but getting out of the way for it seemed to be coming straight at him, this huge roaring fireball. Then as he steadied his machine he watched almost in disbelief as the Zepp crashed earthwards, illuminating the fields and trees with a hellish orange light.

He shouted aloud with wild elation before the shock hit and he realised he was shaking again, as much now from reaction as from the cold. Below him on the ground the Zepp blazed fiercely and with a sense of awe Eric realised that single handed he had been responsible for the destruction of an airship and its crew. The knowledge sobered him. He had done his duty. This airship would not deliver its load of death and mayhem – he had seen to that. But he felt no pride in the achievement, only a sort of numb horror and guilt.

There was nothing left to do here. The people on the ground would take over now. Reacting like some sort of automaton Eric turned his machine for home. He did not feel like a hero. He felt like a murderer. And no-one was more surprised than he when he was awarded the DSO for his night's work.

*

One afternoon in the spring of 1917 Sarah left her office and crossed the courtyard to the old Morse Motors block. She walked briskly and a trifle defiantly but every so often she glanced over her shoulder, a quick furtive glance that indicated she was hoping she would not be seen. The block, and in particular the office towards which she was heading, was supposed to be out of bounds to everyone but the chosen few, for it was there that Max was carrying on his top secret work, drawings for a new aeroplane to combat the supcriority of thc German Albatroses and Fokkers. But Max had not been seen for days on end though a light burned night and day at the window and Sarah was seriously concerned about him for he had taken the death of Annie and little John very badly.

At first, a prisoner of her own grief, Sarah had neither known nor cared very much what he was feeling but as she surfaced to at least some semblance of normality she had begun to realise that Max was experiencing no such relief. He had taken it all inwardly, throwing himself into his work to relieve the pain and succeeding only in burying it deeper so that it bubbled away inside him like the lava at the heart of a volcano. All his friends in their turn had tried to reach him, all had been turned away. He was fine, he assured them testily. He simply had work to do and he would be grateful to be left alone in peace to do it. But as the days and weeks went by and Max became more and more of a recluse Sarah began to fear for his sanity, and she decided that whether he appreciated it or not she must make one more effort to break through the shell with which he had surrounded himself.

The rest of the rooms in the wing which housed Max's office had been shut up when his top-secret project had begun – for security reasons it was not practicable to have any number of people wandering in and out of the building. As Sarah opened the front door it creaked from a winter of disuse and a musty smell came out to meet her. A crack of light showed from beneath Max's door. She tapped and when there was no reply tapped again. After a moment Max called out: 'Who is it?'

'It's me – Sarah. Can I come in?'

She heard him shuffle over to the door and turn the key. the door opened a crack, no more.

'What do you want Sarah?' He sounded impatient.

'To talk to you.'

'No-one is supposed to come in here.'

'Oh for goodness sake surely you don't think I've come to spy on you! Don't be so silly, Max. Let me in – please!'

The door opened slowly and she was shocked by the sight of him – thin, pale, his hair standing on end, his collar studs undone, tie missing.

'Very well then. Come in if you must,' he said grudgingly.

She went in, closing the door behind her and looking around in disgust. The office was a mess. Unwashed coffee cups littered the desks and floor, overflowing ashtrays gave the air a stale smokey smell. On the window sill, surrounded by several dead flies, was a plate with a half-eaten portion of bread and cheese – the bread looked dry and the cheese had grown a dark sweaty crust.

'For goodness sake, Max! This place is like a pigsty!'

A muscle twitched at the corner of his eye, making him wink irritably.

'If that is all you came to say, Sarah, I'll thank you not to waste my time.'

'Of course it isn't, Max,' she said, regretting her lack of tact. 'I've come because I'm worried about you. We all are.'

'There is no need to be,' his eyes darted over her impatiently. 'I am perfectly all right. All I want is to be left alone to get on with my work.'

'Oh Max!' she sighed. 'You can't go on like this.'

'Why not? You don't seem to realise, any of you, how vital it is that we come up with an answer to the Fokker and the Albatros. The lives of our fliers depend on it. And so may our very hope of victory.'

His good hand was working incessantly; she reached out and took it.

'I know how important it is, Max – and I know too that if anyone can do it, you can. But if you go on this way you

420

won't be any good to anyone.' Her eyes flicked disgustedly over the stale bread and cheese. 'When did you last have a decent meal for a start? You would work a great deal better with some good food inside you.'

'Nonsense. I simply go to sleep on a full stomach.'

'And that's another thing,' Sarah said, looking round. 'Where do you sleep?'

'Well there of course.'

'Where?'

'I can snatch all the sleep I need right there in that chair.' He indicated a dilapidated wing chair which like the desk was littered with sketches, calculations and screwed up balls of scrap paper.

Sarah shook her head. 'That is all very well for one night or even two. But certainly not for weeks on end. You will make yourself ill.'

'I'm all right, I tell you.'

'So you say. Oh Max, it would break Annie's heart to see you like this.'

His face changed. Briefly all the pain and naked grief were there in his eyes and she thought she had broken through to him. Then as swiftly as it had fallen the barrier came up again. 'Annie is dead,' he said harshly and it was almost as if he was torturing himself with the words like a monk putting a hair shirt onto skin already chafed and raw. Sarah decided it might be prudent to change tack.

'How are you getting on anyway, Max? Are you any nearer to a design you think will work?'

For a moment he stared at her as if he had failed to understand a word she had said. Then his eyes focused sharply as if his brain had suddenly clicked into gear and he nodded.

'Yes. Yes, I think I am. It's a single seat biplane, you know, better synchronised than anything we have at present and a good deal more manoeuvrable – or so I hope. Have a look. See what you think.'

He crossed to his desk, motioning Sarah to join him and rearranged his board with fingers that shook slightly. 'Speed and manoeuvrability – they are essential for a fighter

421

plane,' he went on, launching into a description of technical detail, totally oblivious to the fact that she was no mechanic – and if she had been he would have been breaking the strict rule of secrecy. But for the first time he seemed to have come alive, his face bright, his voice full and firm, and she did not stop him.

'Well, what do you think?' he asked eagerly when he had finished explaining.

'I think it sounds good,' she said truthfully though she had scarcely understood a word.

'Yes, I think so. Just as long as they give it a fair trial. It will be totally different from anything those boys have ever flown and they will have to learn new techniques in order to gain the full advantage from it . . .' He broke off, making a minute adjustment. 'Still that is not my problem is it? All I have to worry about is giving them what they need to win the war. Learning to fly it is their contribution.'

'It is brilliant, Max,' Sarah told him. 'You are a genius and Annie would be proud of you. But take my word for it you do need some relaxation and a good square meal.'

'I haven't time. I thought I had explained that,' he said, irritable again.

'An hour or two won't make that much difference. Come out to my cottage and I'll make you supper. One of your favourites – liver and onions, perhaps, or bacon with the fat fried crisp.'

'Sarah . . .'

'I won't take no for an answer,' she said firmly. 'I am fond of you, Max, and I don't want to see you run yourself into the ground. What is more, for Annie's sake I am going to make sure you don't.' She crossed to the door. 'I won't press you for a firm arrangement now but you know you are welcome any time at all. Just come when the time seems right to you and I'll have the pan ready for that crispy bacon. All right?'

'Yes . . . yes . . .' But already he had returned to his drawing board. Sarah hesitated in the doorway looking back at him but he seemed unaware now that she was even there. She sighed. How much good had she done? She did not know. Probably no more than any of his other friends. But at least she had tried. For the moment she could do no more. She went out, closing the door after her and leaving Max to his solitary mission.

In the spring of 1917 Adam, who had also been awarded the DSO for his exploits over the Somme the previous autumn, was appointed Flight Commander of a new squadron which was being formed to try to break the supremacy of German air power. Equipped with the fast new Scout Experimentals and staffed by hand-picked pilots, the birth of the new squadron had caused a few raised eyebrows for many of the old guard preferred the old idea of spreading excellence thinly in the hope that it would generate more excellence amongst what might otherwise be mediocre. So-called 'crack squadrons' were not something the British went in for, they proclaimed rather sniffily, being far more suitable to the flash continentals.

Adam, however, felt nothing but enormous relief at the departure. He had become unutterably depressed by the constant stream of inexperienced young pilots the training schools were feeding to the front. Most of them were so green they were unable even to manage their own aeroplanes with any degree of safety if they handled differently to the ones on which they had been trained and when faced with the deadly prowess of the Richthofen Circus they stood no chance. Adam had written too many letters of condolence to next-of-kin which were little more than a fiction – and risked his own life too many times in efforts to extricate some raw young pilot from the dangers into which lack of experience had taken him. It was a relief now to know that the young men under his command would be the cream of those emerging from the flying schools, and the planes were fast enough and manoeuvrable enough to give them at least an even chance against the Bloody Red Baron and his cronies.

But for all that he was no longer under any illusions as to his chances of surviving the war. The earlier gentlemanly comradeship which had existed amongst the flying fraternity even though they were on opposing sides had gone now – fighting had taken on a new and ugly face. Now it was every man for himself – the German spiralling earthwards trailing black smoke and orange flame would not be the one to put a bullet through your own petrol tank – or head. But to replace him there were always a dozen more, well-equipped, well-trained young fighting machines with the legendary names of Immelmann, Richthofen and Boelcke to inspire them and sooner or later even the greatest of aces met their doom – the law of probability determined it. Fly often enough and eventually you would be bound to be shot down, cornered or run into some mechanical trouble. Perhaps you would be brought down by the error of one of your own friends as Boelcke had been, his wing torn off by the wheels of Erwin Bohme as they pursued two DH2s of Major Hawkers 24 Squadron. Perhaps in a state of dangerous elation brought on by fatigue you would simply fail to spot the enemy lurking in the cloud cover until it was too late. Whatever, the risk was high and the odds grew shorter with every mission flown. Death lurked in every shadow and Adam knew it.

The knowledge sharpened his senses making him aware of sights, smells and sounds to which he might have been oblivious before. It made him irritable, impatient with petty inconveniences, intolerant of the boisterous antics of the young fliers who turned the mess into a bear garden and – when he came home for a short furlough before taking up his new appointment – equally impatient of Alicia's shell-shocked officers who seemed to overflow into every room in Chewton Leigh House with the exception of his bedroom.

But it also made him realise how much he wanted to see Sarah and spend a little time alone with her. They had wasted too long already.

When he arrived home Alicia greeted him coolly.

'You won't expect me to drop everything and spend time with you, I hope,' she said off-handedly. 'I am afraid I am much too busy for that.'

'No, I don't expect you to do anything, Alicia,' he said,

424

thinking that if Alicia had suddenly been overcome with a fit of wifely duty it might have been awkward and restrictive to say the least. As it was she was so thoroughly bound up with her war work that it was easy for him to make his own plans and do as he pleased with his short furlough.

Only the thought of Eric acted as a mild deterrent to his plans. He liked Sarah's pleasant, unassuming husband and regretted that he would almost certainly be hurt. But regret was where it began and ended. Eric had had too much of Sarah already. In love as in war it was every man for himself when the chips were down.

Adam's face hardened. Until he had turned his blazing guns on a stricken aeroplane he had not realised just how ruthless he could be. Now nothing mattered but that he and Sarah would have a little time together. God alone knew it might be all they would ever have.

He thought about going to see her in her office at Chewton Leigh and decided against it. They would have no privacy there and he would have lost the element of surprise. No, there were better ways than that. Adam, with just two days to spare before the start of his new appointment, knew exactly what he was going to do.

Sarah had eaten her evening meal and was clearing away the dishes when she heard the knock at the door. She looked up, startled. She seldom had a visitor – unless it was her neighbour begging a cup of sugar. Sarah had hoarded a good supply of sugar at the beginning of the war in case of shortages although she knew it was against the law and she faced severe penalty, perhaps even imprisonment, if it was discovered, but she had never been afraid to take a risk or two and the sugar was her secret, scarcely touched since sweet-toothed Stephen was no longer here to demand it on his stewed fruit and cereal. But once in a rash moment she had whispered its existence to her neighbour, who sometimes came under cover of darkness armed with a small screw-topped bottle and a pleading smile.

Sarah wiped her hands on her apron and went to open the door. She was tired – the days were long and busy – and she

425

hoped her neighbour would not be in a chatty mood. She would have to tell her the sugar supply was almost exhausted, Sarah decided.

She ran a hand across her hair, smoothing a stray end into place, and lifted the latch. Then as the door swung open she gasped.

'Adam!'

He stood there in the doorway, a dark silhouette against the moonlight.

'Hello, Sarah.'

She could not move; her knees had gone weak. She had known he was home, of course – Gilbert had been full of it, but she had declined his invitation to dine at Chewton Leigh. It was too painful to see Adam with Alicia, much as she had longed to see him the reality was simply too much to bear. Now she looked at him wordlessly feeling the uneven beating of her heart that only he could inspire.

'Can't I come in?' he asked.

She stood aside, still afraid to trust herself to speak. He came past her into the kitchen. The lamplight shone on his hair making it molten gold; in his uniform he looked very broad, very strong.

'Why are you here?' she asked. There was a catch in her voice.

'You know why.'

Another moment and she would have been in his arms. A feeling of something like panic assailed her and she turned away, bustling a little to hide her discomfort.

'Would you like a cup of tea? Or perhaps a glass of brandy? You have eaten, have you? I've just finished but I could rustle you up some biscuits and a nice piece of Stilton . . .'

'I didn't come to eat.' There was an amused tone to his voice but also a slightly hard edge. It made nerves flutter in the pit of her stomach.

'No? Come and sit down then!' She crossed to the fire, taking the poker and stirring the logs so that a shower of sparks flew up the chimney. He stood behind her on the hearthrug, arms folded, legs splayed, watching her specu-

426

latively. A pulse leaped in her throat. She replaced the poker and slid into the wing chair beside the fire, forestalling any move on his part to pull her onto the sofa with him. 'Well,' she said brightly, 'you have a new command, I hear.'

'Yes.' He sat down, facing her.

'Are you pleased?'

'As pleased as one is about anything in this damned war.'

'Where will you be stationed?'

'Somewhere in France. It's not going to be any picnic. Sometimes I think I am too old for this game, Sarah.'

'Old? You?' Her eyes betrayed her adoration. 'Max is working very hard on a new design,' she said. 'Have you seen him?'

'I tried to but the door was locked. I presumed that was to prevent people from disturbing him.'

'Oh Adam, I'm worried about him. He really is behaving very strangely. I went to see him a week or so ago and invited him here any time he likes but he hasn't taken me up on it. I haven't seen hide nor hair of him. He is going to crack up you know.'

'Sarah,' Adam said. 'I didn't come here to talk about Max either, even if he is my oldest friend. I came to talk about us. What are we going to do?'

'Do?' she echoed faintly.

'Yes – do. We have already wasted some of the best years of our lives. Are we going to waste the rest?'

'I – I thought we had agreed,' she said helplessly. 'We are both of us married. There is nothing we can do.'

'I didn't agree to anything.'

'But we *are* married.'

'At present. There are ways.'

'You mean . . . divorce?'

'I suppose I do.'

'But Adam, that is impossible.'

'Not impossible.'

'Well – wrong, anyway.'

'And certainly not wrong. I love you, Sarah. You love me. How can that possibly be wrong?'

'Because we are not free.' She twisted her head in anguish. 'What about Eric? And Alicia?'

'Alicia forfeited any right to consideration long ago and there is nothing left between us anyway. I am sorry about Eric. I do feel badly about him. But he has had years of you which he wouldn't otherwise have had – years I have lost. And to be honest fighting has made me selfish. When life expectancy is so short it does wonders for concentrating the mind.'

'Oh Adam, don't say that . . .'

'It's true, none the less. There is no point running away from facts. I love you, Sarah and I want to be with you for however little – or however long – is left to me.'

She swallowed hard. There was a lump in her throat. Oh dear God, she loved him – had loved him for so long. Had there ever been a time when she had not loved him? If so she could not remember it. Ever since the day they had found one another again she had been trying to tell herself that it was wrong, that it could now never be, tried desperately to put him out of her mind and out of her heart – and failed. He had still been there for all her efforts, too much a part of her to be cut out by circumstance or by design or by sheer act of will. She loved him with a love too sweet, too strong, to deny and she knew that in all honesty she had continued to hope secretly that one day they might be together. Now he sat there talking not only of loving her but of dying and the sudden shock of realising that he was speaking nothing but the truth was like a knife thrust through the deepest part of her.

'Adam . . .' Her throat convulsed, choking off breath.

He sat forward, reaching for her hands. 'I have only two more days then I have to go to help with the setting up of my new squadron. I don't know how long it will be before I am home again – maybe not until this damned war is over.'

She nodded. At least now he was talking about coming home – not if, but when. His eyes held hers.

'Will you be waiting for me?'

The pull of love magnetised her. She felt unreal, as if she were dreaming, and in that dreamlike quality was a magic, powerful and potent as any alchemy, and as old as time.

'You know I will.'

He drew her towards him. In the firelight the lines of his face were clean and strong, a familiar face made different by shadows. Beneath his touch her flesh tremored, sweetly sensitised, and her limbs were weak, fluid and unresisting. His lips found hers, kissing her with an edge of desperation that only heightened her longing.

Oh Adam, Adam . . . she wanted him so. Had wanted him through all the lonely nights . . .

'You are so beautiful,' he said softly into her neck and the breath whispered across her flushed skin. 'So beautiful – and you are mine . . .'

'Oh yes,' she murmured back, and it was close to a sob. 'Yes, yes . . .'

They had gone, she knew, past the point of no return. Right and wrong had ceased to matter now; there was an inevitability about what was going to happen and she was no longer afraid but soaringly glad. Then, as their embraces grew more urgent, they were jerked suddenly back to reality by a hammering at the door, and they drew apart, looking at one another.

'It sounds as if someone is rather anxious to see you,' Adam said. His voice was ragged.

Sarah extricated herself and crossed to the door, patting her hair into place with hands that trembled. She opened it and her eyes widened.

'Max!'

'I hope it's not inconvenient. You did say to come round at any time . . .' His voice was hesitant, a parody of his old jovial tones and his thin mobile face was troubled. Somehow he looked a little like a naughty child standing there, dishevelled and expecting a scolding, but that impression too was humour of the blackest kind, for Max had aged so much in the last year. Pity for him overcame Sarah's frustration – she had, after all, invited him. She could hardly now turn him away just because she was aching for a few more minutes of privacy with Adam.

'Of course it's not inconvenient, Max,' she said warmly. 'I'm really glad to see you. I'd almost given you up for lost.

Adam is here. He will be pleased too. He came to see you today, he said, but you were too busy to let him in.'

'Yes . . . yes . . . always busy . . .'

Sarah led Max into the living-room. Adam's face told her that he felt just as she did – frustration mingled with relief that Max had knocked when he did and not a few minutes later and determination that at all costs he must not realise that his arrival was less than welcome.

'Max, my friend! Good to see you!'

'I shall put the pan on to cook your bacon, Max, just as I promised,' Sarah said. 'And I will leave you two alone to talk while I do it.'

When she returned half an hour later with a plate of crispy bacon, eggs and bubble and squeak, made from potato with the cabbage she had cooked for her dinner and not wanted, the two men were deep in conversation, another hour and it became crystal clear they were set to make a night of it.

Sarah smiled ruefully but she was glad to see Max a little more like his old self. If anyone could snap him out of his black depression it was Adam. And there was always tomorrow. Two more days, he had said. Thank goodness for two more days – perhaps the only ones they would ever have.

It was midnight before Max made a move. By this time he had drunk a good deal of Sarah's brandy and was a little unsteady on his feet.

'I'll drive you home, Max,' Adam offered.

'No, old boy, you want to stay here with Sarah . . .' Max was sufficiently rosy to have forgotten that Adam was a married man – and his wife was not Sarah!

'It's all right, you'll need someone to take your boots off and put you to bed by the look of you,' Adam said good humouredly. Except for the fact that he had not had nearly long enough alone with Sarah he had enjoyed the evening enormously. Now he took her aside, pulling her into the dimly lit hall and kissing her.

'I'll see you tomorrow. Is it really necessary for you to go to work?'

'I expect I could find an excuse to stay at home for the day.'

'Good. Do that. I'll come over after breakfast.' He kissed her again, then pulled away, whistling through his teeth. 'No more now. Don't you know what you do to me?'

'No,' she teased. 'What?'

'If you don't know now you never will,' he retorted. 'But I will give you a clue. It is liable to make me stop behaving like a gentleman.'

'Oh Adam, get along with you!' She gave him a little push. 'I believe you are as tiddly as Max!'

'No, it's just the effect you have on me.'

'Adam?' called Max. 'Adam – where are you?'

'I'm just coming.' He grinned at Sarah. 'Goodnight, my love.'

'Goodnight. Take care.'

When they had gone she stood at the door of her cottage staring out into the velvet darkness, at the trees silhouetted against the sky and the myriad of stars which studded it. And for a moment the magic returned, taking away all guilt and frustration, imbuing her only with warmth and love.

Perhaps Adam would soon be going away again. Perhaps the time they would have together would be all too short – a few brief stolen hours. But Sarah believed in that moment that she had never been happier in all her life and wondered if she would ever be quite as happy again.

Chapter Thirty-Five

Unusually for him Adam overslept. Day after day, month upon month of rising before dawn had instilled in him a habit that he had begun to believe was unbreakable – however tired he might be he was awake at precisely the same time. The first day of his furlough had been the same – his body clock was ignorant of the fact that there was no compulsion to leap out of bed and begin the day, and he had been torn between enjoying the luxury of lying for as long as he liked between the sheets and annoyance that he was seemingly unable to take advantage of the opportunity to sleep, sleep, sleep.

Today however was an exception. When he awoke daylight was streaming in through the curtains, daylight several hours old, not the first cold crack of dawn. He stretched, enjoying the sense of well being, and the memories of the previous evening's pleasures came flooding back and with them anticipation for the coming day. He got up, crossed to the window and drew back the curtains to let in the full beauty of the morning then poured cold water into the basin on the wash stand and splashed it over him. Here at Chewton Leigh he could have hot water if he wished – a pull on the bell rope and as much as he required would be brought to him. But he preferred the invigorating cold he was used to.

He was dimly aware of the telephone bell shrilling in the distance but he took little notice and was surprised when there was a tap at his door and the considerate Evans called softly: 'Mr Adam – are you awake?'

He pulled on his shirt and crossed to the door, buttoning it as he went.

'What is it, Evans?'

'Telephone – for you sir.'

'For me? At this time of day?' For some reason Sarah had

flashed into his mind. Perhaps something had happened to Eric.

'I think it may be your aerodrome,' Evans said in his curiously pedantic way.

Adam ran down the stairs and into the hall. Sunlight was making bright patterns on the polished stone floor. He took the telephone.

'Adam Bailey.'

'Bailey – Major Marchment here. Look, I'm sorry to interrupt your hard-earned leave, old man, but we have a problem here. Farrant was killed last night.'

Farrant had joint command of the new squadron with Adam, Major Marchment was the 'desk man'.

'Farrant was!' Adam exclaimed. 'Christ! How?'

'Bit of a mystery. Took up a plane and . . . well, you'll hear the details when you get back. But I'm afraid it's going to have to be sooner rather than later. Can't leave the baby without a nursemaid.'

Adam swore. 'You mean . . . ?'

'I mean you will have to cut your leave short, old man. I know it's a bother but there is no alternative. How soon can you be here?'

Adam passed a hand over his eyes, thinking. 'By lunchtime – as long as the jalopy doesn't let me down.'

'Good. It had better not. I need you here, Adam – and quickly. There are things that need sorting out.'

'I'll be there,' Adam said.

He replaced the telephone and stood glaring at it. Damn and blast. Farrant dead, the whole thing cloaked in mystery. Without knowing a single fact he could hazard a guess as to the reason. Farrant was a brilliant pilot and a daring leader. But on occasions he drank more than was good for him and when he did he could become reckless, juvenile almost. Perhaps there had been a party in the mess last night – and a wager of some sort. If Farrant had taken a plane up for a lark it was unforgiveable, the sort of damn fool thing even a raw recruit should know better than to do. But it was that streak of recklessness that made good fighter pilots. In all likelihood Farrant had been showing off. Now he was dead. The new squadron would have to be reorganised and Adam's leave was to be cut short.

He swore again. Serve him right for looking forward to spending the day with Sarah. Serve him damned well right!

He turned to go back upstairs, returning to the fastening of his shirt buttons as he went. He'd pack now and have breakfast, then it would mean leaving immediately if he was to be back at base by lunchtime as he had promised. Well, he might as well break the news to Alicia right away – not that she would be much upset by it. She had scarcely noticed he was here and probably had not the slightest notion of when he was due to leave.

Voices were coming from the old nursery which Alicia had converted into a day room for her convalescent officers and he looked in. Two young men were there, reading the morning's papers and commenting on the news, one with a fully plastered leg resting on a footstool, the other squinting from a gap in the heavy bandages which covered his face. He had been badly burned and was undergoing a course of operations to rebuild his shattered features. It was a tribute to Alicia that the eminent surgeon in charge of the case had allowed him to come to Chewton Leigh between the various stages.

'Have you seen my wife?' Adam enquired.

The burn case's face was too heavily bandaged to reveal any expression but a dark flush rose in the other man's neck, spreading swiftly up to suffuse his cheeks. He seemed totally lost for words.

Adam felt a twist of irritation. How the heck did Alicia put up with these shell-shock cases? Tragic they might be but for the life of him he could not have spent day after day caring for a man who turned into a nervous wreck every time he was spoken to.

'You don't know where she is?' he asked shortly.

'N–no . . .' Plastered leg shook his head jerkily.

'I think she went downstairs,' the other young man offered. His voice at least sounded quite normal but it was slightly unnerving to hear it emanating from that swathe of bandages.

'Thanks,' Adam said hastily, backing out of the room.

As he did so he heard Alicia's unmistakeable throaty laugh coming not from downstairs but from one of the 'convalescent' rooms. He strode along the landing, knocked briefly on the door and without waiting for an answer threw it open. Then he drew up short with shock. Semi-clothed, her hair loose about her face, Alicia was romping on the bed with a young man.

Not that romping was quite the right word, Adam realised, though it was the first one which occurred to him. To say that Alicia was ministering to him might have been a more accurate description since the young man, another of her recuperating officers, was clearly in no state to actually romp. That he was enjoying Alicia's attentions however was obvious even at first glance.

As the door opened Alicia raised her head. Her lips were moist, her tongue flicked over them lasciviously as it had flicked over the body of the young man. At first she looked startled then a slow smile curved those wet lips and her eyes narrowed like a cat's. Though he spared him barely a glance Adam was aware of the shock and mortification on the boy's handsome face; he lay motionless, only his stomach heaving in shallow ripples beneath Alicia's scarlet tipped fingers. Disgust rose like bile in Adam's throat and without a word he strode out slamming the door behind him.

The slut! he thought furiously. He had never been under any illusions about Alicia's morality but somehow it had not dawned on him that she would sink to this.

He was in his room packing his bag when the door opened and she came in. He glanced at her and away again, as repelled by her now immaculate appearance as he had been by her disarray.

Her eyes narrowed slightly. 'What are you doing?'

'What does it look as though I'm doing? I'm packing.'

'Not because of me, I hope.'

'Don't flatter yourself, Alicia.' He slammed the case shut. 'I have to go back to my squadron. That is what I was coming to tell you when I found you with that . . . boy of yours.'

'Ah.' She crossed to the foot of the bed, reaching for one of the elaborate brass balls that decorated it and running her fingers around it. 'I am sorry about that, Adam.'

'Sorry?' He laughed shortly. 'Since when have you been sorry about anything?'

'Adam!' she reproached him. 'What a horrid thing to say. You make me sound like a monster.' He did not reply and after a moment she went on: 'What I mean is that I am sorry you had to find us. It wasn't very nice for you – or if it comes to that for poor Douglas. But you are quite right, I am not in the least bit sorry for what I did. Why should I be? If I can make a poor boy feel better where is the harm in that? It's not as if you and I . . .'

'Very true. Though you might at least have the decency to be discreet about it. It was perfectly obvious your other guests knew what was going on. It was as embarrassing for them as it was for us.'

'Only because you happened to come looking for me. They wouldn't have turned a hair otherwise.'

'Really? Your affaire is so blatant that it is not only common knowledge but also taken for granted?'

Alicia's mouth opened in surprise, then to his amazement she threw back her head and laughed.

'Darling – how quaint! An affaire!'

'How else would you describe it?'

She considered and her poise was infuriating to him.

'Well?' he demanded.

'Adam, I think we have a little misunderstanding here.' Her tone was soothing.

'Really? You are about to tell me I was mistaken in what I saw?'

'Oh . . . no. No, not in what you saw – the interpretation you are placing on it. Let me explain . . . my officers have been through hell. Some of them are still there. The whole object of them coming here is to assist in their recuperation. I . . . like to do what I can to help them.'

He stared at her, scarcely able to believe what she was saying.

'Help them? You mean . . . ?'

436

She laughed again. 'Oh Adam, don't look so shocked! I thought you of all people would understand. You must know young men very like the ones who come here to Chewton Leigh. Some of them are disfigured, some have lost limbs. They are terribly afraid, most of them, that they are no longer attractive to women – or even capable of . . . well, love. I reassure them if they want me to, that's all.'

'Now let's get this straight, Alicia. Are you telling me that that young man is not the first . . . ?'

'Well, of course not, darling.'

'And . . .' he gesticulated in the direction of the day room, 'the others?'

'Oh yes!' She said it blandly. 'Now don't be cross, Adam. I don't want to quarrel if you are going away. I'm still very fond of you, you know.'

He shook his head. 'I don't believe this. My wife . . .'

'Don't be a dog in the manger. You don't want me.'

'That doesn't mean I don't object to you behaving like a common whore.'

'Oh Adam, don't let's name call. You didn't object to me nursing them. What's the difference? I have spent hours listening to them pouring out their hearts – that helps heal their mind and spirit. The doctors have already done their best to heal their bodies. I just . . . try to make them whole again.'

'Very commendable,' he said drily and almost believed it until he saw the way her fingers were caressing the brass ball on the bedpost, slow, sensuous strokes until her nails touched and scratched the polished surface.

Alicia the philanthropist. For a brief moment it had almost been possible to believe in her. But of course she did not exist – or would not exist if it had not suited her own needs and desires. Her appetite, he knew, was insatiable – in the boys passing through her hands she had found a new and gratifying menu.

'I have to go,' he said.

'Aren't you going to kiss me goodbye?'

The look he gave her was of utter disdain. He picked up his suitcase.

437

'Don't expect me to join the queue.'

'Adam! Don't be this way! You know you are the one person in the whole world for whom such a thing would be completely unnecessary. You are all I have ever wanted. The trouble is . . .'

'Goodbye, Alicia,' he said coldly.

'Goodbye, Adam.' Her tone was regretful. 'Come home safely. Who knows, things may seem different when the war is over. Circumstances may have changed. And perhaps we shall be able to try again . . .'

He did not reply.

Halfway down the stairs he remembered that Sarah was expecting him. Damn Alicia for both distracting and delaying him! He dared not make a detour to see her on his way back to his base for he did not trust himself to make the visit a quick one. Just thinking of her made the blood pound in his veins and his body ache to consummate what they had begun last night; if she were there in the flesh he knew he would be unable to resist.

He went back to his room and penned a note of explanation. As he descended the stairs for the second time he saw Evans in the hall and called to him.

'Have my motor brought round immediately, please. And would you see that this note is delivered to Mrs Gardiner at her home at once?'

Then after the briefest of farewells to those of the family who were still lingering in the breakfast room he ran down the steps, threw his suitcase into the motor, and with a fierce revving of the engine drove away from the house.

'Evans – did I hear Mr Adam asking you to deliver a letter to Mrs Gardiner?' Alicia asked.

'Yes, Madam. I was going to ask Peter to get on his bicycle and ride over with it right away.'

Peter was the gardener's boy, a willing enough lad, but the servant shortage extended to the estate staff and he slaved from morning till night attempting to do the work that had once kept four men busy.

'Don't trouble Peter,' Alicia said. 'He has enough on his

438

plate just now. I shall be seeing Mrs Gardiner myself later. I'll see she gets it.'

'But Madam . . .'

'Not another word, Evans. It's no bother. May I have the letter please?' Alicia smiled sweetly but there was no mistaking her authority. Evans gave a small resigned nod. He did not like having his orders countermanded but then neither did he approve of Miss Alicia's husband sending notes to another woman, even if that woman was Miss Sarah. Miss Alicia was, after all, the daughter of his employer and it was to her that he owed his allegiance. If there was something 'funny' going on then he was glad Miss Alicia would be able to put a stop to it. If not . . . well, it was none of his business anyway.

His expression inscrutable as ever, Evans fetched the note and handed it to Alicia.

Chapter Thirty-Six

The news came at the beginning of August, just a week before Adam was due to come home for fourteen days' leave.

As soon as she reached the works Gilbert called Sarah into his office and the moment she saw his grave face she knew this was no call to discuss business. Something bad had happened. She stopped in the doorway, unable to move for the whole of her body, together with her legs, seemed to have turned to jelly and the dread was like a great dark bird hovering over her and casting a shadow so black it paralysed her.

Adam. She knew without a word being spoken that it had to do with Adam, just as she had known in her bones that last April morning that he was not coming to see her long before the hands of the clock had confirmed it. Then she had felt sick with disappointment and puzzled, now there was nothing but the suffocating terror of what Gilbert was going to tell her.

'Come in, my dear.' His voice was level, his attempt at normality almost succeeding. 'Sit down, Sarah.'

Sit down, Sarah. That is because he wants to tell me something dreadful. I don't want to sit down! If I don't sit down he won't tell me. It will be all right . . . But she sat down anyway, leaning forward onto the desk.

'What is it? What has happened?' *No need to tell me. It's Adam, I know. Is he dead? Please God, don't let him be dead . . .*

There was a letter lying on the blotter in front of him. He glanced down at it, straightening it slightly, then looked up at her.

'Adam is missing. We received this letter this morning from Major Marchment. It seems he failed to return from an offensive patrol over enemy territory.'

Her heart seemed to have stopped beating. But he had said 'Adam is missing', not 'Adam is dead'.

'You mean he is in enemy hands?' she asked.

'We don't know. No-one saw what happened to him. It could be that he had some mechanical trouble and was unable to get back to the British lines. If that is the case then almost certainly he is a prisoner of the Germans. But we must also prepare ourselves for the worst. It seems the formation was involved in a fierce dogfight and Adam may have been shot down.'

'But surely one of the others would have seen if that had happened?' Sarah argued, clutching at straws.

'Not necessarily. The formation was split up and I dare say they were all busy guarding their own tails. But Major Marchment says Adam's kit and trophies are being sent home by way of Cox's Shipping Agency and I have to say I don't care for the sound of that. Though if he is a prisoner and going to remain so for the duration of the war they wouldn't want his things cluttering up the mess for that reason either.'

Sarah nodded but like Gilbert she was unable to escape the feeling that there was something horribly final about the returning of his kit.

'How long will it be before we know anything definite?' she asked.

'Anything from four to eight weeks. I shall set various enquiries in motion at once, of course. And I have to say that if the worst has happened we are likely to know the sooner. The Germans sometimes drop lists of names of those who have been killed over our lines and I should think there might be some mention in the German newspapers where a pilot as well known as Adam is concerned.'

She could not reply. She felt sure that if she opened her mouth her teeth would begin chattering.

'What a time for something like this to happen!' Gilbert drew out his cigarettes and lit one, blowing a thin stream of smoke towards the ceiling. 'Goodness knows what sort of effect it will have on Alicia. She seems calm enough at the moment – but who can tell?'

441

'Alicia is a very strong character,' Sarah said with a flash of irritation.

'Yes but in her condition . . .' Gilbert broke off, flushing slightly. 'I dare say it's not a delicate subject to discuss but perhaps under the circumstances . . . Alicia is going to have a baby.'

'A baby?' Sarah repeated woodenly.

'Yes. It is due in January, I believe. In view of what happened last time, Haley was already concerned about her and anxious that she should scale down her activities as soon as possible. But now . . . well, frankly, a worry like this is something she could very well do without.'

Sarah sat motionless. As yet she could barely register what Gilbert was saying. Already shell-shocked this new piece of information had sent her reeling.

'Does Adam know?' she asked.

'Alicia wrote to him as soon as she was sure herself. He is delighted. Every man wants a son to carry his name and ambitions into the next generation – and I am sure for that reason if for no other Adam will have done everything in his power to take care of himself. So don't give up hope, Sarah. I am confident we will soon hear that he is a prisoner – and I wouldn't be surprised if he managed to escape! In the meantime if you can help Alicia through this difficult time I will be very grateful.'

Back in her own office Sarah closed the door and leaned against it, for now she was alone she did not think she could take another single step without falling. Two pieces of news within the space of a few minutes and both devastating in their way. The first alone would have been enough – more than enough. Adam was missing and if he were dead then she did not want to go on living. In the long dark hours of the night she had faced the possibility often enough and the sheer awfulness of it had made her skin crawl with dread and every muscle in her stomach clench and tighten so that now the reality was a mere echo of it, less real than the precognition. But the second piece of news she had not been prepared for at all and it struck at the very foundations of her world, destroying the base on which it was built.

Alicia – pregnant with Adam's baby. After all that had been between them that April night, after all his protestations of love and talk of the future, after all his denials of Alicia he had gone home and made love to her.

Sarah pressed her knuckles into her mouth, cringing at the thought of it. How could he? No wonder he had not come to see her next morning as he had promised. He had not felt able to face her. Or perhaps he had not wanted to once Alicia had satisfied him. Yet the letters she had received from him in France had made no mention of anything being different – just a brief sentence of regret that he had had to return earlier than he had expected and then words of love – not over-effusive, because that was not Adam's way, but tender and caring all the same with plenty of references to the future. He had written to her in that vein and all the while he had known that he had left her to go to Alicia's bed and now Alicia was to bear his son. The pain of it was a knife thrust in her heart, hurting her more even than the fact that he was missing. Whilst he was missing there was always the hope that he would come back, and even if the worst happened and he was dead then at least there should be memories pure and sweet of a love too great to die. But this . . . this betrayal destroyed them all.

Oh Adam, how could you, how could you? her heart wept. And she knew that whether he came home or not Adam was lost to her now as surely as if he were indeed dead.

As the weeks dragged by their hopes for Adam's safety began to fade. Enquiries as to his fate by the Central Prisoners of War Committee had drawn a blank, the Berlin Red Cross, usually helpful if enquiries were phrased in the right way, were silent, and not even the Crown Princess of Sweden or the King of Spain whose help Gilbert had enlisted had been able to throw any light on the mystery.

The uncertainty imposed a terrible strain on each and every one of the family, and even Max emerged from his cocoon of grief to join in the anxiety for his friend. Gilbert was silent and testy, Sarah swung between wildly differing extremes, sometimes so buoyed up with hope that she was almost intoxicated, sometimes convinced that he must indeed be dead and the coming baby was an omen of it, for didn't everyone say a birth and a death were often closely connected? Only Alicia remained serene, defying all Gilbert's concern for her well being. The more obvious her condition became the more unruffled she appeared to be as if she knew that whatever happened her own position was now totally secure. There was something almost repulsive in her complacency, Sarah felt, but then everything about Alicia either angered or repelled her, and she was honest enough to admit to herself that perhaps she was influenced by a measure of good old-fashioned jealousy.

Adam would come home, Alicia told all and sundry. He was too good a pilot to allow himself to be shot down – and too anxious to be a father to miss the happy event. But things were not looking hopeful. Too many aces had fallen – Albert Ball and Arthur Rhys Davids were dead, as was the great Werner Voss, 'The Flying Hussar'. How dare they hope it might be different for Adam?

At the beginning of November Gilbert went down with a severe bout of influenza – a direct result of the strain, Sarah thought, coupled with work on Max's new aeroplane which he had christened 'The Eaglet' and which was being rushed into production. When he had been absent from the works for almost a week papers which needed his attention began to pile up and one afternoon Sarah motored over to Chewton Leigh to discuss them with him.

Gilbert was up and about now. He received Sarah in his study and she was shocked to see how poorly he looked. To her, Gilbert had always been strong, kindly and distinguished. Now for the first time she saw in him the signs of ageing and the revelation was disturbing.

'How are things going?' he asked, shifting himself in the big leather covered chair as if even the effort of sitting was tiring him. 'I could hardly have chosen a worse time to be ill, could I?'

444

'We are managing,' Sarah said briskly. 'There are just a few things I need to ask you but it shouldn't take too long.'

She got out the papers and Gilbert rallied a little as they discussed them. They had almost finished when she realised he was no longer paying attention but staring out of the window, a strange guarded expression on his pinched face. Automatically she turned to follow his gaze.

A telegram boy was pedalling up the drive, his face a little flushed from exertion under his uniform cap. Sarah's heart seemed to miss a beat. Dear God, what now? In the space of the time it took for him to cycle out of sight and ring the doorbell her mind went racing over the possibilities but neither she nor Gilbert spoke. They simply sat in an agony of tension listening to the footsteps approaching across the stone floor of the great hall and waiting for the inevitable tap on the door. When it came Gilbert called 'Come!' in a voice that echoed his old authority.

The door opened and Evans stood there, the telegram on a silver salver. His face was expressionless but Sarah saw the salver shake slightly in his hands.

Gilbert took the envelope and tore it open. Evans retreated to the door but stood there, his own need to know the worst getting the better of his years of training. For a moment Gilbert's face remained expressionless, then a muscle jerked in his cheek. Still he did not speak and Sarah could bear the suspense no longer.

'What is it?'

He looked up then and his expression was still faintly puzzled, nothing more. 'So Alicia was right,' he said.

'Right about what?'

'About Adam. He is safe. He is a prisoner of war in German hands.'

And in spite of everything the relief was rushing in. 'Oh thank God! Thank God!' she cried. And for the moment it did not matter in the slightest that it was not her that he would be coming home to when the war was over.

Alicia's son, whom she christened Guy, was born with the new year for, this time, in spite of all the traumas around her

445

she had triumphantly carried her baby to full term. He was a strong child with a fine head of hair every bit as black as Alicia's and everyone said he was the image of his father. Sarah could not see it but then as she admitted to herself she could hardly bear to look at him at all.

Soon afterwards Eric came home. Since his brush with the Zeppelin he had been regarded as something of a hero and in the re-organisation leading up to the merging of the RFC and RNAS to form a new service, to be called the Royal Air Force, it had been decided that Eric, whilst retaining his RFC rank of Captain, should be seconded to the works as Chief Test Pilot.

Sarah found it difficult to adjust to having him at home and decided that if she was honest she did not like it. She had developed a routine which was now disrupted, and her tidy cottage looked 'more as if an army had moved in rather than just one man!' as she put it when she was irritated beyond endurance by his boots and flying jacket cluttering the kitchen, his dirty underwear and socks dropped where he stepped out of them in the bedroom and his shaving kit jostling with her neatly arranged jars and pots on the dressing table. Once she had taken these things for granted, now four years of living alone had forged new habits. But it was his intrusion into her privacy which jarred most and she found it more and more difficult to respond to his lovemaking with any pretence of enthusiasm. When he reached for her in the night her feelings ranged between irritation and an irrepressible longing for Adam, which in turn made her feel not only guilty but wretched and angry.

Her only respite came when he had to leave Chewton Leigh to ferry Max to France. Max was now working on an up to the minute version of the Eaglet and he liked to see the original in action so as to be better able to judge what modifications were needed. But since he was unable to fly himself Eric piloted him. When he was away Sarah worried about him a little for in spite of everything she was still fond of him but she prized the few days' freedom.

It was whilst they were away on one of their trips that the newest blow fell. Sarah went bursting into Gilbert's office

446

one morning to see him sitting at his desk looking almost exactly as he had the day he had broken the news to her that Adam was missing. But the lines seemed to have set upon his face now, etched deeply into the sallow cavities between nose and mouth and across his high forehead, and when he looked up at her his eyes were blank and staring, the eyes of a man in shock.

She had thought she had grown used to bad news by now but her blood turned to ice just the same, her mind once more skittering across the possibilities and preparing herself for this latest disaster.

'What is it?' she asked and knew she had used the wrong word. What she really meant was 'Who is it?'

Gilbert's eyes met hers; in them she saw the depth of his shock and pain.

'It is Hugh,' he said. For a moment she did not know what to say. Then the expression in those haunted eyes changed to become clouded and unreadable. 'I only hope,' he said, 'that he died a hero.'

Hugh's death affected Sarah far more than she would have believed possible. He was, after all, the one who had used and abused her, and if she had thought about it at all she would have imagined her emotions would have been confined to sympathy for Gilbert, who had lost all his sons to the war in their different ways – Lawrence struggling on when a spell in a sanatorium might have saved him, James locked up in a prison with the label of coward, however little deserved, to haunt him all his days, and now Hugh. But to her surprise she found herself haunted by the memory of the young man Hugh had been in the days before his lust had poisoned her image of him, tall, straight, handsome, a daredevil always laughing at danger, a superb horseman. Hugh had been part of her youth. Now he was gone and with him a part of her died though she could not grieve for him.

It was some weeks before they learned how he had died.

At long last the high command had been forced to admit that the cavalry no longer had a part to play in battle. Most

447

of the Yeomanry was dismounted and it had been decided that the Life Guards and Blues would take on a new role – they would be trained as machine gunners and be carried into battle not by their handsome long-maned 'black 'uns' but by lorries. This news had been received with mixed feelings. It was good to know the horses would be saved from more suffering but the pride of the regiments could not be tossed aside so lightly and they were glad to learn that every man was to retain his title and badges and even the redundant farriers would still wear horseshoes on their jackets.

In order to prepare for their new role the Life Guards had been sent to the sands outside Etaples for training. It had been a pleasant interlude for the weather was fine, conditions were good and after the hurly-burly of four long years of fighting the training seemed a little like a much appreciated holiday. But the war had intruded rudely into this near idyll. On the night of Whit Sunday the air had suddenly begun to throb with the sound of approaching aeroplanes and the men had almost no time to set up their anti-aircraft guns or take cover before the bombs began to rain down on them. Forty-three men had died that night on the beach and eighty-two were wounded and Hugh was amongst them. In the end he had died not in direct conflict but almost in the same way as so many helpless civilians.

Almost – but not quite. Under the hail of bombs Hugh had managed to fire his gun and continue firing. It was thought he might have been responsible for taking a German aeroplane with him for one had been seen spiralling down out of control and trailing black smoke. The 'kill' was never ratified but it made little difference. Hugh had died as Gilbert had hoped he might – a hero.

It ended just when they had begun to think it never would, the maroons fired at eleven o'clock on a grey November day sounding its death rattle. As the troops laid down their guns the news burst like an unexpected sunrise on a war-weary world and the shout of joy and relief echoed from corner to corner in cottages and castles, in hospitals and munitions factories.

The war is over! The war is over!

Sarah was in her office at the works when it came. She heard the sudden burst of cacophony as the church bells began to peal and looking out of the window she saw the workers come streaming out of the factory, laughing and shouting, dancing and capering and slapping one another on the back. She clapped her hands to her mouth as she watched them, hardly able to believe it was really over. There was something unreal about the scene, something almost theatrical in the wild gaiety. If she believed in it, it would fade away before her eyes and she would know it was just a mirage. For the nightmare had gone on for too long to be dispelled so quickly by a peal of bells and a chorus of excited voices. Then the door of her office burst open and Hazel Rowe, the 'lady typewriter' who now liked to be known as a secretary, came rushing in.

'It's over, Mrs Gardiner! It's over! Come down and let's see what is going on!'

She grabbed Sarah's arm, propriety quite forgotten in her excitement, and dragged Sarah out into the corridor. Sarah laughed because laughter was the only reaction left to her in this state of semi-trance, and Hazel Rowe, quite beside herself, laughed too.

'Isn't it wonderful? The boys will be coming home!' she sang, and Sarah remembered that Hazel had a sweetheart at the front.

The door to Gilbert's office was closed and Sarah's laughter died as she remembered. Not all the boys would be coming home. For too many the end of the war had come too late.

'You go on down, Hazel,' she said. 'I'll join you later.'

She tapped on Gilbert's door and went in. He was sitting at his desk, staring into space. Though he looked much more his old self these days the shadows beneath his eyes told their story – the loss of Hugh had left a pain in him that nothing would ever erase.

'So it's over, Sarah,' he said.

'Yes.'

'And Adam will be coming home.' His voice was so

449

thoughtful, his eyes so penetrating that for a moment she was quite sure he knew her secret.

'Yes.'

They looked at one another, then he gave his head a little shake.

'Nothing will ever be the same though.' She thought he was talking of Hugh's loss and searched for words of comfort, empty though they might be. But he went on ruminatively: 'No, the world as we knew it has gone forever. I always knew I should see great changes in my lifetime – what I failed to realise was just how great they would be. I knew for instance that the time was coming when women would work on more or less equal terms with men – but I failed to realise just how equal. And this industry of ours – from the very moment Adam and Max came to me with their plans I knew a ball had begun rolling which no-one could stop. But how fast it would go was beyond my comprehension. The development we have seen in less than ten years might have taken decades but for the war. And where do we go now, I wonder? How do we capitalise on the progress we have made and use the knowledge we have gained to put it to use for the purposes of peacetime? We have to look forward now, Sarah. We have to plan for the future. For we must ensure that not one of those boys who gave their lives has died in vain.'

'We shall do it,' she assured him. The knowledge that the war was over was at last percolating her numb defences, a kind of slow joy beginning to trickle through her veins.

The shouts in the yard outside had begun to orchestrate now. She looked up, puzzled at first, then comprehending, as the massed voices floated up and through the window, which Gilbert had opened a little in spite of the dark November chill to let some of his cigarette smoke out and the fresh air in.

'They are calling for you,' she said.

'For me?'

'Yes – listen!'

He shook his head. 'Why should they do that?'

'Because they are proud of you and they respect you,' she

450

said. 'We have turned out aeroplanes from this factory that have helped to win the war. And it's all your doing because you had the vision and the foresight to set that ball rolling here. *You* are Morse Bailey International – that's why they are calling for you.'

A small smile lifted the corners of his mouth. He fingered his moustache and went to the window. At once the cheers rose louder than before and Sarah, joining him, experienced a small thrill of pride.

Above the courtyard a flock of birds, startled by the noise, rose and wheeled. Sarah looked up at them. Once the sky had been theirs alone. No longer. Again she found herself remembering what Adam had once said, so long ago, 'The bold will inherit the skies.'

And that is just what we are doing, she thought. Each in our own way we dared to be bold. And now we too share those skies.

As the church bells rang, firecrackers snapped and men and women shouted for joy, Sarah thought suddenly that it was a fitting epitaph for a war that would, so they promised, end all wars.

BOOK FIVE – 1919

Neither be cynical about love, for in the face of all avidity and disenchantment it is perennial as the grass.

Desiderata

Chapter Thirty-Seven

The neat two seater aircraft dropped towards the field at a shallow angle, hovering, dipping, rising and dipping again. May sunshine glinted on the front cockpit where Adam Bailey sat, deceptively relaxed, and the twirling propellers made a shining arc in the clear blue air.

In the rear cockpit Sarah, her face a study in concentration, her hands rigid on the controls, silently talked herself through each move. Easy down, a little more, and a little more still – never mind the instruments. 'Learn to trust your own judgement,' Adam had told her. 'The only one you can't do without is your compass.' But here, with the runway clearly in view beneath her nose and the Morse Bailey sheds visible away to the right there was no need even for the compass.

Sarah caught her lip between her teeth, holding it tightly. A little more . . . no, you are still too high. Ease back on the stick, take her up and go round again. Now . . . down, down, slowly, gently . . .

If only Adam would *say* something! she thought, a word of encouragement to tell her whether she had got it right or wrong. But he wouldn't. He sat there almost nonchalantly, not saying a word, letting her work it all out for herself. Except of course that she was confident he would not actually let her crash. If she got into a really bad mess then he would step in at the last moment.

The wheels touched the ground, bounced once, twice, and then held. The little training aircraft came to a halt, poised at the very edge of the tarmac. For a moment she could hardly believe she was down, then she pushed her goggles up her forehead and laughed aloud.

'I did it! I *did* it!'

'A few more yards and you would have discovered what landing was like in the days before we had the acceptance park and the runways were laid,' he called over his shoulder. 'The Galloping Major had nothing on us, I assure you. It was "bumpity, bumpity, bumpity bump!" all the way!'

'Oh don't be so mean, Adam!' she cried, her voice a little shrill with the exhilaration of her flight. 'I didn't land us in the sewerage pits, after all – or up a tree. You might give me just the teensiest bit of encouragement.'

'You don't need encouragement, Sarah. You do very well without it.'

'So you admit it? I am doing well?'

'Of course you are. I never doubted you would.' He swung himself down easily from the cockpit and came around to help her down. 'I expect you would have learned years ago if it hadn't been for the war.'

'And Eric. I thought he was never going to give in and let me learn.'

A corner of Adam's mouth twisted wryly. 'He should know, just as I do, that you always get your way in the end.'

'I don't think he would have allowed it if you hadn't agreed to teach me. He thinks you are an ace when it comes to teaching. Not to mention flying, of course.'

Adam said nothing. It struck him as extremely ironic that Eric should have chosen him as mentor when Sarah's demands to fly had finally become irresistible. If he had known that two years ago we were on the point of going off together he might have been less anxious to trust me, Adam thought. But Eric did not know and since he had not wanted to teach his wife to fly himself Adam, crack RFC instructor, had been the obvious choice.

'How long do you think it will be before I can go solo?' she asked now without so much as a flicker.

He shook his head. 'For goodness' sake, Sarah, you have

to learn to walk before you can run. You have just landed an aircraft for the very first time. Let's get things right with me there to get you out of trouble if necessary before you start thinking of going up on your own.'

'I suppose so. Though to be honest it *felt* as if I was on my own today.'

'Because you will be a better pilot if you learn by your own mistakes.'

'And it's just three hours' solo flying that I have to do to get my "A" licence – is that right?'

'Yes,' Adam said, 'but don't forget you have to pass tests in navigation and technical knowledge as well. Not to mention a medical examination and eye tests.'

Her chin hardened. 'You didn't.'

'That was because I was flying before the international system of licensing was drawn up.'

She tossed her head, supremely confident. 'It's a nuisance. But I shall make sure I pass anyway. I quite like engines so long as there's someone to deal with the messy bits for me, I don't mind studying and I am as fit as a flea. So there shouldn't be any problem.'

In spite of himself Adam was unable to restrain a smile. Sarah was twenty-seven years old now and still as impetuous as she had been when he first met her. Marriage, responsibility, motherhood and the tragic loss of her son, all had left their mark on her yet there was still a vitality about her and an irrepressible spirit of adventure along with a determination so fierce it was awesome. He had a sudden vision of her as an old, old woman, with the same unquenchable love of life shining out of her eyes and something twisted within him, sharp and painful.

Christ, how he loved her still! Loved her with the same passion she had always stirred in him, part physical, part spiritual. It burned him up, that love, whenever he looked at her, just as it always had. But it seemed that whatever had been between them had died whilst he was a prisoner in Germany. Never had she written one single word to him; when letters had been passed to him by the Red Cross he had always looked for her handwriting on the envelope in

454

vain. And when he had returned he had found her so changed towards him she might have been a stranger. He had sought her out and tried to talk to her but he might as well have tried to talk to a statue. 'There is nothing to say, Adam. It was all a mistake – the sort of thing that happens in war time. I am a married woman and you are a married man with a child. No! Please don't say any more! I don't want to talk about it. Let us just forget it ever happened, shall we?'

Angered by her attitude he had treated her with reciprocal coldness. If that was the way she wanted it then so be it. He had never crawled to any woman and he did not intend to begin now, however much he might want to. Then gradually her aggression lessened so that she was able to laugh and joke with him again, whilst still keeping him very much at arms' length. To the outside world it would have appeared that their relationship was much as it had always been – that of good friends – and he joined her in preserving the illusion. But in reality, he thought, she was as bright and brittle as an icicle – and as cold to the touch. If anything of the old spark was there – and he sometimes thought in spite of everything that it was – then it was well hidden, and if an unexpected touch evoked a response then it was cut off instantly as if by an all-powerful circuit breaker.

He felt it now as he gave her his hand to help her down from the cockpit. Her knees, weak from the drain of adrenaline, gave way slightly as she climbed down and she stumbled against him, but instantly she stiffened, pushing herself away with a little laugh.

'What ever is the matter with me? I feel quite dizzy!'

He made no effort to steady her but turned on his heel. There was only one way to deal with determined indifference and that was to match it.

'You'll get used to it.' A mechanic was hurrying towards them across the tarmac. 'Check the machine over, Perry, will you?' Adam said to him, then undid his leather flying jacket and looked at his watch. 'I'm a little pushed for time, Sarah. We have a board meeting this afternoon – rather an important one. I ought to be getting back.'

'Of course. Thank you for my lesson.' She smiled, that

bright brittle smile. All the spontaneity that the excitement of flying had sparked had been dispelled by that touch and the restraint it had necessitated. 'I'll stay here and watch Perry check the plane. If I am supposed to know about the mechanics of the thing I could do worse than take a practical lesson here and now.'

'Very well.'

'But you never know – you might hear something of me at that meeting.'

Puzzled, he glanced swiftly at her. Sarah was not a director. She did not attend board meetings. But she did not explain herself and he did not ask.

He nodded, raised a hand in a farewell gesture and walked off across the tarmac.

Watching him go Sarah felt an unexpected knot of tears tighten in her throat. She had thought she had grown used to dealing with the emotions Adam had always aroused in her; now she supposed it was the excitement of the last hour, the fierce concentration followed by the exhilaration and the release of tension when she had finally touched down again that had laid her bare.

But it would do no good. If she still loved him that was her folly and her weakness. It was over – over – and had been from the moment she had learned Alicia was carrying his son. For one thing she could not forget that he had left her to go home and make love to his wife; for another the existence of a child changed everything. Remembering her own uncertain childhood Sarah had known she could never willingly be the cause of an innocent child being denied the comforting presence of his father.

Not that Guy seemed to lack for anything, Sarah thought wryly. Alicia, childless for so long, doted on him and spoiled him so that he was fast becoming an objectionable little boy. In the first year of his life two nannies had been dismissed for attempting to bring a little healthy discipline into the nursery. Guy had only to yell for something to be certain of getting it and already he was astute enough to take advantage of this. But he was clearly intelligent and a very

456

handsome child with that mop of jet black hair and the blue eyes that ran in the Morse family. Pity the young women in his circle in twenty years' time! With that wicked combination they would not stand a chance!

But not one of them could be hurt more badly than she had been, she thought, watching his father stride away from her with never a backward glance, sun glinting on his hair and turning it to molten gold, shoulders broad and straight in the bulk of his leather flying jacket, legs long and muscled in those damned flying boots he wore winter and summer alike.

As he reached the corner of the shed and disappeared from view Sarah gave herself a small shake. Pointless to stand there mooning like a lovesick calf. Worse than pointless – a total waste of time and energy when she needed every bit of it for the new ambitions she was determined to achieve and the new horizons waiting to be conquered. Learning to fly was just one of them. Sarah had wanted to do that since she had seen the first flying machine lift clumsily into the air and now that dream was becoming reality. But she had other dreams too . . . dreams that would take them all by surprise when they knew what she had in mind . . .

Sarah lifted her chin and a small smile curved her mouth. She had seen the surprise – and the curiosity – in Adam's face when she had mentioned this afternoon's board meeting. Well, he would be even more surprised when he heard what was to be proposed . . .

'Mrs Gardiner!' Perry's voice interrupted her thoughts and she turned to see him regarding her patiently. 'Did you want to see what makes the engine tick?'

'Hmm?' For a moment her eyes were quite blank when she shook her head. 'No thank you, Perry. Not today. Next time, perhaps.'

She pulled off her goggles and, swinging them between her finger and thumb in cheery arcs, she traced Adam's footsteps across the tarmac.

Afternoon sunshine streamed in through the windows of

457

the Morse Bailey boardroom, sprinkling the crystal decanters of water on the long polished oak table with myriads of sparkling lights, winking on the framed painting of the first Morse Bailey prototype – 'The Eagle' – which hung in pride of place above Gilbert's splendid leather padded chair, and raising the already overheated temperature in the room.

'Can't we have the blinds pulled a bit for goodness' sake?' Leo asked, running a finger round his neck beneath his stiffly starched collar. He looked flushed and moist – hot as well as angry. Already there had been one or two of the usual contretemps – differences of opinion ending in verbal sparring matches and again, as usual, he had had to fight a lone corner. Now the main business of the afternoon was about to begin and he could see it would be yet another fight. The item on the neatly typed agenda in front of him simply read 'Plans for Future Developments' but Leo suspected that this was a camouflage for something as revolutionary as a good many of Gilbert's ideas – some high-handed scheme he wished to introduce and get past the board whilst they were feeling drowsy from the heat of the afternoon – and Leo was determined to see that did not happen. 'The sun – right in our faces – is beginning to be intolerable!' he protested.

'Very well.' Gilbert nodded crisply. 'It is a little distracting, I agree. See to it, Adam, would you?'

Adam rose from his seat and crossed to the window. He moved easily, as if oblivious of the storm breaking around him. For the meeting he had changed out of the casual clothes he wore for flying into a suit, but it was lighter in colour than the old formal uniform of business and unlike Leo he had forsaken the stiff collared shirt for the softer modern lines. At the window he adjusted the blind then returned to the table to take his place alongside his fellow board members.

Besides Gilbert and Leo there were four of them – Alicia, who had taken to putting in regular appearances since Guy had been born – safeguarding the company that would one day be his heritage perhaps, Adam thought; Max; James, released from prison now that the war was over and at home

458

to regain his health and strength; and Joe Isaacs, who had kept the books in the old days and was now accountant for both companies.

'Is that better, Leo?' Gilbert enquired.

'Marginally.'

'Oh, don't be such a pain, Leo,' Alicia said. She looked every inch her new role of company director with her flowing black locks scraped up into a chignon, not loose, full and feminine but scraped away from her face with a severity that only served to highlight the clarity of her features, and wearing a stark black dress with only the merest touch of white at the collar and cuffs for relief which somehow made her look not matronly and dowdy but vital and commanding. 'The rest of us are managing. Why can't you?'

Gilbert hid a smile and straightened the papers on the table in front of him. 'Item Five on the agenda – future development of the company. Now before I come to the main reason for the inclusion of this item I should like to recap on the position as I see it – where we stand at present.' He paused to take a sip of water from the tumbler at his elbow and they waited, all looking at him with the exception of Max, who was doodling absently on his agenda for he considered board meetings to be a shocking waste of time and sat through them on sufferance only. Gilbert set down his glass, wiped away a droplet of water which was clinging to his moustache, and continued: 'Our industry was one of the few to actually benefit as a result of the war. Resources were made available, the order books were full and necessity, as always, became the mother of invention. We went ahead by leaps and bounds, we saw the sort of progress in a few short years which could have taken decades to achieve in time of peace. Now that the war is over, naturally everything is turned on its head. Orders have been cancelled, we have more workers than we can usefully employ, half-built aircraft in the sheds, unwanted, and a proclivity to design fighting planes which hopefully will never again be needed in our lifetime. The situation could well be viewed as serious – many of the companies which leaped on the bandwagon and took up aircraft production during the boom years will go to the wall – some have already done so. As you know we have been fortunate enough to recruit the services of a couple of first rate designers for the Engine Division, thrown out of work when their company failed.'

'A rash move. Extra wage packets to fill at a time like this,' Leo snorted under his breath.

Gilbert ignored him. 'I believe it would be a very retrograde step to draw our horns in now. I fully realise there are tough times ahead – and maybe they will be even tougher than we expect before we're through the worst of it. But we have the advantage of working from a sound base – Morse Motors is, and has been for many years, a successful company which is financially secure and Morse Motors can still be regarded as the parent company of Morse Bailey International – the division which will be most vulnerable if things get tight. And so I firmly believe that we should take the long-term view and look upon the present difficulties as a temporary setback only. We should continue to press ahead, take steps to secure our position in the marketplace for civil aircraft and expand our interests in whatever direction is open to us.' He paused for another sip of water.

'Fine words, Gilbert,' Leo said shortly. 'But I am not quite sure yet where they are leading us. What exactly is this "expansion" you have in mind?'

'I am coming to that, Leo,' Gilbert said smoothly. 'I am about to suggest that we diversify a little and set up a new division – with the same board as we have for Morse Bailey International, I hasten to add.'

A murmur ran around the table.

'Diversify?' Leo pressed. It was totally foreign to his nature to sit quietly and listen without barking questions. 'Diversify, how?'

Gilbert spread his hands on the table in front of him. He looked around, meeting each pair of eyes in turn. 'At the present time no-one wants to buy our aircraft. That will change, I am convinced of it, but in the meantime I have an alternative – rather an exciting one – to suggest. I propose that we create our own market. That we buy some of our own aeroplanes and set up a civil airline for the transportation of freight – and passengers.'

For a moment there was complete silence around the table. Even Max stopped doodling and looked up at Gilbert, an expression of bemusement on his mobile features. Again it was Leo who broke the silence.

'Good God, Gilbert, I guessed you had a shock in store for us but I had no idea what it was. You are suggesting we should actually run a civil air service?'

'I am.' Gilbert's voice was firm and strong now, daring them to disagree with him. 'I believe it is the way of the future. Great Scott, it has to be! As you all know, the first mail was delivered as long as nine years ago, more for show than anything else, I agree, but nevertheless it demonstrated the commercial uses of flying. Think of the ease and the speed with which deliveries can be made over great distances!'

'Freight, yes,' Leo argued. 'But passengers? Who, I would like to know, would be willing to pay to put themselves in a position of danger and discomfort?'

'Plenty will – especially when we have had a chance to modify our aeroplanes accordingly,' Gilbert said with confidence.

'So. We are all to be fully employed producing aeroplanes to ferry presently non-existent passengers from A to B,' Leo said, his tone heavily sarcastic. 'And who is going to run this new venture? Have you thought of that?'

'Yes,' Gilbert said, 'I do have someone in mind – the person who suggested the idea to me in the first place. And I must say I think she will make an excellent job of it.'

'*She*?'

'Yes. The person I have in mind is Sarah Gardiner.'

Again there was a moment's surprised silence and in it Gilbert took the opportunity to assess the impact of what he had said on the members of his board.

Max's face, predictably, was unreadable – the features which had once been so expressive now conveyed only sadness and a vague disinterest in anything which did not directly concern him or his designs. Joe Isaacs too was an unknown quantity. He looked thoughtful, assessing the pros and cons of Gilbert's suggestion with all the thoroughness that made him a good accountant. He is deciding what should go into the debit column and what the credit, Gilbert thought.

The reaction of the others was much clearer, however. Adam's broad grin showed a measure of amusement, whilst Alicia looked thunderstruck. Perhaps outrage was the only word to accurately describe her expression as she sat stiffly erect as if her father's words had turned her, like Lot's wife, into a pillar of salt.

Adam was the first to speak. 'I congratulate you, Gilbert – or perhaps the congratulations should go to Sarah. I had a feeling when I was with her this morning that she had something up her sleeve – she looked like the cat who got the cream, and I thought it couldn't all be due to her acquitting herself so well on her first flight at the controls.'

'Hmm. She is not proposing to *pilot* her airline as well, is she?' Leo enquired coldly but inwardly he was ablaze with anger. What in hell was Gilbert thinking of to entertain such an idea for a moment? At best the project was a risky one, but to set a woman to run it . . . an upstart like Sarah at that . . . well, it was folly in the extreme.

'Sarah would do anything to make an exhibition of herself,' Alicia said. In her own way she was as furious as Leo at the suggestion – why did her father have to fawn over Sarah so?

'That is ridiculous and you know it,' Adam said sharply. 'Sarah does not even have her "A" grade Private Pilot's Licence yet – she would need a "B" licence in order to fly for hire or reward, and they don't grow on trees. One hundred hours' solo flying, mechanical theory, meteorology and navigation, altitude and night flying, not to mention cross-country flights of not less than two hundred miles – it will be a long time before Sarah qualifies for that. Not that it would surprise me if she does it eventually,' he added wickedly for he could not resist goading them a little.

'But she could run a company?' Leo demanded.

'She has had a good deal of experience over the last few

462

years, and she covered for Lawrence very satisfactorily when he was ill.'

'*Lawrence!*' Leo said rudely and drew an annoyed glance from Gilbert. Lawrence might not have been the world's most efficient businessman but one did not ridicule the dead. It simply was not done.

'Well, I shall certainly oppose any such suggestion,' Leo said vehemently. 'Where do you stand on this, Isaacs?'

The little Jew tugged at his beard thoughtfully. 'It is a risk, it's true. We could end up in serious trouble.'

'Exactly!' Leo's tone was triumphant.

'On the other hand if we do not move forward we could find ourselves atrophied. As Mr Morse has pointed out, sometimes to try to stand still is to find oneself slipping backwards. These are difficult times – a wrong move could be fatal. But so could an opportunity lost.'

'So which way do you intend to vote, man?' Leo blustered.

'Give me a chance to make up my mind. I want to work out a few permutations . . .' His pencil was busy, jotting sums on the edge of his agenda and referring back to the financial statement he had presented earlier.

'Well I think it is a splendid idea,' Max put in unexpectedly. 'I shall modify my designs with a good deal more confidence if I know where the finished aircraft are to find a home. Yes, yes . . . and little Sarah too; the challenge will be good for her. She needs her work, just as I do . . .' His eyes clouded and his voice tailed away.

'Adam?' Gilbert prompted.

'I agree. An excellent idea. As Joe has pointed out, it's not without its risks but I believe we should go all out for a place in the aircraft industry of the future.'

'James?' But James's blue eyes were dreamy. He was probably not listening at all but composing a poem, Gilbert thought irritably. Really there was little point in forcing him to sit on the board. Gilbert had hoped that after his experiences as a conscientious objector, involvement with the company might give him a new interest but it had been a vain hope. James would vote with Alicia as he always did,

463

following her blindly. And Gilbert knew from Alicia's expression that she was going to oppose him.

A faint smile lifted his lips. He was proud of Alicia. A woman with a mind of her own. Why had his sons not inherited those same attributes?

In spite of the partly pulled blind the sun was beaming in, making the room very hot and stuffy. Gilbert decided there was no point in delaying the issue. Every mind was clearly made up – with the possible exception of Joe Isaacs.

'Do we want to discuss this matter further or shall we take a vote?' he asked.

'Vote and have done with it,' Leo looked confident. It was not the first time he had opposed Gilbert's will – but if he carried the day it would be the first time he had won. Usually Alicia was at daggers drawn with him . . .

'Those in favour of the new company?' Gilbert asked.

Two hands went up immediately – Adam and Max. Predictable. Gilbert waited, looking at Joe. Slowly, a little uncertainly, the Jew began to raise his hand, then, making up his mind, extended it fully. Three for.

'And against?'

Leo and Alicia raised their hands. This time it was James who at first hesitated then followed suit. Three against. Gilbert knew a moment's triumph.

'Then I have the casting vote,' he said. 'I think you all know which way I shall use it – I would scarcely have raised the issue had I not been in favour. So.' He smiled, a thin smile meant to forestall any suggestion that he might be crowing. 'If our good lady secretary would record the vote – four to three in favour of the proposed expansion – perhaps someone would like to ask Sarah to step inside. Adam – you are nearest the door. She will be anxious to know of our decision and I think she may have a few words to say to you regarding her ideas for the airline. Adam?'

He glanced around looking at the faces of the vanquished. Alicia looked furious still, her face very white in spite of the heat of the room, violet eyes flashing. No matter. A little healthy rivalry would be good for the new company. With Alicia breathing down her neck Sarah was more likely to pull out all stops to succeed. James? James could hardly be counted as opposition. He would float with the tide. But Leo . . .

Leo pushed back his chair and stood up.

'It seems I have been outvoted,' he said. 'But I should warn you, Gilbert, I shall fight you all the way on this. I think we are making a big mistake – and I would like my opinion recorded. Furthermore, if the situation changes at any time I shall oppose.'

'Oh don't be such a bore, Leo,' Alicia said, making it clear that the fact they had voted together on this did not mean they were allies. 'I dare say one day you will be Chairman of this company. When you are I suppose you will have your way. Until then at least have the courtesy to sit down and listen to what Sarah has to say.'

To her surprise he did as she said. But a curious light had come into his eyes. And as Sarah addressed the meeting, putting forward ideas for the new airline, he seemed not to be listening at all.

Chapter Thirty-eight

The trainer plane banked steeply, wing tips angled so that the patchwork of fields below seemed to turn a slow graceful cartwheel, and straightened again. A small air pocket lifted and dropped it like a boat riding a gentle swell, and the breeze on Sarah's face was soft and cool. She flexed her hands on the controls, enjoying herself. She had completed eight hours' tuition now and Adam had said that he thought she was almost ready to go solo. 'Just as long as you remember not to be so heavy handed,' he had cautioned her. 'You have a tendency to go at it like a bull at a gate. The more you try to rush things the longer it will take, you know.'

Sarah had been a little annoyed by the implied criticism. Patience, which had never been her strong suit, was required for everything – and not only in the case of the flying lessons for which she had waited so long, but also for the lengthy struggle to get her embryo airline off the ground, literally as well as figuratively speaking! It had a name, it was true – Condor Airways – and a neat little emblem in the shape of a soaring wing. It had even been able to take on the delivery of some items of freight, using one of the existing aeroplanes, and Sarah had enthusiastically arranged the details of a contract to deliver Cornish cream and freshly caught sea fish for a high-class London restaurant, and another, for the summer months only, to fly in fresh fruit, vegetables and cut flowers. But the launch of the service for fare paying passengers seemed as far away as ever.

In moments when impatience was not making her fume and fret Sarah knew that there was no way the venture could be hurried if it was to be a success. For years now the factory had been geared to building fighter and bomber aeroplanes – there was nothing even remotely suitable for the transportation of ladies and gentlemen of means. The only answer was to produce something purpose built – large enough to seat perhaps ten passengers in reasonable comfort.

The challenge this presented had delighted Max. He had been feeling aimless and curiously bereft since the declaration of peace and he threw himself enthusiastically into plans for the new 'airliner', locking himself up in his drawing office to ensure he would not be interrupted and remaining there for days on end. Now at last the plans for the prototype were complete and the factory was working around the clock to produce it – an impressive conversion of one of Max's most successful bomber designs, with a spacious wooden fuselage to provide a good-sized passenger cabin and a neat enclosed flight deck.

'Personally I don't think that will work,' Adam had said doubtfully. 'Being enclosed is bound to limit the pilot's vision – and besides, I should hate not to be able to hear the wind in the wires.'

At that time Sarah had thought the sentiment oddly romantic and out of character coming from the down to earth Adam but now as she flew the little trainer high above the rolling countryside she found herself remembering his words and knowing exactly what he meant. There was something almost ethereal about the sound, the high pitched constant hum which seemed to surround her, coming from nowhere, going nowhere, just a haunting vibration that might have been the voice of the sky itself. Oh yes, it would be sad not to be able to hear the wind in the wires. How could anyone fly without it? Knowing Max she could imagine the arguments he would put forward for an enclosed cockpit – comfort, protection from the elements, progress – but then he had never known the pleasure of actually flying one of the aircraft he designed.

Sad for Max, she let her eye wander over the expanse of countryside beneath her wing tips, the fields spread out in their patchwork of 'the forty shades of green', a long undulating hillside, a valley golden with corn. The hedges looked like lines drawn with a thick pencil, a river glinted briefly before disappearing into a thick overhang of protective branches. And above it all, around her, the sky deep blue for late afternoon and the sun ready to dip behind the distant hills. Peace, perfect peace . . .

Quite suddenly Sarah caught a faint whiff of burning. She wrinkled her nose and sniffed, wondering if Adam had noticed it and if it was worth drawing his attention to it. Then, to her dismay, the engine began to race. Automatically she pulled back on the throttle. Nothing. Disbelieving, she pulled back again. Still nothing. The whine of the wind in the wires was very loud indeed and she realised it was because the engine had gone silent. She experienced a moment's pure panic, then Adam called over his shoulder: 'I've got it.'

The ground raced up at them, the hedges taking definite shape, the thick reeds along the bank of the river visible to the naked eye. Immediately in front of them was a field of corn, tall, golden, waving gently in the teasing breeze. The wheels of the training plane seemed to skim it and Sarah braced herself. Then with a thud and a jolt they were down, the wheels locking, the nose burying itself in the corn. For a moment Sarah sat without moving, watching Adam climb down from the front cockpit and circle the plane, assessing the damage. Then she leaped up, eyes wide, close to tears.

'What did I do?'

He ignored her, bending down to examine the undercarriage.

'Damnation! I haven't done that much good! What a mess!'

'Adam – what did I do?' she demanded shrilly.

He looked up, surprised by her violent wail of self-condemnation.

'You? Nothing.'

'Then what . . .'

'We lost a propeller – God knows why. Come on, you might as well get down from there. I'm afraid that machine won't be going anywhere in a hurry.' He helped her out of the cockpit. Her knees almost gave way and he steadied her. 'All right?'

468

'Yes.' She nodded. 'What do you mean, Adam, we lost a propeller?'

'Just that. Have a look.' Still holding her hand he led her around to the front of the plane. 'See – it's simply flown off. In one piece, as luck would have it, that's why we scarcely felt it go. If only one blade had sheared off it wouldn't have been so pleasant.'

'Why not?' she asked though she was not convinced she wanted to hear the answer.

'Because it would have thrown everything so out of balance the whole engine would very likely have been ripped out. We were lucky. And lucky not to have had much height at the time. Though I don't think the farmer is going to be very pleased with us when he sees what we have done to his cornfield.

'Never mind his cornfield – it's us I am more concerned about. Corn will grow again but . . . we could have been killed, Adam. How did it happen? How could we just lose a propeller like that?'

'I don't know. I dare say we'll have to wait for the mechanics to examine it before we find out. Let's hope the propeller turns up so that we can take a good look at that too.'

'You think it will?'

'An even chance. I know more or less exactly where it fell off. Well, I suppose there's not a great deal we can do here –except wait for that irate farmer to find us and I can't say that's an idea that appeals to me much. Do you feel up to a long walk?'

She did not. Her legs still felt shaky and cold waves of horror were washing over her as she thought of the narrowness of their escape. But she was too proud to say so.

'I haven't much choice, have I?'

'Nope.' His nonchalance was almost annoying in the light of what had happened. She was tempted to snap at him to ask how he could take it so lightly. Then he said: 'If this was France and it was still war time we'd have to set fire to the plane before leaving it,' and she understood.

After what he had been through in the war this was

469

nothing. An annoying hiccup, no more. Quite apart from the dangers of combat there must have been dozens of occasions when Adam had had to make a crash landing on unsuitable terrain or with a damaged aeroplane. This might be her first brush with disaster, her first 'heavy' landing – to Adam it was almost commonplace. No wonder he was so blasé. It was either that – or become a jangling bag of nerves as so many of the lads had become, their courage spent in the relentless day-by-day conflict over the fields of France, old men though still barely out of their teens. This had not happened to Adam, in spite of having seen out the war as a prisoner of the Germans. Older, tougher, he had been one of the survivors. If he was now hardened as a result she should not blame him.

'Well, what are we waiting for?' she asked lightly and began to plough her way through the waist high corn.

In his office at Morse Bailey International Gilbert was sharing an early evening snifter with Eric Gardiner whilst Eric was waiting for his wife to return from her flying lesson.

Though no-one could ever recall having seen Gilbert the worse for drink there was no doubt that his liking for it had increased over the years – what had once been a relaxation enjoyed at home before dinner had tended to creep earlier into the day and Gilbert needed little excuse to raid the well-stocked cabinet in his office. With the stress of the business weighing heavily upon him he *earned* it, Gilbert thought when assailed by pangs of guilt. The pressures which the war years had begun had not been eased by the ceasefire – if anything they were worse, for the financial problems of an industry suddenly plunged from full production to an almost total standstill could not be taken lightly. And all at a time when he felt drained both mentally and physically. Small wonder he looked forward to a drink as a lifeline – and it was much more enjoyable taken at the office than at home where Blanche made no bones about her disapproval.

Now he sipped his brandy, enjoying the way tiredness

470

seemed to float away on the trickle of warmth, and reflecting on the latest milestone in the story of aviation.

'So – the Atlantic has been conquered then. Well, I can't say I am surprised. They have been practically lined up in Newfoundland to try to be the first for weeks now.'

'I dare say we should be drinking to Alcock and Brown, but I haven't the heart to. I am too damned envious, truth to tell. I only wish it could have been me,' Eric admitted.

'And who knows, perhaps it might have been if we hadn't decided to commit ourselves to starting an airline instead,' Gilbert said. 'I'm sure one of Max's planes would have had just as good a chance as any of the other contenders.'

Eric nodded, recalling the other serious attempts that had been made in the last few weeks. Harry Hawker had been the first to set out in one of Tom Sopwith's machines but he and his mechanic, Mackenzie-Grieve, had been forced to ditch in the sea and had been missing for a week, feared lost, as the Danish tramp steamer which had picked them up had no radio and was unable to report the rescue. Then A V Roe's test pilot, Fred Raynham, had made the attempt, taking off just an hour after Harry Hawker. But he had been caught in a crosswind on take off, his under-carriage had collapsed, and that was the end of that attempt. But now Jack Alcock and Arthur Whitten-Brown had done it, landing in an Irish bog and astonishing the soldiers who found them by claiming to have come from America. At first the soldiers had laughed, then, realising it was no joke, they had begun to cheer.

Eric, however, in spite of his admiration, did not feel like cheering. The Atlantic crossing was one more 'first' achieved – and one less still to be claimed. Eric longed to do something to write himself into the record books – and he had an idea which might enable him to do it and perhaps give the embryonic airline, Condor Airways, a boost of publicity at the same time.

'I'd like to have a go at setting some record or other,' he said now. 'And if I could time it to coincide with the launch of the airline then the press would be that much more keen to give us coverage. Perhaps you might think it sounds cheap but from my days in the ballooning business I believe publicity is invaluable.'

Gilbert smiled wryly. 'You don't have to tell me that. To be honest, I think you have got something, Eric. Max's prototype will soon be ready for a test flight and if there are not too many modifications to be made we could have the first airliner in service before the year is out. But I doubt we are the only ones with such an idea and I have a feeling it will become a cut-throat business before long. We need every advantage we can get if we are to survive.' He paused, sipping his drink, then asked: 'What exactly did you have in mind? An east to west crossing of the Atlantic?'

Eric shook his head. 'The reason the crossing was made west to east was to take advantage of the tail winds. East to west would be much more difficult but to the majority of lay folk it would be just another Atlantic crossing. If we want to capture the imagination I believe we should go for something quite different.'

'I take your point. Well, since such a flight would be advertising for our aeroplanes as well as publicity for the airline perhaps we should be looking towards a country where we have some hope of selling our wares. Before the war we were demonstrating all over the world – India, Malaya, South Africa. Any of those could provide a market place.' He paused, looking at Eric narrowly. 'It would be a long haul, of course, and would make Alcock and Brown's sixteen and a half hours look like a pleasure flip. You would be lucky to do a trip like that in less than a month by the time you put down for refuelling and any running repairs along the way. How would you feel about leaving Sarah for so long?'

'I left her for a good deal longer than that in the war.'

'This isn't the war though, Eric. Then it was unavoidable. This would be from choice.'

Eric was silent for a moment. He could scarcely tell Gilbert that sometimes he wished it was still war time when he had indeed been able to pretend that his separations from Sarah were inevitable. Since they had returned to some semblance of normal life he had become increasingly aware

472

that all was not well between them. They did not quarrel, Sarah was never anything but a dutiful wife, yet there was a distance between them which he found distressing. Perhaps it had come about as a result of Stephen's death, perhaps it was rooted deeper. Sometimes he wondered if it had always been the same only he had been too blinded by love to see it.

'If I don't get on and do it fairly soon Sarah will probably beat me to it!' he said with a smile. 'She is enjoying her flying lessons far too much for my liking and I don't need to tell you about her spirit of adventure. Just think what a stir it would cause for a *woman* to fly from one continent to another! No, I'm game to attempt anything – and the sooner the better!'

'Good.' Gilbert fetched the brandy bottle to replenish both his glass and Eric's. 'Well, if it were left to me I'd whittle it down to a choice of two. Australia or South Africa. We are in with a chance of selling aeroplanes to either – or both. Australia is further, but I believe their government is offering a substantial prize to the first Australians to make the flight. You wouldn't qualify for that – but it might be possible to steal some of their thunder.'

'True. But on the whole I think I favour South Africa.'

Gilbert drained his glass. He felt like celebrating.

'Perhaps I should ask Max to have a look at any special refinements that might be necessary for such a trip – adapting the aircraft for higher temperatures than usual, for instance, or altitude. This would be an ideal time for him to do it, whilst he's kicking his heels waiting for the prototype airliner to come off the line.' He broke off as a telephone jangled in the outer office. 'Who can that be at this time of night? Dammit, I told Hazel she could go half an hour ago.'

'Do you want me to answer it?' Eric asked.

'No, it's bound to be for me. Probably Rose to make sure I'll be home for dinner . . .' He broke off, looking slightly puzzled at his own slip of the tongue. *Rose*? Why had he said *Rose*? Rose had been dead these twenty years. Perhaps he was drinking more brandy than he should. He put his glass down hastily and went to answer the telephone.

Left alone Eric crossed to the cabinet and surreptitiously

refilled his own glass. He had scarcely noticed Gilbert's slip, he was far too excited by the conversation they had just had. If he could be the first man to pilot an aeroplane from England to South Africa that really would be something!

There was a globe on a stand in a corner of the office; he spun it so as to find both England and South Africa and then ran a line from one to the other, plotting a course. Across the Channel, France and the Mediterranean, then south across the African continent . . .

He heard Gilbert re-enter the office and glanced up, ready to describe the route he would suggest, and was alarmed to see how pale and shocked the older man looked.

'What's wrong?' he asked.

'Sarah and Adam.' His voice was expressionless. 'They have crashed.'

'*What?*'

'Oh, it's all right. They aren't hurt. But they lost a propeller. A propeller! Good God, just wait until I find out who was responsible for checking that plane over before they left! I'll have him out of my works so fast his feet won't touch the ground. They could have been killed, Eric!'

'Where are they now?'

'Somewhere in Worcestershire. That was Adam on the telephone. He wants us to send a couple of mechanics and a lorry for the wreckage first thing in the morning. Of course there is nothing we can do until then . . . except find out what damn fool was in charge of the maintenance . . .'

He broke off, passing a trembling hand over his forehead, and Eric realised just how much this had upset him.

'There's no point in trying to apportion blame until we know what went wrong,' he said reasonably. 'These things can happen for all kinds of reasons. Now – would you like me to take you home? You look pretty shaken up to me.'

'No, no, I'll be all right,' Gilbert assured him. 'But what about you? Would you like to come to Chewton Leigh for dinner? Otherwise it looks as if you will be in for a solitary evening meal.'

Eric grimaced, displeased by the thought that Sarah was alone somewhere in Worcestershire with Adam – and would be all night. But since she could so easily have been killed he decided that was a churlish thought. He should be counting his blessings.

'That is a very kind offer, Gilbert,' he said. 'I think I will take you up on it.'

Chapter Thirty-Nine

The private dining-room at the village inn was small and dark – one of its two windows, bricked up at the time of the poll tax, had never been opened up again and since the remaining one faced east it caught none of the setting sun. But the landlord had lighted the oil lamps, one on the window ledge, one on a dresser, and they cast a soft golden glow to warm the fading light.

At the table closest to the window Adam and Sarah sat eating a meal of beefsteak pie, carrots and tiny new potatoes. They were the only diners – the Apple Tree Inn was hardly a mecca for travellers, buried as it was along with the rest of the hamlet in a fold of the Worcestershire hills, but they were glad to be alone at last. There had been too many questions and explanations – first to the irate farmer, then to a horde of villagers who had never encountered an aeroplane before and who treated them with an awe which suggested they thought they had come not from Somerset but from the moon, and lastly to the landlord of the Apple Tree and the woman at the tiny post office from which Adam had eventually managed to put through a telephone call to Gilbert. It had all been trying, to say the least, and the atmosphere around the table was somewhat less than cordial.

'So they are coming for us tomorrow then,' Sarah said.

'I already told you that'

'Did they say what time?'

'No.'

'What time do you think it will be?'

'I really couldn't say. It depends what time they set out.'

'And Gilbert gave you no idea at all?'

'None.'

'Oh, I wish *I* had spoken to him. At least then I would know what is happening.'

'You could have if you had taken the trouble to come with me to find a telephone.'

'But Adam, we had already walked miles. All the way from the cornfield to the farmhouse and then the farmhouse to the village. If I had gone another step I'd have dropped.'

'The Post Office is only just around the corner.'

'Yes, but I was dying to have a wash – the dust from the corn was making me itch all over.'

'Stop complaining then. You can't have it all ways. Besides you would only have complicated matters by wanting to talk to Eric too.'

'Was he there then?'

'Apparently.'

'You didn't tell me that.'

'You didn't ask.'

'It never occurred to me.' She put down her knife and fork. 'Why are you being so horrid and snappy, Adam?'

'I'm not.'

'You are. You can't hear yourself. You said it wasn't my fault we crashed – so why are you taking it out on me now?'

He made no reply, simply shovelled steak pie into his mouth and washed it down with cold foamy beer. He could hardly tell her the truth, he thought, that the prospect of spending the night alone with her under the same roof was almost unbearable, even if they were in separate rooms. Those rooms were too damned close for comfort, next door to one another along the slanting passageway at the top of the old inn. And in spite of the thick walls, when he had returned from telephoning he had been able to hear her quite clearly splashing water in the jug and basin. There must be a connecting door through which sound travelled clearly and the intimacy of it was another irritation to his already frayed nerves. As if it wasn't bad enough to be forced into her company day after day, now this. Christ, was there no end to the torture of it? He could hardly believe that at his age one woman could stir him so – but she did.

He drained his glass. 'I'm going for a walk.'

'A walk! I should have thought we'd walked far enough today.'

'I want to clear my head.'

She pushed back her chair. 'All right, I'll come with you.'

He spun round, bringing his fist down on the table with a thud. 'Christ, woman, can't you see I want to be alone? And don't stand there looking as if you don't know what I'm talking about, because you damned well do!'

'I don't know! What's wrong with you?'

'Very well.' He faced her. She had never seen him quite like this before. He usually took things so calmly. Now the layers of self-control were peeled away and the anger in his face frightened her. 'I have had just about as much as I can take of your games, Sarah. It might seem like fun to you to be married to one man and lead another on but I assure you that way lies certain trouble.'

'I don't know what you mean!' Her heart was beating very fast, pulses echoing in her throat and at her temples.

'Oh yes you do. Don't pretend. Ever since I have known you you have been leading me on. We were going to be married once, if you remember, before you toddled off and wed someone else.'

'Because Alicia was going to see you and Max cut off without a penny.'

'So you say.'

'It's true. It's true!'

'Next I find you with Hugh and you give me another highly coloured story maligning the poor fellow. Then when you think you have me in your pocket again it is time for the protestations of the faithful little wife trying to do her duty by her husband. Yet even then the game is not over. I suppose it has become too much fun. You lead me on yet again then tell me it was all a mistake, that sort of thing happens in war time. But still not prepared to let me off the hook you continually flaunt yourself in front of me.'

Flaunt herself? Suddenly Sarah, too, was angry. 'How dare you?' she blazed.

He ignored her. 'You know how I feel about you. You must. And you know you have not the slightest intention of doing anything about it. Yet wherever I turn you seem to be

478

there. This learning to fly for instance – couldn't you have found someone else to teach you?'

'Eric insisted it should be you. He has touching faith in you. If it had been left to me I'd have steered clear of you, don't worry! But you could have refused. If you hate me so much why didn't you?'

'Because, my dear Sarah, I don't hate you and you know it. I love you.'

She stood motionless, the anger running out of her with the fierce suck of an ebb tide. Something about the way he said it reached for her heart, wiping out all the pain of betrayal. Somehow it was as if all that had gone between was erased and they were back in her cottage on that night when he had come to her. The atmosphere between them was as electric now as it had been then, and if she thought at all of the estrangement the birth of Guy had caused it was only to wonder why she had allowed it to become so important.

'I love you,' he said again, more softly, as though savouring the words, and his eyes held hers. 'And shall I tell you something? In spite of everything, I think you love me.'

A small sob caught in her throat. To be seen through so easily! Yet she could not deny it.

'You know I do.' The words were soft and muffled. 'I always have.'

'Oh Sarah, Sarah, what happened to us?'

'Alicia happened – and Eric.' Even now she could not bring herself to mention little Guy.

'Well they are not here now,' he said. There was a hardness in his voice; when she looked at him it was echoed in his face, a ruthlessness she had never seen before. Then his mouth quirked with a touch of his old humour. 'Neither, come to that, is Max. He is not likely to come around the door interrupting us tonight, is he?'

She laughed a little and shook her head. He stretched out his hand to her. 'Sarah?'

She took a step towards him and her legs felt as shaky as they had done when she had climbed out of the crashed aeroplane. His hand touched hers and the shock of contact ran through her like an electric current. For a moment she thought he was going to take her in his arms right there in the dining-room and if he had done so she did not think she would have had the strength left to protest. But he did not. He led her to the door and out into the passage. The smell of beer and pipe smoke tickled her nostrils, gales of laughter and the comfortable chink of glasses came from the bar, but all those things might have been nothing more than the echoes of another world. It did not occur to her to wonder if they had been overheard shouting at one another or if anyone would look askance now at the half-finished meals and the couple creeping hand in hand towards the stairs. It did not occur to her because it did not matter. Nothing mattered but Adam and the touch of his hand on hers, sure and firm; nothing but the weakness in her legs which was spreading up like an attack of fever into her thighs; nothing but the urgency tingling in her veins.

Up the stairs, the uneven boards creaking beneath their feet, along the narrow sloping corridor – one step up, two down. He threw open the door of his room and led her inside. Then and only then as the door shut behind them did he turn to her, taking her in his arms and pulling her close. The breath came out of her in a sigh. For a moment their eyes held, hypnotising one another, then his mouth covered hers and the hard length of his body pressed against her. Trembling she returned the pressure, her hands spread out across the taut tendons of his back, her lips parting beneath his like a flower opening in the sunlight.

After a moment the pressure of his mouth became more brutal. His hand slid down the length of her back. Then, hooking his arm behind her knees, he lifted her bodily, carrying her to the bed. His leather flying jacket was lying there where he had tossed it; he pushed it aside and the covers with it, laying her gently down on the cool sheet and going down on his knees beside her. He unfastened her blouse, all the while covering her with kisses, pausing at her breasts to draw the rosy nipples erect with his tongue. The tug of his teeth started a fire deep inside her, licking fierce flames into her most secret places and shooting sharp flickers of warmth along paths of nerve endings she had not realised existed.

Oh dear God, she loved him. She had loved him for so long – so long!

She wore trousers for flying, cut loose and floppy. He removed them and she scarcely knew it until she felt his hand on the soft flesh of her inner thigh, then moving with unconscious sensuality she snaked her hips and his hand moved to the very core of her, cupping, moving, exploring and all with an erotic mastery that made her writhe and moan. As he went away from her she almost cried out in protest, stretching her arms out to him, then folding them around herself as she watched him undress, swiftly and without fuss, dropping his clothes and leaving them where they fell.

For a moment he towered over her, lamplight gleaming on his body, colouring it golden and strong and she gloried in the sight of it. Then he lowered himself onto the bed beside her and she turned to him, aching with the desire to feel him close with every inch of her bare skin, to have him around her and within her.

If the touch of their hands had been electric the fusion of their bodies was cataclysmic and all hurt, all guilt, all responsibility to others was forgotten. For a brief moment they hung poised on the brink, then with a thrust he was within her and she closed around him possessively. They moved in unison with the movement of the ocean, rippling gently at first, then rising to a great swell. She cried out at the last, clinging to him, unwilling to relinquish either the moment or the man. And then she was floating down from the crest of that pulsating wave to lie spent and limp in his arms.

A glow of contentment suffused her now, her head nestled against his shoulder so that the slightly salt scent of his damp skin was in her nostrils and his arm lay in a gesture of possession across her stomach.

'Oh Adam,' she whispered.

'Ssh!' His breath tickled her neck. 'Don't spoil it.'

'I wasn't going to.'

His hand traced the outline of her face, tucking her hair back behind her ear and spreading out protectively around the curving fissures of her skull.

481

'I love you,' she whispered.

'Then stay with me.'

'I will,' she whispered. 'Oh, I will.'

He reached out and extinguished the lamp. Darkness had fallen now, the soft darkness of a summer night. He loosed himself from her to reach for the sheet, pulling it up to cover them, and as he lay back against the pillows she curled around him again, snug and clinging as a child. Already she was almost asleep.

His arm went around her, his hand covering her breast. She wriggled once, her mouth forming a small chaste kiss on the hard muscle of his shoulder. But even before her lips had softened back into repose she was asleep.

When she awoke it was morning. Slowly, deliciously, she surfaced through the layers of sleep, only half aware of the reason for the feeling of well-being that pervaded her, and slightly puzzled by her nudity. Then memory returned and she reached out for him to encounter nothing but cool, empty sheet.

'You are awake then!'

She opened her eyes and saw him standing at the wash basin to shave. He was wearing his trousers but no shirt, the sight of his bare back with its hard lines of muscle and his strong upper arms reminded her of the glories of the previous night and made a little imp of desire twist teasingly within her. But his face was covered in a froth of shaving soap into which he was carving flat planes with a foot-long cut-throat razor and curiosity ousted desire.

'Where did you get that razor?'

'Borrowed it – from the landlord.'

'When?'

'This morning. We don't all sleep half the day away,' he teased.

'Oh – you!' She stretched luxuriously. 'What time is it?'

'Eight o'clock.' The razor scythed away the last of the shaving soap and he reached for a towel, drying his face, then crossing to the bed. 'Come here!'

'Adam! It's morning!'

'So what?' The bed dipped beneath his weight. 'Is there any law which says we can only make love at night?'

'Adam!' But he was kissing her, caressing her, turning the sheet back and climbing in beside her, and the protest died on her lips.

He took her slowly, luxuriously, for all urgency had been satisfied the night before, and though it was quite different she enjoyed it every bit as much for she was detached enough to be able to relish his pleasure. When it was over he sat up, pulling on his trousers and looking down at her.

'Well, Sarah, what are we going to do?'

A cloud appeared on the horizon. 'What do you mean?'

'What are we going to do? About us?'

The cloud took shape. They had shared one beautiful stolen night. They had consummated the love they had shared for so long. But now they were back in the real world – a world where she had a husband and he had a wife and son.'

'I don't know . . .'

'You are not about to tell me that last night was just "one of those things that happen", I hope – and suggest we continue as before, because I think I should warn you I won't stand by and see you go back to Eric now.'

Well! she thought with a flash of resentment, what is sauce for the goose is not sauce for the gander, it seems! But she could not bring herself to mention what she still thought of as his betrayal. It was something she wanted to forget.

'We have wasted too long already,' he said and a small treacherous dart ran through her, part excitement, part fear.

'Adam! You don't know what you are saying.'

'Oh yes I do. I am asking you to marry me as soon as we are both free.'

Her heart was beating very fast. 'But Adam – we are married already!'

'Yes, and it could be a messy business. Not that that worries me personally. My shoulders are broad and there are women I could approach who would be willing to be named in a divorce action on payment of a consideration. I don't want to see your name dragged through the mud. But how to manage your divorce is another matter. Eric might be agreeable to do the decent thing and provide you with grounds, of course . . .'

She pulled herself up in bed. The morning air was crisp. She reached for his flying jacket, lying on the floor where he had dropped it the previous night, and pulled it on.

How could something which last night had been so beautiful suddenly become so ugly and sordid?

'I don't think Alicia would divorce you even if you waved a mistress under her nose,' she said. 'Her pride would never allow it and she can be very vindictive. As for Eric . . . I don't know that he would divorce me either. I suppose he might, if he thought it would make me happy . . .' She broke off, biting her lip. 'What a mess!'

'Well we certainly can't go on as we have been,' he said. 'And I am not prepared to carry on a secret affaire either. I don't like deceit. Meeting secretly, lying, cheating, making love in the shadows and never being certain when we would be found out . . . no, I have no intention of living like that. I know if we end our marriages people are bound to be shocked and hurt too, but at least it is honest.'

She tore her eyes away from his. Oh yes, people would be hurt. Eric and Alicia – and little Guy. She recoiled quickly from the thought of the child. But it was the knowledge of how angry and disappointed in her that Gilbert would be that tipped the balance. She could take any amount of flak from the rest of the world. Gilbert's opinion of her was something very precious and very important.

'I'm not sure I can do it, Adam,' she said quietly. 'I'm not as brave as you.'

She looked up, expecting him to argue with her, and saw that he had crossed to the window. His back was toward her and when he turned his face was bland, almost expressionless.

'In that case I shall ask Gilbert to send me to one of the new overseas branches. Oh, it's no use looking at me like that, Sarah. I am not trying to blackmail you. I want you more than I have ever wanted any woman and I think you

484

know that. But if I can't have you openly, without shame and deceit, I would prefer not to have you at all.'

'Adam . . .' She felt like weeping. He was so cold and hard suddenly, all tenderness gone. 'You can't go abroad. Not now . . .'

He shrugged. 'I don't want to go. At least, not without you. But I refuse to stay here to be teased and played for a fool, or drawn into a sordid hole and corner affaire. What it boils down to, Sarah, is that it is up to you now. The choice is yours.'

She could not answer. Her throat was too tight. She lowered her chin, burying it in the leather of the flying jacket and when she raised it again she saw that he had put on his shirt and was combing his hair at the dressing table mirror.

'Well,' he said, 'I am going to have some breakfast and then get out to the plane. Are you coming with me?'

Once again he seemed to have put what had happened behind him, locked it up in a separate compartment whilst he got on with the rest of his life. Easy for him – so easy! Everything black and white – no shades of grey between.

'You go on,' she said. 'I don't think I will come with you.'

He glanced at her over his shoulder but if he was wondering if her words were an indication as to what her decision would be he said nothing and his eyes, cool hazel, did not show it.

'Well, well, look at that, see!' A farm labourer had found the missing propeller in a field, now Perry, the mechanic, was examining it, shaking his head slowly from side to side in wonderment. 'Look at that! Come off clean as a whistle, she must've!'

'Amazing, isn't it?' Adam agreed. 'I've never seen anything quite like it before. What could have caused it, do you think?'

Perry continued to shake his head. 'Well, I s'pose t'weren't fitted proper in the fust place. Not tight enough. That's the only thing it can be. But I can't understand it. I went over that plane meself the day afore yesterday. I should've thought I'd have noticed straight away. I don't know, I'm sure. 'Tis a mystery.'

'A mystery you had better get to the bottom of and make certain it doesn't happen again,' Adam said tartly. 'We could have been killed. You realise that, don't you?'

'Too true! I've already had Mr Morse threatening me with God knows what. But I don't think 'tis my fault and I don't see why I should take the blame.'

'Because you are paid to be responsible,' Adam informed him. 'Well, I dare say there is no point going over it now. Let's get the plane loaded on to the lorry and back to Chewton Leigh so it can be examined properly. Then if you are found to be at fault, Perry, I wouldn't give much for your chances of keeping your job. This is the kind of carelessness we can't afford.'

Perry went pale but he said nothing. There was no point arguing. It was his responsibility. He still couldn't understand it, though. He'd been sure there was nothing wrong with the propeller when he had looked the plane over . . . Ah well. With typical countryman's mentality Perry thought that what could not be cured must be endured.

'Right, Mr Bailey, let's get to work,' he said stoically.

Chapter Forty

'So – what do you think would be the best route from England to South Africa, Adam?' Gilbert asked.

'Sorry, what was that?'

Adam, who was leaning against the great oak desk in Gilbert's office, came back to earth with a jolt. He had been asked in to discuss Eric's attempt at a record-making flight, but he had been only half listening to their plans for his mind was occupied with his own problems.

It was three weeks now since he and Sarah had spent the night together and still she was prevaricating. Not only that, he thought that she was deliberately avoiding him – easy enough now that she had gained her 'A' licence and no longer needed him as a tutor – and he was fast coming to the conclusion that she would never leave Eric. Well, if that were the case, then he had no intention of remaining here like some lap-dog. Plans were afoot to re-establish the South African branch of the company and Adam had made up his mind to ask Gilbert to send him there.

'Which route do you think would give Eric the greatest chance of success?' Gilbert repeated, sounding faintly irritated.

Adam pushed his private thoughts to one side and crossed to the huge map which covered one wall of the office.

'Let me see. France, over the Alps, Italy, across Egypt, down through Africa, Kampala, Bulawayo, Johannesburg – and then south-west to Cape Town.' He traced the line with his finger. 'It's direct and there are plenty of places where you would be able to put down for fuel and water. That's the way I'd go.'

'I think you're right,' Eric agreed. 'But it's a hell of a long way, isn't it – even for a good plane like the Condor. We are bound to meet extreme weather conditions and God alone knows what sort of expertise the mechanics we shall have to rely on along the way will have. The trouble is if the smallest thing is not as it should be it can cause disaster. Take the accident you and Sarah had a few weeks ago – a few nuts not tightened properly and you lose your propeller. If the same thing happened over a desert or jungle it would certainly mean the end of the record attempt and over the sea it would probably be fatal.'

'Thinking of giving up the attempt, are you?' Adam asked, unable to resist a dig at the man who stood between him and Sarah.

'No, certainly not,' Eric said coolly. 'But I could do with a really experienced co-pilot. Why don't you come with me?'

'Me?' Adam almost laughed aloud at the irony of it. 'No, I don't think so, Eric.'

'I suppose you would prefer to stay around Chewton Leigh.' Eric said. His tone was pleasant enough but there were undertones beneath the apparent friendliness and quite suddenly the air was alive with electric tension.

Hell fire – he knows! Adam thought, and then, almost simultaneously, no, it's not possible. No man worthy of the name could suspect that his wife was being unfaithful to him and ignore it. It was all he could do to remain in the same room as Eric and not land a punch on his nose – and he was not the injured party!

'I only hope you can pull the venture off, Eric,' Gilbert said. He seemed oblivious to the atmosphere which had arisen between the two younger men. 'The publicity will be invaluable to the new airline and to the success of the new South African division. We need that new business to get us over this sticky patch.'

Adam turned his back on Eric, speaking directly to Gilbert.

'How bad is it?' he asked.

'Bad.' Gilbert's expression was grim. 'But I am trusting you two not to mention that fact outside these four walls, not even to the other members of the Board. There is nothing like loss of confidence to make things worse.'

Adam's eyes narrowed. 'You don't mean we are going to go to the wall?'

'We wouldn't be the first.' Gilbert drew himself up, summoning the determination that had helped him build his companies into institutions of which he was rightly proud. 'Don't worry. I don't intend to let that happen. We can weather the storms, gentlemen, and the time will come when the name of Morse Bailey will be synonymous with aeroplanes. And I believe this record attempt will herald the beginning of a new chapter in our history.'

By the end of the month everything was well under way. The whole of Chewton Leigh was bubbling with enthusiasm, and the glamour of the project had temporarily eclipsed even talk of the proposed airline. Curly Bowden, an old friend of Eric's from his RFC days, who was anxious to find a niche in commercial flying now that the new RAF was streamlining to meet the needs of peacetime, had agreed to be his navigator and the press came in their droves to interview the pair of them and photograph them beside the Condor.

'We shall never be ready if they don't stop hindering us!' Eric grumbled to Gilbert. But Gilbert was more philosophical.

'Every reporter who comes here bothering you is equal to another few inches of newsprint and the name of Morse Bailey is hammered home yet again,' he pointed out.

'I suppose you are right,' Eric agreed, but he found the constant bombardment infuriating and the lack of privacy worse. Before long one of the newspapermen had unearthed the fact that not only had he shot down a Zepp during the war but also that he had once been a balloonist – and that his wife had been Sarah Thomas, Sweetheart of the Skies. Old photographs of Sarah in her ballooning costume appeared alongside new ones of Eric, Curly and the Condor and the clamour for interviews extended to her.

Sarah could not help enjoying the fuss. It seemed a very long time ago since she had been the centre of attention. And at a hastily arranged meeting Gilbert came up with a suggestion which would satisfy the reporters' interest in Sarah and at the same time exploit it.

'We'll put on a demonstration flight for them,' he informed the other members of the board. 'That way they will get all the pictures they want and we will reap the benefits of the publicity they generate.'

'And how exactly do you propose to do that?' Leo drawled. Since losing the vote on the formation of the airline he had become more and more obstructive, each and every suggestion that was put up Leo was certain to oppose it with such vehemence that he sometimes persuaded one or two of the others to his viewpoint.

'As you know Eric and Curly will actually begin their record attempt by taking off from Brooklands.' Gilbert's eyes were narrowed against the thin stream of smoke from his cigar. 'It is about the closest we can get to the Channel coast. But the Condor has to get there from Chewton Leigh. Now what I suggest is this – we make a big set piece of the departure from here and invite along the press, but instead of Curly in the co-pilot's seat, we put Sarah! Husband and wife setting off on the first lap of the great adventure – it's the kind of story they'll lap up, especially in view of the fact that they used to balloon together. We might even let Sarah take the controls for the benefit of a headline now that she has her licence.'

'Isn't that a little unfair on Curly?' Adam asked. 'After all, he is the one risking his neck along with Eric.'

'Curly will have his share of glory if the flight is successful,' Gilbert said. 'Just look at the reception Alcock and Brown got – mayoral receptions, flags, speeches and cheers in this country and tickertape in New York. If it works out this could be even bigger. But we have to be practical about this. If something goes wrong and they don't make it, Morse Bailey still needs all the publicity we can get. And whether you like it or not Sarah is news. Take a pioneering spirit, a measure of danger and a pretty face, mix it all together and the resulting cocktail will be very potent, I promise you.'

He looked at Leo, throwing out a silent challenge, but

surprisingly the younger man said nothing. He sat thought-fully rolling a pencil between his fingers and it was Adam who voiced dissent.

'Frankly I am surprised at you, Gilbert. The whole idea strikes me as being incredibly cheap.'

'But think of the glut of orders the publicity will produce,' Gilbert said evenly, then broke off, not wanting to mention in front of Leo just how close to the brink they were sailing. 'Perhaps I have become something of a showman in my old age,' he added after a moment. 'Whatever, my mind is made up. When Eric takes off from Chewton Leigh, Sarah will be with him.'

Sarah stood at the window of her office looking out towards the air strip where the Condor stood ready and waiting to leave on the first leg of its historic flight. At this distance it looked so small – incapable of leaving the ground almost, let alone covering thousands of miles over land and sea, and she shivered at the thought of the risk Eric was taking. For years now she had lived side by side with danger and the men who courted it, so that she had thought she had become impervious to the fears that accompanied each new venture. But somehow this was different, resurrecting the anxieties that had haunted her through the years of the war.

The mechanics were buzzing around the Condor like bees around a hive but Sarah knew their activity was show only – all the necessary checks and preparations had been made the previous evening in the privacy of the shed. Today belonged to the press – already reporters were bustling around with their notebooks open, interviewing anyone who would stop to talk to them, and photographers were taking countless shots of the Condor, the mechanics and even the Morse Bailey works. Tomorrow the news-papers would be full of them – together with the photo-graphs of her and Eric. Again the imp of nervousness tugged at her and she wondered why. Perhaps because in the old days the achievement had been her own. This time she was window dressing only.

'Half an hour, Sarah. Are you ready?' It was Eric. Sarah

was surprised to see him – she had thought he would be out on the runway with the mechanics.

'Yes. Are you?'

'Uh-huh.' He joined her at the window and gesticulated towards the throng on the tarmac. 'What a carnival! It's as well everything was checked last night, isn't it? If it had been left till this morning anything could have been missed.'

She was aware of another of those tiny pricks of apprehension.

'They are sure everything is in order?'

'Oh yes. I watched the check myself. You can be quite certain that you will be safe on your leg of the journey at any rate.'

'And what about yours?'

'That, of course, is infinitely more risky.' His eyes met hers, his mouth lifted in a quizzical half smile. 'Never mind, Sarah, you never know, I might not come back.'

'Eric!' she exclaimed, shocked. 'What ever do you mean?'

Again the half smile. 'It would solve everything if I didn't, wouldn't it?'

She felt sick suddenly. 'What on earth are you talking about?'

'Oh Sarah, don't pretend with me any more.' His voice was even. 'I'd like you to know that if anything should happen to me, you and Adam have my blessing. Though whether you will have Alicia's is another matter.'

She stared at him, speechless.

'I've known for a long time how it is between you and Adam,' he said quietly. 'If you think I didn't you must also think I am a fool. But I didn't say anything because I didn't want to lose you. You mean more than anything in the world to me, Sarah. Without you I wouldn't want to go on living.' He paused, then continued. 'I have thought about it a good deal, I can tell you, thought about it until my head spun. I've considered every possibility – even setting you free so that you and he . . . But I couldn't do it. Not even knowing you don't love me. I simply couldn't do it. But of

492

course if I didn't come back there would be no problem, would there? And I have this feeling that I am not going to come back.'

In spite of the heat of the room Sarah was suddenly icy cold.

'Just one thing I would ask of you, Sarah,' he continued in the same level tone. 'Don't make it too soon, you and Adam. I know it is stupid of me but please . . . would you mind leaving me a little pride?'

'Oh Eric, don't say such things! Of course you will come back!' She was trembling, desperately wanting to tell him he was wrong but knowing instinctively that to lie to him would be to add insult to injury.

'It would have been better, wouldn't it, if I had died along with the crew of that Zepp I brought down,' he said softly. 'At least then I would have died believing you loved me.'

'But I *do* love you!' As the words burst from her she knew it was no more than the truth. In her own way she did love him – a totally different love to the passion she felt for Adam but no less real for all that. 'I do love you, Eric, and I will always be grateful to you for all we have shared. It's just that . . .'

'I know,' he said. 'I am not Adam.'

Tears pricked her eyes. There was no way she could deny it.

'Well,' he said, 'I dare say it is time we were going.'

She nodded, reached for him and put her arms around him. He held her briefly, then put her away and she realised the bitter truth. Her touch was hurtful to him now. As long as they were at arm's length he could say these things to her – touch him and his defences were in danger of breaking down.

A wave of dizziness swept over her.

'Ready?'

She nodded. She wanted to say: 'Eric, please take care. In spite of everything, come back safely.' But she could not speak.

He turned and left the office, she followed on legs

suddenly gone weak. Along the corridor, deserted because everyone was out on the airfield, towards the head of the stairs. They spiralled down, those stairs, and suddenly she was dizzy again. She caught at the bannister as her knees buckled – too late. It was not her head that was going round now but the whole world.

In all her life Sarah had never before fainted. She fainted now, her knees giving way, her whole body folding up, then bumping in an untidy bundle down the length of the stairs.

As she came slowly back through the layers of consciousness the voices came at her in waves.

'Sarah! Wake up, Sarah!'

'Is she all right?'

'She fainted. She went from top to bottom of the stairs . . .'

Someone was pressing a handkerchief, cold and wet, to her forehead; there was pressure of a different sort on her lips and her protesting stomach caught the smell of the brandy fumes the instant before she tasted it, burning her tongue, running a trickle of liquid fire down her throat.

She opened her eyes. Eric and Gilbert were there. As consciousness returned she was aware of a feeling of acute embarrassment and struggled to sit up.

'Lie still, Sarah.' Eric's voice, not bitter now, just loving and concerned. 'You took a bad tumble.'

'I'm all right . . .' She tried to move and knew she was not. The whole of her body felt as if it had been run over by a steam roller and the dizziness made her head swim again. The voices became a buzz; when they cleared again she heard Gilbert asking: 'Has the doctor been sent for?'

'Yes. He is on his way.'

'I don't need a doctor!' she said weakly.

'Don't argue, Sarah,' Gilbert said sternly.

The door opened and Leo came in.

'What the devil is going on? What's the delay? The press are getting restless . . .' He caught sight of Sarah and broke off. 'Good grief, Sarah, they are all waiting for you!'

'They will have to wait then!' Eric said irritably. 'Can't

you see Sarah is ill?' He turned to Gilbert. 'What are we going to do?'

Gilbert took out his watch and checked it. 'Leo is right. We can't keep them waiting much longer. But there is no way Sarah can make the flight.'

'But they are expecting her!' Leo protested.

'Good grief, man, surely you can see she is in no fit state.'

'I'll be all right,' Sarah began but he brushed her protest aside.

'Don't talk foolishness. You most certainly will not be all right. No, there is only one thing for it. I shall go in your place.'

Leo drew a sharp breath. From where she lay he was directly in Sarah's line of vision and she saw him whiten.

'But that won't do at all! The whole point, surely, is for *Sarah* to be the passenger . . .'

'It can't be helped.' Gilbert's tone was firm, brooking no argument. 'The press will have to be told Sarah is ill. I am Chairman and Managing Director of Morse Bailey. That should be worth a paragraph even if it does not have quite the same impact as a beautiful young woman in the cockpit. And at least I shall be demonstrating my faith in my aeroplane.'

Leo caught at Gilbert's arm. 'I really don't think you should.'

Gilbert shook him off a trifle impatiently. 'I am afraid that is the way it is going to have to be.' He turned to his secretary who was hovering anxiously. 'Will you stay with Mrs Gardiner, Hazel? See she is all right until the doctor gets here? Now, Eric, if you are ready we had better get out there and make our excuses. The longer we keep them waiting the less gracefully they will accept the new arrangements.'

He strode to the window, pausing for a moment to look out at the milling crowd of reporters. In the bright sunlight his hair shone silver – in the last years the wings had spread so that there was no trace now of the brown. But neither was there any trace this morning of ageing. He looked older, yes, but still handsome and dignified, still very much in control.

'Ready, Eric?' He crossed to the door and stood waiting.

'Yes.' Eric looked down at Sarah and his expression tore at her heart. Love, sorrow, regret . . . she could see them all there. Then he bent to kiss her lightly on the cheek. 'Take care, my love.'

'And you.' Her throat was aching. The goodbye had come before she had expected it and she felt empty inside, torn apart by a mass of conflicting emotions. Then he was gone, pausing in the doorway for just one backward look, then striding away after Gilbert and the emptiness spread until it was a physical pain.

Oh Eric, I have hurt you so and I didn't mean to. But what could I do, when I belong body and soul to another man?

'Don't upset yourself, Mrs Gardiner.' Hazel joined her, looking as if she was enjoying her new-found role of nurse. 'It won't be any time at all before he is back again. And just think how proud you are going to be of him!'

Sarah could not reply and her only consolation was that the secretary had not the slighest inkling of her true feelings.

'They are getting ready for take-off!' Hazel said. She was standing at the window watching what was going on outside and relaying the information to Sarah. 'Yes, the propellers are turning. They will be going at any minute.'

'I want to see them go.' Sarah swung her legs off the chaise and Hazel, realising protest was useless, hurried across to help her. Leaning slightly on the secretary for support she made it across the room to the window and saw that the aeroplane was indeed already moving along the runway. At this distance she could not see Eric and Gilbert clearly, just the brown shapes of their flying helmets as they sat strapped in the cockpit.

The aeroplane moved forward, gathering speed, then the wheels left the ground and she saw it rise slowly until it was above the heads of the spectators. Eric took it around the field in a gigantic sweep, dipping his wings in salute and then turning away towards the rolling skyline.

As the aeroplane shrank to a speck on the horizon the

reporters began to leave the field, eager to rush their stories to their newspapers around the world, and Sarah turned away from the window. She felt weak and sick again and there was a curious emptiness around her heart. She crossed to Gilbert's drinks cabinet – perhaps another brandy would help settle her stomach.

'They are coming back! Why are they coming back?' Hazel had remained at the window; now her puzzled voice arrested Sarah.

'What?' She turned, the brandy bottle in her hand.

'They're coming back!' Hazel sounded really agitated now. 'They're very low. You don't think something is wrong, do you?'

Still clutching the bottle Sarah ran to the window and felt her blood run cold. The Condor was approaching erratically – even at this distance it was obvious Eric was struggling to control it. On the airfield people were running here and there in panic, shouting and waving their arms to clear the runway. Sarah stood mesmerised.

'Oh my goodness!' Hazel cried. She was close to tears. 'They are going to crash!'

The Condor came in low, like a great wounded bird. It tilted crazily as Eric fought to lift it above the line of trees which separated the airfield from the fields beyond, but he could not get even that little extra height. The Condor hit the first of the trees, broken branches and shattered wings and bits of fuselage flew through the air. There was a blinding flash followed by a huge ball of orange flame and a pall of thick black smoke. The screams of the watchers mingled with the fierce crackle of burning wood and Hazel sobbed aloud, almost hysterical with shock. But Sarah stood silent, her hands pressed against her mouth, stunned into a trance of horror.

Dear God, they were dead, both of them. They must be. They had just died before her very eyes, two of the men she loved most in the world. And she was responsible for their deaths.

The family wanted her to return to Chewton Leigh House

497

with them after the accident but she refused, desperate for the sanctuary of her own home. But there was none. She threw open all the windows but still the rooms were hot and airless behind the drawn curtains and the loud ticking of the clock sounded to her like the knell of doom.

During the evening Adam came. She looked at him with a peculiar blankness in her eyes and he went to her, taking her in his arms. For a moment she clung to him but there was no comfort in his touch, no relief in the feel of his chest beneath her cheek, nothing but overwhelming guilt. She had sent both Eric and Gilbert to their deaths. The knowledge was too much to bear; his closeness merely an abomination.

'Don't, Adam, please.'

Not understanding he reached for her again and again she pushed him away.

'Don't, I said! It wouldn't be right. Not with Eric lying dead.'

He went to the big oak chiffonier, taking out a bottle of brandy, pouring a good measure and passing it to her. 'Drink this.'

She made a quick impatient movement as if to thrust it away, then took it and emptied the glass in one gulp.

'It should have been me. You know that, don't you?'

'Thank God it wasn't.'

'Really? You know what they say – "they die young whom the Gods love". They must hate me very much.'

'Sarah, stop this foolishness. It was an accident. Accidents happen.'

'Was it an accident? That's what I keep wondering.'

'What are you talking about?'

She spun round to face him. 'He knew, you know. Eric knew – about us. He told me so – just before he left. And he kept saying he wouldn't be coming back.'

'That he was leaving you, you mean?'

'No – no! That something was going to happen to him. It would solve everything, he said. And that he wished he had died along with the crew of that Zepp he shot down. I think he wanted it to happen, Adam. And now both he and Gilbert are dead and it's all my fault.'

'Sarah – stop this at once! You will make yourself ill.'

'Well? It's no more than I deserve. I don't know how I can face them again – any of them.'

He paced to the window and back again, wondering whether this was the moment to say what was on his mind. Then he thrust his hands into his pockets, leaning against the chiffonier and looking at her steadily.

'There is really no need for you to face them, Sarah – or not for very long, anyway. I had arranged with Gilbert to start up the South African Division and I leave at the end of the month. You can come with me.' Her forehead wrinkled as if she had not understood him and he went on: 'We can start a new life there. Of course, what has happened is bound to set plans for the new division back somewhat. But we must keep the expansion going. Gilbert would want that. And it affords us an opportunity for a fresh start.'

'No!' She shook her head. 'No – I can't!'

'Can't come to South Africa with me? Why not? There is nothing to stop you now.'

Her eyes blazed. 'That is a terrible thing to say.'

He raised his hands helplessly. 'Then I apologise. But it's the truth. I love you, Sarah. I have waited for you so long and now . . .'

'Do you know what Eric said to me?' Her eyes were bright with tears. 'That if anything happened to him he gave us his blessing. But he asked one thing of me – that I should wait a decent interval so as to leave him some pride. How much pride would be left to him if I ran off to South Africa with you, Adam? He'd be a laughing stock – poor old Eric, poor old cuckolded Eric. I can't do that to him and I'm shocked that you should have asked me to. He deserves a better memorial than that.'

Adam nodded. His eyes were bleak. Eric was as much an obstacle to them being together now as he had ever been. Perhaps time would change that. But was he prepared to go on waiting and waiting? Sometimes he wondered if Sarah merely produced one excuse after the other because in reality she did not want to be with him. But she was right, of course. It would be disrespectful to Eric's memory for them to be together too soon.

'I'll leave you then, Sarah.' Adam said. He was aware of the gulf between them and realised this was not the moment to try and bridge it.

She nodded. Most of all just now she wanted to be alone. Perhaps tomorrow when the shock had subsided a little she would feel differently.

But she did not. The next day it was as bad, if not worse, and the next. She could not eat or sleep, the horror was still too vivid. The grief came at her in waves like the swell of the ocean and always in the undercurrent was the guilt. Could she ever go with Adam now, with this shadow hanging over them? Eric, it seemed, was reaching out for her from beyond the grave, holding her more tightly in death than ever he had done in life.

Chapter Forty-One

In spite of the number of people gathered there a hush hung over the library at Chewton Leigh House for the sense of shock at what had happened had crushed them all. For the record attempt to have ended in tragedy before it had properly begun was bad enough. That they had all been there to witness it made it infinitely worse.

Why had it happened? No-one could say with any certainty for the Condor had been totally destroyed in the explosion and fire which had followed. Only a few scattered bits of debris were left and they offered no clue. All that anyone could say was that Eric must have encountered some problem and turned back, but whatever the fault had been it had been so serious that he had been unable to regain the runway.

Max, grey-faced with strain, had sifted every bit of evidence to no avail; it seemed that Eric had taken the secret of the cause of his death with him to his grave.

'There must have been some sort of failure for him to have turned back,' Max had said.

'Not necessarily. Perhaps Eric was taken ill,' Adam had suggested, trying to relieve his friend of some of the weight of blame he seemed determined to shoulder, but both of them knew in their heart of hearts it was unlikely. Eric had been perfectly well when he had taken off, he was young and fit. There remained the possibility that Gilbert was the one who had been taken ill and in bringing him back Eric had been distracted and misjudged his height. But that seemed even less likely. Eric was a good and experienced pilot and during the war he had flown safely with far more than a sick passenger on his mind.

So the mystery remained and with it the sense of numbing shock. Eric and Gilbert had died in the wreckage of the Condor before their very eyes. Now as they gathered for the reading of Gilbert's will each of them in their own way showed the mark it had left on them.

Sarah had been the first to arrive, pale and composed, her eyes haunted behind her small black veil. Max, a tick moving ceaselessly in his eye, had joined her. He had not wanted to come, pleading that the reading of the will was no concern of his, but Percy Dunn, the Morse family lawyer, had insisted – it had been Gilbert's wish that he should be there. He took his place beside Sarah, his good hand plucking nervously at the shirt cuff which hung loosely over his withered one. After a few moments Alicia, James and Adam had entered the library, Alicia walking tall and proud, the whiteness of her face emphasised by the stark black mourning she wore, James following her, looking helpless and bewildered, Adam bringing up the rear. His face was set, his eyes sought Sarah's and when she looked quickly away the lines tightened still more, concealing whatever emotion he was feeling. Last of all came Blanche, leaning heavily on an ivory topped cane, and Leo. The strain of the last days had aged Blanche, yet there was still a proud imperiousness in her carriage as she made her entrance, a refusal to give way to the frailty which widowhood had thrust upon her. Leo guided her to her chair and sat down beside her. Glancing at him Sarah was surprised by the look of him. He was pale, yes, as they all were. But there was something about him which might almost have been suppressed excitement. His eyes darted about the room. When they met Sarah's he looked quickly away but not before she had seen and recognised what looked suspiciously like a gleam of triumph.

Did he know something about the will that they did not? she wondered. He was after all Gilbert's only surviving male relative, apart from James, and of course Adam. But James had not the slightest interest in the business and never had. He now buried himself in his painting and his poetry, whilst Adam was far more a man of action than a businessman. Gilbert had known that, known too how deep Leo's ambition ran. Was it possible that he had decided to put the perpetuation of the business before family ties and make Leo his heir? If he has we must accept it, Sarah thought, for her faith in Gilbert's good judgement was unshakeable. But all the same she could not help hoping that the enterprise she held so dear was not about to fall into Leo's hands.

When they were all seated Percy Dunn looked up from the papers he had been shuffling, eyeing each of them in turn. His expression was suitably grave, his double chin wobbled slightly above the stiff white collar, he licked his fleshy lips and adjusted his pince-nez on his small hooked nose. This was the sort of occasion he loved best. To him it was a little like a theatrical production with the stage set just so and himself the principal player.

He coughed, waiting until all eyes were on him.

'Now – are we all here?' It was a line he delivered regularly; familiarity gave his reedy voice the ring of authority. 'Yes? Good. In that case I will begin.'

The will, a thick wad of cream vellum, lay on top of the pile of papers. With another theatrical gesture he untied the pink document ribbon which secured it and began to read: 'This is the last will and testament of me, Gilbert William James Morse, being of sound mind . . .'

'Just a moment!' Blanche's voice, thin but imperious, interrupted him. He raised his eyes, pained but respectful. 'Do you have to tire us with all the legal jargon, Mr Dunn?' Blanche enquired.

Percy Dunn let the pince-nez fall on their chain. They bounced against his starched shirt front. 'It is usual, Mrs Morse. Out of respect for the deceased . . .'

'I really do not care what is or is not usual and I think on such a painful occasion consideration for the living might be allowed to take precedence over respect for the dead. Surely you can tell us in plain language the terms of my husband's will?'

Percy Dunn looked shocked but Blanche's gaze was piercing and the grip of her thin hand on the ivory top of her cane bore witness to her steely determination. She stared him out, unflinching, and at last he nodded.

'Very well. If that is what you want.'

503

'We do. At least I do and I am sure I speak for the rest of the family.'

'I agree,' Alicia said. 'I too would much prefer you to paraphrase, Mr Dunn.'

He inclined his head, deprived of the opportunity to recite in rolling tones the mysterious liturgy of age old phrases he loved so well.

'If you insist. The provisions as Mr Morse willed them are these.' He replaced the pince-nez, vellum crackled as he turned the pages. 'To deal first with the bequests. Each of the servants in the employ of the family at the time of Mr Morse's death are to receive the sum of one hundred pounds. Miss Hazel Rowe, his secretary, the sum of fifty pounds. To Maximillian Hurst, Mr Morse leaves the sum of one thousand pounds, the like amount to his son-in-law Mr Adam Bailey. To his son, James Morse, will go all Mr Morse's holdings in a number of varied companies in which he has shares, with the exception, of course of Morse Motors and Morse Bailey International. These, I may say, amount to a goodly sum. To his widow, Mrs Blanche Morse, will go the sum of ten thousand pounds. Mrs Morse will also become the owner of Chewton Leigh House.'

A small strangled sound escaped Alicia but she quickly turned it into a cough and Sarah felt a twinge of pity for her. Chewton Leigh House was Alicia's home – she would not care to remain there on the sufferance of the woman with whom she shared little love. But she was too proud to protest in public, however much she might rail in private.

'Now we come to the division of the estate and the shares in the company,' the lawyer continued. 'To take the estate first. When all the bequests and gifts have been subtracted Mr Morse's estate will be divided into three equal parts, that is to say, it will be shared equally between three people. Those three people are his son and daughter, Mr James Morse and Mrs Alicia Bailey and Mrs Sarah Gardiner.'

A ripple ran around the room and Sarah felt the colour rush into her cheeks. She had expected Gilbert would leave her something in his will – though she had wanted nothing. She would prefer to have him alive than to come into any

504

amount of riches. But a third share of his estate – equal with Alicia and James!

Blanche's voice rose above the clamour. 'Are you quite certain that you have that correct, Mr Dunn? We asked you to paraphrase but even so I find it difficult to believe . . .'

'Why?' James interposed. 'Sarah was raised with us. Why shouldn't Father leave her the same as us? After all, Lawrence and Hugh are gone . . .'

'It's all very well for you, James,' Alicia said acidly. 'You seem to have done very well already.'

'There is no mistake, I assure you,' Percy Dunn said reprovingly. 'As for the matter of Mr James being favoured I believe Mr Morse's reason for that will become clear if you will only allow me to continue?'

'Please do!' Blanche said but her tone was more imperious and regal than ever and Sarah's discomfort increased. They had always resented her – now it seemed they had cause.

'We come now to the division of the shares in the two companies, Morse Motors and Morse Bailey International,' Percy Dunn said when he was certain he had their attention once more. 'As you are all aware, Mr Morse held one hundred per cent of shares in each. He arrived at a division of those shares which he believed to be in the best interests of the companies. Before telling you the names of the beneficiaries I will point out that James is not one of them. That is why he was catered for by way of other provision. Mr Morse knew he had no interest in the companies and preferred to leave them in the care of those who have. However, your father wished me to make it clear to you, James, that it is in no way a reflection of his regard for you. Rather he had your best interests at heart as well of those of the companies.'

'Of course – and he has been more than generous,' James muttered. There had been a time when he had been quite certain that he would be cut out of his father's will, but Gilbert had provided for him amply and with some measure of understanding. The knowledge made him feel closer to his father than he had ever felt in life.

'So. The business holdings are to be divided as follows –
and the same division is applicable to both companies,' the
lawyer continued, regarding them over his pince-nez. 'Ten
per cent each go to Mr Adam Bailey and Mr Maximillian
Hurst. Twenty per cent to the widow, Mrs Blanche Morse.
And the remaining sixty per cent to be divided equally
between Mrs Alicia Bailey and Mrs Sarah Gardiner.'

For a moment no-one spoke. It was as if shock had
rendered them all speechless. Then Leo asked sharply:
'What about me?'

Percy Dunn fixed him with an apologetic gaze. 'I am
sorry, Mr de Vere, I am afraid you are not mentioned in the
will.'

'Not mentioned? After all I have done?'

'I am sorry.'

Leo leapt to his feet. His face was suffused with ugly
colour and a muscle worked beneath his eyelid. 'I don't
believe it! I am his stepson and I am not mentioned while
she . . .' he jabbed an accusing finger in Sarah's direction,
'*she* gets equal shares with Alicia! Good God, man, it's
preposterous!'

'Leo – sit down!' Blanche's eyes were gleaming
dangerously behind the hooded folds of paper-dry skin.
'Don't make a fool of yourself.'

'I don't need to do that, do I?' Leo ranted. 'He has done it
for me – him and that . . . harlot! How did you get around
him, Sarah? What went on between you, eh?'

'Hold your tongue, Leo!' Blanche ordered.

'I will not! It's disgraceful!' Words failed him and he
spluttered with impotent rage.

Adam rose purposefully. 'Either sit down and shut up,
Leo, or I will throw you out.'

'Who the devil are you to order me around, I'd like to
know?' Leo demanded. 'You are as bad as she is – worming
your way in with the old man. Bloody upstarts . . . !' He
rushed at Adam, fists flailing. Adam countered the blow
easily, grabbing Leo by the arm and pushing him bodily back
into his chair. For a moment he subsided, glowering, then his
fury got the better of him and he leapt to his feet again.

'Damn you! Damn the lot of you! Who the devil do you Morses think you are?'

'I warn you, Leo . . .' Adam's voice was low but terse.

'All right, you don't need to carry out your threat and throw me out. I am going. But you'll be sorry, all of you.' He blundered to the door, knocking over a chair as he went, then turned to look at them. His eyes were still wild with rage but when he spoke his voice was low and chilling. 'One of these days I'll have your bloody companies, lock, stock and barrel. And when I do don't expect any mercy from me. I'll treat you with the same contempt as you have treated me, I promise you!'

The door slammed after him and he was gone.

'Well!' Alicia said into the shocked silence. 'What a disgraceful performance! I think you might have taught him a little self-control, Blanche. How I pity poor little Emily!' Her face was pale but she was self-possessed as ever and Sarah could only guess at what emotions might be seething behind that ice cool exterior.

Blanche rose, leaning heavily on her ivory topped cane.

'I apologize, Mr Dunn, on behalf of my son. His behaviour was unpardonable. And now, if you will excuse me, I would like to go to my room.'

James leaped up to assist her but she brushed him aside. 'Thank you, James, but I am quite capable of managing by myself.'

Painfully erect, she struggled to the door. Watching her go Sarah felt grudging admiration. She did not like Blanche but without doubt she knew how to behave like a lady. What a pity her son was not more of a gentleman! Sarah was still shaking from his verbal onslaught, still stunned by the provisions of Gilbert's will. She had not fully taken them in yet. All she knew was that between them she and Alicia were now the major shareholders in both companies with all that that entailed. Unbelievable. Absolutely unbelievable. But why had he done it? Why?

Alicia rose and crossed to the lawyer.

'Would you care for some tea, Mr Dunn?'

Sarah almost laughed aloud. Tea! If he was as shaken

as she was a glass of whisky would be more appropriate!

'Sarah?' Alicia's voice was icy but polite.

'No, thank you.'

'You should – and something to eat as well. You are looking very peaky these days.' She paused. 'You know, something occurred to me just now. If you had not fainted that morning we would not be here now for the reading of Father's will. Because it would be you, not he, who died, wouldn't it?'

Again Sarah encountered the naked hatred in her eyes.

'Do you think, Alicia, that I haven't thought of that?' she asked passionately. 'Do you think I don't remember it every day of my life? And now if you will excuse me . . .' She rose and left the library, a small and lonely figure who carried herself tall and straight in spite of the extra weight which the afternoon had laid upon her shoulders.

'What does it mean, Adam? Why did he do it?'

Adam had driven her home. Now, in her little sitting-room she drifted between window and table, idly re-arranging the roses in the cut-glass bowls that she had picked this morning – a lifetime ago – in order to try and bring some colour into the house, for though the curtains were no longer drawn for mourning, darkening the rooms to an eerie twilight, the atmosphere of greyness remained.

'I am grateful to him, of course,' she went on reflectively. 'Eric left practically nothing and a legacy of some kind I would have understood. But to leave me a third share in his estate and so much control in the companies . . . that I don't understand.'

'I think Gilbert knew very well what he was doing,' Adam said. He looked slightly uncomfortable, too large a figure for the minute sitting-room. 'He knew you have the best interests of Morse Bailey at heart – and he had great faith in your judgement.'

'Perhaps – but to treat me equally with Alicia – his own daughter . . .'

'I think there is something you should know,' Adam said. His tone was serious and she stopped fidgeting and looked at him sharply. 'Gilbert had a very good reason for treating you equally with his family.'

'Because he brought me up, you mean?'

'More than that. Have you never wondered why Gilbert took you in, educated you and cared so much what happened to you?'

'Because I went to him for help and he felt sorry for me, I suppose.'

'Possibly. But that is only part of it.' He paused, looking at her directly. 'I thought you might have guessed the truth, Sarah, but I see that you have not. The reason is very simple. Gilbert was your father.'

The air in the room was heavy with the scent of roses. It hung, cloying, in her nostrils. She stood motionless for a moment, almost uncomprehending. Gilbert – her father? It couldn't be! And yet suddenly she knew that it was true. It was as if deep down she had always known yet rejected it as impossible. She had loved him and known he loved her, the bond between them had been so strong, so special that to deny it was madness. Now, everything fell into place and in the quiet room she seemed to hear her mother's voice, weak with sickness, mustering all her failing strength to enunciate the last words she would ever speak: 'Tell Mr Morse! Do you understand? Tell Mr Morse!'

That was it, of course, that was the reason. And she had never guessed it, not even when she had grown old enough to wonder who her father really was. For her mother had been just a lowly seamstress, if a very beautiful one, and Mr Morse was the lord of the manor.

'How do you know?' she asked.

'Gilbert told me. I think he wanted to share it with someone. He had toyed with the idea of telling you but he was unsure how you would take it.'

'Does anyone else know?'

'Not as far as I am aware though I sometimes wonder if Blanche guessed. Now you do know it is up to you whether you keep his secret. It is possible the family will make things difficult for you. If they do then at least you have the knowledge as a weapon.'

'Yes. Thank you.' But her voice was distant.

'It's not going to be easy,' he went on, 'and I don't just mean coping with your inheritance. I have a feeling the company is in financial difficulties. Not Morse Motors – that has a sound basis. But the aeroplane division is a different matter. Similar companies are going to the wall left, right and centre – Tom Sopwith, for all his success with war planes, to name but one. That is why the South African connection can be so important. Not to mention the airline we planned. Now, with Gilbert gone, it is going to be imperative we have a meeting very soon with our financial advisers and get things sorted out.'

She nodded. It was all too much. She felt swamped by it.

'Which brings me,' he said, 'to the next point. What are we going to do?'

A nerve jumped in her throat. 'You mean . . . ?'

'About us.' It was the first time he had mentioned it since the night of the accident. He had respected her wish to wait a little while out of respect for Eric. But it was not in Adam's nature to be patient. 'I don't think there is an easy option open to us any more. We have been left control of Morse Bailey. We cannot go skedaddling off to South Africa and leave the business to fend for itself. I think the Division should still open but with someone else, not me, and certainly not you, to run it. We have to stay here and fight to get Morse Bailey back on its feet. We owe Gilbert that much.'

She nodded. He was right, of course. Going to South Africa with Adam, as she had planned to do when a suitable time had elapsed, was no more than a lovely dream now. He was needed here – and so, she supposed, was she. She shivered slightly in spite of the warmth of the evening as she thought of the enormity of the task before them, all the more important in the light of Adam's revelations, and of the personal animosity they would encounter.

A knock at the door interrupted her reverie and she sighed with annoyance. What a time for a visitor! But she went to see who it was all the same.

'Mrs Gardiner, I'm sorry to trouble you but I wondered if

510

I might have a word?' It was Perry, the mechanic who had been dismissed after her training aeroplane had crashed. He stood on the doorstep, his wrinkled face anxious, twisting his cap between his hands.

'Yes, Perry, what is it?'

'Well, it's a bit awkward-like . . .' He glanced around as if afraid he might be overheard.

'Very well, Perry, you had better come in. Mr Adam is here, though.'

'Oh – is he?' The man hesitated, then appeared to make up his mind. 'Well, p'raps t'wouldn't hurt fer 'im to 'ear what I got to say. It do concern him too and Mr Adam has always been more than fair . . .'

She took him into the sitting-room. Adam, who had overheard the conversation, looked at him curiously. 'Afternoon, Perry. What is all this about then?'

'Well 'tis like this.' Perry shifted from foot to foot, looking ill at ease. 'You know that ther propeller wot come off when you two were up in the training plane? And 'ow we couldn't make out 'ow it come to be loose? Well, I reckon I can shed some light on the mystery.'

'Good. I'm glad you have decided to come clean about it,' Adam said shortly.

The older man bristled. 'It weren't nothin' to do with me. 'Tis my belief the nuts were loosened deliberate-like.'

'Come now! Who would do a thing like that?'

''Tis a bit awkward really. But you know this 'ere crash what's killed the boss and Mr Eric? Well, we was talking about it, me and some of the boys – I do meet 'em still for a pint in the evenings – and one of 'em happened to say he'd seen young Leo de Vere snooping about in the sheds the night afore it happened. Messing about in there all on his own, he were, and mighty awkward he acted when he knowed he'd been seen. Hurried out with just a quick goodnight, as red in the face as a turkey cock.'

'Surely you are not suggesting that *he* tampered with the Condor are you?' Adam demanded.

Perry's own face had turned a dull red. 'That's about the size of it. Now I know on its own it don't mean a lot and I

511

can't think for the life of me why he should do such a thing. But the funny thing is *I* caught him in the sheds the night before *your* accident. I didn't think anything of it at the time but when I come to put two and two together I thought "Hullo – there's some'ut funny going on here." So I thought I ought to let you know about it afore he goes and kills somebody else.'

'You realise this is a very serious accusation you are making, Perry?' Adam said.

'Oh ah, I do. And I couldn't swear to anything in a court o' law or anywhere else, but just the same . . .'

'Well thank you, Perry.' Adam's tone was non-committal. 'Good of you to let us know.'

'I'll show you out, Perry,' Sarah said.

When she returned to the sitting-room she found Adam pacing, deep in thought.

'What do you make of that then? And they say women are the gossips!' she remarked.

'You think it's gossip, do you?' he asked.

'What else? And perhaps a late attempt to get himself off the hook. I don't like Leo, you know that, but I don't think he would deliberately set out to kill anyone.'

'Not just anyone – you,' Adam said grimly and to her amazement she realised he was quite serious.

'Leo – trying to kill *me*? Oh Adam, don't be absurd!'

'Think about it, Sarah.' Adam took out a cigarette and lit it. 'He knew when you were using the training plane – and he knew that you should have been a passenger in the Condor. And as Perry rightly said, there was no reason for him to have been snooping about in the sheds on either occasion.'

'But even if you are right, why on earth should he want to kill me?'

'You were a threat to him and he knew it. You weren't at the board meeting, Sarah, when the idea of the airline was mooted. Leo was furious – particularly at the suggestion that you should run it. I think he realised you were very much Gilbert's protégée – and he was jealous.'

'But surely he would know that such a thing could mean

512

the end of the company? He'd realise that with business already difficult something like that could undermine confidence and sink the boat?'

'I don't think he realised quite how bad things are. Gilbert kept that to himself. It has only come out since his death. Hatred can be a very powerful motive, and I have always thought Leo has a ruthless streak.'

Sarah was silent remembering that long ago day when he had bolted the horses out of pure vindictiveness. Yes, Leo was ruthless. But would he stoop to something so perfectly dreadful?

'I must get back and talk to Max,' Adam said. 'I doubt whether anything can ever be proved, but all the same . . . Will you be all right?'

She nodded.

'Lock the door tonight,' he warned her. 'He'll hate you more than ever now.'

'Adam . . .'

'Now I have to go.' As always he was able to switch from the personal to the impersonal without so much as a flicker. 'I'll see you tomorrow.'

He kissed her briefly and was gone.

Sarah stood for a moment at her window looking out at the fading dusk. She felt calmer now after the shocks the day had dealt her for she had made up her mind on two very important scores.

Firstly she had decided she could not keep the shares Gilbert had left her in the companies. She had done nothing to earn them and the accident of parentage did not give her the right to equal shares with Alicia. All very well to say Gilbert had willed it – he had never acknowledged how deep the ill feeling ran between her and Alicia and he could not have envisaged the trouble such an arrangement could cause. The company needed to be strong now if it were to survive, not torn apart from within. No, much the best thing would be to turn the shares over to Adam. He would know how best to handle them. She would see a solicitor first thing in the morning and have them transferred to his name.

That would satisfactorily defuse one area of dissent, but another still remained – her relationship with Adam himself. Sarah had found herself remembering every word of the conversation they had had and worrying about it. Perhaps if they could have escaped to South Africa it could have worked. But that was now out of the question. They had to be on hand here – or at least, Adam did. And if he divorced Alicia how could he continue to work alongside her? The ill feeling would make it impossible for them to reach the necessary agreements. Worse, the scandal that would surround divorce might harm the company even more.

At last Sarah had come to a conclusion. She needed a breathing space – time to think and assimilate all the new facets of the situation – and Adam needed the same. She would go away for a little while at least. Maybe – just maybe – she would decide never to come back.

And so she had penned a letter to Adam explaining what she was doing though making no mention of where she planned to go – she was not entirely certain of that yet herself. She posted it in the letter box set in the wall opposite her cottage and after she had packed a suitcase she paused for a moment to look out of her window at the familiar rural scene. Would she ever stand here again? she wondered. Refusing to allow herself to brood, she went back downstairs, put fresh water into the bowls of roses and arranged one close to the framed photograph of Eric. Then she took her suitcase and her coat, went out and locked the door behind her.

Her motor car was full of petrol. She tossed the suitcase into the back, cranked the engine and climbed in.

As she drove out of Chewton Leigh darkness was falling.

Chapter Forty-Two

When he left Sarah, Adam did not go straight home to Chewton Leigh House. Instead he drove around for a while for he needed time to think.

Unlikely though it seemed on the face of it yet he had a gut feeling that Perry had not been far out when he had accused Leo of tampering with the aeroplanes. The two incidents were too convenient to be mere coincidence and from what he knew of Leo he believed the man was quite capable of sabotage. He was ruthless, he was ambitious and Adam had no doubt that he would stop at nothing to attain the position he believed was rightfully his. Besides this, he had clearly had the opportunity. But did he have the know how? No reason why not. He was not an engineer but he had been around aeroplanes for long enough to be familiar with them and he had access to the drawings that explained their component parts. He was no fool – quite the opposite. If he set his mind to it sabotage would not be outside the bounds of his ability, particularly sabotage as simple as loosening the fitting of a propeller. What he had done to the Condor no-one would ever know for certain, of course. The evidence had been destroyed and the mechanics, hampered by the presence of the press on that fatal morning, had relied upon the checks they had carried out the previous day – something which Leo had perhaps anticipated and relied upon.

There remained the objection Sarah had raised – the damage that such a highly publicised disaster could do to the company. But as he had pointed out Leo had not known how close to the brink things really were and it could be that he had taken a calculated risk, gambling everything on an all-or-nothing throw. He had known Adam had asked to take over the South African division; with Sarah out of the way Gilbert would have been forced to rely on him as his right-hand man and eventually he could reasonably expect that control would fall into his hands.

It was a wild scheme – insane, almost – but then Adam had thought for some while that where power and position in the company were concerned Leo *was* a little mad.

Not for one moment did he doubt Perry's words. The man was a solid sort, without the imagination to dream up such a story even if he had thought it might help his case, and he had made no request to be reinstated on the strength of his information. What was more Adam happened to know that Perry had found other employment, servicing the engines for a transport concern in Bristol, so he would have been unlikely to go to such lengths even if such a thing had occurred to him. No, on balance Adam believed he had hit on the truth. But proving it would be another matter. Even with witnesses to say they had seen Leo in the sheds at the relevant time it was not evidence enough to take legal action. This was something which would have to be worked out between themselves.

His mind made up Adam turned the motor in the direction of home. With something like this hanging over him all his instincts called for immediate action. At first he had been shocked, now he was angry. He would have the matter out with Leo and do so now. There was no time like the present.

The trees outside Chewton Leigh House were casting long shadows as he turned into the drive. He parked the car in the yard at the rear and went into the house.

The library and drawing-room were empty. The family were all in their rooms dressing for dinner, he guessed. He was about to go upstairs in search of Leo but as he passed Gilbert's study he heard what sounded like a drawer being slammed shut. He turned on his heel and opened the door.

Leo was there, poring over two or three files which lay open on the big leather-topped desk. He looked up, startled, an expression of guilt surprised creeping over his thin features.

'Adam! I was just . . .'

'I can see what you are doing, Leo,' Adam said shortly. 'Snooping.'

516

He went into the study, closing the door behind him.

'Things have to be sorted out – and quickly,' Leo blustered. 'I thought if I were to make a start . . .'

'It is no concern of yours,' Adam said coldly. 'You are not an executor of the will, neither were you named in it.'

Leo's cheeks burned dull red.

'No, but I still hold a position of responsibility.'

'Not for much longer, my friend.'

Leo's eyes narrowed. 'Oh no, Adam, it won't be that easy to get rid of me.'

'No? I wouldn't be too sure of that. I have a few things to say to you and when I have finished I expect you to pack your bags and leave.'

Leo laughed shortly, some of his confidence returning. 'I don't think you are in a position to order me out, Adam. This house belongs to my mother now.'

'I don't care who it belongs to!' Adam brought his fist down hard on the desk so that the ink pot and pens jumped. 'If you don't do as I say, by God, I'll see you charged with murder!'

If he had had any doubts before as to the justice of Perry's accusation they were dispelled now. In that first shocked moment the guilt was all there, clearly written in Leo's face. The dark red flush had drained away leaving his face paper white and the momentary fear in his eyes was unmistakeable.

'You swine!' Adam said. His voice was low and vibrant with anger. 'I ought to beat the hell out of you for what you did. You are responsible for the deaths of two men and you could very well have killed Sarah and me into the bargain.' Leo said nothing. He was too shocked at having been detected to protest his innocence and Adam went on: 'How could you do it, Leo? God, if I had my way I'd like to force *you* up into the skies in a machine that you and I both know is not airworthy. But Morse Bailey couldn't stand another dose of bad publicity just now. And besides, dying is too easy for you.'

'What do you propose then?' Leo sneered with a dash of defiance.

517

'That you do as I say, clear out here and now, or I'll carry out my threat and see you charged with murder – and a host of other things besides. That wouldn't be good for the company either and it is not a prospect I relish – showing up my wife's stepbrother for a common criminal. But I warn you if it comes to the pinch I shall not hesitate.'

As he said it, angry as he was, he wondered if Leo would realise he was bluffing. He was not in possession of the evidence to have Leo charged with anything. But Leo, trapped by his own guilt, did not think to ask Adam just how he would go about carrying out his threat.

'You'll be sorry for this!' he blustered.

'I doubt it. There is going to be a clean sweep at Morse Bailey. I want you out, Leo, as soon as you can pack your things together. I don't know how you will explain to your mother and neither do I care. You can tell her what you please – though I doubt it will be the truth, that you were responsible for the death of her husband.'

'Aren't *you* going to tell her?' Leo asked unpleasantly. 'I should have thought you would enjoy doing that.'

'Unlike you, Leo, I do not gain pleasure from causing pain to others. In fact I feel sorry for your mother. She has done some despicable things in her time and I don't believe she brought much happiness to Gilbert. But I dare say most of what she did was with your good in mind. She is an old woman now. She won't be happy about you going. But it will hurt her less than the knowledge that her son is a murderer.'

'Damn you, Adam!' Leo said softly. 'Damn you all! I hope you rot in hell!'

'Possibly. One thing is very sure, Leo – if we do we shall be certain of meeting you there. Now get out of here before I do what I am itching to and smash that ugly face of yours to a pulp.'

A look of sheer hatred disfigured Leo's features. The evil of him had never been more transparent than it was now. But he was beaten – for the moment – and he knew it.

'Don't think you will get away with this, Adam,' he spat from the doorway. 'I'll have my revenge if it takes me a lifetime. And don't you forget it!'

518

Then he was gone. Adam brought his hand crashing down on the desk again, delivering the blow he had longed to land square on the face of the man who had been responsible for two deaths. Nothing would have given him more pleasure than to see Leo spreadeagled on the floor choking on his own blood. But it would have done no good. This way at least they were rid of him. They could begin to pick up the pieces of the company which meant so much to all of them – and rebuild their shattered lives. His anger spent, he began to put away the files into which Leo had been prying. Tomorrow they would have to be taken out again. Perhaps Sarah could help him sort out the intricacies they contained, for Adam was not a desk-man. But if necessary he would become one. That much he owed to Gilbert's memory.

The lengthening shadows cast a gloom over the study as Adam stood there alone contemplating what was over and done with and what was yet to be.

Sarah's letter arrived with the morning mail. Adam found it in the pile beside his breakfast plate. He recognised her writing and his eyes narrowed. Then as he tore it open and read the contents he swore.

Hellfire and damnation, why had he left her alone last night? He had known she was upset by the traumas the day had brought. But it had never occurred to him she would do something like this . . . Of course it would never have happened if we had had our plans cut and dried, Adam thought. He had let things drag on for one reason and another and it had only made matters worse. Now he knew the time had come to delay no longer. He had to be free so that he and Sarah could make a life together. Better to make the cut cleanly than to bleed slowly to death.

He pushed back his chair and stood up leaving his breakfast untouched, strode into the hall and took the stairs two at a time. The door to Alicia's room was open, he knocked cursorily and went in.

Alicia was sitting at her dressing table mirror putting up her hair and talking to Guy's nanny as she did so. Guy was

519

there too, fiddling with a pile of her hairpins. As he entered the room she looked up in surprise.

'Adam! What brings you here?'

He ignored the question.

'Nanny, would you kindly take Master Guy downstairs? I want to talk to my wife.'

Nanny glanced at Alicia; she was not in the habit of taking orders from Adam.

Alicia nodded briefly. 'It's all right, Nanny. You may do as Mr Bailey says.'

'But Mama, I don't want to go!' Guy had a slightly whiney voice which irritated Adam.

'You, young man, will do as you are told!'

'Go along, Guy. You may come back later,' Alicia said. When Nanny had ushered him out she addressed her husband. 'To what do I owe this visit, Adam? You come to my room seldom enough, and never in the morning.'

He ignored the implication. 'There is something I have to say to you, Alicia, and I will not insult you by beating about the bush. You must know that our marriage has been over for some time now and I think it is high time the situation was regularized. I want a divorce and I want it as soon as possible. The time has come to put an end to the charade.'

She froze, her hands still holding her hair in place. He could see her face reflected in the mirror – it was expressionless but for the widening of her eyes.

'Really? And what has brought it to a head just now?' she asked after a moment and he found himself unwillingly admiring her containment.

'I want to marry Sarah.'

'Oh, I see.' She slipped a pin into her chignon with calm deliberation. 'You want to marry Sarah. Well there is nothing new in that is there? I suppose the only thing that has changed is that now she is as good an investment as me. The same third share in the estate, the same control in the companies. Well, I admire your astuteness, Adam.'

Sarah's letter seemed to burn a hole in his pocket. He was on the point of telling her that if he had wished he could have both – Sarah intended to make all her shares over to him. But he did not. He had no intention of being sidetracked now.

'I will provide you with the grounds for divorce, Alicia,' he said. 'You need have no fear that I will drag your name through the mire.'

'Very commendable,' she said drily. 'But has it not occurred to you that I might refuse?'

'It has, yes. And in that case of course my offer to behave honourably will no longer apply. If you force me to it, Alicia, then I will divorce you. Make no mistake of that.'

She twisted the last strand of hair into place and turned to face him.

'I see. You are determined, aren't you? Is there nothing I can say to make you change your mind?'

'Do you really want me to, Alicia? Surely you know as well as I do that our marriage is a mockery. It is no happier a situation for you than it is for me. You would be far better off free to meet and marry someone who would appreciate you.'

She smiled but it was a hard smile. Was there no softness in Alicia? he wondered.

'Your concern for me is touching,' she said. 'There is, however, someone else involved in this. Your son. What you feel for me is irrelevant to what really matters. If you don't care about disgracing me surely you will continue to keep up the pretence of our marriage for his sake. Think of Guy, Adam. Think of your son.'

Adam's eyes hardened. His mouth was a bitter line.

'Oh Alicia, I did hope you would not try to use Guy to hang onto me. To bring him into it will only make things worse.'

'What do you mean?' she challenged him.

He glanced towards the door, it was firmly shut, no sound of a childish voice coming from the other side.

'Because, my dear, you and I both know that Guy is not my son.'

He saw her eyes narrow; a muscle tightened in her cheek. But she replied with admirable coolness.

'Oh? And whose son is he then?'

521

'His father was one of your recuperating officers, I dare say – probably the one I caught you with. I'm really not very interested. All that matters to me is that I know very well he is not mine.'

'I see,' she said stiffly. 'So now you intend to disown him.'

'No.' He crossed to the window and stood with his back to it. 'I won't disown Guy. If I had intended to do that I would have done it a long time ago, when I came back from my prisoner-of-war camp to find I had miraculously become a father. I decided then that for the boy's sake I would allow everyone to think that what you had led them to believe was true, and I see no reason for changing that now. Guy has handicaps enough without being labelled a bastard as well.'

'You would prefer people to think that you abandoned your own son?'

He shrugged. 'I shall make proper provision for him, now and in the future. And my shoulders are broad. As far as I am concerned the world can continue to believe I am his father just as long as you release me from this charade of a marriage.'

'Oh Adam!' She threw back her head suddenly and laughed.

'What do you find so funny?' he enquired.

She shook her head. 'The irony of it! Our marriage began with blackmail; now it looks as though it will end in the same way.'

'I would prefer to call it an ultimatum, Alicia, but I dare say it amounts to the same. Give me my freedom and I will continue to own Guy as my son. Even he need know no different, though I don't suppose he will thank me for it.'

'And Sarah?' He saw the flash in her eyes, recognised the rivalry that still existed between the two women.

'What passes between me and Sarah is our business,' he said quietly.

Her mouth twisted upwards slightly and for a moment she looked almost wistful.

'You really do love her, don't you?'

'More than anything in the world.'

'Well.' She turned away with a lift of one eyebrow. 'In that case, Adam, I suppose I should no longer stand in your way. I have had my chance – and much happiness has it brought me. Perhaps it is time for Sarah to have hers. Very well, Adam, you shall have your divorce. We will leave it to our lawyers to work out the best way to go about it so that there is as little unpleasantness as possible. And now I suggest you go to her. To be honest, I beg you to go to her. At this moment I really don't care to have you in my room a moment longer!'

'Thank you, Alicia.' He crossed to the door, her back presented to him was very straight, very erect. Even at this moment Alicia was totally the mistress of self-control. 'Thank you,' he said again. 'I am only sorry it has to end this way.'

He went out closing the door after him and only then did Alicia's iron control crack. She snatched up her hair brush from the dressing table and hurled it with all her might at the bed. It bounced off the pillow and lay in the centre of the floor.

'Damn!' Alicia cried. 'Damn! Damn! Damn!'

But there was no-one to hear her.

Chapter Forty-Three

The room at the inn was exactly as she remembered it. Just being there, where she and Adam had made love on that first wonderfu night brought back memories so poignant that she wanted to weep, so vivid that she ached for him with every fibre of her being. She should not have come here, of course. It was stupidly self-indulgent, and yet . . .

Sarah sat on the edge of the bed where they had lain together, recalling every deta'. One night, one glorious stolen night. Perhaps it was all they would ever have. For the good of the company she felt it must be. But nothing could take away from her the happiness they had known.

When she had arrived very late the previous evening the landlord had greeted her with barely veiled surprise – he remembered the lady aviator whose crash landing had caused such a stir in their sleepy village. But Sarah had brooked no questions and today she had spent walking and thinking, and the moment her meals were abandoned, half-eaten, she had left the dining room.

Now it was late afternoon and she was facing the prospect of another night alone. She could not stay here much longer, of course. But at least it had afforded her a breathing space – time to reflect – and so far nothing had changed her view that the only course of action open to her was to leave Chewton Leigh for good.

It would be painful, she knew. She would have to build a new life for herself somewhere. The thought of it was daunting. But left alone Adam would no doubt mend his bridges with Alicia and the two of them would be able to resurrect Morse Bailey from the ashes.

Footsteps on the stairs. Sarah took little notice. Then the door swung open, making her jump and as she spun round breath caught in her throat.

'Adam!'

For a moment she thought she must have fallen asleep and be dreaming. He came into the room, kicking the door shut behind him, and she knew she was not.

'I thought I'd find you here, Sarah. At least – I hoped I would. I couldn't think of another single place where you might go.'

She was trembling with the longing to throw herself into his arms but she remained standing stiffly by the bed.

'Why are you here?'

'Why do you think? To bring you home.'

'But Adam . . . I explained in my letter. It's best if I give you my shares and just disappear off the scene.'

'You little idiot!' he said. 'Did you really think I'd let you go so easily? As for your shares – Gilbert gave them to you because he wanted you to have them. You can't throw them back in his face.'

'Oh – I don't know . . .'

'If I don't mean anything to you at least think about your airline,' he said roughly. 'How is that going to get off the ground if you aren't there to organize it?'

'Someone else can . . .'

'Who?'

'Oh, I don't know . . . Alicia, maybe.'

'Alicia is not interested in the business. It was Gilbert's blind spot to think she might be. And before you say another word I think I should tell you that Alicia has agreed to divorce me.'

'You *told* her?'

'I did. So there is no longer any problem, Sarah, and I am not prepared to listen to your excuses any longer. If I had a fragile ego I would think you dreamed them up especially to avoid me. But I haven't a fragile ego. Now, are you coming with me willingly – or do I have to remove you by force?'

'Oh Adam . . .' Her knees felt weak. Was there another man alive who could make her feel this way?

'Perhaps a little force wouldn't be such a bad thing in any case,' he said harshly. And then she was in his arms and it was a long time before either of them said anything more.

*

525

Darkness had fallen by the time they were back in Somerset, a star-spangled blackness that seemed to draw the last sweet perfume from the hedgerows and lay soft on their faces, and Sarah felt that in some way it was recharging her for all the difficulties of the days ahead, flowing into her, making her strong. It was not going to be an easy road. But that would not deter her now.

Through the lanes, curving and dipping, every one of them with its own special place in her memory. And he had a port of call to make before he took her home.

The works made an unsightly blot against the skyline. The windows were darkened now, like blinded eyes, but as he stopped the car on the drive the lights caught some of the panes of glass, bringing them to sudden sparkling light and in the rattle of the idling motor she seemed to hear the hum of an aero engine.

How I love this place! she thought. It must not fail – I will not let it! Especially since Gilbert had put his trust in her – whatever the cost, she would fight on as long as there was breath in her body. Much as she loved Adam the company was bigger and more important than any of them. And yet in some strange way they were inextricably bound – now that Gilbert was gone Adam *was* Morse Bailey. In fighting for one she would be fighting for them both.

There in the darkness Sarah took on the mantle of responsibility – and took it gladly. This was where she belonged, here where the smells of engine oil mingled with the fresh scents of the countryside. Here her past, her present and her future were bound up together in the heritage of Morse Enterprises. And she knew she would never willingly leave them again.

BOOK SIX – THE PRESENT – 1965

Take kindly the counsel of the years, gracefully surrendering the things of youth.
. . . in the noisy confusion of life keep peace with your soul. With all its sham and drudgery and broken dreams it is still a beautiful world.

Desiderata

Chapter Forty-Four

Alicia, Countess von Brecht, had slept late.

Every morning for the past ten years Irene, her maid, had awakened her at seven with a pot of Earl Grey tea and whilst she was drinking it Alicia planned her day, beginning with the decision whether or not to take breakfast in bed, which clothes she should ask Irene to lay out for her and where and with whom she would lunch. Then she would open her mail, scan the headlines of the *Telegraph*, and take a leisurely bath.

When Irene tapped on the bedroom door on the morning after the catastrophic meeting at Rules, however, there was no immediate reply and when she opened the door, balancing the tray expertly on the flat of her hand as she did so, Alicia, who was still wearing her midnight blue satin sleep mask, gave no sign of having heard her.

Irene's heart almost stopped beating and with a great leap of panic she wondered if Alicia had died in her sleep. She had not been herself yesterday and at her age one never knew . . . As she hovered anxiously in the doorway she saw Alicia's hand move in a gesture of dismissal before it dropped back once more onto the soft fawn fur of Ming, curled up on the bed beside her, and Alicia murmured:

'Leave me a little longer, Irene. I haven't slept well.'

527

Relieved but puzzled Irene withdrew. She was exceedingly curious as to what had happened yesterday to upset the Countess so. There had been no mistaking her distress when she had returned, much earlier than expected, from her luncheon appointment and she had spent the rest of the day pacing her small sitting-room, smoking so many Black Russians that Irene had had to open all the windows to clear the fug out of the air after she had gone to bed, and merely picking at the dainty supper Irene had prepared for her. It was all very unlike the Countess and Irene would have given a good deal to know what was wrong. But she was not paid to ask questions. In all the years she had been with her the Countess had never encouraged the slightest familiarity and Irene knew she would not do so now.

An hour later she made a fresh pot of tea and tried again, this time with more success. As she set the tray down on the bedside table Alicia stirred, removing the sleep mask and blinking as the cold light of the March morning struck her eyes.

'Thank you, Irene. Leave it there would you?' She raised herself on the ivory silk pillows, massaging her face awake with scarlet-tipped fingers.

'Yes, Madam.'

'And then you can run my bath. God, how I hate sleeping late! It makes one so wooden!'

Irene thought that few women of seventy-five would have considered sleeping until eight to be an extraordinary thing to do but of course she did not say so. Her friends thought it odd that after all these years in her service Irene had not struck up something of a relationship with her employer but Irene was a solitary soul herself and the situation suited her. The Countess did look very pale and strained though . . . Irene experienced another stab of anxiety. Quite apart from a genuine respect she had developed for Alicia over the years – one did not use the term 'fondness' in connection with the Countess – Irene knew she would be out of a job if anything happened to her employer and positions as ladies' maids were few and far between nowadays. Irene sighed inwardly. Just a few more years and then she would be able to retire herself . . .

'Is there any mail for me today, Irene?' Alicia asked, sipping the aromatic tea.

'Yes, Madam, on the tray . . .' Irene caught at herself, frowning slightly. 'I am sorry, Madam, I must have left them in the kitchen . . .' She hurried out. The letters had certainly been on the first tray as they always were, she must have forgotten to replace them when she made the fresh tea. How unlike her – especially since she knew only too well the Countess's habit of opening her mail as early as possible in the day. At one time the postman had changed his round so that the first post was several hours later in arriving – but a telephone call from Alicia to the Post Office had soon set that to rights! Clearly her anxiety about the Countess's health was affecting her more than she had realised.

She fetched the pile of envelopes and took them back to Alicia who leafed through them immediately. Most of them, Irene suspected, were in connection with the various charities Alicia chaired, and several, well-disguised though they were, suggested accounts. But when sorting them Irene had noticed that one was handwritten and bore an Australian stamp, and now Alicia homed in on this envelope, putting the others down on the counterpane beside Ming's enquiring nose and ripping it open with the narrow bladed paper knife which lay on her bedside table.

Irene smiled to herself as she went into the bathroom and emptied a sachet of salts into the stream of scalding water. She had recognised the writing at once. It belonged to the Countess's grandson, David Bailey. After a short spell as a total drop-out – a 'hippy' Irene believed she had heard the type referred to – he had joined the Countess's family firm of aeroplane manufacturers and had spent the last year in Australia, home of one of the overseas divisions. Whilst he had been there he had written periodically to his grandmother and the letters never failed to put her in a good humour. Perhaps this one would make her snap out of whatever was troubling her, Irene thought hopefully.

Above the rushing of the water she thought she heard a cry. Alarmed she hurried back into the bedroom in time to see Alicia turning back the covers and getting out of bed whilst a disgruntled Ming, resentful at being disturbed so suddenly, yapped furiously from the centre of the Chinese rug.

'Madam! What is it? Not bad news, I hope?' In her agitation Irene almost forgot the unwritten rule of impersonality.

One glance at Alicia's face told her she need not worry. The Countess no longer looked tired and strained. There was a sparkle in her violet eyes and her lips, still stained from the scarlet lipstick she always wore, curved up into a wide smile.

'Bad news? Certainly not! The only bad news is that I have overslept. Is my bath ready, Irene? Good! I haven't a moment to waste. My grandson is coming to visit me – this morning, probably. And I would hate him to find me looking like a tired old woman!'

Irene smiled, turning off the taps and testing the foamy water.

'But I thought your grandson was in Australia, Madam.'

'He was, Irene, he was. But not any more. He flew back to England yesterday. Today he is going down to Bristol to our main works. And before he goes he is stopping off to pay me a visit. The water is not too hot, is it? You know if I have it too hot it will make me feel faint. Good. Now you may get my breakfast ready downstairs – a grapefruit and some dry toast, I think. I will be down in approximately half an hour. Well, what are you waiting for? Didn't you hear me say there is no time to waste?'

'Yes, Madam,' Irene said, unable to suppress a smile of relief.

That was much more like the Countess! Perhaps whatever it was that was worrying her was not so serious after all – or at least not serious enough to spoil her pleasure at the prospect of seeing her grandson again. Crusty she might be, difficult and autocratic she certainly was, but Irene was only too pleased to have the old Alicia back!

The ornate anniversary clock, one of the few pieces of

Klaus's collection which Alicia had kept, began to chime and Alicia, seated in the wing chair with Ming curled up on her knee, glanced at it. Eleven o'clock. Surely David would be here soon? Of course it was possible that like her he had overslept – and with more reason for he was probably jetlagged after the long flight from Melbourne. But she could not imagine that jetlag would bother a young man of his age unduly, and if he was expected in Bristol today then he should be leaving London fairly soon. He would be flying down in his own light aircraft but even so . . . Alicia cast her mind back again to his letter, remembering it word for word, for in spite of her age her memory was as good as ever.

'I tried to telephone you, Grandmother, but you were out – at one of your charity functions, I expect,' David had written. 'Anyway, I arrive at Heathrow at 10.30 pm provided the flight is not delayed and I shall stay overnight at the Post House. The following day I am expected in Bristol but I shall have a few hours to spare and should like to call on you if it is convenient.'

Alicia's lips curved a little at this. Convenient! Just as if it wouldn't be! She was always ready to see David – he was one of the few people with whom she never felt impatient or irritable – and really his visit today could not have been better timed. David was the one person who might have some idea what his father was up to and whether there was any truth in what Sarah had said. In fact, now that she came to think of it, the very fact that David had been recalled seemed pertinent. Perhaps there *was* something afoot – and Guy wanted David here when things developed.

Alicia's eyes narrowed, the anxiety that had kept her awake half the night closing in again. All very well for her to have taken umbrage and walked out on Sarah – with all the years of hatred to goad her that part had been easy. What was not so easy was to dismiss her allegations. A determined, dangerous woman Sarah might be, Alicia had never known her to make trouble for trouble's sake. In all these years whilst she and Guy had worked side by side on the board Alicia had never so much as set eyes on her. There had been differences before – she had sometimes heard of them second hand – but never had Sarah approached her in this way and although Alicia had tried to tell herself that Sarah had called the meeting for some ulterior motive of her own yet she knew in her heart that this was not the case. Sarah had had a good reason for appealing to her, deep down Alicia knew it, and it was this certainty that had kept her awake through the long hours of the night.

Unthinkable that Guy, her own son, should betray her by selling out to her old enemy Leo de Vere! Unthinkable! Yet why should Sarah invent such a story if there were no truth in it?

Alicia's brows drew together in a fine straight line and a tiny frown puckered her smooth forehead. Why was it that every encounter she had ever had with Sarah had proved to be so upsetting? Whenever she put in an appearance trauma followed – it had always been so and it seemed it always would. But this latest was more than mere emotional stress. It rattled not only at the foundations of her own personal world but at those of the company. And the company, like the great living beast it was, must be protected.

The doorbell jangled, the sound carrying clearly up the stairs to the sitting-room, and Alicia brightened, listening eagerly for the sound of her grandson's voice. At her wrists and temples her pulses had begun to race and she realised how afraid she had been that something might have occurred to prevent him coming. Ridiculous! she thought with that hint of self-deprecation that had always leavened her character. Ridiculous to set so much store by one little visit. But then at her age the pleasures left to her were fewer than they had once been and most of the visitors who came to her sitting-room now were elderly ladies like herself but without any of her wealth of experiences to make them interesting. Alicia had joined their ranks gracefully but her outward appearance of gentlewomanly respectability hid a spirit as free as it had ever been and a yearning for just a little excitement in what was now an uneventful life. David was young and vigorous – the prospect of an hour of his company cheered her as it offered a vicarious window on his world.

When she heard the footsteps on the stairs she put Ming down so as to go and greet him but in telling Irene he would see himself up then taking the stairs two at a time he was too quick for her. As she rose from her chair he appeared in the doorway and the fast beating pulse arrested for a moment.

'David!' she said warmly and thought: my God, how like Father he is! for indeed it might almost have been a young Gilbert standing there in the doorway.

The resemblance had always been there, of course, undeniable even when he was a child, but it had been masked somewhat during what Alicia referred to as his 'hippy phase'. Now however with the return to conventionality the likeness was almost uncanny in spite of the casual sweater and denims, and the once flowing locks, trimmed to a neat and almost Edwardian style, actually heightened the illusion.

'Grandmother!' He came towards her, almost sweeping her off her feet with a great hug and the happiness welled in her once again. Nobody but David had hugged her for years. Certainly not Guy, his father, who kissed her politely and dutifully but with a slight impatience that told her he had many other things on his mind, all ranking far higher than her in importance.

When he released her she took his hands, holding him there for a moment.

'David, it is so good to see you! And just look at you! You seem to have grown even taller – or perhaps it is me shrinking. That happens to old people, you know.'

'Old? You?' He laughed.

'I am over seventy,' she reminded him.

'But certainly not *old*. And not shrunken, either.'

'If you say so,' she conceded, pleased. 'Now, Irene will be bringing us coffee at any moment so let's sit down, shall we? I want to know all about Australia. What did you think of it?'

'It's a wonderful country.' He waited until she sat down then settled his long frame into the matching wing chair opposite. 'The works is in Victoria, of course, but I managed to fit in a spot of travelling whilst I was there. I had

533

a couple of weeks up in Queensland, enjoying the surf beaches and exploring the Great Barrier Reef and I got over to Sydney for a couple of trips. Oh – and the Red Centre, of course. I couldn't spend a year in Oz and not go to the Red Centre.'

'The Red Centre?' Alicia raised one eyebrow questioningly.

'The outback, Grandmother. Real desert outback where it never rains. Midway between Darwin and Melbourne and several days' drive from either. I never did get time to do everything I wanted to, of course. I'd have loved to spend a couple of weeks in a camper van exploring the Territory and I never managed to get out west, to Perth, and it's reputed to be beautiful over there. But primarily I was working so I was lucky to get about as much as I did, I guess.'

'And how is Morse Bailey Australian Division?' Alicia asked.

'Alive and well. It certainly managed to keep me busy. And I learned quite a lot.'

'Such as?'

'Such as you have to let your blokes go in time for them to grab a few beers in the pub before they go home.'

'David!'

'True. Closing time is six o'clock so if they didn't make a dash for it they'd be too late. The six o'clock swill, they call it.'

'Disgusting – and I hardly think relevant to the running of an international company.'

'Wrong, Grandmother. It's very important indeed. You have to keep the workforce happy or you'd never get anything done.' He grinned, a young and mischievous version of Gilbert's smile. Alicia's heart turned over. 'Here's the coffee,' he said.

'Oh yes. Thank you, Irene. Put it down there.' Alicia indicated the low table that stood between them.

'Shall I pour, Madam?'

'No, thank you. We'll do it ourselves.' Alicia felt jealous of every second with her grandson. As Irene withdrew she leaned forward to set out the cups, smiling at him.

534

'And now you have come back to put all you have learned into practice in Bristol,' she said.

'Yes. Dad thinks it's time I did a stint here. And sorry though I am to leave Australia I suppose he is right. After all I am his son and heir.' He said it unself-consciously, without the slightest suggestion of swagger or even pride. To David it was just a simple fact with which he had lived all his life, much as an heir apparent to the throne does. There were his uncles, of course, Roderick and Miles, but Guy had always treated them as an irrelevance and naturally his assessment had passed without question to his son. He liked Roderick and Miles, but Roderick he saw as a pale inferior to his own father and Miles was, by his own admission, happiest in the testing sheds. Without a doubt it was David who was being groomed for great things, David who would one day head the empire. Unless, of course . . .

Unless it falls into Leo de Vere's hands, Alicia thought, and was again struck by a feeling close to disbelief. Surely Guy would not deliver the company into the hands of their oldest enemy? Quite simply it was incredible. And yet . . .

Perhaps Roderick and Miles are getting too big for their boots and threatening David's eventual succession, Alicia thought. Roderick, after all, now had twin sons of his own, even if they were as yet little more than babies, and Miles had recently married a very pretty but very ambitious young actress – a social climber, in Alicia's opinion, and just the sort to cause trouble. Perhaps Leo de Vere had promised what the Morse Bailey board no longer could – or would – eventual autonomy for David. If that was the case then she could scarcely blame Guy.

'Do you have any idea at all why he chose this moment to bring you back to England, David?' she asked. Her voice was deliberately casual but she was watching his reaction closely and was disappointed by his shrug.

'Because he thinks a year in Oz is enough, I suppose.'

'Yes.' She poured the coffee, passed him a cup and tried a different approach. 'Has your father talked to you about developments in the business?' she asked.

535

Again his expression was ingenuous. 'Developments? What developments, Grandmother?'

She hesitated. Clearly he knew nothing. Well, it would be a pity to spoil his visit with fruitless discussion on a subject that was repugnant to her.

'I really don't know, David,' she admitted. 'You know I have practically nothing to do with the business these days. Your father manages my interest in it for me. But sometimes I think I should know a little more of what goes on. In fact I was just wondering . . . you are going to Bristol now, you say? I was just wondering whether I could come with you.'

She saw the surprise in David's face and understood. He knew she almost never went to Bristol. But he did not mention the fact, nor ask what was behind her unexpected decision.

'Of course, if you don't mind flying in a little plane I'd be delighted,' he said, sipping his coffee, and she thought again: how like his great grandfather he is! So equable, so smoothly in control, so charming, yet somehow leaving one in not the slightest doubt that beneath that charm is undeniable strength. If only Guy had inherited more of those qualities! But somehow most of them had skipped a generation. The pang of regret she experienced made her feel oddly disloyal to her son and when a moment later David asked: 'Does Dad know you are coming?' she answered quite sharply.

'No, he doesn't, but I am sure he won't object. I shall not impose on him. I'll have Irene telephone and book me into a hotel. The Grand Spa, perhaps – that is within striking distance of both your father's house and the city, and I adore the views over the Avon Gorge. All in all it makes leaving London that little less painful.'

'I'm sure there is no need for you to stay in an hotel at all,' David said. 'Dad has three bedrooms, after all. That's one each.'

Alicia shook her head.

'No, David, I would much prefer to be independent. Besides, your father has no live-in servants and I don't find

536

the prospect of having to get my own breakfast a very appealing one.'

'I'll get your breakfast, Grandmother, if that is all that is worrying you.'

'It is not. You and your father will go off to the works and I shall be left to cope with that dreadful uncouth daily woman of his. I have not forgotten the last time I stayed with your father – she banged around until she had given me a migraine and then attacked me with the vacuum cleaner.'

'Attacked you?'

'As good as. She pushed the thing at me as if she expected me to lift my feet up so she could clean underneath them! And she was exceedingly rude when I admonished her. She said she was only employed for three hours and what wasn't done in the time wouldn't be done at all and would Mr Bailey be very pleased to find crumbs under his favourite chair.'

David laughed. 'Mrs Freeman is all right, Grandmother. Her bark is worse than her bite.'

'*Mrs* Freeman? You address her as *Mrs* Freeman?' Alicia gave her head a small shake of disapproval. 'No wonder she is so disrespectful. And as for her bark being worse than her bite – I certainly would not employ anyone who so much as *yapped*!'

'Then perhaps it is as well you aren't staying in Dad's house. He wouldn't want you upsetting Mrs Freeman. He says he is lucky to have her.' He stretched his long legs, deftly avoiding the priceless Aubusson rug with his brown leather cowboy boots which were, Alicia noted with satisfaction, polished to a high gloss. 'Of course it's not quite what you were used to in the old days, I suppose.'

'You could say that,' Alicia returned drily, remembering the army of servants who had run Chewton Leigh when Gilbert and Blanche had been master and mistress, and she and Sarah and the others had been children. There had been no nonsense then such as maids refusing to do more than their hours and certainly no impertinence or insubordination. She wondered briefly how Sarah managed

537

with the servant problem at Chewton Leigh these days and reflected that she did not envy her. When Adam and Sarah had bought the house after it became too much for Blanche alone she had been hurt and angry – Chewton Leigh was after all her home. But when she had left Somerset to live in London she had decided that it had been all for the best. She no longer wanted to live in the country – let Sarah and Adam have Chewton Leigh and all its attendant problems. In the intervening years she had given it scarcely a thought; now when she did she felt nothing but relief that it was Sarah, not she, who had to bully gardeners, chivvy maintenance men and cope with a whole regiment of Mrs Freemans. Poor Sarah! As if it were not enough to have the cares of the business, to have the house to worry about as well . . .

'Well David,' she said now, 'Perhaps it's wrong of me to sit here chatting when I shall be seeing plenty of you in the next few days. I don't want to keep you waiting. Have another coffee and one of those delicious Chocolate Oliver biscuits while I ask Irene to pack a case for me. Then I can be ready to go with you just as soon as you wish to leave.'

She rose and the slight frailty which had worried Irene earlier had miraculously disappeared now. Her shoulders were straight, her carriage erect, and there was a touch of natural colour beneath her rouge.

'Grandmother . . .'

She paused in the doorway looking back at him. 'Yes, David?'

'Tell me to mind my own business if you like, but why have you decided to come down to Bristol out of the blue?'

Momentarily she hesitated. Should she tell him at least something of the reason? There was after all no question of him 'minding his own business' as he put it. This was his business – more, almost, than it was hers, since whilst it was her past, it was his future.

But the habit of secrecy was too strong and in any case she did not as yet know the whole story herself – whether there was any truth in what Sarah had told her and if there was, what lay behind Guy's decision. Best to keep her own counsel for the moment. And besides . . . she smiled faintly, David might no longer be the little boy who had once loved nothing better than sliding down the ornate and very steep banister here in her London house but he was still very young, inexperienced in the ways of business and of the world. There would be no point in confiding her worries. There was nothing he could do.

He was still looking at her questioningly but she replied to him without so much as a flicker.

'I feel like a change of scenery and company, David. Isn't that a good enough reason?'

For a moment his eyes narrowed. Then his brow cleared and he smiled back at her.

'Of course, Grandmother. It's the best reason in the world.'

Chapter Forty-Five

Kirsty Rowlands applied a touch of mascara to her eyelashes, filled in the outline of her generous mouth with pearly pink lipstick and moved a little further away from the mirror, surveying her reflection with a critical eye.

Not bad. Not bad at all. The mascara made her blue eyes look large and sparkly beneath her deep fringe and the lipstick emphasised the width of her smile. She moved back further still from the mirror, twirling to get a full length view of her suit – sky blue bouclé with a cropped collarless jacket and neat knee-skimming skirt – and nodded with grudging satisfaction. Yes – a definite improvement on her usual uniform of jeans and oversized sweater – at least for the purpose she had in mind.

'Good grief, the girl's got legs!' a voice from the doorway exclaimed. 'What's this in aid of, Kirsty, hon?'

'I want to look halfway decent for once in my life.' Kirsty twisted to glance over her shoulder at Martha Kallinski, the bouncy American girl with whom she shared a flat. 'What do you think – will I do?'

'Depends what for.'

'Seduction.' She said it lightly but Martha heard the serious undertone. She leaned against the doorpost, hands stuck into the waistband of her jeans beneath the voluminous smock she wore, and pulled a face at the back of Kirsty's head.

'Seduction! And who the hell are you setting out to seduce? Not your tutor in the hope of getting better grades, I hope?'

'Certainly not!'

'Who then?'

'Oh Martha, it's a very long story.'

'I'm in no hurry.'

'No, but I am.'

'Just tell me the name of the lucky fella.'

'His name is Guy Bailey. He's a sort of cousin of mine.'

'Guy Bailey? Not the Guy Bailey who runs the aircraft companies?'

'Yes.'

Martha whistled softly. 'What are you after? I didn't have you marked down for the materialistic sort.'

'I'm not. It's not like that at all.' Kirsty glanced at her watch. 'I can't stop to explain now, Martha. I really do have to go.'

She took another look at herself in the mirror, flicked her fingers through the shoulder-length fall of nut-brown hair and crossed to the door. Martha moved aside to let her pass, sighing and shaking her head.

'Just watch it, kid. Take care.'

'I will.' But Kirsty sounded a good deal more confident than she was actually feeling. As she let herself out of the flat and ran down the stairs to the street she shivered and knew that it was not just the gust of cold March air that chilled her but the prospect of her meeting with Guy.

She did not like the man – she never had. There was something about him she could only describe as reptilian – though he was rather on the large side for a snake. A python, Kirsty thought, that's what he reminds me of – a python who has just swallowed his supper, sleek and fat and full – and yet still on the look-out for more. But it was that very quality she hoped to play on – the greedy self-indulgent side of him which she sensed was there co-existing with the ruthless businessman. He liked her, she knew. There was no mistaking the naked lust that glinted in his eyes when he looked at her. Perhaps if she could play him along a little, massage his ego, dangle a promise or two in front of his rather fleshy nose, she might be able to discover exactly what was going on at Morse Bailey, if not actually do something about it.

Sarah would be furious of course if she knew what Kirsty was up to. She had made it clear that under no circumstances did she expect her granddaughter to involve herself with Guy Bailey. But Kirsty knew just how worried Sarah was – and knew too that her meeting with Alicia had not been a success. If Granny was seriously concerned about the future of the companies then there was cause for alarm, Kirsty thought. Granny did not take fright easily – she had been around the world of big business too long for that. And loving her as she did Kirsty was determined not to simply stand aside and do nothing. Granny might be experienced and still very much in command – she was also not getting any younger. Worrying would do her no good at all.

I shall do what I can to sort things out, Kirsty thought, and Granny never need know I had anything to do with it. But even while her conscious mind formed the bold thought she was shivering inwardly again as she wondered just how far she would have to go to achieve her aims.

Guy Bailey's house stood on the edge of the Downs, tall terraced Regency elegance with magnificent views across the Avon Gorge. On either side the dwellings had been made into flats but Guy, because he sometimes entertained at home, had retained the house in its entirety although he lived alone. Outside Kirsty paused for a moment wondering even now if she should turn back, then giving herself a small shake. Stupid not to go on now when her mind was made up to it. And besides, today was Saturday. She knew enough about Guy to know that Saturday afternoon was the best, perhaps the only, time to be sure of catching him at home. Give up today and it would mean waiting another week. Give up today – and perhaps it would be too late. The vote Granny was so concerned about might very well take place at the next full meeting of the board – delay and risk losing the opportunity to make at least some small alteration to the stakes . . .

Kirsty ran up the steps and rang the bell. She heard it jangle somewhere in the magnificent house, echoing up to the high ceilings. For a moment there was silence and she wondered with a sinking heart if today of all days Guy had broken his routine and gone out. Then she heard footsteps on the tiled floor within and the heavy lock turning. She took a deep breath and arranged her face in a smile of greeting. Then as the door swung open she experienced a small stab of surprise.

542

Not Guy but a young man, perhaps twenty or twenty-one years of age, good looking, dark, with piercing blue eyes. Momentarily she could not think who he was or what he could be doing here, then recognition dawned.

'David!' she said, surprise at the change in his appearance and dismay that she had not found Guy alone evident in her voice.

'I'm sorry . . .' He smiled but the blue eyes were puzzled. 'I'm afraid I don't . . .'

'Kirsty,' she said.

'Kirsty!' His eyes ran over her, appraising. 'Good lord, you've changed! I didn't recognise you.'

She laughed. 'I'm not surprised. The last time we met I think I was in pigtails.'

'Not pigtails – a pony tail. And jodhpurs. You'd been riding, I seem to remember.'

'Probably. Mummy used to make me ride pretty often. As for having changed, I'm not the only one. I'd never have known you either except that seeing this is your father's house I didn't think it could be anyone else.'

'Hmm.' He suddenly remembered himself. 'Sorry, Kirsty, how rude of me! Would you like to come in?'

He opened the door and she followed him through the vaulted hall and into the drawing-room which was starkly furnished in dark leather. The pictures on the walls were original cartoons and hunting scenes, there were no vases of flowers to lend a touch of colour. It was very much a man's room. A nerve jumped in her throat.

'Actually I called to see your father.'

'The old man? Sorry, you're out of luck. He's out at the moment and I don't know how long he will be. Would you like to wait? We could have a coffee or something.'

'Well – I don't want to put you to any trouble . . .' She glanced at the papers spread out on the low table which he had obviously been working on when she had rung the doorbell. 'I'm interrupting you, aren't I?'

He smiled. 'Quite a welcome interruption. I've been buried in all this stuff for hours. I've joined the company – did you know? I've just come back to Head Office from

Australia and there are reams of information I have to familiarise myself with. But I can only take in so much at a time and I was just thinking I'd have a break and a coffee. So why not share it with me?'

'All right. Thank you.'

'Let's go through to the kitchen.'

He led the way back along the hall. The kitchen was down two steps on another level – again a typical man's kitchen with used crockery piled in the sink but no feminine clutter. 'If I can find some clean cups . . .' He opened cupboards, peering inside. 'Sit down, Kirsty.'

She perched herself on a stool trying to jerk her skirt down to a decent level over her long legs.

'Dad has gone out with Grandmother,' he said, spooning instant coffee into mugs. 'She's staying in Bristol for a few days. I brought her down with me when I came.'

'Alicia is staying here?' The dismay was there again in her voice. All her plans, it seemed, were going awry – now she had not only David but also the redoubtable Alicia to contend with.

'Not staying here exactly. It's not luxurious enough for her, I'm afraid. She's taken a suite at the Grand Spa.'

'I see.' Kirsty's eyes grew thoughtful. 'Does she often come to Bristol? I didn't think . . .'

'Not often, no. In fact I was pretty surprised when she said she'd like to come down with me – especially in my cramped little kite. She seldom leaves London these days. Do you take milk with your coffee?'

'Just a splash.' Her mind was racing. Did Alicia's visit have anything to do with the problems at Morse Bailey – a direct result perhaps of Sarah contacting her? And if so what did it mean?

'What are you doing these days, Kirsty?' David asked, putting the mug of coffee down on the ledge beside her.

'I'm at art college here in Bristol – studying graphic design.'

One of his eyebrows quirked. 'You don't look like most of the students I know!'

Colour rose in her cheeks. She glanced down, acutely

544

aware of her long nylon clad legs and high heeled shoes.

'Well, I . . .'

'Do you often come to see my father?' he asked shrewdly.

'No . . .' Kirsty fought an almost irresistible urge to get up and run, away from this cold house which could never in a million years be termed a home, away from the extremely attractive stranger who was David, and whom she felt suddenly horribly sure could see right through her. But to leave now would not only be to admit defeat it would also make her look very foolish. Kirsty did not like looking foolish. There was nothing for it, she decided, but to stay and brazen things out.

'I think he will be as surprised to see me as you were,' she admitted. 'It was just that there was something I wanted to talk to him about.'

David took a drink of coffee to give himself time to think. There was something going on here that he did not understand. First his grandmother had asked him to fly her down to Bristol – an almost unheard-of request – and been rather mysterious about her reasons. He had taken that on board, although it had puzzled him. His grandmother had always been a person who enjoyed her secrets. But now here was Sarah's granddaughter, obviously ill at ease, also seeking an audience with his father, uninvited and clearly unexpected. David glanced at her over the rim of his coffee cup. In the years since he had last seen her Kirsty had become a very attractive young lady. Under other circumstances he might very well have chatted her up and perhaps asked if he might see her again. He still felt an urge to do just that – and if he began questioning her he might spoil any chance of success on that score. But all his instincts were telling him that something odd was going on – something he knew nothing about – and curiosity and not a little concern were getting the better of his reluctance to spoil what might turn out to be a very pleasant interlude.

Making up his mind he set down his mug and looked at her directly.

'Has it anything to do with the business, Kirsty?' he asked. 'If so perhaps I can help. As I told you I am working for Morse Bailey now. I'm not an authority yet, far from it, but I am anxious to learn. And if Dad is going to be a long while perhaps I can give him a message.'

As he spoke he saw the high spots of colour in her cheeks deepen and saw too the look of wary indecision in her eyes. 'Well?' he said.

What do I do? Kirsty was thinking. Clearly I am not going to be able to see Guy alone – if I am going to do anything to help Granny I have to find another line of attack. And David seemed very nice – totally unlike his father. Whereas Guy only made her want to squirm there was something about David which inspired trust. It was unlikely of course that he knew what was going on and if he did he was probably too young and inexperienced in the ways of business to be able to do anything to help even if he wanted to. But it would be good to have an ally or simply someone to talk to, someone of more or less her own age, someone who might just conceivably understand . . . Kirsty drew a deep breath.

'Have you ever heard of Leo de Vere?' she asked.

Dinner in the restaurant at the Grand Spa Hotel was almost over. Some latecomers were still eating but the music wafting in from the ballroom indicated the lateness of the hour and at their table in a secluded alcove David and Guy, his father, lingered over their coffee and brandies. Alicia had dined with them but now she had excused herself, pleading tiredness, and they were alone.

'Well, David, do you have any plans for your Saturday evening?' Guy asked drawing on a panatella cigar. 'If you do I shall quite understand.' His tone was smooth and it crossed David's mind to wonder if his father had any plans of his own. But he dismissed the thought. This was the moment he had been waiting for – the opportunity to discuss the matters that had been bothering him ever since his talk this afternoon with Kirsty.

'No, I've no plans,' he said. 'I haven't been in Bristol long enough yet to make any friends.'

'Hmm. We shall have to do something about that. A

pretty girl, David, would do you the world of good. There is nothing like a pretty girl for putting hair on your chest, though I dare say you don't need me to tell you that. And Bristol is full of pretty girls, one way and another, if you go out and look for 'em.'

And sometimes when you don't, David thought with a smile. Aloud he said: 'I'm in no hurry, Dad.'

'Let's have another brandy then.' Guy signalled to a passing waitress.

'Not for me, thanks, Dad.'

'Yes – have another, my boy. Don't want girls, don't want brandy – what the hell sort of son have I raised? I thought at least Australia would have made a man of you. Two brandies, please – doubles,' he instructed the waitress who had answered the summons with the alacrity he always commanded.

David felt his cheeks burn with annoyance but he controlled himself. No point antagonising his father – better to keep him in receptive mood. When the brandies arrived he sipped reflectively.

'I spent the afternoon reading up on the business, Dad,' he said.

'Good. The more you know the better placed you will be to take your rightful place. I have great plans for you, David, when I feel you are ready for the responsibility.'

'In that case perhaps you could enlighten me on one or two things I don't understand.'

'Of course. Fire away.'

David set down his brandy balloon. Soft reflections of the muted overhead lights danced in the amber liquid.

'Why are you planning to merge with de Vere Motors?'

If David had struck him the older man could hardly have been more surprised. He almost choked on the smoke of his cigar.

'What sort of a question is that?'

'A very simple one. The company is in good shape, isn't it? So why are you planning to sacrifice our autonomy?'

Guy's paunchy face gave nothing away but his eyes blazed furiously.

547

'Have you been talking to your grandmother?'

'As a matter of fact, no. But I am right, aren't I? Merger is on the cards?'

For a moment Guy said nothing, merely drew harder on his cigar. He seemed to be debating with himself. Then he wafted away the haze of smoke with a be-ringed hand and nodded.

'Yes, David, it is true I have been having talks with Leo de Vere.'

'Why?' David asked directly.

'Why? Because I think it would be advantageous, of course. What other reason could there be?'

'In what way advantageous?'

Guy laughed a little derisively.

'It is quite obvious, David, that you are new to the world of business. Merger would give us control of an empire.'

'I should have thought we were quite big enough already.'

'One can never be big enough. Large fish will always gobble up smaller ones, David. In spite of our size we are still a privately owned company. I want to make quite sure we are invincible.'

'I understand that. What I don't understand is – why Leo de Vere?'

'Why not? De Vere Motors is a healthy company, most compatible with our own.'

'The company, maybe. But not its founder. Everyone in the family hates Leo de Vere. The very mention of his name has always been enough to put Grandmother in a foul temper.'

A muscle tightened in Guy's cheek. 'Your grandmother's prejudices are rooted in the past. They should not be allowed to influence important decisions half a century on. When you meet Leo de Vere, as you soon will, you will discover him to be a most charming fellow and an excellent businessman. I have had dealings with him for some time now and I assure you we are on the best of terms.'

David sipped his brandy and tried a different approach. 'Is this business the reason Grandmother is in Bristol?'

'Yes, it is. I expect the whole matter to be sorted out at the board meeting this coming Wednesday but that damned trouble maker Sarah is against the idea and decided to go running to your grandmother to try and throw a spanner in the works. She is a menace – more of a threat to our continued stability than Leo de Vere could ever be. It's time she retired and left the running of the company to those of us who understand progress.'

David said nothing. This was hardly the moment to mention the high esteem in which Sarah Bailey was held by everyone he had talked to – in Australia she was regarded almost as a candidate for canonisation by the management – but he knew to say so would antagonise Guy.

'So what has Grandmother to say about the proposed merger?' he asked after a moment.

Guy ground out his cigar. 'As you so rightly say she has a blinkered dislike of Leo de Vere and at first she was cautious of merger. But I have talked to her and I believe she is coming to see the sense of what I propose. In any case she is an old woman now and has had nothing to do with the running of the company for the past forty years. I have her proxy vote and I am quite confident she will allow me to use it as I think fit. In her heart she knows that ancient rivalries have no place in the running of a modern business, and I am sure when you have had time to give the matter some thought you will realise I am right. One day you will head Morse Bailey. I am grooming you to that end and I want to ensure that you inherit a healthy company, not an atrophied dinosaur. So let us hear no more talk of old enmities. Your future depends on what I am doing.'

David was silent. Seeing his thoughtful expression Guy moved impatiently.

'Shall we go? I have a good bottle of port and plenty of brandy at home.'

David hesitated. 'I think if you don't mind I will do as you suggested and go in search of a little night life.'

Guy laughed, somewhat relieved. He had found the conversation with his son heavier going than he had anticipated.

'Good. That sounds more like it.' He slapped David's shoulders in a gesture of bonhomie and was surprised to realise that almost unnoticed the boy had grown into a man, taller than he was by some two inches. 'You'll ease into the business gradually, David. In the meantime take the opportunity to have some fun. I'll see you in the morning.'

'Yes, Dad,' David said and knew his father had no idea of what was in his mind.

For almost an hour David drove his Mercedes sports around the streets of Bristol, avoiding an accident through sheer instinct, for he was totally preoccupied with his thoughts.

He wished he could have gone to his grandmother's room and talked with her but he knew she would be asleep by now, drugged by her sleeping tablets, and in any case he was not sure what he would have said to her.

Everything his father had said was so plausible – the need to keep the business alive and expanding, the fact that old enmities should not be allowed to live on to the detriment of development, even the unpalatable statement that Alicia was now an old woman who should leave important decisions to the younger generation. He knew that his father had held the reins of power for a good many years now and under his guardianship the company had flourished – who was he, a mere novice, to question what he proposed now? And he was flattered that he should be considered a worthy heir to the empire even if Guy's decision did smack heavily of nepotism.

But nevertheless he was disturbed by a gut feeling that something was wrong here. There was more to the so-called 'merger' than Guy had admitted, he was certain of it. Sarah had been to see his grandmother – a visit that in itself must have been a move born of desperation – and as a result his grandmother had been sufficiently concerned to have left London and flown with him to Bristol. Perhaps his father was right and Sarah was nothing but a troublemaker but somehow he did not think so. There was no love lost between her and his grandmother and never had been, it was

550

true, but since they had both been married to the same man that was hardly surprising. It did not make Sarah a monster, far from it. She had the respect and affection of the entire workforce whilst the things he had heard of Leo de Vere had been less flattering. And it was impossible for him to reconcile the image of a ruthless opportunist with a woman who could inspire such love and loyalty in a granddaughter – who could actually *be* the grandmother of a girl like Kirsty if it came to that.

He swung the car into a vacant space at the kerb thinking of the girl who had come to see his father this afternoon and ended up pouring her heart out to him. Perhaps he should not allow himself to be swayed by appearances, he thought, but in his short life he had come to trust his own judgement and without doubt first impressions almost always turned out to be correct. Kirsty was not only pretty, though she was certainly that, there was an innate honesty about her that was impossible to deny.

'Granny told me a long time ago that Leo de Vere vowed that one day Morse Bailey would be his and it looks as though he is going to get his way,' she said and there had been nothing melodramatic or vindictive in the way she had said it. She had simply been stating facts as she knew them and he suddenly knew that he would prefer to believe her rather than his father.

The knowledge was disconcerting – to distrust his own father went against the grain, against everything he respected and held dear. Yet he knew that in the past there had been occasions when he had come close to thinking the same way about other things – the wreck of his parents' marriage, for one thing. His mother had never tried to turn him against his father, on the contrary it was his father who had squirmed and blustered and made excuses and as David had grown older he had formed his own opinion as to what had gone wrong – an opinion that was not wholly complimentary to his father. Now, however, faced with the possibility that Guy meant to betray what was almost a sacred trust, he found himself torn between filial loyalty and his own high standards, a painful and destructive conflict.

After a moment he started the car again, driving without any real idea of where he was going, and it was almost a shock to him when he realised he was in the street where Kirsty had her flat. He had driven her home this afternoon after their talk and she had pointed out her window to him; now he looked up and saw that a light was still burning.

Christ, he wished he could talk to her again! It was too late, of course, much too late – past eleven – and yet . . . An inner compulsion seemed to take hold of him. She had come visiting unannounced this afternoon – he would return her visit. Before he could change his mind he parked the car, went to the house and pushed the bell marked 'Rowlands'.

In the few moments he had to wait for her to answer he almost changed his mind. Then just as he was about to turn away the intercom crackled and he heard her voice, distorted but sweet and just a little nervous.

'Hello?'

'It's me – David,' he said, feeling foolish. 'Can I talk to you?'

'David?'

'David Bailey. I know it's late but . . .'

'I'll open the door,' she said.

He heard the lock click and when he pushed it the door swung open. He found himself in a bare hall and started up a flight of stairs. On the first floor a sliver of light showed beneath one of the doors. As he went towards it it opened a crack and he heard her say: 'David – is that you?'

'Yes.'

She opened the door fully. She was wearing a towelling robe now, floor length, and her face, devoid of make-up, was a little flushed. Tendrils of damp hair clung to her neck as if she had just got out of the bath and he noticed that she had scooped most of it up into a pony tail so that she looked ridiculously like the little girl he had once known – almost but not quite for now she was not a little girl but a beautiful young woman. His throat constricted; for a moment he almost forgot why he was here. Then she said: 'Come in, David. What has happened?' and he recovered himself.

'Nothing really. I just wanted to talk. I'm sorry it's so late.'

She gave a small impatient shake of her head and the pony tail swung enticingly.

'It's all right. It's quite early really. I shan't be going to bed for hours and if I did I don't believe I'd sleep. I'm too worried about all this. Do come in so that I can close the door. I know it's silly to be nervous but there was a Peeping Tom round here not so long ago and I'm on my own tonight. Martha, my flatmate, is out with her boyfriend and likely to be very late – if she comes home at all.'

He followed her into the living-room, all cushions and comfortable clutter, flattered and yet at the same time ridiculously slightly offended that she should feel he posed no threat.

The television was on full blast – a chat show. She went over and turned it off, cleared a sketch pad and a pile of reference books off the low chintz-covered sofa and indicated that he should sit down.

'My turn to offer you coffee,' she said. 'Or would you prefer cocoa?'

He smiled. He did not think anyone had offered him cocoa since he was a child. It sounded rather nice.

'Why not cocoa?' he said.

She disappeared into the kitchenette.

'No point asking you to join me,' she called as she clattered pans. 'There's simply not room for two people out here. I won't be a sec.'

'I'm fine,' he called back, glancing at her sketch pad – evidently some kind of design for an advertising poster that she was working on. The lines were clear, the message bold. She was good, he thought, and called out: 'We could use some of your designs in the company, you know. They are every bit as good as the agency we used in Melbourne.'

'Do you think so?' she asked, reappearing with two mugs of cocoa and a packet of biscuits on a tray. She looked pleased.

'I do indeed. You have a great future.'

'Tell my tutor that!' she said ruefully. 'I've only been

553

getting 2.2s and 3s this term and I do so want to get a good degree.'

'Either they are trying to spur you on to even greater heights or they don't know what they are looking at.' He grinned. 'They're probably all high on pot.'

'Don't talk about my tutors like that!' She smiled back. 'You establishment types think all artists are the same.'

'Ah, but I haven't always been establishment. You might be surprised if you knew some of the things I've done.'

'Go on then – surprise me!'

He shook his head. 'Not tonight. I'll save that for another time.'

'You weren't an artist too?'

'No. Why do you ask?'

'Because it's in the family, isn't it? Uncle James was an artist – you remember Uncle James . . . ?' She broke off. He was looking at her with a faintly puzzled expression and she realised what she had said. 'Ah! I'm sorry, David. My tongue does run away with me sometimes.'

'I don't quite follow you,' he said.

'No, I can see that you don't. You are wondering why I should allude to your Uncle James in the same breath as my flair for art. I suppose that means you don't know.'

'Know what?'

She sighed, spooning sugar into her cocoa.

'I've rather put my foot in it, haven't I?'

'For goodness' sake, Kirsty!' he said, a little shortly. 'Do tell me what it is I don't know.'

'All right.' She looked at him squarely. 'I don't suppose your grandmother will be very pleased with me though. She does like her secrets.'

'What secret?'

'That she and my grandmother are half-sisters.' Her tone was matter-of-fact now. 'Gilbert Morse was Sarah's father too. She was illegitimate, of course.'

He sat silently for a moment digesting the information. Of course. Why had it never occurred to him? It explained everything – the rivalry, the jealousy, the reason why Sarah had equal shares with Alicia. Yet somehow he had never thought of it for himself. Sarah – Alicia's half-sister. Born on the wrong side of the blanket, as they used to say. His grandfather must have been quite a man.

He shook his head slightly. 'Well, well. I must be pretty dim not to have thought of that myself. But no-one has ever said anything – not grandmother, not Dad . . .'

'I'm not sure how many people know,' Kirsty admitted, 'though I should imagine there was a certain amount of speculation at the time. Granny told me, but then it's different for your grandmother, isn't it? She probably wouldn't want to advertise the fact.'

'Probably not. Though in this day and age I don't suppose anyone could care less.' He sipped his cocoa. It tasted good – hot and sweet, a taste evocative of cosy childhood days. He wished there was no need to bring up the subject that was on both their minds. It would have been so pleasant to treat this as a social visit to an attractive girl. But there was no avoiding it any longer.

'I talked to my father,' he said.

Her fingers gripped her cocoa mug more tightly, 'And?'

'Everything you said is true. Except that he puts a different interpretation on it, of course. That it is for the good of the business and so on.' He could not bring himself to mention that his father had also said it was for the good of his own future.

'The good of the business! Ha! Leo de Vere does nothing except for the good of Leo de Vere.'

'Dad thinks he's built up to be an ogre because of things which happened a long time ago – things that should be forgotten.'

'There are some things it is impossible to forget.' Her lips tightened, eyes narrowing, and something in her expression disturbed him. There was something else she knew that he did not, just as she had known about the relationship between their grandmothers, something from the past which cast this long dark shadow across the years.

'What did he do?' he asked. 'Why do Alicia and Sarah hate him so?'

'You don't know?'

555

He shook his head. Her eyes came up to meet his, clear honest eyes. 'They believe he was responsible for the death of Gilbert Morse.'

'Responsible for his death? But he was killed in a flying accident wasn't he?'

'They don't believe it was an accident. They believe he tampered with the aeroplane in some way.'

David looked incredulous. 'That's a bit far-fetched, isn't it? Why should he do something like that – assuming he could.'

'He always wanted control of the business, even then. I don't think they believe he set out to kill Gilbert. It was Sarah he wanted to get rid of. She was Gilbert's protégée and getting too much power for his liking – taking over the position he believed to be rightfully his after Lawrence died and Hugh was killed. And you see it should have been Sarah in the aeroplane that day, flying the first leg of the record-making journey they were attempting to South Africa. As for the how – he was seen the night before, snooping around the sheds – just as he had been on a previous occasion when something went wrong with an aeroplane Sarah was learning to fly in. Oh, I know nowadays it sounds an impossibility but things were different then, far more primitive. A nut loosened here, a bolt removed there – I don't know. No-one really does – the aircraft was totally destroyed. But there was very real suspicion directed at Leo. He was told to get out and never come back, and as he did everything was hushed up. But you see that is why they will never forgive him.'

David sat silent, stunned by the story.

'It wasn't just Alicia and Sarah who disliked Leo either,' Kirsty went on, anxious that he should not think she was over-dramatising some unlikely plot. 'Gilbert couldn't have trusted him either because when his will was read Leo was not mentioned. It was then he vowed he would one day control Morse Bailey. It seemed impossible at the time, Granny said, and certainly it has taken him a lifetime to reach the position from which he can attempt it. But now he's done it, hasn't he? Somehow he has wormed his way

556

into your father's confidence, used his wiles to make the deal sound attractive enough, and there it is, *fait accompli* after all these years. We can't allow it to happen, David. We can't allow the family firm – *our* family firm – to fall into the hands of a man like that.'

David set down his cocoa mug. The feeling of well-being had gone now, totally destroyed by what Kirsty had said. He could not believe his father had not known the story – he would certainly have heard it from Alicia. So how could he disregard it and dismiss the ill feeling so lightly as 'old enmities', trivial as some children's quarrel? Presumably because there was enough in the deal for him to enable him to overlook Leo's treachery. Enough for him – and for David. But David wanted no part of this. A position of authority in the company might be something he would be prepared to accept – if he had worked for it and earned it. He could never take it if it were the prize for a dishonourable ploy, his principles were much too high for that – too high for the world of business altogether, he had sometimes thought and certainly too high to betray the memory of the man who had founded their empire, his great-grandfather, Gilbert Morse.

There was only one thing for it – much as he loathed the idea he would have to work against his father and do what he could to prevent the merger going through. Guy would be furious – worse, he would consider him a fool, for by doing so he would be turning his back on a joint fortune that could make him rich and powerful beyond his wildest dreams. But so be it. There was enough of a hippy still in David to make him contemptuous of too much money, and power for its own sake did not attract him either. Integrity was, he considered, a good deal more important.

'You agree with me, don't you?' Kirsty asked. She sat forward on the ottoman facing him, arms wound around her knees, small chin jutting with determination. 'It would be terrible if Morse Bailey fell into Leo de Vere's hands. But from what Granny says the only person who can stop it is Alicia. And will she? From what you say she was concerned enough to come to Bristol but your father has run her affairs for so long that habit may be too strong. If he pulls the wool over her eyes, convinces her that we are taking over de Vere Motors or something of the sort, then she will very likely allow him the proxy vote just as she always has. Especially if he can convince her that what he is doing is beneficial for her side of the family.'

He nodded, surprised by her perceptiveness.

'Yes, Dad knows how to get around Grandmother. He has had plenty of practice at it. And from what he said to me tonight he is fairly certain, I think, that he has allayed her fears. He has had too much power for too long, that is the trouble, and he is bolstered up by Leo's own share in the company which he inherited from his mother. I dare say unbeknown to anyone they have been scratching one another's backs for years.' He broke off for a moment, finding the idea distasteful in the light of what he now knew.

'So what are we going to do?' Kirsty sounded desperate. 'If Leo de Vere gets control of Morse Bailey it will kill Granny, I know it will. The company has been her whole life.'

'There is only one thing to do,' David said. 'Your grandmother talked to mine without success. Understandable, I suppose, considering the ill feeling between them. Now it is up to me.'

She looked at him steadily, hardly daring to hope.

'I'll talk to Grandmother. I'm not sure how much influence I have with her but I can only do my best – and the trouble is we haven't long. The all-important meeting is on Wednesday. Dad is wasting no time. I'll see Grandmother tomorrow and try to persuade her to use her votes to keep Morse Bailey independent.' He glanced at his watch and stood up. 'It's late. I'd better be going.'

She nodded, curiously reluctant to see him leave. Whilst he was here nothing seemed so bad. He crossed to the door and she followed him.

'Good luck, David.'

He smiled crookedly. 'I may need it. Think of me tomorrow.'

'I will.'

When he had gone she sat for a long while deep in thought. Perhaps it would be all right. For everything her grandmother held dear, it had to be!

Chapter Forty-Six

For years Mondays had been Grace's afternoon off and it was her custom to leave a cold supper for Sarah ready for when she returned from the office. As usual there was a good selection of cold meats, cheeses and salad, but tonight Sarah had no appetite and as she carried the tray through into her sitting-room she wondered if she would be able to manage more than a mouthful.

Dear God, this business had upset her more than anything had done for years. The thought of the business falling into Leo de Vere's hands was a terrible one, yet she was powerless to do anything about it. The dread had settled into Sarah's stomach like a leaden weight and the sense of utter helplessness fermented in her veins making her unable to rest. Sarah had always hated being helpless. It was totally foreign to her nature to sit back and let fate take its course. But on this occasion there was nothing, absolutely nothing, she could do except wait and pray that perhaps others would be able to open Alicia's eyes to the seriousness of what would happen if she remained with the status quo and allowed Guy to make her decision for her.

Yesterday she had experienced a flash of hope, a little light at the end of the tunnel. Kirsty had telephoned to say she had talked to David, who in turn was going to talk to Alicia. Sarah was not well acquainted with David but Kirsty, whose judgement she trusted implicitly, had spoken of him in glowing terms and when she had last seen him when he had come to look around the Bristol works on joining the company Sarah had been struck forcibly by how like Gilbert he had grown – a point which had given Sarah an instant affinity with the young man. Perhaps, she thought, he could succeed where she had failed and make Alicia face up to her obligations after all these years. The thought had been something to hold onto but since then she

560

had heard nothing and she was beginning to be doubtful of his success. Moreover, Guy had been as full of himself today as he always was – a sure sign that he felt his position to be secure.

How I dislike the man! she thought. And what a bitter moment it will be to see the triumph in his eyes when he carries the day . . .

The thought took away what little of her appetite remained and Sarah put the tray down on the low table beside the chair. Grace would probably scold her tomorrow when she discovered the food untouched but Grace's scolding was the least of her worries just now.

Sarah poured herself a glass of Chablis and sipped it but even the fine wine tasted bitter in her mouth.

The telephone began to shrill, jangling on Sarah's nerves. Who could it be – one of her sons, perhaps, who had got wind of what was going on and wanted to discuss it with her? Or Kirsty maybe, still concerned about her grandmother and wanting to check that she was all right? The thought warmed her a little. Kirsty was a darling. If she lost everything else, there was still Kirsty. She got up and crossed the room to the telephone, limping a little on her stiff knee.

'Sarah Bailey.'

'Sarah.' It was Alicia's voice – she recognised it at once and her hand tensed on the receiver. The two of them had not spoken since that day at Rules and though she knew Alicia was in Bristol she had not seen anything of her. But in spite of her need for Alicia as an ally she was unable to restrain the feelings of antagonism that autocratic voice always excited in her.

'Alicia.'

'Yes, it's me. Please don't hang up, Sarah. I should begin by apologising for having left you so abruptly at our last meeting.'

Alicia – apologising? Unheard of! But then of course for all her faults Alicia was well-bred. The least she could do was reciprocate . . .

'I quite understand, Alicia. What can I do for you?'

561

A slight pause. Then Alicia said smoothly: 'I understand there is to be a very important meeting on Wednesday afternoon. I am not sure if I shall be able to be there myself but I would like to take the opportunity of talking to you before it takes place. I am staying at the Grand Spa Hotel in Clifton. Could you possibly come to see me tomorrow evening?'

She doesn't change! Sarah thought. She still issues her invitations as if they were commands. Aloud she said: 'At your hotel, you mean?'

'Yes. It would be easiest, I think. I have no transport.' Alicia hesitated, then continued smoothly: 'I should warn you it will be something of a gathering. I have also asked Guy and David to come along.'

Sarah lifted a hand to pat her cap of silver hair into place with a movement that those who knew her well would have recognised as defensive. What is she up to now? she was wondering.

'Very well, Alicia,' she said, then added: 'Perhaps you would have no objection to my bringing Kirsty along with me? If she can make it, that is. She does have college commitments to consider.'

'Of course I have no objection,' Alicia said and instantly Sarah felt a little foolish. She must be getting old, to feel in need of some moral support!

'What time will you expect us, Alicia?' she asked.

'Oh – seven perhaps? I'll have some sandwiches sent up, or we may indeed be finished in time to dine in the restaurant. Though I feel sure it would do Guy no harm at all to go without his dinner for once. All the business lunches he consumes have done no good at all for his waistline.'

And all the bottles of spirits he puts away, not to mention the fine wines, Sarah thought.

'Very well, Alicia,' she said. 'Until tomorrow.'

'Until tomorrow.'

It was perhaps the friendliest farewell the two women had shared in a lifetime of antagonism and it was only when she had replaced the receiver and found herself trembling slightly that Sarah thought: why is she gathering us together like a spider in her web? Just what has she decided?

And knew that, trying as it would be, she would have to wait until the next day to find out.

Alicia's suite was perhaps the finest the Grand Spa had to offer, overlooking as it did the magnificent sweep of the Avon Gorge and the countryside beyond so that it was impossible almost to realise that it stood in the heart of a bustling city.

Sarah arrived at seven on the dot and Kirsty was with her.

'Of course I'll come with you, Granny,' she had said when Sarah had telephoned her.

'Are you sure it's not imposing dreadfully on your time?' Sarah had asked, feeling guilty, and Kirsty, bless her, had insisted it was not. Now, grateful for her presence, Sarah took her arm as they walked along the carpeted corridor from the lift and was grateful for the youth and strength that seemed to flow into her.

'What can she have decided, Kirsty?' she wondered and the girl turned to smile at her with the sparkling blue eyes that were so like her own had been before time had faded them a little.

'We'll soon know, Granny.'

'Yes, we will, won't we?'

As she raised her hand to knock Sarah heard voices coming from the other side of the door. Clearly Guy and David were here before them.

David answered the door and once again Sarah was struck forcibly by how like Gilbert he had become – the likeness was almost uncanny, taking her across the years as if she had been caught in a time warp. Except, of course, that this young Gilbert wore a casual open necked shirt and a sweater in a bright red, a colour that a man Gilbert's generation would have considered totally unsuitable for anyone of the male gender.

'Come in. It's good to see you.' His voice was easy, less formal and clipped than Gilbert's had been but with the same underlying firmness. I like him, Sarah thought, and noticed in spite of her anxiety the flash of communication that passed between him and Kirsty. And Kirsty likes him too, she thought, pleased.

Alicia and Guy were standing together by the window with the wonderful view of the Gorge. They had obviously been deep in conversation and Guy turned to nod curtly at Sarah and Kirsty, as if annoyed by their interruption. But Alicia was the perfect hostess. She swept across to greet them, her lack of natural warmth completely hidden by her impeccable manners.

'Sarah – Kirsty – thank you so much for coming. And at such short notice too.' She spread her arms and for a startled moment Sarah thought she might be going to kiss them in greeting but at that Alicia drew the line.

She looked magnificent as ever, Sarah thought with grudging admiration, tall and straight as she had ever been in her simply cut dress of coral wool with a black shawl arranged elegantly around her shoulders. But she did look paler than she had done at their last meeting, her skin almost blue-tinged ivory, drawn tightly over her cheek bones, and the merest hint of dark circles beneath her eyes.

'Isn't there anything to drink in this place, Mother?' Guy asked rather rudely from his place by the window. 'I asked for brandy to be sent up but it hasn't arrived.'

'And I cancelled the order, Guy,' Alicia said smoothly. 'You drink far more than is good for you and I would like you to be stone cold sober whilst you hear what I have to say.'

Guy tutted but did not argue. In some respects he was still slightly in awe of his autocratic mother.

'Well, let's get on with it,' he said impatiently. 'You have got us all here – and I for one am anxious to know why.'

Sarah heard the undertone in his voice and thought: Guy is worried. Perhaps this is a good sign. But she was afraid to hope too much. Even now Alicia was a total enigma.

'Very well. Why don't we all sit down?' It was not so much an invitation as an order. They did as she bid, Kirsty taking her place on the small sofa at Sarah's side, David

564

coiling his long frame into the matching chair, Guy plumping for a straight-backed upright. Only Alicia remained standing. When he saw this David half rose, offering her his seat, but she shook her head.

'Thank you, David, but I would prefer to stand. I find it easier to talk – and I have a good deal to say. I suppose it would be naïve of me to imagine you don't know, any of you, why I asked you here – it concerns, of course, this proposed "merger", I think you called it, Guy, with de Vere Motors.'

'I realise that, Mother, but I don't know why you are continuing to worry your head about it,' Guy said, raising his voice slightly. 'You have allowed me to manage your affairs for a long time now and I don't see why this should be any different.'

'Kindly do not interrupt me, Guy. Yes, you have managed my affairs – and very satisfactorily as far as I am aware, for many years. This is different.'

'Different how?'

'Different because it strikes at the very basis of the firm my father founded.' She glanced at Sarah, a faint flicker in her violet eyes. '*Our* father,' she amended.

'But I still don't see . . . Mother, I have given the matter a great deal of thought and it is my considered opinion . . .'

'I know your opinion, Guy. Now I have asked you here so that I can acquaint you with mine. As you so rightly say you have had my proxy vote for a very long time now. I have called you all here tonight to tell you that this time I intend to come to the meeting tomorrow afternoon and vote for myself.'

There was complete silence in the room. Then Guy leapt to his feet.

'You intend to humiliate me, Mother, is that it?'

'No, Guy, I don't want to do that. For that reason and that alone I called you here this evening so that I can tell you privately what I intend to do.'

'Privacy?' Guy gesticulated angrily at the others. 'This is hardly privacy.'

'A great deal more private than a board meeting surely?'

Alicia said. She had circled the chair and now held tightly to its upright back with her be-ringed hands. 'Sarah I asked because in spite of all our differences I believe she has a right to know what I intend to do. We are the original Morse Bailey, all that is left of it, Sarah and I:' She smiled faintly in Sarah's direction. 'Kirsty is here because Sarah wished her to be and I saw no reason to deny her request. David . . . David is here for a different reason, which I will come to in a moment. You, Guy . . . you are here because I wish to tell you that I believe you have betrayed my trust.'

'Mother!' Guy was white.

'You know, Guy, of the enmity there is between myself and Leo de Vere. You must have known I would never agree to him gaining control of Morse Bailey. When Sarah first told me of it I must tell you quite frankly I could not believe such a thing would enter your head. I told her so. But I was wrong, wasn't I?'

'You have got it all wrong, Mother. I thought I explained to you – this merger would eventually give *David* control of de Vere Motors.'

'You coloured things, Guy, for your own ends. You attempted to pull the wool over my eyes. It's not that at all, is it? I have been doing a little investigation myself and find that in fact you are indebted personally to Leo de Vere to the tune of a great deal of money. How you got yourself into this mess I don't know, but the result is that you were quite prepared to sell out to de Vere in order to save your own skin. Deny it if you can!'

'Mother . . .'

'I have discovered a great many things in this past week, Guy, which I would have preferred never to know. But now I do know I must warn you I do not intend to stand by and see you sacrifice Morse Bailey to the one man who has spent his lifetime – a very wicked lifetime, I might add – with the sole purpose of getting us where he wanted us. That is why I shall vote myself tomorrow – and why I shall vote with Sarah.'

Guy was almost purple now.

'Don't you realise what you are doing, Mother?' he

566

raged. 'Don't you realise that to pull back now could ruin us?'

Alicia shook her head. She was trembling now, her face deathly pale, her hands clamped to the back of the chair as if her life depended on it.

'No, Guy, I don't think so. If it costs me every penny I have I won't see that happen and neither I believe will Sarah. If we personally lose everything we own we won't let it happen.' She turned to Sarah, extending one hand in a gesture that was curiously theatrical. 'Sarah? Will you stand with me?'

In the hush that followed Sarah got to her feet. Her eyes were very bright. Kirsty stretched out a hand either to help or restrain her, Sarah was unsure which, but she ignored it. This was something she had to do – and she had to do it alone. Slowly, a little stiffly, she crossed to Alicia and took her outstretched hand. For a moment they looked at one another, two women who had spent their lives in rivalry, united at this moment by the one thing they both cared about more deeply than any past quarrels or wrongs.

'I am with you, Alicia,' Sarah said.

'Good.' Alicia smiled faintly and her voice was lower. 'I knew you would be. As you can see, Guy, you may as well withdraw from this plan of yours as gracefully as you are able. In the knowledge that you have disappointed me. I hoped you would be strong, like me. You are not. Ah well, *c'est la vie*.' She laughed bitterly but there was an odd strangled note in the sound. Lost in their own thoughts they failed to notice it. Alicia drew a deep shuddering breath. Her free hand went to her throat, loosening the shawl, and Sarah saw a look of pure glazed fear and pain come into her violet eyes.

'Alicia!' she cried. 'Are you all right?'

Alicia did not reply. She groaned, a small throaty gargle, and swayed on her feet.

'Grandmother!' David leaped up, rushing to her side, and caught her as she fell, still holding tightly to Sarah's hand and dragging her down with her. 'Grandmother! For goodness' sake – she's ill!

He scooped her up, carrying her to the sofa. Kirsty relinquished her place, drawing to one side, frightened by the sudden turn of events, and he laid Alicia down on the sofa, loosening the collar of her dress.

'Get some water!'

Kirsty ran to obey, Guy, still shaken, stood helplessly by like a bull elephant who does not know which way to turn.

'Why didn't they bring the damned brandy?' he muttered. 'She could do with the damned brandy!'

David was in control now.

'Telephone for an ambulance, Dad – quickly!'

Alicia's eyelids flickered. They looked heavy and bluish but when she saw Sarah bending anxiously over, her lips curved in a faint smile.

'Friends, Sarah?' she murmured, her voice choking away. 'Friends at last?'

'Don't try to talk, Grandmother,' David urged but Sarah clasped again the hand of the woman she had spent most of her life hating.

'Friends, Alicia – and sisters.'

Alicia nodded, an infinitesimal movement, then her eyes squeezed shut and her features convulsed, the faint blue tinge to her skin which Sarah had noticed earlier intensifying.

'Grandmother!' David shouted, as if by calling her name he could somehow revive her. 'Dad – get a bloody move on!'

'It's too late,' Sarah said. Her voice was calm and quiet but very sad. 'I think she's gone.'

She turned. Kirsty was in a huddle, her hands pressed to her mouth, eyes huge with horror. But Guy stood holding the telephone and the expression on his face might almost have been one of triumph.

'Oh Kirsty, Kirsty, I never thought the day would come when I would shed tears for Alicia,' Sarah said.

It was all over and Kirsty – a Kirsty much subdued by her first brush with death – had driven her home. They sat now in the sitting-room at Chewton Leigh, taking a little comfort from each other's presence, for Kirsty had insisted on staying with Sarah though Sarah suspected it was as much for her own sake as for her grandmother's.

'It was so awful, Granny,' she said now, wrapping her arms around herself to try to stop the trembling which seemed to start deep inside her, reaching her skin as only a faint but uncomfortable prickling sensation. 'One minute she was standing there so much in control, the next . . .' She broke off, squeezing her eyes tight shut as if to erase the indelible vision of Alicia's collapse.

'She overdid things, obviously,' Sarah said. Upset as she was she was less overwrought than Kirsty. She had lived too long, seen too much, to be shocked any more. 'Poor Alicia. It was her heart, I should think. She must have had a weakness perhaps even she didn't know about and the stress of the last week proved too much for her.' She shook her head sadly. 'It must have been terrible for her, discovering the truth about Guy and his entanglement with Leo de Vere, and it took a great deal of courage to do what she did. Not that I ever doubted her courage, of course. That is one thing I never accused Alicia of lacking. But to actually denounce her son – in front of me, of all people – and then to offer me an olive branch . . .'

'You're right, Granny, it was a very brave thing to do.'

'And to think it was all in vain!'

Kirsty looked up sharply. 'What do you mean?'

'Well, darling, the game is lost, isn't it? Didn't you see the look on Guy's face when he knew his mother was dead? Not grief. Not shock. Just utter relief – and a rather nasty twinge of triumph because I suppose he knew in that moment that it was going to be all right for him after all. He had won.'

'Won?'

'The right to do whatever he pleases with Morse Bailey. Alicia had just told him she intended to use her votes to negate the proposed merger instead of allowing him to use his proxy. That no longer applies, does it?'

Slow horror dawned on Kirsty. 'You mean . . .'

'I mean Alicia's votes will now be Guy's by right, Kirsty. I suppose she has left everything to him. He is, after all, her only son.'

569

'Oh no!' Kirsty said, appalled. 'That is really awful, Granny. It was bad enough before but now . . . when we know he will do something with them that is totally opposed to what she wanted . . . oh, we've got to do something about it. We can't just sit back and let it happen!'

Sarah shook her head.

'Oh Kirsty, Kirsty, there is nothing we can do.' She reached for her granddaughter's hand. 'I'm afraid this is one time, my dear, when we are going to have to admit defeat. But one thing I am decided upon. I won't have anything more to do with the company when it comes under the control of Leo de Vere. I shall go in to the office tomorrow and begin packing up my things. Then I shall hand everything over to your uncles. They can fight what battles they think necessary. I have had enough. I am too old to fight any longer.'

'Don't say that, Granny!' Kirsty protested passionately.

Sarah squeezed her hand.

'Don't look so sad, my dear. I wish it had ended differently but there it is. As Alicia said – *C'est la vie*. At least we were friends and allies in the end. And I have had a good run with Morse Bailey. My part in it has kept me going. But now it is time for me to bow out unless I want to finish up as Alicia has. No, I don't relish the thought of what will happen, but since there is nothing I can do to stop it I shall retire gracefully and live out my days . . .'

'Doing *what*, Granny?'

'I don't know,' Sarah said. 'But I expect I shall think of something.'

Chapter Forty-Seven

Perhaps the shock of Alicia's death affected Sarah more than she realised. Next morning she felt unwell and Kirsty insisted she remain in bed.

For once Sarah did not argue. It was as if with Alicia's passing all the spark had gone out of her. She remained obediently in her room and when Kirsty had to leave to go to college she instructed Grace that her grandmother was to be coddled and fussed and treated as an invalid, and not bothered by any phone calls unless they were from herself.

By the end of the day however Sarah had begun to feel that the enforced inactivity was worse for her than any possible stress she might encounter at the office and she wondered anxiously how she would cope with retirement. All very well to tell Kirsty she would think of something to do with her life but in all honesty it would not be that easy. Morse Bailey had been her entire world for so long now and many of the things she had used to enjoy were hardly suitable for a woman of her age. Ballooning, flying, tennis – they were all activities for the young. But traditional pastimes for the elderly appealed to her not at all. The thought of days filled with nothing more exacting than flower arranging, embroidery and a little pottering in the garden filled her with dismay. She could not paint or draw and though she enjoyed reading and listening to music, she was shrewd enough to realise that the main reason they were a pleasure to her was because she had always looked on them as luxuries to be relished in her rare moments of relaxation. If there was nothing else they would quickly lose their charm.

Many an old horse only drops when it is finally taken out of the shafts, Sarah thought ruefully. Perhaps that will happen to me.

But there it was – she could not, would not, continue to

be associated with Morse Bailey when it came under the control of Leo de Vere. She would simply have to adjust to a new lifestyle – there was no choice. And the sooner she cleared out her office and handed over all her ongoing work to Roderick and Miles the better. They could keep the wheels turning until Leo de Vere took over and reorganized the company to suit himself.

Next morning Sarah rose at her usual early hour, sweeping aside Grace's protests, and breakfasted not in her room but downstairs as she always did.

Sitting at the table in the breakfast room, picking without much appetite at her toast and marmalade, it crossed Sarah's mind to wonder whether perhaps she should dispose of Chewton Leigh. It was, after all, much too large for her now. Roderick had his own home, a comfortable converted farmhouse on the other side of the valley, and Miles, though he nominally still lived at Chewton Leigh, spent most of his time in his bachelor flat in town. If she was no longer going to need Chewton Leigh for business entertaining then to keep it on seemed folly. Why not bring the whole era to an end by selling the house and moving out to something small, manageable and a little more central?

But even as the thought passed through her mind she knew she could not do it. Too much of her life was bound up here – she loved the place too much. Her lips curved slightly as she remembered her joy when Blanche, feeling perhaps much as she did at the moment, had put it on the market, and Adam had bought it for their home. Even then Chewton Leigh had been the place she loved best in all the world and the years had only deepened that love. There were memories now in every room, every corner, wonderful memories to eclipse totally the bad things that had happened. Here she had raised her family and it seemed to her that even now the corridors echoed with the laughter of her children and later her grandchildren. She remembered the shared teas in the nursery when she had taken them on her knee, reading to them until they fell asleep in her arms; she remembered how the boys romped through the endless rooms and slid – though they knew it was forbidden – down the sweeping banisters to collapse in a giggling heap in the great hall below, and how they decorated the drawing-room for Christmas with a huge tree and holly and mistletoe gathered from the estate. The stables had become for her not the place where Hugh had raped her in some far-off distant past but the haunt and refuge of Sheila, who had spent every spare moment there with her beloved horses. And best of all the house had become the home which she and Adam had built together, filling the rooms with love and companionship, enjoying a life which had once seemed beyond her grasp.

The decor was theirs – gone were the sumptuous but somewhat overbearing Victorian overtones. The gardens rioted in the way she and Adam had liked them and the deer in the park were there because it had been her idea. No, the thought of leaving Chewton Leigh, however sensible, was a terrible one. I couldn't bear it! Sarah thought. And besides, I would be depriving my descendants of their heritage. For, one day . . .

She did not continue the line of thought but it was there all the same, a small comforting warmth within her and an almost unacknowledged hope for the future. One day in the not too distant future Kirsty would marry and when she did Sarah hoped that Chewton Leigh would become her home. Sarah would have to move out, of course, perhaps take over one small wing or a cottage on the estate, but at least she knew that Chewton Leigh was safe in the hands of someone who loved it as much as she did.

Glancing through the window she saw the Rolls was ready and waiting for her. She finished her coffee and gathered her things together. Grace, still wearing an expression of disapproval, was ready with her coat and Sarah snuggled into the soft cashmere gratefully. Stupid how cold she still felt – she did not think she had been completely warm since this whole dreadful business began.

It was a fine clear morning, the sky clean-washed blue above the new growth of trees. Sarah watched the hedge-rows slip past, busy with birds. Beyond them, on the grassy hillsides, new lambs skipped and Sarah experienced a sudden sharp sadness to think that Alicia would never see them again. Dear God, how depressing it was to see the passing of one's peers! Not tragic in the way that so many deaths she had known were tragic, but laden now with inevitability. Sarah gave her head a small shake. *Come on, Sarah, this is not like you* . . .

There was an air of industry about the works in spite of the fact there were few people to be seen, a feeling that behind the closed windows and doors work of the utmost importance was going on. Sarah dismissed the Rolls and went into the main block and along the corridor to her office – on the ground floor now to facilitate her stiff knee.

Like Chewton Leigh House Sarah's office was very much her domain, decorated to her instructions, functional yet also displaying touches of femininity with photographs of the family placed where she could see them and a vase of daffodils on the corner of the desk. I shall miss it, thought Sarah. She took off her coat and buzzed for her secretary.

'Jenny, could you organize some coffee, do you think?'

'Oh, you've come in, Mrs Bailey. I thought you were ill . . .' The girl sounded concerned.

'I'm fine, Jenny,' Sarah said briskly. 'But please don't pass on the news to anyone yet that I'm here. I shan't feel ready to deal with Mr Bailey or anyone until I have had that coffee.'

She settled herself at her desk, glancing quickly through the pile of messages that awaited her. A few minutes later Jenny appeared in the doorway bearing a tray – freshly percolated coffee and a plate of biscuits.

'Bless you, Jenny,' Sarah said.

The girl regarded her anxiously. 'Are you sure you should be here, Mrs Bailey?'

'Quite sure. Don't fuss, Jenny.' She wondered if she should tell her about her decision to retire and decided against it. It was Guy's right to be the first to know. 'Now, is there anything urgent I should know about?' she asked, sipping her coffee.

'I'm just going through the mail, Mrs Bailey. Yesterda

was a bit odd, of course – all comings and goings and nothing as it should be.'

'The meeting, of course, was postponed.'

'Of course. Mr Bailey was out for most of the day.'

He would have been, Sarah thought. And not only making funeral arrangements. No doubt he had some reporting to Leo de Vere to take care of.

'There is one thing,' the girl continued. 'I know you said you didn't want to see anyone yet but David has been most anxious to speak to you. He tried to telephone you yesterday afternoon but your maid refused to put him through.'

Sarah smiled. 'She was under orders. My granddaughter can be quite bossy, you know. Is David in this morning?'

'Yes. He's been down here once already enquiring after you and I told him I didn't think we would be seeing you this week at least.'

'Oh did you?' Sarah said amused and thought: perhaps it is not only Kirsty who can be bossy – perhaps it is the entire younger generation!

'Shall I let him know you are here now?' Jenny asked. 'Or shall I stall him again?'

Sarah considered. She had not wanted to face Guy yet but David was a different matter. His similarity to Gilbert had made her warm towards him and besides after what had happened she felt she owed it to him to treat him with complete honesty. 'Very well, Jenny,' she said. 'I'll see David, but no-one else. You may as well call him now and he can share my coffee.'

The girl departed and Sarah returned to reading through a pile of messages. But she was unable to concentrate on any of them. How on earth can I close the files on a lifetime's work? she wondered edgily.

A few moments later she heard footsteps in the corridor, followed by a knock at the door.

'Come in,' she called.

It was, of course, David – a David who resembled Gilbert more closely than ever this morning, dressed as he was in a well-cut dark suit.

'David!' she greeted him. 'Come in. My dear, I did not have the chance to tell you the other night how dreadfully sorry I am about your grandmother.'

He nodded. He looked drawn yet strong. Thank God for the young, she thought.

'It was a shock, it's true. Grandmother has always seemed so fit. It just goes to show, doesn't it?'

'It does indeed.' Jenny had provided another cup and she offered it to him. 'Have any funeral arrangements been made yet?'

'Yes, Dad is dealing with those. A small private funeral next week to be followed by a memorial service later.'

'That is much the best,' Sarah approved. 'It's what I would prefer, certainly, when my time comes. A service to celebrate my life rather than one to mourn my death. If there is anyone to mourn,' she added with a touch of her old wry humour.

David said nothing but his face remained grave. This has all been a terrible shock for him, Sarah thought, and I believe he was genuinely fond of Alicia.

'It is a difficult time, David,' she said sympathetically. 'And of course it is not made any easier by the problems with the business. Terrible though it is to say it I am afraid your grandmother's death carries far greater implications than simply losing someone you love. It also means presumably that your father has the control of Morse Bailey that he wanted. The merger, as he called it, is certain to go through.'

'No,' David said.

She set down her cup, a small frown puckering between her eyes.

'What do you mean, no?'

'I mean the merger will not be going through.'

'But – why not?' Sarah asked, puzzled. 'He was so set on it.'

'And still is for all I know.' David thrust his hands into his pockets, looking at her directly. 'It is no longer up to Dad though.'

Sarah had begun to tremble. She pressed her hands tightly together.

'Why, David? Why is it no longer up to him?'

A tiny smile lifted one corner of David's mouth.

'Because it is up to me. I have been trying to get hold of you since yesterday afternoon. She did not leave her shares in the company to Dad. She left them to me.'

'What?' Sarah could scarcely believe her ears. 'She left them to *you*?'

He nodded. 'I haven't taken it in yet, either. Naturally we all thought that Dad would be her heir and so he was – until last Monday afternoon. Apparently Grandmother summoned her solicitor to her hotel suite and changed her will in my favour. It seems she totally disapproved of what Dad proposed and wanted to make sure he did not gain control of Morse Bailey.'

'But why didn't she tell anyone?' Sarah asked.

'I think she intended to tell us on Tuesday evening. Do you remember she said something about having had a reason for asking me to be present? I think she was coming to it. But she . . . well, she collapsed before she could say anything.'

Sarah touched her fingers to her lips. They felt deathly cold.

'This is yet another shock, David – but I must confess a very welcome one. I take it you are still with us – you are against the merger?'

'Even if I weren't I would make sure Grandmother's wishes were adhered to. I regard what she has done as a very special trust. I don't know what I have done to deserve it but I can promise you I mean to make quite sure I don't let her down.'

'Oh David . . .' Tears were pricking at Sarah's eyes. I could tell you, she thought – I could tell you why I am sure Alicia trusted you, but it would only sound like empty flattery.

'So you see you need not worry any more,' he was saying. 'That is what I wanted you to know.'

She could not reply. Her throat was aching. Then another thought struck her.

'David – suppose your father contests the will?'

577

'I don't think he will. He won't risk a family rift. Besides on what grounds could he contest? Grandmother was quite obviously in possession of all her faculties – more than most, I'd say. And he hasn't been cut out entirely. Her house in London and what little money that wretched second husband of hers left to her all go to him. It's just the voting shares that come to me. And I know what I have to do with them.'

Sarah nodded. Her heart was full. She held out her hands to him and her eyes sparkled, bright with unshed tears.

'David,' she said softly, 'I know she would be proud of you.'

Chapter Forty-Eight

Alicia was laid to rest in the churchyard at Chewton Leigh, a stone's throw from the house where she had been born and the fields where she had galloped so long ago on her beloved Baron. It was a cold grey March day and the mourners shivered slightly and huddled into their coats as they stood around the graveside watching her coffin lowered into the dank Somerset earth.

'Ashes to ashes, dust to dust . . .'

No, thought Sarah, whatever our differences Alicia will never be dust and ashes to me. She was always too vibrant, too alive, even to the end, and if she was sometimes spiteful and scheming then, God knows, so do we all have our faults and Alicia paid dear for hers.

She glanced up from the coffin, looking at the other mourners. Max was there, frail now and coughing a little in the biting wind, leaning heavily on the arm of his second wife, whom he had married some ten years after the death of Annie, and who had borne him two fine daughters. Max had pulled the threads of his life together; when his time came he would be remembered by his family with love and by the public as a genius. Sir Maximillian Hurst – who would have thought the Max I knew would one day be a Sir? she wondered. Then there was Guy, the very epitome of the successful businessman, though the high colour in his cheeks owed more perhaps to the brandy bottle than to the wind, and in some ways he looked like a man with a weight lifted from his shoulders. Whatever his private debt to Leo de Vere at least his loss of power meant that the wicked old man no longer had a hold over him – or if he did he must know it would do no good. Guy would continue as Managing Director but never again would he be in a position to jeopardise the future of Morse Bailey and it looked as if the knowledge had come only as a relief to him.

Next to Guy stood her sons, Roderick and Miles, Roderick's wife, Susan, and Sheila and her husband, Clive. Sheila was the only woman not to be wearing black – she could not spare the time to go shopping for something special, I imagine, thought Sarah, looking at Sheila's country tweed suit and knee-high brown boots. But who am I to criticise? There are more important things in life than outward appearances.

Her gaze flickered on. Gwen, David's sister, perhaps the most fashionable of the party, with her television director boyfriend, then David, standing beside Kirsty. Sarah's heart softened with love. Oh Kirsty, my dearest grand-daughter. And David – so like Gilbert it makes my heart miss a beat. It is possible . . . am I hoping too much . . . that perhaps one day they might . . .

The vicar had reached the end of the service. Sarah looked at him, arms raised to bring a blessing to them all, and thought: soon it will be my turn. Soon they will be gathered here to bury me and in all honesty I am not sorry. I have lived my life – and what a life! How can I regret one moment of it? But I am not quite ready yet. Last week when I thought I had to leave Morse Bailey to its fate I might have been. But not now. There are still things I want to do. Oh no, I am not quite ready yet.

The service over, the mourners began to move away.

'Granny – are you all right?' That was Kirsty, anxious as always for her welfare, touching her elbow. She nodded.

'Yes, Kirsty.'

She moved to the edge of the grave. In her hand she held a single white rose. Leaning forward she dropped it in so that it fell on the coffin.

'Goodbye, Alicia. Perhaps we shall be better friends in the next world than we were in this one,' she whispered silently. 'And if I caused you pain, my dear, then I am truly sorry. But we stood together in the end, didn't we? Gilbert would have been proud of us.'

'Granny?' Kirsty whispered anxiously.

'It's all right, darling.'

'But . . .'

'I'll take your grandmother home.' Miles's hand was firm beneath her elbow.

She let him lead her away across the soft turf. At the gate she turned, looking back, and saw Kirsty and David holding hands. A faint smile touched her lips and she let her gaze flicker over the other graves, well kept and flower-decked, where her loved ones slept.

'You were right, Adam,' she said softly. 'You were right. We did indeed inherit the skies.'